D0504057

THE LEGACY OF THE MERCENARY KING

THE
TWO-FACED
QUEEN

A Novel

Nick Martell

SAGA PRESS

LONDON SYDNEY **NEW YORK** TORONTO NEW DELHI

SAGA PRESS

AN IMPRINT OF SIMON & SCHUSTER, INC.

1230 AVENUE OF THE AMERICAS, NEW YORK, NEW YORK 10020

Copyright © 2021 by Nicholas MacDonald-Martell

First Saga Press trade paperback edition July 2022

SAGA PRESS and colophon are trademarks of Simon & Schuster, Inc.

For information about special discounts for bulk purchases, please contact Simon & Schuster Special Sales at 1-866-506-1949 or business@simonandschuster.com.

The Simon & Schuster Speakers Bureau can bring authors to your live event. For more information or to book an event, contact the Simon & Schuster Speakers Bureau at 1-866-248-3049 or visit our website at www.simonspeakers.com.

Manufactured in the United States of America

1   3   5   7   9   10   8   6   4   2

Library of Congress Cataloging-in-Publication Data is available.

ISBN 978-1-5344-3781-4
ISBN 978-1-5344-3782-1 (pbk)
ISBN 978-1-5344-3783-8 (ebook)

For my grandparents,
Douglas and Mary Martell

DRAMATIS PERSONAE

KINGMAN AND ROYALS:

Michael Kingman: Middle child of the Kingman family.
                            Known throughout Hollow as a king killer and a
                            Dragonslayer.
                            Bonded Kingman to the Princess of Hollow.

Gwendolyn Kingman: Youngest member of the Kingman family.
                            Bonded Kingman to Adreann Hollow.

Lyonardo Kingman: Oldest child of the Kingman family.
                            Bonded to the deceased Davey Hollow.
                            Engaged to High Noble Kayleigh Ryder.

Juliet Kingman: Head of the Kingman family.
                            Widow of David Kingman.

David Kingman: Known as "the Kingman Who Murdered the Boy
                                Prince."
                            Deceased.

Davey Hollow: The murdered boy prince. Former heir to the Hollow
                                throne.
                            Bonded to Lyonardo Kingman.
                            Deceased.

~~Serena~~ Hollow: The Princess of Hollow.
                            Heir to the throne.
                            Bonded to Michael Kingman.

Adreann Hollow: Second in line to the throne.
                            Known throughout Hollow as "the Corrupt Prince."
                            Bonded to Gwendolyn Kingman.

Isaac Hollow: Former King of Hollow.

                               Bonded to David Kingman.

                               Deceased.

HIGH NOBLES OF HOLLOW:

Charles Domet: Much-appreciated patron of the Hollow Library.

Alexander Ryder: Head of the Ryder family.

                               Close friend of David Kingman.

Kayleigh Ryder: Firstborn of the Ryder family.

                               Engaged to Lyonardo Kingman.

Kyros Ryder: Third-born of the Ryder family.

                               Known as "Kai."

                               Blind.

Joey Ryder: Youngest child of the Ryder family.

                               Mute.

Danielle Margaux: A High Noble from Michael's childhood that he's

                                   forgotten.

                               Eldest of the Margaux family.

                               Known as "Dawn" and "the Girl in Red."

Maflem Braven: Head of the Braven family.

Edward Naverre: Head of the Naverre family.

Edgar Naverre: Eldest child of the Naverre family.

Patrick Naverre: Second-eldest child of the Naverre family.

Katherine Naverre: Middle child of the Naverre family.

Edgill Naverre: Second-youngest child of the Naverre family.

Evelyn Naverre: Youngest child of the Naverre family.

RAVENS AND MEMBERS OF SCALES:

Efyra Mason: Captain of the Ravens.

                               Mother of Chloe Mason.

Chloe Mason: Single-feathered Raven.

                               Daughter of Efyra Mason.

Karin Ryder: Two-feathered Raven.

                               Second child of the Ryder family.

Rowan Kerr:	Three-feathered Raven.
Michelle Cityborn:	Four-feathered Raven.
Hannah Hyann:	Five-feathered Raven.
Jasmine Andel:	Six-feathered Raven.
Bryan Dexter:	Commander of the Evokers in Scales.
	Father of Naomi Dexter.
Naomi Dexter:	Former member of the Executioner's Division of Scales.
Angelo Shade:	Foster father to Michael, Gwen, and Lyon Kingman.
	Commander of the Watchers in Scales.

ORBIS MERCENARY COMPANY:

Dark:	Recruiter for Orbis Company.
	Known as "the Black Death."
Tai:	Commander of Orbis Company.
Imani:	Second-in-command.
Alexis:	Gun Master.
Beorn:	Poison Master.
Haru:	Weapons Master.
Cassia:	Sailing Master.
Gael:	Explosives Master.
Otto:	Magic Master.
Jade:	Memory Master.
Nonna:	History Master.

OTHERS:

Symon Anderson:	Known as "the King of Stories."
	Known throughout the world for his charm.
Treyvon Wiccard:	Best friend of Michael Kingman.
Jamal Wiccard:	Younger brother of Trey Wiccard.
	Deceased.
Sirash:	Michael's con artist accomplice and former Skeleton.
	Real name is Omari Torda.
Arjay:	Sirash's younger brother.

Jean Lorenzo: Sirash's girlfriend.

                                 Student at the College of Music.

Olivier Comar: Leader of the refugees.

Rian Smoak: Dragon Historian for the Church of the Eternal
                                    Flame.

The Archmage: Author and Master Surgeon.

                                 Immortal.

Drisig Tiro: New Reclaimer for the Church of the Wanderer.

Zain Antoun: Ambassador of the Gold Vein Casino in Goldano.

Champion Prasai Alareata: Champion of Ancients of the Thebian Empire.

Emelia Bryson: Leader of the Hollow rebellion.

                                 Known as "the Emperor."

                                 A former sacrifice.

THE STORY SO FAR

Michael Kingman is an obnoxious, arrogant child with delusions of grandeur who should've died—leaving me to dictate his family's legacy and story—but the bastard lived. And so, regrettably, I must continue to chronicle his miserable life.

If you missed the first volume of his story, let me save you the trouble of hearing his whiny explanation for ending up on trial for the murder of King Isaac. Michael Kingman is the middle child of David Kingman, the infamous traitor who murdered the boy prince ten years ago. Since his father's execution, Michael spent his time conning noble visitors to the city of Hollow—being the only ones stupid enough to fall for his rudimentary schemes. After the rebel army attacked the Militia Quarter on the East Side and murdered one of his friends, Michael finally got a proper job when his sister, Gwen, found him work with High Noble Charles Domet. While in Domet's employment, Michael tried to learn how Fabrications worked—ignorant of the fact that he's been using his Fabrications for years—while participating in the Endless Waltz. An outrage! The grand event is reserved for the nobility to court and develop lasting alliances in Hollow, not for angry young men to posture and refuse to slay dragons. Using the Endless Waltz, Michael earned an invitation to the king's birthday party, where he attempted to determine whether his father had truly murdered the boy prince through a misguided attempt to steal the king's memories. His attempt ended in disaster—and his pistol-dueling against his best friend.

After more whining about his legacy, a Mercenary kidnapped one of his friends and held him to ransom, to reclaim an item Michael had foolishly stolen from him. To give him some credit, while attempting to save his friend, Michael discovered that the Mercenary possessed a revolver that was a twin of the one used to kill the boy prince. This piece of evidence finally proved there was more to the boy prince's murder than previously thought. In his desperation to learn the truth, Michael snuck into Hollow Castle and confronted the king about his father's trial. According to Michael, the king would not accept his father's innocence, but the king's grief ~~lit its apex from losing his son and forsaking his kingdom and . . . and the King~~

I heroically made a deal with Michael: to exchange his story for my aid in saving his mother from a Forgotten's fate. I must admit, even now, I'm not sure how we managed it. Perhaps it was a combination of our magical abilities? Regardless, with his mother safe, Michael turned himself in and prepared to die to protect his family . . . until the last moment, when he escaped his execution and hid in a church, where he was saved by Orbis Mercenary Company.

Now Michael Kingman is apprenticed to the Mercenary Dark. And being hunted by every organization in Hollow until it can be proven beyond doubt that he didn't murder the king. At the time of writing, I doubt he'll survive much longer. Not when even his Royal is out for vengeance . . .

Symon Anderson crossed out what he had written with a single stroke, hesitated, and then tried to write the ending to Michael Kingman's story again. He made it four words before the tip of his quill lingered too long on the page, leaving a large black blob of ink where a period should have been. He cursed, shoved it aside, and put his hands behind his head to control his breathing. Something was wrong with the story. He just didn't know what. Had Michael lied to him about something? And if so, why?

What had he tried to protect? And why had he run into the Church of the Wanderer during his execution?

The single-feathered Raven walked through the door to the Archmage room, plate armor clanking until she stopped on the other side of the table from Symon. "Recorder," she said, holding her metal helmet against her side. "I have a few questions I hope you might have answers for."

"About?" the King of Stories asked, perking up.

"Commander Angelo Shade."

He deflated. "Oh. I have some information on him. But wouldn't you rather know more about the king killer?"

"No."

Symon wanted to crumple up the papers around him and throw them at the walls. What was the point of getting access to the King of Imbecile's story if no one wanted to hear it? Right now, it was about as useful as the Thebian Empire's champion of war's poetry collection.

"Why do you care about the Commander of the Watchers so much?"

"I think he's manipulated history."

"I oversee the archives," Symon said with a chuckle. "Do you really think some muscle-brained—"

"Do you know of the Mercenary company that used a broken crown as their symbol?"

"A broken crown? What does a . . ." Symon trailed off, gears clicking into place at words that held no previous meaning. Pressure welled in his throat, his nails scratched the table, and he glared at the Raven as if she had slapped him. "How did you figure it out?"

"I overheard something in the Church of the Wanderer I wasn't meant to."

"Maybe it was a blessing Michael lived after all." The King of Stories motioned for the Raven to join him. "Shall we discover the truth together?"

BOUND BY FATE

It was our birthday, and for the first time in a decade the Princess of Hollow invited me to celebrate it with her.

My mother told me not to go. That it would be a trap. That the princess would use any and every opportunity to get revenge, since I was the primary suspect in her father's death. But my siblings Lyon and Gwen both knew what I would do before I admitted it.

From the very beginning of our lives we had been together. The Princess of Hollow and I had been born on the same day. She was early, while I was late. It had occurred on the last snowfall of the year when spring was in sight, coating the entire city in a heavy white blanket that had kept the midwives from reaching our mothers, forcing our fathers to birth us instead. Fate had decided to replicate that day, as I trudged through the snow toward my destination, wishing it wasn't so far away. The merchants tried to maintain the roads in the city, but in the Upper Quarter it was the Royals' responsibility to clear the snow, and ever since King Isaac's death the castle had gone silent. It might as well have been a mausoleum, because no gossip, rumors, or whispers had come out of it since I had escaped my execution. No doubt the princess was determining whom she could trust and whom she had to dispose of.

According to stories I had heard in my youth, most considered our dual birth to be an omen of good things to come. There was only one other time in Hollow history that a Kingman-and-Hollow bonded pair had ever entered the world together, and it had been Montagne the Remembered and Yuri the Unneeded. They had created a golden age in Hollow together, and without meaning to . . . we had been born with the pressure on our shoulders to do the same. Even if we weren't the heirs. And maybe that was why we became obsessed with our legacies and ancestors.

Because of this supposed destiny, our parents had never been surprised how close we became, even for a bonded pair. There were times that we could communicate without speaking, glances and smiles substituting instead. We were perfect together, inadvertently covering each other's flaws and highlighting our strengths. The princess was intelligent and artistic but quiet and nervous in large crowds, while I was confident and talkative, drawing in people with what she had affectionately dubbed my poisonous tongue. She had also been the only person able to see through my lies—no matter how big or small . . . She always knew the truth. And now, with me being blamed for the king's death, she was about to be my greatest enemy.

If I didn't convince her quickly of my innocence, it was only a matter of time before whatever revenge she had planned came to fruition. My hope was this invitation would prove a chance for me to explain what had happened. So long as she could still see through my lies, she might believe what had happened with her father as the truth. But if this was a trap . . .

I stopped in front of the gates to the King's Garden. The snow was higher here than it was in the rest of the city, with only a single-file line of footprints to follow inward. They were smaller than mine and whose feet they belonged to were clear. The princess had come to the gardens.

And judging from the lack of other snow prints . . . it would just be the two of us.

I followed the trail the princess had left behind for me through the snow and slush and flurries around me. Her path led me to a circle of old birch trees, the leaves having been stripped away back when I was an immature brat who couldn't remember anything about his life and thrived on basic things—anger, selfishness, and delusions of grandeur. But I wasn't the same as I had been a month ago. I felt reborn, as if the weight on my shoulders had finally gone away.

Yet, the thing about consequences was that they always caught up eventually. The princess—never one to celebrate in vain—had left me a gift for my birthday. A grave and headstone, to be exact.

There was a large pit big enough to fit my body and then some, along with a crudely chiseled headstone of marble with the words *Here Lies Michael Kingman* carved into it. There were endless groups of four finger marks along the edges, along with dried blood flakes of frozen skin. In the middle of winter, with the ground as hard as diamonds, the princess had dug me a grave with her bare hands. The headstone had been her handiwork, too—bits of marble that hadn't been turned into a fine powder littering the nearby ground. A bouquet of Moon's Tears slightly coated with snow rested at the bottom of the pit. The flowers were pristine and bright, still giving off a faint white glow. They had been picked recently. A few hours ago at most.

I went to the headstone and sat on top of it after brushing off the snow that had accumulated on it. Taking a deep breath, I steadied my heartbeat until I was certain my voice would come out clear and calm. There was no point in shouting at the sky. The princess was around here somewhere. She wouldn't miss the opportunity to watch me admire her threat and declaration of war. But if she wasn't going to stand in front of me herself, I'd take the opportunity to speak uninterrupted.

"Thanks for the gift," I began, running my fingers along the edges of the marble. "It must have taken a long time to do. It definitely makes up for not getting me anything the past ten years." I exhaled and watched as my breath came out white and wispy. "I'm sorry I didn't get you anything as good today. Gift giving has never been a strength of mine—except for Lucky. That gift I was proud of."

The wind answered me, blowing against my face as I returned to my feet. I trudged over to a nearby tree that was just a little bigger than the others, hands still bundled into my pockets to fend off the cold. "But I was good at everyday things, wasn't I? The big moments were always hard for me to get right. Too much pressure. Too many eyes on me. I felt as if everything I did was being watched . . . dissected." I hesitated. "I remember that on your seventh birthday I got you a black leather-bound book that smelt of hidden secrets and bone dust. Everyone I asked for their opinions told me it was a proper gift for a Kingman to give their Royal. It was practical and showed I understood the nature of our bound relationship. That I was maturing and no longer overstepping into something beyond duty."

I kicked at the base of the tree I was standing in front of and watched as snow fell from the branches to the ground. It landed with a soft plop. "It was a lousy gift. Too impersonal for what we were. Even when you smiled sweetly and said thanks through gritted teeth, I knew you hated it. We were best friends, and being a bounded pair was only a part of our relationship—not the base." I took a deep breath. "I should have given you a heart-shaped glass necklace like I wanted to. That was the right gift back then. And although I never got the chance to give you your ninth birthday gift officially . . . better late than never, right?"

Words were carved haphazardly on the tree's trunk in a childish scrawl. *Michael and the Princess—bound by fate but chose each other anyway.*

"That's one birthday gift I missed. Forgive me if it's childish. I was eight when I did it." I returned to the edge of the pit, toes dangling over as if I were about to jump. "Nothing I say right now will make you forgive me or make you believe that I had nothing to do with your father's death. So keep watching until you're satisfied. You won't find the monster you're looking for. Just the foolish boy you once knew."

A voice came from everywhere and nowhere. "I am going to kill you, Michael Kingman."

Unlike my memories of Dawn that returned in a torrent all at once and nearly split my head open . . . my memories of the princess trickled back to me like an offbeat rhythm. It made me wonder if my memories of her had been manipulated or forgotten, or if I had simply pushed them to the back of my mind as a child to save myself from losing another loved one after my father.

I answered her threat with a smile as something in my mind turned open, her name returning to me after a long absence. "Come at me with everything you've got, Serena Hollow." The scrawl on the tree changed. The princess morphed into "Serena." "I promise you that I'm not going anywhere ever again."

There was no response—not that I expected one. Serena had never been good at comebacks under pressure. Actions were her strength and words were mine, and if we were going to be enemies, this would be the last chance I'd have at being in a position of relative power or safety. Serena wasn't careless. I'd have to be better than ever before if I was going to survive her war.

Under the shattered moon and scattered stars I began my walk back to Kingman Keep.

Serena haunted me as I walked through the city she would one day rule. When I passed sweetshops, I recalled how she used to hoard pastries filled with strawberry jam in her room to remind herself of summer. I heard her laugh in my mind whenever I passed Wanted posters of myself, knowing she would have made fun of how they depicted my nose jutting out like a bad wart. I smelt her favorite perfume—oranges and lemongrass—as Low Nobles shouted obscenities at me from the windows of homes in Justice Hill. And sometimes I saw her out of the corners of my eyes, close enough to feel her breath on the nape of my neck but gone by the time I turned around.

I was so lost in my thoughts . . . I almost didn't notice something that hadn't happened in more than two decades.

There were refugees at the gates of Hollow, begging to get in.

Everyone in the area was caught off guard as a horde of people staggered into the city. Most of them were groaning and fell to their knees clutching at the legs of Advocators. What initially seemed like a dozen or two soon became a few hundred and people were still coming. Some were bandaged, some bleeding, some had fresh red and flaking burns. Others were missing limbs. A few with red lines covering their bodies spontaneously caught fire the moment their feet touched the cobblestone streets. They died screaming for Celona's mercy while those around them shouted that the Corruption had arrived in Hollow, that a Goldani curse turned magical infection was killing the refugees from the inside out with flames.

There was no indication where they had come from—another city, or a different country entirely. Hollow citizens who had initially stood back to let the refugees pass were suddenly shoving past the healthier ones to reach those more critically injured. All the order had vanished in a singular moment.

Wherever the prince and princess were within the city, they were probably more shocked than I was. It was one thing for King Isaac to deal with the rebellion, and now this—he had had decades of experience on the throne. The princess had a month.

What would she do? Would she let them stay? Would she kick them out?

Suddenly I doubted I was Serena's top priority anymore.

MEMORIES OF INK

Morning only brought pain. Whether it was the light in my eyes, the dull ache that covered my body, or the cold that lingered in my bones after a night under a thin, scratchy blanket. I couldn't remember the last time I had slept through the night. Nightmares of the king's suicide usually plagued my mind. They were worse than the ones about the Kingman Keep riots and left me looking for distractions while the city slept. The only good thing to come out of my restlessness was that I had spent that time getting better at shooting guns. I was the scorn of painted-on targets everywhere.

Normally I could take my time getting up, but not today. My mother wanted us to have breakfast together. I realized why the moment I stumbled out of the room I shared with my sister, rubbing sleep out of my eyes. In the middle of the sunlit great hall was a massive maple table that could easily sit thirty. It stood out against the rotten wood, dust, and ruin that was everywhere else, and it was vastly different to the table that had stood here in my youth, but as I ran my fingers over the smooth wood it still made me remember my father and the elaborate toasts he would give before every meal. I would've cried if I wasn't so tired.

"The Ryders brought it after you fell asleep last night," my black-haired and sun-kissed-skin sister said. She had a blacksmith's body with forearms more defined than most soldiers' and had rolled up her sleeves so the crown brand on the back of her left hand was visible. Our mother's red scarf was around her neck. "They said that if we were going to live here, we might as well have a place to eat dinner. Ma and Lyon cried. A lot."

"I forgot how important family meals were to Ma and Da."

"I don't know how you could've," my mother declared, entering behind Gwen. Lyon was at her side, carrying a steaming pot. Unlike Gwen, the brand above his eyebrow was obscured with the ends of a knit hat. "Without them, none of you would've learned anything about our family history. I don't think I need to say how important that was and how important it'll be in the future."

Lyon put the pot down on the table, gave each of us a spoon, and then took a place at the table near me and my sister. My mother stopped behind the chair at the head of the table. It had been my father's seat, and now it was hers. After steeling herself mentally, she looked at her amber-eyed children and said, "In the upcoming days, we'll have to make a lot of hard decisions. Some of them none of you will like, and others all of you will."

"Will those decisions include getting beds?" I asked. "Because sleeping on the floor is a pain."

"Michael."

"Sorry, Ma."

Gwen was smiling ear to ear. "It's good to be home again."

"I'm just glad for once it's not me scolding Michael," Lyon said.

"It wasn't that bad, Lyon."

"You two rarely went a day without getting into an argument," Gwen said as she played with her spoon.

"We couldn't be in the same room together," Lyon added.

"That's a little dramatic, don't you think?" I said.

"No," they said in harmony.

"You're both being—"

"Enough," my mother said as she took her seat. "We're all aware of Michael's selective hearing. He's had it since he was a child."

"Ma!"

There was laughter at the table as I flushed.

"Everyone, dig in. After beds, I promise we'll get some plates and bowls."

None of us moved our spoons toward the pot's mysterious red contents. Noticing our hesitation, my mother said, "What?"

"Who made this?" I asked. "And what is it?"

"I did. It's beetroot porridge. Your grandmother made it for me when I was a girl," my mother said. "I was a great cook before I married your father and relied on . . . Just give it a chance."

Bravely, I dipped my spoon into the pot and tried it. "Wish we had some bread to go with it, but I think I like it."

"Seriously? There's no comparison to Ange—" Gwen caught herself before she said his full name, clenching her fists instead.

"Are we going to talk about what he did to us?" Lyon questioned quietly. "Or just keep delaying the inevitable?"

"It's not delaying. It's just . . . we can't move against Angelo openly yet," my mother stated. "So long as the Royals and Efyra think Michael killed King Isaac, they'll react violently to any move we make against them. And that includes Angelo, so long as he works for Scales. They might not be able to come for Michael, but we aren't as lucky."

"What do we do, then?" Gwen asked hesitantly.

"We prepare," my mother said. "After Michael is proven innocent, we'll be able to deal with Angelo Shade. But until we know who he is and what his goals are, we're treading water. Let's use this time to learn."

"*I* know what his goals are," I said. "He wants to destroy all the High Nobles because they did something to his wife and unborn child."

"But what does 'destroy' mean, exactly? Does he want to burn it all down and make himself king? Does he want to stand on the ruins and then walk away? Both have the same end goals, but one is vastly different."

Lyon's face was red, and he picked at a scab on his forearm until it was bleeding. "This is ridiculous. We lived with this man for ten years. How do we know nothing about him? How did none of us realize that we were being manipulated?"

"We were all focused on ourselves," I said. "We have to do better."

If there was anything that could embarrass my siblings, it was when their selfish brother admitted he had been too focused on himself. We all started to eat while my mother got up and walked around the table to strengthen her muscles. Every so often she would eat, too, she'd lost too much weight over the past decade to miss a meal.

Lyon filled the silence: "I have a matter to bring to you all. Kayleigh and I will be hosting an event at Ryder Keep in a few days to formally announce our wedding and forthcoming child. I would like you all to attend. It'll be a social event. But a small one. Hopefully."

Talking about Angelo had soured my mood, so I didn't have a joke. I simply said, "I'll be there. No question. Family looks after family."

Gwen and my mother expressed similar sentiments, and Lyon let out a heavy sigh. I realized how much of a burden that simple question must have been on his mind. Having me at the event wouldn't be easy.

The princess was likely to be there. As children, Serena and the Ryders' daughters had been an inseparable group whenever the princess's duties allowed. Clearly their bond had been strong enough to compel Karin Ryder to join the Ravens and protect her close friend. The group had seemed so intimidating when I was a child, regardless of how confident I had appeared to be when I approached them. Something about a group of girls huddled close to each other seemed more impenetrable than a vault.

Before anyone else could speak, Lyon asked, "Michael, can you walk with me on my way to get a new tattoo?"

Gwen glared at me, silently asking what I had done this time. But all I could do was shrug. For once, it had seemed Lyon's and my relationship was improving. We were still at odds as a decade's worth of arguments took time to reestablish trust, but whatever he wanted to talk to me about alone was a mystery. We made our way out of Kingman Keep together as my mother and Gwen cleaned up what remained of breakfast. Neither of us spoke until we had crossed the western bridge and headed toward the Student Quarter.

"How many refugees do you think there are?" Lyon asked as he kicked at hard snow that had formed in the gutters of the road. It barely moved.

"Hundreds, if Hollow is lucky. Thousands if we're not."

"Kayleigh says her parents are starting to notice the dwindling supplies. Fewer Mercenary companies are willing to protect the shipments we need. Greed or boredom, it's hard to tell why they're refusing the contracts. If the High Nobles start to pay attention and pressure the princess to end this rebellion decisively, maybe we'll all avoid starving to death."

"If the princess could end it with one blow, don't you think King Isaac would have?"

Lyon tilted his head to the side until his neck cracked. "War redirects hate. It can make a tyrant look like a hero if they play it right. The princess isn't loved. She's been too absent to be. Everyone just hates her less than her brother and is angry at . . . well, at you."

"That isn't going to change anytime soon."

"Not as long as Efyra is breathing."

"Wonderful," I said with a shake of my head and a small laugh. As if the princess wasn't bad enough, now I had to deal with the leader of her maniacal guard. Just because I had defeated Chloe in the Church of the Wanderer didn't mean I was foolish enough to think I stood a chance against any of the others.

"So," I began, trying to fill the silence, "have you and Kayleigh found a date for the wedding?"

"Spring. Maybe summer. Hard to know for certain. Even though I'm a . . . less-than-ideal suitor for Kayleigh and our child could be perceived as a scandal . . . our wedding is still political. At least our love isn't."

"Does it bother you?"

"All the politics?" he asked. When I nodded, Lyon continued, "No. I knew what I was getting into. The only thing I didn't take into consideration was . . ."

Lyon trailed off in a way that suggested he didn't lose his thought but simply didn't want to continue. So I did for him.

"Was me messing everything up? You're heir to the Kingman family again."

"I was always the heir," Lyon said. "The heir to a lost legacy and a cobweb keep, but always an heir. The High Nobles never let me forget it."

"Do you want to forget it now?"

"Does it matter?" he countered. "I am Lyonardo Kingman, heir to the most infamous family in history, from now until my dying day. And one day my child will be forced to take up this burden, too."

"You could renounce your position as heir if you wanted to. Then it would be my responsibility."

"If only it were that simple. You're a part of Orbis Company now. If they wanted to, they could claim all the Kingman assets as their own, since you're one of them."

I scratched my head, watching as a hooded man who had been leaning against a wall ran away from us as we turned into an alleyway. "That's ridiculous."

"It's the law. We know Dark saved you, but we don't know why he did. Until we do, I doubt Ma wants to give them any opportunity."

"That means if you're determined to take the Ryder family name, then I'd have to renounce all rights to the Kingman name, to protect our assets. By law I wouldn't be a Kingman anymore . . . and Gwen would be the future head of the family."

I'd spoken the words without understanding the implication. If that happened, I might be allowed to keep my family name but surrender everything else, including land and inheritance rights. If not, they could wipe every trace of me from my family's history. Trading my legacy to Recorder Symon had been hard to do, but I had known I would still be a Kingman. This move could take that away.

"Are you still going to . . ." I couldn't finish the sentence, too scared to know the answer.

I wanted to ask more. To unravel who my brother thought he had to be, as opposed to who he was. To learn why he had the name of every person he had executed tattooed onto his body. No one had told him to. He had done it on his own, and I never understood why. Who wanted to remember all that pain?

But I couldn't. Lyon was standing in a doorway beneath a shoddily painted sign that read *Voluntary Stabbings* in reddish brown that looked too much like blood to be accidental. Classy.

"Wait here. It won't take long. Names never do."

"Why did I come if you were just going to make me wait outside?"

"Because I don't want you to see how many other names are on my body."

Lyon entered the building. When the door closed behind him, I sat down on the ground against the wall and watched people pass by. It was early, so everyone was still getting ready for the day. A hooded woman who seemed to be emulating Domet's drinking habits teetered back and forth before falling against the wall next to me. She reeked of the sewers.

The drunk woman offered me a sip from her bottle, but when I rejected it, she shrugged and swigged it herself, then threw an arm around me and leaned her head against my shoulder. I was about to shove her off when she asked, "Did it feel good?"

"Did what feel good?"

She slid her sharp nails against the side of my neck. A shiver went down my spine as she placed the end of a flintlock pistol against my skin, concealed by her baggy clothes. "Killing King Isaac, of course. What else could I mean?"

Emelia Bryson, the Rebel Emperor, was sitting next to me. She had cut her hair short, shaved the sides, and used makeup to cover the very distinct scar that ran below her right eye, along her jawline, and then disappeared at her neckline. She was still frighteningly beautiful and batshit crazy if she was willing to wander into Hollow like this.

"Emelia," I said.

"You remember," she said softly, running her nails up and down my neck, gentle enough not to break skin. "I was worried after our meeting in the cemetery. You seemed so cold, so distant, so . . . lost."

"You killed Jamal."

"Who?"

"Jamal Wiccard, the boy that was with me in the cemetery. You ordered one of your rebels to shoot him."

"Hmm, I don't remember."

"You don't remember that you—"

"Ah-ah-ah," Emelia said as she pushed the gun into my side. "Don't be impolite, Michael. It would only take a squeeze of the trigger to kill you. If you were unlucky, taking a bullet from this angle would only paralyze you from the waist down."

"Do it," I goaded. "Shoot me. Make me the martyr you seem so obsessed with becoming."

Emelia scrunched her face but remained silent with the gun still pressed against my side.

"If you were going to kill me, you would have in the graveyard. Did you think I'd forget your words? For whatever reason, I'm too valuable for you to kill. So if you're here to talk, let's."

"You remember my words! That makes me *so* happy." The Rebel Emperor whistled. Two men opened nearby window shutters, rested their forearms against the frame, and then stared at us from above. Both had the rebels' closed red fist tattooed above their left eyebrows. And then, with a smile on her face, she shoved the gun into my hands. The trigger was missing, the wood was splintered, and all the inner mechanics were rusted. It wouldn't shoot and would barely work as a club if I got desperate. "My guards will watch and make sure all you do is talk. Fair?"

"Fair," I admitted. Her nails remained around my neck, traveling up and down the muscles. I bit back all the names I wanted to call her. "What do you want, Emelia?"

"To see how my second-favorite Kingman is doing. I heard you tried to save my father from the Corrupt Prince's wrath. Despite the anger between you, I'm thankful you were good to him before his death."

"I didn't try to save him. I hesitated before murdering him myself. The Corrupt Prince simply did it faster."

"That hesitation is love, Michael." She put her head against my shoulder again. "It makes me wonder if you're ready to join the rebellion. Believe it or not, I don't normally come into Hollow. But there was someone I had to meet, and this encounter might be fate's way of drawing us together."

"You murdered my friend. Do you really think I'd ever join you?"

"Why not?" she said with more levity than she ought to. "You killed King Isaac. My rebels hold your name in higher regard than they do your father's. You're an icon. A symbol. A legend of defiance." She bit her lower lip. "A perfect representation of the new generation."

I wanted to provoke her, but there was something I wanted to ask her more. "Why didn't you try to kill King Isaac when you had the chance after your trial? There was no way you could have foreseen what happened."

She giggled as she ran her nails along the back of my neck. "What makes you think the king was the rebellion's target?"

"In the graveyard, you said—"

"That the rebellion is here to rid the world of a tyrant whose regime will never end. The king, although corrupt, was not a tyrant. He did not shape history. He was not important. He was nothing but a man who could never step out of his dead sister's shadow."

"Then who—" I stopped myself.

She couldn't know about *him* . . . could she? It was impossible.

As if she knew what I was thinking, Emelia leaned close and whispered in my ear, "You weren't the only one who overheard something they weren't supposed to that night. We inherited your father's legacy. But I wonder, which of us will be remembered as a hero? And who will be the villain?"

"You're spouting nonsense," I said, voice shaking.

She said it quietly, but I heard it so very clearly: "Charles Domet is immortal."

Domet had been wrong. There were others who knew his secret. But how did she? Her, of all people?

"Do you want to know how I figured it out?" she teased. "I'll tell you if you ask nicely."

"I don't know what you're talking about."

"Liar. Want to know his real name? It's quite interesting."

I hesitated, and it put a smile on her face. As much as I wanted to know, I couldn't admit it. It would only give her more satisfaction. I had to escape this conversation with some of my dignity intact. Sadly.

"Do you really think you could stop him? When no one else could?"

"I'm the only one who can." Emelia moved to kneel in front of me, and then put her lips against my ear. "If you ever grow tired of being on the losing side, come to my camp. They'll escort you straight to my tent. We'd be the perfect duo to rule a new generation, wouldn't we? Think about it."

She was enjoying this too much, so I said the only thing that might ruin her mood. "Does it bother you?"

Emelia hesitated and then said, "What?"

"That you can't convince me to join you? I hate Domet, yet I would rather kiss his feet than help you. You wanted a Kingman, and now you have one. No matter your plans, they didn't account for me."

A smile. "You know where I live. Now, Michael, don't try to follow me. My business in Hollow is personal."

I motioned to her guards above. "Are you going to hurt my brother if I do?"

"No." Something softened in her persona as she looked over her shoulder. "His time in this war is fleeting. And I have no desire to hurt someone who once looked at me with hearts in his eyes." She turned, outstretched her arms, and jogged away from me in reverse. "Stop me if you can, Michael."

I ran after her once she rounded the corner and was out of sight, only to emerge in a road crowded with people dressed identically to how she had been. They circled around me as if I were the center of a whirlpool and bumped me all over the place until I lost sight of Emelia somewhere near the Hanging Gardens. Then they dispersed like flies and left me alone.

I couldn't help but laugh at how she had outplayed me. I had assumed Emelia had lost control once I called her bluff, but it was just to lull me into overconfidence. She had an army to help her escape from my sight. The next time we met, I wouldn't let her get away again. I'd need allies to stop her. Whoever Emelia was planning to meet in Hollow, I could only hope they weren't planning another attack.

I tossed the useless gun into the gutters, and was back before Lyon emerged with his new memory tattoo. He was rubbing the skin around it, a small smile on his face. In flowing cursive, the tattoo over his left wrist simply said: *Kayleigh*.

"I had the tattooist match a sample of her handwriting," Lyon said. "Kayleigh was against it. Too embarrassing. But I convinced her otherwise."

My run-in with Emelia had left me annoyed and bitter, and I was running a thousand scenarios in my mind, all ending with Emelia dead or chained up. Preferably in that order. But I did my best not to show my emotions and said, "It looks great."

"Doesn't it? Now I'll have a piece of her always with me."

"I'm glad you're so happy."

"So am I." Lyon paused, focusing on me for the first time since he left the building. "Are you, Michael?"

"Am I what?"

"Happy?"

How was I supposed to respond to that question?

"There's still time, you know, for you to fall in love and build a life outside . . . before . . ." Lyon looked toward Kingman Keep. "Before we become what we were raised to be. I've always wondered if love would make the burden easier."

I shifted, and so did the invisible weight on my shoulders. "Do you think it will?"

Lyon gently ran his fingers over his left wrist. "I hope so."

We said our goodbyes before it could get more awkward. Lyon went off to show his fiancée his new tattoo and I returned to Kingman Keep.

———————

Only my mother was there, sitting at the table with a half-eaten loaf of bread in front of her.

"Ma?" I said as I approached her.

At the sound of my voice, she perked up and turned to me. "Michael! I was hoping you'd be back soon. I had a few questions for you." A pause. "This bread is yours if you want it. Gwen and I already ate."

I sat down and began to eat. "Is this about succession?"

"No," she said firmly. "Lyon and I are still discussing that. I was hoping you knew some other details. Such as why our vaults are empty."

"Taken. Mainly by the Royals, but rioters helped, too."

"What about the Cutter, Page, and Harbour families? They must have protected some of our assets for you three to inherit."

Around a mouthful of bread I said, "They cut ties with us soon after Da was executed."

My mother tapped her fingers against the table. "So Lyon wasn't exaggerating when he said the Ryders may be our only allies in the city."

"For now, they are."

"Oh?" she said with a chuckle. "Are you planning on changing that?"

"I am."

"As thankful as I am that your Mercenary company saved your life, I don't trust them that much."

"Neither do I. But I have a plan to fix everything."

"Michael—"

"I'm serious," I said, voice growing harder. "I know Lyon and Gwen have probably told you how inconsiderate I've been, but I've changed. There's a lot of people I have to make things right with and I'm working on it."

My mother smoothed her hands over the table. "And what is your end goal?"

All I had was my new goal of becoming a Mercenary King, which was naïve, and I certainly had no clear target to proceed toward. Until this morning. To convince Serena of my innocence, I had to do something that would force her to acknowledge me as a loyal Kingman. And I knew what.

I was going to kill the emperor and end the rebellion.

My family had created it, inadvertently, so there was no better person to destroy it.

"For now, it's making amends with people," I said. "Then I'm going to prove to Serena that I'm not a king killer."

My mother smiled slightly. "She was an incredibly stubborn child. That won't be easy."

"I know. I have a lot of work to do," I said as I left my seat. "Thanks for the bread, Ma."

"You're welcome. And, Michael? I want to meet Sirash and Trey. Invite them to dinner."

The last time I had seen Sirash, he was about to murder someone. While Trey and I realized we were heading in different directions, in the graveyard. I doubted either would be wise for me to find and bring to dinner. I didn't tell my mother that and simply said, "I'll do my best."

Before I could kiss my mother goodbye, we were interrupted by Chloe, the single-feathered Raven. She was wearing her familiar plate mail and walked toward us with her hands up. My mother, who hadn't shown much emotion over even our father's murder, put her hand over her mouth to contain a gasp. "Chloe Mason? Is that really you?"

She stopped in place. "Yes, Juliet."

My mother ran to her and embraced her in a tight hug. Chloe tentatively returned it as I stood staring at them, dumbfounded. Where had this relationship come from?

"You've grown so big!" My mother pulled back to get a full look at her. She frowned at the sight of the peacock feather in her frizzy hair. "I see you've joined the Ravens like your mother."

"It's what I was born to do."

"Fate can be defied. Didn't I tell you that repeatedly?"

Chloe looked away. "Regardless. The castle demands your presence. I am here to indicate how serious this request is."

My mother tensed. "The princess or the prince?"

"Neither."

"It's not Erica, is—"

"Efyra."

"Ah," my mother said before she exhaled loudly. "I should have expected that. Surprised it took her this long. Does the captain of the Ravens want me now?"

"Yes. I am to escort you there."

"I am curious how the past decade has treated her," my mother said with a raised eyebrow. "Michael, are you ready to go?"

"What?" I said.

If Chloe was surprised, she didn't show it. "Juliet, this was a singular invitation. Commander Efyra would not appreciate it if you bring Michael to the castle. For obvious reasons."

My mother patted Chloe's shoulder. "There's no need for that, Chloe. But if your mother is going to command my presence like she's the queen, after all the history between us, I'm going to make her regret it. I could cite the laws and regulations that would allow me to bring Michael, or we can save ourselves the time, since you know them as well as I do. Your choice."

For someone overly obsessed with duty, I was surprised when Chloe cracked a smile and said, "I've missed you, Juliet."

THE STONE THRONE

During all my adventures in the castle throughout the Endless Waltz, I had never entered the throne room. For most it was the only thing they ever saw, but for me . . . I could count on one hand how many times I had been here. The first time my father had brought me there to teach me why the throne could never be mine, but how it would be my duty to protect whoever sat on it.

The second visit had been right after my father's execution. With the brands still flaky and fresh, the king had lined me and my siblings up to warn us that if we so much as shat in the wrong alleyway on the East Side or knocked a noble's hat off, we'd be brought back here and our situation reevaluated. It didn't take a mastermind to realize that meant losing our heads.

This was the third time. And since my mother looked like she was out for revenge, I had a feeling it would be the most entertaining trip by far.

The golden throne room was opulent and pristine, except for one small flaw: the plain stone throne that the castle had been built around. My father had told me that it was deliberate, because a Royal should never enjoy having that much power, and to flaunt it only made madmen and tyrants. He had always added, with a laugh, that it being incredibly uncomfortable only made it better.

But Efyra didn't seem to mind it.

The fifth- and sixth-feathered Ravens, Hannah Hyann and Jasmine Andel, flanked her while she rested her ass on the throne. Otherwise there was no one else in the room but my mother, me, and Chloe. I would have tried to make a joke about the absurdity of it all, if not for the fact my mother was seething. Her face was red as a ruby with light being shone through it, entirely because no one without the last name Hollow was supposed to be there.

My father would have denounced Efyra as a traitor and murdered her on the spot if he had still been around. I couldn't help but wonder if Gwen's dislike of Efyra was wiser, not the simple pettiness of disliking her in our father's place beside the king that I had always considered it to be. Was there a chance Efyra had been working with Angelo Shade this entire time to get herself closer to the throne?

"Efyra," my mother said, voice strong and clear, a distance away from her.

"Juliet," she answered, making no move to rise. Efyra wore heavy plate armor with a curved sword over her knees, frizzy black hair framing her narrow face. And whether it was to save face or to control her anger, she never acknowledged my presence.

"I see you're just as tasteless as I remember you to be. Still cutting food with the same sword you use to slaughter?"

"At least I didn't bed a child killer and give birth to a king killer."

"Caught me," my mother said with a feigned look of embarrassment. "I'm *so* happy to hear that you finally got over that stutter of yours. It was probably necessary once you could no longer hide behind me or Erica."

"I've never hidden behind anyone."

"Liar. You've only ever been confident at the king's side." My mother gestured at the Ravens next to her. "That's why this spectacle is happening. We could have talked in private, but you wanted spectacle, so here I am to deliver one," she snarled. "Sorry. Did you think years in an asylum would make me meek and powerless?"

"So that's where you were." Efyra drummed her fingers on the throne. "I should have searched the entire city for your body rather than foolishly believe you were dead." She paused. "I won't make that mistake again."

"You won't get the chance. I'll outlive you."

The Ravens next to Efyra drew their weapons. "Threaten me again and I'll cut you down where you stand."

"Try it," she said. "I've put you on your ass so many times, I wish I were a Fabricator. Then I'd have a use for all those useless memories."

"The past is the past. And you are nothing like you were."

"Pretty sure I'm still a bitch."

"Apparently time can't fix everything."

If my eyes had been closed, it would have been hard to determine if it was my sister or my mother next to me. They were both fearless. I wondered if Gwen knew how similar they were—as close as I was to my father. We had inherited their personalities, not just their looks.

"What do you want, Efyra?" my mother asked. "Still seeking revenge because I almost got you removed from the Ravens? Or do you have something worth talking about?"

Efyra cracked her neck. The sound was loud and distinct. "For once, you're correct. There are other matters we must discuss. You are violating Hollow law by dwelling in what was formerly known as Kingman—"

"We are Kingman. We have the right to be there."

"You did ten years ago, before King Isaac stripped the Kingman family of their High Noble titles. Keeps in Hollow are merely loaned to the High Noble families by the crown—"

"Except Kingman Keep. To ensure our family could never be controlled by an ambitious Royal. Clearly the Mother didn't predict the captain of her Ravens would rise far enough to be considered a Royal in everything but name."

Efyra was calm and expressionless, while the Ravens next to her glared at each other. Both looked more frazzled than they ought to appear, willingly standing by an impostor on the throne.

"Fine," the Captain of the Ravens said as she rose, staring into my mother's eyes. "If you want to follow the rules, then let us. You claim the Kingman family is back—you must prove it. You have until the princess's coronation to restore your family's honor."

"Be clearer, Efyra. I won't let you claim we failed because your requirements were vague."

"You will determine who was responsible for King Isaac's death. With insurmountable proof."

"So you want us to do your job for you?"

"Yes," Efyra said, clawing at the back of her hand. "And I want you to kill them. Personally. No matter who it is."

"What if the investigation takes longer?"

"Then you and your family will leave Hollow forever, and Michael will sign an agreement that if he ever sets foot in Hollow again he can be killed. Without repercussions from Orbis Company."

My mouth felt dry. There was no way my mother would agree to those terms. If Efyra was this desperate, then she likely didn't have anything tangible on me . . . which probably meant she was one step away from ignoring the laws. I wondered who, or what, they'd send after me. Hopefully Evokers, Wardens, and tweekers would be the worst of them. I would have to fight to survive. But with no allies, no money, and no way to prove that King Isaac had killed himself, taking this deal was mad—

"Deal."

Oh, no.

"I want a blood oath," Efyra said.

Clearly the Captain of the Ravens wasn't as experienced a historian as I was. Blood oaths had been broken so many times that the only period they had been effective was around Hollow's foundation . . . and suddenly it became quite clear to me why Domet had suggested one to me when we had begun to work together. Hopefully Efyra wasn't another Immortal. One was enough of a nuisance.

My mother seemed annoyed by the suggestion. "Seriously?"

Efyra took a dagger from her belt. "Seriously."

The two women cut the backs of their forearms with the dagger, wiped the blood up with their palms, and then shook hands. It was a simple, unsanitary gesture, over in a few moments, and we turned to leave with Chloe as our palace escort. There were no more words exchanged until we were out of the castle and had reached the Conqueror Fountain, near Domet's house. My mother and I sat down on the edge of it and watched some Low Nobles and merchants wander the Upper Quarter. Some were going out for a meal, dressed for a High Noble party, while others meandered to and fro as they basked in the dim winter light. As I debated sticking my fingers in the nearly frozen fountain's water to calm down, Chloe turned her attention to me.

"I'm going to make you an offer, Michael," she said, a hand on the sword at her side. "One that will save your life and give the princess time and space to grieve. Maybe when her head is clear she will be able to see other scenarios."

"Oh? So you accept I'm innocent?"

"I accept King Isaac's death wasn't as simple as everyone believes." A pause. "But the truth is irrelevant. I want you to leave Hollow. And if you go tonight . . . I'll give you this." She reached into her armor, pulled out a small box, opened it, and then twisted it around. Inside was a piece of moon-fall that shone a dull blue. "It may look unremarkable. But this is one of the sparkling pieces that the Institute of Amalgamation thinks may hold the secret to who or what shattered Celona. If you find the others, you could solve one of the world's greatest mysteries."

"Chloe," my mother whispered. "Did you steal that from the royal vault? Put it back before someone notices! Hollow nearly went to war with the Skeleton Coast over one of them!"

"It's war I'm trying to avoid." Chloe wiggled it at me. "Will you do it? It may be hard to leave Hollow, but it really will be for the—"

"I can't."

Her face fell. "Are you really turning down the chance to get a legacy that could surpass any of your ancestors'?"

"It's not about my legacy." The words felt bitter on my tongue. "I literally can't leave Hollow yet. I'm an apprentice Mercenary. I go where Dark goes, and until he says we're leaving, I'm here for better or worse."

"Would you leave if you could?"

I shook my head. "I don't want to run away from my problems anymore."

Chloe snapped the box closed. "Then nothing can change your fate. Serena will slit your throat and throw your body in that grave she dug with her bare hands."

"I'm glad she hasn't lost her flair for the dramatics."

"Michael, if you treat Serena like she's the same child you once knew . . . you have no chance of surviving."

My mother put her hand on my shoulder. "It's good he's not alone anymore, then. We'll convince her of the truth together."

"For your sake, I hope you do."

As Chloe walked toward the castle, I said, "Is there any chance you'll let me hear what that moon-fall says? It was my birthday yesterday."

A laugh. "Goodbye, Michael. Goodbye, Juliet."

Once Chloe was out of sight and I made sure there were no Advocators around us, I asked my mother, "Care to explain what all that was about in the castle? I felt like I'm missing some context."

"Efyra and I have never seen eye to eye," my mother said. "But Chloe and I have always been close. She didn't have many friends growing up, since Efyra forbade her from playing with you or the Royals. The other High Nobles saw her as less than them and the Low Nobles were too scared to be relaxed around her, so she was alone for most of her early life." My mother exhaled. "I tried to be someone she could confide in. More like an older sister than a mother."

"Chloe was forbidden from playing with us? Seriously?"

My mother hesitated, hands folded in front of her. "Efyra thought it was best she never become overly familiar with you all."

"That's stupid. All children deserve to have some fun. Davey could disappear for hours on end without anyone worrying, and he was the heir!"

"Ravens aren't supposed to have children," my mother said slowly. "So there wasn't a standard for Efyra to follow when Chloe was born. She took extreme measures to make sure her daughter had a future . . . even if it was a strict one."

"Why didn't Chloe live with her father if being with Efyra complicated things?"

"The identity of Chloe's father is one of the great mysteries of Hollow. Your father . . ." She closed her eyes for longer than a standard blink. "Your father knew. But I didn't and—"

"You don't have to tell me if it makes you uncomfortable."

She gave me a gentle smile and brought me in close for a hug. "As much as I dislike Efyra, this secret doesn't just affect her. I don't want Chloe to find out from you or someone else if she doesn't know. That would be cruel."

"I get it."

"Thank you, Michael. I'll tell you his identity if it ever becomes necessary." My mother stared at the castle. "But I can't imagine it ever will . . . Some secrets don't need to be revealed if all they'll bring is pain."

I drummed my fingers against the stone and wondered if there would ever come a time when I hid the truth to protect the people I loved. Because if the truth didn't set people free, what good was it?

THE GIRL BEHIND
THE CURTAIN

After kissing my mother goodbye and telling her I had people I needed to see, I left her in the Upper Quarter and went to Margaux Keep.

The last time I had visited, it had been to tell a friend the worst news of his life. But as I returned, it was with a newfound treasure trove of previously obscured memories. It was truly amazing how little had changed in the past ten years.

When I was a child, it had been a game to get to Dawn's room without being seen—I went so far as to climb up trees and walls to avoid the patrols. Dawn's father, High Noble Antoine, found it amusing and let me test their security—never fearing a child. Her stepmother never enjoyed it quite as much and would call the Wardens or the Ravens if I was caught today. But I was willing to take that risk to make amends to Dawn. It might show how sorry I was for what had happened.

The walls themselves were a respectable height, but the general layout of the keep provided the best security architects could create. In the center of the grounds was a multi-tiered triangular structure surrounded by a hedge maze and a circle of trees that obscured the lower levels of the keep. Visitors were forced to traverse the maze to reach the main entrance, and anyone foolish enough to try to cut through the hedges was greeted with a face full of stone. Thankfully, there were other ways in and out of the keep for those who lived and worked in it, though I wasn't going to use them. I was going to take the exact same path I did as a child.

The northern entrance to the hedge maze always had the newest guards, since it faced the Upper Quarter. After waiting for an opportunity, I climbed over the outer wall and descended into the maze. From here it was right, left, right, right, left, right, left, straight, and then right to get to the main entrance. I followed that path almost exactly, but instead of the final straightaway I turned left and snuck through an opening through the hedges that only Dawn, Sebastian Margaux, Davey, Serena, and I ever knew about. Ten years later it was still there. Just as the great oak tree with its thick, twisted branches right outside of Dawn's bedroom was.

From there it was an easy climb.

I knocked on Dawn's window, waited, and, when nothing happened, I decided to force up the window. It was simple, and soon I was tumbling into Dawn's room.

Her room was largely unchanged except for the bigger bed, newer paintings that hung on the walls, and dozens of vases holding cut flowers. Yet, it still looked more like a painting exhibit in a museum than a bedroom. A trail of clothes stretched from a wheeled chair that was partly hidden by a blanket in the corner of the room. Dawn must've left in a hurry. There was also something . . . odd about her room. As if the air was permanently stale, and a breeze hadn't touched the walls in years.

The single most interesting thing in here was the painting that hung opposite her bed. It depicted five children—three boys and two girls—playing in a garden. The boys were running around, swinging sticks as if they were swords, while the girls sat on a blanket making faces and laughing at their playmates. I was one of the children in this painting. With Davey, Kai, Serena, and Dawn.

No wonder she hadn't forgotten me. She had seen me every day.

Before I could decide whether it was wiser to go or to wait for her return, someone began to jiggle the doorknob. I dove under the bed, put my hand over my mouth, and waited to see who it was.

When the door to the room opened, I could only see a pair of magically defined legs and the silver flats that accompanied them. The feet stopped in front of my hiding place as a voice said, "Michael, you can come out. There's no one else with me."

Dawn didn't have to tell me twice. My childhood friend was waiting for me with a warm smile and took me into a tight embrace. She was dressed as lavishly as she had been during the Endless Waltz, if not in red, and I did my best not to wrinkle her clothes as I returned her hug.

"You remember," she whispered.

"You'd be amazed at how often I've been hearing that lately." A circlet of white roses was around her head, an obvious sign that all eyes were supposed to be on her and no one else. Dawn picked at the stems as if the thorns hadn't been removed before she wore it. "You look beautiful."

Dawn let me go and kissed me on the cheek before making her way over to the wheeled chair. "Thank you for not making this awkward."

"I've been told I have a way with words. How come you're all dressed up?"

"I was meeting more potential husbands." She threw the blanket off her wheelchair and took a seat. The definition in her legs seemed to melt away once she did. "Sadly, I do not think any of them are interested in seeing a loudmouthed open-mouth chewer and incessant giggler like me again."

"Not trying to be subtle anymore, are you?"

"No. My father is getting more desperate and I'm getting more defiant. Either he'll let me do what I want or he'll push me away."

"Push you away?" I asked as I crept closer to her. "What does *that* mean?"

Her face was flushed. "It doesn't matter. So, how'd you remember?"

"It was a Darkness Fabrication, meant to make me forget a conversation I overheard before my father's execution. Your name was mentioned in it . . . I couldn't be allowed to remember you."

"Ten years," she muttered. "You lived with Darkness Fabrications altering your memories for half your life? Oh, Michael."

"It explains my immaturity. I never had a chance to grow up . . . always stuck in the past," I said with a laugh. "Some things are still spotty. And sometimes it's hard to juggle two different sets of memories for a single event, but I'm recovering."

Dawn was busy smoothing out her dress.

"You want to know what happened with the king, don't you?"

"Everyone does."

I took a deep breath. This story was becoming easier to recount in detail. How many times had I explained what happened already? A dozen? It didn't take long to tell her what had happened. But it was still a few painstakingly long moments before she said anything.

"The king . . . killed himself?"

"You don't believe me?"

"I'd be lying if I said I did completely. There's never been a—"

"I know," I interrupted. "Trust me, I know. If I hadn't been there, I doubt I would believe it. The only reason my family does is because they're family."

Dawn laughed and I was caught off guard. Before I could ask why, she said, "I realized that separately none of it makes sense. But together it's all too crazy to be anything except the truth. The right hand of the king kills the child prince. The king kills himself. And you claim it's all the mad plan of someone who wants to destroy Hollow, and yet you won't name them."

"It's better if you don't know that part."

"Why? Scared I'll betray you to them?"

"Honestly? Kind of."

After what Angelo Shade had done to me, it was hard to trust anyone.

Dawn always seemed to have my best interests at heart. But so did Angelo Shade until I had the evidence in front of me. If she had been willing
to accept me back when I didn't remember her, I hoped she'd trust me
even as this hung over us.

Thankfully, she did. "You have your reasons," she said. "But I expect
to know eventually. If I'm the last of your friends to find out, I'll cas-
trate you."

A smile. "Noted. My mother has been asking me to invite friends
over for dinner, do you want to—" Too late I remembered her legs and
how she had to use Fabrications simply to walk. Inviting her to something
felt like I was taking memories from her and smashing them on the floor.

"Do not treat me differently because of my legs. I don't want that,"
she stated. Her eyes were narrowed. I had struck a bigger nerve than
intended. "I make my own choices."

"But you lose memories every time you walk. Is that price worth it?"

"No, but I'd gladly pay it to ensure people see more of me than my
inability to walk. Before I learned how to use my Fabrications, I was
trapped in this room like one of those pathetic princesses who wait
around to be saved. I wanted to see the world. I wanted to dance at night
with attractive partners and laugh and forget that by morning my bones
will break if I put any weight on them. I wanted someone to fall in love
with me without knowing my condition. You can't even imagine some of
the looks strangers gave me when I was younger."

"What if you become a Forgotten?" I asked softly.

Dawn looked into my eyes. "If my memories are the price I must pay
to be known as something other than a cripple, then so be it."

"That's shortsighted."

"Maybe. But I've set up my own precautions," she declared. She
wheeled her chair over to an old trunk, opened it, and motioned for me
to look inside it. There were dozens of journals in there, labeled with
dates, all stacked with the utmost care. It made the Archmage room in
the Hollow Library seem amateurish.

"I record the events of every day," she explained. "I haven't missed a day since I've been able to write on my own. I may become a Forgotten, but at least I'll be able to look back and know I lived a fulfilling life. Hopefully my future husband will understand."

"For someone who gave me so much shit for initially forgetting them . . . it seems like one day *you'll* forget *me*."

Dawn wheeled herself back. "We're all hypocrites when we want to be."

"And if I don't forgive you for being a Forgotten one day?"

"Relax, Michael. I have no intention of letting that happen. So there's nothing to worry about."

"Intentions and reality aren't often the same."

A shrug. "I've always envisioned a different fate for myself."

Arguing any further would be pointless. I'd have to try again later. Instead, I shifted topics. "So, want to be my date for this family event two nights from now, for Lyon and Kayleigh?"

"I've already been invited," she said with a roll of her eyes. "Most of the High Nobles have been. No one would miss it. The Kingman family and Kayleigh's pregnancy are the hottest topics in noble society."

I wonder if Lyon knew how big this small event was about to be. Or how dangerous it could be for our family. "You could still be my date. Makes it even easier if you've already been invited."

"It does, but that means I would have to tell the beautiful High Noble Raine Solarin I can no longer accompany her. She asked me so sweetly, and I don't want to break her heart. No offense, Michael, but she's much more attractive than you are."

High Noble Raine Solarin had been the subject of affection of nearly every noble child when I had been younger. When we were seven, Kai had written a sonnet to invite her to the summer festival, only to find she had already accepted another's invitation. It was children's games and children's priorities. And yet it had meant everything back then.

Someone knocked on the door to Dawn's room, and she motioned for me to go to the window. So much for our bonding time.

"High Noble Danielle!" a voice said from behind the door. "Your guests are wondering where you went. Do you need assis—"

"I can get there on my own," Dawn interrupted. "Once I've washed the slime off my hands from having to interact with all these star-chasers."

There was a hesitation, and then the voice said, "I will let your father know, High Noble Danielle."

Dawn held up a hand and then counted down from five before letting out a sigh. "I'm sorry we were unable to . . ." She trailed off, sadness turning into a playful smile. "Actually, is anyone expecting you?"

"Not really. Why?"

"Any desire to come join the party out there with me? It's me and a bunch of suitors, and I could really use a friend to lean on."

"Kai isn't there?"

She shook her head. "My parents aren't dumb. They know I wouldn't interact with anyone else if he were. We've been so platonic that they didn't even bother having a chaperone watch us when we were alone once we were of age. That's how little they were worried about us doing something scandalous in private." She folded her hands together. "Please, Michael?"

Her tone made her request seem more forceful than the words let on. "Isn't someone going to notice me?" I tapped my brand. "It's not as if I'm really inconspicuous."

Dawn reached under her bed, rummaged around, and then tossed me a full face mask. It was pitch-black, with ornate gold lines around the eyes and mouth hole.

"Is everyone in masquerade?" I asked.

Dawn nodded with a smile. "Except me."

I turned the mask in my hand. If I put my collar up, I could hide my face and brand. "You really want me there?"

"Stay for a bit," she said. "Watch my signals and steal away any unwanted attention. That's all I'm asking."

"Only for you." I held out my hand to help her up. "To make up for lost time."

Dawn took my hand and pulled herself to her feet, legs becoming unnaturally defined once again. "How charming of you." She reached into one of her dress's pockets, pulled out a pin with a forget-me-not etched onto it, and then stuck it onto my lapel. "This will keep you from being bothered. It's a sign of my favor."

"How generous of you." We left the room with arms locked together and made our way down a lavish hallway toward the source of excessive noise. "So while I imagine you hate them all, are any of your potential husbands at least slightly interesting?"

"Not really. But, to be fair, most of them aren't at fault. Right now you could pluck the partner of my dreams out of my mind and I'd still find them dull. Choice is half the allure of falling in love, and arranged marriages strip that all away." She paused to run her tongue over her teeth. "Part of me hopes someone who's longed to talk to me will sneak into this event and steal me away and I can have one of those romances you read about in books."

"I thought you didn't want to be saved."

We stopped in front of the large door to the ballroom where the courting event was being held. "It's not about being saved. It's about having an adventure . . . and who doesn't want that?"

I said nothing, donned the mask, and watched as she opened the door. Dawn slipped away from me almost instantaneously as suitors caught sight of her and approached with a ravenous fervor.

Everyone was dressed extravagantly, way beyond what I had experienced during the Endless Waltz. Despite the fact that everyone was masked, it was easy to determine where some were from based on their jewelry, accessories, and even the style of clothes they wore. The Goldanis wore flashy jewelry that glittered in the light and could be taken off with ease to be used as collateral should a bet become too alluring to resist, while those from the Gold Coast wore looser clothes that showed off more of their skin. There were even a few from New Dracon City, as evidenced by their formfitting vests, striped trousers, and outrageous headwear. And there were even Mercenaries here.

Why were all these people from other countries here? Most High Nobles preferred to marry other nobles in Hollow to consolidate power rather than develop connections with foreign powers. Usually those were reserved for the Royals. Dawn must've chased off more nobles than I thought she had. Good for her.

With little to do but wait for a signal, I drank wine by myself as I watched Dawn interact with anyone brave enough to approach. She danced with them all and even went out of her way to approach those who stared from across the room. She was a woman of the people and it was the closest thing I had ever seen to someone emulating the behavior of a proper Royal. Only the guilt of watching her feet glide across the polished flooring and knowing what it cost made me unable to fully appreciate the moment.

"She's captivating, isn't she?" a handsome man at my side said. He had short black hair and bigger-than-normal ears, held his glass of wine like a proper High Noble between his middle and ring fingers, and had half of his face covered in a snow-white mask. The other half had intricate bone tattoos. A Skeleton. And one who had earned Dawn's favor. The forget-me-not pin was on his lapel.

"She is," I said as I took another sip of wine.

"It's a shame her brother doesn't have half the grace she does," the man said. "Anyone who mingles with the Corrupt Prince is little more than scum in my eyes."

I nearly choked on my drink. He definitely wasn't from Hollow if he was bold enough to insult a High Noble and the Corrupt Prince in the same sentence. "I don't think it's wise to insult the brother of the person you're looking to marry."

The Skeleton shrugged. "I doubt she thinks differently. But she may be in denial about it. People rarely see the bad in their family until it's too late." He examined the table of food we were leaning against. "So, call me curious, what did you do to earn her favor?"

"We're childhood friends. And you?"

"Rich and powerful. The usual. It's not that interesting. But I'm a little shocked. I didn't think she had many childhood friends. Well, besides the obvious ones."

" 'The obvious ones'?"

"Those Kingman traitors." The Skeleton took one of the decorative slices of lemon and sucked all the juices from it. "Have you ever met one? I've wanted to but haven't had the chance yet."

"No," I said levelly. "I haven't."

"That's a shame. I thought you might be able to help me."

"Why do you want to meet one so badly?" I asked, curiosity getting the best of me.

The Skeleton looked at me, something in his eyes turning hard and venomous. "Isn't it obvious? I want to—"

A short man tapped me on the shoulder and interrupted our conversation. He had the posture and air of someone who'd had the same haircut since they were ten and the suggestion of getting something different would send them into an unstoppable fury. He stared at me with his arms crossed behind his back.

"Yes?" I said cautiously.

"Can I get your name, profession, and origin?"

"Ren Arsenius," I began, relying on an old childhood alias. "I'm a Mercenary of Machina Company. Does it really matter where I'm from?"

"Another Mercenary? Ridiculous. What were they thinking?" The short man rolled his eyes. "Follow me, Mercenary."

I put my wineglass down at a nearby table as the Skeleton waved me goodbye. I didn't want to cause a scene and create further problems for Dawn, so I followed the short man with the plan to sneak away the first moment I could. I didn't have any chance until he ushered me into a plush side room filled with cushions, wine and food, and an almost see-through black curtain separating the room in two. Someone moved on the other side of the room, but I couldn't identify anything about them. The door was locked behind me with an audible click.

"I'm sorry you got dragged into this," the woman behind the curtain said. There was a sound of a liquid being poured into a cup. "There's wine nearby if you want something to drink." And then, under her breath, she added, "I know *I* need it."

"What is this?" I took a seat on a cushion so big I sank into it.

"Surveying for potential suitors." The woman sat down somewhere with a *plop*. "High Noble Danielle Margaux's family was generous enough to hold this event for the both of us. Even if I would rather be anywhere else."

"You must be pretty important to have this be so secretive." I pushed my tongue against the inside of my cheek. "Are you Princess Serena Hollow?"

"God no," she said quickly. "No offense, but she's a bitch. I don't know what her nobles think of her, but everyone outside of Hollow hates her and her manipulative tendencies. I like to think I have a little more tact and grace."

Nothing the woman on the other side of the curtain had said convinced me it might not be Serena. Insulting myself would have been exactly what I would have done if I had been trying to remain hidden when confronted with my true identity. But since she seemed to be talking freely, I might as well take advantage of the opportunity. Especially since she had no reason to suspect I would have been able to get in here unnoticed.

"Fair," I said. "So, besides your name, can I ask whatever I want?"

"Pretty much."

"If a suitor brought you a gift, would you rather it be flowers, sweets, or jewelry?"

"What kind of sweets?" she asked without hesitation.

"Sun drop cakes." It was Serena's favorite as a child.

"Sun drop cakes. No contest."

More evidence to support my theory. "What was your favorite game as a child?"

"Hide-and-seek," she said happily. "And I was the absolute best hider in the whole wide world."

So was Serena. One time we played, it took me all day to find her in the castle, only to discover she had been following me the entire time. And since I was so focused on going forward, it never occurred to me to look behind. She was clever like that. Always hiding in plain sight.

"What kind of stories do you like?"

"Tragedies," she said firmly. "There's something hauntingly beautiful about a story that can make me cry."

"Like what happened to Goro Lafette?" I clarified.

"No, not like that at all. That's a romantic tragedy, not a heroic one." She huffed. "That story just makes me mad. What woman wants to be left a note on their wedding day from their beloved saying they can't go through with it? Especially when it's rumored Goro Lafette left because he was in love with another woman."

Another similarity with Serena. I had once caught her reading a story about Goro Lafette and asked that very question about the difference between heroic and romantic tragedies. I had received a similar—yet much longer—rant about why they were very different and why the distinction was important. A heroic tragedy was a good cry, while a romantic tragedy was a bad one.

If this really was Serena—and I was all but certain it was—she hadn't changed much since childhood. She still had the same taste, but, just to make sure, I asked a more blatant question. "Have you ever had someone you would consider a best friend?"

The woman behind the curtain made a ticking sound with her tongue. "People like me don't get to have best friends. It's an occupational hazard."

"Not even when you were young? Children don't normally care about crowns."

"No, they don't, but . . . wait, I . . . I never said I wore a crown."

"Crowns, thrones, legacies, and last names . . . it's all the same. Every important person in the world has at least one," I said evenly, heat rising up my face. "I may not know who you—"

"You're lying."

I couldn't suppress my smile. Even without seeing my face, Serena could still always tell when I was lying. At this point, there was nothing I could do but tell the truth. "You're right. I am." I exhaled and feigned as much courage as I could. "Hello, Serena."

Silence.

"Do you need me to say my name, or do you already know who I am?"

She rose from her seat, right hand gripped tightly around her left wrist to ease the shaking. "How?"

"We have mutual friends."

"God dammit, Dawn," she muttered under her breath. "You should leave. Before I lose my temper."

"Don't want to listen to what I have to say?"

"Leave," she growled.

For once, I listened to royal instruction and left, apologizing to the poor sparrow-masked fool who was about to wander into Serena's room after me. Dawn skipped over to me from across the room with childish glee when she saw me emerge.

"You set me up," I said.

"Did I?" she asked. "What reason would I have to do that?"

"I don't know, but you did. Those pins weren't signaling your favor, were they? You were choosing candidates for Serena." I massaged my temples, wondering whether the screams I could hear behind me were Serena's or not. "Are you and Serena friends or something?"

Dawn lost her smile. "No. Not anymore, at least. We haven't talked more than a few sentences since she was a child. To be frank, apart from her Ravens, I don't know if she has any friends. I handed out the pins from the goodness of my heart. The courting process is a nightmare for me . . . I can't even imagine what it's like for her."

"Why did you give one to me, though? You know she hates me."

"She hates what she thinks you did," Dawn corrected. "If you're to have any chance of convincing her otherwise, you have to catch her off guard. She needs to see the real you—the fool—not the king killer or the villain you pretend to be."

I was getting a headache—no fault of Dawn's. Everything when it concerned Serena made me pause and go over our interactions, searching for something or anything that would calm my beating heart. As always, nothing did. "I don't know how to do that."

"Just be yourself." Dawn shifted from one foot to the other. "Are you annoyed at what I did?"

"No, you did the right thing. Serena and I have to keep interacting if there's any hope of us repairing our relationship." I scratched at my brand. "Do you have plans for dinner? We could continue to catch up then, since I think Serena might come for my head if I stay here much longer."

"I was planning to see Kai before Joey's surgery tomorrow and eat at Ryder Keep . . . but maybe I should let them have some family time." A pause. "Will you be there for the surgery? Kai mentioned he told you about it."

"Wouldn't miss it for anything."

"That settles it, then. I'll come to Kingman Keep for dinner after I see Kai. It'll distract me. Do you need anything?"

"Bowls. We don't have any."

"Bowls?" she questioned.

I cupped my hand as if I were holding a ball. "They look like this."

"Oh! Soup holders!" She smiled broadly and rubbed the back of her head. "Sorry. I must've forgotten that word at some point because of Fabrication use." She hesitated again. "Do you have anything in Kingman Keep?"

"We have a table."

"Let me see what I can do."

I left Margaux Keep the same way I entered, savoring the time alone to collect my thoughts about Serena. Once out of the maze and over the outer wall, I had the day to myself . . . until I saw Dark leaning against the wall, waiting for me.

My Mercenary mentor kept his hair tied back with the sides shaved, his cool grey eyes never revealed his thoughts, and he openly wore a hatchet and one of the twin revolvers. He was tall and made of hard muscle, and overly optimistic: dressed for summer rather than the end of winter. His shadow was nowhere to be seen, absent in the dim light.

After having my memories manipulated by Darkness Fabrications for over a decade, I had begun to take note of everyone's shadow. If only to make sure no one I cared about was suffering the same trauma and fate I had been. My family's shadows were whole and healthy—unlike mine, which had flickered in and out—but since Dark's was currently missing . . . I couldn't know for certain about his own memories yet. The last thing I wanted to do was work with someone who was blind to the truth. But could Darkness Fabricators even have their memories manipulated? I didn't know, but I'd find out soon enough.

"How'd you find me?" I asked as I approached him.

He moved off the wall he was leaning on. "You're predictable."

I'd have to work on that. "What do you want?"

"Did you get the company tattoo?"

I nodded. The skin was no longer raw, but I could still feel Orbis Company's symbol of an ever-burning torch on my inner bicep. Just like the brand of treason on my neck, I had another mark that would shun me from certain circles. I was a Mercenary and would be for the rest of my life . . . whether I liked it or not.

"Do you need to see it?"

Dark shook his head. "Lying about it would only get you killed."

"Always so kind. Are you going to tell me where you were this past month? Or why you made me send a letter about myself to someplace near New Dracon City?"

"Where I've been is my business," he said. "But the letter was for Nonna. It's best not to question her demands. She probably wanted information that would help her catalogue the natural order of events. That's all she ever cares about."

"'The natural order of events'?"

He glanced over his shoulder. "What? You didn't think the Archivists were the only people who tracked the truth through Hollow's lies and Fabrications, did you? How ignorant."

I hated how he could disappear for a month, then make me feel like a moonstruck fool in a few sentences. Was nothing I did good enough for him?

"You're a Mercenary now, Michael. Focusing on Hollow and its struggles will cloud your judgment. People will take advantage of that," Dark said. "Do you know what lies beyond Eham in the Eastern Sea? Or what the title of the leader of the Thebian Empire is?"

I didn't, but I assumed he already knew that.

"You should," Dark said as we reached Refugee Square. "We expect you to up your game, Michael. Consider the Endless Waltz your initiation ritual into Orbis Company. You've proven your worth, but now you need to prove you belong. Which means impressing Orbis Company enough to vote you a full-fledged Mercenary."

"How do I do that?"

"By helping me complete the contract a High Noble wants to offer us."

"Which noble?"

Dark looked at me like I was a child. "Does it matter? Come, it's time for you to start acting like a Mercenary."

5

A GAMBLER'S FOLLY

There's a saying in Hollow: that anyone can rise above their station if they're willing to put the work in. It is, of course, bullshit. A honey-coated lie meant to sedate the masses. If anything, the Goldano saying is closer to the truth: that anyone can become rich and famous if luck is on their side and their soul is for sale.

The Goldani like to think themselves honest, but in reality, they were professional gamblers always seeking the next great thrill. No stakes were too high or morality too shaky for them to take advantage of. And as a result their district was filled with compassionate moneylenders, efficient bonesetters, and fools who knew the taste of gold.

Like our soon-to-be client: High Noble Maflem Braven.

From what Dark told me, High Noble Maflem loved spending his days in the Hollow Gold Vein Casino, betting on whatever suited his fancy. Whenever he wasn't tending to his important religious or noble affairs. Which was most of the time.

The Gold Vein Casino in Hollow had been meticulously designed.

Upon entering, I didn't smell a thing. Which was something that had never happened before. Hollow was on a river, and the smell haunted the city. Except in here. But that wasn't what unnerved me. This place ran with a streamlined efficiency the Royals would kill to have a fraction of.

Burly men with eyebrow piercings transferred chinking sacks of coins to and from tables while attendants made sure no one was without a drink in their hand. All the tables were filled and every game imaginable was here. From roulette and five-finger fillet to whiplash and three brothers.

I stopped briefly to watch as two Low Nobles played a war game and gamblers looked on around them. One was clearly more skilled than the other, but only the Goldani attendants had realized. I knew because they had begun pushing gamblers to bet on the weaker player by proclaiming that the birthmark on his hand was lucky. Judging by how the game was going, the casino would soon make a fortune from their lies. I may not have been the best con man in Hollow, but even I knew easily influenced prey when I saw it.

"Where is High Noble Maflem?" I asked, looking away.

"He'll be surrounded by imbeciles," Dark said. "But we need to find the second-in-command of Orbis Company first. We can't negotiate terms without them."

"Where are they?"

Dark pointed toward a large crowd in one of the corners of the casino. "There."

"How do you know?"

"Because she always makes a scene in public."

I pushed through the crowd to the front. There were two people within the circle. A familiar Goldani ambassador who would shout out a number between one and six and a black woman with her eyes closed, who was stabbing the corresponding spot between her fingers with a knife. She was moving faster than she could be told where to go, and not a speck of blood stained the wooden table below. I held my tongue and watched in awe.

The Mercenary slammed the knife into the table, between her middle and ring fingers. Everyone around us began to clap. Zain Antoun, the ambassador for the Gold Vein Casino in Goldano, the loudest of them all. Can't say I had expected to run into him again.

"Imani," Dark said amidst the cheering. "Isn't this a little excessive?"

She opened one eye, looked up at Dark, and smiled. "Live a little, Dark. Everyone needs some fun now and then. We're Mercenaries, not soldiers."

"I'll remember that line next time you yell at me."

While everyone continued to congratulate Imani on her impressive performance, Zain saw me among the crowd and ran over, embracing me in the tightest hug I had ever received. He smelt of sharp perfume and his blond hair was slicked back with something wet and shiny.

"Michael Kingman! Fate has brought us together once again!" he exclaimed as he kissed my cheeks in quick succession. "What are you doing here? I've been looking for you."

I doubted that was a good thing. "I'm with the Mercenaries. On business."

His smile turned to a frown and he edged us out of the crowds, who were returning to their games. Dark and Imani were talking privately as Zain kept me focused on him.

"I suppose I can't interest you in a game or drink, then?"

"Sadly, not this time, Ambassador. Another day, perhaps?"

Zain ran his fingers through his beard. "I wish, but I return to Goldano tomorrow for the Fate Selection. The new ruling class must be determined, new ambassadors must be chosen, and who knows where I'll end up when it's all said and done. This is a tragedy."

"I'm sure we'll see each other again at some point."

"Oh, we will, Michael Kingman," Zain said slowly. "The only question is when and where. How do you feel about the Night Market in New Dracon City?"

"I don't think I'll be there for a while."

He patted me on the shoulder. "Goldano it is, then. Find me at the Gold Vein Casino."

"If I'm ever there, I will," I promised, and part of me even meant it. Goldano wasn't a place to be without an ally, even if it was Zain Antoun, the man who kept a Skeleton and had sliced out his tongue.

"Good! I wish you well, Michael Kingman. May Lady Luck keep you in her favor until we meet again."

Zain gave me another hug, awkwardly, and then dashed off after someone else. I tried to sneak up on Imani and Dark to overhear their conversation, but Imani caught me before I could with a smile and a firm grip on my shoulder.

"Michael, I see you're in better shape than I last saw you. Shame it had to be under such dire circumstances. Has the wound on your chest healed well?"

"It's fine," I answered. It still hurt when I moved certain ways, but the cut itself had disappeared a long time ago. I didn't scar easily. "My apologies, but who are you?"

Imani turned to Dark and playfully punched him on the shoulder. "Have you been teaching him nothing? What have you been doing for the past month? You were—"

"I've been busy," Dark said forcefully.

"Ah, yes, your infamous trips to lands unknown. How could I forget about those?" she said with a roll of her eyes. Looking at me, she said, "I am Imani Orbis, one of the few people in the world who can tell Dark what to do. Occasionally he does it. Do you have any questions about Orbis—"

Dark crossed his arms. "Imani, can we give him the introduction later? I want to get in and out of here as fast as possible."

Since when did Dark openly show how he was feeling?

Imani thought the same and spoke before I could. "Not a fan of the Goldanis, Dark?"

"They're fine. Maflem Braven, on the other hand . . ."

"I see."

Imani pushed Dark toward a room guarded by house soldiers who wore the Braven family symbol: three cups in a triangle formation.

They let us in without question or direction, and without much delay we walked down a tacky hallway decorated with paintings of past High Noble patrons of this place.

"Both of you remember not to look at his eye," Imani said. "Beorn forgot last time I was here and nearly ruined the whole deal."

"What's wrong with his eye?" I asked.

"He claims he sacrificed it trying to protect his followers from the flesh-eating ticks in the Azilian rain forest," Dark said.

"What actually happened?"

Dark smiled, but it was Imani who answered me: "His mistress stabbed him in the eye with a rusted spoon. He's lucky to be alive."

"Do people actually believe the infection story?"

Imani had her hand on the handle of the door. "Some people will believe in anything if it's said with authority."

We knocked and entered the room. A very slender man who wore robes that seemed absurdly big on him was putting logs into a small fireplace. There were piles of coins on the nearby gambling table, and I saw he had a gaping hole of discolored flesh where his right eye ought to be, and a smile that seemed to be more silver than bone.

Imani stepped forward and motioned behind her back for Dark and me to remain still. "It's a pleasure to see you again, High Noble Maflem Braven."

The High Noble raised a piece of wood toward Imani. She took it from him and placed it in the fire. After the wood had begun to smoke and crackle, Maflem Braven sat down with Imani in a set of plush chairs. We remained by the doors.

"Imani, you do me a great disservice by bringing the king killer here unannounced," High Noble Braven said as he picked up a full teapot. He filled his own cup and then Imani's. It had a strong flowery smell, and Dark's face soured when it reached us. It appalled him so much that he tried to discreetly hold his nose. Even at the risk of insulting our client.

"My apologies, High Noble Braven. But, given the initial details of the contract, it seemed wise to bring the Mercenary who was the most familiar with Hollow customs."

He took a sip from his porcelain cup. "Still. You put me in an awkward situation. Commander Efyra, the Corrupt Prince, or Princess Serena could charge me with treason for associating with him."

"No one will be able to accuse you of such an outlandish idea," she said. "And Dark will be accompanying Michael to any meeting he's at with you."

"How comforting," Maflem said. He picked up a plate filled with tiny cakes and delicacies. Imani took a piece of toast with a sea urchin on it and nibbled at it as he continued, "But I must still ask for some insurance. This is a sensitive task and I require evidence that the king killer won't go around spreading lies about me."

"Dark," Imani said.

Dark grabbed my arm, twisted it up behind my back, and then pushed me down against the back of Imani's chair. I cursed, loudly. I hadn't even seen him move. It seemed that even with Nullify Fabrications, I would always be outmatched by Dark.

Imani finished her toast. "Dark is more than capable of keeping Michael in check. Or do you require further proof?"

Nonchalantly, Dark took the hatchet off his belt and held it against my cheek. Blade inward. The hairs on my neck stood straight.

High Noble Braven waved him off and I was released from my hold. I rubbed my arm and said nothing as I returned to my spot near the door. Dark stood silently next to Imani.

"You were about to explain the details of the contract, High Noble Braven."

"So I was," he said. "Hollow is in a fragile state, between the death of the king and the ever-growing rebellion outside our walls. Supplies are limited, work is scarce, and the High Nobles are doing everything in our power to maintain peace in these troubled times."

Neither Dark nor Imani said anything.

"Thus, sadly, it falls on my shoulders to make sure our city survives. I need you all to determine where these refugees flooding into Hollow are from and whether their arrival is a rebel plot to undermine us or if they truly are upstanding citizens from the outskirts of our country."

Imani reached for the milk and put a few drops of it in her tea. She tested it, nodded to herself, and then said, "To clarify, you want us to determine the origin of these refugees and their allegiance, correct?"

"Correct."

"Is there anything else? Investigating some refugees hardly seems worth the price you're paying us. An Evoker would be cheaper."

"An Evoker," he said, drawing out the name, "has their own allegiances. Country, queen, and all that nonsense. Orbis Company does not, and will do as I wish. Even if the tasks are unethical."

"So you want us to kill them if they're not Hollow citizens," Dark snapped.

"What?" I said without thinking. "You want us to murder the refugees? That's no—"

Dark's hand slapped over my mouth. Imani didn't miss a beat and said, "That's not possible without a sizable further payment. But since you initially said you want us to determine where they're from, I assume we would discuss further actions once we have more information."

"Precisely. At heart, this is a labor dispute. My guilds don't want to employ newcomers when work is already rare enough. We wish to be sure they are who they say they are."

"Completely understandable. Do you have any information for us concerning where they are or who their leaders are?"

"From what I understand, most of them have taken up residence in the remains of the Militia Quarter."

Of course they'd chosen that quarter.

I hadn't spent much time there since Jamal had died. If only I had remembered who Emelia was, maybe I could have saved him. Maybe he'd still be alive. It was my greatest failure, and one I wasn't sure I could ever forgive myself for.

"And their leader?" Imani asked.

"No one has come forward for them. Another reason the High Nobles are suspicious. Who doesn't have a leader?"

"Barbarians," Dark said with a smirk.

"Clearly we're in agreement, then."

"I think we are, High Noble Braven," Imani said as she rose from her seat. "We'll return with more information about the refugees or if we need further clarification about your requirements."

The High Noble remained where he was. "Good. One of my house guards will get half of what we agreed on from the casino. They will allow you and Dark to see me at any time. But not the king killer."

High Nobles always thought they were so clever and cautious.

With nothing more to say, we left. There were no words spoken as we did, only a few hand gestures between Dark and Imani, who pointed to me, then looked as if she wanted to wring my neck with her hands. Hard not to understand what that meant. Thankfully for me, Imani left us before she could follow through with her hand gestures.

Once outside, Dark stretched his arm behind his back and tilted his head to the side. "Do I need to lecture you or can we both pretend I did?"

"Pretending is fine with me."

"It better be. I don't have the energy to deal with an imbecile day in and day out. Be grateful Imani didn't dock you pay after your little outburst in there."

"Wait," I said, "I'm getting paid?"

Dark turned slowly to face me. "Did you think Mercenaries work for free? Remind me, why did I save your stupid life again?"

"I don't know. You never told me. I assume it has something to do with wanting to oppose your father. I'm ready to have that conversation if you are."

He scoffed and shook his head. "I'm not. We don't have the time anyway. I want this job over quickly so I can focus on more important things."

"We have to discuss it at some point."

"Not if I don't want to."

"But I have the right to—"

He moved so quickly, the next thing I knew, his forehead was pushing against my own and I was staring into his grey eyes. "You have been given the right to live this long because of my generosity. I could have let you die in that church. Don't forget that."

I swallowed my pride and anger in that moment. Nothing I could say would make him talk before he was ready. I needed something he wanted, or something on him, before he'd spill any of his secrets. For now, I'd be patient.

Feigning being flustered, I looked away from Dark and edged away slightly. "Militia Quarter, then?"

WAYLAYERS

I don't know why I had expected the Militia Quarter to be in better condition than the last time I had been here, but I had.

How naïve.

But it had changed. What was once a district that showed obvious age and history had now been leveled and replaced with a makeshift city of tents and straw-roofed houses that did little to keep the rain and cold out. It was a good thing winter was nearly over and spring was just a dream away.

My best guess was that the tents that surrounded large black cauldrons and sturdy firepits housed Hollow citizens, while those surrounding freshly dug holes filled with ash and stone circles held the refugees. That was only reinforced when I realized that there were few, if any, tent circles near the destroyed colosseum. After all, who from Hollow would want to live near it? How many had lost friends or family . . .

Dark was doing a better job of keeping himself composed than I was as we walked by all the citizens who had once had homes in the Militia

Quarter. He paid no attention to the wary children who scattered when we drew close, or the piles of half-rotten food people were eating. And the flies, there were flies everywhere.

"How are we going to figure out where the refugees are from?" I asked as I sidestepped a hole in the road.

Dark kept his eyes straight ahead. "We ask them."

"They could lie to us."

"Everyone lies."

"How are we supposed to trust them, then?"

"For a child who figured out who my father really is, you ask a lot of stupid questions."

"Forgive me for wanting to hear something more than 'Come here,' 'Go there,' and 'Follow me,'" I said.

We were close to the colosseum walls. "When you deserve to know more, you will."

I held my tongue as we entered the area that had suffered the most damage during the rebels' attack on Hollow. The rubble and bodies had been cleared out of the colosseum, and most of the dangerous areas had either been blocked off or given a shoddy repair that would hold for a few months. There were tents around the hole left by the initial explosion, and the hole itself was filled with murky water.

How bad was wherever they had come from that they thought this was better?

If it were possible, I would have . . . No, I wouldn't have left Hollow. I'd had the option, before turning myself in following King Isaac's death, to walk away from it all. It was pointless to think this wasn't exactly where I wanted to be.

We made our way over to a circle of refugees sitting on the dirt around an elderly man in faded clothes. They were all very different: some pale, some sun-kissed, some dark, and some with olive skin. But they were all wounded. The luckier ones were missing limbs. Others, like the girl with the hazel eyes to the left of the elderly man, were so covered in bandages, only their irises showed.

Dark broke the circle and stood in front of the elderly man, all eyes on him. "My name is Dark, of Orbis Mercenary Company. Are you the leader of the refugees?"

The man looked up at Dark. His hands were shaking but he said nothing.

Dark repeated his question, this time flashing the pistol obscured by his coat, but still received no response.

"He can't understand you," the bandaged girl next to him said.

"What language does he speak, then?"

"Familial," she said with a slight accent. "But it doesn't matter."

"Why not?"

The bandaged girl tapped the elderly man on the shoulder and made a gesture with her hands. His eyes lit up and he opened his empty mouth. Everything that should have been in there was missing: tongue, teeth, and tonsils included. Only rot remained.

Dark winced and glanced away to the bandaged girl. "He's not your leader, then."

"No, he's not."

"Then who is? Are you?" I asked.

The bandaged girl held herself in a hug. "No."

"We just need to know. We won't hurt you," Dark stated to the circle of people.

Silence, except for the hum of flies.

"That's what they always say," a woman said. "That's what we were told before we fled from our homes."

"Where are you from?" I asked.

Silence. Dark clicked his tongue and looked around at all the refugees. Likely he was trying to determine who would be the easiest to coerce into giving us information. He settled on a pregnant black-haired woman.

Dark knelt in front of her. "If you tell me what I want to know, I can help you. Your child, too. I don't make empty promises, not like the others."

"I know," she said softly. "You're worse. All you want is—"

There was a gunshot, and half her head exploded in a red mist. Dark's eyes widened as bits of the woman's skull spattered his hair and his face. The refugees around us hit the dirt, screaming, and Dark shouted something. I couldn't make it out, but saw him stomp his foot against the ground and a barrier of ice rose to envelop us.

There was another gunshot before the ice roof was fully formed. A bullet ricocheted off a wall, then hit the tongueless elderly man in the back. He took in a sharp breath and went rigid. The inside of our ice dome began to smell like iron.

"Who's shooting at us?" I asked, hearing my heartbeat in my ears.

Dark put his hand against the ice dome he had created. Another bullet lodged in the wall, splintering the ice but not breaking it. "I don't know."

"Shouldn't we be able to see them?"

"Theoretically," Dark said. He turned to me. "I've heard of long-range guns, but I've never seen one until now." A pause. "They're probably shooting at us from the top of the colosseum. Best vantage point in the area. They must be pretty skilled, too."

All the refugees had huddled together in the furthest corner. Part of me wished I could join them.

"How are they so accurate?" I said with a noticeable tremble in my voice. The ability to kill people with a pull of the trigger was terrifying enough. If it became possible for people to shoot at us from a great distance, what was there to stop Angelo from doing that while I wandered through the city?

"Uncertain," he said.

A third bullet hit the ice wall directly in front of where Dark stood. It continued to crack, but Dark's ice held firmer than I thought it would.

"What do we do?"

Dark ran his fingers over the ice. "For starters, don't use your Nullification Fabrications. If you do, I'll get a bullet in the heart. I don't need to explain how annoying that will be for both of us."

Even under constant gunfire, Dark still managed to be a gloating asshole. Remarkable.

To calm myself, I twisted my father's ring around my finger. It lulled me into a sense of familiarity and my breathing began to normalize. I went to Dark's side and looked out toward the shooter. Two more shots struck the ice while I stood by him.

"So," I began, "if you're right, and our gunman is up there, we'll need to reach him to stop his barrage."

"Correct," Dark said. "We're limited with what we can do, Fabrication-wise. Unless you're in close range, your Nullification abilities are useless, and my Darkness Fabrications aren't much better under a midday sun."

I opened my mouth to question about Fabrications, then realized there was a better time to worry about the details. Like when I wasn't being attacked.

"So we're relying on Ice Fabrications," I said.

Dark nodded and crossed his arms. Bullets were sporadically hitting the ice now. The gunner was trying to break the ice with sheer force rather than the precision that had killed the woman and elderly man, and the cracks were spreading rapidly. Unless Dark strengthened it, we didn't have much time.

"Could you create an ice path up?"

"Yes, but we'd have no cover," Dark said. "Given this gunner's accuracy, we'd take a bullet or two to the chest."

I didn't respond, focusing on the remaining colosseum walls. They were cracked and broken, and wouldn't support our weight if we tried to climb up. If Naomi were here, she would be able to get up there with a single hop, just like she had last time. But she wasn't, and we'd have to figure out—

I had an idea.

"Let's knock it down."

"Elaborate," Dark ordered.

"The walls are unstable. It wouldn't take much to bring them down and force the gunner to us. They'll lose most of their advantage without the high ground, and if we can get in close range, we'll take them."

"That plan assumes we don't get shot the moment we leave the dome."

"Do you have a better idea?"

Dark exhaled through his nose. "On three. Don't blink.

"One.

"Two.

"Three."

What Dark did made the attack on the Militia Quarter look like child's play. The ice dome melted in an instant, water splashing down. A bullet whizzed past my head, hit the dirt behind us, and kicked up dust. Dark clapped his hands and then slammed them against the ground, raising a wall of protruding ice and throwing it toward the colosseum walls. It collided with what little of the structure remained with a seismic thud. Ice and stone toppled together as if two titans were locked in a stalemate. But the difference was that one was controlled by Dark, and he was not easily swayed.

Dark clenched his fists, regrowing the parts of the ice wall that had been damaged, and then whipped his hand to the left to destroy the ruins. He kept the ice wall fully formed and constantly renewing until every single trace of the colosseum was gone. Debris fell like crumbly pieces of Celona. As the last of it hit the ground, a wave of dust blew over us, and we heard an ear-piercing howl that got softer and softer as if falling into a bottomless hole.

"Think the gunner is alive?" I asked.

Dark breathed shallowly. His grey eyes flashed red for an instant, just like a tweeker's did while they were high. "If they are, they're hurting right now. They'd have to be . . . unique to survive that."

The word Dark was looking for was "immortal." I would never have believed it if I hadn't seen Domet carve out his guts with my own eyes. I couldn't help but wonder if Dark had met others like Domet. There couldn't be that many out there . . . could there?

"Should we check the rubble?" I asked.

"I'll do it. Check on the refugees. Use the attack to get some information out of them. We need it."

Gun drawn, Dark wandered over to the rubble where our suspected shooter might be. If I heard a gunshot, I'd run to help him. Until then, I went to the bandaged girl, who was checking the elderly man for a pulse. He was gone. The others were dealing with the woman's body. One of them had already begun gathering wood for a pyre.

"Were you close to him?" I asked the girl.

"Not really," she said. "We met on the road coming here. But he was nice. He helped me change my bandages when the burns were still fresh."

"Where'd you come from?"

She shifted and winced afterward. Her every movement brought more pain than I initially realized. How long and how far had she walked to come here? Just to live in a city under siege, drink dirty water, and see a friend die in front of her. Eventually she said, "Why does it matter where we came from? We're here now."

"Someone hired us to find out."

"Are they going to hurt us if they don't like the answer?"

"I don't know. But they definitely will if they don't get it."

"Celona's mercy," she muttered. "So what makes you different from those threatening us?"

I took a deep breath. It was time to see how far-reaching my family had been. "My name is Michael Kingman. Like Dark, I'm a member of Orbis Mercenary Company. But, unlike him, I . . . I promise I'll help you. I've made some mistakes in the past, but I won't let Hollow ignore or bully you when all you need is a little help. You have my word."

The bandaged girl's eyes grew wide. "The person who led us here talked about your family. He said the Kingman were titans among others. That you could catch lightning and divert moon-fall with a wave of your hand." A pause. "Your family is the reason we came here. But everyone here said you were gone, broken, dead, mortal, and incredibly ordinary. That's not true, is it?"

"No, it's true."

The girl's face deflated, but before she could speak again, I continued, "My father was executed for treason and my mother was locked away in an asylum. But we're back now, and we're going to do our best to make things better. Now, please, where are you from? And who led you here?"

"We're from the Warring States," she said, voice firm and clear. "We were driven out by the Sleeper Cultists, and Hollow was our only chance. Olivier Comar brought us here. He'll want to meet you. He'll want to know there are still Kingman."

My heart sank into my stomach. The Warring States were a nightmarish landscape from the mind of daemons. They were a former empire ravaged by loyalists, cultists, and harbingers that was separated into four provinces all vying for control of the greater region after the capital had been petrified. Most of the former rulers had gone missing or died or were encased in obsidian. From the rumors I heard, nothing flourished in that country but despair.

The refugees weren't from Hollow, and High Noble Maflem might force Orbis Company to get rid of them by any means necessary. But maybe he wouldn't . . . and I told myself that lie as I thanked the bandaged girl.

Dark returned with a broken lantern in one hand and what looked like a bag filled with iron balls and vials of gunpowder. There was a scowl on his face.

"No body?"

"No body," he snapped. "I think it was a Waylayer."

I almost scoffed at him. The Waylayers were a mythical league of international assassins. Most, myself included, thought they were as real as dragons or titans. But if Immortals were real, I supposed a league of assassins wasn't much harder to believe in. Though meeting a Toothless Wyvern had proven to me that dragons could stay where they belonged: in imbeciles' imaginations.

"What makes you say that?"

Dark held up the broken lantern and then flipped it over. Scratched in small, scattered letters was the name *Famine*. "It's one of the code names Waylayers use. They like the calamities and downfalls of mankind. But why would there be one here? Attacking me, or the refugees, makes no sense. Which means he was after—"

"Me," I interrupted. "I wonder how much Famine cost Efyra."

Dark laughed and tossed the lantern away. "More than I would have to put a bullet in you." A pause. "Imani needs to know there's a Waylayer operating in Hollow as soon as possible. Come, Michael."

I did as I was told, giving the bandaged girl a wave goodbye before trotting after Dark. Once we had left the ring of debris where the walls had been, Dark said, "Where are they from?"

"What makes you think she told me?"

"You're an imbecile, but you're not inept."

"Fine," I said as we passed a group of gawkers pointing toward the fallen colosseum wall and a vast cloud of dust. It made my eyes water. "I'll trade you the information."

Dark stopped walking. "When you say things like that, I seriously question your sanity."

"You have information I want and you're not giving it to me willingly. What other option do I have? Insult me first if you must, but it won't change anything. Unless you're willing to go back to Imani and tell her you couldn't get any information out of the refugees."

"Well played, Michael. Ask your question."

That was unexpected. I'd thought he would hit me or threaten me, like he had in the past. To have him compliment me, let alone agree to my terms, made me wonder if I was starting to understand how Dark operated.

I'd have to choose my question carefully. Did I ask him about his father? What he wanted, where he came from, or how they had fallen out? Or did I ask him how he was able to use multiple Fabrication specializations? The possibilities were endless, but there was only one thing I was sure Angelo hadn't lied to me about. And that was his wife.

"How did your mother die?"

It was hard to tell if Dark was caught off guard with my question. Statues were easier to decipher than he was. Without looking at me, he said, "My grandfather murdered her by accident. He was trying to kill my father."

"Wait, which grandfather?"

"My mother's father. Edward Naverre. You may have heard of him. Consider that information a freebie."

My mouth hung open. "Wait, you're a Naverre. You're a High Noble! But they were all burned alive in the Annexation of Naverre. That's imposs— Who are you?"

"A Mercenary," he whispered. "Now, where are the refugees from? I want to tell Imani before Lights Out so we can plan our next move."

"The Warring States. Their leader is called Olivier Comar."

"Good. I'll find you tomorrow, Michael, so don't get into any trouble tonight. I don't want to start my day saving you."

Dark left for Little Eham, on the East Side. Who knew why. It was a great place to find rare, exotic goods, though it was cheaper to chop off an arm and a leg than to buy anything there. Alone, and still shocked by his revelation, I began my long walk back home to Kingman Keep. There was still time before dinner, so I took the long way, to understand exactly what this part of the city was going through.

Most of the businesses in the Militia Quarter were closed, large X's painted across the doors to signify their owners had perished. Some were also marked by flowers. But the tweeker population was less prominent than it had been. Only a few dimmers sat on the curbs of the road with Blackberries under their lips, eyes flickering red. I was happy something was going right in this quarter. Even if it was simply that the addicts had found darker places to loiter.

The rebels' attack had left scars on this place that were unlikely to ever recover fully. If I only understood *why* they had chosen to attack this quarter. Why had they killed civilians and Militia members rather than nobles or members of Scales? The attack had done nothing to garner sympathy to their cause. If anything, it had pushed those on the edge to the nobles' side of this rebellion. So what was the purpose? How did it help Emelia stop Domet?

After I crossed the eastern bridge to the Isle, I passed by the abandoned buildings around Kingman Keep. Most were rotting and missing either a wall or roof. Uninhabitable. If my mother wanted to house people in them again, likely they'd have to be torn down or extensively repaired first.

Despite the turmoil of my own life, I dwelt on what I had learned about Dark. His family seemed to be the opposite of mine: filled with murder and betrayal instead of love and loyalty. Even when Lyon and I were at each other's throats, we—I—had never thought of hurting him. That desire was something I never longed to understand, though I still intended to learn more about Dark and Angelo. I'd have to study the Naverre family when I could. Knowing even a little more about Angelo might be useful.

I was deep in thought when I entered Kingman Keep, and it was only as I neared the great hall that I heard the laughter coming from it. Dawn had clearly gotten there before I had, and I wondered how much flak I would get from Gwen for arriving late after having invited someone.

"Sorry I'm late, every—"

I cut myself off. There was an extra guest at the table, one in a similar state to the refugees. My mother was sitting next to the older gentleman, who had wispy salt-and-pepper hair and a nose that was slightly too large for his face, just like Lyon's. There were two guards in the far corner of the room sitting on the floor, eating from bowls. Likely Dawn's house guards.

When my mother noticed me, frozen in the doorway, she left her seat and came to my side. The old man accompanied her, and Lyon, Gwen, and Dawn fell quiet.

"Michael," my mother said, "I'd like to introduce you to Olivier Comar. Your grandfather."

A SICKNESS OF EMBERS

"Grandfather? Grandfather," I repeated, tone changing. "Explain."

"It's pretty self-explanatory," Olivier said with a smile. "I'm your mother's father."

I wouldn't have believed him if he didn't have Lyon's nose and Gwen's weird half smile. And his skin and hair coloring were identical to my mother's. This man, with wrinkled skin and the tips of the fingers of his left hand missing, was my family. It was clear from the way he looked at my mother. The same way she looked at us when she thought we weren't paying attention.

"If you're family," I began, "then where have you been? Where were you when we needed help?"

"Dying," he said. It was hard to tell if he was being serious or not. "Surprisingly, the world does not revolve around the Kingman family. Now, come join everyone at the table. Your mother made dinner and I don't want it to get cold."

Olivier returned to his seat. My mother ran her hand gently down my back before doing the same, and I reluctantly took a seat next to Dawn, across from my sister. Dawn, true to her word, had brought bowls with her to dinner, and Olivier dished out a peppery stew to us all with a smile on his face. We'd have to use bread as cutlery. Although it wasn't exactly proper dining for a High Noble, no one at the table seemed to care.

Once we all had food in front of us, I said, "Why are you here?"

"I came here with the refugees," Olivier said simply. "We've been fighting a losing war for over a decade. Finally realized there was no hope and got as many as I could out."

"Only cow—"

"Michael," my mother growled, "be polite. Father, where's Quinn? Did she choose not to come with you? And is she still married to Bernard? I imagine they must be grey by now with seven sons to take care of."

"Your sister is dead. So is Bernard," Olivier said. "Happened about two years ago. They were fighting the Sleeper Cultists. Died honorably."

"I hope my husband greeted them in the afterlife as family," my mother whispered. "Their children?"

"They all left years ago when they had the chance. I have no idea where they are or if they're still alive."

My mother nodded solemnly.

"So, Olivier," I said as I chewed, "you're the one who led the refugees to Hollow, aren't you?"

He dipped his bread into the concoction in the bowl. "I am."

"Why'd you bring them here? Hollow can't be much better than the Warring States."

Dawn elbowed me in the ribs. I wasn't sure why, but my mother stopped eating and waited for Olivier to answer. I must have struck a nerve.

"Hollow has rebels outside the walls and a shortage of food, water, and life." He finished chewing. "But though our country is on the edge of disaster, the Warring States have already succumbed to it. In the summer province, the duke kidnaps girls and sends them away to a military school that specializes in training poison resistance. For every girl taken, a boy is fed to the wildlife to maintain balance."

"That's barbaric," Lyon declared.

"The summer province is the tamest of the Warring States," Olivier responded. "In the autumn province, where the land is overgrown with jungle, anyone not a parent by their twentieth birthday is forced to clear the rain forest. Most don't last a year. They're taken by an insect-borne disease that turns their blood to stone. If someone is lucky enough to survive five years, they get transferred to the autumn army. You can imagine how that ends."

"And I thought there was no place more brutal than Hollow," Gwen muttered.

"The Warring States were named for a reason," Olivier stated. "Whether you believe it or not, those who made it to Hollow are the lucky ones. There's hope here."

"Not for the people who've been here for years," Lyon said softly. "Especially not after the king's death."

Everyone but my mother had finished eating. She hadn't said much during this conversation, but she had listened intently.

"How come we never knew we were from the Warring States until now?" Gwen asked suddenly. "I'm proud of being a Kingman, but . . . it would have been nice to know that wasn't all I was."

My mother rubbed the back of her neck. "Your father and I made the decision to hide that I was from the Warring States before we returned to Hollow. We were worried that some High Nobles might use my past to undermine your father's position. Especially with how chaotic my home was becoming after the cultists began to take over."

"That doesn't explain why we were never told," Gwen said.

"The Kingman legacy is overpowering," my mother said softly. "When people asked me where I was from, I told them that I had given birth to Kingman children and dined with the Royals like equals, so I was a Kingman and nothing more. I must've said it so many times that I believed in the lie that the person I was before didn't matter and that the world revolved around the Kingman family."

"But it doesn't," Lyon declared.

"It doesn't," she repeated. "But right now it does. We can't walk away from Hollow. Your father gave his life to make sure all of us lived. We owe it to him to protect this city. Once Angelo is in the grave, we can decide what to do about the Kingman legacy together as a family, but until then we are Kingman and we will have our vengeance."

"Spoken like a true daughter of the Familial Empire," Olivier said.

My mother glared at him. "If any of you have questions about the Warring States, I'd advise you to talk to your grandfather. He's the expert. No matter what your grandfather says, I might as well have been born in Hollow."

Neither Lyon nor Gwen seemed satisfied with my mother's explanation about why we had been kept from learning about her side of the family. But rather than dwell on that any longer, I had one more question, and it was going to be the most uncomfortable. "Olivier, what did you mean when you said you were dying?"

"That I am," he said without hesitation. Olivier pulled up his dirty sleeve and laid his right arm out on the table. At a distance, the markings on his skin could have been mistaken for tattoos. However, the red lines on his skin were moving and wiggling as if insects had burrowed into him, multiplied, and were now struggling to get out. It was hard to tell exactly where the lines ended, but they easily went past his elbow.

"What is that?" Gwen asked.

"My doctors in the Warring States called it the Corruption. It's incurable. When these red markings cover my face, I'll die."

"The doctors here are better than those in the Warring States," my mother said at once. "We'll try everything. We won't give up on you on their say-so."

"Thank you, Juliet. But I've already tried everything. Only the Church of the Eternal Flame seems to have any idea how to cure it, but they're being evasive—"

"We'll do whatever it takes, Papa."

I had to hide my smile by looking down into my bowl. Even Olivier was powerless to struggle against my mother's concern and commands. It was nice to see it wasn't just me and my siblings she could do that to.

"I warned you about Michael's questioning nature. Now there are other concerns we must address while the entire family is in attendance. High Noble Margaux, if you're not comfortable with hearing this, you can leave. Otherwise, I'll assume you're with us," my mother said as she rose from her chair at the head of the table. When Dawn didn't move, we had our answer. As quickly as she could, my mother recounted our meeting with Efyra earlier in the day. Out of everyone, only Lyon looked visibly uncomfortable with the news. Maybe his succession conversations with our mother recently hadn't gone very well.

"How can we possibly get enough evidence to prove Michael didn't kill King Isaac?" Gwen asked no one in particular.

My grandfather stared at me. He must not have heard this detail when he arrived in Hollow. How many more times would the shadow of a dead king fall across me? "I didn't do it. The king killed himself," I said flatly.

He seemed to accept that.

My mother placed her hands on the table. "Our first concern is to restore Kingman Keep to its former glory. I'm currently searching for people willing to work for us. Once we have enlisted some help, we'll need to repair the houses outside. Wait. Father"—she turned to him—"what are you planning to do in Hollow? I just assumed—"

My grandfather simply crossed his arms, nodded, then motioned for her to continue. Even our extended family seemed to share the traits I had spent my life living: family looks out for family.

My mother continued with a smile. "To ensure we don't repeat mistakes we've made in the past, I think we should . . ." She trailed off, staring at the two guards who had been sitting in the corner as they approached Dawn. One of them whispered something in her ear that made her sigh dramatically. "I apologize, everyone," she said. "It seems I must excuse myself. My guards have been instructed by my father to bring me home before Lights Out. He is nervous of rebel attacks, it seems."

"I'll show you out," I said. Before anyone could question it, I had gently taken Dawn's hand and we ran out of Kingman Keep together. I only let her go once we had emerged into the cold night air, having left her guards behind temporarily. We would only have a few moments of privacy.

"Subtlety isn't your strength, is it, Michael?" Dawn said as she straightened her shirt.

"Not really."

"What's wrong?"

"It's compli . . ." I trailed off into silence, remembering all that had happened to me recently and how much easier things would have been if I had been truthful to my friends. "Orbis Mercenary Company has been charged by a High Noble with investigating the refugees. Now I learned their leader is my grandfather. I'm worried the investigation will end in violence if we can't convince the High Noble otherwise, but if I disobey my company's orders, they'll abandon me and the princess will execute me shortly after."

"Oh," she said.

"Exactly."

Dawn thought for a moment. "Can you change the rules?"

"What?"

"Change the contract. If you're sure it's about to end in disaster, convince your company to side with the refugees instead of the High Noble." A pause. "The noble isn't either my father or stepmother, correct?"

"No, it's not."

"Good, then see if Orbis can change sides."

"But how? The High Noble will have access to far more money than the refugees," I said. Her guards had caught up to us, and neither looked happy about their sprint through Kingman Keep.

"It's not always about—" She swallowed her word. "It's not always about coin, Michael."

"It is to Mercenaries."

"Is it? Even to Dark?" she questioned as she began to walk away with her guards. "You like to think you're clever. Find another solution."

That was easily one of the nicest compliments I had received in a long time. It was amazing how, once I started thinking before acting, people actually treated me like I was capable of impressive feats rather than just insulting me for my stupidity like they had during the Endless Waltz. I deserved it, but it still stung.

By the time I returned to the great hall, it was deserted but for Olivier, who was cleaning up the bowls and pot. He looked up, saw me, and said, "Everyone retired for the night. Your ma wanted everyone to get a good night's rest. There will be a lot to do tomorrow to begin to rebuild."

There always was. I bid him good night and went to the room I shared with Gwen. She had already lit the fire and was curled up in front of it. I pulled a blanket across the floor to do the same. I waited for my sister to say something about dinner, but she was already asleep, snoring slightly.

Though I tried, sleep never found me. I was too worried about how I was going to save my grandfather from High Noble Maflem Braven to rest. And at some point in the middle of the night, when the fire had died and Gwen slept haphazardly spread out, the screech of a chair across flagstones rang through the empty keep.

Already awake, I went to investigate.

———————

My grandfather was sitting near the table in the great hall with a lit lantern and a jug of water in front of him. I took the seat across from him.

"Couldn't sleep?" I asked.

"Never tried to," he said. "Water? No cups. You'll have to drink from the jug."

No cups. No paintings. No beds. And it still felt more like home than Angelo's ever had. I took a drink of water, the coolness easing a minor headache, then said, "What were you doing if not attempting to sleep?"

"Meeting with the people I led here. A few of them were staying by the colosseum when one of the walls collapsed. Two of them even died."

"My condolences."

"Thank you," he said. "It truly is a shame. Especially when I learned they had been shot, not crushed by falling debris. It seems two Merce-naries came to interrogate them and brought an assassin with them. One of them even matched your description. Anything you want to tell me, Michael?"

I shifted in my seat and folded my hands on the table. "We didn't bring the assassin with us. We were just there to learn where you all were from and to make contact with the refugee leader. I believe the assassin was there to kill me. Saw an opportunity and took it." I rubbed my brow, a familiar weight on my shoulders again. "Two people died because of me."

"The assassin killed them, not you. But the rumors I heard weren't exaggerated, then. Everyone really is after your head."

"The bounty is two hundred suns," I said. "I can't really blame any-one who tries to collect it."

"Why is Orbis Company interested in refugees? A Mercenary com-pany only takes an interest if they're looking for recruits or have been hired to."

"It was the latter."

My grandfather leaned back in his seat and closed his eyes, hands behind his head. "Who?"

"Does it matter? I'll protect you. Family looks after—"

"What about the rest of the refugees?"

I didn't respond at first, the hoot of an owl outside the windows the only noise. "Why do they matter to you?"

"Because they put their trust in me," my grandfather said quietly. "I won't abandon them just because I'm safe. They look to me for protec-tion and I will not abandon them simply because that isn't convenient anymore. That's not how leaders operate. Your father should have taught you that much. Or maybe he was still as hopeless a teacher as he was when we met."

Throughout my childhood men had tried to act as my father figure with the intention of manipulating me into the person they wanted me to be. And after what happened recently, I didn't trust any man who wanted to give me friendly advice. Some childhood traumas were like sunburns, others like broken bones, the most extreme like scars—faded but not forgotten.

"My father gave his life to protect our family." I clenched my knuckles and felt my face get hot. "Don't you dare belittle his memory. Family or not, I'll slam your head against the table if you do."

"Then don't tarnish his memory by acting like a child," my grandfather snapped. "Family is family, but that doesn't mean you can abandon everything else in the world to protect them. If anything, your ancestors knew the importance of putting the rest of the world first. They did what had to be done, regardless of how much they would lose."

"You talk like an observer to history, not part of it, old man."

My grandfather coughed up ash and spat embers, as if a strong flame were ablaze in his belly. It was an awful wet hacking sound, as if he were about to choke up his lungs. He was easily loud enough to wake others, and it was then I realized why his veins were so red and protruding. They were inflamed by whatever was going on in his body. It wasn't a Fabricator's body, rather something twisted and corrupted, and a clear death sentence. Maybe medicine couldn't heal him. Was he being truthful when he said only the Church of the Eternal Flame might know of a cure?

"Old man," he repeated. "I like it. No one's ever called me that before. My own children were too respectful, but not my grandson, it seems."

"I'm nothing if not entertaining."

"And I'm nothing if not truthful. If you don't believe me, clearly you've been spoon-fed lies for a majority of your life."

I stood up, hands on the table, and leaned toward him. "A truer statement than you probably realize."

My grandfather mimicked my stance. "Do you want to hear more? What else didn't your father teach you? Do you know he—"

"Father."

We both turned toward my mother, who stood at the other end of the table, hair disheveled and an expression that was not one of patience in that moment. Some of the tension bled out of us.

"Father," she repeated. "Go to bed. You, too, Michael. Don't wake me up again."

She left, confident neither of us would disobey her. But my grandfather couldn't help but give one last piece of advice: "If you only protect those who you consider family, you have no right to call yourself a Kingman. That wasn't their legacy, but it may be yours. Be better, Michael."

His words stung, and I stayed at the table even after he was long gone. Choosing to die to protect my family had been easy. Living up to the legacy of my ancestors would be much, much harder.

What was I going to do?

There was only ever one thing *to* do: move forward. I may not have had the answers as to what I was going to do with the refugees if we were ordered by High Noble Braven to . . . drive them off, but I knew I needed to know everything about the Naverre family as soon as possible to see whether Dark had been lying to me. Maybe if I had leverage against him I could convince him to save Olivier and the refugees. It was a desperate plan, but it was the only one I had.

Since I was already wide awake, I might as well use my time wisely and visit the only man who could help me.

Symon Anderson, the self-proclaimed King of Stories, and the man who held my legacy to ransom. What a joy this conversation was going to be.

A TRANSFER OF TRUTHS

The Hollow Library had changed little since my last visit as a runaway king killer bartering my story to a man obsessed with destroying my legacy in exchange for a chance to save my mother. In the end, the risk had been worth it. My mother was cured. But my survival had been unforeseen. Who knew how Symon had taken that.

I snuck through the library as I had before, following exactly the same route. None of their security had changed, much to my relief, and soon I was at the door to the Archmage room.

I had barely cracked the door open when Symon called, "Enough dramatics, Michael, come in."

"For the self-proclaimed King of Stories, you don't seem to like them very much," I said as I closed the door behind me. Symon was sitting at the table in the center of the room, surrounded by dozens of journals written by an Immortal. He was wearing the trademark red robes, his hood down and revealing his receding hairline. His fingertips were stained black from ink, and the pen in his hand moved across the page with a speed many swordsmen would be jealous of.

"Take a seat, Michael. As always, we have much to discuss."

Once I was seated, I said, "I thought you'd be angry that I survived."

"Oh," he laughed. "I am. Furious, actually. You're lucky you didn't come by earlier. I'd considered putting a knife through your eye rather than deal with your nonsense any longer."

"The princess might make you a noble if you do."

"I'm aware. It's a shame those kinds of achievements mean nothing to me. It's history itself I want." He paused to set his pen down, then gently fanned the sheet of paper to dry the ink and moved it to the stack beside him. "That's the last page of your story. Written into the narrative I seek to tell about you and your family. Do you want to read it?"

"Not really," I said. "I doubt it's very pleasant."

"Not pleasant in the slightest," he said with another laugh. At least Symon finishing transcribing my story explained why he seemed so happy. It was unsettling. "I was planning on distributing it after your execution. You've forced me to delay that, which is an inconvenience, but I have greater plans now."

"No doubt they involve me."

"They do, but I won't ruin the surprise." Symon showed all his teeth in another freakish grin. "Why are you here, Michael? I thought I'd have to chase you down."

"I need information."

"Of course you do," Symon said, running his tongue over the gap in his teeth. "What about?"

"The Naverre family."

Symon's eyes narrowed. "Interesting choice. What do you have to barter with? Remembering that I already have one question over you."

"What do you want?" I asked.

"Isn't it obvious?"

There was no way I was going to like his clarification, and yet I said, "Clarify it. To be sure there's no mistake."

"I want your story, Michael. Every scrap of it. I control one part of it already, but I have a feeling it's just the beginning. You're a Kingman Mercenary in a period of unforeseeable political unrest. You're going to be in the middle of it all until you either die or . . ." He trailed off.

"Or what?"

"You prove my predictions right and take the throne for yourself."

It was almost unheard of to insinuate that a Kingman would sit on a throne. For most of my life, even after my father had been executed and we had been branded, I had thought the same. Then I remembered swearing to Trey that I would help the princess retain her throne so long as she deserved it . . . and that if not, a Mercenary King would be crowned. It was the only way I could think of to save Hollow. Desperate times called for desperate measures.

But Symon didn't need to know that, so I recited a famous phrase: "Kingman stand beside the throne."

"In the past, yes. When Kingman weren't also king killers. Or Mercenaries. Before you."

I leaned back in my chair and crossed my arms. "For someone who hates my family, you seem to have a lot of respect for me. Which is novel. Everyone hates me."

Symon brushed his finger over the stack of papers at his side like a jailer making sure their prisoner's chains were tight. They were his words but my story. A curse for both of us. "I value the potential of your story. With my help, it could become the greatest story ever told. Rather than a forgotten footnote in history when you are no longer the name on every-one's lips."

"I only gave you so much because I was desperate. I'm not desperate today. Name something else."

"You don't have a say in that matter, Michael. Either you give me your tale willingly or I will take and twist it until people are unable to tell fiction from fact," Symon said as he rose from his seat. He moved to a bookcase, hesitated, and then took a journal from the shelf. After turning to a page, he put the book in front of me so I could read it. "Second-to-last paragraph."

I pulled it close.

> *Whatever Michael Kingman has been, or will be, his path*
> *toward a king killer was set at an early age, and completely*
> *and utterly unavoidable. He might like to claim that he did only*
> *what was necessary to survive in a city that wished to see him*
> *dead, but how true is that? Michael likes to present himself*
> *as a gallant rogue. Is that merely a façade for something more*
> *sinister? There's strong evidence to suggest so. Because when we*
> *look at his actions as a child, the answer is clear.*

"This meant to be a threat?" I asked.

"Clearly."

"How do I know you're not bluffing?"

"The green-and-white-striped house."

I closed the book and said nothing. I desperately wanted to pull at my collar to get some air on my skin. Symon had found the absolute last thing I had wanted him to. The insufferable prick.

"Here's what I propose, Michael," the King of Stories began. "A question for a question for as long as answering is beneficial for both of us. No lies or omissions. Only the absolute truth. If you try to conceal something or paint your actions in a kinder light, I will write your story as I see fit. Whether you like the way it's presented or not."

"What about the question you already have over me?"

"You'll know when I decide to use it," Symon said. "Ask as many questions as you desire. I'll ask an equal number of my own once you're done. No need to go back and forth when we've both accepted how much we need each other."

I hadn't expected to get out of this encounter with Symon without losing something that I valued. So far, it was going about as well as possible. He was still holding my story—my legacy—hostage, but I would have input into it. Maybe I could influence what he wrote without his knowing. Paint me and my family in a better light than he necessarily wanted it to appear. Was there a way to manipulate him while telling the truth? I was going to find out soon enough.

"Who were Edward Naverre's children?"

"Does Domet's book not have information about them?"

"No," I said. "Which, in hindsight, should have made me suspicious. But I was too much up my own ass to realize what isn't said is more important than what is."

Symon picked up a quill and started writing on a fresh piece of paper. When he was done, he slid it across the table to me. I read quickly.

Edgar Naverre—Eldest. Son of Georgina Boleyn—Suicide by extreme distress

Patrick Naverre—Second eldest. Son of Georgina Boleyn—Suicide by hanging

Katherine Naverre—Middle child. Daughter of Jane Cityborn—Poisoned

Edgill Naverre—Second youngest. Son of Elizabeth Cleves—Burned to death by rebels

Evelyn Naverre—Youngest. Daughter of Elizabeth Cleves—Trampled by a horse

I had never known the name of Angelo Shade's dead wife. He had never mentioned it and none of my siblings had ever pushed him to find out. We refrained out of respect. What a mistake that had been. I needed to narrow it down between Katherine and Evelyn.

"Was either Katherine or Evelyn married?" I asked.

"There's no record of either of them ever being wed."

That was unsurprising. It would have been too easy a way to determine which of them was Dark's mother. But with every question I asked, Symon would be able to ask just as many. His would be much more dangerous than mine.

"Were either of them mothers, or with child, at the time of their deaths?"

"Both were," Symon said. "High Noble Katherine's pregnancy was nearly complete when she died. The records show the doctors tried to save the child. The Archmage himself was brought in from Hollow for aid. But, in the end, neither mother nor child survived."

"And Evelyn?"

"High Noble Evelyn took an arrow in the back while riding with a suitor, High Noble Elliot Castlen. She might have survived the arrow, but her horse crushed her head in her fall. Her pregnancy was only discovered after death."

Both women fit the little information I had about Angelo's wife and Dark's mother, and, with pregnancies outside wedlock, both had their secrets. I didn't have another way to narrow it down between them, so I would have to regroup at a later point when I had more information. Thus I said, "I'm done with my questions."

"My turn," Symon said with a smile. "First question: the boy you claimed to see as you were drowning fits the description of Davey Hollow. Was it Davey?"

I crossed my arms. "Yes, it was."

"Interesting. Second question: What is your noble nickname?"

"My noble nickname?" I repeated.

"Save me your feigned ignorance. All you High Nobles have them. 'Kyros' to 'Kai.' 'Gwendolyn' to 'Gwen.' 'Lyonardo' to 'Lyon.' 'Cyrus' to 'Cy.' There are only two of the new generation I don't know. Yours is one of them."

"Because I didn't have one."

"I don't believe you."

"Don't you think someone would know it if I did? Everyone always called me Michael no matter how—"

"The other I'm missing is Princess Serena's. Strange coincidence, is it not, that a Kingman and Royal who were bound together seem to be the only two who didn't participate in a long-standing Hollow tradition?"

I leaned toward Symon, smiling. "We were always the exceptions to the rule. We thought it would make us special. Unique. That means more to a Kingman and Hollow than you could ever know." I sat back. "Ask Serena if you don't believe me. I'm sure she'd love to talk about her childhood memories of me."

Symon muttered something rude under his breath and then continued. "Last question: What is your current relationship with your former foster father, Angelo Shade?"

It's a clusterfuck.

Instead I said, "Strained. He's not adjusting well to not having us around. Think he thought of us as his children."

"That's a lie," Symon snapped. "I know most of what happened in that church. You were going after him. Why?"

Since Symon already knew everything that had led up to that point in the church, I filled in what he was missing. Like a true Archivist, he never commented or added his own bias, only nodding and asking for clarification once or twice. He didn't seem surprised by any of it, which made me wonder how much he knew. Or suspected.

"That's all I have," Symon said when he had finished writing. "For now."

With all the animosity between us, I may have underestimated Symon. He wasn't one who waged wars with swords and guns like the Corrupt Prince or the emperor. Even Domet, with all his money and status, wasn't comparable to him. Symon's power lay in the past, present, and future. History was his to control, and that was more frightening than most realized. Everyone says history is written by the winners. But in Hollow it was written by this man. This self-proclaimed King of Stories who could erase families and events from the records simply because he didn't like them. Knowledge was power, and he had unlimited access to all of it. I would have to start taking him more seriously.

"As pleasant as this has been, I should go," I said. "You know me: kings to kill, children to terrorize and all that."

Surprisingly, that elicited a small laugh from Symon. And people didn't think I was funny. "That's fine, Michael. I have more to do before normal operating hours begin. If you don't mind, have someone prepare a room for me in Kingman Keep."

"What?"

"I told you. So long as you live, I will be watching. Living in Kingman Keep only makes that easier for me and harder for you to hide. I'll need a room close to yours."

"You do realize how decrepit Kingman Keep currently is?"

With a shrug he said, "Sometimes one must suffer in order to achieve greatness. You should sympathize with that."

"Less than you may think."

"I'll see you tonight, Michael."

With nothing left to discuss, I left the Archmage room and snuck back out of the library. The sun was rising, the city was covered in a soft orange light. Not wanting, for once, to disappoint my Mercenary mentor, I took the most direct route back to Kingman Keep through the Hanging Gardens. I hadn't been back there since the night it all began, but as I passed under the trees that cast this area in darkness, through the reek of rotten flesh, I couldn't help but glance up at all the bodies hanging from ropes, most of them as purple as morning glories. Some of them innocent and some guilty. I seared this scene into my mind, a memory I would never forget.

This wasn't my city. It hadn't been mine for nearly a decade. It had been warped and twisted into something that was nothing like the splendor and beauty I had heard about in childhood stories. I owed Hollow nothing. But if I didn't act, there would soon be refugees hanging next to these rebels simply because some people said they didn't belong.

Being a Mercenary didn't mean I had to be inhumane. It was time to change the city and rewrite the rules as I saw fit.

Symon could control history all he wanted to. I would control what he wrote about.

As was tradition.

A MERCENARY'S OATH

"Say that again. With less idiocy this time."

"I think we should protect the refugees regardless of what the High Noble says today," I said, hoping Dark didn't notice that my voice cracked as I made the plea. I was more than a little nervous.

Dark stood over me, arms crossed as he pressed his tongue against the inside of his cheek. "I said without the idiocy. Try again. I know you're slow."

"We should protect the refugees."

"Are you an imbecile?" Dark snapped, grabbing me by the collar and slamming me back against the wall. My breath was short and brought pain. Dark glowered at me. "We're *Mercenaries*. We work for money. We don't get a say in what we do and you knew that when you signed up. Don't make me regret saving your life. Whatever it is you're after, try again."

"What if the refugees had something more valuable than anything High Noble Braven could offer us?"

"That's unlikely," he said, turning away.

"But what if they did? Then would you listen?"

"Yes," he said, and I knew he meant it.

"Then I think we need to talk, Mercenary," a familiar rough voice said from behind us.

My grandfather was standing in the open doorway of the room where Dark and I had met. I'd suggested this to him when I'd returned, now I could only hope it worked. Dark had already agreed to consider a better deal. My grandfather would just have to offer him something more valuable than a hoard of gold.

"Who are you?" Dark asked.

"Olivier Comar, leader of the refugees." He paused and glanced at me. "And that boy's grandfather."

"My condolences."

"I appreciate it," my grandfather said. "Can we talk like gentlemen?"

Dark made a dismissive noise with his tongue. "If we must."

Olivier motioned for Dark to sit on the ground with him, and he did so cross-legged. "Let me get to the point, Mercenary. My grandson tells me that when your High Noble employer learns we're not from the outskirts of Hollow, there's a chance he will order you to get rid of us using whatever methods are necessary. Is that correct?"

Dark nodded. I had cautiously taken a seat on the floor between them. I wasn't going to choose between family and being a Mercenary. No matter what, I was going to make sure I could be devoted to both. My father's ring felt heavy on my finger and I knew I had done the right thing. I had no idea what Olivier would offer Dark, but hopefully he could pull this off.

"Is there any chance you would lie and say we are from Hollow? None of these High Nobles knows anything about the more rural areas of this country. If you say it, they would believe it."

"Orbis Company is known for its honesty. I won't change that."

"I understand," my grandfather said. "Then let me make an offer. I have reason to believe I know the identity of the Waylayer that attacked

you and murdered two of my people. We picked up a few stragglers between the Warring States and Hollow. Likely, Famine was one of them."

"What proof do you have?" Dark asked.

"They went by the name Mocking Bird, and I can identify them for
you."

There was no fluctuation in his voice when Dark said, "A name isn't
proof of anything."

"Quite right," my grandfather said. "It was the stories that they told
that raised eyebrows. They spoke of meeting with a man in Hollow who
sought to defile God's creation and reverse death itself."

"They planned to meet my father," Dark muttered as he stood.
"I've heard enough. Come with me, Michael. We will meet High Noble
Braven this morning and discuss further steps now that we know where
the refugees are from."

Dark was back to treating me like a dog, it seemed. Some things were
eternal. We left in such a hurry that I had no chance to share a parting
word with Olivier or tell my mother where I was going. Thankfully, I had
already told Olivier early that morning while relaying to him what Orbis
Company had been tasked to do that we would soon have another guest
at Kingman Keep. He found it humorous and agreed to give Symon a
room close to mine whenever the renovations were complete. Perfect.

We didn't speak as we walked toward the Gold Vein Casino, only
stopping so Dark could piss in an alley. Dark's silence was almost eerie,
and I wondered if Olivier had struck a nerve with my Mercenary mentor. If so, I'd have to take notes. The best I'd ever managed was to elicit
a snarky comment.

When the casino was in our sight, Dark snapped at me, "Say nothing
while I'm talking unless directly commanded to."

For once Dark didn't ask me if I understood, assuming that I did. He
was behaving oddly today. All his mannerisms were off, and as we crossed
the casino floor to meet High Noble Braven, I had absolutely no idea what to
expect. Maybe that was for the best. Dark knocked at the door to the inner
sanctum, heard a response, and entered. I was directed to wait by the door.

High Noble Braven was breaking his fast when we arrived. There was a large tray before him bearing toast slathered with butter, oats in milk and honey, a grilled peach, and bacon charred almost to death. It was enough food to feed multiple people, and yet I doubted he was going to share with any of the people starving in Hollow.

"Mercenary Dark, a pleasure to see you so soon. Do you have some answers?"

"Yes, sir," Dark began. "The leader of the refugees is a man named Olivier Comar. He's a spring man from the Warring States. The people with him are a mix from each province, intent on escaping the war that encompasses everything there."

High Noble Maflem set down his cutlery, tearing a piece of toast with his fingers instead. I could see the melted butter glisten off them from where I was. "What a tragedy for them. If only Hollow were in a better place to support them."

"If it informs your decision, sir, I don't think they're of a violent nature. They just need a place to stay."

"But living in the city is costly, Mercenary," Maflem said as he stuffed the toast into his mouth. He sprayed crumbs as he spoke. "Where are we supposed to house them? Who will employ them? We have enough trouble supporting our own people. The refugees will only drag us down further. Hard decisions must be made."

"What would you like Orbis Company to do, sir?"

The High Noble took a sip of water and swallowed whatever was in his mouth. "We must get rid of them."

"Sir," Dark said, "I'll need confirmation that Orbis Company won't incur the wrath of the Royalty or the other High Nobles in carrying out your wishes regarding the refugees. We are a secular state and do as we wish, but the Kingman has earned us more than enough enemies recently."

"Orbis Company will come under no scrutiny," Maflem declared with a smile. "Sadly, it is better to ask forgiveness rather than permission where the Royalty is concerned, and I will bear this pain to be sure Hollow survives this blight on our economy. The Archivists will understand I did what had to be done."

Not if I had any say in it. I would make sure this pathetic excuse for a man was remembered exactly as he ought to be, if he commanded us to do the unspeakable.

"Understood, sir," Dark said. "What would you like us to do with the refugees?"

"Order them to leave Hollow within the week," High Noble Maflem said. "To show them we're serious, kill anyone who openly opposes your orders. Their leaders will probably have to be hanged, but some members of Scales owe me favors. They can have the leaders in the Hanging Gardens within a day. If there is a single rumor of the refugees joining the rebellion in retaliation, we may have to take more drastic measures."

High Noble Maflem took his napkin from his lap, set it down beside his tray, and continued. "Upon further consideration, any man or woman of a sufficient standard of beauty may stay. I'll have to send one or two of my own servants down to inspect the stock and pull out the best of them. There are a great many places and uses for beautiful things."

"And the children, sir?"

"The children," he said to himself. "How many are there?"

Dark shook his head slightly. "It was hard to tell which were citizens of the East Side and which were refugees. Likely a decent number."

"The East Side will overrun us if we're not careful," he said with a snarl. "A problem for another day. If the children run, let them. The ones that stay will leave if their families do. That seems reasonable. Do you have any further questions of me, or should we move on to payment negotiation?"

"I have enough information, sir," Dark stated. "I regret to inform you that Orbis Company declines the updated contract you have presented. It does not suit us. You will be charged for the work we've done so far."

I pushed my tongue hard against the roof of my mouth to mask my smile. Olivier's information had been enough to bring Dark to our side.

High Noble Maflem wasn't pleased. "What?"

"I think I made myself clear, sir."

"You work for me, you cannot—"

"We have completed the job initially offered to us," Dark interrupted, standing straighter. "My commander agreed we would discuss further instructions once the first stage was complete. We have decided to reject your further proposal."

High Noble Maflem slammed his hands down on his desk, shaking toast to the floor like the overblown villain in a story. "Imani will hear of—"

"Imani will agree with my decision. You have nothing sufficient to offer in exchange for driving the refugees off. We're not Regal Company, and this is not Vurano."

"Fine," he said as he collapsed back into his seat. "I will find others who will accomplish what I desire. Leave. Immediately."

"With pleasure. An officer of Orbis Company will collect the payment already owed," Dark said.

High Noble Maflem ignored him, stuffing his face with his remaining breakfast. He was flushing bright red, and when the door closed behind us, he screamed in annoyance and threw something against the wall. Two of the guards in the hallway rushed to his aid.

Once we were out of the casino, it was hard to contain my excitement, and I said the only thing I could to Dark: "Thank you."

"Don't," he said as we walked through the streets.

There were beggars on the street asking for food and money. I gave them what I could. The effects of an open rebellion outside the walls were beginning to be visible even in the wealthier parts of the city.

"We were opposed to the contract from the beginning. Imani left it up to me to handle. Your grandfather only made my decision easier."

"So do you think the Mocking Bird was talking about meeting your father, then?"

"Ever since my mother died, my father has been determined to bring her back to life. If he had to, he would destroy the world to do it, and he'd sit with her among the ruins with a smile on his face," Dark explained. "His love for my mother is catastrophic."

Did I know anything about Dark or Angelo that might indicate who his mother was, Katherine or Evelyn? Any detail . . . and then I realized I knew who it was. How had I been so blind to miss it? The only thing I knew for certain about Angelo was how much he hated the smell of tea. And, like many things, Dark shared the trait with his father.

"Your mother was Katherine Naverre, correct?" I asked. That was why he and Angelo had such an aversion to tea. Katherine must've died by drinking poison in some.

Dark put his hands in his pockets. He didn't look in my direction. "Lucky guess."

"I've done my research. You might as well tell me what happened. The more I know about your father, the better."

Dark made an exasperated sound. "Angelo and I were struck with a terrible stomach sickness while we still lived in Naverre. My mother was nursing us back to health despite her pregnancy, and my grandfather made us tea that was supposed to ease our stomachs. She tried it, to test the flavor, and when she didn't like it, went to brew some more while we slept. When we woke we were told that she had been stricken with a sickness so terrible, she had begun to bleed from her eyes and nose. A week later she was dead. My prematurely birthed sister died a day later. My father was grief-stricken and suspicious, and when he learned the truth, he swore his revenge on the entire Naverre family."

"But they're dead now. Why does he continue his vendetta against the High Nobles? Just because of what one family did?"

"When the people who are supposed to love you unconditionally betray you . . . it twists your humanity. It makes you see enemies everywhere you go. To find love afterward is hard. Revenge is easy," Dark stated.

But he didn't say it as if he were remembering his father's actions. He spoke as I had, before my execution. Like a dead man who had resigned himself to his fate, intent on doing one last thing before departing. What had I missed with Dark?

"But that doesn't explain—"

"Enough about my family," he said. "I need to confer with Imani, and you have errands to do."

Dark handed me a list with places and things written on it, from determining whose Wanted posters were hanging in the Upper Quarter to getting three bottles of Thebian wine. It was nothing of vital importance, which meant Dark was trying to keep me preoccupied or out of trouble. Probably a little of both. I took the list without complaint and watched as Dark's face scrunched at my silence. Little did he know I was already scheming about how I was going to get it done quicker than he wanted me to.

"Finish before we meet up at Kingman Keep. I must meet with your grandfather—today or tomorrow, whenever I have time—and make sure he remembers he owes me what he promised. Be aware, unless we get another contract in Hollow, we may depart within the month."

"Depart Hollow?"

Dark nodded. "How many times, Michael? We're Mercenaries. We go where the work is. What? Did you think you'd spend your entire life in Hollow? Even when you joined Orbis Company?"

"I was just—"

"I don't care. Make sure your affairs are in order. There's no place like a new place."

10

YLWE HVBJ YLWE
LJ VLKFS

Dark's errands took less than an hour to complete rather than half a day like he probably expected them to. Rather than go to the East Side and check up on the refugees, I went to a nearby bakery and learned as much—if not more—in a single conversation with the baker's daughter, Em, than I would have all day. And she gave me half a loaf of black bread for free when I shared some High Noble gossip. Getting three bottles of Thebian wine was a little trickier, but with runners not having much post to deliver, it was easy to convince one to retrieve it from the embassy for me. It didn't even cost that much.

After finding out whose Wanted posters were in the Upper Quarter—mine, Dark's, Emelia's before it was revealed the emperor was a woman, and that of a rather eccentric-looking man who wouldn't stop harassing nobles about a man being on the moon—I was left with a little bit of time before I had to go to the hospital to check up on Joey's surgery.

And since I was so close to the Church of the Eternal Flame, I would have felt like a hypocritical dick if I didn't try to investigate whatever was killing Olivier.

Rian Smoak, Domet's friend, or enemy, or whatever, was at his office even if the rest of his church was taking a midday rest, dreaming of flames licking at heathens' heels. Scholars always seemed to sacrifice sleep for potential breakthroughs, and I was happy to see that Rian followed that trend.

When I swung the door open, I was greeted by a potbellied man with mismatched-color eyes writing in a journal at his desk. Dozens of diagrams of Celona and Tenere covered his walls.

"Michael!" Rian said cheerfully. He hobbled to his feet, knocking over two of the towering stacks of books near him. He cursed, tried to stack them again, and quickly gave up. "What an unexpected treat!"

"I'm not sure many others would consider my appearance a treat."

"Well, I've never been one to think like others do," he said with a jolly grin. "I try not to meddle in anything that isn't related to dragons. Keeps my life less dramatic. And people leave me alone to read. Which I adore. You can never learn enough."

"I suppose," I said, closing the door. This office looked messier than the last time I had been here. Which, frankly, was impressive. "But it doesn't look like you're currently doing research on dragons. Taken an interest in the moons or something?"

Rian deflated. "Ah, no. Just doing a favor for the Whisperer. He is obsessed with the night sky. And there's only so many times you can turn your better down before you run out of excuses why." He scratched at his teeth with his long nails. "But what can I do for you, Michael? I doubt you decided to sneak in for no reason."

Questions and thoughts ran through my head at an alarming speed. I took a deep breath, reminding myself there was a reason I did the talking while Sirash did the shooting.

"I was curious if you'd heard about the second event of the Endless Waltz, the hunt?" I said. "Prince Adreann has a Toothless Wyvern in captivity."

Rian's lip twitched, but it came and went quickly. "I heard."

"Are you going to claim it? Last I saw, it was still alive."

Rian sucked his teeth, and the sound was disgusting. More animal than human. "It's been sent away already. To the Gold Coast. To Vargo. To the queen's city, one of the few places out of my and the church's reach."

"How tragic," I said, carefully making my way further into the room. Simply because I was here for one thing didn't mean I was going to waste an opportunity to learn more about what he was currently researching. But I couldn't make out anything, since his handwriting was so bad. "If only you knew someone who could go anywhere."

"What do you want, Michael?"

I made my way over to his desk, leaned on it as Rian stared at me from behind his chair, his own hands on the back of it. "Information."

"I'd be concerned if it was anything else," he said. "More about Domet? I thought I'd told you more than enough. A shame what happened to the Shrine of Patron Victoria. Quite the coincidence, don't you think?"

"Quite. But, no, I'm not here for information about Domet. That relationship has . . . finished for the time being."

"Does Domet know that?"

"I imagine he's aware." A pause. "What information would you offer in exchange for helping you retrieve the Toothless Wyvern?"

"Fishing, Michael? I expected better from you." He reached for his unlit pipe on the desk, sucked in a deep breath, and then exhaled a puff of smoke. It washed over my face and made my eyes water, but I refused to concede and cough as I slid my hand across his desk. "I could offer something valuable. If you promise to help me reclaim the Toothless Wyvern when you are no longer an apprentice Mercenary."

"And that is?"

He put a hand on my shoulder. "Come back when you're no longer an apprentice. You're useless to me right now."

I clenched my fists, swallowed my pride, and said, "I need information about the Corruption."

Rian stopped mid-motion. "The Corruption? Why do you . . . Who has it?"

I stared at him and hoped my hands weren't trembling.

"Where are the markings on their skin? And have they begun to cough up embers yet?"

"It's at their neck, and, yes, they have."

Rian gently sat in his seat. "Then it's already too late. As much as I enjoy all these games we play for information and power, you deserve to know the truth, since their time is limited." Rian took another drag from his pipe. "At most they have a week."

His words echoed in my head. "A week? That's . . ."

"I'm sorry, Michael. But it's the truth. I don't lie about death."

"Why should I trust you? Domet is your friend. And that man hasn't told the truth since he learned to speak."

Rian's eyes looked red in the dim lantern light. "Domet omits. He doesn't lie. But you have every right to be suspicious." He leaned toward a nearby stack of books, removed a small red journal from it, and sent the stack crumpling to the ground. Then he handed it to me. "Flip through this. It contains firsthand accounts of the infection."

I did, and quickly learned Rian was telling the truth. The Corruption's origin was unknown. Some claimed it came from Goldano, but they vehemently denied it, saying it was nothing more than Thebian propaganda. Once it infected someone it slowly turned its host's organs to ash before they exploded into flames. The markings on someone's skin determined how long they had. But once it covered the face, they would die within the day.

"Is there a cure?"

"Not one we know of," Rian said softly. "And the church has exhausted every potential cure from magic to science, but always comes up with nothing. Our members think fires are purifying and holy, so having a disease in the world that kills its victims by engulfing them in flames born within them is bad for our reputation." He exhaled more smoke. "As you could imagine."

"So it's already over for him," I muttered.

"Sadly."

"Thank you, Rian." I went to the door. "I'm sorry for bothering you."

I left before he could respond, craving the sun against my skin. Once outside, I went to an alleyway and screamed as I kicked at the walls. My grandfather was going to die and there was nothing I could do to save him. And my mother didn't know how little time he had left. How was I going to tell her? *Could* I even tell her? Dammit. Olivier had made it sound like his time was limited, but not *that* short. Why hadn't he been clearer? Did he want us to randomly find his body one day or something? Or did he not know himself?

A nearby bell rang and interrupted my thoughts. If I didn't run, I would miss Joey's surgery entirely. I'd figure out what to do with Olivier later. So I slapped myself and continued on my merry way, wondering why it always felt like I was powerless to protect the people I loved.

11

FIELDS OF AMARANTHS

It was always that smell that got me in hospitals. So fake, so sharp and sweet and overwhelming. I nearly gagged on entry, and it made me long for the ever-present stink of fish guts I was used to in Hollow. But I was at the Hawthorn Medical College to support a friend and would have to make do.

A receptionist directed me toward Joey Ryder's surgery, in an area away from the other patients' rooms. It was a small stage in the middle of the hospital with floor-to-ceiling glass walls that allowed people to see inside. There was even a balcony where people could wait directly above the surgery area. Dawn was watching through the glass with Kai, his parents, Kayleigh and Lyon, and Karin. They were all holding hands.

Below them, four people in white surgical robes were mid-procedure, handing tools to each other with a terrifying efficiency. I couldn't see any of the intricacies of the operation. Joey was completely covered except for his face.

I tapped Dawn on the shoulder. "How's it going?"

With one hand on the glass, she continued to watch. "Almost done. So far, so good."

"What's the surgery for?"

"He has a bad heart, so they're replacing it."

"They're *what*?" I questioned, flabbergasted. "They can do that?"

"It's complicated. Beyond my understanding. It's only been done once successfully before and only one surgeon can do it. Alexander Ryder had to call in every favor he's ever been owed to get the lead surgeon here," she said. "But it's the only option. He'll die in a few months unless this works."

I collapsed against the glass, my back to the surgery. "I never knew Joey's condition was that bad."

"They kept it quiet."

I closed my eyes. "I've been such an insensitive asshole."

"So be there for Kai afterward," Dawn said, looking at me for the first time since I had arrived.

"I will. So who's this super-skilled surgeon?"

"It's the Archmage."

I jumped to my feet and put both of my hands against the glass, then asked, "Which one?"

Dawn pointed to the one in black robes. Every part of him was covered except for his eyes, and he looked nearly identical to the others on either side of him. But just seeing him from up here made my heart race. Another Immortal. Though I'd never articulated the thought, part of me had always wondered if the Archmage and Domet were the same person. But he was thinner than Domet, and the way he carried himself was different. More relaxed.

"Part of me thought he was a myth," I said in barely a whisper.

"We've met once before," she said. "Back when I was in the hospital a lot. He tried to help me recover the use of my legs. But nothing worked. He was the one to tell me my Metal Fabrications would be strong enough to support myself if I wanted to walk that way."

"Did he warn you about becoming a Forgotten?"

"Only once. He told me not to squander my life if I chose that route."

"You could always stop before it's too late. Like now. Why stand? Why not just sit in a chair or on the floor?"

Dawn wouldn't look at me. "You don't understand."

"Understand what?"

"The looks I get from people who will never see me as anything but a cripple once they know about my condition." A pause. "Think of it like those that can't see beyond your father's actions when they see you. It's relentless."

"Kai tried to explain it to me once. I kind of understood."

"All I want is freedom. To decide who I am, who I'll be, and how the world views me."

She exhaled, and she reminded me of my sister. I wanted to give her a hug and tell her everything would be fine. "I'm worried about you."

"I know," she said. "And I appreciate it. But my fate is my choice."

I leaned back so my head was against the glass. "If you forget me, I promise not to hit you."

Dawn smiled, then straightened up. "The Archmage is leaving. The surgery must be almost over."

"He doesn't stay for the entire thing?"

"No," she said. "Only for as long as he thinks he's needed."

I hesitated.

She looked at me. "Do you want to meet him?"

"Can you introduce me?"

"It's not . . . I mean . . . Yes, I can. Come with me, we'll be quick."

I followed Dawn down a set of stairs into a small room beside the surgical theater. A dark-skinned man was sitting down in front of a small basin of steaming water and washing his hands slowly, making sure no blood remained beneath his nails. A constant breeze fluttered around him as if we were outside, and every exposed part of his skin seemed to be covered in ink. His face was still obscured with a cloth mask, except for his eyes. A bluish grey.

He didn't notice us until Dawn said, "Archmage. I'm patient Seven-White-Lilac, can I borrow a moment of your time?"

The Archmage stopped what he was doing, pulled up his right sleeve, and looked at the words tattooed there. From a distance it looked like a chart, but I couldn't make out any of the words.

"Seven-White-Lilac . . . Bone. Surgery. Child. Few in that category. Are you dying?"

"No. I use Fabrications to strengthen my bones so I can walk."

"Ah," he said, and nothing more.

"I want to introduce you to my close friend, Michael Kingman," Dawn said, pushing me forward.

The Archmage pulled his mask down, exposing a shadow of a beard and thin lips. For someone who had lived over a century, he barely looked older than me. "Are you dying?"

"No, I just wanted to talk to you. I read a lot of your journals."

"Do you wish to become immortal?"

I didn't respond at first, wondering how much to say in front of Dawn. I trusted her, but I didn't know if I wanted to burden her with this. But, in the end, I thought if she didn't want to be a part of my life—in full—she wouldn't be here. Not after what happened in Kingman Keep or with the king.

"No, I want to know how to kill one."

Dawn was silent, but I could feel her staring at me.

The Archmage massaged his neck, as if what I had said was routine. "Do you want to kill me?"

"No. Another."

"There are two kinds of immortality. True and Beast. Beast Immortals don't die of age or sickness or time but can be killed like any other mortal. Guns work best on those. Aim for the head."

"And for those with true immortality?"

A shrug. "Don't remember."

"Liar."

His eyes sharpened as he cracked his knuckles one by one. "I'm a Forgotten. There's plenty I don't—"

I repeated his own words. "'Maybe I've lived so long I've forgotten what it's like to fear death. Maybe my atonement should be finding a way to kill Immortals. Certainly if I have reached this state, others have, too, and humans are not supposed to live forever. We live our lives to their fullest and then die, hoping we did something memorable in our brief time alive.'"

"You've done your research," he said. "That's good. Makes you more prepared than most of my apprentices. Find me again before the coronation and we'll talk. I'm too tired right now to focus on anything but rest."

"How do I know you won't forget me?"

The Archmage stood and yawned. He strolled over to me, hands in pockets. "What's your name again?"

"Michael Kingman."

"Mi-chael. King-man," he repeated. "When we meet again, ask me about . . ." He trailed off and checked the chart on his right wrist again. ". . . amaranths."

"Where will I find you?"

He walked away and with a wave said, "I'll be wherever the past can be seen."

When it was just us, Dawn asked, "Care to explain?"

"It's a contingency plan."

"Do you know something about Immortals that I don't? Is the person who framed your father one?"

"No."

"Then who is?" she pressed.

"Trust me when I tell you this is one secret you don't want to know."

Dawn paused, trying to figure out who could be worse than the man who had framed my father. There was only one option, and I saw the moment she realized who I meant when her eyes went wide. Softly she said, "Are they a current threat?"

I shook my head. "Not as long as I'm around."

"Will you come to me if you need help?"

"Of course. But we should get back. Check on Kai."

She didn't protest, and we walked back up to the balcony, where Kai was alone, leaning against the glass, eyes closed. He was dressed in his family's colors but much less formally than anything I had seen him in before. As we approached, he said, "Surgery was a success. Doctors feel good about his recovery. He's already awake, too. Tired and groggy, but awake."

"Already?" Dawn asked.

"Or he was, at least. Might have slipped back to sleep by now."

"That's a rather . . . quick recovery, isn't it?" I questioned.

"We're all surprised. Except for my father. He's claiming he knew Joey was stronger than the rest of us. But we'll see what the Archmage thinks and what recovery plan he suggests. He's the expert."

It made no sense to me that Joey could recover so quickly. I'd had infections that had plagued me for longer than his surgery seemed to have. But it wasn't my place to question a good thing, so I held my tongue.

"Thank you both for coming," Kai said as he hugged us both. "But I need to be with my family. You're both going to Lyon and Kayleigh's party tomorrow?"

We nodded.

"Good, good. I will see you then. And thank you both again. I appreciate it so much."

"So," I said as I watched Kai hurry away, "got any plans for the rest of the day?"

Dawn had a hand on her hip. "I'm going to paint. Likely in the King's Garden. Some lovely winter jasmines have bloomed recently near the lake that I want to eternalize. The fact the servant my father sends after me sneezes uncontrollably near them is all the better."

"Sounds fun."

She nodded, and then tears started streaming down her face.

I reached for her. "Dawn, what's wrong—"

"I'm fine," she snapped as she wiped them away. "Sorry. I guess I'm a little more emotional about Joey's surgery than I thought. Ignore me."

I hesitated, wondering if I should press about why she had suddenly started crying, but decided not to. Kai and Dawn were close. Her having a small outburst after putting on a brave face all day for him wasn't too concerning.

Once she painted on a smile, she resumed our previous conversation. "What about you?"

"Unsure."

"Go find your friends. You must have others besides Kai and me."

"It's complicated."

"If there's anything you should have learned by now, Michael," she said as she patted me on the back, "it's that any problem with friends can be solved with an apology."

"What if it doesn't work?"

Dawn was walking away backwards so she could face me as she said, "Then maybe they weren't really your friends to begin with."

She was right. She was always right. I hated that about her. But with so many people left to make amends with, if I didn't start, I would never get to them all. And there was no better person to start with than Omari, whom I had manipulated and abandoned in his time of need.

Would he be able to forgive me? I hoped so.

I really was delusional sometimes.

12

A REQUIEM FOR
THE DEAD

I could hear the music before I saw the college.

The slow wafting tune of a masterpiece played for the thousandth time, accompanied by a singer who could moonlight as a torturer. And yet, they brought their own style to the song and made it beautiful to listen to. For some reason, it reminded me of the singer Red.

The College of Music was in the corner of the Student Quarter, away from public view. Most of the locals, myself included, tended to stay away from the attendees as much as possible. It was hard to have a meaningful conversation with them when all they wanted to talk about was the conductor's brilliant decision to compose the piece in blah blah blah. They would go on and on about nothing.

Music was the least important thing to me with rebels outside the walls, kings killing themselves, and assassins coming for my head. But the collegians never cared about anything else. Jean had been the only one

I could ever get along with. Probably because, unlike most of her class-mates, she'd had to work to get there instead of having a family member make a sizable donation. No one liked to admit it, but it was widely con-sidered to be where the nobility's reject children went. And their bas-tards. Plenty of bastards made it their home.

Although I had seen and heard the College of Music plenty of times from a distance, I had only been within its walls once: a long time ago, when I had been stupider and even more careless, and had attempted to steal a one-of-a-kind composition by some famous musician. The entire attempt had been a complete failure—my life the only thing I had escaped with that night—but Omari and I had bonded over our colossal fuckup. It had been the starting point of a friendship I still cherished.

After everything that had happened, I just wanted him, Arjay, and Jean back in my life. Family looked after family, and I was closer to them than my grandfather. Omari didn't have to forgive me for what I had done, but I hoped he would.

There were plenty of students on the grounds, just outside the long rectangular building, playing instruments in small groups. Jean was likely to be with the other flautists. As badly as our last interaction had gone, I had no other way to reach Omari. They had abandoned their old home and I suspected they were all living in the College of Music together, de-spite the risks. Jean wasn't the kind of person to let the people she loved out of her sight—especially after everything they had gone through with the Last Knight and Omari's captivity.

I did my best to evade any of the musicians trying to get passersby to join their celebration of life. Not only were they harassing me, they were annoying the workers who were preparing for another concert by the singer Red to be held two days before Serena's coronation. It was a miniature civil war no one not in the college's ten-block radius cared about. Eventually, and after nearly punching a musician who claimed that my life would be changed if I heard Fat Sun's rendition of "The Angels of Naverre" played on a washboard and harmonica, I entered the college and approached the attendant at the reception.

The attendant, an older musician with short cropped hair, didn't notice me until I tapped a hand against the table and cleared my throat. Loudly.

"Careful, friend," the attendant said. "I'm doing delicate surgery here."

No, he was fumbling with the strings of an instrument. What was with these musicians? It was like they lived in another world where dragons flew the skies and mischievous monsters lurked in the baths.

"I'm looking for Jean Lorenzo," I said after a deep breath to calm myself. "Could you direct me toward where she's staying?"

The attendant made a sound that would have gotten him hit anywhere else in the city. After the painstakingly long time it took for him to put his instrument down on the table between us, he swung his legs around the chair to face me and opened the big book in front of him. It was a list of names with information about them scribbled in the same line.

"What was the name of your friend, friend?"

"Jean Lorenzo."

With his finger pointed at me and a half-assed smile on his face, he said, "I know her! She's a beauty. The way she holds her flute makes a man want to . . . you know?"

"I don't care."

"I'm saying I want her to hold my—"

"Just tell me where she lives."

The attendant shook his head. "Just trying to make conversation, friend." He paused to flip through a few pages of his book. "Jean lives on the third floor in the Woodwind Wing of the building. Room fifty-three. Would you mind asking her if she wants to get dinner with—"

I left before he could finish his sentence. Thankfully, the entire building was well organized and had signs up everywhere directing people to the Wind Wing, Torture rooms, Woodwind Wing, or whatever else this freakish place offered its prisoners.

I'd have to remember to hold my tongue when I saw Jean again. It would be a mistake to insult the place she lived and hoped to thrive in. It would be the equivalent of someone insulting the Kingman family to my face.

Despite having to avoid more musicians in the hallways, I found room fifty-three in the Woodwind Wing easily. There was a sign hammered into the door that simply read *Jean Lorenzo, Flute, rank six.* I played with my father's ring on my finger before knocking on the door.

Two voices mumbled behind the door, and then there was a clamor and the door opened. Jean, Omari's thin dark-haired girlfriend, saw me there. She didn't say anything immediately and didn't look like she was going to.

"Jean," I said. "Hello."

"What do you want, Michael?" she asked. Her arm was across the doorframe, preventing me from entering the room.

"I want to see Sirash."

"Oh, color me surprised. It's only been two months. I thought you'd forgotten about us. Too busy letting children kill your enemies for you?"

My instinct was to snap back. To say I'd never have wanted Arjay to kill someone just to save my life. But I didn't. I did the one thing my family and friends rarely ever saw me do. I apologized. Profusely.

Jean, much to her credit, never showed any emotion on her face. When I finished, she said, "If you're so sorry, how come you didn't tell Sirash as soon as you saw him? Because he found out. We all did."

"Because I was selfish and needed his help to break into Hollow Castle."

"And you still think you have the right to call him—any of us—a friend?" Jean sneered.

"We love despite a person's flaws, not for their lack thereof."

As Jean opened her mouth to yell at me, from within the room Omari said, "Let him in, Jean."

Though it was clear she didn't want to, Jean listened to Omari and let me in. The room was small and cramped, a bed big enough to fit one person in one corner of the room. Arjay was in a hammock in another.

He didn't look at me. There were clothes stacked against the walls next to a desk, a wardrobe, and a chair. The rug in the center of the room was discolored, the original white reduced to a muddy tan.

Omari sat on the edge of the bed. He looked better than the last time I had seen him. His burns and cuts had healed, leaving only scars behind. Half of his face was still visibly wrinkled and discolored, and I suspected it might be that way for the rest of his life. But it did make his green eyes flaked with gold much more prominent. He was also wearing a necklace with a silver lantern attached to the end. It looked incredibly familiar, though from where, I couldn't remember. Jean took a seat next to him, and all three of them waited for me to speak.

"I'm sorry," I said. "Omari, I'm sorry for abandoning you in Kingman Keep. For not checking in on Jean and Arjay before it was too late. For letting Arjay kill someone. For not telling you what had happened sooner. For everything. I was a shit friend. I'm so sorry."

"Was it worth it?" Omari asked. "If you could go back and change things, would you lie to me again to break into Kingman Keep?"

Not breaking into Hollow Castle might have prevented Isaac from killing himself, but then Angelo Shade might not have revealed himself to me. Because he had, we had an opportunity to stop him. Was that worth it? It was hard to know, but I could only imagine how much harm he could do without opposition. I said the only thing I could.

"I . . . I don't know."

And that was the truth, bought and paid for in my suffering.

Omari stared at me. "I don't hold you responsible for Arjay. You saved him. It's the lying I have an issue with, Michael. You were supposed to be my family, and you manipulated me as if I were a stranger."

"Omari, I—"

"Enough," he said as he rose.

My heart was pounding so hard, I could hear it in my ears. This was too familiar. For a moment, the flesh on his tattooed hand seemed to melt away, exposing the yellowish bone underneath. But it returned after a standard blink and left me wondering if the panic of losing Omari had made me imagine things. I could only hope history didn't repeat itself. Not with Omari. Please, not with Omari. I would do anything.

"Never come here again, and keep my real name out of your mouth," Omari said, voice like striking lightning. "From now on, everything in public between us will be backwards. Regardless of how you wish it were different. And it will remain that way until the Reaper themselves cease to breathe. Understand?"

Sirash ushered me out and slammed the door behind me. I was already wiping tears from my eyes.

When Trey rejected me, after Jamal died, it had nearly destroyed me. And now Sirash was doing the same. I was a monster. I was worse than Dark. I'd deserved to die in front of the church . . . I should have joined King Isaac after all . . . No, no. I couldn't dwell on that. There was still too much to do. I had lost Sirash, Arjay, and Jean because of my selfish decisions.

There were people who still needed me, and I wouldn't let them down again.

I had to be better.

13

BURNT FAITH

The Kingman family has always been an enigma to the average citizens of Hollow. They exist within a weird space in society. They have as much influence as the Royals but act as if they come from the East Side . . . despite living in one of the most prominent keeps in Hollow. It's the only one on the Isle for a reason. Hollow is a city of permanent statements and everlasting memorials. Yet, in light of the actions of Michael Kingman—the king killer, the Dragonslayer, the whatever-he-is—we have an opportunity to examine the Kingman family again, and to ask whether we want them to return, or if we're better off without their forced care.

While many Archivists like to examine the more famous members of the Kingman family—the Conqueror, the Noble, and the Mother—I want to examine two lesser-known ones. The Domestic and the Kingman-Who-Walked-Away.

The Domestic earned his title and place amongst his legendary family for perhaps the most asinine reason: he did nothing. The Domestic was one of the four children of the Unnamed, and while his siblings went on to become the Gambler, the Explorer, and the Seafarer, he stayed in Hollow, got married, and had two children. Without him the Kingman family would have ended. Each of his siblings' lines eventually died out, well before they were expected to. It's interesting to think, for all the praise we give the actions and heroics of the Kingman family, that they would have died out if the Domestic had chosen to do something more with his life than stay at home.

The Kingman-Who-Walked-Away is a different case. Unlike her siblings, she refused to choose a Royal to support during the War of the Bloodlines. Instead, she simply . . . left. Which is unheard of in Kingman history. They never run away from the conflicts of Hollow to the point that even the Peaceful Kingman—

———

My mother pulled my head back and looked down into my eyes, averting them away from what I was reading. "I have an errand for you, Michael."

"You always told me I needed to read more. And the one time I am, you want me to stop?"

She took the handwritten journal from my hands. "This is one topic you're well versed on. Where did you get this, anyway? It looks new."

"Stole it," I said with a smile. "I'm in it. It's only right I know what the Archivists are publishing about me."

She put the journal down between us. There was no one else in the great hall, everyone else busy, and after seeing Sirash I had wanted to relax. Try to get my head back into a better place. From my mother's expression, I doubted I was going to like this errand. I told her as much.

"I need you to go to the Shrine of Patron Victoria."

I took a moment to compose myself and asked for further explanation.

"Your grandfather—"

"What does he have to do with this?"

"Michael," she said sternly. "If you don't blame me for being absent these past ten years, then you can forgive your grandfather. We are family, and you will not hold a stupid grudge against him. Understand?"

"Yes."

"Good." She sat down next to me. "Now, I need you to go to the Shrine of Patron Victoria. I need someone I can trust there."

"Why? What's happening?"

"As a symbolic gesture to High Noble Domet, Adreann is reconstructing the shrine. They're breaking ground today and the prince is in attendance. Your grandfather has gone to plead with him to allow the refugees to stay and to give them the basic supplies they need to survive."

"Is that man fucking stupid?"

"Michael! Language."

"Sorry, Ma."

"Your grandfather isn't stupid, he's just . . . honorable to a fault. Things are done differently in the Familial . . . in the Warring States. We didn't have Fabricators there, so the nobility was never predisposed toward manipulation or lying to get their way. Every conflict was handled with integrity. This is him doing what he was taught to since birth."

"You'd think fighting in a civil war would have corrected that thinking."

My mother tapped a finger against the table. "Knowing you'll die soon changes things. Makes you want to go out on your own terms."

Not only did I have to deal with my naïve grandfather, but he was in denial about his life, too. Wonderful. "You want me to get him and drag him back before he does anything stupid?"

"Yes. I would have asked Lyon, but he's . . . indisposed with obligations to the Ryder family, and Gwen, I understand, is the last person who should be interacting with Adreann right now."

"She's probably the only person the Corrupt Prince hates more than me."

"The Corrupt Prince? What is it with you and all these useless titles? All it does is give petty people more authority. If you want to insult him, call him Adreann."

"If you say so, Ma. I've been dealing with him my way pretty well so far." I stretched my arms and then shook out my legs. "I'll have him back before dinner. Do you know if Domet will be there?"

"Not to my knowledge. But don't be brash, Michael. Remember, we're trying to make allies in the city, not give them more reasons to hate us."

I waved goodbye. "Making friends is what I do best."

My mother laughed and clearly didn't agree with me.

———————

I felt uneasy about returning to the Shrine of Patron Victoria, since the last time I had been here, I had . . . well, I had burned it to the ground in revenge. It had once been a lush green oasis in a desert of grey. Now it was unrecognizable. All the vegetation in the area was gone, all the wood was ash, and the marble pathway was scorched blacker than a starless night. Even the pond was now topped with a green algae that was slicker and thicker than fish guts. The shrine itself had collapsed in on itself, a few snow-topped wooden timbers the only indication of where it had once stood.

There was no trace of the statue anywhere, and maybe, just a little, I was thankful for that. It would have hurt to see it. What I had done was inexcusable . . . but it was done. There was no point dwelling on the past. Let the consequences come at me as they would.

The Shrine of Patron Victoria had about a dozen workers muddling around, examining the damage the fire had wrought. There were a few guards pacing back and forth near the entrance, there to intimidate and drive off any misplaced wanderers or nobles seeking an audience with a Royal.

My grandfather was nowhere to be seen, and that worried me more than confronting the Corrupt Prince. I hoped I wasn't already too late. So I did the only thing that made sense.

"Adreann!" I shouted as I strolled into the clearing. I patted the guards at the entrance on the shoulder and was met with visible confusion. "Miss me?"

The Corrupt Prince gave me a sideways glance from the middle of the bridge. It was the only thing that hadn't been obliterated. There were two Ravens at his side. Michelle Cityborn, the four-feathered one, and Karin Ryder, the woman who wore two feathers. They were dressed in the typical Raven garb: plate mail armor, intimidating stances, and their preferred weapons strapped across their backs. A spear for Karin and a shield tower and short sword for Michelle.

Adreann was monstrous, as always. A man who outweighed and over-shadowed everyone around him. He was nearly perfect except for the raised scar in the shape of a crescent moon on his right cheek—a parting gift I had given him before my self-presumed death. I was glad to see it.

"Michael," he said, much quieter and more composed than I thought he'd be at seeing me. "Must I fake pleasantries, or can we just skip to the part where we openly show our contempt for each other?"

I stopped in front of the bridge, just out of arm's reach. "After every-thing we've been through, I think we can be truthful with each other. How's the cheek?"

"Painful," he said. "But I appreciate it. It keeps me focused."

My brand was throbbing. When was the last time that had happened? "I can relate."

"I imagine you can," he said as he cracked his neck. "Why are you here, Michael? Are you trying to give me a reason to crush your head like the maggot you are?"

"Bold of you to threaten a Mercenary. Do you want another war? One you have no chance of winning? Or is the rebellion not enough for you?"

"How dare—" Michelle growled, about to draw her sword.

The Corrupt Prince grabbed her wrist and stepped in front of his Raven. "Anyone can be killed in the right circumstances, Michael. You. Me. My sister. My Ravens. Death does not discriminate. You may have outplayed me, but you are mortal and you will die. And when you do, I will be there smiling and laughing and enjoying the view."

For some reason my chest felt tight, and all I could mutter was "We'll see."

"We will." He returned to leaning against the railing of the bridge.

"Get on with whatever brought you here. I have things to do and would like you out of my sight as quickly as possible."

"I'm looking for an old man. He's one of the refugees that arrived in Hollow recently. I was told he was headed in this direction."

"Why do you care about an old man?"

"He's the leader of the refugees. High Noble Maflem Braven has tasked Orbis Company to investigate them. This is me doing my job," I said. It was the truth, albeit a little selective.

"He came and went without incident. I had no intention of listening to a nobody beg for favors. As if I were someone he could approach casually." The Corrupt Prince sucked on his teeth. "It was disgusting."

"That's unlike you. When did you stop killing people who bother you?"

"When I realized how juvenile it was," he declared, and a shiver went through my spine. "Why should I kill those who do not matter and cannot harm me? They will all be my subjects eventually, and I need them to serve me. Bake my bread, dye my clothes, and whatever else they do to fill the void of their meaningless lives."

"That . . . that's . . ."

"Did you think you were the only one who could change, Michael? How naïve of you."

It was. It had never occurred to me that Adreann could mature. He'd been an obnoxious brute with ambitious goals since childhood. The last thing Hollow needed was for him to learn restraint or guile or strategy. If he did . . . he might actually have a chance at taking the throne from Serena.

"If you'll excuse me, I have places to be and allies to acquire," the Corrupt Prince said as he walked past me. His Ravens were close behind. "I would say we'll settle this another day, but, alas, you have Serena's full attention. Your fate is already sealed."

"Everyone keeps telling me that. Yet, here I am, still breathing."

The Corrupt Prince looked over his shoulder. "Not even I want to openly oppose her. She terrifies me, and you have no idea what she is capable of. She will kill you, and you won't see it coming."

"If you say so."

He let out a small laugh and then waved goodbye. "Tell Gwen I cannot wait to see her again. Our next meeting is all I dream about."

I let him and his Ravens leave. As much as I wanted to get the last word in, to show he hadn't shaken me, it would only do the opposite. It didn't take a genius to realize Serena was . . . Serena was . . . Serena was special to me. In more ways than being bonded as Kingman and Royal. She had been my best friend, and . . . and back then she'd probably known me better than anyone else.

If I was going to have any chance at convincing her King Isaac had killed himself, I was going to have to . . . ah, fuck. I had no idea what I'd have to do. Hopefully it would come to me.

On my way back to Kingman Keep, I found my grandfather in Refugee Square, staring at the statue in the middle of it. He didn't notice me until I was right next to him. I watched the sunset, waiting for him to speak.

"Did Juliet send you after me?" he asked eventually as the wind howled through the gaps between the buildings.

"Sadly. Got to the shrine after you did. Expected to find blood and guts and bone. Imagine my surprise when I didn't."

"For someone called the Corrupt Prince"—he stopped to cough and hack up wet clumps of ash—"he was rather calm."

"He's lying low while the princess is in the city. Gathering allies and promises while he waits for an opportunity to strike. Probably the smartest thing he's ever done."

"That's a more dangerous tactic than you may realize," he said. "There is no more vulnerable moment for a country than during a transfer of power. The Familial Empire fell in a month after the last empress died."

"The Familial Empire?"

Before he could answer, a bell rang out. Celona moon-fall. I looked toward the sky, searching for the falling rock to see what color its tail was. I couldn't see much, the setting sun painting the sky an orangish red. As always, I wouldn't run until I heard that third or fourth bell.

"Celona watch over us," Olivier recited as he made a gesture with his hands.

That wasn't a prayer I was familiar with. Did my grandfather follow one of the lesser-known prophets rather than those of the Wanderer and Eternal Flame? I asked him that.

"It's just a personal prayer. The moon I could see and respect. God I could not." He paused to scan the sky but saw nothing, as I had. "The Familial Empire was the name of the Warring States back when they were unified." He looked at me. "Did your mother ever tell you how she met your father?"

"No." I paused. "Can you?"

"Absolutely," Olivier said, without dramatics. "Your father was secretly brought in to investigate a death during the Empress of the Familial Empire's funeral. We were concerned the murderer might be a member of the ruling family. Your father worked with Juliet and . . . and they attempted to find the killer. But they failed and a god returned, destroyed the capital, and created the mess we've been fighting to prevent ever since."

"What?" I asked in disbelief.

The first bell stopped ringing as the piece of Celona flashed over Hollow for a moment, bathing the city in a red glow, before disappearing to the west. Unless there was a second moon-fall, which was incredibly rare, the pieces of Celona wouldn't be causing me any more problems this week.

My grandfather continued our conversation. "After that, your parents worked with one of the branches of the ruling family to stop the inevitable civil war from occurring. It didn't work, but they did their best. Tried to save the Familiar Empire for—how long was it again?—a little less than five years."

That explained where my father had gone after the Day of Crowning and how he had met my mother. I just hadn't expected them to have found each other in the middle of a war. Were Kingman all destined to spend our lives on a battlefield?

"When your family was murdered by New Dracon City . . . something in him broke," Olivier continued. "He was a pacifist until that moment. Afterwards he only wanted revenge and death, and to embrace the inheritance that he had run from. We were in a better position back then, so we let them go. From one war to another, taking their place as the next leaders of the Kingman family, and the world saw it."

I crossed my arms. "Why do I feel like this story is about to become a morality lesson?"

"Because it is. I'm pushing you to be better. It's why I came here—despite running out of time." Olivier looked into my amber eyes as he said, "You, Gwen, Lyon, and whatever friends and family you choose will soon be the leaders of this world. I'd rather not have you plunge it further into war, as the previous generations did."

"Nothing can change until the problems we inherited are resolved."

"I have faith that my grandchildren will emerge victorious."

There was a weird feeling swelling in my chest, and I didn't want to be here anymore. "You can find your way back to Kingman Keep, right?"

"I'm old, not stupid."

"Good," I said as I began to walk away. "Tell Ma I'll be a little late to dinner."

"What's more important than dinner with your family?" he shouted at me as I took off in a light jog toward the southern part of the West Side.

The streets weren't very busy or crowded. Spring would be coming soon, but until the warmth didn't rely on the sun, people would be enjoying the comfort of their homes when night came. I found my way with little effort, walking sideways down tight alleyways rather than risk getting seen on the main streets. I had lived in Angelo's house for half my life and knew each and every way there. And where I could see inside. Without him knowing.

I leaned against an alley wall of the Narrows and watched the shadows move within the house. He was alone at the table reading a book, a single lantern illuminating the entire room. He read and then he went to bed. When he disappeared, I waited until my fingers were numb with cold and the suspicion he might try to sneak out was eased.

I wondered if I would ever be able to let my anger at him fade. And if I could, did I even want to?

14

A TOWER OF BLOOD

I spent the rest of the night and the following morning in Kingman Keep helping my family repair some of the damage caused by the Kingman Keep riots. Olivier had the wonderful job of repairing any cracks and holes in the roof and walls. Lyon was off with his soon-to-be wife, while Gwen and I had been directed to clean out the rooms connected to the great hall. Our mother was trying to determine the best way to repair the towers and houses outside the keep. Gwen and I had the easiest task. It helped that Gwen was probably stronger than I was from her work as a blacksmith. There was nothing we couldn't lift together.

As we heaved half a shattered table over the balcony into the great hall, watching it drop into the woodpile below, Gwen said, "How many more rooms left?"

It landed with a *crack* and *snap*. I wiped some of the sweat off my forehead. "Two or three. Shouldn't be too bad."

"Spoken like a man who doesn't have to pull a night shift at the asylum later."

"Why are you still working there, anyway?" I said as we entered the next room. It was more dusty than cluttered, broken glass and a few broken chairs scattered over the floor. "Ma isn't a patient anymore."

Gwen swept the broken glass into a pile with the side of her boot. "My plan was to stay until I could help Blackwell more, but . . . I don't know. The asylum is giving me pushback on whatever I try to do."

"Who's Blackwell?" I asked.

Gwen stopped what she was doing and stared at me as if I had two heads. She muttered nothings as she blinked rapidly and then, very quietly, said, "Just a friend. He helped me out and I wanted to repay his kindness."

"What's he in for?" I swatted cobwebs out of my face. "Memory loss?"

"Kind of. It was more like memory manipulation, but, uh, it's not important." Gwen gulped audibly. "Once I run out of options to help him, I'll leave. I always hated it there. And with everything going on, I think it's time for me to find my own way, especially after the blacksmith told me not to show up for my shift anymore. He was perfectly fine with my masquerading as a boy, but apparently a Kingman was too much. King Isaac's death probably brought up bad feelings again."

"Sorry."

"Don't apologize," she said. "Neither job was my dream."

I broke down a wooden chair into small pieces of wood good for tinder. "What do you want to do, then?"

Gwen hesitated. Suddenly she looked so young and vulnerable, the crybaby sister I remembered from the Kingman Keep riots. But it lasted only a few moments before she steeled herself and said, "It doesn't matter what I want to do. I must be ready in case Lyon abdicates his position as heir of the Kingman family and I have to take over. It can't be you."

"No," I said with a chuckle. "Definitely not me. But say you didn't have to worry about that. What would you do?"

"Live on the Gold Coast in one of those nude bathhouses and spend the remainder of my life being fed grapes by beautiful men and women."

I threw a piece of wood at her. She dodged it and then threw it back at me. I wasn't as lucky. "Real answer this time."

Gwen's eyes lingered on an old, discolored painting that still hung in this room. The frame was broken and parts of it had been torn off, but it was still clearly a painting of the two women who'd been meant to guide Hollow: our deceased aunt, Gwyneth Kingman—the woman whom Gwen had been named after—and the king's elder sister, Charlotte Hollow. They were smiling, with their arms around each other. A simpler time.

"I need a favor," she said, her voice softer than I had ever heard it before. Without waiting for my response, she moved toward a pile of furniture and pulled an oddly familiar wooden box from it. "I need you to test my blood."

"What're you . . ." I paused. "Is that what I think it is? How did you get that?"

"Found it," she said as she took a seat on the floor. "Is it really important how? Or just that I have it?"

I sat across from her and the box. She had already begun to pull the vials and copper bowl out of it. "I thought you already know if you were a Fabricator or not."

"For years I thought I wasn't . . . but recently I've been wondering if I was like you . . . that I didn't understand how it was manifesting." She was putting various liquids into the bowl. It was as if I were watching Domet do it again. If anything, she seemed quicker. "I need to know for sure."

"Doesn't seem like you need my help to find out."

Gwen glared at me as she tied a tourniquet around her bicep before drawing blood from the vein. When the syringe was full, she handed it to me and said, "I don't know what to look for. You do."

"Liar. I told you what happened."

She looked away, a blush creeping up her face. "Just do it. Don't make me beg."

"Are you scared about what the results might be? Because—"

"Michael, get on with it," she interrupted. "Please."

I wanted to make her talk about what she was feeling, but maybe it would be easier to discuss once we had the results. I squirted the blood into the bowl and waited for the tower to form. I didn't remember exactly how long it had taken, and it felt like an eternity as we watched the blood fall to the bottom of the bowl like rocks.

There was no tower. Not for Gwen.

"Maybe you messed up the quantities? Domet said they had to be precise or—"

I looked up at my sister and found her crying. The tears fell without dramatics, like drops of rain as she stared blankly at the bowl. Despite them, she didn't look sad or angry, just accepting of what she was and could never be. I don't think I would have taken it so well if the positions had been reversed. I would have broken something.

"That's the third time I've tried," she said, tears continuing to fall. "The results were the same. I told myself that if it happened again I couldn't run from the truth anymore. I'm not a Fabricator." She wiped her face on the back of her sleeve like a child. "I didn't expect it to hurt this much."

"Did you want to be one?"

"I wanted the option," she muttered. "To use my powers as I saw fit. I don't get to make a lot of choices. I won't choose to be the heir. I didn't choose to be a Kingman or be bound to the Corrupt Prince. But I thought . . . I thought this might be the *one* thing I could control."

I stayed still, knowing that if I moved to comfort her she might push me away and snap that she was fine. "What do you really want, Gwen?"

"I don't know. That's the problem," Gwen said. "Have you ever felt like we were raised to be a Kingman, and nothing else?"

"That's because we were."

"Did you never want to be something else?"

No, I'd never wanted to be anything but a Kingman. Even when I believed that my father had murdered Davey Hollow. My youthful dreams had been about leading armies against insurmountable foes, being remembered as the ideal hero, and eventually dying to save the world. Reaching old age had never seemed desirable to me as a child. Mainly since I had correlated it with being a useless coward. Kingman never lived to have grey hair. They were always dead before that. Somehow I doubted I would be any different. But Gwen could be.

"Do you?" I countered.

"If it comes to it, I'd be honored to lead the Kingman family, but . . ." She trailed off.

"But?"

"But I don't know if I can," Gwen said. "And maybe that's the problem. I wanted to prove Da was innocent. And I want to punish Angelo Shade for manipulating us and killing Davey. But some days I wonder what I would do if I could do anything."

"Would you leave Hollow?" I asked, scooting closer to her.

"I don't know. I always wanted to see New Dracon City," Gwen said. "I've read the accounts about how they slaughtered our family and Isaac's older sister. I want to walk the streets. See the Thousand Steps, where it happened, and see the Night Market, which only appears when all of the merchant princes and princesses are in the city." A pause. "I want to dictate my own life, not have others do it for me."

"Gwen," I said, voice growing stern and taking her hands in mine. "If you want to travel, then you should. Leave the family to Lyon. He's not going to abdicate anytime soon, if he ever does. Take the time you need to be happy. Find yourself. Just like Ma and Da did."

"I have obligations."

"This Blackwell isn't more important than your happiness."

"He's not. I did something that—"

"Michael! Get out here!"

It was Dark. But why was he here?

Gwen and I went over to the railing and looked down into the great hall. Dark was standing below us with the bandaged girl from the colosseum at his side. She looked different—less frail—though her head was down. She was rubbing one of her hands up and down her arm. Something had happened.

"Where's Olivier?" Dark shouted.

I put my hands on the railing. "He should be outside repairing the roof. What happened?"

"There's been a murder."

THE GREEN-EYED MONSTER

It was the stench that I noticed first. Musty wood and rotten eggs.

The blood was the second thing. The amount of it nearly made me gag and puke up whatever was in my stomach. It would add a little more color to this bloodstained portrait at the very least. The only thing that wasn't covered in blood in this boarded-up Militia Quarter house was a very carefully laid pathway of wooden planks. Sticky ankle-deep pools of blood lay everywhere else. A single body hung from the ceiling, suspended on a meat hook. It was flat like a discarded snake husk, the organs neatly placed in glass jars below. Only the heart was missing. Written on the wall in blood above the body were the words *Run and Hide*.

I had seen death before. Held bodies in my hands and felt the blood of my friends dry on my face. This was not that. Creating this scene was a pleasure for the murderer and nothing I felt could ever justify this savagery. I thought I had seen it all before. What a fool I had been.

"Sleeper be damned," Olivier said before he put his hand over his mouth. "What kind of monster could do something like this?"

"It's a serial killer," Dark mumbled next to me. The bandaged girl was behind him, her pale green eyes locked on the horror in front of us.

"This has to be High Noble Maflem," I said. "He said he was going to get rid of the refugees without our help. He wasn't lying."

"But it's been less than a day since we turned him down."

"So explain how this happened!" I shouted. "This wasn't accidental. This isn't just a murder, it's a *message* to someone. And I would love to hear a reason for it, other than scaring off the refugees we helped."

Olivier had his arm around the bandaged girl to comfort her. I couldn't tell if it was working, she wasn't looking at anything in the room or at anyone. Hopefully she didn't know whoever had been brutally murdered, even though she had been the one to find this grisly scene. I could only imagine her pain. No family. No home. And now being targeted by a killer. How did she find the strength to keep going?

While I dealt with the haze in my mind, Dark had begun to investigate the murder scene. He lifted the lids of the jars that held the organs, smelled their sickly scent, and then replaced them. He ran his fingers over the blood on the wall, rubbing it between two of his fingers before it flaked off. Finally, Dark inspected the area where the heart had been. The organs had been removed with surgical precision. What was Dark looking for? Was there something I was . . .

"What if . . . ," I said. "What if we were the backup plan?"

Dark turned to me, waiting for me to continue.

"We assumed we were the Waylayer's primary target in the colosseum. But what if we weren't? You said yourself that the gunner was extremely skilled. Yet missed. Before either of us knew they were there. What if High Noble Maflem had already hired the Waylayer to scare them? For all we know, he may have wanted for us to turn him down so he could have evidence that he attempted to find a peaceful solution before resorting to violence."

"That's a lot of what-ifs, Michael," Olivier said from behind me.

"I'd love to hear another explanation."

Neither Olivier nor the bandaged girl said anything.

"As much as I hate to say it," Dark began, "Michael could be right. It would make a twisted kind of sense."

"Can I get that in writing?"

"Quiet. We can't do anything until we have more evidence," Dark said. "I'll let Imani know about this and she'll alert someone in Scales. Just in case the High Nobles want to make a move against us because Michael wasn't executed like they planned."

"What am I supposed to tell my people?" Olivier asked.

"Not to die."

The bandaged girl broke down, falling to her knees, sobbing loudly. I made a gesture to Dark and Olivier that I could take care of her. Olivier would fill me in on anything important later. He hadn't kept anything from me yet, and I would have to trust that he wouldn't.

As they left I knelt next to the bandaged girl. "I'd love to say it'll get better, but I don't think it will. Do you have anyone in Hollow you could stay with until we can find the killer?"

"No," she said between sobs. "My father was murdered. He was shot by a coward."

I remembered the tongueless old man. I hadn't realized they were related. This poor girl. So much suffering, and she was no older than I was. How strong would I be without my family?

"I can't promise you much, but if you want to, you can come live at Kingman Keep with my family. There's a lot of work, but you'll be safe there."

"I can protect myself. Besides, there's something I must do," she said, suddenly defiant. Her sobbing ceased, and she met my eyes. Hers were pale green. When I had first met her, they had been hazel.

Oh, shit.

She smiled like a fox who had caught her prey. My body felt very, very heavy and I suddenly found myself sprawled out on the floor on my stomach. None of my limbs could twitch, let alone move. My boots and fingertips were in the blood, and my face was sideways on the floor as I was forced to watch the bandaged girl slowly unravel.

"I've been thinking about how to do this for the past month, Michael," she said. "I'd thought about posing as a beggar in front of Kingman Keep until you gave me an opportunity. But that required time I didn't have. And I doubted you would be very trusting of strangers."

Her hair was loose now, strands of auburn coming undone from the bun. It contrasted with her naturally tan skin and the few freckles over the bridge of her nose.

"That's why I was so thrilled when this bandaged-up girl came to the castle begging for help. Claimed a boy called Michael inspired her to ask for aid when she needed it. From there it was simple. She'll spend the rest of her days working in the castle, with the best doctors attending to her injuries, and I . . . well, I get this."

The Princess of Hollow and future queen, Serena, squatted down in front of me as she began to braid her hair. She was dressed simply: black pants and a brown shirt that did nothing to show her physique. But even so, I could see what she had tucked between her skin and waistband. When she noticed me staring and was finished with her hair, she pulled it out with another wicked smile.

Serena put one of the twin revolvers against the side of my head.

It was an odd thing to think, but, for the first time in ten years, I saw her. Not the child I had gone on adventures with and stolen glances at when I thought she wouldn't notice. Serena had grown up, her hate sharpened to a fine edge that wouldn't dull in the foreseeable future. And it was all directed toward me. The man she believed had killed her father. The son of the man she believed had murdered her brother.

I had been a fool to think we could reestablish our relationship as it had been before my father's execution. That she would even listen to me. That she would still feel even a fraction of what she had once felt. And yet, lying on the wooden planks and in pools of blood, I longed to ease her pain. We had been bonded once . . . and some obligations were hard to forget.

"After I watched you escape execution because of a loophole," the princess said, "I realized there was only one fitting end for you. For me to kill you with this gun. The gun that stole my brother and father from me."

"Serena," I whined, the invisible pressure pushing down on me even harder. "Please. Don't."

"'*Please*'?" she mocked. "Did my father beg for his life before you shot him? Did my brother whine at your father? I imagine they must have. No one wants to die."

My breath was fading. Everything hurt. I was going to die soon enough even if she didn't shoot me. "We." A breath. "Didn't." Another. "Kill." And another. "Them."

"You don't even have the decency to tell me the truth in the end? God, what a waste of air you are," Serena said. "I hope death hurts. So you feel a fraction of the pain your family has caused me."

"Es. Please. Wait."

"Don't call me that! You have no right to!"

Blackness was creeping at the edge of my vision. It had been so long since I had taken a breath. Maybe a bullet through my skull would be less painful. She wasn't going to end this easily. I did all I could think of. I said, "Sorry."

"'*Sorry*'?" she screamed, back on her feet and waving the gun around frantically. "That's it? You're *sorry*? Do you even understand what you've done to me? I'm ending this. Goodbye, Michael."

Serena pointed the gun at me.

At least this time my family knew I loved them.

A gun went off and the pressure on my back lifted. I waited for the pain to resonate in my body. It never did. Instead, what came was the very familiar voice of my Mercenary mentor. The Princess of Hollow turned to face him.

"Excuse me, Princess," Dark said with his gun drawn and still smoking. "He's not yours to kill."

Serena pointed her gun at him. "Do you really want to try and stop me?"

"Michael, use your Nullification Fabrications."

My breath hadn't returned fully, and the only response I could give was a half-assed wheeze.

"Now," Dark grumbled. "Before I join you on the floor."

Deep within myself, I found the warmth and let it coat my body like a jacket. It still hurt to breathe, but gradually I was able to roll over and sit up. What had the princess done to me? What kind of Fabricator was she? I had never seen or heard of anything like that.

"I think we have the upper hand, Princess," Dark said. "Your Fabrications won't work on him now. And if you're still considering shooting either of us, then be aware I won't miss. Will you?"

Serena lowered her gun, and Dark did the same. "If you had been a little later, you would have found a second body here," Serena said. "Shame I couldn't make that happen."

"Sadly, I need him," Dark responded.

"Why?" she asked. "Why would you and Orbis Company save his life? He's an unremarkable Fabricator. Not smart. Or clever. Or strong. Or anything noteworthy, really. Why not let us have him? What does Orbis Company gain from letting him live?"

"He's an investment."

"An investment? What are you planning for him?"

"Nothing you can replicate."

"No one else will value his death as highly as I do. I could give you anything you want. All you have to do is name it."

"Asking a Mercenary to name their own price never ends well. Ask Michael."

Serena hesitated for a few heartbeats. "I wouldn't be offering it if I wasn't willing to pay the price."

"Fine," Dark said as he returned his revolver to its holster. "Your throne. Abandon it. Abdicate."

"What? That's impossible. I ref—"

"You know my price. Do it, and Michael is yours. Nothing less."

"Very well," Serena said to Dark. To me she said, "Run and hide, Michael. Enjoy spending time with your family while you can."

Serena holstered her revolver and left in a hurry. The door slammed behind her before I had even returned to my feet. When I did, Dark let out a giant sigh of relief. I had never seen him do that before.

"Thank you," I said.

"You imbecile," Dark said, his voice dripping with venom. "You had an advantage over her and almost wasted it. Now she knows you don't fear her even when she has a gun to your head."

"I don't understand."

"That's always your problem, Michael!"

It caught me off guard. Had Dark ever shouted at me like this before? No, it was only ever a disappointed voice and a shake of his head. Whatever had just happened, this had launched him into a new territory of anger. But why?

"Then enlighten me."

"The Princess of Hollow is a . . . unique Fabricator. She may be the first of her kind," Dark said with his arms crossed. "The best way we can describe it is to create a force pressing down on you. That's why she's called a Force Fabricator. You, as a Nullify Fabricator, are the only Fabricator with a natural advantage over her. Even I would be helpless against her."

"Well, I know for the future, then."

"You still don't understand," he sneered. "You're a Nullify Fabricator. Your body will sometimes involuntarily use a Fabrication when you're in a dangerous situation. She just learned your body doesn't consider her a threat. Even when you're suffocating because you're pressed against the ground with a gun to your head." He clenched his fists. "Why did you not nullify her Fabrications?"

"I forgot."

"You forgot? Are you that—" He screamed like a rampaging beast. "Do you realize the danger you've put us in? I swear, if you say you can't view her as a threat because you think she's pretty, I'm going to rip out your heart and crush it under my boot."

"A little dramatic, don't you—"

Dark pulled out his revolver and I was silent. After aiming it at my chest for a few moments, he exhaled and returned it to its holster. His finger had been on the trigger the entire time, but I was going to pretend I hadn't seen that.

"Get your shit together, Michael," Dark said. "Your enemies are mine and mine are yours. We're intertwined. And I don't want to die because a woman has you wrapped around her finger."

"That woman you speak of is the future Queen of Hollow and my best friend and . . ." I trailed off, unable to admit that Serena had meant more to me than just the Royal I was bound to. No one knew except Lyon. When I told him, he hadn't yelled or chastised me, just held me close and said he was sorry that I had fallen for the only person I could never be with.

Kingman and Hollow weren't allowed to be engaged romantically and have children. One of the many laws we followed to preserve our place in society. My ancestors would likely rise from the dead and come for my head if we were. Certain lines were never to be crossed.

"Figure out who's an ally and who isn't," Dark said. "It may cost us our lives if you can't."

I was already trying to do that. "And what about all of this? Are we just going to wait around for more people to die?"

"Would you rather I stood in the Great Stone Square and shot whoever looks suspicious?" he asked. "No? Didn't think so. All we can do is make sure Imani and Scales are aware of the situation."

This conversation was going nowhere. "Is Olivier still outside?"

Dark shook his head. "He went to check up on his people. This has scared him." With his voice lowered he added, "Rightly."

I'd have to catch up with him in Kingman Keep. With nothing left to do here and neither of us wanting to be found at this grisly murder scene, we left for separate destinations. Dark went to Orbis Company's headquarters in Hollow, while I went to the Rainbow District.

It was time to see Trey.

STONE THROWING

Change had come to the Rainbow District.

Instead of the destruction that had plagued other districts on the East Side, it had begun to look . . . cleaner and more put together than ever. Trees had begun turning green instead of the seemingly permanent shade of mud brown they had been before, and there were cats lounging on rooftops and over the sills of doorways. It would have been unprecedented to see any of that a few months ago. The tweekers and dimmers had gone from the streets. In the past, there had been five for every non-addict and it had been hard to go a block without one sizing someone up for what valuables they had on them.

That was no longer the case, and there were more children running around and playing than ever. For every two of them, there was only one adult. Something amazing had happened here. And I had every intention of finding out what.

If someone was willing to talk to me, which none was. The children would be cordial at first but, once they noticed the brand on my neck, would scatter faster than dandelion seeds in the wind. The women didn't even respond to my questions. And the men . . . well, the men were the men. Every topic was more important and readily able to be discussed than how this district had changed for the better.

The only thing I got out of anyone was that Big Brother had taken over this district. And that name was only given out by chance, in a long-winded rant about how things used to be better before they came around and made changes. Pride had a funny way of clouding judgment and blinding reality if it didn't fit their perception. Even here, where Fabricators were rarer than bottled wine.

It wasn't long before I might as well have had boils on my face and blood coming out of my ears, because everyone avoided me like I had the plague. Despite being the unfortunate carrier of a king killer title, I didn't understand why it would particularly manifest here, of all places. The East Side rarely cared about the affairs of those on the other side of the river unless it brought further pain to them. Who was I to them but another delusional noble?

I would have been able to understand if it were simply the inhabitants of the Rainbow District that wanted nothing to do with me. Everyone feared strangers on some basic human level. But when the merchants refused to sell to me and the bartenders politely refused my orders, I knew I had been purposefully boxed out from this district. Whether it was because of the brand on my neck or my once-noble blood, or simply because I didn't look as if I belonged here. It could have been all of them or some fourth reason I was unaware of.

By the time the sun set and people had begun to hang lanterns outside their doors, I was no closer to finding Trey. Rather than admit defeat, I went to the edge of the eastern split of the river and skipped rocks across it. I'd have to be home soon to get ready for Lyon's party, but I wanted to calm myself down first. Months ago I had thought the destruction of the Militia Quarter by rebels was the worst thing imaginable. No longer.

Serena was likely going to be there tonight.

As much as I would have liked to avoid her and the event, I owed it to Lyon to attend. He was going to be a father soon, and as bad as our relationship had been for years, we were making progress in repairing it. I didn't want to ruin it just because I feared being murdered by Serena. I had already escaped once with my life today, what were the odds she was going to attempt it twice?

"Cure-alls! Get your cure-alls here! Sure to clear your hangover or clear out your stomach! No refunds! We ain't a charity!"

I turned toward the voice. A dark-skinned boy with his hair braided into locks was pulling a small cart down the road. It was filled with bottles of different-colored liquids and had the words *Soopa meracl cur al 4 sal* scrawled on the side. For some reason he looked familiar. But, considering the only boys I knew from the East Side were Jamal and Arjay, I was uncertain why I recognized him.

"You there!" the boy shouted toward me as he drew closer. "You look like a man who needs a little confidence. Can I interest you in a drink that'll make your prick— Oh, no, not you."

I was more confused by the boy's sudden change in tone than anything else. He started spouting nonsense as he attempted to turn his cart around in a hurry. If he wasn't careful, it was going to tip over.

"Let me help you," I said as I went over.

"Please don't! I remember what your help is like."

I hesitated with one of my hands on the cart. "What're you talking about?"

The thin boy opened his mouth, paused, and then said, "Nothing. Nothing at all. Clearly I took a hit to the head at some point today. Let me give you a free sample of my wares for all your trouble." The boy reached into his cart and pulled out a small vial of a perfectly clear liquid with the label *Dangr* on it. It was barely a gulp. "One of my best wares. Guaranteed to make whatever pain you're feeling go—"

"This is poison, isn't it?"

"What? Why would you say that? I'm deeply offended."

"It has the word 'danger' on it."

The boy blinked and stared at me as if I had said one of the moons wasn't shattered. "For some reason I assumed you couldn't read. That was a mistake. Big mistake."

"Why are you trying to poison someone you just met?"

"Because you're Blunder."

"I know I tend to . . . Wait . . . Rock? Is that you?"

The boy sighed and slumped down on the ground next to his cart. "Why didn't I just go home? I made enough money today. But, no, I had to be greedy and think I could get a little bit more, and then I run into you again. Terrible day. Should've stayed bundled in my blankets."

"I'm glad to see you haven't changed," I said as I pocketed the vial. "Moved on from selling rocks to . . . What's in the other bottles? I'm assuming it's not all poisoned."

"You assume correctly. It's a bad habit for a merchant to kill off their customers," he said. "Had to switch to dust water after a few of my previous customers went to bed for the eternal night. Turns out selling addicts rocks is a bad idea. A lot of them choke on them. Probably should've seen that coming."

"Probably."

"Yeah, well, we can't all be the perfect Michael Kingboy, can we?"

"Kingman," I said. "My last name is Kingman."

"Then why do you act like a child? Kingboy makes more sense."

I let that one go. "Whatever. If you're willing, I need some help with—"

"No," Rock said as he climbed to his feet.

"You didn't even hear my offer."

"Last time I helped you, someone was murdered. Some tweekers who used to work for that knight still stare at me when I pass. I want nothing you're selling."

"Fair," I said. "But are you sure you don't want to hear my offer? I'm just looking for someone."

"That's what you said last time. Remember how it turned out?"

"If it helps, I didn't bring a gun this time."

Rock's eyes narrowed. "I hate you."

"Listen to my offer, at the very least."

Rock considered my words, mindlessly moving bottles and vials around in the back of his cart. I wondered if this was what he'd bought with the money I had given him last time. Likely. "What're you offering?" he asked softly.

"Something no one else can give you . . . a safe home and a future with unlimited possibilities."

Rock laughed. And laughed. And, seriously, what was with people laughing at me? First Dark, then Dawn, and now Rock. When he was done, Rock said, "Stop lying."

"I'm not," I said. "I want you to work for me. I want you to join my family."

"Why?"

Because Rock reminded me of Jamal. They were different in many ways: Jamal had been quieter than Rock was, and they looked very little alike. Rock was wider and taller than Jamal had ever been. But there were more similarities than I had been able to admit to myself when we first met. And the eyes . . . something about the eyes made me remember the friend I couldn't protect. Maybe it was their determination to rise above their lot in life. I had failed to help Jamal do that, but I could still help Rock.

Rock didn't need to know my intentions. So I told him a sugarcoated lie. "I owe you for what happened in the Tweeker Keep. Consider this my formal apology."

"Money is a better apology."

"What I'm offering lasts longer."

"Not if I die or get branded," Rock declared. "Which seems to be common with your family, Kingboy. I've heard about the riots."

"The riots were a fluke. They happened because my family was unprepared for an enemy. It won't happen again."

Rock considered my words, one of his hands against his chin as he paced back and forth. "What would I do if I worked for you?"

I had him. He was going to join me. The conversation was simply a formality.

"You'd be my man," I said. "You'd be responsible for maintaining my affairs when I'm away, making sure I get to appointments on time, and keeping me well-informed on what's going on in the city. And spying on two specific people for me."

"Sounds like a Skeleton," he responded. "I don't want to obey—"

"I'm not asking you to dress me or wash my back. This is something greater. If it helps, none of my family would be able to command you. Not even my mother, the head of the Kingman family. You'd work for me and me alone. If things continue to go the way they are currently . . . you'd likely be the second most influential man in Hollow. My family is on the rise again and you could rise with us. Will you?"

Rock stared into my eyes and then glanced at what surrounded us. This was his home, he had likely been born here and had assumed he would spend the rest of his days in this district on the East Side of Hollow. I knew from talking to Trey and Sirash that the West Side had sometimes seemed like hostile territory when they were younger. Although the Rainbow District was recovering, Rock couldn't turn down the opportunity to drastically change his standing. This chance wouldn't happen again, and he knew that.

"I don't have to kiss your ass or call you some fancy title?"

"No," I said. "Michael is fine. And it's not as if anyone else is polite to me."

Another pause. "I want a feather bed. One as big as the room I'm staying in."

"It'll take time, but that can be arranged."

"Then we have a deal."

We shook on our agreement. Then Rock made fun of my sweaty palms. I took hold of his cart and began to pull it down the streets toward Kingman Keep as he rode in the back. Bells rang out in the distance and I knew if I didn't get home soon, I would be late.

"So, what's my first job? You wanted information on someone, right?" Rock asked.

"I need you to find a man named Treyvon Wiccard. He used to live in the Rainbow District. I tried all day and no one would talk to me, let alone answer my questions about him."

"That name sounds familiar," Rock said. "I'll see what I can do."

I trudged over the eastern bridge, the pale light that emitted off Kingman Keep finally coming into view. Out of the corner of my eye, I saw Rock's eyes widen at the sight. It was his home as much as it was mine now.

"Any chance you'll tell me what your real name is, Rock?"

Breathlessly, he said, "Adrian Julius Westbrook the Third."

I stopped the cart. "Seriously? Westbrook is a Low Noble last name. Are you—"

"I'm messing with you. I'm an orphan. 'Boy' was the only name I knew until I started selling rocks. Everyone in the Rainbow District knew me as 'Rock Boy.' I shortened it to Rock. It was the first thing I earned, so it's mine till I die."

With a smile I said, "You're a prick, Rock."

"You too, Blunder. You too."

17

THE KINGMAN HEIR

Lyon and Kayleigh's little event turned out to be not so little. More akin to the late king's birthday than the quiet family gathering we had been led to expect. Clearly, for the nobility, whether the king had died recently or not, whether we were still under constant threat of a rebel attack or not, the parties had to continue.

Because neither I nor my sister had been warned, we had shown up wearing clothes only slightly fancier than our everyday attire. And that was only because our mother had insisted. I should have realized Lyon had underestimated the size of this affair when we discovered Symon had an invitation, too. It turned out the Recorder's red robes were appropriate for any occasion, and Symon's gap-tooth smile was making me angry. My sister was similarly annoyed at her predicament. At least she was wearing a red dress. I was wearing none of the family colors, and neither of us had gone to the baths recently. Likely we smelled more like body odor than rose water.

"You could have warned us," I said as I focused on the crowds attempting to squeeze into Ryder Keep in an orderly fashion. There were hundreds of them. Who knows how many were in the ballroom.

"I'm an observer, Michael. Influencing events isn't my job."

"You're still an asshole, Symon," Gwen said as she played with her hair. "The baths in the Student Quarter should still be open. I could rush there and back and not be too late. Probably arrive the same time as Mother and Olivier."

"You're going to make me go in there alone?" I questioned. "Bold move."

Gwen stopped fiddling with her hair and put her hands in the pockets of her dress. "I want to look good for these nobles. Just in case I become the head of the family. Nearly killing the Corrupt Prince and showing up to a party looking like a vagrant is a terrible first impression."

"Are you sure it's not because you're nervous about seeing the Corrupt Prince again?" Symon asked.

"Symon," my sister said sweetly. "If you don't stop being an asshole, I swear to my ancestors I'll murder you in your sleep, then throw your body into the river with weights attached to your feet. Understand?"

Symon kept that smile plastered to his face. We all knew he was right, even if my sister wasn't going to admit it. And having known her my entire life, I wasn't stupid enough to agree with Symon openly. I'd have been the one taking a dip in the river instead of the King of Stories.

Thus I offered a third option. "We should find Kai quickly once we arrive," I said. "Maybe one of his servants can help us clean up a bit. Or find some perfume to mask our smell."

Gwen wasn't happy with the situation, but it was the best we could do. Neither of us wanted to come back later. Our plan had been to arrive early, trade a few compliments with Lyon and his future wife, and then leave before either the Royals or Domet arrived.

I had no idea what kind of terms Domet and I were on after the trial and my near execution, and I really had no desire to find out. Domet hadn't tried to avenge the Shrine of Patron Victoria yet, but that didn't mean he wasn't planning something. What else would an Immortal do but wait and plan for a perfect opportunity, after all? Or maybe Domet had been serious about no longer being an observer to history. Maybe he was planning on changing things in Hollow. But what would that look like? What made a perfect world to an Immortal who had seen with his own eyes the Wolven Kings overthrown and my ancestors rise to power?

Domet might have even helped them do it.

"Not that I don't enjoy standing outside in the cold," Symon said as he strode toward a side entrance with his hands behind his back. "But I'd appreciate if we went in. I have questions for High Noble Kyros and I imagine you'd both like to ask for his assistance before he's surrounded with guests."

"Symon," Gwen said as she walked after him. "Remember what I said about being an asshole?"

I followed them. Instead of going through the main entrance, we entered Ryder Keep through one of its many side entrances, the same one I had used on my last visit. A straight shot to the upper area of the ballroom. Upon sight, the guards waved us through without bothering to check our invitations. Even Symon's. I was hoping they would stop him and make him wait in the main line. The headache he was giving me might have been delayed that way. Alas, I wasn't so lucky.

Since there was no other way for us to go but straight, we did so quietly. The last time I walked these corridors was as a former noble from a disgraced family about to make his debut back into high society. Now I would appear as a supposed king killer. And yet I didn't feel as nervous with Gwen and Symon by my side. There was no one I could disappoint. I had already hit the bottom.

The ballroom was louder than it had been during the first event of the Endless Waltz. We could hear the orchestra playing and laughter resonating from the hallway we were walking through. Pushing open the door to the balcony, I half expected to be announced. I even paused for it, but nothing happened. The party continued as it had been.

"Smart," Symon declared as he looked down into the ballroom. "They've put nearly half a dozen guards on the stairs separating family from everyone else. Someone would have to charge them to get up here."

"Since when were you a part of our family, Symon?" my sister asked.

Another gap-tooth smile. "Since Michael bartered his legacy for a chance at saving your mother. We're intertwined till death now."

How dramatic . . . if true. My sister, having already known what I had done, didn't respond on the off chance Symon had been the reason our mother's memories had been restored. It was hard to know for certain whether my Nullification Fabrications had been enough or if it truly had been a combined effort that had saved her. I'd already paid the price in return for his help that day, but some actions were hard to forget. Some things could take an eternity to repay.

Gwen and Symon took their seats at a group of couches around a table. There were already pitchers of ice water, white wine from the Gold Coast, and purple wine from the Thebian Empire. Instead of joining them, I leaned against the rails and took in the view. From up here we could see the entire party and choose to participate as much or as little as we liked. Considering our attire and cleanliness, we weren't going down there unless it was absolutely necessary.

Below, the party continued in full force. Most of the High Nobles were distinguishable by their family colors and the sigils on their clothes. High Noble Kayleigh was wearing a sleek black dress that did little to hide a slight bump in her belly. Unlike the last time I had seen her, she had chosen to wear her dark blond hair down with two golden hoop earrings. My brother looked like a slob in comparison. They were surrounded by a horde of people all intent on complimenting High Noble Kayleigh and doing their best to barely acknowledge Lyon.

High Noble Emily and Alexander Ryder were near the happy couple but occupied talking with various doctors from the surrounding hospitals. The rebellion was making resources scarce in the city and countryside, forcing the number of Mercenary escorts to increase to maintain some semblance of normality. If I put in a good word with Kayleigh and her parents, they might use Orbis Company. That would keep me in Hollow until the war was over.

"A lot of people, is it not?" a familiar voice said from behind me.

Kai Ryder and his brother Joey approached us. Always the gentleman, Kai bowed in the general direction of Symon and Gwen. Gwen gave him her hand and he kissed it. Joey, still so thin and pale with his wispy blond hair, took a seat next to my sister. He looked incredible for someone who had just had heart surgery. Together they played with a few of the wooden toys he was carrying. Joey chose to use the two soldiers while Gwen had been graciously given the wooden dragon. A great honor.

Kai joined me at the railing. Symon followed suit. No introductions were initiated by either, so I did it for them.

"Kai, this is Symon Anderson. He's the Recorder for the Hollow Library. The self-proclaimed King of Stories."

"A pleasure to meet you," Symon said. "I've heard stories of the blind Ryder. Many say you've been practicing the Broken Hilt style of spear fighting rather than the trident style your family is famous for. Some claim it's because of an ever-growing rift between you and your father. I would love to hear your side of the —"

"Thank you, Recorder," Kai said firmly. "But let's save the questions for later, if you do not mind. This is meant to be a celebration, not an interrogation."

"Asking questions is my idea of fun, High Noble Ryder. But I will respect your request."

"Here I thought I was the only subject of your interest, Symon," I said dramatically. "How am I supposed to get over this heartbreak?"

Kai chuckled as Symon glared at me. "Mockery doesn't suit you, Michael. I much prefer when it's the other way around."

I smiled and returned my attention to Kai and the ballroom below. Although Kai couldn't see himself, he tracked the various sounds that rang out. It was hard not to be jealous of the fact that, unlike me, someone told him how fancy this event was going to be. He was wearing a yellow-and-black military jacket with gold buttons with black trousers and black boots. Even his hair was neatly trimmed and the shadow of a beard was beginning to form.

"Glad to see you're still standing, Michael. Despite the Corrupt Prince's rants about how you shouldn't be," Kai said.

"His bark is worse than his bite," I said. Having faced the princess, it was hard to be intimidated by a brute I could hear coming. When his brain caught up with the strength of his muscles, maybe I'd fear him again. "Have you heard that he has a scar on his cheek from the execution?"

"Yes. Rumors say the royal maids are being trained to use creams to cover it. His poor Highness."

"Tragic. And he probably thought Gwen putting him on his ass was the worst a Kingman would do to him." A pause. "Do you know if the prin—"

"We're not supposed to call Serena that anymore. She's the queen-in-waiting until her coronation," Kai explained. "But the guards know that you two are to be kept separated at all times. Kayleigh even went as far as to ask our Raven sister, Karin, to do everything she could. So long as you don't approach her, we should all escape this without incident."

As much as I didn't want Symon to hear, Kai had to know what had happened earlier in the day. Luckily, Symon didn't have anything to write on or with, and this was my best opportunity for the information to come out. "The princess found and confronted me earlier today. She had a gun. She's blind with rage. It may not be as simple as my avoiding her any longer."

Symon took a vial of ink and a quill from one of the pockets of his robe. He dipped the quill in ink and prepared to take notes on his skin. I should have known. As if Symon wouldn't be prepared for an emergency.

Kai, on the other hand, was alarmed by the news and didn't know what Symon was doing. "What?" he said loudly. Lowering his voice, he continued, "How? When? I saw her schedule. My father had a meeting with her that lasted most of the day. When would she have had the chance to slip away and find you?"

"Serena's been good at that since we were children. If she doesn't want someone to find her, they won't. Remember when the royal maids tried sewing bells into her clothes so she couldn't disappear? She attached them to Davey's clothes instead. Serena is craftier than anyone I know."

There was a silence as we listened to the orchestra play a quick-paced song and I watched Symon scribble notes, muttering to himself as he did.

"She really wants to kill you for what happened to King Isaac, doesn't she?" Kai asked.

"I think so."

"Do you have a plan?"

"Not for this. I was hoping to talk to her before she decided to carry out my execution personally. If I'm lucky—"

As always, I wasn't.

The music broke off and trumpets blared. Everyone turned to the main entrance of the ballroom. A stiff woman shouted, "Presenting the Queen-in-Waiting and Prince of Hollow, Serena and Adreann Hollow!"

Everyone was kneeling before the announcer finished her sentence—Kai and Symon included. The only ones who weren't were Kayleigh, Lyon, Gwen, and myself. Three of us had a storied history on our side, and Kayleigh had law. Pregnant women never had to bow before Royalty. It was one of the few goods things the Regretful King had put in place during his very limited and critiqued reign of Hollow.

This was the first time the princess had made a public appearance in Hollow Court for years. Suddenly I understood why Lyon had underestimated how large this party was going to be. If the princess was supposed to make an appearance, then everyone else wanted to be here. The king was dead and the princess was in charge. Laws were hers to create and destroy as she desired.

This was a new day in Hollow. And everyone wanted to be on the winning side.

The Ravens entered first. Six women in plate mail surrounded the two Royals. Each carried their weapon of choice openly, and after everything that had happened, no one could tell them not to. Adreann Hollow, the Corrupt Prince, was still his loud and boisterous and monstrous self.

And there she was, standing next to the Corrupt Prince. Serena Hollow looked nothing like I had seen her last. A simple gold crown adorned her head, and she was dressed in a pristine blue dress with a train so long, two maids had to carry it behind her. Her shadow was as perfect as she was. Seamlessly, Serena had been transformed from a commoner into a Royal. Based on how well she was able to disguise herself, I couldn't help but wonder if I had seen her before today and not even realized it.

The Royals and Ravens made their way toward Kayleigh and Lyon, the crowds parting for them. Serena took Kayleigh's hands in her own and smiled sweetly. Her voice carried throughout the entire ballroom in the way a singer's would onstage. "I am so happy for you, Kayleigh. I hope your future child has a fraction of your charm and beauty."

"You honor me, Your Highness," Kayleigh answered. Her hands moved to her stomach.

"Personally," the Corrupt Prince said, "I hope you are blessed with a boy. With open war with the rebels on the horizon, we need all the soldiers we can get. The Ryders are a legendary family with a storied past, and we need every loyal noble in these troubled times."

From above, I could see my brother clench and unclench his fists. He wasn't doing a good job of hiding his anger. The Ravens had noticed but didn't consider it a threat. What was more concerning was how happy the Corrupt Prince was. Even if he hadn't seen me yet, he must've known I was here. I had embarrassed him. My sister had embarrassed him. His father was dead. What did he know that I didn't?

Kayleigh, ever poised, answered the Corrupt Prince. "Thank you, my Prince."

"You are welcome."

Princess Serena lightly tapped Kayleigh's hands. "Kayleigh, you know I consider you as a sister?"

"Yes, Your Highness. I am eternally grateful for—"

"I have a gift for you," Serena interrupted. "It's not common to give a gift until the child is almost due, and you're not even wed yet, but, as the queen-in-waiting, I wish to give you this in thanks for your many years of true and loyal friendship."

I had a feeling that I wasn't going to like what was about to happen. My sister had joined us at the railing with Joey in her arms. She was as nervous as me.

The princess continued, "This gift is unprecedented in Hollow. I will give your child a future they may not otherwise receive."

For the first time since arriving, Serena turned to my brother. "Lyonardo Kingman. Your father murdered my brother, and your brother, Michael, is the lead suspect for the murder of my father. Your position in Hollow Court is precarious, and the captain of my Ravens has informed me your mother wishes to restore your family to its once-honored position in society. You are the firstborn. As is Kayleigh. One of you will have to step down from your position once you are wed."

"Indeed, Your Highness," Lyon said flatly.

My heart was beating rapidly. This was bad. Where was my mother? Could she stop whatever was coming?

"This is my gift to you both: Lyonardo, I will exonerate you from all the crimes and presumed crimes of your family. No one in Hollow will associate your child with the Kingman family, by Royal command. Kneel to me now, and when you rise, it will be to a new last name. Continue to associate with your family if you wish. I would not divide a family. But accept this gift of a new beginning."

"Wanderer have mercy," Kai whispered next to me. "Who knew she would go this far?"

Symon had stopped writing, mouth agape.

My sister was frozen in place. Joey, who wanted to understand what was going on below, was poking her but got no response. A scene that had everyone transfixed on my brother. The dog of the nobility. The Kingman turned into an executioner. A man who had been given the opportunity to walk away from his legacy and family to protect his unborn child from what I had done.

"Your Highness," Kayleigh said, flustered. "Lyon and I have not spoken about the succession yet. Allow us some time to discuss this and give you our answer."

"No," the princess declared as she rubbed her left wrist. "My love is not eternal. Accept this gift now, with all of Hollow Court to bear witness. I will have it no other way."

The princess's first act as the queen-in-waiting was a power play. A bold statement of what was soon to come to her enemies if they didn't fall in line. A personal warning to me. She knew I was watching this.

"Your Highness," Kayleigh repeated, sterner than before. "You said I am like a sister to you and yet you come into my home and threaten my beloved before the court? How could you? Having a crown sitting upon your head doesn't give you the right to be a bitch."

There was an audible gasp that echoed throughout the room. Kai nearly fell over the railing. Symon fumbled to keep his ink bottle from toppling to the ground. Only the Corrupt Prince was laughing. Five out of the six Ravens had tightened their grips on their weapons. No one spoke like that to the Royals. Especially not when one had been buried only a few days ago. Especially not when the presumed murderer was in sight.

"I will forgive you for that statement," Serena said. "Emotions can run wild during a pregnancy, and I know your beloved can speak for himself. Make your choice, Lyonardo, and accept the consequences of your words. Of your actions."

Lyon had his head down. He couldn't look into the princess's eyes. Or maybe he was simply trying to avoid his siblings' glares from above. Either way, he was alone.

Lyon believed me about what had happened to King Isaac and our father. We were united in our desire to take down Angelo Shade. To avenge all the people he had hurt. But having others believe our story was another thing entirely. Having the princess believe us most of all. Because if she didn't, his child would be in constant danger, regardless of whether they had the Kingman last name or not. They would carry our blood.

This decision came down to whether he thought I could convince the princess that King Isaac had killed himself and that Angelo Shade was responsible for Davey's murder. After what had happened today, I didn't know if I could. She had made her stance quite clear. But he didn't know that. His decision was about how much faith he had in me.

Steeling himself, Lyon took a deep breath and met the princess's gaze. "Your gift is an honor, Your Highness."

"That doesn't sound like an answer."

"I'm getting there, Your Highness. Your gift is an honor, and I would be a fool to not accept it."

"Are you a fool, Lyonardo Kingman?"

Lyon didn't answer her question. "I never wanted to be the firstborn and inherit the Kingman legacy. Not even when I was a child growing up in Kingman Keep surrounded by legends. But I was prepared to accept it, as my father had before me. Did you know that, Your Highness? My father never wanted to be a Kingman. He took up the mantle only after his sister, his parents, your aunt, and your grandparents were murdered by New Dracon City."

"I admit," Serena drawled, "I did not. But what is your answer, Lyonardo?"

"My answer is that I would have been bad at it. Carrying the Kingman legacy on my shoulders. But neither of my siblings will be. They will restore the Kingman family's place in this city, end the rebellion, and prove to you that no Kingman has ever murdered a Royal."

Serena spoke through clenched teeth. "Give me your answer this instant before I rescind this gift."

"Lyon, don't!" Kayleigh pleaded. "Let's talk about this, we don't have to—"

Lyon brushed a strand of hair away from Kayleigh's face. "I made my decision the moment I knew we were going to have a child. My mother returning changes nothing. My family will forgive me. Because making sacrifices is what a father does for his child."

My brother, a Kingman, knelt to the Princess of Hollow and simply said, "I accept your gift, Your Highness. With my thanks."

"So be it," Serena said as she swept her hand above Lyon. "Rise, Lyonardo Cityborn."

When my brother did, everyone in attendance cheered and hollered for the reborn noble.

"Michael," Gwen said next to me. "Does this mean . . . ?"

"Yeah," I answered. "I'm the heir to the Kingman family."

18

THE ROYAL CONSPIRACY

As applause drowned out everything in the ballroom, Serena Hollow looked up and met my eyes. She hadn't glanced up here before this moment and yet knew exactly where I was. This had been a show for me. A demonstration of what she was capable of.

I had never been so scared. Domet, Angelo, and the Corrupt Prince all seemed manageable. Beatable. Now, without meaning to, I might have created someone with the potential to be worse than Angelo Shade. I couldn't protect my family against the Royal that sat on the throne. How was I supposed to survive the week?

And now I had to do it all as the potential successor to the Kingman family.

"History," Symon said slowly, "was written here tonight. This is unprecedented. Unimaginable." A pause. "I love my calling."

"Kayleigh isn't going to be happy about this," Kai said to no one in particular. "I can't believe he agreed without consulting her."

"Lyon did what he had to," I said. "My father gave his life to protect us. Why wouldn't Lyon give up his position? It's nothing in comparison."

"I knew he had doubts . . . ," Gwen said, trailing off. "But I didn't . . . Michael, we have to get out of here. Mother needs to know what happened."

"Agreed. Kai, it's been nice to catch up with you. You're always invited to dinner. Symon, are you coming with us?"

Symon shook his head. "Doubtful there's anything you can do tonight that rivals what just happened. History has been made. Someone needs to record it. Let it be my words that do so."

The King of Stories didn't wish any of us goodbye as he ran down the stairs to interview people. Lyon, Kayleigh, the three Ravens that hadn't disappeared, and the Corrupt Prince were probably his primary targets. They were everyone else's. I hadn't seen where Serena had gone, but wherever she was, she'd vanished.

We left quickly, back the way we had come in. Joey had been disappointed to see us go so soon, but I promised him I would return another time to play with him.

———————

The princess sat in a chair in front of the side entrance, three Ravens at her side. Chloe was to her left, while Karin and Rowan were to her right. All were openly armed. The guards we had seen earlier were gone. Serena was eating nuts, cracking the shells with her fingers before sucking out the insides and discarding the rest. She hadn't looked up at me yet. Remembering Dark's warning, I nullified my body in preparation for a fight.

"Did you two enjoy the show?" the princess asked.

"It was surprising, to say the least."

"I thought it might be," Serena said. "He folded more easily than I expected. Some resistance might have been nice. Alas, cowardice must run in the family."

"And this isn't cowardly?" Gwen countered. "Sneaking out to intimidate us with your Ravens as we leave a party? If you want to talk—"

Serena stared at Gwen. "I want your brother's head on a spike. We're past the point of talking."

"This is how you're going to do it?" I asked. "Stab me in the dark, cut off my head, and call it done?"

The princess ate another nut.

Thankfully, my sister was smarter than me. "Don't do anything stupid, Michael. She's trying to taunt you into a fight. Then she can claim you attacked her if Orbis Company asks. It's a ploy. Walk away. She won't do anything."

"How confident of that are you?" I whispered.

"Enough to risk it."

"Please risk it," Serena said with a smirk. "Try me."

Neither Gwen nor I moved. We had grown up with the princess. We knew what she was capable of, and knowing that made us fearful of more than her powers as a strong Fabricator. Growing up in the shadow of the Gunpowder War had taught us all hard lessons. That pride could blind us. Force us into situations that could lead to disastrous consequences. But following her father's death, she had forgotten it all. Only revenge was on her mind.

I closed my eyes and took a deep breath. "How do you want this to go, Serena? You want me dead and I want to talk. One of us will have to compromise."

"Do you remember the games we used to play as children, Michael?" the princess asked. "There were a few. Court . . . tag . . . even that game, Star-chaser, that you made up. How about we play a game?"

The Corrupt Prince liked to make bets, and the princess liked to play games. Unless I wanted to die here tonight, I'd have to go along with it. So long as I was breathing, there was a chance I could convince her King Isaac had killed himself. Until then, I would have to do what I was best at: survive.

"What kind of game?"

"Tag," Serena said. "My Ravens will be it, and you will be their target. If you make it to Kingman Keep—half a city away—without their catching you, you win. If not, you lose your head."

"That's pretty lopsided, Serena," my sister declared. "Give Michael something if he wins."

"Is his life not enough?" she questioned.

"No," I said. "I want something else. If I'm about to wager my life, there should be something in it for me."

"What do you want?"

"A meal. An opportunity for us to catch up. I'll come unarmed and you can bring as many Ravens as you want. That, and no harm comes to Gwen while we play our game. Deal?"

"Deal," Serena said. "Your sister stands witness to this arrangement so Orbis Company knows you agreed to these terms. I wouldn't want them to think I murdered you without cause." To the Ravens, the princess said, "Whoever catches him tonight will be well rewarded. Do not fail me."

The city darkened around us, Lights Out coming to the city as if those responsible had been listening to our conversation. There would be no one else in the streets while I ran for my life. I looked up at the sky, staring at the shattered moon and the orange-blue marble next to it. Everyone followed my lead. When nothing happened, I shrugged and said, "Hoping a piece of Celona might fall and save me from this mess. Odds aren't in my favor after last night."

"Are they ever?" the princess asked. "Even as a child you were unlucky."

"You only have luck because of Lucky. Do you still—"

"Don't mention Lucky to me," she said before I could finish.

"Why not? I gave—"

"You have until I count to thirty as a head start. Any last words?"

I knelt and picked one of the early-blooming flowers growing between the cracks in the pavement. It was a small and delicate yellow thing, likely to succumb to the lingering cold before spring arrived and saved it. I rotated the stem between my fingers before throwing it to Serena.

She let it hit the ground and then stomped it into nothing. "Ten years overdue."

I shook my head. "Nothing is too late for us."

"Say goodbye to your sister. I hope I never see you again," Serena stated. "One . . . two . . . three . . ."

And I was off running down the main road, mouthing "I love you" to my sister before I did. Gwen would give me a piece of her mind when she got back to Kingman Keep. But I hoped she was sly enough to use her opportunity to our advantage. She was about to be alone with Serena. Something that was unlikely to happen again. But there was no time to think about that, I had to escape these Ravens.

If there was any quarter I had the best chance in, it was the Student Quarter. The quickest way to Kingman Keep was through Refugee Square. But that entire area was too open. Widely spread buildings, open squares for markets, and trees that could make a toothpick look fat. I'd have no place to hide if they caught up to me. Whereas the Student Quarter was tight, crowded, had meandering roads, and got darker than the other districts during Lights Out.

It would give me a chance. All I had to do was outrun three incredibly skilled women who wanted to kill me to please their princess. Karin might go easy on me, because we were almost family. Who knew what Chloe would do. I knew nothing about Rowan besides her name and a little bit about her family. But I was faster than they were and I knew this city better than anyone else. There was no way they would be able to catch me dressed as they—

Lightning struck in front of me, blowing me into a nearby gutter. My focus blurred for a moment, but the warmth over my body brought me back quickly. I looked over my shoulder and saw two Ravens. It was impossible to tell which ones in the dark, but one of them had to be Chloe, given the lightning that had nearly struck me. I doubted the Ravens would have two Lightning Fabricators in their ranks. And where was the third?

I nullified my body again, ignoring the small voice in the back of my mind wondering what I was giving up in exchange for this power. How long would it be before I lost something that was impossible to replace?

The Ravens approached me slowly. One had a spear in their hands and the other had a great ax that was probably heavier than I was. I had . . . my fists. Shit. With nothing to lose by taunting them, I said, "I don't suppose I can interest either of you ladies in a bribe not to do this?"

No response. Only the howl of wind through the buildings, children scattering, and the slamming of doors echoed around us. If there was anyone else in the district, they were getting out of here or hiding as best they could. Three Ravens and a Kingman in a staring match was about as close to a forewarning of disaster as a piece of Celona falling from the sky.

"I was thinking, what if I—"

I never finished my sentence, the Raven with the spear *leapt* toward me. She flew at an unnatural speed. In a fraction of a second, she zoomed past me. Her spear caught my shirt and ripped it. The Raven skidded past me, cut off my escape, and suddenly I was surrounded. Brilliant. The only person I had seen do something similar was Naomi. The spear Raven was a Wind Fabricator, then. I wouldn't be able to outrun her.

I'd have to fight.

I cracked my knuckles, put my back to the nearest wall, and then raised my fists. My body had never been warmer. With their armor I'd have to aim for their faces. Those were the only parts of them that weren't covered. It was that, or try to replicate what had happened in the church. I caught lightning once, could I do it again?

The Raven with the great ax charged me wildly, screaming as she did. Her footwork was sloppy, her motions erratic . . . I had faced better than her and won. I had seen Chloe win a fight against someone very similar. It was a shame she hadn't learned from her own fight. This was going to be easier than I'd feared.

I sidestepped her first attack, a powerful swing that caused the great ax in her hands to *bang* against the ground. I twisted my body to get a better angle and then punched her face. But I never connected. The Raven disappeared, smoke replacing her body but leaving the metal ax floating in the air. I fell forward, off balance, rolling at the last minute to prevent myself from landing face-first.

Not Chloe. I was facing Rowan and Karin. So where was she?

The Raven reappeared out of the smoke in the blink of an eye. Within arm's reach. A Smoke Fabricator. If what I had read was to be believed, they were the opposite of Metal Fabricators in every way. One made their body hard, and the other made their body soft. Smoke Fabricators were rarer, and I'd never seen one before. It explained why Rowan had been chosen to join the Ravens. Another piece of the puzzle filled in, from my ten-year absence from Hollow Court.

As often as I had been in awe of Serena recently, she continued to amaze me. She had chosen two Fabricators I had no natural advantage over. One was too fast and the other was too hard to hit, and Chloe must still be waiting somewhere for an opportunity to strike. Likely from above. I had already shown that I could catch lightning once, and now the princess had found a way to make sure I would never have the chance again.

I was so fucked.

Karin and Rowan crept closer, hunters trapping their prey into a corner.

What were my options? Stand and fight? I was out-armored and un-armed. Run? They'd catch me and skewer me before I even realized. I had to be clever. I had to be smarter. I had to give myself an opening . . .

The Ravens struck in unison, a spear thrust from the left and a horizontal ax swing from the right. One was going to hit me, so I did the only thing I could. I stepped into the spear attack, sacrificing my side to take the brunt of the thrust. It cut my flesh and skin and blood and oh, fuck, it hurt like hell, but I didn't fall to the ground and scream as I wanted to. Instead, I grabbed the pole of the spear, yanked it closer to me—making my wound bigger—then smashed the Raven in the face with my elbow. No amount of training can erase the instinct when you're hit hard enough in the face. It was only for a heartbeat, but the Raven let go of her grip on the spear and I took control of it myself.

I passed the spear behind my back from my left hand to my right. The other Raven didn't have time to realize what had happened to her sister, and I used my momentum and weight to hit her in the chest with it.

She exploded into smoke.

I threw the spear away and took off running down the streets, clutching my wounded side. Although it wouldn't be long, it would take time for the Wind Fabricator to recover and for the Smoke Fabricator to re-form. How far could I get? Would a blood trail lead them to me anyway? I didn't have time to think. Just run. And run. And run.

My vision was fading. I was losing too much blood too quickly, and only rage and fear were keeping me going. I had to find a place to hide. I went down an alley, shouldered open a door, slammed it closed with my foot, and then fell against a wall.

I wasn't one to pray. My family had been at war with God since before Hollow was founded. But in that moment I hoped for a chance. I couldn't die yet. Not yet. Not—

The door next to me opened. I was too weak to do anything but groan and turn to see a Raven with a sword drawn in her right hand. She was breathing steadily. Her black frizzy hair was tied back in a ponytail that looked like crackling lightning.

Chloe.

She stared, voices calling out behind her.

"Is he in there?"

No response.

"Chloe!" the voice repeated. "Status!"

Chloe sheathed her sword. "If you survive, I'll do what I can to help you. Don't die, Michael," she whispered. Much more loudly, she shouted out the door, "Kingman isn't in here! He must've doubled back!"

She closed the door behind her.

Everything hurt. Nothing seemed to be working right. But I couldn't die here. I had to stand. Get back to my feet. Get out of here. I had to—

19

A NEW REBELLION

The darkness returned to me. An old, toxic friend that I wanted nothing more to do with but wouldn't let me go until it dragged me into the abyss with it. It was hard to know if I was dead or not. Considering my mind still wavered, I doubted I was. This wasn't the same place I had been after watching the king kill himself, no, this was more akin to what had happened after the Militia Quarter's explosion.

So I was alive. But barely.

I found the warmth I had relied on so many times before. A beacon in the darkness. There were days I wondered how I could take this much abuse and still get up again. Was it because my mind could push past the pain better than most? Or were my Nullification Fabrications somehow responsible? I didn't know for certain. I might have figured out broad strokes of what my Nullification Fabrications were capable of, but I didn't understand the specifics. That would have to change soon. Maybe Dark could help me.

But as always there were more pressing concerns now. Like where was I? And how was I still alive? I had lost a lot of blood before passing . . .

Wait. I knew what to do.

I took a deep breath and opened my eyes.

Pain came first.

Terrible shudder-inducing pain that took my breath away as I sat up on the raised wooden board I was lying on. My shirt was off, and a sticky green leafy poultice covered my wound. It reeked like it was decomposing. My shirt had been turned into bandages to keep it in place. The room I was in was windowless, cramped, and seemed wetter than it ought to be. I wasn't in Kingman Keep, that was for sure. This was a makeshift prison cell.

So who was my jailer?

I scooted backwards so I could lean against the wall. This was the second time in less than a year I had woken up shirtless in a bed without remembering what had happened. It was becoming a habit. I cursed. At least I hadn't nearly drowned in the river again. Small victories.

The door to my cell opened. A girl with extremely long black hair was standing in the doorway. She was missing part of her right ear. "Can you move?" she asked.

I swung my legs over the side of the bed, groaning as I did. "Where am I? And who do you work for?"

"Big Brother said not to answer any of your questions."

That answered both of them. Big Brother had taken over and improved the Rainbow District. And now they had saved me, too.

"Do you have a spare shirt? Mine seems to have been repurposed."

The little girl looked up at the ceiling. "Big Brother says we ain't a charity for little Kingboys and . . . um, I forgot the rest. Sorry."

At least she was polite. Hopefully that "Kingboy" nickname wouldn't stick. What an embarrassment. Realizing I wasn't going to get any more out of her, I followed her into the corridor, walking slower than someone with a broken leg, carefully keeping pressure on my wound. The hallway was lined with children of all ages sitting on the floor, playing with mismatched decks of cards and broken toys. As I passed, they all glanced up at me and then returned to whatever they were doing before. None of them feared me. In a city where I was known as a monster, that was unusual.

My guide brought me to a bright little kitchen with a table and two chairs, lit by a concentrated ball of light in the center of the table. I didn't know that was possible to do. But Big Brother had clearly figured it out. I wasn't too surprised, Trey had always been testing the limits of his Fabrications.

Even when I warned him not to.

Trey hadn't changed much since I had seen him last. His black hair had grown slightly longer, and he was wearing an old Scales uniform with the jacket unbuttoned to show off the butts of four flintlock pistols strapped to his chest. There were thick-lensed goggles around his neck, more commonly used by Fabricators who fought fires in the city than teenage deviants. But it was obvious even in how he positioned himself at the table—legs crossed, fingers drumming against the table—that he had grown more confident. A man who had his eyes set on change with a fire in them that would never go out.

"You're awake," Trey said as he signaled for my guide to leave. "That's good. I was worried."

I took a seat at the table next to Trey. "How'd you find me?"

"My siblings came running to tell me that a Kingman and three Ravens were fighting in the Student Quarter. Hard not to come see what was going on. Imagine my surprise when I found you passed out in a pool of your own blood."

"And you saved me."

"And I saved you," Trey repeated. "You probably want to know why."

"A little. You made it clear that I chose my path and you chose yours and that they were headed in opposite directions. I never thought we had to be enemies, but you . . . you saved me because I was fighting the Ravens, didn't you? Enemy of your enemy is your friend and all that nonsense."

"The only people I hate more are the rebels." He reached under the table and put a bottle of rum and two cups on the table. He uncorked it and then poured a sizable amount into each glass. "Cheers."

"Cheers," I said, and we drank. The first taste always burned. Some things were eternal. "'Big Brother,' eh?"

Trey cursed and poured more into his cup. "I hate it. After the grave-yard I didn't know what to do with myself. I was alone, angry, and lost. I missed Jamal . . . I even missed you. Thought I would try and do some good. Gathered orphan children on the East Side and gave them places to live where they didn't have to worry about skull-branded assholes, tweek-ers, dimmers, or any other abusers. Any who tried got a late-night visitor."

"So why are residents of the Rainbow District saying you've taken it over? Where have the tweekers and dimmers gone?"

"Michael," Trey said with a smile. "Since when do you visit the Rain-bow District?"

"I was looking for a friend."

"What friend do you have . . . Oh."

We drank to ease the silence. Water went *drip drip* from the ceiling onto the floor.

"What happened to all the tweekers?" I asked.

"The Berry Field . . . the Tweeker Keep . . . the Starless Observatory. They're in their dens, out of sight. The only reason they ever left them was because they ran out of their drugs. I've simply dealt with that prob-lem for them."

"Seriously?" I said. "You're supplying them with Blackberries? The amount you would need to keep them content is ridiculous. You'd have to know the supplier, and why would you . . ." I trailed off as Trey wouldn't meet my eyes. "You know the supplier, don't you?"

Trey finished his drink. "I've known who's been making Blackberries for years. Even knew how. Turns out when you have nothing to lose, you can make offers that are incredibly hard to turn down. In that business, exposure isn't a good thing."

"So you're going to let them keep filling your district with drugs? After what they did to your moth—"

"They're on my list to deal with, but the tweekers aren't the biggest threat to me right now. And don't mention *her* to me again."

That was still a sore subject, clearly. "Tell me your plan, if you're so confident in it."

"No," Trey said, unwavering. "You may be fighting with the Ravens, but when you convince the princess the king killed himself—and you will—you'll return to her side and become much, much more dangerous than you are now. Then you'll be a problem. Then I'll have to destroy you. So I'm not sharing anything. I'm sorry."

"You're acting like I'm a noble," I spat. "That I want to be a part of that world again. I don't."

"Says the man who is currently the heir to the Kingman family. Whose mother is doing everything in her power to restore her family to their once-prestigious position."

It was my turn to be caught off guard. "How'd you hear about what happened at Ryder Keep already?"

"It's nearly dawn. Everyone knows. You're the talk of the city."

Which meant an unpleasant conversation with my mother and sister was incoming whenever I returned home. Disappearing all night after making a deal with the princess for my life was only going to make them worry more. Until they saw me. Then they would just be angry at my moonstruck tendencies.

"What are you, then? Clearly you don't want to work with the nobility and especially not the rebels after what they did. Are you just going to form a third faction?"

"Yes," Trey said. "Let the nobility and the rebels fight over the throne and ignore the East Side as they always do. Whoever takes it will find me leading all the citizens. Change will find its way to Hollow. Whether those in charge like it or not."

"With what army? With who backing you?"

"Leave that to me," he said with an air of finality around him. "As much as I enjoy this conversation, we're done here. There's nothing more to discuss."

"I'm always here for you if you need to talk. My mother says you're always invited to dinner."

"Your mother is too nice," he said slowly. "I doubt she remembers me, but that time you introduced me to her, when you weren't looking . . . she told me how happy she was to meet her son's best friend, since it meant that he wasn't alone in the world like she feared. At the time I simply nodded, unable to express how it felt to be called someone's best friend. It made me realize I had someone more than just Jamal for the first time in my life." Trey stared at the wall behind me. "I never thought she would recover. But to hear she has is . . ." And he trailed off, likely thoughts of his own mother and her fate making him unable to speak.

"None of us really thought she would."

"Except you never stopped trying to save her."

I said nothing, unable to come up with anything that wouldn't make him feel guilty about what he had done.

"Are we good people, Michael?" he asked softly.

"I don't know." I exhaled. "I hope we are."

"One day we'll find out." Trey was silent and took the ball of light on the table into his hands. He held it carefully, tenderly, as if it were a child that he feared hurting. "That woman . . . the one who was shot by the Corrupt Prince . . . have you seen her recently?"

What an odd question. "No, I haven't been able to find her. Why?"

"Just curious."

"Have you had any luck finding your father yet?" I asked as I stared into my empty cup, wondering if I should have another drink before leaving.

"No. I don't even know where to start looking. He left nothing behind for me to follow, and it seems only Shadom knows the answer."

I motioned for Trey to fill my glass. "I wouldn't advise asking him. The answer won't come cheap."

He poured some more in. "I'm not going to. I'll find out who my father is on my own. Somehow."

"Smart choice." I gulped down whatever was in my cup. I'd need the liquid courage for the conversation that was coming. "So where's the exit?"

"The children will escort you out of here and leave you close enough to Kingman Keep that you'll be able to get back there safely. The Ravens have given up the hunt and retreated to the castle anyway. There's no danger."

"Don't want me to know where your hideout is?"

Trey smashed the ball of light in his hands, plunging the area into darkness. I wouldn't have been able to see my hand if it was in front of my face. In a disembodied voice, Trey said, "Not in the slightest. Give your family my best, Michael. They'll need it."

IGSEW HVBJ
IGSEW LJ LTE

The children guided me through a series of tight, wet corridors where the dripping drowned out all other noise except for the wet *slap* whenever one of us stepped in a puddle. It was impossible to know how long I walked, my senses lost. When we got closer to the exit, they wrapped a blindfold around my eyes. Only after I felt the sun's heat on my skin was the blindfold ripped off and a door slammed behind me. They slid the deadbolt closed and that was it. With a hand still on my side, I looked at the building I had come out of. Small, windowless, and made of brick. Located on the edge of the East Side in the Underside. It was incredibly plain and a perfect place to hide.

At least now I had some idea where Trey was if I needed him. If our conversation was proof of anything, it confirmed my fear that we were headed down different paths. But he still cared about me. No matter what Trey said his reasons were, he wouldn't have saved me otherwise.

From what I'd heard of his plan, it relied on no one knowing about him until it was too late. Saving me from the Ravens could have exposed him. And why would he do that if he didn't still feel something toward me?

All I had to do was make sure we were never forced to fight. If I could do that, Trey might stand by my side again. In the end, that was all I wanted. To have my family whole. Well, that and to have my revenge against that spineless coward Angelo Shade. That was just as important.

I slowly walked back to Kingman Keep, doing my best not to aggravate the wound in my side. Whatever Trey or the children had done to it had lessened the pain and swelling. I should've asked what it was when I had the chance, and I'd probably still need to have Gwen check it. I knew my life well enough to understand what a stupid idea it was to walk around the city with an open—

Kingman Keep was within my sight. I would have relished my victory over Serena more and begun to plan how to make the most of the dinner we'd be forced to have soon if I wasn't mentally preparing myself to be yelled at by my family. I entered through the servants' entrance and made my way to the great hall. Everyone was eating breakfast at the table, except for Lyon and Olivier, and turned their heads toward me when I entered the room.

"What's for break—"

I was cut off by Gwen giving me a hug, squeezing the curses out of me as she hugged me tighter. Noticing the dried blood on my bandages, she pulled back and said, "Where were you all night? I expected you back by midnight. Not this dawn crap. What happened?"

I took a seat at the table. Olivier—wherever he had come from—put a spoon and a bowl of porridge of some kind in front of me. The Archivist had already taken out the needed instruments to record what I was going to say. How long before I tired of his endlessly recording of my life? Soon. Much sooner than I had expected.

"Serena was ready for me. She'd chosen Ravens knowing my Fabrication specialization. I should have—"

"Which Ravens and what were their Fabrication specialties?"

"Symon," Gwen growled. "Now is not the—"

"Gwen," my mother interrupted. "The Recorder might have other interests, but it's good we all know the answers to his questions. Unless everyone at this table knows what Fabrication specialty every Raven has? Because I don't."

My sister opened her mouth to respond but then didn't. Instead she returned to her breakfast, shoveling whatever was in her bowl into her mouth.

I continued my story. "The Ravens were Chloe Mason, Karin Ryder, and Rowan Kerr. They are Lightning, Wind, and Smoke Fabricators, respectively. I couldn't outrun them. They cornered me. I fought back and received this"—I motioned to my wound—"and got away. But I was wounded. I passed out from blood loss somewhere in the Student Quarter. One of the Ravens spared me . . . I . . . forget which, but without their mercy I wouldn't be here. Then a friend found me and saved me. Only woke up recently. Came straight here."

"Father," my mother said without context.

Olivier appeared next to me wearing black gloves. Kneeling at my side, he unraveled the bandage and inspected my wound. He poked around it and then said, "It's already been taken care of. Very well, in fact. Gwen, do you want to look, too?"

Gwen did so. She ran her hands over my skin much more carefully. "Grandfather is correct. This has been professionally done. I don't think I could have done the stitches this uniform. But what is . . ." She paused as she smelt the green mixture that had been put on it. "What is this? It smells like marigold and chilis, but I think . . . I think, whatever it is, it's helping repair the wound. It's already scabbed over, and I can barely see the initial cut. That's incredible."

"Take a sample of the mixture and get fresh bandages for Michael," my mother said. "And a clean shirt."

Olivier scraped some of the mixture off me with the edge of a knife and then disappeared. "So," my mother began, "who was this friend with extensive medical knowledge that saved you? Was it Domet—"

"No," I said as loud as I could without screaming. "It *wasn't* Domet.

I haven't had any contact with him in a long time. Trey saved me. I have no idea how he did this, though."

None of them said anything. Not even Gwen . . . They thought that I was lying. That I had broken my promise to Lyon about not making another deal with Domet. They all knew what had happened during the Endless Waltz, I had told each of the family members individually about it. To think that they were still holding it against me instead of moving forward . . .

"I haven't talked to Domet in months," I stated. "I haven't *seen* him in months. Trust me, I want nothing to do with him and he wants nothing to do with me."

"You disappeared the night you became the heir to the Kingman family, Michael," Gwen said. "Domet hasn't been seen in Hollow Court since the trial. We know he has an interest in you, and we know he's planning something."

"So you assumed we were together."

"Yes," my mother said from the head of the table, her fingers interlocked. "We need to talk, Michael. Last night you became the heir to the Kingman family as well as a Mercenary."

My heart started beating faster. "You want me to abdicate, too, don't you?"

My mother's eyes answered my question.

"I wouldn't be a Kingman anymore," I said to no one in particular.

"There's a chance of that."

I couldn't hear what she said next. The words never registered, despite the fact her mouth kept moving. Gwen ran her hand up and down my arm. This was my nightmare. I was about to lose everything. And there was nothing I could do to stop it. I simply had to accept my fate, I couldn't run—

"Michael!"

It wasn't God intervening to save me, it was Dark. A monster in human form. The last person anyone wanted to see coming toward them.

But as he strode into the great hall dressed all in black with a hatchet in his left hand and a revolver in his right, Dark was the only hope I had.

"Michael," Dark repeated as he clicked his tongue. "With me. There was another murder last night. It was another refugee with no heart. We're going to go find out how credible your theory is."

"What?" Olivier said as he returned from the kitchen. "Where?"

"Little Eham. Scales is already at the scene. Check it out yourself if you want to. Come on, Michael. There's work to be done."

I was out of my seat before he finished his sentence. Olivier was nearby with a new shirt and an apple in his hands. I took both and followed Dark out of Kingman Keep.

"Michael!" my mother shouted. "You can't run away from this conversation! It's for the good of the family!"

And we would have it. Later. What I was doing would only delay the inevitable. I wanted to be a Kingman, just for a little longer.

21

THE LIGHT OF HIS LIFE

Dark told me the gist of what had happened last night as we made our way to meet High Noble Maflem Braven, who was walking the battlements. One of Orbis Company's informants in Scales had tipped Dark and Imani off when they discovered a similar murder scene like yesterday's. Dark had checked it out and discovered a picturesque replica. The only difference was the words painted above the body: *The forest is plentiful.*

Not wanting this to get worse, Dark had, oddly, decided to find out if I had been right. If High Noble Maflem had hired a Waylayer to start this, we were going to end it. Orbis Company didn't want a Waylayer operating in Hollow and I didn't want more refugees to get murdered. A win-win situation for all of us. Assuming High Noble Maflem was truly behind it.

High Noble Maflem spent every morning on the battlements blessing the brave soldiers who were the first line of defense against the rebellion. It was a largely useless gesture. But it was done to convince the commoners that High Noble Maflem was a friendly, down-to-earth man. Even though he spent every night gambling away more than they would make in a lifetime and eating the richest foods imaginable. His morning rounds were the only time of the day he wasn't surrounded by an army of house guards, a small honor guard with him instead. It was our best opportunity to get answers.

"Can you fight with that wound?" Dark asked me as we climbed the ladder to reach the battlements.

"Not well. Just doing this hurts enough."

Dark cursed. "Why did I bring you, then?"

"I don't know. Why did you?"

"Because it'll make the fanatic freak fearful. You've already killed a king in his eyes, how's he to know you aren't there for him?"

"We *are* here for him," I said as Dark was about to pull himself onto the battlements. "Is there something you're not telling me? You seem off."

"Shut it," Dark snapped as he swung his legs over. "Stay behind me and don't get in my way."

"Yes, master. Whatever you say, master."

Dark ignored me.

The sun was in my eyes briefly as we climbed onto the battlements. Dark was already marching toward the sounds of bells and chatter, and it wasn't more than a five-minute walk. Since Dark didn't seem to be the best conversationalist right now, I stared out at the horizon. At the world beyond Hollow's walls. But whatever was out there—be it New Dracon City or the Sea of Statues—a rebel army blocked it off. Their numbers had easily doubled, dozens more banners flying over their encampment. Based on their size, position, and the fact that the emperor had escaped Hollow's justice system, it wasn't a question of whether a High Noble would join forces with them anymore. Only of which one would join first.

"You two there!" a soldier shouted as she cut off our path. "What're you—"

Dark drew his revolver and aimed it at her. The end of the barrel was touching her forehead. So much for stealth. "Who's your commander? And is that High Noble Maflem up ahead?"

The soldier was younger than me by two years, maybe three. She was about as bright-eyed and green as anyone can be. She didn't even have anything to indicate her rank on her hand-me-down Watcher's uniform. This might have been her first patrol. "W-what? Are you two rebels?"

"Answer the questions."

Her hand was resting on the butt of the sword hanging at her side. "I'm not supposed to disclose that information."

"Let me make this clear," Dark said. "I am a Mercenary, not a rebel. I do not follow the same rules you civilians do. If you feel obliged to keep your commander's secrets, then take my advice: Don't. Because after I cut off your hand and you tell me what I want to know, it won't be Angelo Shade visiting you in the infirmary."

"How do you know the commander's name?" she asked without thinking, and realized her mistake as Dark started smiling.

"I'll assume that's High Noble Maflem up there, too."

"They're going to hang me for treason," she said, defeated.

"No they won't," Dark stated. Then he punched her in the sternum, hard. I could've sworn I heard a *crack* as she fell to her knees. Dark took her sword belt off her and then handed it to me. "Tell your commander that a dark-haired Mercenary with a revolver and a hatchet did this to you. You'll be honored."

Dark stepped over her and I followed, tying the sword belt around my waist. I hadn't used a blade in years . . . well, except for those brief few moments when I had taken Chloe hostage at my execution. But that hardly seemed memorable. As injured as I was, I could swing it if I needed to. Hopefully, I wouldn't, and if I did, I hoped I wasn't too rusty.

"Was that necessary?" I asked as we continued walking toward the sounds of a crowd.

"I saved her life," Dark said. "And learned my father has been promoted. We're not on the battlements near the Narrows. Which means he likely has control of all the walls on the West Side. Upper Quarter excluded. Valuable information."

As much as I wanted to, I couldn't disagree with that. The more I knew about Angelo, the better. And Dark was right, he had saved the soldier's life. Angelo might even promote her once he learned she had survived a run-in with Dark. A broken rib or two for a promotion? Worth it.

"Do you have a plan?"

"Get the information we need out of the fanatic freak. However necessary."

We entered an area of the battlements that was wider than the rest of them, three or four could pass instead of two. A group of soldiers were lined up along the barriers, kneeling and waiting for High Noble Maflem to bless them. The pious noble was walking back and forth with a bowl of ashes in his hand, dressed in his black robes with a flame trim. High Noble Maflem sprinkled ashes over one before continuing. There were three guards near him, frightening looking in a normal situation. But compared to Dark they were mice before a lion.

"Morning, boys!" Dark shouted once we were close.

Everyone turned to us, drawing their weapons, and High Noble Maflem looked like he was going to piss himself. Judging by the sudden sharp smell, he may have.

"Let's get right to business," Dark said. "I want to talk, High Noble Maflem. Alone. Anyone who's still here after a count of five will experience the full extent of my wrath. If you're lucky, I'll shoot you and not throw you over the barricade to fall to your death. Any questions?

"I'm Dark, by the way," Dark added. "A Mercenary of Orbis Company. The Black Death. You know who I am, so you know why you don't want to be here."

The defenders of the wall scattered like flies. Only High Noble Maflem and his three guards remained. Dark was enjoying this too much. A cat playing with its toy.

"Should I bother counting?" Dark asked. "Or is honor going to compel you to lay down your lives for that fool?"

"Kill him!" High Noble Maflem shrieked while backing away from us. "Whoever kills him will be promoted! Money! Women! Men! Whatever you want!"

Dark holstered his revolver. "Three on one isn't enough for me to use my gun. Don't be imbeciles."

They were. All three rushed Dark at the same time. A solid plan for anyone else. Not for Dark. With his hand pointed toward them, Dark shot ice out of his palms. Sharp and long and deadly shards of it. An icicle hit one of them in the heart and he dropped to the ground with a heavy *thud*. Another was hit in the knee and he followed the other one to the ground. The third wasn't hit by ice, avoiding the shards at the last minute. Instead the guard slipped on his comrade's body, lost his balance, and then went over the side of the battlement. He screamed one last time and then there was nothing. Not even a crash.

"I always feel for the people that don't listen to my warnings," Dark said as he approached High Noble Maflem. He stepped on the only surviving bodyguard's ankle as a reminder to stay down.

During Dark's surgical destruction of all the guards, High Noble Maflem had fallen and tried to crawl away from us. It hadn't worked. Dark picked him up by the collar, slammed him against the low battlement wall, and held him there so half his body hung over the edge. Like a dog, I followed quietly.

"Let me go!" High Noble Maflem screamed. "I'm a High Noble and an Igniter in the Church of the Eternal Flame! Do you know what I'm capable of?"

"Michael," Dark said. "Does High Noble Braven's family control any of the provincial armies? I forget."

I doubted he forgot anything. "No. Law prevents the Braven family from overseeing one of the provincial armies due to their close ties to the Church of the Eternal Flame. The four that do are the Solarin, Morales, Hyann, and Castlen families."

"Ah, so I'd only have to deal with the Church of the Eternal Flame if my fingers . . ." Dark trailed off, letting High Noble Maflem slip a little more off the edge.

High Noble Maflem was pale. "What do you want? Let me go and I'll give it to you!"

"Refugees are being murdered. Two so far," Dark said. "Are you responsible?"

"What? No!"

"Are you sure?" Dark asked as he pushed High Noble Maflem further over the edge. Dark was holding on to his legs to keep him from falling. Everything else was over the edge and his robes had fallen, covering his face and exposing his bare ass.

"I'm sure! I'm sure! I was going to order you two to do it! I didn't hire anyone! I swear to God! I swear on my faith! My church!"

"I don't believe you," Dark said. "The murderer of the two refugees follows a pattern of killing that was used years ago. Coincidentally, also to kill enemies of yours. Rather lucky for you, isn't it? That your problems would go away like that?"

"It wasn't me! I have not been able to organize any killings yet! It's been barely two days since you broke off our agreement, and I haven't had the chance to find someone else to do what I want. It's difficult to find discreet, immoral killers in Hollow!"

Dark began to shake High Noble Maflem as he hung, and the pathetic noble sobbed loudly. "What about the original murders? Your father, Eternal Sister Laurel, Merchant Reo, and Evie Dexter?"

Dark hadn't mentioned those to me before. And there was a pattern? Why was this only coming up now? For two people who were supposed to be working together, he really did enjoy keeping secrets from me while insisting I told him everything.

"I had nothing to do with their deaths! You really think I would order the death of my own father? What kind of heartless monster—"

"I know he didn't approve of your mistresses and was considering disowning you. Killing him first would preserve your position in Hollow. And the others? Well, what's a few more murders once you've given up your humanity?"

"Please, don't do this," High Noble Maflem said between sobs. "Spare me."

"Dark," I said softly. "I think he's telling the truth."

"And what makes you say that?"

"What does he get from lying to us now? All that would guarantee is that you drop him."

High Noble Maflem screamed for mercy, but I ignored him and continued, "If he was behind these murders, he'd be smart enough to realize he could trade us the identity of the killer for his life. It's not him. And pushing him further might give the Braven family a reason to side with the rebels over there. They may not be in charge of the eastern provincial army, but they'd still be a pain in the ass to deal with."

"The Kingman is right! I would tell you if I knew, and there is no honor in dying like this. Falling to my death in robes I've pissed myself in. Not even being purged in fire could restore peace to my soul."

Dark glared at me and said nothing. "And if you're wrong? If more people die and this asshole hired the killer—you know their deaths are on you."

I laughed and shook my head. "I'm a Kingman and now the heir to the family. All my life I've carried the weight of living up to my ancestors' legacy. To be a fraction of the people they were. What's a few more people relying on me when a whole city waits for me to save it?"

"So melodramatic," Dark said with a roll of his eyes. He hesitated for a few heartbeats before pulling High Noble Maflem up. Dark made sure to bash the noble hard against the wall as he did, but he was alive and standing on the battlement soon enough.

High Noble Maflem straightened out his robes as he said, "Thank you for saving my life, Kingman. Know that I would not say those words if I did not mean them. Especially after all you have done to this country I love so much."

"Don't thank me."

"So be it," he said, and turned to Dark. "Mercenary. I had nothing to do with those deaths. Truthfully, they are one of the few things I wish I could have prevented. As you can imagine, I make few mistakes and—" He stopped, staring at Dark with wide eyes. Perhaps seeing the monster in front of him for the first time. "It's you. Davis. Davis the Black Death. How didn't I recognize you sooner? Oh, God. Oh, no."

"Don't say another—"

"Or what?" High Noble Maflem countered. "You'll kill me? How many times did you threaten that, years ago? No wonder you want to know about those deaths, you always blamed my family for what happened. But it wasn't us. It never was. If there are similar deaths now, then the Heartbreaker Serial Killer has returned, and I hope they come for you, like they should have all those years ago. I hope they take everything you love."

"Enough."

"It was *your* fault!" Maflem screamed. "*You're* responsible for their deaths! Brooks, Evie, and even your beloved Zahra. It should have been *you. You* killed them all in your endless pursuit of power and revenge. What a fool Zahra was to love a man as selfish as—"

High Noble Maflem never finished his sentence. Dark grabbed him by his robes and threw him over the edge before I understood what was happening. There was no scream as he fell. But there was a crash when he landed. A *splat* and a *crack* and a *crunch* that seemed much louder than it had any right to be.

"What was that? Why did you just do that? Dark, they could blame me for that and make it grounds for execution!" I paused. "Or should I call you *Davis*? High Noble Maflem seemed to be pretty sure that was your real name."

Dark pointed his revolver at me. "My name is Dark, and I killed a liar for his lies. Understand?"

"You just murdered an innocent man. Don't try to justify your actions."

"I've killed better men and women for lesser reasons. He spoke nonsense and I put him out of his self-inflicted misery."

"I don't know, Dark," I said as I stepped closer to him. His gun was touching me now. "I'm pretty sure he said whoever this Waylayer is who's killing the refugees, they have a personal connection to you. That they killed the person you loved. Likely the person who wore the ring you were so desperate to get back from me during the Endless Waltz. Zahra, wasn't it?"

"Michael," he said, voice cracking and eyes slightly red. "If you say her name again, I will destroy everything you love until there's nothing left but memories."

We were interrupted by four dozen Scales with crossbows and torches and a man neither of us wanted to see: Angelo Shade. He looked much as I remembered: well-groomed, immaculate clothing, and three rings on his hand. Although there was a difference. He had more medals on his Scales uniform. Angelo Shade had been promoted. I could only imagine what for. He stood behind his soldiers with a sickening grin. "Good morning, boys. Congratulations, you're both under arrest for the murder of High Noble Maflem Braven. If either of you move, my soldiers will shoot. I'd love to see you try to dodge all of them."

AN OATH OF VENGEANCE

Dark wasn't stupid, and even he realized he couldn't avoid that many bolts aimed directly at him. A few were sure to hit. And it would only take one to the heart to make sure neither of us got up. We had no option but to drop our weapons and submit to Angelo. And because Angelo knew us so well, he took every precaution. Dark was gagged and blindfolded, and had his arms and legs shackled before any of the guards lowered their crossbows. They merely bound me with chains. I would have been insulted if I didn't know the difference in our strength.

All four dozen soldiers escorted Dark through the city and into the Upper Quarter. Angelo Shade held my chains personally and smiled every time he made me stumble. He brought us both to the castle and held us outside of the throne room, waiting for an audience with either the princess or Efyra. It was hard to tell who was in there. All I could hear from outside was yelling. A lot of yelling. Which was better than the snickering from the man next to me.

"What a glorious morning this has been so far," Angelo Shade said quietly. All the guards were out of earshot, too focused on Dark to pay us any attention. "A High Noble died, I've humiliated and arrested one son in front of dozens of my soldiers, and another son will have his head cut off before dusk. I don't know how the day could get any better."

"Don't call me your son."

"Oh, why not? I raised you for the past ten years. Shame I could never get you to call me Father. That would have been wonderful."

"I'm going to enjoy destroying you."

Angelo Shade only laughed in return. "Always the comedian, Michael. How do you expect to get out of this predicament?"

"I wasn't responsible for High Noble Maflem's death, Dark was. And last time I checked, it was legal for a Mercenary to kill someone, given sufficient reason to."

"I can't wait to hear this reason. The princess might even let you finish your sentence before ordering your execution. You know it doesn't even need to go to trial? One mistake and you're done."

I wasn't worried. This was one situation I knew I could get out of. I had learned enough to justify High Noble Maflem's death, even if I had been against it. But this opportunity to press my advantage over Angelo Shade was something I had no intention of squandering.

"Good thing we didn't make a mistake," I said. "Now, did Edward Naverre have justification for murdering your wife and your unborn child? I wonder how he avoided the ax. Care to enlighten me?"

Angelo was like a statue, emotionless and stiff. "Just because you have a piece of the puzzle doesn't mean you see the entire picture."

"I will in due time. You wanted a Kingman to destroy this city, and now you have one coming for your head. Run and hide, Angelo. I'm coming for you."

That elicited a small laugh from my former foster father. "The more you discover about me, the more you'll realize I am the hero of this drawn-out story. My son is the villain. And once you learn what he's done . . . I imagine you'll decide to kill him yourself, to end his reign of terror once and for all."

"Desperation doesn't suit you, Angelo."

"You're correct," he said. "But the truth does. When you learn it, you know where to find me. I'll even help you kill the whelp. It's only fitting I take him out of this world, having played my part in bringing him into it."

One of the castle guards opened the door to the throne room and ushered us inside. All four dozen soldiers and Dark went first, followed by me and Angelo. The throne room was as immaculate as it had been the last time I had been here, but instead of an impostor on the throne, the queen-in-waiting was. Two Ravens flanked her. Serena wore a regal purple dress, one befitting the woman who would lead Hollow for decades to come. Yet, there was no crown upon her head and that seemed odd to me. Why would she wear it at the party but not on the throne?

"Commander Shade," the princess said. "Why have you brought Michael Kingman and a Mercenary to my throne room?"

"Your Majesty." Angelo bowed quite formally. "It is my unfortunate duty to inform you that High Noble Maflem Braven was murdered. He was thrown from the battlements by these two. I was too late to save him, but I was able to capture his killers. Knowing Michael Kingman is only one strike away from death, I thought—"

"Take the blindfold and gag off the Mercenary," she demanded.

"Your Majesty, that is unwise. The Mercenary is quite skilled with Fabrications."

"I'm aware, Commander Shade," Serena said. "If the Mercenary tries anything, I will deal with him. Michael may nullify my Fabrications, but even then they'd both be outnumbered and unarmed. We'll be fine."

Angelo motioned for his soldiers to do as the princess commanded. Once Dark was able to speak again, he spat in the nearest soldier's face. The princess gestured for them to leave the room. Now it was only her, four Ravens, two Mercenaries, and a bastard who needed to be shot.

"Princess," Dark said, calmer than I expected. "Do I need to explain why arresting two Mercenaries was a mistake or can we skip to the point where you apologize and let us go?"

"Why did you murder one of my High Nobles?"

"We had reason to believe that High Noble Maflem Braven hired a Waylayer to murder the refugees that arrived in Hollow recently," I said. "We were interrogating him."

"I can only assume he was behind it if you two killed him."

"We were unable to obtain proof either way before he died."

"How unfortunate," Serena said in a strange tone. "Did you discover anything that you can share with me?"

I glanced at Dark out of the corner of my eye. "We have the name of the killer."

Serena drummed her fingers on the armrest of the throne. "And that is?"

"The Heartbreaker Serial Killer."

Silence. Next to me, I could have sworn I heard Angelo Shade curse.

The princess leaned forward and said, very slowly, "Michael, if you're lying to me, I will kill you where you stand and welcome the consequences. Are you telling the truth? The Heartbreaker Serial Killer is in Hollow?"

"He is," Dark said with his arms crossed. "Compare the artist renditions of the old crime scenes to those of the past two days. They're nearly identical."

The princess left her throne and walked down the stairs until she was within arm's length from me. Her Ravens remained next to the throne, hands on their weapons.

"You said High Noble Maflem Braven may have hired a Waylayer to kill the refugees. Does that mean the Heartbreaker Serial Killer is a Waylayer?" she asked me.

"No," Dark said as he came closer. "The Waylayer is after us. The Heartbreaker Serial Killer is after something else. If we were his target, he would have killed us already. Not making some of the refugees his first target."

"That suggests both the Heartbreaker Serial Killer and a Waylayer are operating in my city. Without my knowledge."

"I'm not suggesting anything. I'm telling you they are."

Silence.

"GOD DAMMIT!" the princess screamed.

Everyone in the throne room fell to their knees, an invisible weight pressing all of us down. The chandeliers in the room buckled and swayed as every candle in the room went out. The princess continued to scream in anger, but before I could nullify my body, she stopped, and the invisible force disappeared.

Serena took a deep breath and then pushed the strands of hair that had fallen loose back behind her ears. Her face was bright red. "My father was buried a month ago. I haven't had my coronation yet . . . and you're telling me I am dealing with the most notorious killer in Hollow history and a member of a professional league of assassins that many consider to be a myth?"

"Yes," Dark and I said in unison as we returned to our feet.

"Why should I believe either of you?" she asked.

"Can you afford not to?" I countered.

The princess glowered at me. "No. Not with a rebellion going on as well. It seems I am forced to do something I do not care for." She turned her back to me and returned to her throne. "Mercenary Dark. Many claim Orbis Company is the best Mercenary company in the world . . . Are you genuinely better than Regal Company?"

"Yes," Dark said without hesitation. "One of us is worth a hundred of them."

"Bold claim," Angelo said behind us.

"A very bold claim," Serena said. "But one I may have to take advantage of. Let me be blunt. There are rumors that the rebels have tried to hire Regal Company to help them attack Hollow. I want to hire Orbis Company to stop them. As you can imagine, that's not looked upon very favorably in Hollow after one company destroyed Vurano during the Gunpowder War."

"Let me guess: You want us to catch the Waylayer and Heartbreaker Serial Killer so you can justify hiring us to defend Hollow from Regal Company?" Dark asked.

"Yes," the princess said from her throne.

"Your Highness!" Angelo exclaimed as he stepped closer to her. "I implore you not to do this. Do not hire these monsters. Let me attempt to contact with Regal Company discreetly. I have a long-standing contract with them. Their contract price will no doubt be high, but it would be better than catering to these inhuman assholes."

"You may contact them so long as you keep Captain Efyra updated with your progress," she said. "But that doesn't solve the issue that the High Nobles would never let Mercenaries aid us without a reason. Dark and Michael can give us that opportunity."

"And if we die in the process, no sleep lost, correct?" I questioned.

Serena crossed her legs. "Correct."

"What are you willing to pay for this?" Dark asked.

"I am sure we can agree on a monetary sum for—"

"No," Dark interrupted. "I'm not asking what you're going to pay Orbis Company, I want to know what you're going to give me for doing this. Orbis Company will either accept or reject this contract on my word. If you want it done, I want more than just money."

"What do you want?"

Dark ran his tongue over his upper lip like a feral animal. "I want the gun that killed your father and Davey Hollow."

She shifted in her throne. "Why?"

"I like owning things that have shaped history."

That had to be a lie. Dark had to have an ulterior motive for wanting the gun. But what it was, I had no idea.

"Can you stop both killers before my coronation?"

"Easily," Dark growled.

Angelo was tapping his foot on the floor.

The princess rubbed her left wrist.

Chloe put her hand on the princess's shoulder and said, "Your Highness . . ."

Serena put her own hand over Chloe's. "Sacrifices must be made for the greater good. You have a deal, Mercenary. Bring me the heads of the

Heartbreaker Serial Killer and the Waylayer and I will give you the gun. Send someone from Orbis Company to negotiate payment."

"As you wish, Your Highness," Dark said with a bow. "We should go. These killers won't catch themselves."

We turned away from the throne and departed, making sure to give Angelo a smile as we did. It really was the small victories that were the sweetest. Before we left, the princess said loudly, "Michael. This doesn't change anything between us."

I didn't face her as I said, "Not yet it doesn't. Remember you owe me a meal. I like chicken, and you can bring Lucky if you want to."

"Leave, Kingman."

We did, without any further incident. They even returned our weapons to us at the main entrance. Once we were away from any eavesdroppers, I turned to Dark and said, "I have questions."

"I'm sure you do. But I'm not going to answer them."

"How are we supposed to work together if you keep me in the dark about everything?"

Dark looked down at me. "As long as you do what I say without question, we'll be fine. You're my apprentice, not my partner."

"If I'm your apprentice, shouldn't I meet everyone else in Orbis Company? Because apart from Imani, they might as well be strangers."

Dark opened his mouth to object, then calmed slightly and said, "You may regret it, but fine, let's have you officially meet the family."

THE NEW MONSTERS

Dark was, in the minds of many, the ideal representation of a Mercenary. A monster disguised as a human who cared little about killing those in his way. Considering how often he used his Fabrications without thought, he didn't care what memories were lost, either, so long as he got what he wanted. He was the living nightmare that mothers warned their children to avoid. The other members of Orbis Company were polar opposites: goofy, without a serious bone in their bodies.

Orbis Company had chosen to congregate at an old inn called the Lone Wolf in the Sword District. The outside was as unremarkable as the inside was—everything battered and wooden and chipped. Despite how unimpressive it looked, the sour-smelling bartender made it quite clear upon arrival that they had the absolute best steamed rice cakes in the city and a long-storied history of serving Mercenary companies. There was even a plaque with indistinguishable print that was supposed to represent how the first Mercenary company in history—Void Company—had been formed in this inn.

Like all stories told by drunkards, I didn't believe anything he said without proof. Regardless of how insistent the moonstruck fool was, I was just trying to get a word in to ask for their names. It wasn't going well.

Two of the Mercenaries at the table were snorting and spitting at an alarming and uncomfortable rate. The third was a small, slender girl a few years younger than me with short white hair and pale green eyes. Azilian. Unlike her unarmed compatriots—their weapons hanging on hooks nearby—she had two flintlock pistols strapped to her side and four more over her chest. She smelt like gunpowder and sulfur and citrus and seemed completely uninterested in me. Instead, she was focused on knitting a brightly colored scarf with a mismatched ball of yarn.

Just her appearance raised a flurry of questions in my mind, but the other two Mercenaries were wasting my time with drivel.

"—and that's why I chose this tattoo," the lanky Mercenary said as he showed me the underside of his right wrist. There was a tattoo depicting a man hanging from a tree by his foot. The lines were dark and heavy and perfectly straight. "Why was I telling this story, again?"

"I don't know. I only asked for your name."

"My name?" he questioned as he put his arm around me. "Well, my name is another thing entirely. I can't simply tell you my name. That would ruin the entire ballad of lost love, heroic greatness, and endless adventure that gave it meaning. No, I must tell you the entire story. Now, where do I begin? At the true beginning? Somewhere in the middle and let you interpret it as you will? Or at the end and then retrace my steps? You must understand a story's beginning is more important than the ending, Michael."

What a mistake it had been to come here with Dark. I just wanted to know their names and who I would be spending the rest of my life working with.

"If you start that story again, I'm going to get some beauty sleep instead," the stocky Mercenary said with an overexaggerated yawn.

"Understandable. You do need it." A pause. "Because you're ugly, Beorn. And fat."

There was one name.

Beorn, the stocky Mercenary, leaned toward his friend. "Oh, really,

Haru? I'll have to remember that the next time you need someone to shave your entire body after you get a lice infestation."

And there was the second name.

"We said we would never talk about that again."

"That was before you called me fat and ugly!"

The conversation slid into indistinguishable yelling. But since I had the names of two out of the three people at the table, I turned to the white-haired girl, and said, "I'm Michael, pleasure to meet you."

She didn't stop knitting. "Alexis."

"I have to know, are they always like this?"

Their argument had devolved into splashing wine into each other's faces. It was like watching children play. No one else in the bar, owner included, seemed to care. This must have been commonplace.

"No," Alexis said. "Sometimes they're drunk."

"I thought they already were," I said with a smile. "Would you be able to answer a few questions for me about Orbis Company? Dark hasn't really told me anything yet. Says I'll learn in time. But I'd like to at least know something."

"Dark said you'd have questions. Said I could answer them at my discretion."

"Really?"

"Sadly." Alexis sighed loudly and stopped knitting. "I'll give you the quick version. We were one of the first Mercenary companies to form— but not *the* first, that's important—and we have the smallest number of Mercenaries. Each of our members are experts in their chosen field. You will be expected to continue that tradition."

My focus returned to the Mercenaries having a wine fight next to us. "Even them?"

"Beorn and Haru Orbis. Poison and Weapons Master respectively."

"Seriously?"

Alexis nodded. "Beorn knows every plant, fish, and animal that has poisonous qualities and how to extract them cleanly, so it has the most potency. Haru is the one who defeated Nox the Undefeated in single combat. Needless to say, the Thebian Empire doesn't want that story to get out." She pointed to the guns on her person. "And I'm Orbis Company's Gun Master. I'm the best shot this side of the Iliar mountain range. If I can't make the shot, no one can."

It became quite clear to me why Dark had been so surprised that the Waylayer had attempted to shoot us from the top of the colosseum. He knew the limitations of what a gun could do and knew what it meant for someone to surpass them.

"What are Dark and Imani?" I asked.

"Imani Orbis is the second-in-command of Orbis Company. Before that she was known as a Spear Master. She created the Broken Hilt style. You've likely heard of it."

I had. The Broken Hilt style of spear fighting was widely considered to be unstoppable once mastered. It had been created only a few generations ago but had still changed how wars were fought on a large scale. Even with gunpowder rising to prominence.

"What about Dark?"

"Dark is Dark."

It didn't take a genius to see she wasn't going to give up anything about Dark. Even if it was odd that she had told me about Imani.

"So how does this vote for my advancement happen? Dark hasn't told me much besides that it'll occur once everyone is in Hollow."

"It's a vote," she said. "Rather self-explanatory, I thought. If a member of Orbis Company thinks you're qualified, they'll vote for you, and if not, they won't."

"How am I supposed to convince people to advance me if I haven't met them before?"

"Most will ask you questions about things they value in a fellow Mercenary. Could be about anything. Our chef usually asks about your favorite dish, and so long as you have one he respects, he'll vote for you. Our historian asks questions that are nearly impossible, but she does it to see your reaction." A pause. "There is one person who won't vote for you no matter what you do."

"How come?"

"You're a Kingman from Hollow."

That Mercenary must've been from New Dracon City. The hatred between our two countries wasn't one-sided. "Can I count on your vote?"

Alexis stared at me as if I was the least-interesting person in the world. "Are you a master in something? Have you done anything to impress me? Or anything I've asked you to do?"

"No."

"Then why would I vote for you?"

Before I could say anything, Beorn's body landed on the table. Their wine fight had turned into a full-on brawl. Still no one moved to do anything about it.

With a body between us, I asked, "Why do you keep saying everyone's first name and then 'Orbis' after like it's their last name?"

Alexis shoved Beorn off the table and gave him the momentum he needed to tackle Haru into a nearby table. Splinters rained down on us. "Because it is. Most of us give up our families' names once we join Orbis Company. Whatever circumstance drove us to join usually isn't worth remembering. So we don't. We embrace the family we chose instead of the ones we came from."

I didn't respond, tapping my finger against the table instead.

"I imagine you won't do the same," she said rather . . . oddly.

Considering that I was going to have to abandon my family name so my sister could become the heir, I might as well become Michael Orbis. But . . . it sounded unnatural, strange. Like an unfinished story. Could I be someone other than Michael Kingman?

"You might be surprised," Dark said as he and Imani approached the table.

Alexis stood quickly, hands perfectly straight at her sides and a slight flush on her face. "Dark. Imani. I was just going over the basic information about Orbis Company with Michael."

"No need to be so stiff, Lex," Imani said as she rubbed her head and then took a seat at the table. Dark and Alexis followed. Neither of them went to stop the brawl, which had devolved yet again. Haru and Beorn had taken their weapons off the wall and were mid-duel. An endless *clang* rang out in the bar. Maybe once blood fell freely someone would step in.

"Dark's informed me of the agreement you two made with the Hollow princess," Imani began. "Even though our commander isn't here, I've decided to accept the contract. Assuming the price is agreeable. Perhaps it will restore some of the goodwill we lost by welcoming you into the company."

"Where is everyone, anyway?" Dark asked.

"Otto is on his own in the Low Grounds. Everyone else is with Commander Tai in Goldono except for Nonna, who's with the Archivists. They're all dealing with easy contracts. Whoever I take with me will help them finish up so we can have Michael's advancement vote."

"I'd appreciate it if you could leave someone with me," Dark said. "Michael's Fabrications are advantageous in some situations, but I could use some backup against a Waylayer and whoever this Heartbreaker Serial Killer is."

Imani leaned back in her seat, arms crossed with a slight smile. "Never thought I would hear you asking for help, Dark."

"Clearly the Heartbreaker brings out the best in me."

"Clearly," Imani repeated. "I'll leave you Beorn. His knowledge of poisons might help figure out how the killer is getting their victims to isolated places before killing them."

"I don't think that aspect is too important," Dark declared. "Likely the Heartbreaker Serial Killer is able to trick his victims into coming with him with promises of food, shelter, water, or whatever. When the Heartbreaker has total control over the situation, he kills his victims."

"That wouldn't explain why no one has ever heard anything when they die. I've checked the records. The last time the Heartbreaker was in Hollow, there was a murder in Scales headquarters, right next door to a meeting with the head of every division in attendance. That's not just luck."

"The victim was Evie Brown."

"And?" Imani questioned.

"And I don't think I'll need Beorn. I'd rather have Lex. She's more skilled in a fight and could help me determine how that Waylayer took a shot at us from such a long distance. Because it shouldn't have been possible."

"Imani," Alexis began. "I'm fine with helping—"

Imani put her hand up to silence Alexis without looking at her. To Dark she said, "I need Alexis. There's an entire army outside Hollow's walls and I don't want to travel with two close-range combat specialties. If Haru and I run into a gunner, archer, crossbowman, or Weaver, we would have to solely rely on his Lightning Fabrications. That's too risky."

"Since when did you become a coward?" Dark asked.

Imani stood, put her hands on the table, and said very, very softly, "Since learning what goes bump in the night from you. I don't underestimate anyone anymore."

Dark clicked his tongue in response and that was it. The man had more secrets than a child with strict parents. How long would it take me to learn all of them?

"Haru! Beorn!" Imani shouted. The brawl that the two imbeciles had been engaged in stopped immediately. Haru still had his arm around Beorn's neck in a headlock, but their focus was on the second-in-command. "New orders. Beorn, you'll be helping Michael and Dark catch the Heartbreaker Serial Killer and a Waylayer in Hollow. Haru, you'll be accompanying Alexis and me to reunite with the rest of Orbis Company. We'll leave at midnight to minimize the chances of the army outside the walls detecting us. Any questions?"

"Can we finish this before leaving?" Beorn and Haru asked together.

"Pack up your stuff first," she ordered.

With a huff and the exaggerated movements of sulky toddlers, Haru and Beorn stormed off upstairs. Alexis followed them, after giving me a long stare.

"What're we going to do?" I asked Dark. "How do we catch a serial killer who has evaded justice for so long and a Waylayer trained to avoid capture?"

"We follow the clues we have," Dark said without looking at Imani.

"We know the killer is skilled at surgery. The cuts on the body were too precise to be amateur. So we'll need to check the hospitals for anyone new. Second, the bodies and blood had a sickly-sweet smell associated with them. The only time I've seen that is in correlation with Blackberry use. Tweeker dens should be searched as well. Lastly, we'll check out refugee gathering points, see if we can find out where the killer is finding his victims. The Church of the Wanderer is a start. Nothing like fear and hopelessness to send people to a godly power."

"There's a lot of uncertainties in those clues, Dark."

"Yes," he said. "But it's all we have. I'll take the hospitals on the West Side and you can take the Blackberry dens. We'll gather before the Pathfinder service and search the Church of the Wanderer together."

"Why do I have to search the drug dens?"

Imani glared at Dark. "That's an excellent question."

"Because I said so," Dark snapped.

"What about the Waylayer?"

"Let's assume that he'll come for us. No point in tracking him down. We'll just have to be vigilant. Any other great questions, Michael? Or can we get to work?"

I stood up from my chair. "Nope, I get it."

There was nothing else to discuss, so I left the Lone Wolf inn. The amount of broken furniture all over the floor from Beorn and Haru's duel was ridiculous. Once I was back on the streets of Hollow, a voice called down from above. "Michael."

I looked up. It was Alexis. She was sitting on the edge of the window, half of her body out of it. "Yes?"

"If any harm comes to Dark while I'm gone, I'll kill you."

Alexis dropped back into her room and closed the window before I could respond. What a weird little family I now found myself a part of. Though it wasn't any more extreme than the family I had known all my life. The family that I would soon have to dissociate with. I pushed those thoughts to the back of my head and pressed on.

Time to hunt down some drugs.

SCARRED SKIN

Turned out walking around the Rainbow District, asking people where to find drugs, was rather stupid, and my efforts were rewarded with a lecture by an elderly woman about how Blackberries would ruin my life. She didn't let me leave her sight until I agreed never to try them, and then gave me an apple as a reminder of my promise.

After she was satisfied and walking away, her husband gave me directions, a description of the building, and a warning not to have anything valuable on my person when I entered the Blackberry den.

Sometimes love makes no sense to me.

The name of the place was the Berry Field, and it was widely known as the largest tweeker den in Hollow. But despite what my preexisting bias might have led me to believe, it was in the Militia Quarter and not the Rainbow District. A broken three-story stone building that was covered in tarps and wooden boards to keep the cold air out. The roof had a man-made skylight in the center of it. It looked as though someone had made the hole but then given up and slid a pane of glass over it. But it was the large black palm print that told me I was in the right place. It was the universal symbol that tweekers used to mark a safe place. At one point in time the entire East Side had been covered in them, but because of Trey they were slowly disappearing from the area entirely.

I had no idea what was waiting for me in there. It would only take one tweeker to associate me with the Last Knight's death, and to hold a grudge, for things to get ugly. And although I still had the sword I'd taken from the battlements at my side, tweekers didn't go down easily. Dark might be easier to kill than one of them.

After toying with my father's ring to steady myself, I approached the Berry Field. The metal door was brand-new with a heavy-duty lock on the outside. Designed to keep people in rather than to protect those inside. After opening the door and closing it behind me, I entered the tweeker den fully. It was cold, a painful cold that was harsher than it was outside with the wind blowing against my body. This den had seen better days. The floor was dirt and mud except where a few well-placed rotted wooden planks had been placed to make a direct path to the stairway. All the walls had scrapes and holes left by fighting. And the smell was something else. Pungent and rancid and familiar. Like a decomposing body that had been left out in the sun for a month.

As I held my nose, I took a quick peek into the rooms as I passed. Men and women were lying on blankets around burned-out fires with their bright red eyes wide-open. Piles of Blackberries were next to them. A dozen tweekers couldn't go through the amount of drugs in a single room in a year. Trey had done exactly what he'd said he would: completely immobilized the addict population that had tormented his district for years and damned his mother.

I saw only tweekers on the first and second floors. Once I saw those red eyes, I moved on to the next room, hoping to find a dimmer. They were tweekers who weren't fully gone, missing the red eyes that used to strike terror in the hearts of those brave enough to wander the streets after Lights Out. They still had the ability to think about something else that wasn't Blackberries, and as I worked my way up to the third floor, I hoped I would find someone who could help me.

There was only one room on the third floor. The door to it had been broken in half, but the lower part was still attached to the hinges. The top half was lying just outside the room. I could hear someone rummaging inside. Carefully and slowly, I crept into the room. A woman with wild brown hair and dressed in a dirty Scales uniform was searching under a bed, cursing and mumbling as she did. The room was a mess, a breeding ground for maggots. A hoard of heavy, lumpy Blackberries sat in the corner.

"Should be here," the woman mumbled. "Thought I left it here. Why isn't it here?"

The fact that the woman wasn't looking for Blackberries was a better sign than anyone else in the house had given me. And since this was the last room, I might as well try. If it went badly, I could be out of this house before anyone noticed.

"Excuse me," I said as I crept toward the woman. "I was wondering if—"

Wind blew me back and my body hit the lower half of the door and took it off its hinges. My body was warm and in pain, an aching back and neck. I'd nullified a moment too late. I pushed myself off the ground, drew my sword, and faced the—

Oh, shit.

Naomi Dexter smiled sweetly, her electric-blue eyes shining brightly. She had a handful of Blackberries in her left hand. "Michael Kingman," she said, every syllable drawn out dramatically. "I'd apologize for the rude welcome, but I don't really care. What are you doing here?"

Cautiously, I entered the room again. My sword stayed in my hand. "I could ask you the same thing. Are you . . . ?" I didn't know how to finish that sentence. She clearly wasn't well, but I didn't want to imply anything more. Not to her. Not after she had been shot by the Corrupt Prince trying to protect me.

"Can't say the word, Michael? Let me help you. It's spelled A-D-D-I-C-T."

"So you are?"

"Obviously," she said with a raised eyebrow. I watched her take one of the Blackberries and slide it between her teeth and lower lip. Naomi sucked on it loudly and then shuddered with her eyes closed for a few heartbeats. When she had returned to reality, she said, "It makes it much more bearable when you've lost everything and endure unbearable pain after being shot in the stomach. Want to see the scar? Why am I asking? Of course you do."

Naomi lifted her shirt so I could see her stomach. There was an ugly, bright red circular indent on the left side. There were raised, jagged lines around it as if worms had burrowed into her skin and taken up residence there. "Blackberries take the pain away. My life may be intact, but who cares when it's like this?"

"Last time I saw you—"

"Last time you saw me," Naomi mocked as she covered herself again. "I had given you up to the Royals after you turned yourself in. For a moment I was important again. People stopped whispering behind my back. The princess even invited me to dinner. Life was returning to some semblance of normality . . . right up until you escaped your execution, and no one knew how. Without knowing, they blamed everyone who had had any contact with you. Me included. They kicked me out of Scales and told me I was lucky not to get a branch in the Hanging Gardens."

"What about your father? He couldn't protect you?"

"My father," Naomi said bitterly as she crept closer, "seems so noble, doesn't he? But he isn't. He's a work-obsessed fool. When the Corrupt Prince shot me, I was an embarrassment to him. Not a daughter. If he seemed to care, it was only to mitigate the political damage I'd done to him."

"Naomi, I'm sorry."

"Don't act like you're any better than me," she growled. "Most people want nothing to do with me, but I have a new job with perks. As you can see, I babysit the addicts below and take delivery of drugs from the kids. It's easy. I'm supposed to get a new delivery today. Blackberries are always best when they're fresh."

"What happened to the woman who wanted to be queen?"

"She's dead." She started to unbutton her clothes, exposing the bare skin beneath. "But I've been thinking. Since everyone already calls me the Kingman Whore, we might as well fuck. At least then the rumor will be real. I imagine you'll be halfway decent."

I was stuttering, unable to form complete sentences in my surprise. Then she put one of her hands on my inner thigh and squeezed. I jumped back and cursed, face redder than a tweeker's eyes. Naomi was laughing now, still halfway between clothed and naked. "What a prude. Can't even do the thing I've been damned for."

"Fuck you."

"That's more like it," she said with a wink before buttoning her shirt again and taking a seat on the bed. "You never said why you're here, Michael. Want a taste? It goes down *so, so* sweet. I'll even share mine."

Naomi stuck out her tongue, presented her prize, then tucked it away in her lip again and waited for my answer.

"I'm good."

"A shame," she said with a roll of her eyes. "If you're not here to fuck me or share a Blackberry with me, why are you here? I can't wait to hear your hypocritical noble bullshit reason. Please don't say you're here to save me. I'm not in need of saving. Especially not by you."

"I'm not," I said. "I'm looking for information, and you're the only one relatively conscious here."

"What a joy for me. What did you want to know?"

I heard a commotion downstairs but ignored it. Tweekers were always getting into useless fights over Blackberries. That wasn't going to stop even if they had a lifetime supply. Thus, I said, "Information about refugees. Whether you've seen any of them come here and then leave under strange circumstances. Their killer is targeting the weak and vulnerable and, well—"

Naomi chuckled and crossed her legs. "Some noble asshole is targeting the refugees?"

"It's not a noble. We already investigated that angle. It didn't end well for our suspect."

"Who else would care about some dirty, useless refugees?"

"A killer who preys on the helpless. One called the Heartbreaker. That's what Dark . . ." I paused, noticing the change in Naomi's expression. She was pale, the Blackberry she had been sucking on forgotten. I had a sudden feeling that I had forgotten something extremely important about Naomi.

"Michael. Are you lying to me?"

"No."

Naomi gripped the edges of her bed. Hard. Knuckles whiter than the snowcapped Iliar Mountains. "The Heartbreaker Serial Killer took me hostage, murdered my mother, and made my father one of their playmates for their grand finale. My father won, barely, and I became the only person to ever escape from the Heartbreaker Serial Killer. Now you're telling me they're back? And that you're investigating them? How many victims so far?"

"Yes, Dark thinks the serial killer is back. Yes, we're investigating the murders. And we think there have only been two victims so far."

"You imbecile."

"What did I—"

Naomi reached under the bed and took out a flintlock pistol from a hidden place. She made sure it was loaded and then stuffed a handful of Blackberries into two of her jacket's pockets. "The Heartbreaker is coming."

"How do you know that?" I questioned.

"The Heartbreaker Serial Killer finds opponents to play their game with them. Gives them a chance to save those who have been taken. My father always believed that they liked the thrill. Liked the competition. Sometimes they're the relatives of the victims that have already been chosen. Sometimes they're the investigators of the previous murders that were a warm-up for the grand finale. Just like my father. You've definitely been chosen. You're a Kingman. And you brought them to me. The one who got away. We're the ideal candidates."

"That's rid—"

I didn't finish my sentence, cut off by screams from the lower floors. Long, pained wails of tweekers clawing at the walls to escape whatever was going on. But that shouldn't have been possible. Tweekers didn't feel pain. Blackberries numbed their senses once they had ingested enough of them. Whatever was going on was making them remember what it was like to feel.

All the lanterns and candles in the tweeker den went out and we greeted the darkness like an old friend. There were no creaks in the wood or flapping of the tarps from the wind. Just silence.

Endless silence.

A giggling voice sang from below, "Na-o-mi."

We froze in place, unsure what to do or where to go.

"Mi-chael."

Naomi was right. The Heartbreaker was here for us.

The hunters had become the hunted.

THREE FLOORS
TO FREEDOM

"Skylight. It's our only way out," Naomi snapped. "Lift me up and I'll break the glass."

I hesitated, staring at the staircase, waiting for someone to walk up it. Where were they? Why hadn't they come up here after taunting us?

"Michael!" she screamed.

I snapped back to reality, sheathed my sword, put my hands together, and moved to lift her up. We had done this once before, so it was familiar. Naomi gave herself a slight running start and leapt as I threw her upward. My side burned with pain as I did, but I gritted my teeth and pushed through it. Now wasn't the time. Naomi glided in the air, changing directions as only a Wind Fabricator could, then grabbed hold of a protruding lip below the pane of glass. Hanging from one hand, she hit the glass with the butt of her pistol in her other.

Boom, boom, boom.

The glass wasn't breaking.

"Why isn't it working?" I asked, glancing between the stairs and Naomi.

"I don't know!"

"Try hitting the center of it."

Naomi grumbled something, shuffled along the edge she was hanging on to, and then tried beating on the glass in a new spot.

Boom, boom, boom.

Still nothing.

"Why isn't this working?" she whined as she continued to hit the glass.

"We might have to fight," I said, my full attention on the staircase and the darkness below now. I couldn't hear anything anymore. Even the screaming had stopped.

"Pointless," Naomi said breathlessly. "No one can beat the Heartbreaker when they fight them on their terms. Only survive. We need to—"

Naomi stopped talking. There was a hooded figure in a long, loose black robe standing above us. In one movement they slammed their palm against the glass. It shattered instantly. Naomi fell, soundlessly screaming as she did. Glass fell from above like snow. I nullified my body and moved to catch Naomi—dropping my sword away in the process—and I did catch her. With my chest. We both hit the ground with a *thud* and a groan. The pain from the cut on my side was worse than ever, joined by dozens of small glass shards poking me.

The figure remained above us. Watching.

"Na-o-mi Dex-ter. I. See. You."

"Get up," I moaned. "Get up, Naomi, we have to run."

We helped each other, every movement slow and painful. Naomi had her arm wrapped around my waist and together we limped away from the figure in black and down the stairs—nearly tripping down the length of them.

"Mi-chael King-man," the figure sang. "Play. With. Me."

There was another loud *thud* from the room we had just been in.

"Windows?" I suggested.

Naomi shook her head, steering us toward one of the rooms on the second floor. "Boarded up. Very well. Tweekers would have broken them if they weren't."

I cursed and then gagged at the sight we had walked into. Four tweekers were dead and Blackberries littered the floor. Two of them were slumped against the walls—eyes wide and blood dripping out of their ears. Another had his head smashed into the now-smoldering fire, smoke wafting out around him. The fourth was sprawled right in front of the doorway. All his fingers were missing. And his tongue . . . I couldn't recognize what I was looking at anymore.

But there was something coming from the room. A soft, steady sobbing from under a pile of blankets. Naomi let go of me, moved toward the noise, and then threw the blankets up into the air with a flick of her wrist. She revealed a boy, maybe less than ten years, with bloodshot eyes and a small kitchen knife in his hands. His entire body shook as he pointed the knife toward us, eyes closed.

Naomi knelt and then stroked the boy's hair. "Jay. It's Naomi. I'm not going to hurt you."

The boy grabbed her in a tight embrace, the knife tumbling to the ground next to him. Like a mother would, Naomi gently stroked his hair and very softly whispered, "Shhhhh."

"Not to ruin this moment, but—"

The Heartbreaker Serial Killer's voice cut me off instead: "Na-o-mi. Mi-chael. Where. Are. You?"

Naomi beckoned me toward her and then threw all the blankets over us when I was close. We were completely hidden, but I still nullified my body. Somehow it calmed me. Naomi held the boy tightly.

"Let's. Be. Friends," the killer said as they stalked closer.

Shadows darted and twisted in the room we had hidden in. I couldn't hear the killer's steps but felt them in the ground with my face pressed against it. The killer moved from the doorframe to the center of the room. We were off to the side under a pile of blankets, holding our breath.

"I. Know. You. Mi-chael. Won't. You. Play?"

A centipede fell out of the dirty blanket and onto Naomi's forehead. It crawled down her face toward her mouth, edging at the corners as if trying to pry her lips open. She didn't scream or squirm at the bug creeping over her face with its dozens of legs, keeping her hand over the boy's mouth.

"Na-o-mi," the killer continued. "What. About. You?"

The centipede squirmed fully into Naomi's mouth, over her teeth, and onto her tongue. Rather than risk the crunch, Naomi let it slither down her throat—a bulge visible as it did—and into her stomach. Her eyes watered from pain. Yet she remained utterly silent.

The killer made an exasperated click with their tongue. "Shame. Shame. Shame. None. Will. Play."

The Heartbreaker Serial Killer left the room, and after waiting a few heartbeats to make sure they were gone, Jay and I exhaled in relief as Naomi dry-heaved. Even after hearing the voice so close, I couldn't distinguish an accent or gender or anything tangible. Their weird speech pattern made it impossible.

"The front door," Naomi whispered after she recovered. "It's our best chance, short of trying to break down the walls."

I nodded and crept toward the stairs. Naomi carried the boy, pistol hanging at her side, one hand over the child's mouth. We could hear the Heartbreaker singing from another room on the second floor. One of those endless sticky tunes that always seemed to play in bars and never ran out of new verses. It sounded like "The Rabble Rouser's Riot." People hadn't sung it in Hollow in years. A decade, maybe.

We crept soundlessly down the stairs. It was a miracle that they didn't squeak or creak and give us away, and then the front door was only a straight hallway away. We walked rather quickly toward it and then attempted to open the metal door.

It didn't budge.

"Locked," I muttered, continuing to try to push it open.

"It only locks from the outside," Naomi said. "I don't understand. The killer would have had to kill everyone inside, leave, and then climb the building to enter through the skylight. There wasn't enough time to do all that."

"But they did," I said as I put my head against the cool metal. "What do we do?"

The Heartbreaker Serial Killer answered my question instead of Naomi, and sent shivers up my spine. "Play. With. Me."

The figure in all black was waiting at the bottom of the stairs. No part of them was visible except for their thin lips and hairless chin. The darkness distorted their skin, giving me no clue what they were or where they were from. If we escaped, I still wouldn't have any solid information about them. Great.

"Naomi, give me the gun."

She did, and put Jay on the ground behind her.

My body was already nullified in case the Heartbreaker was a Fabricator. If I could get close with the gun, I might be able to put an end to this. It was a small chance, but I didn't have many options. Dark wasn't coming for me. No one was coming for me. No one knew I was even here.

Naomi and I were on our own.

I still tried to stall for time. A fool's fallacy.

"You're the Heartbreaker Serial Killer, aren't you?" I asked.

"Yes," they said as they crept toward me with painfully slow steps.

"What do you want?"

"Doesn't. Concern. You."

That was something. If it were some urge, or for an entertainment factor, they would have said so. But their reaction suggested a deeper motive was at play. Something they didn't want me to know. If only I could figure out what it was before it was too late . . .

The Heartbreaker was two arms' lengths away. I only had one chance at this, and I wanted to be sure . . . When they came in arm's reach I'd shoot for the head. Unless they were immortal, we'd have them. Or that's what I kept telling myself.

There was a pounding on the metal door and everyone in the hallway froze. The Heartbreaker included. Had Dark come after all?

The door swung open and I threw myself over Naomi and the boy, my nullified body protecting them.

A figure surrounded by blinding light charged into the Berry Field. Guns were strapped to their chest. They fired one, threw it aside, drew another, and then resumed firing until smoke filled the hallway and the smell of sulfur overpowered everything.

Treyvon Wiccard stood triumphant in the doorway as the smoke began to clear, a loaded gun in each of his hands and the light emanating from his body lit the hallway. The killer was gone. "Go!"

He didn't have to tell us twice. Scrambling and hunched over, we all left the Berry Field in a hurry. Trey backed up carefully, guns still aimed down the hallway. Once he was clear, he slammed the metal door and locked it with a key from his pocket. Only after Trey had tested the door—to make sure it was secure—did he holster his guns and turn toward us.

The sun was still high in the sky and citizens of Hollow walked past us without a care, blissfully unaware of what had just happened. That a serial killer had returned to Hollow and would soon kill again.

"Big Brother!" the boy yelled in excitement, jumping into Trey's arms.

Trey said something to Jay, moved his goggles off his eyes, and then turned to Naomi and me. "Let's get some distance away from the Berry Field before we talk."

We did, walking multiple blocks to a small murky pool of water that people used to wash in. We all stopped and collected ourselves. Naomi was shaking slightly and sucked on a fresh Blackberry. Trey did little to hide his disgust.

"How'd you know we were in trouble?" I asked.

Trey put down Jay, instructed him to clean off, and then said, "I don't let the kids make deliveries unsupervised. I was waiting outside and when it took him too long to come out, I suspected something was wrong."

"You saved us. Thank you, Trey."

"It's nothing," he said dismissively. "Tweekers aren't that hard to deal with once you know how. They'll cool off after a few days of solitude and then I'll even be able to collect my guns again. Thought you would handle them better, Michael."

"We weren't running from tweekers," Naomi said, shaking her head. "It was the Heartbreaker Serial Killer. They killed all the tweekers, left their bodies out like it was an art exhibit."

Trey didn't look at Naomi. "Is the addict telling the truth, Michael?"

"Yes. And her name is Naomi. She was the one who got shot by the Corrupt Prince because we wouldn't shoot each other."

"I remember," Trey said. "But if this is her fate, that Mercenary should have left her to die."

Naomi laughed. "No argument here."

"So what is the Heartbreaker after?" Trey asked. "Are they just killing addicts? Because I have no complaints if they are."

"They've begun by killing the refugees in Hollow," I said.

"But it won't stop with them," Naomi declared. "The refugees' deaths are only to set the stage for the main event. With every passing day the killer will kill more important people until the grand finale. They'll pit two people against each other. Usually the two they deem the worthiest to be their opponent, forced to fight because someone they hold dear is being held captive. Only one of the combatants will survive, and if they fail, then everyone else dies. Until my father. Until me." A pause, and she looked at Trey. "And guess what, asshole? Having saved us, you might be one of the Heartbreaker's chosen ones. Or at the very least someone they won't kill until the end."

"It's funny you think I have anything left to lose," Trey said. "My mother and brother are dead. I don't know who my father is. And I've already accepted that Michael will die soon enough. Be it by my hand or another's."

That was news to me.

Naomi pointed toward Jay. He was busy washing his feet, twisting and bending in angles only children could. "What about him? Or any of the other children that look up to you . . . Big Brother."

Trey exhaled hard. "How do we stop the Heartbreaker?"

Naomi closed her eyes for a moment. "We talk to my father. He's the only person to have beaten the Heartbreaker at their own game." A pause. "I can't believe I have to talk to that asshole again."

COMMANDER OF
THE EVOKERS

I had to meet with Dark at the Church of the Wanderer at the end of the day. Not wanting to give up the opportunity to spend time with Trey and learn more about the maniac who had slain their way through a house of tweekers, we made our way to Naomi's old residence. Just the thought of talking to her father again made her agitated. She had already gone through one Blackberry before we crossed over the eastern bridge and was likely to finish another before we made it to Scales Headquarters in Justice Hill.

The building was the pride and joy of Justice Hill. It had been built recently and was free of the wear and tear that characterized other parts of the city. But the real reason everyone loved it was because it had raised the value of the property around it. A few families had bought their way into the Low Nobility after selling their residence at a premium. Yet even this place couldn't escape the disaster of mud and ice between the beginning of spring and the end of winter. The roads were caked brown, slushy snow clogged the gutters that caused everything to reek of old fish guts, and every bit of green shined translucently from the frost.

At least it wasn't snowing.

Naomi was braiding her hair as we approached the entrance to Scales Headquarters. The guards at the door drew their weapons on seeing us. Something about a Kingman and suspected king killer, a dimmer, and a kid from the East Side must've made them nervous. Trey and I let Naomi do the talking. Despite her untidy appearance and the obvious bulge in her lower lip.

"I'm looking for my father, Bryan Dexter," Naomi told the two guards.

They glanced at each other and the female guard said, "Commander Dexter isn't taking any visitors today. He's busy."

"Too busy for his daughter?"

The other guard said, "*Especially* for his daughter."

"I have the best father," she said with a shake of her head. "Well, tell that asshole I have information he'll want. About the Heartbreaker. You two imbeciles must know what he'd do to you if that message gets lost. Let him punish me himself if I'm lying."

Naomi walked away from them and took a seat on a bench with me and Trey and Jay under a leafless tree. We were all bundled tightly in our clothes, the cold creeping under our skin and into our lungs. The guards were whispering to each other but had yet to move.

"We should have waited for him at your house," I said.

"No," she countered. "My father lives at Scales Headquarters. Even when we were on better terms he only came home for dinner once a week. Who knows if he's even been there since I was let go from the Executioners."

"Who doesn't have time for their family?" Trey asked.

Naomi sucked on her Blackberry as one of the guards went to give her father the message. "A man whose daughter reminds him of his murdered wife and his greatest failure . . . being unable to catch the killer who did it." A pause. "Some days I wonder if he wishes I had died, too.

So he could fully immerse himself in his work rather than being bothered with a child."

Neither Trey nor I had a response to that. As dysfunctional as our families' lives had been, I doubted even Trey could say his mother—whom he had murdered—had wished he were dead. We were, at the end of the day, our parents' children and bore the scars to prove it.

It wasn't too long before the guard returned with a muscular man with a heavy beard and permanent dark circles under his eyes. His Scales uniform was sloppy and stained. Only a commander could get away with looking like that.

Bryan Dexter was unarmed, his hands in his pockets. A small locket around his neck swung back and forth as he walked over. It didn't look as if he had smiled in decades.

"What attention-seeking waste of time is this, Naomi? Drawing me out by mentioning the Heartbreaker? Pathetic." After looking at me, he continued, "Still giving people a reason to call you the Kingman Whore?"

Naomi put her hand on my thigh and squeezed dramatically. "I was considering fucking him in public to help solidify my reputation. Where do you think would be better? Conqueror Fountain or in the middle of the Great Stone Square before a Pathfinder service?"

"What do you want, Naomi?"

"Information," she said sweetly. "I wasn't lying. The Heartbreaker is back."

"Unlikely. I would know if they were."

"There have been two murders so far," Naomi snapped. "Both missing their hearts. Along with other things. Things no one except those who've seen the Heartbreaker's work would be able to re-create."

Bryan Dexter cracked his knuckles. "Where?"

I rattled off the locations for him. His face soured.

"I've heard about those murders. I haven't had the time to investigate them yet, but I will today. If the killer has returned . . ."

"Must be embarrassing to have missed connections to the one thing you're obsessed with finding," Naomi mocked.

Trey shifted away from her on the bench. He was looking at anything that wasn't the scene in front of us. The blackbirds in trees, the Advocators walking past, the refugees begging—literally anything else.

"Mistakes happen." Bryan Dexter exhaled loudly. "So you came here for information about the Heartbreaker? Why? You never cared before."

"Sorry I tried to honor my mother another way," Naomi snapped.

"Says the addict who can't remember what she looked like."

Naomi clenched her fists and said with gritted teeth, "The Heartbreaker attacked Michael and me today. Trey here saved us. They're targets for the grand finale now. As am I. Again."

"It won't get to that point. If the Heartbreaker Serial Killer is back, I'll stop them. I won't fail again."

"If you say so, Father."

"I do," Commander Dexter declared. He reached into one of his jacket pockets and pulled out a small black book. It was faded and old and had likely been used hundreds if not thousands of times. "This book holds everything I learned about them. They murdered twelve people in Hollow. Take it. I've memorized it. Not even using Fabrications could take those memories from me."

Bryan Dexter turned away from us and then continued, "And, Naomi . . . don't let me see you with that poison in your mouth again. It's disgusting."

Naomi let him leave without a word. She hesitated to put a fresh Blackberry in her mouth for a few heartbeats, tapping her foot against the stone below, until she did. Four Blackberries in a morning. At the rate she was going, she'd be a tweeker soon.

Trey slapped his hands against his knees and then rose from his seat with Jay. "This was a complete waste of time. Can't believe I actually went with you two to Scales Headquarters."

"You don't want to know what's in here?" Naomi asked as she waved the book.

"I don't read as fast as you two do," Trey said. "I'll send one of the children by Kingman Keep in a few days to get the gist. At least he reinforced what you told me earlier. I doubt I have much to worry about until this grand finale anyway."

"The children might."

"Over my dead body," Trey declared. There was no mistaking that he meant it.

"You could always get the information in a few days yourself," I said without looking at him. "My mother did invite you to dinner. She wants to meet you. Wants to meet my best friend."

"No," Trey said, and that was that. He left, hands in his jacket pockets to draw it close and hide the bulges from the guns strapped to his chest.

"He's a bit dramatic," Naomi said when Trey was out of sight. "Not that I'm any better. You'd think his life was one long tragedy by the way he acts."

That's because it was. Trey was right: he had already lost everything he had held dear, to either rebels or Blackberries. And now there was a fresh threat to the new family he had built. All the people he had helped. It was amazing he had the willpower to keep marching forward.

But I didn't tell Naomi any of that and instead asked, "How long will it take you to read through your father's notes? Dark will want to read it, too."

"A day or two?" she said. "Hopefully, Kingman Keep won't be too distracting."

"Why would you go to Kingman Keep?"

"Well," Naomi said with a smile and a brush of her hand down my shoulder. "My former abode is filled with dead bodies, and I'd rather sleep in the streets than in my father's house. He's going to kill himself trying to catch the Heartbreaker Serial Killer, and I have no desire to watch it happen. I'll see him at his funeral. That only really leaves one place for me to go. Especially with this book."

What kind of messed-up community was I beginning to build? Of people who either wanted something from me or wanted me dead. Brilliant.

"Fine," I said, resigned to my fate. "Tell my mother I'll be there for dinner. I have to meet Dark at the Church of the Wanderer first."

Naomi met my eyes. A sickly sweet smell came from her mouth and lips. "May your adventures be fruitful. But I would hurry back, Michael. Or else I might tell everyone we're engaged to be wed. Do you think they would take that well? A whore turned wife?"

"Goodbye, Naomi." I left her sitting on the bench.

"Bye, sweetie," Naomi said. "It'll be cold in bed without you."

The joke was on her, we still didn't have beds in Kingman Keep.

A SMOKY CELLAR

A blizzard came out of nowhere, one last *Fuck you* before spring arrived. The wind howled down the streets as snow fell in large clumps, settling on the ground. It was nearly whiteout conditions, and while everyone else around me did the smart thing—went home—I still had to go to the Church of the Wanderer. But it was cold, so I took the secret entrance to it the former Reclaimer had shown me.

Imagine my surprise when I entered the cellar and found Rian Smoak there, the dragon Historian for the Church of the Eternal Flame, hovering over a bucket fire. He was dressed in his typical black flame-trimmed robes that did nothing to hide his protruding belly. His mismatched eyes went back and forth as smoke fluttered up from the fire. It made the entire basement smell. There was a book in his hand, and he tried to hide it as he greeted me with a big smile.

"Michael! What a pleasure to see you again so soon."

"Rian," I said as I rubbed my hands together. "What are you doing down here? Forget what church you belong to?"

He beckoned me over to the fire. I couldn't see the flames themselves, but the smoke was warm enough. Tingles went through my hands and fingers as they began to warm up. It almost made me forget that book. Almost.

"Are you going to answer my questions?" I asked.

"Potentially," Rian said. "Would you believe me if I said an Eternal Sister sent me here to spy on the new Reclaimer?"

"I saw you try to hide that book."

Rian made an exasperated sound. "Shame. That story would have been more fun to talk about." He tossed me the book. "Look at it if you want."

I did, once I could feel my fingers again. The book was titled: *The Anatomy of Myths*. It was old and musty, and part of the once-vibrant blue cover had been ripped off. The pages felt brittle and I flipped through them slowly. It was written in a foreign language—Thebian, maybe—but I was able to get some context thanks to the animal sketches that littered it. They were all done in charcoal and, judging from the shading, a professional was responsible.

The sketches were methodical and detailed, labeling each individual muscle group of whatever was being displayed. The animals depicted ranged from elephants and whales to ever-changing foxes and glowing jellyfish. But as I flipped to the last page, I saw why Rian had tried to hide this from me. It was a drawing of a Toothless Wyvern, the closest living thing to the imaginary dragons that plagued myths and legends.

I closed the book and handed it back to him. "Did you steal it from here?"

He stashed the book in his robes. "Unlike you, I don't admit if I commit a crime." He paused and stared into the smoke. "But I did happen to find it after being forced to take shelter from the blizzard. I was very fortunate."

"I hope it's worth it."

"It is." Rian blew into the fire pail, and more smoke filled the basement. It made me cough and my throat burn, but I was warm, so warm.

"So, Michael . . . is there any chance I could hear more about the Mercenary with two Fabrication specializations?"

All the smoke made my head feel fuzzy, but I blinked rapidly to regain clarity. "I already told you everything I know."

The smoke seemed to swirl around me, an intoxicating little tornado. Rian stared at me with his mismatched eyes—one bright blue with a ring of red and the other a hazy green. "Are you sure? Try to remember. I would really like to learn about him."

"I wish I could help," I said tentatively. All the smoke in such a small enclosed space was making me meek. I tried to wave it away, but it seemed to hover over me. Rian wasn't as bothered by it as I was. "Aren't there others you could ask?"

"No. Just you." He ran one of his long nails down his wrist. "His name is Dark, correct? From Orbis Company?"

I nodded. My stomach was on the verge of purging itself all over that fire.

"Do you know where he might be? Is he staying somewhere in the city?"

He was probably upstairs waiting for me. But instead of telling the truth I decided to lie. "I'm not sure. He comes and goes. The only time we ever meet up is when he decides to. But I saw him go to Little Eham on the East Side once or twice."

"Little Eham?" Rian repeated. "I will have to investigate. Thank you so much for the information. Are you well, Michael? You look a little sick."

"I think I'm going to puke," I said, clutching my stomach. "It's all the smoke."

Rian's hand pierced through the smoke and ran down my back. The small comfort made me feel safe, despite the fact everything was blurry and unfocused. Had I inhaled too much smoke? I needed fresh air as soon as possible.

I wobbled to my feet using the walls as support.

"Michael," Rian said. His body was lost in the haze of smoke, so it seemed like his voice was everywhere. All I could see were red eyes staring at me through the veil. "Let me help you. I didn't realize you inhaled so much smoke."

"Air," I wheezed. "I need—"

I was sick straight into the fire bucket. The fire was smothered, and the smoke vanished almost instantly. What was left in the air wafted away through the cracks in the walls and ceiling and I found myself on my knees looking up at Rian. From down there, he looked bigger than normal. More . . . more animalistic. Had his tongue always been that long?

"Better?" he asked.

"Yes." I wiped my mouth. "A lot better. What were you burning to create that kind of smoke? It was . . ." And I trailed off, wondering how assertive I wanted to be.

"Just some coals I found down here," Rian said as he kicked the bucket. The black ovals at the bottom were covered in my puke and soot. They didn't look hot to the touch, and I would have examined them more if they weren't . . . well, covered in my vomit. "I think it was just too much smoke. It can happen sometimes. I smoke a lot while working or I might have realized. I apologize for not seeing what was happening sooner."

I mumbled polite nothings, trying to lessen the ache in my head rather than his guilt.

"We'll see each other again soon, Michael." Rian patted my back. "I guarantee it."

The Historian walked toward the door I had come in through. As my head cleared, I realized I could have asked him about suspicious strangers and about the refugee murderers, but when I looked back he was gone. Not even a trace of him remained. If he had left through the secret entrance, I would have felt the cold wind on my back. But it was as if he had vanished, and it sent a shiver up my spine.

THE RECLAIMED

Dark was already in the church, near the doors, when I emerged from the cellar. He glared at me as I made my way through the chaos over to him.

The pews and floor space were filled with refugees in various states of injury. Poppy flowers were strewn everywhere to mask the scent of death. The faceless statue had hundreds of wooden talismans hanging from its arms, a crown of winterbloom on its head, and some hooligan had painted an overly friendly face onto it. All the monks were too focused on whoever needed the most aid to care about the vandalism. Some carried water and food, and others were armed with saws designed to cut bone and bandages to repair what was broken. Volunteers marked with white bands around their foreheads were plentiful, too. Even days after arriving, most of the refugees still looked as if they had come straight from a battle, not a long march across the country.

"How did you get in?" Dark asked, voice stern.

"Cellar," I said, rubbing my hands up my arm. It was colder up here than it was in the cellar, thanks to the boarded-up hole where the stained glass had once been. Flurries of snow were blowing through it, dusting everything below. "I was trying to get out of the cold."

"Pathetic. Did you find anything useful in any of the tweeker dens?"

"You mean besides the Heartbreaker? Who tried to kill me and Naomi?"

"What?" Dark lowered his voice. "Are you positive it was him and not the Waylayer?"

"They knew who Naomi was, and she's the only person to ever survive the Heartbreaker's grand finale. Her father, Bryan Dexter, was the only person ever to defeat them. So, yeah, I'm going to say it was them and not the Waylayer."

"That girl I saved at the castle . . . her last name was Dexter?"

"Yes," I said.

"Today must've been a trap," Dark mumbled. With more clarity he continued, "The sickly sweet smell on the bodies was probably intentional, to lure us into the tweeker den. To see what we're made of. I wonder if they knew Naomi would be there."

"That would go against the pattern, wouldn't it?" I asked. "I thought the Heartbreaker only went after their combatants during the finale. Why would they risk exposing themselves too soon?"

The shadows seemed to be moving around him, twisting his features. "Because some urges are harder to resist than others. Correcting a failure most of all."

"That implies Naomi's survival was a failure," I said.

"It was." The area around him lightened as Dark looked around the church, hunting. His target was a woman in all white in mid-surgery. Considering how many people were coming up to her, she was likely the replacement for the Reclaimer who had died trying to save me. "She'll have the answers we want."

We made our way over. She was a thin, pale woman with a shaved head and a whale-tail tattoo on her wrist. Her left arm was missing at the shoulder, but she deftly wielded a scalpel as she attempted to drain pockets of blood all over the patient's body.

"Can we have a moment of your time?" Dark asked as we stood over the operation.

The Reclaimer didn't look at us. "Are you pregnant?"

"No."

"Then you're not a priority and can wait until I'm done."

We didn't wait long. She was so fast with her incisions and cuts that the patient only winced in pain after she was finished. A monk brought her a tray of leeches and she placed them carefully to drain the black-tinted blood that was oozing out. That action alone made it clear she wasn't from Hollow—leeches weren't used in the hospitals anymore. Their overuse had led to too many deaths.

Once she was done, she wiped her dirty hand against her robes, staining them a light red. "How can I help you two? You're not bleeding, hungry, thirsty, or dying, and yet I imagine you're about to become a pain in my ass regardless."

"We're here to ask about the refugees," Dark said.

The woman swept her hand in front of her. "Well, there they are. Anything else?"

"We're here to talk about the murders," I clarified. "Two have been killed in the past two days and we were wondering if you've noticed anyone or anything suspicious. Maybe someone who started coming around recently. Anything, really."

"This church has been overwhelmed with people that need assistance," the woman said. "I don't have time to investigate every single person that volunteers for help or record who is here one day but not the next. I wouldn't get anything done if I did."

This was a complete waste of time.

"I didn't get your name," Dark said.

That was odd. Since when did Dark care about people enough to ask for their names?

"Probably because I didn't give it," the woman said. "Call me Reclaimer. I know who you two are. Dark from Orbis Company. Nicknamed the Black Death. And Michael Kingman. The king killer, Dragonslayer, and now heir to the legendary family. I want nothing to do with either of you. Only ruin lays ahead for you two."

"And here I thought it was all sunshine, rainbows, and sex," I muttered.

Both were smart enough not to engage with me.

Dark continued, "Don't you want to help stop a serial killer?"

"I do," the Reclaimer said. "I just don't want to be involved in whatever nonsense you two will create. I'm not heartless. If I had information, I would give it to you. But I don't."

"How do I know that's true?" Dark asked.

The Reclaimer leaned close to Dark and said, "Because I'm a better person than you are, Black Death. If you don't believe me, talk with the refugees. They'd have more information than me anyway."

"Then I'll do just that."

"Beautiful," she said, handing us both bandages and waterskins. "Take these with you. Try to do some good while you're bothering those in need."

I hadn't felt as conned in a long time as I did in that moment as the Reclaimer went off to a different group of people. She had just tricked Dark and me into helping her. And, judging from Dark's grimace, he wasn't too fond of the idea of being taken advantage of either.

"She's a prick," Dark growled.

"A smart prick."

"Get as much information as you can out of these people. Word of anyone who might be missing. Anything might be useful. We're not going up against an imbecile. The Heartbreaker is in a league of manipulation matched only by my father."

That was a compliment I wasn't expecting to hear from Dark. And one I had no comeback for. So I did as I'd been told to do and began to help the refugees, learning as much as I could. As I bandaged non-life-threatening injuries and gave water to those who couldn't move, the refugees spoke freely. Most of them seemed happy to have someone to talk to who would listen without interrupting.

I heard stories of a place I had never seen or cared about before. Of a place I had never considered connected to me before I learned my mother and her family were from the very same place. They told me of the war that had shattered the Familial Empire into the Warring States, and the lunatic nicknamed the Cripple who had started it. Of a divide in leadership even among families. Of arrogance and everyone believing they were the best choice to lead. How a civil war could last for over thirty years with no end in sight, and how many of them had been forced to admit it wasn't going to get any better and find a new place to call home.

Not a single person was able to say their entire family was with them when I asked if they knew anyone was missing. Even when I clarified that I meant only those that had come to Hollow with them, it was no easier. People had disappeared on the road, upon arrival in Hollow, and in the past two days. It was chaos for them, and normality for everyone else living in a city under siege by rebels.

Once I ran out of supplies, I sat by a dirty child with shoulder-length hair who had wanted me to hold his hand while he fell asleep. I'd been unable to say no, and now couldn't move lest I risk waking him. Dark was on the other side of the church, in the middle of a conversation with two monks.

"Your mother is worried about you," Olivier said from behind me.

Of course he was the one to find me. Great.

"I'll be home for supper," I said, still trapped by the small child.

"I knew you would," Olivier said as he pulled a chair over to sit next to me. "Do you have an answer yet?"

"About my abdication?" I asked in little more than a whimper.

"No. About being better. About caring for more than just those you see as your family."

"I've had more important things to deal with! I'm trying to catch a serial killer and a Waylayer all while protecting our family. Save your noble-esque bullshit for another time."

Olivier crossed his legs and arms in one motion. "Why don't you like me, Michael?"

I didn't respond.

"I'm trying to pass on some wisdom while I can. I'm not trying to be your father."

"Could have fooled me," I snapped. "Giving me all this advice about being better is pretty fatherlike, isn't it? My father is my hero. The person I strive to emulate, as he's always been. And based on recent events I'm skeptical of people who try to talk me into their point of view."

"Ah, Angelo Shade. I should have realized you'd have an aversion to father figures. He did attempt to manipulate you for . . ." He trailed off.

"Half my life."

"I'm not trying to manipulate you, Michael. Just to make you wiser. Help you see other point of views. You're my family and I don't want to see you fail. The world is changing, and we all need to evolve with it. If you want the Kingman family to survive."

"It's hard for me to trust anything you say when you've been lying to us from the start. You told us you were dying, but you didn't say you had less than a week before the flames overtook you."

Olivier hesitated, mouth slightly agape. "How did you find out? Did you . . . ?"

"I have a connection in the Eternal Flame."

"Ah." Olivier looked away from me. "I thought it would be better to die without warning than burden you all with trying to make the most of my limited time left. Did you . . . did you tell your ma?"

"No," I said. "Only because I hoped you would say something before I could."

"I'll tell her soon. I promise."

"You better," I said as I let go of the boy's hand. The child stirred, but before he woke I took Olivier's hand and had the boy hold his instead. The boy was peaceful and comforted again.

Olivier simply looked at me and said, "Seriously?"

"Gotta do what I gotta do to survive."

"You're being childish."

I shrugged as I walked away. "It's a family trait."

Dark was waiting for me, his conversation over. He didn't look happy, not that he ever did. "Learn anything?" he asked.

"Not about the Heartbreaker Serial Killer. People are barely able to take care of themselves, let alone keep track of everyone else. It's probably like picking apples for the killer right now."

"This was a waste of time."

"It's been a long day, so I'll take this respite." I stuck my hands into my pockets to warm them. "Maybe Bryan Dexter's notebook has something useful in it."

Dark looked at me suspiciously. "You have Bryan Dexter's notes from the original Heartbreaker investigation? Why didn't you tell me sooner?"

"I'm your apprentice, not your partner," I mocked. "How am I supposed to know what's important and what isn't? If only I had more information that would make it easier to make decisions on such complicated issues . . ."

"Do you want me to shoot you? Because it's quite tempting right now."

"I have a right to know what you know, Dark," I declared. "The more you keep hidden, the less I can help. Unless you don't want to catch the Heartbreaker and avenge Zahra."

"I told you never to say her name," Dark said through gritted teeth.

"You're right. And I've always listened to everything you've told me to do in the past, so this insubordination is totally unlike me."

Dark hesitated, then took a deep breath and said, "Read Bryan Dexter's report. I'll answer any questions you have after that."

"Seriously?"

"Seriously. I may not like talking about the past . . . but I understand if we are to catch the Heartbreaker you'll need to know as much as possible. I've been foolish to think otherwise. I admit that. But you'll also need to have a better grasp on the limitations of your Nullify Fabrications. We're not going up against children who can be easily tricked."

"Does that mean—"

"Yes," Dark answered before I could finish my question. "Expect me at dawn. Dress in warm clothes. I'll be using Ice Fabrications against you and I'd rather you not lose a finger or limb to frostbite while we're training. Maybe if you're lucky you'll be able to replicate what you did at the king's party and in the Church of the Wanderer."

Considering the monsters we were going up against, I didn't have any option but to get better control over my Nullify Fabrications. Dark wouldn't be willing to train me otherwise. He wasn't known for his charitable tendencies, only his murderous ones, and despite the risks, this was an opportunity I couldn't pass up. Hopefully, Dark was a better teacher than Domet.

Dark cracked his neck. "Now it's time for me to go hunting. See if I can find any other leads."

"In the middle of a blizzard?"

"The Heartbreaker might be using it as an opportunity to stalk their next target. Footprints will be easy to follow. So whoever's at the end of them will die."

"What makes you think you'll be able to find the Heartbreaker's tracks and not some random person's?"

"I don't." Dark opened the heavy wooden doors with one hand and let the snow blow in. "But this might be my last chance to strike back before the finale begins. Then it's kill or be killed. I know which side I fall on. Do you?"

The blizzard obscured him from sight within a few heartbeats. But, honestly, for once in my life I was glad to be within the walls of this church . . . Dark was looking for blood tonight, and I didn't want to be anywhere near him when he found a way to quench his bloodthirst.

Only monsters could stop monsters.

WINTER NIGHT

I paced in front of the servants' entrance to Kingman Keep until my ears were so cold, they might have snapped off. The blizzard had calmed into a heavy snowfall, but the cold had lingered like a knife wound to the gut.

There was no part of me that wanted to go home. Only pain and suffering waited for me, and being forced to give up my last name and my place among my ancestors for the better of the family. It had been one thing to sacrifice it all when I was going to die. I never thought I would have to experience a life where I wasn't seen as a Kingman anymore. And yet, now I would. I'd be Michael Orbis, the king killer.

All because Lyon wouldn't . . .

No, I couldn't blame my brother for this. He had done what was best for his unborn child. My father had given his life to protect us. Lyon was only following that precedent. We were both paying the price for surviving—and getting the opportunity to avenge our father.

I would have hesitated longer, coming up with excuse after excuse not to go home, but if this was to be my last action as a Kingman . . . I might as well be brave. As I approached, I could hear laughter and conversation in the great hall. Each was distinct. From Gwen's awkward childhood giggle to Naomi's overexaggerated laugh that seemed more and more rehearsed every time I heard it.

Not wanting to subject my family to Naomi's antics without aid any longer, I entered the great hall. My entire family, minus Olivier, and all the strays I had picked up recently were there. And Beorn. The poor man was sitting next to Naomi, holding a bottle of Thebian wine as he attempted to flirt with her. If looks could kill, hers would have already put him in a grave. Unlike Dark, he didn't seem to want to keep his distance from my family. Or maybe he had been sent to watch me while I was still the heir to the Kingman family. Keeping an eye on their investments and all that.

The laughter subsided when they all noticed me. Except for Beorn. Beorn kept going. For whatever reason. My mother came over to me. It was hard to tell if she was angry that I ran out earlier. Or if it was because people kept moving into Kingman Keep. Who knew what they'd said in my absence?

"Michael," my mother said so, so sweetly that she might as well have been shoving candied pastries down my throat. "Have you had a good day? You left rather abruptly this morning after having come home wounded. Are you feeling better?"

I touched the wound on my side. It didn't hurt as much as it had this morning when I woke up. And I was able to move freely, albeit slightly stiffer than normal. I told her as much.

"Good, good. Now I won't feel bad for smacking you upside the head for this morning. How dare you run out after we were up all night worrying about you?"

Oh, shit.

Naomi was hiding a smile behind her hand, elbow on the table. Rock was eating candied nuts. Everyone else was staring at us.

"Mother," I said, "can we talk somewhere in private? This is a little—"

"Embarrassing? I'm glad. Because if you're going to act like a child, I'll treat you like one. Right now you are the heir to the family. You will lead the family if something happens to me. You cannot run away from your problems. Your hardships. You are a Kingman and you will act as such."

"I won't be for much longer," I muttered. "I know what has to happen."

My mother did something unexpected. She grabbed me by the back of my head, pulled me close, and then kissed my forehead. Then she whispered so only I could hear, "You silly child. Did you really think we wouldn't look for ways that you could remain a Kingman?"

I hadn't. And in hindsight it was even more embarrassing to think that my family wouldn't look out for me. Family looked after family. My mother led me to the table and sat me next to the head, across from Gwen and next to Symon.

Once we were seated, and Gwen had served me a plate of potato cakes with apple mash in front of me, my mother said, "Symon, would you explain what we've learned about succession to Michael?"

"There's a way you can remain a Kingman and Gwen can become the heir to the family."

"Really?" I asked.

"Yes. It's been done before," Symon said. "Multiple times. Even once in the Kingman family. Before the War of the Bloodlines began, the first-born son, Vincent Kingman, abdicated his position to his younger brother, Marcus Kingman. Of course, ultimately it didn't matter, since at the end of the war three out of the four Kingman children were dead and succession wasn't complicated anymore. But it's happened. Which is the key part."

"But how?" I asked around a mouthful of potato cakes.

Symon hesitated.

"The current King or Queen of Hollow has to approve it," Gwen said from across the table. "In our situation, it would be the princess."

I nearly choked, coughing and then pounding my chest to get some air. Gwen came to my side to see if I needed any help. I didn't, and when

I could speak again I said, "There's no chance she would agree to help me. In any capacity. She's already tried to kill me twice in the past few days."

"We'd already agreed to a deal to present convincing evidence that the king killed himself—" Gwen was cut off by an audible gasp from Naomi. Guess no one had told her that yet. "This just gives us another incentive to convince her to trust us."

"We have time to get it done," my mother added. "Thanks to your friend . . . what was your name again, Mercenary?"

"Beorn!"

"Yes, thanks to Beorn, we know Orbis Company can't seize your assets as their own until you go through the advancement ceremony and become a full-fledged Mercenary. We know that's unlikely before Serena's coronation. That gives us plenty of time."

Serena's coronation was going to be one to remember. Everything was going to come to a head then. My family either succeeding or failing to meet the requirements to return to their High Nobility status; my formal initiation into Orbis Company; the deadline to catch the Heartbreaker Serial Killer and Waylayer; and now the day when I would either be allowed to remain a Kingman or sacrifice my place in the family for the greater good. What fun.

Nothing serious was discussed for the remainder of dinner, and we all reveled in a conversation that had nothing to do with the hardships to come. Olivier returned to Kingman Keep halfway through the meal, making a flimsy excuse as to why he was late, staring me down as he did. Beorn continued trying to flirt with Naomi, who, with more self-control than I'd expect, never slapped him. She stared at me while my mother and I listened to Rock recount stories about the various cons he had pulled on the East Side. Sirash and I were amateurs compared to him. My mother liked Rock a lot, treating him as she had us when we were younger.

When everyone was done for the evening and ready to head to bed, Olivier approached me with a lantern to ease the creeping darkness. Most of the others at the table had gone off to their respective rooms. It was just me, Rock, and Olivier.

"Michael," Olivier said, "the First Tower is ready for you. The main room has been cleaned out along with the room for Rock. There are even beds, courtesy of the Ryders. From Kayleigh, to be specific. No doubt she feels some responsibility for what happened and is trying to make amends."

So we'd traded Lyon for beds. I'm not sure we got the better end of that deal. But, regardless, the First Tower was where the heir to the Kingman family lived. Lyon's room had been there as a child. The fact that Olivier was saying it was mine only reinforced my awkward position. Worse, last I checked, the tower was too dangerous to occupy. The stairs were unstable and the walls were riddled with holes from the riots. I asked Olivier what had changed.

He looked at me without blinking and said, "What do you think I do all day? Wait to die? I've been preparing Kingman Keep with your ma. I am grateful you took it upon yourself to find a man to support you. As young as Rock is, he learns quickly and brings a lightness to the work I haven't experienced in years."

I didn't know how to respond and simply said, "I'm glad. Have you and Ma had any luck finding others to help you?"

"No, sadly, not yet. But we're using your ma's connections to the other High Nobility to see if they have anyone that might be a fit for our household."

"Is it common to ask other houses for help?"

"It depends on the families. The Margauxs and Ryders have been helpful, but as you can imagine, the Andels and Castlens are telling us to kiss hot rocks."

So the Castlens hated us, too. I'd have to remember that for the future. "Thank you, Olivier."

"Family looks after family."

I hesitated. "Sorry about what I did in the church."

"It's fine. We all can be childish sometimes." He coughed embers into his palm. "Now go get some rest. We'll talk more after I tell your mother what's happening to me."

I went toward the First Tower as Olivier began to clear the table, with Rock's assistance. It had been a decade since I had been in the First Tower. Memories of the riots filled my mind as I climbed the stairs toward the main room. I stepped around where bodies had once fallen forever, as if scared to trample on their final resting places. Kingman Keep was my home, but even though we were rebuilding it, nothing could erase what I had seen happen here. It was just another part of the Kingman family's history that was drenched in blood.

I climbed until I couldn't any longer, and then managed a few more steps to the main room of the First Tower. It was large, much larger than most of the other rooms in the keep and only smaller than my mother's room. The only light was from a dwindling fire in the hearth. There was a trapdoor in the corner of the room that led to Rock's quarters. His room would have access to everything else in the tower: the escape tunnel, the secret food storages, and the water well. From what I remembered, that room had more doors in it than walls and floors.

I was delighted to see a feather bed against one of the walls. One of the scratchy blankets Gwen had stolen from the asylum was draped over it, and three pillows sat fat at the head. It was perfect. Or would be if Naomi weren't sitting on it, smiling at me. She was wearing only a nightshirt. Some of the higher buttons were undone, showing some of her . . . ahem.

"Hello, sweetie," Naomi said.

"I expected Gwen to be here, not you."

"I told her you wouldn't be scared of the dark with me around, then shooed her off."

"I'm scared of being trapped in small, dark spaces after what they did to me in the dungeons—not the dark. There's a difference." I kicked off my boots. "Don't you have something better to do than torment me before I sleep?"

"Torment? I would never do that. I was just waiting for you to come to bed."

"Very funny," I said as I massaged my aching shoulders. "Go to whatever room Olivier told you to use."

"That's the problem, Michael," she sung. "No one was expecting both Beorn and me to be living here, and there seems to be a bed shortage. Either Beorn can have his own bed or I could. Someone has to share."

"Or you could just sleep on the floor."

Naomi made a feigned expression of shock. "You would make a lady do that?"

"Since when have you ever acted like a lady?" I scooted her over and sat on the bed. "It's not as if you've ever used courtly manners on me. Seems pointless if I suddenly did to you."

"Fair. But don't expect me to give up this bed so easily."

I rolled over onto the other side of the bed, threw the blanket over my body, and then placed one of the pillows in the center of the bed. "I'm not. You stay on your side and I'll stay on mine."

Naomi huffed and then joined me under the covers. "Don't you have any interest in romance?"

"Not really. There's too much to do."

I closed my eyes and thought of nothing, wishing that lie could be real.

THE KING'S SCRIPT

Rock woke me up in the middle of the night with a gentle shake as he whispered four words: "Angelo's broken his pattern."

I was alert in a heartbeat. After getting dressed without waking Naomi, I followed Rock out of Kingman Keep to the King's Garden. The city was asleep, both moons high in the sky, so we moved through it quickly. There were no guards at the glittering gate—for some odd reason—so we ventured deep into it until Rock brought me to the royal crypt.

The white marble entrance towered over us and wasn't guarded. The only protection it had from grave robbers and scoundrels was the golden gate that had been left ajar and a warning engraved over the doorway: *Those Who Disturb the Dead Will Be Forgotten for All Eternity.*

"You're sure Angelo went in there?" I asked, still staring at the warning.

"Yah," he said. "I followed him from his house and everything."

I was about to ask if he was still in there, but a missing lantern just inside the crypt gave me my answer. Angelo was still in the royal crypt. And I would never know why unless I followed. I knew so little about the man that I couldn't waste any opportunity I had to learn more about his life, his goals, and why he was so obsessed with destroying the nobility.

"Get Gwen if I'm not out by sunrise," I ordered as I pushed open the gate. "Maybe Dark, too. Or Beorn. Really, anyone capable."

"You're seriously going in there?" Rock asked. "Crypts are a big no-go for me. Who wants to be surrounded by that many dead bodies?"

"Kingman Keep is built above crypts, Rock."

The small boy's face soured. "Seriously?"

"Seriously," I repeated, staring into the dark halls that awaited me. Hopefully, being a Kingman would protect me from the curse. "If Angelo comes out before me first, run. Understood?"

Rock saluted me. "Aye, master, sir."

At least he was entertaining.

I took the second lantern off the wall, lit it from another, readied myself, and descended a steep set of stairs into the royal crypt. The air down here felt colder than it did outside, and my breath plumed every time I exhaled. The walls on the way down were marked with a repeated string of letters—*HWEHGWE YQW SFE WESBWX QY IQVPEX OLXKJ*—that flowed as naturally as water, and the light from my lantern turned everything golden. When the stairs ended, I emerged into a large hallway that had dozens of offshoots. Each one was marked with the name and title of a former Royal who had sat on the throne. The strange script was also there but had a different string of letters now—*HWQSETSQW QY TEVQXG*. I couldn't make any sense of it.

All the gates to the final resting places of the Hollow kings and queens were locked tightly, so I continued down the hallway, hoping for a clue to where Angelo had gone. I didn't find any signs of a disturbance until I'd passed every King and Queen of Hollow—from King Isaac to Sophia the Summer-End Queen. Only the gate at the very end of the hallway had been busted open. It belonged to Adrian the Liberator, the first King of Hollow.

If any king was going to forgive me for disturbing him, Adrian might be the one. Despite my hesitation I followed Angelo. The walls grew narrower as I ventured farther in. It was so bad, I had to draw the lantern close to my chest to avoid knocking it against the stone walls, my shoulders scraping against them instead. I didn't know what I would do if something happened to the lantern. I'd probably have to crawl out. What a sight that would be for Rock.

But as I grew more frantic, shadows dancing in the corner of my vision, a large tomb came into focus. I could see something was protruding from it, but before I figured out what it was, I fell. Sliding down a tunnel I hadn't spotted, I screamed and landed—less than elegantly—on my ass—hard. The lantern shattered, and I should have been plunged into darkness, except there was a light on the far side of the bone-filled room I had landed in.

A shadow of a man leaned against the wall. And as the lantern swayed, a sharp jawline and cool grey eyes came into view. Angelo Shade, who smiled and drew back his long coat to expose the flintlock pistols strapped to his hips.

"You really need to stop venturing into strange places, Michael. Were you following me?"

I gritted my teeth and got to my feet, mentally berating myself for not bringing any weapons. "Do I really need to answer that?"

"No," he said. "Honestly, I should have expected this. You were never good at listening to me. Why should I have expected anything different, given your mother? But I'm curious: Did you come here to kill me or to learn something?"

"Whichever opportunity presented itself," I said, pacing back and forth. There were no sharp rocks or stones or anything I could attack him with. The bones would probably break if I hit him with them. If I tried anything, I'd have to use my hands. "But this might be the best chance I ever get to kill you. No one would find your body. And it would be fitting."

Angelo yawned overdramatically and set his lantern on the floor. "Do you really think I don't have a dead man's letter in case something happens to me?"

"Liar."

"I'm not," he said casually. "Regal Company is hidden just outside Hollow, out of sight of both the Watchers and the rebel army. If they don't get a signal from me every day, they have instructions to raze this city to the ground and salt the earth. Because even if I die . . . I made sure Hollow suffers."

"There's no way an entire Mercenary company could be hiding out there."

Angelo crossed his arms and tilted his head slightly. "Can you really take the chance?"

I had enough to deal with, and we both knew it. "Why would Regal Company be outside of Hollow?"

"You'll understand soon enough. But let's just say . . . No, never mind, I don't want to ruin the surprise."

I hated this man more with every passing day. Worse, I was coming to realize I was trapped in here with him. I glanced around again to confirm it: there were no exits. Just to make sure, I asked, "We're stuck in here, aren't we?"

"Kind of."

"'Kind of'?" I repeated.

"Yes." He pointed his thumb at the wall behind him. "See all the images on this wall? They unlock a secret pathway. I just haven't figured out how yet." He bit and then spat out a piece of his nail, leaving the remains jagged and pointy. "Would you care to help me escape?"

"Not in the slightest. Someone will come for me eventually."

He continued to smile, and it made me suppress a shiver. "Before the princess comes to pay her respects to her father? She visits every morning at dawn. Isn't grief a terrible thing? I'm sure she will see the missing lanterns and investigate. Do you think she'd believe me if I told her I followed you in here? Rather than the reverse?"

I stared at him and said nothing.

"You were right that this would be a great place to hide a body. She might agree."

"People know I'm here," I growled.

"Yes, but your relationship with the princess is ever so fragile. Violating her family's crypts might be the act that finally causes her to"—he made a fitting gesture—"snap."

I played with my father's ring. "What were you trying to do down here?"

Angelo picked up his lantern, and his coat obscured his guns from sight. "Help me escape and you'll find out. Or do you think you already know enough to stop me?"

I bit back my desire to shout out the one ace I had up my sleeve. Instead, I cracked my neck and said, "Move the lantern so I can see the images clearly."

He did.

The wall was separated into five-by-five grids. Each section had an image on it, ranging from fire and lightning to clouds and swords. There was no obvious pattern and—after Angelo moved far enough away—I ran my hands over the wall and found no clear indentation for my father's ring. The same trick wouldn't work twice.

"Do you know how old this room is?" I asked.

"It was likely built before Adrian the Liberator died," Angelo said with his arms crossed. "It's built in the same style as the building above, and I can't imagine them building an extension down here after he was buried. You Kingman and Royals are too scared of insulting your ancestors to disturb their rest, even if it's to keep grave robbers out."

Judging from all the bones and moldering clothing scattered over the floor, they had clearly worried about keeping people out. "Do all the other Royal tombs have traps?"

He shook his head. "Only Adrian's does."

"Just because he's the first king?"

"No," he said. "If I'm right, there's a very good reason for it."

He didn't elaborate further, so I went back to trying to solve this puzzle. First, I tried pressing all of the symbols, but none of them buckled. Then I examined the grooves of the walls, hoping that some of them could be removed to reveal a tunnel, but without tools I wouldn't make a dent. My attempt at kicking the wall had shown me as much.

Nothing I could physically do would break it, so I put my hand against the wall and closed my eyes. There was still one power I had left to try. I gathered the warmth in my chest and then concentrated it on my hand, before letting it slither over the wall until I could feel all the images covered with my magic.

The wall crumbled into pieces and revealed a staircase hidden behind it.

Angelo whistled. "Well done, Michael. Good thing you followed me down here, else I may have been stuck here *forever*. What a shame that would have been."

I gritted my teeth and followed him up the stairs. I hated being here with him—my eyes still looking for anything pointy—but the fact that I had just sacrificed my memories to help him made me feel sick to my stomach. Only the need to be strong in front of him kept me from puking.

We emerged from our cell into King Adrian's tomb. The walls of this room had streaks of a bright green crystal that seemed to give off a faint glow. The lantern wasn't necessary to see, so Angelo set it down. The tomb itself was a massive piece of marble with images depicting King Adrian's life carved into it. Most of them were weathered and vague, barely recognizable. A strange stone stool was to the right of the tomb, out of place in this hallowed space. But of everything in the room, my eyes were drawn to the ornate bow protruding from the tomb like a wayward flower. It was all white, curved, and engraved with a single phrase: *For the People*.

Angelo plucked it away and threw it to the side, where it shattered into a thousand pieces.

"Angelo!" I shouted, face hot. "Why did you do that?"

"It was old and useless. Who cares?" he asked as he ran his fingers against the groove of the tomb. "Help me move this."

"I'm not helping you do anything."

Angelo stared at me with his infamous grey eyes and pointed back to the crypt. "Then leave."

"Not until I know what you're after."

"So childish," he muttered. He took a deep breath and then began to push the marble top off the tomb. He was able to move it alone, slowly, and it wasn't long before the whole lid fell off and smashed against the ground.

When the dust settled, a skeleton covered in shards of moldy wood was staring at us. It was dressed in rags—the clothes having wasted away hundreds of years ago—and wore a single band of silver around its head. There were dozens of books at its feet and a key beneath its hands. Angelo instantly seized the key from the skeleton king. My nails dug into my palm so hard, I could feel blood drip to the floor.

Angelo held the silver key up. It was very old, small, and lopsided, as if it were handmade. "Interesting," he said. "So they thought this far ahead."

"All this for a key?"

"Yes." He tossed it back into the crypt. "But this one is a decoy. I must've been wrong. It might not be here."

"What might not?"

Angelo shrugged. "I've learned when I should talk and when I shouldn't. The only way you were going to learn what I wanted was if I found it. Which, sadly, doesn't look like it's happening." He looked down at the skeleton king. "For all the hate I have for the Royals, he might have been the smartest of them. He set a precedent none were able to match."

I was well aware of that. There was a reason there was such a weight on my shoulders. As Angelo muttered nonsense to himself, I made my way around the tomb toward an out-of-place stone stool. Without knowing why, I sat down on it and leaned forward as if in prayer. I hoped King Adrian could forgive me for—

One of the walls rumbled to life, slithering out of the way to expose another hidden room.

Angelo's eyes and smile went wide. "How naïve of me to forget how the Royals think. Of course the true path would only be clear for a Kingman."

I rose again. "What're you talking about?"

Angelo took the lantern and entered the hidden room, and I followed. While the previous room had been a pristine memorial to the first King of Hollow, this one was far, far different. There was a stone sarcophagus in the center with more than fifty barbed swords stabbed into it. A person-sized hole was in the middle of it, and there was dried blood everywhere, all over the walls and the floor. It looked like an old murder scene.

"Why is there a hidden burial chamber behind Adrian the Liberator?" I asked out loud. "How does someone honor the dead like that?"

"Who said this was meant to honor someone?" Angelo looked down into it. "No bones . . . only blood. I wonder . . ." He knelt in front of the sarcophagus and wiped away some of the dirt and grime with his sleeve. It was hard to make out any of the words written there, even with the glowing crystals and lantern illuminating everything. "So, this was all for you, Alphonse . . ."

"Who's Alphonse?"

Angelo looked back at me. "Just an old fool."

"You're lying to me."

"Am I?" He got to his feet. "You have the same clues I do and enough knowledge to put it all together. What reason would there be to hide a sarcophagus so completely? Why skewer a dead body with so many swords?"

Only one reason came to mind. "This was to trap an Immortal."

"Here I thought you would be coy. That's refreshing. And while this is a rather crude one, it was a trap. As for who the Immortal was . . . do you have any idea?"

Was this for Domet? Was Alphonse his real name? Had Emelia found this chamber and learned Domet's real name from the sarcophagus? There were too many questions running through my head. So instead I asked, "Is this what you were looking for here?"

"It's no fun when you don't answer my questions. No, it isn't. I learned something interesting, though, and we got to spend some quality time together. I can't be too upset."

I clenched my fists. "Whatever you're planning won't work. I'll stop it. I'm smarter than you ever gave me credit for."

Angelo Shade laughed. "No you're not. I raised you, Michael. I cared for you. I was your confidant. I know all your tricks, thoughts, and abilities. You will never impress—"

"Katherine Naverre."

Something changed in him as I said that name, the mask he always wore finally falling away. I saw the true Angelo Shade for the first time in my life, and it was something unhinged, chaotic, and angry. There was a monster in him, just like his son.

"Never say her name again." Angelo drew out every syllable for emphasis. "Do not say it as if it were common. As if it wasn't above you, your family, and all those you support. Do not take it in *vain*."

I steeled my resolve. "I'm sorry, I didn't know God's name was Katherine Nav—"

"Enough!"

His voice echoed through the crypt and stole my voice. I took an involuntary step away. It shook me to my core, but I took a step toward him again. His shadow seemed to envelop me.

"I'm figuring out more of the story day by day. Without Dark's help." I paced in front of him. "How long before I figure out your plans? Do you really think you can stay ahead of me forever?"

"Yes," he said matter-of-factly. "I know how to pull people's strings to get what I want. I did it with a king, do you really think I can't manipulate the other High Nobles and the princess?"

"The princess is stronger than the king."

"She is. But I know what's written on her skin, what silly fantasies prance around her head, and what duties compel her. If anything, she is easier to direct than the king was. He doubted everything and rarely acted, preferring to keep the status quo."

"She'll figure out what you're planning—"

"No she won't." He looked down at me. "She's too obsessed with you."

"For now. It'll change when she learns the truth about the king."

"She already knows, Michael. Do you really think any child will admit their parent killed themselves? She will reject even a mountain of evidence and search for an alternative. Otherwise she will have no place to redirect her hate for not being able to help him. Should I remind you of your determination regarding your father?"

I held my tongue and glared at him.

"In this city, hate is easier to inherit than blood."

"Things can change."

Angelo walked away from me. "Not soon enough. But I wish you luck, *son*."

I stayed in the crypt for longer than I should have after Angelo left. I examined the key, Adrian's tomb, and his sarcophagus again to make sure I hadn't missed anything. But instead of the name Alphonse, all I found was a string of letters: *GVHRQXJE*.

When I emerged from the crypt, it was still dark, and Rock was waiting for me as he napped against a tree. Part of me was angry that he had ignored my instructions, but he was a child and deserved to act like one every now and then. So I didn't wake him, rather taking him into my arms and carrying him back to Kingman Keep.

Once I was in Kingman Keep, I dropped Rock off in his bed and I returned to my room. Naomi was still snoring softly. I slipped in as quietly as I could, only to have her throw an arm around me. The warmth felt nice, and I didn't move it, drifting off to sleep feeling comfortable and safe instead.

THE KING OF STORIES

In the early morning light, Michael was dragged out of Kingman Keep by his ankles as Symon finished chronicling the events of Lyon and Kayleigh's engagement party. The amber-eyed boy shouted obscenities, asinine quips, and even a singular plea for food at the Black Death as they passed the table most of the members of Kingman Keep were eating at. All were ignored—by not just the Mercenary but the members of his family as well—and it was only a few heartbeats until his shouts became echoes down the halls before turning into nothing.

Watching Fabrication training was not something Symon would enjoy—no matter how delightful it would be to watch Michael get knocked down repeatedly—so the Recorder would have to find another way to entertain himself today. Was anyone around here worthy enough of being remembered in writing? Or were they all a waste of ink?

"I tried to wake him up, but he kept groaning about needing more sleep," Naomi said. She had her feet up on the table as she read Bryan Dexter's journal. Symon had tried to sneak a peek at it earlier, but the addict was always surprisingly adept at keeping it within her eyesight and out of his. "You'd think he'd learn not to give the Black Death a reason to hurt him."

"You'd think." Symon's eyes were drawn to the elder Kingman as she entered the great hall. Before Juliet had a chance to ask, Symon explained, "He overslept and was late to meet the Black Death."

"Ah," she said. "Gwen, I need your help with an errand, then."

The youngest Kingman stared into her bowl as she lifted her spoon and watched as the sloshy contents fell back in, splashing the edges. She was dressed as a boy again with her hair hidden by a cap and in Michael's old threadbare coat and trousers that had been washed too much. Symon had assumed she had stopped her masquerading tendencies after her stint as Low Noble Dolyn Woodsman during the Endless Waltz. So what was the special occasion today?

"Gwen," Juliet repeated. "Can you hear me?"

Gwendolyn's eyes snapped open as if she had awoken from a sweet dream. Her spoon clanged against the table. "Sorry, Ma. I was lost in my thoughts. What do you need?"

Juliet put a small brown package wrapped in twine down on the table and pushed it toward her daughter. Its size and shape made Symon certain it was a book. He always was able to spot one regardless of how well or badly it was wrapped.

"I need you to take this to the new Reclaimer. Her name is Drisig Tiro. She's a winter woman who was thirtieth in line for the throne of the Familial Empire. We used to be fellow initiates in the Church of the Wanderer, and I was hoping this could be an excuse to talk again after a rather . . ." She trailed off. "It's not important. Once you're done, I'll need help with—"

Juliet Kingman was once a member of the Church of the Wanderer? Did she leave before or after she married into the Kingman family? Or did it have to do with the Familiar Empire's collapse? Symon would have to investigate that further. These Kingman were like rats: always scurrying out of sight, carrying secrets like a plague.

"Sorry, Ma," Gwendolyn said quickly as she rose, chair screeching behind her. "I have to be at the blacksmith's in the Sword Quarter all day for work. But I can take this on my way there."

That was a lie—Gwendolyn hadn't been allowed to work at the blacksmith's recently. And, barring Royal intervention, Symon was positive a lowly blacksmith wasn't going to get mixed up in a feud the queen-in-waiting had a personal stake in. No apprentice was that valuable.

Now, there was potential that it could be an innocent lie meant to avoid hard work in exchange for a peaceful day reading as she often did, but it was a lie, nonetheless. One that had come from the youngest Kingman herself. And that was all Symon needed to know to decide where his priorities would be today. He had spent so much time focusing on Michael that he had let the other Kingman's lives avoid his all-knowing gaze. This was a story of the Kingman family, not just Michael, and so he would make sure all their secrets were exposed. Then he would be able to finally destroy their legacy. As they so deserved.

Juliet was not one to push her children, so she accepted Gwendolyn's lie as the truth and turned her attention to Rock and Naomi, eager to make use of the others who had begun to call this place home. Symon followed Gwendolyn, forgoing most of his instruments for only the essentials to record a story, if the opportunity presented itself.

It always did.

Gwendolyn, unamused, was waiting for him at the exit on top of a pile of snow that had turned brown and hard. "What do you want, Symon?"

"A new sword," he said as he slipped quills down his red sleeves. "I thought I might get one from your blacksmith."

"Try again."

"Fine, you caught me." Symon playfully put his hands up. "I want a new iron quill. The one I currently use is deteriorating. And what finer craftsmanship could there be than Kingman-made?"

Gwendolyn turned on her heel and started walking away, and so Symon followed, matching her pace. They walked through the broken-down houses surrounding Kingman Keep with an efficiency that made

Symon question whether he kept too many bottles of ink in his Archivist's robes. They jangled like bells as he struggled to keep up.

"You're quite fast," he said, breathing heavily.

"You're just slow." Gwendolyn stopped suddenly and Symon almost ran into her. As he caught his breath, hands on his knees, she said, "Are you going to tell me what you want now? Or should I start running?"

"I . . . ," Symon wheezed, ". . . was curious about you."

"Curious about what?"

"Whether you've ever been in love or not."

Gwendolyn instinctively took a step back, a blush creeping up her face like a bad encounter with itchy clover. "Love? Why are you asking me about that?"

Symon was a storyteller at heart, which made him a formidable liar. After all, what were stories but long, exaggerated lies? "Because I think you're in love with someone right now. How else could I explain the longing looks at your bowl of porridge and your instantaneous refusal to help your mother with her errands?"

The youngest Kingman regained her composure quickly, relaxed, and then held up the package. "I *am* helping. Just not with everything today. I have a job."

"A job that's more important than regaining the Kingman family's position in Hollow?"

Her answer was interrupted by a rat.

Appearing out of nowhere, Michael Kingman dove out of one of the nearby house's front windows, rolled, and then sprinted past them as he shouted more profanities. Dark appeared moments later, destroying the front of the house as he sped after Michael on a slide of translucent ice. The noise of Michael's cowardice was gone before the ice had an opportunity to thaw.

Gwendolyn rubbed her brow. "Do whatever you want, Symon. Just don't get in my way."

"I'd never dream of it." They barely made it past two houses before he did. "So have you ever been in love?"

"Question for a question?"

Symon nodded, agreeing to the terms. It wasn't the question Symon would have chosen to lead with, but it might be the one to get Gwendolyn to start divulging her secrets. Love, as he had discovered, was a topic everyone liked talking about. Regardless of whether it had ended badly. And sometimes, especially if it had.

"I was in love once," she said softly. "They were a friend. Someone I confided in when I struggled with my feelings concerning my treasonous father. But we grew apart once my days became busier with work in the asylum and in the smithy. Last I heard, they were in New Dracon City, trying to invent a gun that shot bullets faster." She paused. "You must have similar problems. I can't imagine being a Recorder leaves much time for romance."

"Who cares about people when I have books to read, legacies to write, and history to shape?"

"As long as you're happy." They entered the Great Stone Square and passed the numerous food, game, and entertainment stalls that would be open from dusk until dawn the night before the queen-in-waiting's coronation. Symon debated bargaining with a festival vendor for freshly made pomegranate pastries, but he didn't imagine Gwendolyn would wait for him. Sadly, his stomach would have to suffer for the greater good. "Symon, tell me the truth, why are you so obsessed with my family?"

"Because you Kingman represent everything I hate."

"Oh?"

"Do you know where the village of Trivo is, Gwendolyn?"

She shook her head.

"It's located on the Clockwork River near the ruins of Vurano. Besides for me, its only claim to fame is a copper mine, but even that's not enough to put it on most maps. So it languishes in mediocrity as New Dracon City soldiers disguised as bandits raid it for supplies every new year, childhood lovers become mates for life, and the citizens forget the sun's warmth from working underground their entire lives like good, obedient nobodies. But would you like to hear the worst part of what it was like to grow up in that idyllic little town?"

"No, but I imagine you'll tell me anyway."

"It's that they idolize the Kingman family," Symon sneered. "Rather than teach us how to read or write or mathematics, our elders regaled us with stories about your family. We learned generosity from the Mother, bravery from the Explorer, and order from the Conqueror. Your family's legacy was my childhood. I can recite every Kingman story from memory with ease. In Trivo, you are a god. And do you know what good god-fearing citizens do to those that try to be something more than what they see around them? They beat the oddity into submission until they either give up or die." The numerous scars that covered Symon's body throbbed in unison. By his estimate, there were over a hundred. None of them were silvery and sleek. Most were black and scabbed over, a reminder that burns never become marks of pride or honor. "I did neither."

The sounds of people chatting and moving boxes was the only response Symon received. Gwen stood in the shadow of the Church of the Wanderer, a work of master craft from one of the Builder's many disciples. In another life, Symon would have become an architect. Both professions created things to last for eternity. All that differed was the materials used.

"When I came to Hollow—broke, hurt, and alone—I searched for you Kingman with all my might and discovered mortals rather than the untouchables my village revered. So, in revenge, I sought to bring the heavens down and destroy your legacy so that even my *brother* would be forced to admit that his gods were nothing more than my playthings."

"Petty," she said. "But understandable. We deserve your hate."

Symon held a clenched fist to his mouth and exhaled loudly. "Regardless. My turn. Who are you meeting?"

Gwendolyn yawned with her hands behind her head. "My employer."

"Liar. You don't work in the smithy under Master Ama anymore. So wherever you're going or whatever you're doing, it doesn't involve him."

She skipped up the steps of the Church of the Wanderer. At the top, she lingered in the spot where her father—and almost her brother, too— was executed for treason. The indents in the stone were still there, hidden by slushy snow. She spat at it and waited for Symon to catch up, admiring the view of the rest of the Isle. It was nice of her, and instantly made Symon suspicious of what she would say next.

"I wasn't lying," she said, hands on her hips. "I am meeting with my employer. Just not my master in the forge or the asylum."

"A third job?"

Gwendolyn pulled her scarf over her chin. "Technically it was my first."

"And what is it?"

"I can't say," she said quietly. "Part of the job is secrecy."

"Are you a New Dracon City spy? Or perhaps a hopeful trying to get into the Thebian Empire's military school? I heard they always offer merit tests to those without their eyes." Gwendolyn stared at him without blinking. "What do you want for the information? One truth that can be redeemed at any time? Two?" Symon hesitated, balancing the worth of the answer in his head. "Three?"

Gwendolyn turned away from him, stopping in front of the doors to the Church of the Wanderer. Ever since the arrival of the refugees, it was covered in letters from desperate families looking for loved ones, Wanted posters for various criminals in the Warring States, and a long list of names of those who had died on the trek to Hollow from the Warring States. There were over three hundred on the list.

"When I was a kid, I thought it was my family's job to protect the innocent," Gwendolyn said, staring at the list of the dead. "I understand how foolish that is nowadays. We were nothing more than a lie to reassure the masses. That if they believed in us hard enough and held us to high-enough standards, we may become mortal gods who would protect them from evil." She chuckled to herself. "Ridiculous, right?"

"Correct," Symon answered with a slight stammer. A nuanced statement about the Kingman family's position in society was the last thing he expected to hear from Gwendolyn. The only thing more shocking would have been if it had come from the King of Imbeciles himself. "Not that I don't enjoy this conversation, but who are you working for?"

Her answer was to push open the doors of the church and slip in as if touching the sides would kill her. And Symon followed, irritated that she still evaded his question. Just who was her employer if she went to such lengths to avoid mentioning them?

There was nothing but sickness and death within the church. Two out of every ten refugees were infected with the Corruption. Most of them had resigned themselves to their fate, choosing to aid others while they could. Those who were close to death traded stories with each other in the corner of the church near the lockless door. Symon considered recording their stories before it was too late . . . but he couldn't let Gwen out of his sight. He hoped they would forgive him.

The one-armed Reclaimer was sitting in the pew closest to the faceless statue, smoking rolled fireleaf. It was clear she was in charge even without all the people constantly going up to her, asking for guidance, prayer, or offering thanks. Reclaimers were identified not by their loose-fitting white robes like most assumed but rather the way they styled their hair and the tattooed lines that ran down their left arms. Short hair meant they had recently reached the rank, while the number of lines dictated how difficult their quest had been. Most Reclaimers—this one included—kept their arms covered to avoid letting others see their marks.

"Reclaimer," Gwendolyn said as she approached, "I have a package for you."

The Reclaimer blew out pungent white smoke and then extinguished the embers of her rolled fireleaf on the side of her boot. She took the package from Gwendolyn, examined the flimsy wrapping, and then tore it open with two fingers. It was a brown-paged book that someone had affectionately painted yellow, orange, and pink flowers on.

The Reclaimer riffled through the pages without care. "It's full of lullabies and childhood rhymes. Who wanted you to give this to me?"

"My mother, Juliet Kingman."

"Ah," she said. "Give her my thanks." She looked away from them toward two refugees who were arguing over a scratchy blanket. "We'll have to talk once things settle down."

She put the book down on the pew and then walked away to deal with the newest crisis.

"That was a rather cold response from a childhood friend," Symon said.

"Friendships don't last forever. Even if we wish they did," Gwendolyn muttered. "Did her appearance seem odd to you? Winter women from the Warring States are known for their fair skin and light-colored hair. That Reclaimer was as sun-kissed as someone from the Gold Coast or Eham."

"Maybe she changed her appearance. It would be a logical decision if she wanted to eradicate any indication she was once in line for the throne of the Familial Empire."

"That's true, but . . . do you mind if I take a moment to collect myself over there?" She pointed to the room reserved for quiet reflection on the left side of the church. "Something doesn't feel quite right, and I don't want to lose my thought."

Symon waved her on. The room used for reflection didn't have any windows in it and the only exit was through a door he would keep his eyes focused on. There was no danger in leaving her unsupervised for a few moments. He would get the answer to his question. As always.

Gwendolyn disappeared into the room and Symon sat next to it, taking the quiet moment to write notes to himself on his skin. There was no point in wasting paper until his thoughts were fully formed. He watched the refugees meander to and fro, trying to distinguish those who were from the spring provinces and those who were from the winter, autumn, or summer. If those distinctions even mattered anymore. The Warring States was one of the few territories that Symon didn't consider himself an expert on. Their history was in a constant state of change, thanks to revolution and the Sleeper Cultists—fools who thought a sleeping god was responsible for the petrification of the former capital of the Familial Empire. He would have to consult Archivist Laetia's book *The Fall of the Familial* when he had the chance.

Symon's quill snapped in mid-stroke.

It was an unparalleled omen for Archivists, and Symon immediately jumped to his feet, opened the door to the reflection room, and tripped over a pile of rocks at the entrance. Symon scraped his knees as he fell, cursing at his own stupidity. The room was empty and Gwendolyn was gone. How had she escaped? As fast as he could, Symon searched the candle-filled room for a trapdoor, hidden latch, escape tunnel, or brick-colored window that might explain how she had vanished. Yet all he found was the pile of rocks near the entrance.

"Dumb," Symon said as he stood in the middle of the room. "I am so dumb. Why did I trust a Kingman?"

———

Gwendolyn had vanished, and rather than waste the rest of his day searching for her—which Symon assumed would be impossible—he turned his focus on a former Kingman, Lyonardo Cityborn. It helped that he was easy to find. Lyonardo hadn't left Ryder Keep since his ascension at his and Kayleigh's engagement party. The guards at the front of the entrance were courteous and polite, leading Symon to a stylish yellow-and-black room with plush furniture and a soot-stained fireplace. A picture of the entire Ryder family hung over it. Lyonardo wasn't in it, and Symon wondered whether a new one would be painted once he was officially married into the family.

Lyonardo arrived with a plate of cut pears before Symon had a chance to examine the bookshelves. His hair had been recently cut short and styled upward, he wore fine Ryder-colored clothes, and it looked as if he had recently gained weight. Maybe the loss of his Kingman status affected him more than he openly expressed. Lyon motioned for Symon to take a seat opposite his.

"Recorder," Lyonardo said, leaning forward with his fingers interlaced. "How may I help you today? Do you need something clarified?"

"No, your interview recently was more than enlightening." He crossed his legs, trying not to sink into the overly soft chair. "I've come to ask you a question about one of your siblings."

Lyonardo deflated in his seat. "What did he do now?"

"I'm not here about him," Symon said, enjoying the confusion on Lyonardo's face. "Your sister is working for someone not in the asylum or the smithy. Would you happen to know who?"

"No. Gwen has always been independent. I always trusted her to make smart decisions that I may have . . ." He hesitated. "I don't even remember the last time we had a conversation that wasn't about our family."

"*Her* family," Symon clarified.

"*Her* family," he repeated slowly. "Yes, well, I don't know who else Gwen is working for. Is that it?"

"That's it." Symon returned to his feet and readjusted the vials of ink in his pockets. He hadn't needed to take them out during this conversation with Lyonardo, and the sides of the bottles had pressed against old scars and irritated him beyond belief. "Thanks for your help."

"There's nothing else?" Lyonardo asked.

"Why? Do you want there to be?" Symon smirked at the former Kingman. "Getting bored, Lyonardo? Do you miss the Kingman lifestyle? Do you crave adventure?"

"No," he said. Lyonardo's words weren't nearly as firm as he had hoped they would be. "I just want to help."

"You are." Symon walked to the exit and turned the doorknob. "You're helping me weed out those who are important and those who aren't." Symon clicked his tongue. "I know you once said you'd be fine with your legacy being known as the Cowardly Kingman if it meant protecting your family, but . . . I'm not sure you deserve that title anymore. You're just a footnote."

"And you're just a historian."

"No, I'm *the* Historian." Symon looked over his shoulder. "The world will tell my stories to each other until the sun shatters alongside Celona. But you? I hope your child's love makes up for the prestigious place in the world and the family you abandoned."

The dog of the nobility didn't rise as Symon left. And so he continued, juggling in his mind who would be next to interview. Who would entertain him? Who could give him what he needed to tell the greatest story ever told? And who would help him discover what Gwendolyn Kingman was hiding?

Juliet Kingman was the logical answer, but she was not the one Symon chose to go to. Juliet knew nothing about Gwendolyn's lies—just as Michael didn't—and so he decided to expand his horizons and search for her friends. Which, frankly, was nearly as impossible as figuring out how she had escaped from a room with only a single exit. Symon quickly discovered that she didn't indulge in relaxation with any of her coworkers in the asylum or the smithy she had worked at. Every person told the same story when they were interviewed. That Gwendolyn did her work quickly and efficiently and then left as soon as she could to either return home or check in on her mother. What she did in her free time was a giant mystery.

So Symon was forced to consult the only person who might have an idea: Angelo Shade.

The Recorder found his former foster father in Scales Headquarters after a meeting with the other division commanders had ended. The Commander of the Watchers was nothing if not astute and walked over to Symon upon seeing him waiting outside the room. Bryan Dexter, the Commander of the Evokers, was at his side. Both men were wearing military-style coats dyed in their factions' colors—silver and black, respectively. But that was where the similarities ended.

Angelo's appearance was tidy, pristine, and formidable, while Bryan looked as if he hadn't bathed since his last shave weeks ago. The only thing that wasn't up to standard for Angelo were the rings on his fingers, and yet Symon didn't see the infamous crown ring that had indicated to Michael he had been the previous leader of Tosburg Company. Had he disposed of it? Or did he only wear it when he was certain no one would recognize it?

"Recorder," Angelo said as he approached, "I assume you're here for me. What nonsense has the king killer been spreading about me now?"

"Nothing that isn't quickly dismissed," Symon lied. "I'm actually here for information on one of the other wards you looked after: Gwendolyn Kingman."

Bryan Dexter raised an eyebrow and looked at Angelo as if offering to shoo Symon away if desired. But the Commander of the Watchers simply smiled and shook his head slightly. "I'll be fine. Do let me know if anything tangible comes up about the Heartbreaker that you need aid with."

The Commander of the Evokers yawned, mumbled thanks, then meandered down the hallway with his hands in his pockets.

"Would you be fine with talking in the central gardens?" Angelo asked, pulling at his tight collar. "I've been inside all day and I would love to get a bit of sun before it disappears."

Symon agreed and they entered the winter gardens in the direct center of the building. It was an open-air design that was very popular on the Gold Coast but had never received the same amount of respect in Hollow. Most of the High and Low Nobles so strongly preferred walls or obscuring nature that kept a barrier between them and everyone else that the thought of something so easily infiltrated was ridiculous to comprehend.

Most of the vegetation had been planted with the intention of having the gardens bloom in winter with red bark trees, small purple fruits hidden by pine needles, and small pink winterblooms that poked through the snow as if defying death, turning a grey monotone landscape into a canvas of colors. Symon and Angelo walked along the paths until they reached a half-frozen pond filled with long, brightly colored fish that swam under the ice. Angelo closed his eyes, letting the cool winter air blow against his exposed skin. Symon just dug his hands further into his pockets to protect what little warmth he still had.

Angelo yanked him back from the edge of the pond. "Don't let your toes touch the water or you may lose them."

"What?" Symon asked incredulously. "Why?"

"It's Bandit's territory," Angelo said with a chuckle. "That's the name of the snapping turtle that lives in there. The old prick must be at least a few hundred years old and as entitled as any Hollow High Noble." Angelo's breath was white and fleeting in the cold. "He usually claims a toe or two from every new recruiting class. Even got one of mine when I was a fledging Advocator."

Symon investigated the pond. Its depth was impossible to tell from where he was, but he doubted a three-hundred-year-old turtle would be able to live in there comfortably. The story must've been a lie or an exaggeration to lure Symon into a false sense of security. "A turtle stole your toe and you let it live? Mercy is rare in Scales."

"Revenge isn't the solution to every problem. Knowing when to walk away is the sign of the smarter man." Angelo's eyes grew focused. "What do you want to know about Gwendolyn?"

"While she was living with you, do you know if she had any jobs that weren't with the asylum or apprenticing under a blacksmith?"

"Gwen worked in the dye pits when she was younger," Angelo said. "But she wasn't there for long. Why? Is she under suspicion of something?"

Symon hesitated. "No, I'm just trying to fully understand the complicated dynamics of the Kingman family."

"Liar," he whispered with the same intensity as a scream. It sent shivers up Symon's spine and made him very aware of how alone they were. Not even birds bore witness to their conversation. "Be direct with what you want, or this conversation is over. Understood?"

"Perfectly," Symon said. "I believe Gwendolyn is working with someone who is going out of their way to remain hidden not just from the Kingman family but from all of Hollow. Do you know who that might be?"

Angelo reached into his pocket and pulled out a small knife that looked more useful for sharpening blades than stabbing or slicing. He used it to extract the dirt under his fingernails. "Let me say, I admire your tenacity in deciding to approach me for information. It's quite bold." He flicked dirt and blood off the point of his dagger. "So let me give you some advice. Don't try to hunt wolves simply because you're pretending to be one." Angelo stared Symon down with his grey eyes. "Because—"

"Commander Shade!" an Advocator shouted as she ran toward them. "Someone's just broken into your office!"

His demeanor changed. The calm and focused man was gone, and only someone overwhelmed with anger remained. Angelo sprinted past Symon and the Advocator, knife in hand. Symon chased after him, refusing to let this opportunity go to waste. Had Michael broken into Angelo's office in Scales Headquarters? Did he even know his foster father had one here? And if it hadn't been Michael, who had it been? The Black Death?

Angelo's office had been ransacked. Potted plants had been knocked over or torn out at the stems, loose papers were strewn across the floor, a painting of a noblewoman on the bow of a ship had a fist-sized hole where her face had been, and all the books had been thrown off the shelves and half of them had been torn in half, forcing Symon to swallow bile that tried to come up at the sight. There were two kinds of people in Symon's mind: those who respected books and those who didn't. And anyone who fell in the second category would be lucky if they were erased by history rather than dehumanized.

The Commander of the Watchers stood in the doorway, hand extended to the other side of the frame to prevent others from entering. There were about a dozen Scales members behind him from all the six branches of Scales, except for the Judges. Without words he motioned for two Evokers to get their commander and for the Watchers to prevent anyone from entering his office while he investigated. They tried to keep Symon back, but he didn't need to be pushing his body against them to get a good look at what Angelo was doing within the room. He was used to watching from a distance. If anything, he liked it, as it allowed him to see the entire scene rather than get lost in the minute details.

His skin was his paper and his backup quill was his instrument as he recorded.

Angelo started with the dirt on the floor. The perpetrator hadn't left behind any footprints or marks or blood. From there he picked up one of the destroyed books and examined it. Its tear was ragged and crooked, as if done by an animal's teeth rather than a person's hands. The hole in the painting was similarly bizarre. It had been clawed out from the front rather than punched out from the back as Symon had initially assumed. And as Angelo checked his desk's drawers, he said to all those watching, "Nothing's been taken. Where's Commander Dexter?"

One of the Evokers behind Symon shouted, "We can't find him!"

"What do you mean you can't find him?" Angelo asked, eerily calm. "That man barely leaves this place to eat and bathe. Did you try the training grounds or the Archives?"

"We checked everywhere. He must've left," another added. "The guards at the entrances didn't even hear or see him leave. He just vanished!"

"How does a Commander of Scales vanish in our headquarters?" Angelo pressed, voice slightly rising. "Wait. Have someone check the Heartbreaker murder scene we found today. He might have gone back to it." Two Advocators ran off at his command. Angelo pointed at Symon. "Someone also escort the Recorder out of here at once. I apologize that we couldn't finish our conversation, but there are more pressing matters to attend with."

"I understand," Symon said as he put away his quill and ink. "Another time."

"Another time," Angelo repeated as he gently ran his fingers down the ruined painting's frame.

Advocators escorted Symon out of the building, making sure he was unable to wander off in case he decided not to follow Angelo's orders. But Symon was more than pleased with what he had come across. Not only did he have the opportunity to see Angelo Shade's true persona for a heartbeat, but he had also learned that his office had been ransacked. Had Michael done it? And if not, how much would he be willing to give up to learn about it? Maybe using Michael was the way to uncover what Gwendolyn was hiding. Would she lie to Michael about whatever it was she was doing, too?

Kingman Keep was newly dark when Symon entered the great hall. Naomi was still at the table as she had been in the morning, all that differed were the dirty bowls in front of her. Rather than porridge, dinner must've been something that left brown rings around the insides of the bowls. Symon joined her and emptied the vials of ink and quills from his pockets. Neither Gwendolyn nor Michael nor Rock nor Juliet was anywhere to be seen. He asked for their whereabouts.

"Michael is already asleep," Naomi said. "He looked like death when he got back from training with Dark. Barely took off his shirt before collapsing." She licked her thumb and turned a page. "Claimed he knew how to catch lightning now, though."

"I'll believe it when I see it." Symon leaned back with his arms crossed. "And the others?"

"Gwen hasn't returned yet and Rock disappeared a little after midday. Told me he'd be gone for a few days." She turned another page. "Juliet is walking through the Upper Quarter with Olivier. They wanted some quality daughter-father bonding time." She tried to say the last sentence without bitterness interlaced with her voice but was left wanting.

"I saw Bryan Dexter today."

Naomi looked up from the journal. "Oh? And what did you need with my caring father?"

"I was visiting another commander in Scales Headquarters and ran into him."

"Angelo?"

Symon nodded.

Naomi hesitated and then said, "Were you investigating whether Michael was telling the truth? That he was responsible for Davey's death and framing Michael's father?"

"Do you think Michael is lying about that?"

"I think he believes it's the truth."

"That was very carefully worded."

Naomi put the book down and popped a Blackberry in her mouth. She moved it around until it was under her tongue behind her lower teeth. "What were you after, then?"

"Nothing. I just had a gut feeling I might find something interesting if I talked to him. And I did." Symon paused for dramatics. "Your father has vanished."

Naomi was unfazed. "Unsurprising. He once disappeared for a month when he thought he found a clue that might help him determine the Heartbreaker's identity." She sucked on the Blackberry. "He'll appear again eventually. He always does."

"What if the Heartbreaker has him?"

"Then he'll die doing what he loves."

Symon nearly knocked over one of his vials of ink. "At least we won't have to worry about you being a target. You don't have a heart to lose." Naomi shuffled in her seat uncomfortably. "Do you truly hate your father so?"

"It's hard not to hate when you've never known love." Naomi grabbed her book and walked away from the table and toward the room Michael and she shared. "Good night, Symon."

"Good night, Naomi."

The Recorder twirled one of his quills as he stared at all the notes covering his skin. While Symon didn't have answers to the questions he had started the day seeking, he had found something quite tantalizing. Symon wrote Gwendolyn's name repeatedly on the back of his hand and smiled wickedly.

Symon was going to determine who the youngest Kingman was working for and why she was so bent on keeping it a secret. She had had her chance to come clean with him, but now the truth was going to come out whether she wanted it to or not.

THE MORNING AFTER

Nothing felt right when I woke up the next morning.

I wasn't wearing a shirt, I wore different pants than I had gone to sleep in, and there were new aches and bruises all over my body. The stiches in my side were gone, with no indication I had ever been cut. Whatever position I had slept in the night before clearly had been the wrong one.

Two dresses—one blue and the other gold—hung over a chair. The only table in the room held three shirts that looked like my size, neatly folded. Likely Olivier's handiwork. It was too precise for Rock. Naomi was nowhere to be seen in the room or on the balcony. If it weren't for the dresses and the Blackberries scattered on the table, there wouldn't have been a trace of her.

There was a letter written in a messy scrawl on the wall closest to my bed:

Four things:

1. Get up! You're meeting Trey in the morning outside Ryder Keep

2. You have a new tattoo over your ribs—left side

3. Stop staring at Celona

4. I'm sorry

What was that supposed to mean? Who had written it? And why was it wrong? I was meeting Dark today, not Trey. What was going . . . ?

The sun shone through the nearby window, blinding me. It was way past dawn, which meant I was very, very late to meet Dark. I wondered why he hadn't stormed in to get me himself. Flustered and aching, I grabbed my shirt and jacket off the table before running down the stairs toward the great hall. If I was lucky, Dark would let me eat before subjecting me to some brutal Fabrication training. It wasn't going to be fun. "Mercy" wasn't a word I associated with him.

My sister, Symon, and Naomi were the only ones at the table when I arrived. Olivier was likely in the area. Somewhere. I didn't have the time to catch my breath before I asked, "Dark? Here yet?"

"Is he supposed to be?" my sister asked as she dunked a piece of bread into her runny eggs.

"Yes," I said, hands on my knees. I really needed to get into better shape. "We're supposed to be training today."

"More Fabrication practice?"

"More? We haven't started yet."

Symon and Naomi stopped reading from their respective journals and looked at me, focused. They whispered something to each other and Symon shook his head.

"Michael," Naomi said, "what did you do yesterday?"

"You mean when I wasn't with you?" They were all staring at me. It was unsettling. "What's going on?"

"Congratulations, Michael," Symon said as he drew out every word. "You've officially become a Fabricator. You've forgotten an entire day of your life. Yesterday, to be exact."

I felt pale. "What?"

My sister guided me to a chair. The world was spinning around me . . . This had to be a joke. I recalled yesterday in detail. Being attacked by the Heartbreaker, meeting with Dark, and our useless trip to the Church of the Wanderer. I couldn't have forgotten an entire day, right?

"You three are messing with me, aren't you?"

Gwen shook her head. "No. Dark came by yesterday to train you in Nullify Fabrications. It was memorable: you woke up late and he dragged you down the stairs by one ankle."

That explained the new aches and pains all over my body. "How do we know that my memories weren't messed with again?"

"I would know," Symon said.

"You've made mistakes before."

"'Before' is the key word in that sentence, Michael. It won't happen again." Symon shifted dramatically. "Besides, memory loss from Fabrication use doesn't occur until someone sleeps. So it makes sense that you'd only realize some of your memories were gone when you awoke."

"What?" I said, caught off guard. "What do you mean it occurs when I sleep? I thought it happened when I used Fabrications."

Symon shook his head. "Becoming a Forgotten happens instantaneously after Fabrication use. But otherwise, consider it a debt. For every Fabrication you use in a single day, you'll lose exactly that many memories when you sleep. Did you really not know that, Michael? Almost everyone in Hollow does. Even non-Fabricators."

"We were taught it as children," Gwen said softly.

"I . . . I . . ." And I trailed off into nothing. "I guess I must've misunderstood when it was explained to me."

"That's not surprising, considering how dense you are," Symon said. "And if you truly don't believe us, look at this."

Symon flipped open one of his notebooks and handed it to me. In clear, flowing handwriting was an account of a day I didn't remember:

Michael began the day training with Dark the Mercenary to get a better understanding of his Nullify Fabrications. They were gone from dawn to dusk. When Michael returned, he claimed to have a basic understanding of what his Nullify Fabrications were capable of and was able to reproduce what he had done at the king's party, where he nullified a large group of people. He also can apparently catch lightning again as he did in the Church of the Wanderer at his execution. Will need to follow up about that.

There has been another Heartbreaker murder, raising the total to three people in three days. If history repeats itself, it won't calm down until another nine have been murdered. One for each day of the week.

Otherwise, the day was largely uneventful. Naomi sucked on three Blackberries throughout the course of the day and helped Juliet clean up Kingman Keep. She debated taking more when she was stressed. A typical addict conundrum. The only oddity of the day was that Rock left very early in the morning and hasn't been—

I put the journal down. "That's beyond creepy, Symon. Do you write notes like that every day?"

Symon took his journal back from me, holding it quite gently. "I wouldn't be doing my job if I didn't. Or have you forgotten what my goal in life is?"

"Symon, stop taunting Michael," Gwen said.

"As you wish, future heir."

I wanted to punch Symon in the jaw but grabbed the edges of the table as hard as I could instead. "I knew this would happen eventually. Every Fabricator does. I just . . . I just . . ."

"You didn't think it would really happen to you," Naomi said. "Everyone thinks they'll be the exception. No one is. It's one of the two great equalizers in the world."

Naomi was right, but I didn't want to openly agree, so I said nothing. "What does this mean for the training I did yesterday with Dark? If I do it again, who's to say I won't just forget that day again? I could be stuck in a cycle of learning and then forgetting."

"Maybe, but now you know how your Fabrications work," Naomi said. "Imagine a building. Once it's been built, it's there until it gets destroyed, even if you lose the blueprints that created it. Your body remembers your limitations even if you don't. You'll just have to experiment with your powers, remember what you did in the past, and see if you can do it again."

"That sounds dangerous," I said. "An easy path to become a Forgotten before I turn twenty."

"Then come up with a different solution. Because it sounds like fate doesn't want you to have a complete understanding of your powers. I'd bet that if you trained with Dark again, you'd wake up the next day with no memory of it."

Knowing my luck, it was hard to argue with her. "Did I do anything else of importance yesterday I should be reminded of?"

"We slept together last night," Naomi said.

Not even my sister responded to that. Naomi sighed loudly and then crossed her arms like a child who'd been told to behave.

Thankfully for us all, Symon answered my question. "Not that I'm aware of. But given your habit of visiting people in the middle of the night . . . I can't say for certain."

Great, not even the Recorder who had come to Kingman Keep to record the history of my life knew for certain what I'd done yesterday. Had I left that message next to my bed for my future self? Was there something I didn't want to risk forgetting? And why did I warn myself about looking at the moon? Wait, it said I had a new tattoo, did that mean—

I pulled up my shirt and found a name etched over the left side of my ribs: *Jamal*.

"He deserves not to be forgotten," Gwen said as I put my shirt down.

"I've been thinking about getting it for a while," I muttered. "I guess the me of yesterday decided to do it."

"Maybe you should consider keeping a journal," Symon said as he handed me one with the Kingman family crest on the cover. It was small enough to fit in my pocket. How long had he been holding on to that? Definitely longer than I wanted to know.

I tucked it away in my jacket. "Never thought of myself as a writer. Maybe I should start a painting or get more tattoos."

"Michael," Gwen said, sounding like our mother when I was in trouble, "you're a Fabricator. You need to take it seriously. Or you'll become Forgotten and have no way of remembering anything."

"Write in it every night if you can," Symon suggested. "It may not prevent every memory loss, but it'll help you more than you'd imagine."

"We'll see."

Writing down my own story would make me an observer of my own life. Someone constantly stuck in the past rather than moving forward. And considering I was already making progress moving forward, I didn't want to be that lonely child ever again. Who knew if I would actually use this journal or find another way to record what was important to me?

No way to know until I tried.

I pushed the fears I had about losing memories to the back of my mind lest they try to overwhelm me. Instead, I wondered where Olivier was. This was the longest he'd ever taken with breakfast, and everyone else's plates were making me jealous. As if I could foresee the future, Olivier and Rock rushed into the great hall. They were visibly flustered.

"Michael . . . Gwen," Olivier said between breaths. "Where is your mother? We have a problem."

I looked to Gwen for an answer. "She left early this morning. She didn't say where she was going or when she'd be back."

Olivier and Rock shared a glance that might as well have been a curse.

Gwen stood from her seat. "What's the issue? How can I help?"

"Some workers with hammers and Steel Fabricators are here to tear down the houses around Kingman Keep. Claim their benefactor told them to. Want to replace the houses with new houses and a memorial garden for King Isaac."

"Don't most of the locals still think Kingman Keep is haunted?" I asked. "Why would someone do this?"

"It's clearly a declaration of war by someone," Olivier said. "Although Kingman Keep is large enough to house a well-sized staff, the surrounding area is just as important. It'll be hard to recruit people unless we can house them. We won't be able to attract business to settle there, either."

I rose to my feet. "Let's go and talk to them."

All of us, minus Naomi, who decided to continue eating her breakfast, left Kingman Keep in a hurry. There was a crowd of men and women in dirty clothes with old tools in their hands. The Fabricators were easy to identify. They were the only ones not dressed for construction and demolition. Their leader was a man with the owl sigil on his clothes right above the heart. The Castlen High Noble family oversaw development in Hollow. Maybe they were making a power play against us at the princess's suggestion?

"I don't see how bringing more people here is going to change what we've been instructed to do," the leader declared.

"Just hear them out before you begin destroying all these houses," Olivier said as he made a sweeping gesture toward Gwen and me. "This is Michael and Gwendolyn Kingman. While the head of the household isn't at home, I'm sure these two will be able to negotiate in her absence."

Shockingly, the leader pulled a face and drew a letter from his pocket, which he handed to me. "Consider me proven wrong. Didn't realize who you were, Kingman. I was told to give this to you if I saw you."

It was a plain envelope with nothing written on it. I opened it and took out the letter inside of it. It was longer than I thought it would be.

Michael,

It has been far too long and we have much to discuss. Consider this a formal invitation to my house for a midday meal. The typical time. You should remember where it is.

*Bring a guest. I have prepared a feast and it would be a shame
for it to go to waste.*

*If you choose not to attend, these fine workers will
continue as instructed. I own the land around Kingman Keep.
Don't make me prove it. If you will attend, tell the workers
they have the rest of the day off and I will contact them with
further instructions tomorrow morning.*

Yours truly,
Charles Domet

Of course this was his doing. Charles Domet loved to interfere with
my life, and this was so in line with things he had done to me in the past,
I was surprised I didn't realize it sooner. Or at least expect him to try
something.

"Domet?" my sister asked.

"Domet," I confirmed.

I showed the letter to the leader of the workers. They left with a
smile and without a fuss, and would clearly be back tomorrow morning
to continue what they started unless told otherwise. It was hard to tell
where my relationship with Domet stood, but it felt like I was about to
walk into an obvious trap that I wouldn't escape without sacrificing something. Assuming I went.

"What're you going to do?" Gwen asked.

I crumpled up the letter and put it into my pocket. "I don't know."

"Any idea who you'll bring?"

I didn't respond and followed Rock, Olivier, and Symon back into
Kingman Keep. My sister stayed at my side. "Seems like you think I
should go."

"Be honest with yourself. You're going. Ignoring Domet would only
hurt us in the future. The only question is who you're taking with you."

"You'd be my first choice. You know him. But I probably shouldn't.
Future heir and all that."

Gwen opened her mouth to object but sighed instead. "I don't want to be treated like some fragile thing that might break in a strong gust of wind."

I put my arm around her shoulders and held her close. "Please. Everyone knows I'm the weakest Kingman these days. You're a force of nature who fought the Corrupt Prince, and Lyon was brave enough to sacrifice everything for his unborn child. While my ego gets bruised daily. Along with my pride. And my body. Really, everything associated with me."

"Always so dramatic."

"Some things are eternal."

Gwen leaned her head against my shoulder for a moment before pushing away and composing herself. "I don't want it, you know."

"I know. Ironically, I'm the only one who ever did, and I'm the one who never can."

"Life's a bitch."

"It's better than dying."

We walked into the great hall. "Are you sure? I've never tried it."

"I have," I said with a smile. "It hurts."

"Another thing to be disappointed about."

My sister went off to talk to Olivier while I went to talk to Naomi. Her plate was empty and she was licking her fingers. I doubted it was the eggs she was hoping to savor. I put my hands down on the table and then said, "You, me, and a crazy rich man obsessed with my family are having a midday meal."

"You want the Blackberry addict to accompany you? Why?"

"Because Domet will be expecting Gwen, not you. It might catch him off guard."

Naomi put her hand over her heart. "You really know how to sweep a girl off her feet."

"And to think I'm still this romantic after we've already slept together."

"Clearly it can only get better from here," she said with a wink. "Actually, I have a question for you. How well do you know Dark?"

"He's an immoral asshole who murders anyone that gets in his way. Why?"

Naomi showed me a page out of her father's journal without saying anything.

My initial investigation into the serial killer we're nicknaming the Heartbreaker is going nowhere. We know little, if anything, about their motive, gender, method of operation, or anything else. My only point of investigation are sightings of an Orbis Company Mercenary named Davis who has been loitering near the murder scenes. We are unable to determine if they are cleaning up evidence or searching the area for clues themselves. Considering the brutality and efficiency of these kills, a Mercenary would have the skills necessary.

Davis will be at a party High Noble Braven is hosting tonight with his partner, Zahra of Azil. I'll have to make contact and determine what his motives are for myself. Hopefully he makes a mistake and gives me the information I need to end this case before any others are harmed.

When I was finished reading, I clicked my tongue. "Zahra was the name of Dark's lover and Davis is Dark's real name. Are these notes trustworthy? Because they suggest Dark was a suspect."

"These notes are the only thing I would ever trust from my father."

"Wonderful," I grumbled as I put my hands behind my head and began to pace in front of the table. "He said he would answer my questions after I'd read that notebook, but . . ."

"Do you trust him enough to tell you the truth?"

"Not without some other leverage," I said without hesitation. "But why would I suspect Dark? He wants to catch the killer more than I do."

"Could Dark be involved in some way? It wouldn't be the first time someone close to you has deceived you."

I paused and glanced at Naomi. She wasn't being as erratic as she had been in the Berry Field. It was hard to tell whether she was feeling the effects from Blackberries or not. "You really want to catch the Heart-breaker, don't you?"

"More than you realize," she said. "I suggest we start by learning more about Zahra. She was Dark's one weakness, which makes her our best tool to learn more about him. Women don't fall in love with monsters. They only watch them turn into them. Maybe her death made him what he is."

"That's a great theory. How do we get information about her?"

"Luckily, there's a mention of a place that might know more about her."

Naomi flipped to a different page in the notebook and then showed it to me.

> *Although I haven't had much time to assess the other*
> *combatant—because I don't want to get attached to people*
> *who must die for my daughter to live—one of my colleagues*
> *investigated them. There is very little out there about the*
> *Mercenary named Davis. All we can determine is that he is a*
> *member of Orbis Company. His captive, Zahra, is a prominent*
> *member of the Hollow Castle community, serving as the lady-*
> *in-waiting to the princess. One that was recommended by the*
> *Thebian embassy through their Azilian placement program. It's*
> *a shame her life will be cut short at such a young age.*

"Dark was a contestant?" I said breathlessly. "How did this not come up sooner?"

"Since when does Dark tell you anything?" Naomi questioned.

I bit down on my tongue. I needed to know what he did. At this point it was putting people in danger. What possible reason was there for keeping this from me? What was he hiding?

"At least we know where to go next," Naomi said as she rose from her seat. "I'll get changed into something more appropriate for noble affairs and then we can go."

"I have an errand first," I said. "I have to go meet Trey."

"Why?" Naomi asked.

"I have no idea. It was one of the notes I left for myself last night, and it seems wrong to ignore my own advice."

"Guess I'll meet up with you later, then."

I nodded. "Thanks for understanding. But care to explain why you think anyone is going to let me set a single foot in Hollow Castle? Or how we're going to find someone who knew Zahra?"

In answer, she poked a finger through one of the holes in my shirt. "Who said we were going to Hollow Castle? The Thebian embassy is responsible for her getting the job in the castle, so that's where we're going. I have an aunt who works there that can help us. But do me a favor and deal with this . . . stench. We may not be about to seek out nobility, but that doesn't mean they don't have standards."

As Naomi left, I pulled my shirt away from my body slightly and took a big whiff.

Just this once, maybe she wasn't wrong.

THE SUPPLIER

"You're late."

I slowed down in front of Trey, put my hands on my knees, and tried to catch my breath. "Sorry. Had to stop by the baths first. And I didn't know I had to be here or I would've woken up earlier."

Trey moved off the lamplight he had been leaning on. "How? We talked about it repeatedly yesterday when—" His eyes widened. "Memory loss?"

"The entire day is gone." I stood up straight and put my hands behind my head. "Did we talk about anything important?"

"You told me your plan to end the rebellion and asked me to help you."

"Wait, I finally came up with a plan? Can you tell me about it?"

Trey hesitated. "Help me with an errand first."

I didn't really have any reason to argue, so I simply nodded and asked, "What do you need me to do?"

We walked through the Upper Quarter in silence, taking in all the oddities that only seemed to exist in the morning. There were Low Nobles sitting at food stalls eating simple dishes—or attempting to—after a long night of excess. Vendors had callers outside of their shops to entice anyone passing about the rare goods within their stores, from slivers of moon-fall to foreign perfume and silk clothes. Birds rarely liked to make this place their home, but the few that did sang short songs on the rooftops before flying off to warmer places. Because no matter what season it was, the Upper Quarter always seemed to be cold.

Trey pointed to a nearby building with columns and ornate silver lettering around the door. "That's the place we're going." He reached into his jacket and handed me a flintlock pistol. "You'll need this. That place is where I get Blackberries and it's always better to be prepared for a fight."

I cursed rapidly as I took the gun from him and shoved it between my back and trousers. "Dammit, Trey. Not even trying to be subtle anymore, are you? And what do you mean that place is your supplier? We're in the Upper Quarter."

He looked at me as if I were an imbecile. "Did you think the person who controlled the Blackberry trade would be on the East Side? That's the place they poison, not live in."

"Does that mean the supplier is a noble?"

"It doesn't, but they are."

"High or Low?"

Trey walked toward the house. "Who cares? All nobles are the same in my head."

"They're not to me."

"That's your problem, not mine."

"Maybe I could stop them if you tell me who they are."

Trey's knuckles hovered over the door. "*I* would stop them if I wanted to. But for now they're useful to me. Their poison corrupted my mother, so I might as well use it for my own ends while I can."

Before Trey knocked on the door, it edged open on its own. Without saying anything and in unison, we drew our guns and crept into the house. A Blackberry supplier wouldn't leave their door unlocked. Even in the Upper Quarter. I was expecting a disaster . . . and we found one.

Tables were flipped, glass was shattered, Blackberry powder covered the floor, and four bodies were strewn across the main room, looking as if they had been torn apart by an animal rather than by swords or axes. Two of them were missing their faces, one had both of their arms torn off, and the fourth was huddled in the corner wholly intact but with a look of complete and utter terror on their face.

The smell of this room made me long for sun-soaked trash.

Trey held his nose and put away his gun. "Whatever did this has come and gone a while ago." He squatted to look at one of the bloated bodies. "Multiple days at the earliest. A week at the latest."

I walked through the room. "None of them seem to be missing their hearts. So there're no signs that this was the Heartbreaker." I kicked over a bucket and found nothing in it. "It almost looks like they were interrogated. Could this have been an attack by someone wanting to take over the Blackberry trade? Because whoever did this destroyed all the drugs in here."

"Doubtful," Trey said. "I would've heard if the attack came from someone on the East Side. I suppose a noble could have done this, but . . . the current Blackberry supplier has gone to extreme lengths to make sure every part of their involvement is hidden. Attacking them like this is too brutish to be effective."

"Could it have been a warning to stop what they're doing?"

"Maybe. I just don't . . ." He slapped his thighs and returned to his feet. "It doesn't matter. This is annoying—nothing more. There may not be as many Blackberries in the dens as usual this week, but it should be fine, since there's one less to worry about now."

We left the house and made sure the door was closed tight behind us. That first breath of fresh air was more satisfying than clouds parting on a rainy day. Not wanting to get caught at the scene of multiple murders, we went to a nearby bench to talk. None of the locals so much as glanced in our direction. It was as if they had decided shunning us because we didn't belong was better than making a fuss.

"Can you tell me what my plan for ending the rebellion is?" I asked once we were settled.

Trey was staring at the castle in the distance. "For your own sake, it may be better if you don't know. That way you'll be more genuine when it happens."

"Genuine? Why does that matter?"

"Because you're going to turn yourself in to the emperor and convince her you're there to join them."

"I'm what?"

"If you think it's stupid, you only have yourself to blame."

I made an exasperated sound. "Guess I do. So what happens after I do that?"

"That's where I come in," Trey said.

"Are you going to explain? Or at least tell me when this plan is happening?"

"Nope," he said with a slight smile. "Just know that I'll be there to help whenever you need me." He conjured a small ball of light and then twirled it in his palm. "I'll make the rebellion an offer to join they can't refuse. Just as I did with the Corrupt Prince." He crushed the ball, twinkling light falling through his fingers. "I may be nobody, but I know how to present myself to somebody."

I looked at my friend. "Can I ask why you're doing this? Is it to avenge Jamal or . . . do you think we can be friends again?"

"We'll always be friends." He paused. "But that doesn't mean we'll be on the same side. Right now we are, so we should enjoy this reprise while we can and avenge the person we both loved."

"And when we're not?"

"We'll face that day when it comes."

Trey left me on the bench to collect my thoughts. I didn't wallow in my misery for too long. There were other things to do. And if I didn't continue to move forward, I would never have the chance to defy the fate Trey thought we were locked into.

WEAVERS

The Thebian embassy had a dozen carts in front of it, all piled high with boxes and furniture. Various people were moving around the building, tossing papers into makeshift bonfires or carrying more things to the cart. Naomi was standing in front of it with her arms crossed, dressed in clothes fit for a meeting with Domet . . . or a funeral. She saw me approach and was already in mid-sentence by the time I could hear her: "—and they're leaving! Can you believe it? Just because it's been a month since King Isaac died and Serena is still the queen-in-waiting. They claim they'll have to reassess Hollow's standing with them. That we may be currently too volatile and instable for diplomatic relations."

"All of them?"

"All of them," she repeated. "Including my aunt."

"Has she left yet?"

Naomi shook her head and walked up the steps to the entrance of the embassy while I followed. We pushed our way past the group of refugees getting old coats and boots from Thebian soldiers with bone whips and swords that had their blades dyed black. "Not yet. But she is tonight." She clicked her tongue. "Doubt she would have said goodbye."

I stopped. "You don't have to do this if you don't want to. I'm sure I can con—"

"Michael," she interrupted, her voice so calm, it sent shivers up my spine. "If you suggest that I run away from my problems one more time, I'll slap you. Understood?"

"Perfectly."

Naomi and I reached the top and stopped in front of a Thebian guard. Without saying anything, Naomi pulled down the skin below her left eye so her electric-blue iris was even more visible. The guard ushered her in without a word, and in we went to the most secure embassy in Hollow.

"That's all it takes to enter?" I asked.

She nodded. "All Thebians have these electric-blue eyes. The Divine General calls it the empire's biological conquest because all it takes is a drop of Thebian blood to make sure someone's descendants are marked as one of them forever."

And here I thought my family's amber eyes were a strong inherited trait.

"Is the Divine General the leader of the Thebian Empire?"

"Kind of." Naomi paused. "The Divine General is the spokesman for the Imprisoned One. They're the one who's actually in charge, but . . . well, they've been dead for three hundred years." At the sight of my scrunched face, Naomi added, "It's complicated. Most citizens think the Imprisoned One will return one day and lead the empire into a golden age."

"Doesn't that make the Thebian Empire a necrocracy?"

"Please don't remind me."

Like all the other countries, I had been taught about the Thebian Empire as a child. But because of their distance away from us, it was, frankly, about as minimal as possible. New Dracon City and Goldono were between us and them, which gave Hollow a buffer from their . . .

sometimes erratic tendencies. They weren't zealots, focused on conquering the world to spread their religion or beliefs. They were just orderly to a fault and didn't like to see anyone—their own citizens or not—suffer. Which meant they often went to war for the good of the world, or so they claimed. The Thebian Empire hadn't always been as vast as it was now, but if they were really pulling out of Hollow, then there was a fair chance that they would deem us unworthy to govern, and an army would be approaching from the west in due time. And there was no doubt in my mind that they would win. Even my ancestors had barely been able to hold them off in the past.

But I tried to quell those thoughts as we stood in the main entrance of the embassy, watching and waiting. Naomi tried to get various people's attention, half shouting out her questions as they passed, only to get ignored without so much as a glance or a pause. She had looked more composed talking to her father than she did here in this building.

"I'll have to go find her," she muttered. "Why did it have to be this annoying? Why is it always so stupidly complicated when it comes to my family?"

"Story of my life."

Naomi didn't appreciate the joke, and probably would have jabbed me in the side if it was worth the effort. "I'm going to go find my aunt. Wait on those benches over there and try not to draw attention to yourself."

"Wait," I said with a laugh. "You're going to make me wait here? Alone? How is that better than having me come with you?"

"Because deeper in there are very, very delicate and important documents that the Thebian Empire would start a war to prevent from getting out. At least here—while you may say something stupid that could anger someone—I don't think you'll start a . . ." She moved the Blackberry from one cheek to the other with her tongue. "Actually, pretend you're a mute. Or deaf. And put up your collar. Try to be inconspicuous. Please."

I adjusted my jacket so my brand wasn't quite as visible. "Why'd you bring me here, again?"

"I don't know," she muttered as she headed up the nearby stairs. "What was I thinking, bringing Michael dumbass Kingman to a place he could start a war with a single comment?"

Clearly the Blackberries were affecting her judgment more than I realized. But since I was sober, and smart enough to take Naomi's warnings to heart, I sat down on the benches. And waited. And waited. And almost fell asleep sitting where I was, only to slip, overadjust my position, and then bang the back of my head against the stone wall behind me. It sent a wave of pain through my head, concentrating in my forehead.

The laughter that quickly followed it eased my pain. Light and childish.

A child was standing in front of me in loose-fitting clothes and with a shaved head. It was impossible to tell their gender, the child thriving in that time before a decision was made for them. Every visible part of their body was covered in scars. From faded burns and missing teeth to bite marks on their arms and dislocated fingers. The child looked as if they had been tortured for their entire life—worse than I could ever imagine, even after what had happened to me in the dungeons—and yet still they had a smile on their face and levity in their laughter.

"Are you hurt?" I asked the child, leaving the bench. "Do you need help?"

The child shook their head.

"Are you sure? Because if you need help, I can give it to you." I hesitated, creeping closer. "My name is Michael Kingman and I—"

A hand gripped my shoulder, freezing me in place. "You should not get any closer to that child. It may hurt you."

A Thebian man strode past me as another man kept me in place. He wore a long silver robe with slits in the side that made it flow whenever he walked and golden gauntlets that went past his elbows. His eyes were the same electric blue as Naomi's, but his gaunt face was paler, as if he hadn't seen the sun in many months. The Thebian squatted in front of the child and said something to it in a different language that I didn't understand. Except for two words that were impossible to miss or mistake: "Michael Kingman." So much for keeping a low profile.

As the Thebian man took the child's hand in his own, he glared at me. "Was what we heard true? You are a Kingman?"

I nodded, still stuck in place by whoever was holding me.

He looked me up and down. "I knew the stories had been exaggerated, but I did not realize to what extent. Kingman, like you, are truly so important to Hollow society? Maybe we overestimated this place for too long."

"Don't you dare—"

The person holding me put a hand over my mouth and said, "Champion Prasai, perhaps you should introduce yourself before saying anything else." He let me go. "That way this Kingman doesn't say anything out of line and regret it."

"Yes, I suppose that is necessary. I am Prasai Alareata, the Champion of the Ancients. As one of the nine noble champions of the Thebian Empire, I have been selected by the Imprisoned One themselves to enrichen the empire's knowledge of the Wolven Kings' reign." He scoffed at his surroundings. "Hence why I am in this sulfur-ridden city. This is my ward." The champion gestured to the child. "And the man holding you is—"

"If it's alright with you, Champion Prasai, I'd prefer to remain nameless. I'm not supposed to be here right now, and if it were reported back to my peers, it could be disastrous." The man behind me stepped into view. It was the Skeleton from Dawn's courting event. He had two swords strapped across his back and a pistol at his side and kind of reminded me of Dark. "So I did meet a Kingman after all. Call me Skeleton if you desire, Michael."

"Who are you? Especially if you're bold enough to carry a pistol in Hollow."

The Skeleton shrugged. "I imagine you'll find out eventually. Isn't that right, Champion Prasai?"

"Very much so." The Thebian gestured for the child to take hold of his shirt and then crossed his arms. "So, Kingman. Why are you in my halls? Come to see us off?"

"I'm here with a friend who was visiting family before they left," I said. "Do you want me to leave?"

"No, you are not a big enough concern that I feel I must banish you." He looked at the Skeleton. "You may disagree, but I have never seen them as you do."

"What can I say? My father raised me on Kingman stories," he said with an easy smile. "But I never really worshipped them like most kids did. I always wanted to defeat my heroes. Smash their faces into the dirt and make them acknowledge me instead. Idolization is such a waste of time and breath and lets those undeserving cling to power."

My body nullified itself without me realizing, but I held the warmth steady over me, hoping this wouldn't turn into a fight. Naomi would kill me herself if I accidentally started a war here.

"Say, Michael . . . you're not busy, so how would you feel about a friendly duel?" the Skeleton asked, hand rubbing his chin. "A one-on-one spar. No weapons or guns. Just magic and fists. First to fall down loses."

"Why would I want to do that?"

"To see another country's magic," Champion Prasai said. "The Skeleton is right. I may think little of you, Kingman, but I do not think little of Fabricators in Hollow. Prove me wrong. Do you think you can defeat my country's magic users? Or will you run away?"

"Fine," I said, remembering Dark's words in Kingman Keep. Hollow wasn't an empire for a reason, but the Thebians were. What could they do that we couldn't? And maybe seeing another magic user would give me an idea if I was being hunted down by one. Part of me had assumed the Heartbreaker was a Fabricator, but I had no proof. "Who am I fighting?"

The child stepped forward.

I relaxed. "I'm not fighting a child."

Champion Prasai snapped his fingers. "Who said you had a choice anymore? *Bomarhki Ras.*"

The child bent back their index finger until it made a sickening snap. Pain overwhelmed the child, forcing them to their knees as I asked in disgust and confusion, "What are they doing?"

"Winning," Champion Prasai said.

My feet sunk into the ground as if swallowed by quicksand. I tried to lift them up and out, but I met solid stone rather than the sticky movable material I had expected. I kept sinking as I struggled to get out, clawing and scrabbling forward in vain. The child kept staring at me, moving their hands in small consecutive circles. They were doing something, but I just didn't know what yet. The ground was changing beneath my feet . . . which was impossible for a Fabricator to do. We could create, but not manipulate things already in nature. So if they could, did that mean that physical pain was their cost to use magic?

Manipulation and physical pain compared to creation and mental loss.

This was the magic that existed in other countries. So what were the chances I could cancel their magic, too? Having my body nullified wasn't enough to stop me from sinking—I was already up to my waist—but I stood a chance if I could do what I had during the Endless Waltz and cancel all magic around me.

I let the warmth flood to my core, concentrating there like a pit in my stomach. Now all I had to do was let it out. Pushing it out of me like an invisible force only I could direct and control. I took a breath, concentrated, and then repelled it out of me as I let go of a deep breath. The earth that held me captive crumbled away and I climbed out of the pit. The child went wide-eyed as I did.

"Magic nullification," the Champion of the Ancients breathed. "We do not have those in Thebes."

"They're a pain," the Skeleton said. "A lot of people shoot them on sight."

"This duel is over," I declared, walking toward them. "I win. So what do you call your—"

The child bit at the skin between their thumb and index finger, drawing blood. They pushed their hand forward, as if trying to throw something, before making a pained whine and scratching at their forearms with a ravenous ferocity.

"Stop! Stop!" I screamed. "It's finished. Champion Prasai, tell them the duel is over! Their magic won't work! They're hurting themselves for nothing!"

The Thebian champion said nothing as I sprinted toward the child, grabbing them in a tight hug and stopping them from harming themselves. They squirmed in my arms like a worm avoiding the hook.

"How long do you think the magic nullification lasts?" he said as I continued to restrain his ward. "This is all new territory for me. I am not sure how to make the most of it."

"It lasts long enough to be annoying," the Skeleton answered. "But you should call off your ward. It might kill itself. At least now it'll have experience against Nullify Fabricators."

"A bittersweet taste." Champion Prasai snapped his fingers and the child went limp. "But information is information. The Divine General will be interested to hear about it. Thank you for your invaluable aid, Kingman."

I let the kid go and they ran to Champion Prasai's side, fingers still swollen and scratches festering. In due time they would harden and heal and join the hundreds of other self-inflicted scars on their body. How had they ended up like this? What had they gone through? And still at such a young age . . .

"Are you going to take them to a doctor?"

"Obviously. They are my ward."

"Then why are you letting them hurt themselves like that?" I asked, voice rising.

"Pain is merely a sheath to unleash the sword. Without pain, there can be no magic. My ward may bear their scars on their body for the world to see, but is it truly any worse than hiding the cost like you Fabricators? At least they know what is happening to them."

I didn't respond, realizing I had lost one or two memories just because of this little duel and had no idea what they were. Was being a Fabricator any better than being . . . whatever the child was?

"This has been fun," the Skeleton said with an air of finality. "But we should be going. Michael, very exciting to learn who you really are. And I'm sure we'll see each other soon. The moon is a-changing."

"Whatever. But tell me, what do you call your magic users?"

The Champion of Ancients scowled at me. "Why would I tell you—"

"Wee-vars," the child said with a whistle. There was a gap where their front teeth should have been. Ignoring the looks Champion Prasai and the Skeleton were giving him, they repeated, "Wee-vars. Wee-vars."

"It seems the child has taken to you. I will respect their judgment. They did fight," Champion Prasai said, taking the child into his arms. "Goodbye, Kingman."

The Champion of Ancients and the Skeleton left the main entrance with the child. I debated whether I should chase after them and try to save the child from a life of pain and suffering . . . but was starting a war and killing thousands worth more than a single life? In another life that child could have been Jamal or Arjay. I was damning them to pain . . . and yet I did nothing. I was such a hypocrite. Would I ever not be?

"Why does something happen every time I leave you alone, Michael?" Naomi said as she descended the stairs with a similar-looking woman at her heels. "It's something, but at least you didn't seem to start a war."

I wasn't really in the mood for jokes after seeing the child. "Is that your aunt?"

"Sadly," the woman answered, stopping in front of me. She had the same blue eyes as Naomi, a thin face, and long black hair. Despite minor differences, there was a decent chance this was how Naomi would look in a decade or two. Her looks wouldn't hinder her ambition if she chose to seek the crown once again.

"Michael, this is my mother's sister, Astra Browne. She is a steward of the Thebian Nation. Aunt Astra, this is Michael Kingman. And, no, the rumors aren't true. Either of them."

I did the formal thing and bowed. "It's a pleasure to meet you, Astra."

Naomi's aunt looked me up and down like I was a statue on display.

"I thought he'd be taller. And what's with the hair? So messy. You can do better, Naomi."

Naomi rolled her eyes. "Auntie, can we ask you a few questions? It's important. There's someone you likely knew in the past that we need information on."

Astra stifled a yawn and rubbed the back of her neck. "I don't really have the time for this. But . . . I suppose I must. Who did you want to know about?"

"A woman named Zahra. She was the lady-in-waiting to the princess a few years ago."

"You really are your father's daughter, aren't you?" Astra snapped. I unconsciously flinched away from her, but Naomi didn't so much as blink. "Some stories deserve to stay in the past."

"The Heartbreaker is back," Naomi said levelly.

"Ah, so that's why you came here. I should have known." She crossed her arms. "Zahra was the lady-in-waiting to Princess Serena. The princess acquired her after she saw her perform in the Azilian circus years ago. They only performed for one night and it was the talk of the city, from what I remember. Long before the rebels began their siege. Back before open rebellion. Zahra was a tightrope walker. Went by the name White Rose."

"Wait, Zahra was the White Rose?" After calming down, Naomi continued, "I was there. Ma took me to see it. Da was off working. It's one of the last good memories I have of her. White Rose was incredible. I had never seen a female Azilian before and I was in awe of her beauty."

"She was astonishing," I added.

They both looked at me. But it was Naomi who asked, "You were there?"

It was one of the few real family moments I'd had since my father's death. All of us were there: Gwen, Lyon, and Angelo. Angelo had gotten the tickets as a surprise, and, oh, how surprised we were. It was one of the few luxuries we experienced and we never wanted it to end. Gwen most of all. She had grown up hearing stories about the Azilian circus and dreamed of joining them as a fire dancer, or tightrope walker, or beast tamer. Anything. She would have been willing to feed the animals and clean up their shit if she got to watch them perform every night.

Lyon had been given the unfortunate pleasure of explaining why her dream was impossible. At thirteen, she hadn't taken it well, and I always suspected she never let that dream go. During the circus performance, she had been so happy—forgetting about all our troubles.

The circus pulled out all the stops for their one-night show: the acrobatics, the displays of strength and precision, and the exotic animals that had never set foot in Hollow until then. Looking back, it was like a dream. Only two things had stayed solid in my memories from that night. The first was an interaction with an old man with eyes as black as night who had whacked me across the back of the head when I stepped in front of him by accident. Angelo stepped in when the man began to insult my family. It was the first time I had seen him as a protector and a . . . a . . . a father figure. Despite having lived with him for six years, he had only been a jailer in my mind. Without that moment, I might never have begun to trust him.

The other moment had been watching the tightrope walker, White Rose. Zahra. She was the last act that performed. And they had saved her for the finale for a reason. She was high up in the air, walking along a length of rope barely wider than her big toe. Yet she danced on it. Insulted it. At one point she balanced on one leg and leaned back until her back touched the rope. Partway through she sat down in the middle of the rope cross-legged to yawn. It was so impressive to watch, not a single person seemed to take a breath during her performance. They exhaled only after she took a step onto the platform . . . after completing seven crossings.

Some feats were impossible to forget. Hers was one of them. The fact that she was a female Azilian only made it more of a spectacle. From what I remembered from history lessons, the birth rate of females in Azil was extremely low, and each one was a rarity. All of them became leaders in their society, had large families, or left forever. It was evident what Zahra had chosen to do. The question was how she met Dark.

"I was," I said to Naomi and her aunt. "As was my family. Do you know why the princess recruited her as a lady-in-waiting? That's not usually a position foreigners hold."

"It's not," Astra said. "From the rumors I heard, many in the royal staff were displeased about it, too. But we helped her get the necessary paperwork and the late King Isaac made it so at Serena's insistence. Zahra had no previous experience and messed up nearly everything. If she had worked for a stricter Royal, they would have let her go within a day."

"If she was so bad, why would they keep her around?"

"Because she was training the princess in secret. Hard to tell what exactly Princess Serena learned from Zahra, but a year later she joined the Evokers. A year after that she went off to study with the Berserkers at the Thebian Military Academy. Where she was right up until King Isaac died."

That explained why the princess was so good at deception and manipulation. The Evokers were the spies and investigators of Hollow, and the Berserkers that belonged to the Thebian Military Academy spent decades memorizing and examining war stratagems. Learning from those two groups had likely given the princess the skills of a master spy. Our history aside, with that training, how was I supposed to convince her that I didn't kill her father?

"I had no idea she was so . . ." Naomi trailed off.

I finished her thought. "Frightening."

"Which is surprising to hear," Astra said. "Don't you two know what everyone outside of Hollow calls her? Or has she been able to contain that better than I thought?"

We both shook our heads. I had no idea what she was hinting at.

"We call her the Two-Faced Queen. No one knows her true intentions. Some claim she's as rotten as her brother but is able to hide it better. She shifts between a regal smile and a stare that makes you feel like scum without warning. How else do you explain why she doesn't have any friends? It's not normal that none of the High Nobles want to interact with her. Only the Ravens who are sworn to do so."

The Two-Faced Queen and the Corrupt Prince. What a pair they made. I couldn't help but wonder what Davey's nickname would have been if he had lived long enough to get one. As it was now, the only title he carried was the Murdered Boy Prince.

But, more importantly, I had been working on the idea—the naïve hope—that I could convince the princess that I hadn't killed King Isaac. That we could work together rather than fight. The only thing that I had to back up my belief was the history we shared and the vow all Kingman made to their Royals. If she was what she now appeared to be, then it would be war. And I would break the promise I had made to King Isaac before he killed himself.

Did any stories have happy endings? None of mine seemed allowed to. What was I thinking? I was a Kingman. There was no lifetime of happiness to look forward to, only duty.

"Do you know anything else about Zahra?" I asked when my thoughts had calmed down.

"Only that she was murdered by the Heartbreaker, and the princess gave her a funeral that could rival some of the Royals'. First foreigner in history to receive such a distinction."

"Where was she buried?" Naomi inquired.

Astra looked taken aback, her eyes narrowing at the question. "Do you children know nothing these days? Or have you lost all your memories using Fabrications? You must know how Fabricators honor people."

"Aunt Astra, what're you—"

"Dammit," I said out loud. Both turned to me. I began pacing back and forth, trying to contain my laughter. "Fabricators don't think like normal people. It's about a legacy. Doing something so you'll be remembered. When a life is cut short, they find other ways to make sure whoever it was isn't forgotten."

"So?"

"So the princess cared for Zahra. Thus, she honored her the only way she knew how." A pause. "Refugee Square. There's a statue in the middle of it. That's her tomb. It was constructed about two years ago. Right around when she would have died. Now it's a place where people leave offerings before their travels. A good luck charm."

"That's ridiculous," Naomi said, and faced her aunt. Astra was smiling slightly, and we both knew I was right. "Wait, you're telling me there's a statue of a *foreign servant* in the city? Just because the princess liked her? What did she do except die? What right does she have to be remembered in the same way that—"

Astra flicked Naomi in the forehead to stop her tangent. "Naomi. Don't forget where you came from. *You* are a foreigner. You may have been born in Hollow, but your mother was Thebian. You have our eyes and were raised in these halls before your foolish father thought you weren't experiencing enough of Hollow customs and forbade us from teaching you about your homeland."

Naomi gritted her teeth and then said, "I am a citizen of Hollow. This is my country. No matter what you say."

"Then you will die alone on foreign soil once we leave this place," she stated. "Are you sure that's the path you wish to go down?"

"Yes," Naomi said, and there was no hesitation.

"So be it. Enjoy the rest of your life in Hollow, Naomi. The empire will never welcome you again."

Naomi didn't look her aunt in the eyes, preferring to study the ground as she gave a nod to acknowledge what was said. After getting all the information we could from Naomi's aunt, we bid her farewell—or at least I did—and we left the embassy in a hurry as the last of the boxes were packed away. Upon feeling the sun against my skin again, I began to walk in the general direction of Refugee Square with Naomi by my side, silent.

I started to walk faster. Which turned into a jog before evolving into a full-blown sprint toward Refugee Square. Naomi had to take off her shoes and jog barefoot to keep me in sight, but I lost her as we turned onto the royal path. For some reason I had to see the statue in Refugee Square as soon as possible. Nothing else seemed important.

There weren't many people in Refugee Square. The markets were still as empty as they had been during the Endless Waltz. Zahra's memorial was in the direct center of it, covered in half-melted candles, wax, and incense. The statue itself was rather plain compared to others—a nondescript woman with long hair staring toward the west. Toward Azil. Toward home.

Unlike the last time I had been here, only one person was asking the statue for luck. Or perhaps paying respects to a lost love.

Dark.

I went to his side.

"I hate it," Dark said. "But I was a nobody when the princess wanted to erect this memorial. A Mercenary who thought he was stronger than he was. I couldn't stop its construction, just like I couldn't save her. It would be different now."

"Is this such a bad thing?"

"If you knew her, you'd understand. She had no desire to be celebrated. One of the few I've ever met who didn't want power. She just wanted to live her life her way. Free. And now she's immortalized. I can barely look at this . . . thing. Alexis can't look at it at all. Avoids it at any cost."

"Why would Alexis . . . ?"

I realized the answer mid-question. Alexis was Azilian, too, and likely Zahra's younger sister. No wonder she had been so fiercely protective of Dark. He might be the closest thing to family she had left besides Orbis Company.

"What happened? Why did the Heartbreaker go after you and Zahra? And how did High Noble Maflem know you two? You said you would tell me."

"If you're still asking those questions, then you haven't finished Bryan Dexter's journal."

"Why not save me the time and tell me?"

"Because once you know the truth about my family, you'll want to put a bullet in my head. Learning it in small pieces might stave off that feeling. I'm not a fool and am painfully aware the only reason you're working with me is because my father set yours up for regicide. If you'd never found that out"—and he said this last part looking down at me, eyes locked—"you'd be working with him, trying to take down his monstrous son."

I didn't know how to respond to that. Angelo had said almost exactly the same thing when we spoke. I hadn't believed him . . . but maybe I should have. I already knew Dark was a monster, but I didn't want to kill him. What had he done that would make me want to despite the fact he had saved my life?

Dark spared me the trouble of having to come up with a response and left with a promise I would see him again whenever another murder happened.

Naomi reached me by the time Dark was too far away to talk without shouting. She wasn't nearly as sweaty as I was. One of us had been smart enough not to get too smelly before our meal with Domet. "I see he didn't feel like catching up. Shame. Never did get the chance to thank him for helping remove that bullet from my stomach."

"Another time." A pause. "Naomi, how far are you into reading your father's journal?"

"Halfway through. But most of it isn't important. It's just a lot of small details about each crime scene. That passage I showed you today was the first mention of Dark or Zahra. Did he mention something?"

"Only that something in that journal would make me want to kill him."

"Doesn't Dark murder people for no reason? What could be worse than that?"

"I don't know, and that's the problem."

Bells tolled off in the distance. It was almost time for our meal with Domet.

"Let's walk this time," Naomi said as she slipped back into her shoes and locked arms with me. "I wouldn't want Domet to be too overpowered by our smell when we arrive."

Another day, another crazy asshole to appease.

But Domet wouldn't get the better of me this time.

34

LUCKY

I only rapped the metal knocker on Domet's front door at Naomi's insistence. I had been here enough times to expect him to either be passed out on the floor, surrounded by empty bottles, or not hear my attempt at being polite.

Imagine my face when the door opened and a servant stood at the entrance. "Heir Kingman, can I take your jacket? May I take your name, madam? Master Domet only advised me that Heir Michael would be bringing a guest. No name was accompanied with it."

"Excuse me?" I said, flabbergasted. This had to be a joke of Domet's. "Formal" and "fancy" and "proper" weren't words I would have used to describe anything about him in the past.

"My name is Naomi Dexter," Naomi said as she handed the servant her jacket. Then she nudged me in the side and urged me to do the same.

Once the butler had both our jackets, he invited us into the house properly. "If you two would follow me, Master Domet is waiting in the dining room."

Naomi and the butler spent the length of the walk discussing what was for lunch—a bunch of fancy things that usually didn't taste as good as cheaper things soaked in butter and garlic—while I took in the changes to Domet's house since the last time I had been here.

It was still immaculate, but in a much more orderly way. There was no sense of lingering dust on the tops of paintings and behind pieces of furniture that hadn't been moved in, well, generations. Everything was still colored azure and pink, and I made a mental note to determine why at a future date. Domet wasn't someone to do something without reason. For all I knew, it could be a clue about his past before becoming an Immortal.

As we entered the dining room Domet was in the middle of a conversation . . . with Serena and Chloe. I must have looked a mess for Domet to smile quite as widely as he did. Serena, in a dress very similar to the one she had worn the last time we met, wasn't pleased. Neither was Chloe. She was wearing her Raven's armor. Not even dinner with Domet was a good enough reason to wear something else.

Domet rose from his seat, arms open wide, and then said, "Michael, such a pleasure to see you again. I am glad to see you are doing better, Connoisseur Dexter. You gave us all a fright when Prince Adreann shot you."

Naomi opened her mouth to respond but was cut off by Serena stabbing a knife into the table. She wasn't even attempting to hide her displeasure. "Domet, what is the meaning of this? You invite me to lunch knowing full well *he* was attending, too? I should have you hauled up for treason."

"Frankly, my dear, you couldn't even if you wanted to," Domet stated as he looked down at her. "Hollow is in debt to me. Wars aren't cheap. Do you really want to threaten the man who is helping you fund it? If you want to try to win it on your own, I am positive the emperor will accept my aid. No matter the conditions I demand."

Serena kept squeezing the knife lodged in the table until her hand paled.

And if I am not mistaken, you owed Michael a meal, having lost a bet. This is simply an opportunity to keep your word in neutral territory. Aren't I helpful?"

There was no point in asking how Domet knew about the agreement the princess and I had made. It was Domet. He knew everything. Thus, Naomi and I took our seats at the table. Naomi across from Chloe, me across from the princess, and Domet at the head of the table, presiding over perhaps the most awkward and angry lunch in decades. The waiter brought Serena a new knife without being prompted to.

Domet set his napkin on his lap before holding up a crystal goblet filled with a clear liquid. Probably vodka. Everyone else's glasses held red wine. "To forgiveness, death, and everything in between."

Instead of toasting, Serena placed a revolver on the table next to her plate. Naomi snorted. Chloe sighed. And I just stared at it as Domet drank. We were off to a great start.

"You are all probably wondering why I invited you here," Domet said. "It's quite simple. I want to end this feud between the Kingman and Hollow families. You two are the most likely to make that happen."

"Nothing I say will change what Serena thinks," I said. "She's made that quite clear."

"If it makes you feel better, I'll forgive Gwen once you're dead and your head is mounted above my throne."

"That does, actually." I reached for my wineglass and took a sip from it. I was going to need something to keep me sane throughout this meal. "Aren't you a little curious about what I have to say regarding what happened with your father?"

"Not in the slightest. I know you, Michael. I see you. The real you. Not the one wearing the heroic mask that you show to the world. Whatever you claim to justify killing my father"—Serena's voice was rising—"it doesn't change the fact that he's dead. Nothing can bring him back. You want so badly to be remembered, but at the end of the day you're just a loser trying to emulate your ancestors, and failing. I bet you're still acting like the weight of the world is on your shoulders despite being a pathetic crybaby whose only impact on this country will be the patch of ground that's disturbed when they bury you."

With a wink she added, "Hopefully sooner rather than later."

Everyone's mouth, including Domet's, was agape. I took another sip of my wine. Besides my siblings, Trey, and Sirash, the princess knew me better than anyone. It was hard not to after we spent the first years of our lives together. She wasn't going to insult me the same way Dark or strangers did. She aimed for the heart.

"Maybe you're right," I said. "Maybe I'm a pathetic loser who fails at everything he tries. But by that logic, isn't it shocking that I was able to kill King Isaac? A fool like me? Unless—and bear with me for this shocking thought—I didn't kill him." I rose from my seat and slapped the table. Everything on it shook slightly. "King Isaac killed himself. With that gun you like to parade around with. It wasn't me. It *wasn't* me. But your head is so far up your own ass, you couldn't see the truth if you tried."

Silence.

Serena picked up the revolver and aimed it at my chest. "Speak to me like that again, Michael, and I will shoot you right here and call it self-defense. Forget the consequences."

"Do it and become like all the kings and queens before you who disposed of records in favor of their manufactured truths. Rewrite history and make me the villain. This is the clearest shot you're ever going to get. Do what you must." I paused. "Tell my family and friends I love them."

Serena stared at me, gun steady in her hand. There was no flush on her face or hesitation in her eyes. She wanted to kill me. To get revenge. To act once and for all on this hatred she felt. But it wouldn't go away so easily. Just as mine wouldn't have if I had killed King Isaac when I had had the chance.

Hate was a drug. Stronger than anything sold in Hollow. It could also be a gift. An energy that allowed people to push forward. And there always seemed to be a well full of it to draw upon. A onetime fix marketed as a miracle cure-all. But no one remembered that until it was too late.

Until it festered and burrowed into people's brains to lay down roots. Corrupted them.

I had experienced that level of hate. It had nearly destroyed me. It *should have* destroyed me. The only thing that saved me from it was my family's and friends' love. Something I was grateful for to this day. Now here was the princess, stuck in the same situation. Without a family to save her.

Serena likely thought that if I were dead, it would end. All her troubles. All her pain. All her anger. And it would, for a time. Until Gwen came for her and the endless cycle took another turn until only one side remained. If this was going to end in anything but bloodshed, she would have to end the dance we were both unwilling participants in.

"Princess . . . ," Chloe whispered.

"Michael deserves to die, Chloe."

"If he does, do it the right way. Use the law. Be better than this. Don't become the thing you hate, not for him."

Serena's hand started shaking and her grip on her gun became more strained, forced.

"Queen-in-Waiting Serena," Domet said. "Think of the consequences if you kill Michael like this. Orbis Company may not be as renowned or big as Machina or Regal Company, but they would burn the castle down all the same. Mercenaries like to make examples out of those who cross them."

Serena began to breathe more shallowly, less focused. Less certain. "I hate you, Michael Kingman."

"I know."

She slammed the revolver on the table and ran her hands over her face, breathing deeply. Then she began to rub her left wrist over and over and over again. That was a habit of hers I wasn't familiar with. She must have gained it sometime after my father's execution.

"That was a riot," Naomi said with a laugh before downing her glass of wine in a single gulp. "Who needs Blackberries when you can get that kind of rush?"

The princess, to her credit, only glared at Naomi rather than pick up the gun again. No war would start if Naomi died, yet I doubted she backed down willingly anymore. Not after being shot.

Domet snapped his fingers and looked over his shoulder. "Let's skip to the main course before we lose anyone. If everyone is still here, we can have the soup before dessert."

The headwaiter balanced five different plates that he brought to the table. He placed one in front of each of us. It looked like a piece of art rather than dinner. A large piece of steak was in the middle, with barriers of green beans cooked in garlic around it and a large spoonful of the butteriest mashed potatoes I had ever seen. The smell was divine.

"Enjoy the meal," Domet declared with fork and knife in his hands. "I supervised the preparation myself. It is fit for a princess, a king, an emperor, or Patron Victoria herself."

Serena stabbed her steak in the middle with a fork. Like someone who had never been taught civilized manners, she ate it without attempting to cut it, ripping big bites out of it instead as if it had come off a stick over a campfire. Only Naomi was caught off guard by it.

"Still eating like that when you're angry, I see," I commented. "Surprised you never grew out of that habit. It isn't very regal."

"Fuck off, Michael." Her mouth was full of steak and it was not proper in the slightest.

"The princess does not have time for useless customs and traditions," Chloe said as she cut her own steak into small, bite-sized pieces. "She is busy, and manners are a necessary sacrifice when she isn't trying to impress anyone."

"That explains why the princess was smiling and using a knife when we had dinner," Naomi muttered.

Serena put her steak back down on the plate, leaving the fork in it. Miraculously, she even swallowed her mouthful before she said, "Naomi Dexter. I forgot about you. A shame what happened. What my brother did was inexcusable. Powerful women like us deserve better."

"That's almost word for word what you said last time."

"Forgive my memory, and let us make a deal. You want to be a Raven, is that right? I can make that happen. All I ask is that you kill Michael Kingman."

I glanced at my date, wondering if I had made a mistake bringing her instead of Gwen.

Naomi licked some mashed potatoes off her fork. "Tempting offer—"

"You can do it now if you like, or later. I really don't—"

"—but I'm going to have to decline," Naomi said with a smile. "I prefer it when the people trying to fuck me don't disappear the morning after. Strong women like us deserve better, and you and your brother don't care what happens to me once I'm no longer useful."

"Naomi . . . ," Chloe growled.

"You are a generous person," Naomi finished with a clarification. "But the answer is no. I did want to be a Raven, but Michael is helping me achieve something you cannot. I need him. Sadly."

"You need him?"

"Yes." Naomi put her hand on my thigh. My face turned red, though I doubted anyone else at the table knew where it was. "I *need* him."

"Chloe, we're leaving." Serena took the napkin off her lap and put it on the table as she stood. "I lost my appetite."

"What about dessert?" Domet urged. "My man has made the most wonderful fruit tarts. You must have one."

"Another time," the princess said. "When the company is better."

"Say hi to Lucky for me," I said as I removed Naomi's hand.

The princess was about to respond with something probably rude and insulting, but Chloe put her hand on her shoulder and quelled her rage. Then they left in silence. Naomi excused herself to go to the bathroom shortly afterward, and, without his having to orchestrate it, Domet and I were alone for the first time since he had learned I had burned down the Shrine of Patron Victoria.

"That was a little more chaotic than I expected," he said with a nearly empty goblet in his hand. It was amazing he hadn't moved to refill it or instructed his servant to already. "I wish Serena had stayed longer. You two seemed to be making some progress repairing your relationship."

"If that's your idea of how someone repairs a relationship, you've forgotten what normal ones are like."

"Perhaps. But have no fear, I haven't forgotten what you did."

"Nor have I."

We ate in an uncomfortable silence.

"Why do you want the land around Kingman Keep?" I asked.

"Because *you* want it," he said very matter-of-factly. "I have no need of it. But having it hurts you. I would have Kingman Keep torn down if I could. Alas, some things are beyond me."

"It's nice to be reminded that you're mortal. Oh, wait, no you're not."

Domet's knife scraped his plate. "Always with the insightful insults, Michael. So what do you want from me?"

"Nothing."

"Liar," Domet said as he leaned closer toward me. "You wouldn't be here unless you wanted something. My threats have never worked on you in the past. Deep down you're here for selfish intentions. Be it the land around Kingman Keep or something else. Let's negotiate."

My plate was nearly as empty as my glass of wine. Until Naomi returned, maybe it wouldn't be the worst thing in the world to talk with Domet. To learn from him. He might know something about the Waylayer or the Heartbreaker. Lives were at stake . . . and as long as I didn't accept another deal with him, I wouldn't be breaking my promise to Lyon. Maybe I'd even figure out why Domet felt the need to bring Serena and me together.

I started with that question.

"You ask the stupidest questions, Michael," Domet said. "I told you I've decided not to be an observer anymore. I have a goal, and it requires you and the princess to be on speaking terms. If you hadn't destroyed the shrine, maybe I would have told you what it was."

"I see you're still bitter."

"Always," Domet said softly and slowly. "But despite my . . . anger, I kept my side of the bargain. None of your friends or family were implicated in your trial. I have atoned for not saving your father."

"How noble of you."

"Only because I thought it would help me in the long run. And it has. You live, and my quest for death can continue uninterrupted."

"Still can't die? What a shame."

Domet drained the dregs in his goblet, then said, "Soon I will. But you know how it is, Michael. So many things to do first. All these mistakes I must fix."

"You said the same thing when I first learned you were immortal. Is it true? Do you actually have to fix the mistakes of your past before you can die? Can no one kill an Immortal?"

"Some secrets you'll have to learn on your own, Michael. I wouldn't want to make it too easy. You and me, we're in this together for the long run. The true Endless Waltz."

I gripped the sides of the table and focused on my father's ring to distract myself from the insane Immortal in front of me. He wasn't my main concern right now. As twisted and manipulative as Domet was, he wasn't going around killing people like the Heartbreaker was. I could deal with him later. There were other priorities right now.

"There's a Waylayer operating in Hollow. Came in with the refugees. The Heartbreaker Serial Killer has also returned. Do you know anything about either of them?"

Domet tapped his index finger against the table in a steady, rhythmic beat. "Do you know the title of the Waylayer?"

I hesitated, trying to remember the word Dark had discovered on the underside of the lantern. "Uh, Plague. No, wait, it was War. No, no, I think it was Death."

"Have you forgotten? Or have you *Forgotten*?"

"I don't know," I groaned. "I think I just forgot. Non-magically."

"Good thing for you, I know everything. Even where the Waylayers are. But that information will come at a cost, as all things do."

"Consider me surprised you're on a first-name basis with a league of assassins." A pause. "What do you want for information on both the Waylayers and the Heartbreaker?"

"Smart phrasing," Domet said. "Good to see you learned something from me."

"Only to trust no one."

"A very important lesson. Now, let's see . . . what would be a fair trade? Your firstborn child? A sample of your blood? Perhaps I should extract one of your most important memories and put it in a jar to watch as I see fit. Wouldn't *that* be entertaining?"

"Domet."

He sighed dramatically. "You're no fun, Michael. Humor me a little."

"Name your price and let's get on with it."

"Dangerous words," Domet said as he adjusted himself in his seat. "Thought you would be more careful following your near execution."

"Just name your price already."

"I want to return to our old arrangement. Without the money. Come by my house once a week, so long as you're in Hollow, so we can talk."

That was surprising. "That's what you want? Get another servant. I'm sure someone is desperate enough for money to sit and talk with you every week."

"No," Domet said. "I want you. Only you."

"I'm flattered. Who knew burning down the Shrine of Patron Victoria and wanting to kill you would make you want to talk to me more."

"I have my reasons, Michael. And better the monster you know, after all. You have a general idea of my goals. Can you say the same of this Waylayer? Or the Heartbreaker? Or even Dark?"

That was a cheap shot, but I let it go. At least I wasn't starting a new deal with Domet, only continuing an old one. I wasn't breaking my promise to Lyon. And truly, so long as war was on the horizon, I needed Domet as much as he needed me. We couldn't do nearly as much alone as we could together. A bitter truth I had accepted a long time ago.

"As long as we never interact in public . . . fine. Now tell me what you know about the Waylayer in this city and the Heartbreaker."

Domet smiled in a way that sent shivers down my spine. Something purely monstrous about it. Inhumane. "Excellent decision, Michael. Excellent decision."

"Get on with it."

"As you wish. I regret to inform you I know nothing about the Heartbreaker. I was . . . occupied with drink when they terrorized Hollow years ago. If I was mortal, alcohol poisoning would have killed me every day. Dark days. I remember little, if anything, from that period."

"You'd better have some information about the Waylayer or I'll call off this deal."

"Patience, Michael. I have what you want. What exactly do you know about the Waylayers?"

Truly, I knew next to nothing. They were a league of assassins that may or may not exist. That may or may not have committed some of the highest-profile murders in the past three hundred years, including killing Golden Calico, one of the original crew members of the first pirate crew in Eham, who became a renowned pirate captain with a fleet of over a hundred at its peak. Some called them the counter to my family, a group of individuals who thrived on chaos where mine tried to bring order. The Waylayer leader was the Reaper, rumored to be able to taunt death and not suffer its consequences. For most of my life I had thought them to be imaginary. A story created to entertain and scare the masses, like dragons and daemons.

If the Waylayer order actually existed, then I would do what I did best and expose the truth behind the lie. The myth and the reality weren't going to match. Just like it hadn't with dragons and the Toothless Wyvern. So far immortality was the only exception. It was real, and I wished it wasn't every day.

I relayed as much to Domet, minus the snark.

"I'll start with the basics. There are thirteen of the Waylayers, including their leader, the Reaper. Upon joining, each member takes a title. They are: Plague, War, Death, Famine, Love, Gluttony, Sloth, Pride, Greed, Lust, Envy, and Wrath."

"Love? What a lame title."

A laugh. "If you met the one who holds it, you might think otherwise. Thankfully for you, I've been around long enough to have met a decent number of them and learn what countries they operate out of. Most stay close to home unless they're forced to travel. They all have lives that they do their best to maintain."

"Which ones operate out of Hollow?"

"Pride and Wrath. War used to. But they disappeared a few years ago, so I doubt it's them. It's most likely someone killed War, but the Reaper hasn't determined who did it or invited them to claim their new title and invite them to join the Waylayers."

"What?"

"Ah, yes. I suppose that wouldn't make sense to a Kingman. The Waylayers are a *meritocracy*, Michael. Survival of the strongest. The only way to join their ranks is by killing an existing Waylayer. It ensures they're constantly improving themselves. No one can rest easy with impending death looming over them."

I drummed my fingers against the table. "Do you know who Pride and Wrath are?"

Domet shook his head. "No. They have been careful to ensure I don't know their true identities. Others were more relaxed."

"Why should I honor this deal if your information was useless?"

"Patience isn't one of your virtues, Michael. Do you really think I wouldn't attempt to learn more? Because if you do, you vastly underestimate me."

I waited for him to continue.

Domet did so with a smile. "Wrath, to the best of my knowledge, works in the castle. Whenever I met him—yes, Wrath is a he—he was always dirty yet smelled like lavender and wore a lantern necklace. Spoke quickly and informally. Probably a servant to someone important, especially since he was never able to meet during the Endless Waltz or other courtly events in Hollow. I know very little about Pride. They changed how they spoke every time I met with them. Dressed differently, too. I always assumed they worked for Scales in some capacity."

"What makes you say that?" I asked.

"Because whenever I wanted someone dead and they were handling it, there would be a convenient noble execution a few days later. Or a new rebel sympathizer would appear in the Hanging Gardens. Corruption at its finest."

I'm not sure I would ever associate corruption with being fine, but whatever. Domet had given me enough information to learn something—anything—about the Waylayer that was coming after me. A servant in the castle and someone with authority in Scales. It narrowed down my search slightly.

"Are you still able to contact them?"

"No. Both burned bridges with me after the king's death. Wrath stopped responding, and Pride took the expression literally and burned down the tree I used to leave requests in." Domet looked over his shoulder, suddenly growing concerned. "I was so focused on our conversation, I just realized that Naomi has been gone for quite a long—"

"Apologies," Naomi said as she returned. "I discovered mixing Blackberries with good food upsets my stomach quite severely."

"That's why I always stuck to alcohol," Domet said. "The comedown always seemed to be better than the alternatives."

Naomi raised her wineglass before taking a sip from it. "I'll remember that for the future."

The rest of the conversation was an odd mix of anecdotes and Domet and me exchanging insults. Naomi joined in whenever she thought necessary. Which was often. Once we finished the fruit tart, we left. Domet made sure to remind me to attend lunch with him next week and that I had better come with an appetite. And so long as I appeased him, his men wouldn't begin tearing down all the houses around Kingman Keep. I shrugged his words off.

Naomi skipped down the stairs of Domet's house, smiling. "I'm amazed that went as well as it did. All things considered."

"Says you. I was the one stuck talking to Domet. And the princess caught me off guard."

"Yeah, well, so did Domet's staff. Thankfully his men were so focused on making sure everything was perfect, they didn't pay any attention to me." A pause. "Want to see what I found while you two were talking?"

I pointed to Conqueror Fountain and we took a seat on the edge of it. "Something on the Heartbreaker?"

"No, but I found this. He was using it as a bookmark," Naomi said as she pulled out a folded-up piece of paper from her cleavage.

Shadom,

Famine will be operating in Hollow until further notice.
You'll know when they arrive. I can't reveal the target, but it
involves a Kingman, and you've asked to be kept informed of
our interactions in the past. If you want to discuss the contract
with them, we have alerted Famine to make themselves
available to you. Go to Lip Service and order a Honeysuckle.
They'll find you afterward.

Sincerely,
The Reaper

"Domet lied to me," I muttered out loud.

"For someone who spends so much time with him, you always seem to be surprised about that. Domet does what he wants however he wants. The truth is a lie he simply hasn't distorted in his favor yet."

"It is what it is. What're the odds if we go to . . . Lip Service . . . and order a Honeysuckle, we can find this Waylayer?"

"Slim to none? They probably know what Domet looks like and they'll definitely know how you look. They've already tried to kill you once."

I gave her a smile. In my mind, there was only one thing to do, and she knew it. This was a golden opportunity to strike back that we might never get again. She didn't have to come, but I knew she would. Naomi didn't walk away when things got rough.

With a sigh and a curse she said, "Fine, let's go."

35

SHADOWS

It was harder to find Lip Service than either of us initially suspected.

We tried asking a spice merchant to no avail. They just went on and on about how high quality their product was and how it had been imported from the Pillar Islands past Eham and blah blah blah. After narrowly escaping that torture, we tried asking a drunk pissing into the Western River if they knew where Lip Service was. He did not. Hadn't even heard of it. Which was concerning. Usually drunks of his caliber knew all the good spots in the city. Even the places outside of their price range. The fact that we had to hunt around before one had an idea of where Lip Service was made us uneasy. No establishment should have wanted to remain that well hidden. Even those with exclusive entry requirements made sure everyone knew what they were and who was allowed in.

We finally found Lip Service on the outskirts of the Rainbow District. It was unremarkable in many ways and had no sign to distinguish it from the dozens of oddly colored buildings around it. If we hadn't been told to look for an unmarked bright pink door, we could have walked by it a thousand times without ever realizing. Upon entering, we saw that its décor was . . . interesting.

Most brothels had a large central area for business and relaxation—maybe a musician off in the corner if it was trying to be fancy—and a set of private rooms for personal festivities. Everything was out in the open here. All the guests were sitting around a circular stage in the middle of the room that scantily clad men and women were dancing on. Every so often one of the patrons would point to someone onstage and the staff would escort them elsewhere.

I suspected Honeysuckle wasn't a drink.

Naomi was staring at the dancers onstage. "I like this place."

"Do you think the Waylayer is one of the dancers?"

"Only one way to find out." Naomi dragged me closer, pushed me down in one of the seats closest to the stage, and then sat on my lap. A few of the patrons started to take notice of us.

Wonderful. So much for laying low.

"Oh! Look at how she dances," Naomi said as she pointed to a black-haired woman being spun by a man from Eham. "And I didn't know men could be *that* flexible."

"We're not here to take in the sights, Naomi."

She turned to me, pure joy disappearing. "We're in a brothel surrounded by beautiful people. Enjoy it. Stare if you want to. Stop acting like you have a stick up your ass."

"We're not here for fun, Naomi."

"Can't we be here for both?" she asked with a raised eyebrow. Instead of allowing me to continue talking, Naomi beckoned the dancing woman onstage toward us with a curl of her finger. Naomi whispered something in her ear that caused the woman to giggle and nod. And then she kissed her. It lasted longer than I expected, and I had to look away to hide the blush creeping onto my face.

The woman walked back toward the man and Naomi turned to me. "See? Easy to have both."

"Was that necessary?"

"Absolutely. I wanted to know what the glistening on her lips was, and now I do. It was honey, if you were wondering."

"I wasn't."

"C'mon, Michael." Naomi put her hand on my thigh. Not this again. "You must have some interest in sex. Have you ever fooled around with someone? Or has it just been the solo dance for you? No judgment if it has been. I can't imagine many people were lining up to fuck a traitor's son."

I took her hand off my thigh. "Enough, Naomi."

Others in the brothel were staring at us now—staff included.

"Did I strike a nerve? Let me make up for that lapse of judgment."

Naomi snapped her fingers to call over a man in black with long hair pulled back into a ponytail. He was too poised and well-groomed to only be a servant here. I wondered if the staff alternated between stage and floor.

"How can I help you, mistress?" the staff member asked.

Naomi put her hand back on my thigh and it took all my self-control not to yank it off again. Very sweetly, Naomi said, "I'm looking to expand my darling's sexual prowess. I've heard good things about Honeysuckle. Would we be able to participate together? I'm worried he may not rise to the occasion unless I'm there."

She was asking about . . . what?

The staff member didn't skip a beat. "Honeysuckle usually only takes one customer at a time."

"Could you please check if they could make an exception?"

The man looked toward someone making hand signals in the corner of the room. It was impossible to memorize them from this angle. Too many nearly naked bodies in the way.

"We can make an exception today," the staff member said. "But it'll be triple the price: nine suns. Finer details will be worked out with Honeysuckle."

Naomi took out nine suns from her dress pocket and handed it to the man. "That sounds perfect."

He led us from our seats down a hallway with the minimum light needed to make sure we could see without tripping. Passionate sounds came from the rooms we passed, and Naomi had a firm hold of my hand to make sure she could direct me as needed. And to stop me from running away. We were brought to a room with silk pillows and blankets spread across the floor. Jasmine-scented incense was burning slowly in the corner of the room. If I hadn't known what Naomi had paid for this, I would have thought it looked rather cheap and been even less impressed.

Naomi sat down on one of the overly plush pillows and said, "You make it too easy for people to trick you if they know where the cracks in your façade are."

"A little warning would have been nice."

"And miss the spectacle and blush on your face when I tease you like that? Never. You should have realized what I was doing. How else were we going to convince anyone that we were here for fun? I doubt who or what we ordered is very common if a Waylayer is keeping tabs on it."

I crossed my arms and paced from one end of the room to the other. "Whatever."

"Still annoyed? I apologize if I struck a nerve. You don't actually believe in true love or something, do you?"

Silence.

Naomi leaned closer to me. "Do you? You? Of all people? And here I thought your heart was as twisted as all your other views on life."

"We all have to have something to believe in, don't we?"

"A romantic! Literally anything else would have made more sense," Naomi drawled. "So how will you recognize your one true love? Will you catch them when they fall from the sky or slay a dragon to save them?"

I exhaled a deep breath. "Something like that."

Her eyes went wide. "Wait, it's not—"

A Goldani woman in a see-through white lace dress entered the room. There was nothing else on her person, and I knew that with, um, absolutely certainty. As she closed the curtain behind her, I thought she was the most beautiful woman I had ever seen before and wondered whether it was okay to tell her that.

Naomi did it for me. "Wow."

"Thank you," she responded. Her voice was deep and smooth, a calm river. "I'm Honeysuckle. But you already know that. Who are you?"

"Michael Kingman."

"Chloe Mason."

It took all my strength not to shoot Naomi a look. Why did she give Honeysuckle the wrong name?

"Pretty names . . . It is not every day I'm requested by strangers. How did you hear about me?"

I opened my mouth to lie, but Naomi was quicker. "Charles Domet."

"Charles Domet," she repeated as she drew closer to us. "I've only ever seen him once. It was a short session. I'm honored that he would speak so highly of me afterward. What did he say?"

Honeysuckle ran her hands down my chest. I said nothing. My mind was fuzzy, and I had no faith that the truth wouldn't come out of my mouth if I spoke. What I said surprised even me. "He said you were wonderful. Very relatable."

"'Relatable' is a description for a mother who is friendly to your mates. Escorts don't want to hear that they're *relatable*. Sexy. Striking." And she leaned toward me to whisper the last word: "Powerful."

I gulped. Audibly.

"Am I powerful, Michael?"

I couldn't focus on anything but her mismatched-color eyes. "I . . . Yes, you are."

"Would you do anything I asked of you? Would you kill for me?"

"Of—"

"Michael! Nullify!"

Her words were like a slap to the face, and I found the warmth of nullification almost obscured by a different kind of heat in my body. Once I had it, I embraced it and raised my fists. What had just happened? Honeysuckle seemed ordinary, rather than the captivating figure she had just been.

Honeysuckle backed away from us, straightened, and then smoothed her outfit. She looked at her hand as she moved her fingers slowly. "Nullify Fabricator. Interesting. I haven't used those in a while. I'll miss wind, though." Her attention returned to us. "What gave away what I was doing, girlie?"

"Do you know how many times I've tried to seduce this fool?" Naomi put her hand on my shoulder. "I don't know what you were doing, but it had to be something magical because—no offense—you're not getting through to this thickheaded romantic fool without a little help."

"Confidence," she said. "I like that. But, to be fair, I did think you were here for fun . . . so I acted appropriately." She took a silk cover-up off the back of the door and put it on. "Clearly you're not. So why are you here?"

My body still felt hot and my mind fuzzy, so Naomi took the lead in the conversation. "We're looking for Famine."

"To kill or hire?"

"We want information," I croaked.

"About?"

"Who their target in Hollow is."

Honeysuckle snorted. "As if I'm going to tell you that. I'll give you points for trying to get the information out of me, though."

"What do you have to lose?" Naomi asked. "We can pay well."

"And lose my well-earned reputation as a confidential assassin? As if."

"Wait, that means you're—"

Honeysuckle pointed her fingers at me as if they were a gun. "Nice to see you again, Michael. You're rather handsome close up."

Honeysuckle was Mocking Bird, the Waylayer who went by the code name Famine. I held Naomi's hand out of fear I had finally made a mistake we wouldn't be able to come back from. She returned my feelings with a tight squeeze of her own as my warmth covered the both of us.

"This is how it's going to work, Michael," she said as she crept closer. "You made a mistake. And mistakes are like bullets—it only takes one to kill. So you're going to come with me and answer some questions or I'm going to kill your friend Chloe." She gestured to Naomi. "Usually I don't jump straight to threats, but after you and the Black Death embarrassed me in the colosseum, I find myself out of patience and will take what I need with force."

I continued to steady the warmth in my body. She had no weapons or armor, but I doubted that would be a big advantage when this devolved into a fight. And she . . . could she please put more clothes on? This was getting ridiculous. Who fought in just a cover-up?

"Are you refusing to do as I say?" Mocking Bird asked. She was between me and the door. "I'll take that as a no."

I lunged toward her, guard up. Naomi hit her in the backs of the knees while I threw my elbow into her face. It hit true and blood sprayed out of her nose. Mocking Bird hit the ground with a thud as I leapt over her. I grabbed Naomi's hand and we sprinted out of the room and down the hallway.

We were bursting out of the door of Lip Service when she screamed, "So be it, Michael! You and your friend's life are now forfeit!"

We left the brothel before Naomi stopped and looked back at the pink door. "Why aren't we being chased?"

"Does it matter? I have no desire to get into a prolonged fight with a Waylayer right now."

Naomi nodded and we kept going, eventually stopping in an enclosed area with no angles for a long-distance shot. Naomi slumped down against a wall to catch her breath. I kept pacing, hands behind my head.

"I think we made a mistake," Naomi said between breaths. "We were in control. She was naked and unarmed. Why did we run?"

"She's a Waylayer, we don't know what kind of Fabricator she is—assuming she is one and not something else—and it's not as if we were armed, either."

Naomi ran her hand over her mouth. "We caught her off guard, Michael. That was our one chance at ending this quickly. What was the point of going there if we were going to run away?"

"We can get Dark and come back."

"You really think she'll still be there? Because I don't!"

I didn't know how to respond. We hadn't run into the Heartbreaker, but Naomi was acting as if we had. As if not stopping Mocking Bird was worse than dying. Something was off with her, but what caused . . . Oh. "Chloe will be fine. I doubt the Waylayer will go after her just because you used a false name."

"It was a stupid thing to do, and I don't know why I did it. I just couldn't stop thinking about Chloe when I saw her." A pause. "But what if Mocking Bird does? Chloe is important to me. I don't know what I would do if I was responsible for her getting hurt."

"Go and warn her, then. Apologize, even."

Naomi bit her lower lip and looked off to the side. Moments later she had a Blackberry in her mouth. "Maybe you're right."

"More people seem to think so nowadays."

"Quiet." She slapped the back of her neck. "Tell your mother I won't be at dinner. It might take me some time to make contact with Chloe."

"Do you want me to come with you?"

The Blackberry nearly fell from her mouth in shock. "What did you say?"

I repeated it, word for word. Her shocked expression didn't change.

"Don't you have better things to do than come with me to apologize to someone you don't know very well?"

I shrugged. "Not really. Besides, after everything we've been through, I'm starting to see you as family. And family looks after family."

Naomi hesitated, sucking on the Blackberry. Not one to be openly emotional, she composed herself and then rose to her feet. "Fine, come with me. Chloe is usually training when she's not on duty."

Just like that, I had an excuse to see Chloe again. After the excitement of lunch, I was going to need every possible ally to convince the princess I hadn't killed her father.

36

CRUSHED

If asked, I would've assumed the Ravens trained somewhere in the castle. Or maybe in the Shattered Stones if they wanted variety. Or with the Wardens if they wanted to test themselves against other elite warriors in the city. In actuality, it was the last place I would've ever guessed.

I stared at the top of the great redwood trees in the Hanging Gardens. "You're joking, right?"

Naomi was tying her hair back. "Nope. It's hidden by the needles, but their training ground is up there."

"Why would they choose here of all places to train? This seems . . ."

"Unexpected?"

"Yeah," I said. "I thought they never came down this far into Hollow. I wonder how much they've seen from up there."

"A lot more than they reveal." Naomi slipped out of her dress and into more practical clothes. I did my best not to look. "I only know they're up there because of Chloe. Normally, it's a secret only the Royals are privy to. But we followed her mother here one day on a dare and found out together. It was a childish thing to do."

"I didn't realize you and Chloe were so close. She seems so formal, it's hard for me to imagine her sharing secrets. How do you know each other?"

Naomi shook out her legs, stretched, and jumped up into the air. She flew higher than any normal person could, landing on a thick branch a distance above me. "I'll tell you as we climb, unless you'd prefer to wait down there?"

"You're going to make me climb this on my own? Can't I get a little help from your Fabrications?"

"It's a Raven tradition. They do this every day as part of their training, so it should be no problem at all for a Kingman. But I'll help a little. I might catch you if you fall."

I threw my jacket down next to the trunk of the tree. "How comforting."

She laughed and then climbed higher. Not wanting to be left behind, I stretched and then began to climb behind her. There were plenty of holds for my feet and hands, the natural grooves in the bark giving me a path upward. The tree limbs were also big enough to rest on and catch my breath whenever I needed to. Yet my muscles still burned the further up we went. When I was halfway there, I saw Naomi waiting for me on a branch, swinging her legs back and forth.

"Tell me why you and Chloe are such good friends," I said as I climbed past her.

"There's not much to tell," she said. "We met because our parents are obsessed with their work and they thought leaving us with each other might alleviate some of our loneliness. It kind of worked. When the princess was away, we did everything together. Both of us were preparing to take the Ravens exam."

"So what changed?"

Naomi looked offended. "Why do you assume something changed? People naturally drift apart and . . . who am I kidding? If I'm going to tell anyone the truth, it might as well be you. I applied to join the Ravens.

Openings are rare, and since we didn't want to compete against each other, she let me apply for Siggy's place after she was murdered and—you heard how Siggy died, right?"

I had heard. Rebels had snuck guns into the city and opened fire as she had stepped out of the public baths in the Narrows. Four others had been killed in the cross fire, including a young couple planning to be married the following day. It had been the talk of the city for months. Raven deaths were rare, and despite the fact the rebels had already annexed Naverre and burned a Raven alive, for most citizens Siggy's death was the first indication that the rebellion would continue until the Royals were overthrown or the rebels exterminated.

"Horrible way to go. Worse, as you know, my application was denied. They thought I was there for the wrong reasons, even though I was the strongest applicant, and that doubt was strong enough to bar my entry to the Ravens. Can you guess who the loudest voice against me was?"

"Efyra?"

"Efyra," Naomi repeated with a growl. "I had the numbers on my side, but not her, and her vote was enough. I handled rejection badly, and I blamed Chloe. Said her mother had blocked my application to make sure she got the position whenever she applied. It wasn't pretty. But the worst part of it was she never yelled back. She just took my anger like it was actually her fault and not her mother's." A pause. "I hated her for that. It felt like she was pitying me. I don't like being pitied by strangers, but to have her pity me was . . . was heartbreaking."

"Why?"

Naomi avoided my gaze, cheeks reddening.

I stared at her, confused. Why was she blushing? Naomi never got embarrassed. Yet here she was acting like a kid with a cru— *No way.* My next thoughts came out of my mouth unfiltered. "You're in love with Chloe! That's why you took it so personally." I snickered to myself. "And here I thought you were only attracted to brutish assholes."

Naomi's scowl was like music to my ears. "You're not the only one who's ashamed of how they acted during the Endless Waltz."

I stopped on a branch to wipe away some sweat. "Have you apologized?"

"Yes. After she convinced the Mercenary to save my life. It's difficult to be angry at someone—or their mother—when they're willing to oppose a prince for you. But our relationship is still fragile. It's hard to see someone accomplish their dreams when you can't. Even if it's someone you care for deeply."

"Do you know if she feels the same way?"

"No," she said softly. "And I doubt I ever will."

"I bet she does," I said. "Ravens don't oppose Royals for their friends."

Naomi turned redder than a rose, and was about to reply when she took off higher into the tree instead.

I followed, slowly, with a smile on my face.

She was waiting for me near the top, where the thin needles obscured nearly everything. She pulled me up onto a branch that had the top cut off, deliberately shaping it into a walkway. Up here the branches were closer together, and the trunk was oddly shaped. As if there was a door to open it. My suspicions were confirmed when Naomi rapped her knuckles against certain parts of it before opening the door.

"After you, Michael," she said.

"You first. Do you know what the Ravens would do to me if they caught me in their training facility?"

"We'll find out, coward. Fine, follow me."

We walked into the tree together. The walls were smooth and had been carefully carved so there was enough room to stand. It was hard to tell which parts of this area were natural and which had been hollowed out to give it more room. The same light-emitting cylinders used in Hollow Library ran the length of the ceilings here, too.

When we reached another door, the sounds of a quiet conversation and the *thwap* of metal hitting wood behind it, Naomi put her hand on the doorknob and then said, "Depending on who this is, you might need to run."

"Run where?"

"If it's Efyra, I'll be right behind you."

"What about the others?"

"Some of them still like me. Just not the older ones." Her eyes lingered on the door, and the long drop beyond it. "It'll be fine."

That did little to comfort me as she opened the door into a wide, open area. The wooden walls and floors were rough, and there were training dummies, large stones, and a hole in the center where the tree trunk continued upward. Names were carved into it, and I recognized some of them as former and current Ravens. I heard another door open and close, and I saw Jasmine Andel, the six-feathered Raven.

Sweat dripped down her face as she held a great-ax in both hands. She wasn't in her armor and had her hair tied back but still looked ready to kill us the moment she saw us. She reminded me of a carrion crow with a slightly bigger-than-average nose and a surgeon's eyes. But before she could question us, Naomi said, "Chloe's in trouble."

Jasmine stared at us, eyes narrow, still holding the great-ax to the neck of the training dummy. With little effort, she brought it back and cut it cleanly in two. It was hard not to gulp at that sight.

"Is that why you two are here?" she asked. "To warn her?"

"Yes," Naomi declared, voice like striking thunder.

"I don't believe you."

"You voted for me to join the Ravens. You trusted me then, and nothing has changed. My loyalties—"

"Your loyalties are to yourself, Naomi," Jasmine interrupted. "You proved that by conspiring with a Kingman while flirting with the prince. No one loyal could have done that."

"Thankfully my loyalty to the Royal Family isn't in question right now. I'm here for Chloe. She saved my life. Do you really think I could remain silent if I thought she was in danger?"

The wind blew through the branches around us, and we could hear the rustle from inside.

Jasmine sighed and placed her great-ax against what remained of the dummy. "Did you really have to bring the Kingman here?"

"I needed a backup plan in case you arrested me for trespassing and ignored my worries," she lied.

"Smart. Because I considered doing that."

Naomi cracked her neck, and I could see the relief come off her as her shoulders relaxed. "Where is she?"

Jasmine Andel moved over to the pitcher of water and poured herself a drink. When the cup was empty she said, "Tell me about this threat first. Does it put either the prince or princess at risk?"

"Not directly. We have reason to believe a Waylayer will target Chloe."

"And what reason would that be?"

To her credit, Naomi didn't look away from Jasmine as she said, "Because I stupidly used her name during the investigation."

"That sounds less about loyalty and more about righting a wrong."

"Can you tell me where she is or not?"

Jasmine hesitated, then looked at me. "Weren't *you* supposed to dispose of the Waylayer? The princess hired you to do a job, and so far you seem to be . . . failing."

I knew the mask I had to wear at that moment. "I'm working on it. The only reason we're here is to warn Chloe. Naomi believed it more important than continuing our searching."

"Are you going to tell us where she is or not?"

Jasmine took the great-ax up again, then hefted it across her shoulders as if it weighed nothing. "Justice Hill. A blue house with a metal knocker and a bed of scorpion grass beginning to bloom in front of it. We received word that another victim of the Heartbreaker was found there, and she went to investigate."

"What? No . . . that can't be right," Naomi whispered. "Are you—"

"The report is credible."

Naomi took off running. What Jasmine had described was Naomi's home. If there really was a body found in there, it was her father's.

"You should catch up with her, Kingman," Jasmine said. "She'll need friends."

"Why didn't you tell us sooner? Why all the games?" I asked, fists clenched.

"It was a lesson."

"A lesson? What did Naomi ever do to you to deserve to be treated like that?"

"I wasn't trying to hurt her, Kingman." Jasmine advanced closer to me. "It was for you. I've heard the lies you've been spreading all over the city. That the king killed himself."

I didn't back down. "He did. He was distraught, there was nothing—"

"Save your sweet lies for another," she said, voice rumbling. "The bitter truth is that you killed him. I saw you, Kingman. I saw you push his body off the balcony. I saw him hit the ground. And then I saw you . . . bloodstained and holding a gun. The way you smiled haunts my dreams. I should have climbed the walls and killed you then and there."

"You sure expressed your anger the night I was arrested."

Jasmine smiled. "I was wondering if you remembered that."

"I will never forget how you tortured me. What you did was inhumane."

"Perfect. I wouldn't want you to forget what you deserve." Jasmine pinched my cheek with her free hand. "Good luck, Kingman. It's a long, difficult climb down without Wind Fabrications."

I cursed under my breath and chased after Naomi, who was nowhere to be seen. Only the howl from the increasing wind kept me company as I made my way back down the great redwood trees, hoping Bryan Dexter was still alive.

INHERITANCE

I arrived to see Naomi trying to shove Chloe out of the way, and her friend standing firm, arms encasing her in a tight hug. Tears flowed down Naomi's face as she screamed, the wind picking up around us, blowing nearby shutters open and then slamming them shut. A small twister was beginning to form around them as the nearby trees swayed violently, as if about to snap. Snow and slush whipped at my face, and it was impossible to hear anything but the howl of the wind and Naomi's cries.

Bryan Dexter's fate was clear.

I had seen this once before and knew what to do.

Despite the wind trying to keep me away, I put my forearm in front of my face and step by step made my way toward them. When I could, I put my hand on Naomi's shoulder and let my warmth envelop her.

The harsh wind stopped, and she fell to her knees, sobbing, and Chloe sat on the ground with her, still holding her.

"Is there anyone inside?" I whispered to Chloe.

"Mercenaries."

I couldn't offer Naomi comfort, so I entered the house to see what had happened.

Bryan Dexter had not died without a fight. Everything was shattered or torn, from the vases and tables to the paint on the walls and the tiled floor. Every step I took into the house crunched. The walls were covered in vicious-looking scrapes, and Naomi's father was in the center of the carnage. I could tell it was him only because of the two names written over the left wrist: *Naomi* and *Evie*. His face wasn't nearly as intact. Strangest of all, his heart had been left behind. Removed, but then crushed in the center of the room like a tomato under a bootheel. There was a message written in blood across one of the walls: *Watch as I fix mistakes from the past.*

Dark was staring at the message while Beorn examined the body. He stuck his fingers inside Bryan Dexter's mouth, moved it along his gumline, and then smelled it.

"No discernible poison administered orally, Dark."

"Check his skin for marks," he ordered. "We need to be sure."

I focused on the body. Impossibly, Bryan looked as if he'd been crawling toward his heart before it had been crushed. But how? Had the killer positioned the body to make it appear that way? It . . . it . . . it was all so monstrous. What kind of person could do that? At least when Dark killed people I could understand his reasons. What could this be but the killer having fun?

"We're out of luck, aren't we?" I said to no one in particular.

Beorn didn't acknowledge me, but Dark did, looking over his shoulder. "Where were you?"

"With Naomi."

"Ah. Is she outside? Is that what all the commotion was?"

"Yes. She's with Chloe, the Raven. I think she may have snapped."

"To be expected."

Dark carried on inspecting the crime scene, looking for any scrap of information about the Heartbreaker. At this point, a piece of thread could be the difference between life and death.

"What does it mean, 'Watch as I fix mistakes from the past'?" I asked.

"It means we're going to die," Dark said. "The Heartbreaker isn't taunting us from a distance. He knows we're coming for him and is striking first. Maybe tomorrow. Depends on who he wants to participate in the grand finale."

I clamped a hand over my mouth to prevent myself from losing what little I had in my stomach.

"Our best approach is to try and determine who the Heartbreaker will choose for the grand finale. Everyone close to him is a potential victim and should be kept under close watch until the coronation," Dark said.

"Trey might be a target. He stopped the Heartbreaker from killing us in a tweeker den."

"Naomi might be, too," Dark said as he lifted and examined Bryan's hands and arms. Beorn was taking off his boots to check for anything there. "Along with you, me, and anyone who currently lives in Kingman Keep."

"Lyon?"

"Doubtful. Not after the stunt he pulled in Ryder Keep."

That was comforting, in a small way. "Do you think we can stop them?"

"Us? No," he said without hesitation. "But all together? Maybe we have a chance."

"Waiting around to die is a stupid plan."

Dark glared at me. "And what would you rather do? We can limit his options if we gather everyone who could be a target or potential participant in the grand finale. Force him to make a mistake. But if we play his game, well . . . more will die. Bryan Dexter never understood that. It's why his wife died."

"But his daughter lived."

"Because of me. Not him."

"What do you—"

Naomi walked through the door with Chloe's hand on her shoulder.

No one spoke until she reached her father's body, fell to her knees, and then asked, "Can I touch him?"

"Yes," Beorn said. "There's no poison on the body."

Naomi brushed her fingertips over Bryan's blood-soaked, slicked-back hair. "Was it painful?"

"Yes," he answered. "But unlike the other victims, he died fighting. I don't think the Heartbreaker got away as cleanly as they normally do. That's evident from the way they treated the heart."

Silence.

Chloe moved to my side, hand on the hilt of her sword. Dark watched Naomi with his arms crossed. We all waited for her to say something.

"Am I next?"

"Based on the message left for us," Dark said, "either you are or I am."

"Guess dying young isn't too bad." Tears were trickling down her cheeks. "I mean, who wants to live forever? Who wants to get married or have children? Who wants to be anything more than a Blackberry addict who was banished from Scales? Who wants redemption? Not me."

"Naomi . . ."

Naomi emptied her pockets of Blackberries and smashed them to powder with her fists until they disappeared completely. "If I'm going to die, I might as well die free."

Dark made his way over to me as Naomi continued to mutter to her father's body.

"We should head back to Kingman Keep, there's nothing else for us here," Dark declared. "And we should get Trey on the way. Where is he?"

"Somewhere the Heartbreaker will never find him."

"Are you positive?"

"Absolutely," I said, and my heart knew it was true.

"His death is on you if you're wrong. But, fine. Grab Naomi and let's go."

"She needs more time to grieve," Chloe said.

"We don't have more time, Raven. Not if she wants to live."

"I'll stay with her," I said. "We'll catch up. Go and make sure everyone in Kingman Keep is safe. Protect my family."

"You'd risk your own life to make her feel better? We're chasing a serial killer, Michael. There's no time for sentimental bullshit. It's life or death."

My voice didn't waver. "She deserves a chance to make amends with her father on her own terms. Or do you disagree?"

Dark didn't look at me. "Do what you must. But be quick about it. You'll ruin my plan if you're caught."

The Mercenaries left soon after that, the door slamming behind them.

"Don't pity me," Naomi said with clenched teeth as her tears continued to fall. "Don't feel bad for me. Don't see me differently because of this."

"We won't," Chloe and I said together.

"Good." She tore her father's locket from his neck and opened it. A very small scrap of paper tumbled out of it. "He said he would leave a note for me when he died. And the bastard actually left me one. Time to either die free or get revenge."

"Naomi, what are you talking about?"

She shoved the scrap into my hand as she put her father's locket on. The note had five words scrawled hastily on it in blood: *Heartbreaker on the Isle. For* . . .

Chloe spoke before I could. "Naomi, what are you planning?"

"I'm going to search the Isle and kill the Heartbreaker before they kill me."

"You don't know who they are! You'd be a perfect target. Just go with Michael to Kingman—"

"I'm ending this. Are you two with me or against me?"

A familiar weight returned to my shoulders as Naomi stared at me. This was a crossroads and I was lucky enough to be able to see that in the moment, rather than in hindsight. Returning to Kingman Keep with Dark to watch over my family was the smart choice. It was the plan. And before my misadventures with the king and Angelo, it was what I would have chosen to do in a heartbeat. But if I let Naomi go off on her own, I'd be abandoning a friend who had always stuck by me. We may have started off as . . . something between enemy and friend, but now she was firmly a friend in my mind.

My grandfather was right. I had to be better. If I was going to be a Kingman like my ancestors were, I had to protect everyone. Not just my family. It was time to make the world stop and stare.

Let history remember this.

"Did your father leave any information about who the Heartbreaker might be?" I asked.

"Michael," Chloe said. "Are you serious? Your family—"

"My family will survive. Kingman don't die easily. Don't think they're as foolish or lackadaisical as I am. But, more importantly, Dark was right. We can't beat the Heartbreaker if we play their game, and they don't know Bryan left that note. This is an opportunity for us to strike. It would be a shame to waste it. Don't you agree, Chloe?"

"Not in the slightest."

"You don't have to come with us," Naomi said, her tears drying. In their place was focused anger. "I won't blame you if you don't. You have a duty to the Royals, not to me."

"I . . . I'll join you two," Chloe said. "The princess wants the Heartbreaker dealt with, and I can open some doors for you." A pause. "We'll also stand more of a chance against them if it comes to that."

Naomi hugged Chloe, and nothing else needed to be said as the front door opened behind us. I didn't have time to respond before I felt a slap against the back of my head. Chloe electrified her arms as I fell to the floor, and I wondered why I had heard the door open here when I hadn't in the tweeker den.

SIGHT

When I was younger, I used to have nightmares. Terrible, crippling things that made me wake up in the middle of the night shaking and sweaty and counting numbers until the sun returned and the darkness receded. My father stopped them by showing me there was nothing to fear in the darkness. Things were only different—unique—and that I would be a fool not to appreciate them in darkness as I did in the sunlight.

For years after that, I slept through the night without problems and only woke up in order to go exploring without anyone watching.

After my father's execution, the nightmares returned. Twisted and changed. No longer did I fear unseen things in the darkness. Instead, it was people that I feared. With their subtle lies and twisted truths and bloodstained hands.

Now, as I woke to darkness after being knocked out, it was hard not to tremble as I had after my childhood nightmares many years ago.

My head throbbed as if it were being beaten like a drum. Everything was hazy. When I wiggled my legs and hands, I found them bound to a chair with rope. Tightly.

No chance of escape.

"Hello. Michael."

Fuck.

It was the Heartbreaker. They had found us. Or maybe they had been watching the whole time.

I heard the floorboards creak as someone made their way over to me. Their breath was hot against my ear. "Miss. Me?"

"Not in the slightest. Where are my friends?"

"Here," the killer answered. I heard two chairs screech against the floor and muffled screams. Naomi and Chloe were bound and gagged in the same room as me.

Double fuck.

"What do you want?" I asked as I tried to wiggle free from my bonds. If I could stall them—

The Heartbreaker tightened the restraints around my wrists.

"Not. Smart. Enough."

"At least I don't talk like I get winded walking up stairs."

They backhanded me with a ringed hand. I was almost certain I spat blood onto the floor, but I couldn't be sure. Because of the blindfold. How inconvenient of it to get in the way of my ability to see my injuries.

"Are you going to kill me or not? Because I've already done the whole waiting-around-to-die thing, and let me tell you—it's really boring."

No response.

"I'll take that as a no. After all, if you wanted to kill me you would have done it already. What're you waiting for? Or are you keeping me for your grand finale?"

The Heartbreaker didn't respond. Instead, I began to hear muffled sounds coming from above me. Instruments being played. Singing. Cheering. Clapping. And then, as clear as the sun on a cloudless day, I heard someone shout, "Presenting Red, and her rendition of 'The Angels of Naverre'!"

I heard the singer cross the stage above me, exactly as she had when I had seen her perform during the Endless Waltz. Maybe the Heartbreaker was playing tricks on me—but the College of Music wasn't supposed to have their pre-coronation performance for another day. It was scheduled two nights before Serena . . . Oh.

I'd lost another day. This time due to captivity. No wonder my throat felt so parched and my stomach remembered what the king's diet had been like.

"Ah, planning on killing us and presenting us after the show is over, then?"

"No," the Heartbreaker said. "Need. Something. First."

"My love and affection don't come cheap."

The Heartbreaker dragged one of the other chairs closer to me, the muffled screams intensifying. "I'm going to cut out your tongue if you continue to make those stupid jokes, Michael."

There went the odd speech pattern. A victory.

"You are going to answer my questions, or I'm going to slit Naomi's throat and make you experience what it's like to feel someone's warmth leave them. Do you know how long it takes for a body to become cold after death?"

"No."

"Half a day." They breathed loudly, and then ran the back of their ringed hand down my face. "And if you try to be a wiseass, you will experience it firsthand. Understand?"

"Perfectly."

"Where are Bryan Dexter and the Mercenary known as Dark?"

That was an interesting question to ask. "Bryan Dexter is dead. Shouldn't you know that? As for Dark, have you checked the Church of the Wanderer? He's quite relig—"

They backhanded me again. "Do you think I won't kill her, Michael? Must I prove it?"

Everything was hazy. Those rings hurt.

"If you wanted to kill us," I said, "you would have done it already. For whatever reason, you need or want us alive. So why would I tell you anything? Hit me as much as you want. I promise you I won't break."

The Heartbreaker ran a hand down my chest and then whispered into my ear, "You're right, Michael. But that doesn't mean I can't maim, cut, and scar this beautiful woman. As I do, remember, we could have done this in a much more civilized way."

The muffled screams were getting louder, as did the singing from above. Red was in the middle of her song and nowhere near completion. It was only going to get more intense from here, and I didn't know which performance was going to be louder.

"There's an art to torture. It's a lot like sex," the Heartbreaker said. "Most people think it's best to strike hard and fast. But it's better to know the body. Know its curves and how to use motion and precision for maximum results. Take the eye, for example. Soft. Squishy. Vulnerable. Perfect for playing with."

Muffled screams and whimpers echoed around me.

"Wait. Hold on. Let's talk. You're right, clearly I don't know when to hold my tongue."

The Heartbreaker ignored me. "What you want to do is move your index finger into the hollow above the eye, then press your thumb against the bottom as if about to rub something between them. Of course, the extraction is easier if your nails are longer. And mine are. So convenient."

"Wait! Please!"

"You had your chance. Listen to this."

There was a *pop* and I nearly threw up. I couldn't see the eye or the blood, but Naomi was screaming as loud as she could with a gag in her mouth.

"Such a lovely shade of green, Naomi. What do you think, Michael? I know you can't see it, but take a feel. I have to wipe the blood off it anyway."

The Heartbreaker put Naomi's eye against my cheek, soft and moist.

There was a wet cordlike thing attached to it, and I turned to my side to puke. The Heartbreaker was laughing hysterically.

Now everything smelt like porridge and eggs.

"That's disgusting, Michael. Have you no manners?"

I was still dry-heaving and didn't respond. All the hairs on the back of my neck were standing straight up.

Above, Red was reaching the climax of her song.

What was I going to do?

Thunder boomed and lightning chirped simultaneously, and my reactions weren't fast enough to avoid taking a bolt to the chest. It blew me back, chair included, into a nearby wall behind me. The chair shattered and, groaning, I took the blindfold off. The music had stopped.

Lightning was still flickering off Chloe as blood trickled down her face like tears. She was missing her right eye. Naomi was untouched in the corner of the room, unconscious with the remains of her own chair around her.

Our captor was pushing herself off the ground slowly, a long gun strapped to her back. I had never seen anything like it before, and when she rose to her feet I saw who it was. Mocking Bird. My gut was telling me it was impossible, she couldn't be the Heartbreaker, if only for the simple fact she had confused Naomi and Chloe. The Heartbreaker had known what Naomi looked like back in the tweeker den after not seeing her for years. So why hadn't she known down here if they were the same? The Heartbreaker was still in the city somewhere. Mocking Bird was just mimicking them here.

I screamed and leapt toward her.

We grappled and tumbled and rolled on the floor, each trying to get the advantage. I punched her in the face and she scratched mine with ridiculously long nails that broke my skin. After knocking me off her, she kicked me in the side and then took off up a nearby set of stairs.

I was slow to stand and recover, and limped straight over to Chloe to take the gag out of her mouth. She spat and said, "Leave me. Get the bitch. The princess might be in danger."

Even without an eye she was worried about the princess. Was that true loyalty or stupidity? "The princess will be fine in the castle. You don't—"

"No," Chloe interrupted. "She's not. *Red* is the princess. She's onstage right now, and in danger."

"What?"

"The singer Red is the princess Serena. *The singer Red is the princess Serena.* You of all people shouldn't be surprised, Michael. 'The Angels of Naverre' started off as a lullaby she used to sing all the time as a child. It even has the same tune. Did you never really connect the two?"

Suddenly, some of the oddities during the Endless Waltz made more sense. I had always assumed that Domet had ensured none of the nobility came after me directly during the Endless Waltz. I wasn't so sure of that now. Especially when I realized how infatuated I had been when I heard Red sing. I might as well have been enthralled.

"Get her out of here. Tell the other Ravens what happened," Chloe said as she tried to stand, instead falling to her knees in pain. She was still bleeding. "Please."

"They won't believe me. Even if the Waylayer is—"

Chloe ripped the peacock feather out of her hair and then handed it to me. "Find a Raven. Tell them: *We fly unfettered.* Then give them my feather. Understand?"

"Understood."

"Hurry." Chloe put her hand over her lost eye, voice wavering. "Go!"

I took off after Mocking Bird. The stairs led to a hallway filled with musicians hurrying back and forth with instruments. All of them were dressed as faux nobility with a lot of gaudy jewelry.

I didn't have the time to falter or get lost in the crowd backstage. Chloe was severely injured, Naomi was unconscious, and a Waylayer was running loose. What were the odds that she was going after the princess? It was impossible to know, but until I could be certain she wasn't, I would have to assume she was. Mocking Bird was unique looking, but I couldn't distinguish her from any of the other able-bodied women in sight.

How was I going to find her?

Maybe finding the Ravens was my best option.

"Michael? Michael."

Unless someone found me first.

Sirash approached me. Out of anyone that it could have been, I was glad it was him. Some of the tension in me left my body. "Sirash."

"I thought I was clear that we wanted nothing to do with someone so selfish ever again."

His words struck harder than Mocking Bird and made my chest tighten. "Trust me, I wouldn't be here willingly. Don't believe me? A Raven and my friend Naomi are down below the stage. Go and check on them if you want."

Sirash stared at me, unblinking. "Truly?"

"Yes. I'm chasing a Waylayer who may or may not want to kill the princess. She's here tonight. She's masquerading as the singer Red. Who knew, right?"

"What? A Waylayer? Are you making this up?"

"You know me, Sirash. I'm not smart enough to come up with anything original on the spot. I only twist the truth as I see fit. What a great leader I would make."

Sirash cast a sidelong glance as Arjay approached us and then said, "Do you need help?"

Those were the last words I expected him to say. My jaw was nearly on the floor, and he saw my astonishment.

"A Waylayer attack here changes things. Even with you."

I wasn't going to question his sudden change of mind, not when I needed all the help I could get. "I need someone to get Dark from Kingman Keep, I need to alert the Ravens to what happened below stage, and I need a weapon. Preferably a gun or a crossbow."

Sirash looked down at Arjay. "Run to Kingman Keep. Tell whoever you find first that Michael is at the College of Music and a Waylayer is trying to kill him. Then return to our room and don't leave, understood?"

Arjay took a last look at me and then took off running.

"Have you seen any Ravens?" I asked.

"Not in a while," Sirash answered. "One was patrolling before the performances started. But I haven't seen her since."

"What about Red?"

"No one sees her until she walks onstage, and then she disappears soon after."

"Is she still onstage?"

Sirash nodded. "Can't you hear her? She's performing her final set. Earlier she declared she will be in semiretirement until further notice. Which makes sense if she's truly the princess."

I looked around us. Women in plate mail should have been easy to spot, even among the crowds. I was backstage, so where would they be? What would be the most tactical spot in a theater to watch a performance? From one of the balconies? From the front row? Or were they disguised as the princess was? If they were, what would they be wearing?

"What would be the best place to reach the stage but still be able to see it?" I asked.

"Probably the stalls."

Brilliant. Too large an area to cover quickly. But the Waylayer was skilled at shooting from an extremely long distance. Would she try that here?

"What's the farthest and highest place in the theater that can still see the stage?"

"The upper box. Have you never been to a theater before?"

Should have seen that one coming. "Fine. What about weapons? Where can I get—"

Sirash reached behind his back and pulled out a flintlock pistol. He offered it to me butt-first. I took it, and from the weight I could tell it was loaded. "You carry a gun now? Since when?"

"Since I was tortured by the castle educator and my little brother murdered someone to save your life."

"Fair."

"Do you have a plan, Michael?"

"Kind of," I said as I walked toward the stage. "If I can't find the Ravens in time, I'll do the next best thing: I'll bring them to me. If anything happens to me, head to Kingman Keep. My mother will protect you there."

History is defined by moments. Moments of bravery. Moments of foolishness. Moments of compassion. Moments of hate. These moments are impossible to identify when they happen, and usually only seen in hindsight.

Except for this one. Symon would be annoyed he missed seeing it in person. I looked forward to learning how it would be seen. As foolishness, or bravery.

I walked onstage mid-song.

No one saw me.

Red sang "The Minuet of Memories" beautifully. A true master of her craft.

As I stood behind the princess with my body nullified, I raised my gun, then shot.

The bullet hit the roof as everyone screamed and ducked into their seats.

Serena turned around, her red mask obscuring her reaction.

Four elegant women rushed the stage from all angles. The Ravens I'd been unable to find.

I stood still, my gun aimed at the sky while the other held out Chloe's feather.

"Sorry to bother you, but I need a moment of your time."

39

HEARTBREAKER

I was surprised they didn't immediately stab me.

The four Ravens surrounded me carefully, unsure if my gun was still loaded. It wasn't, but most people erred on the side of caution with guns, since they lacked practical knowledge. Ignorance wasn't an excuse for not knowing something so vital, but people always tried to claim it was.

Serena, to her credit, didn't drop her façade. She strolled toward me, every step careful and precise. Since the audience was filled with nobility, it wasn't too much of a surprise that Ravens had rushed the stage.

"What're you doing here, Michael?" she said, quietly enough that only the people in the immediate area could hear her. "Hand-delivering a death wish?"

The audience had fallen silent, rapt by the unfolding drama.

I handed her Chloe's feather. "*We fly unfettered.* Chloe's injured below the stage. We were kidnapped by the Waylayer that's been operating in Hollow recently. Naomi is with her."

Serena rubbed the feather between her fingers. "Hannah, check below the stage."

"But, Prin—"

"Now."

The five-feathered Raven sheathed her sword and left the stage, making sure to take Chloe's feather with her.

Serena motioned to her Ravens to lower their weapons. "Was all this a show to draw my Ravens out? Could you not have managed something more discreet? Or do you enjoy being a thorn in my foot I cannot be rid of?"

"Thorn. Definitely thorn. But you would know all about that, wouldn't you? How often were you keeping an eye on me during the Endless Waltz? Because I'm starting to remember an auburn-haired woman who sung me a familiar lullaby after Jamal died. Among other mysterious women."

Her mask limited my ability to read her expression. I could only watch her eyes, which were staring right through me. "You always did enjoy telling ludicrous stories."

"This is one of the few times I'm telling the truth."

"If you say so, Michael."

I looked up at the upper floor of the theater. Someone was moving up there. Was it the Waylayer? Or was it simply someone leaving?

"I'm leaving," Serena said. "Be thankful I'm not here as the princess or I would consider this an attack on my life and act accordingly."

She turned her back to me but didn't begin to walk away.

"Serena," I said in nearly a whisper. "Will you trust me?"

"Nev—"

I tackled her and put my nullified body over hers as a shot went off in the upper balcony and the four-feathered Raven cried out in pain moments later. The bullet had gone through her armor and now she was struggling to stand, let alone move.

The audience had turned into a mob that wanted to get out of there as soon as possible. The screams made it impossible to hear the Ravens as one of them leapt toward the upper balcony with the help of their Wind

Fabrications. Another stepped in front of Serena and me, her body chiseled and hard like metal, as she took aim with the crossbow in her hands.

It was pure chaos. Women trampling men, men trampling women, and children crawling over the crowds, all to get away from the shooter.

Another shot went off and the bullet bounced off the Raven standing in front of us and hit a Low Noble in the leg. His companions grabbed him and helped him flee. Good to see not everyone was selfish in Hollow.

Serena rolled me off her. "Is that the Waylayer?"

A third shot bounced off Rowan and splintered the wooden stage. For whatever reason the Waylayer didn't seem to be as accurate as she had been at the colosseum—which was the only good luck I'd had recently, since the Raven in the upper balcony was struggling to get through the crowds. She hadn't seen where the Waylayer was shooting from. Neither had I. It was all darkness from the stage.

"Serena! Use your Fabrications! There are too many people moving around and we can't—" Another shot went off. "—you and I will be the only ones who can move. We can end this quickly together."

A fifth shot. How was Mocking Bird reloading so quickly?

After taking the impact, Rowan backed up slightly. The bullet might not penetrate, but the pain was still there. How many more shots would she be able to withstand without falling or canceling out her Fabrications?

"No way," Serena said. "What's to protect me from you with that kind of opening? I am not a fool, Michael. They call you the king killer for a reason."

"I didn't kill your father!"

A sixth shot. The crowds were thinning now, leaving only a few stragglers who hadn't made it out.

"Stop lying to me! I know you killed him! Your father killed Davey, my father killed yours, and you killed my father in revenge! I would be a fool to ever think otherwise!"

"Then I'll be the fool for the both of us!" I screamed as I stood. "Watch me save your delusional, misinformed ass like all my ancestors have saved Royals in the past!"

The Waylayer shot and missed, and the bullet hit the ground near me. I leapt down into the stalls. "Aim better! Or else I'll think you want me alive!"

She didn't like that, and Karin—the Raven searching the balcony—was thrown off the upper balcony by the Waylayer in an attempt to take both of us out in one shot. She crashed into the middle of a set of chairs nearby. I crept up, felt for her pulse, found it slow and steady, and moved on without hesitation. The only way up to the upper balcony would be by climbing one of the columns to the side. At least I knew I would be good at that. Assuming I didn't get shot.

I took a deep breath to steady myself as shots continued to ring out around me. My body was still nullified, but it took focus to make sure I remained so. Rowan was shielding the princess with her body, while Michelle was still onstage, crawling toward an exit.

I was on my own. Hopefully, Sirash was safe backstage.

Here went nothing.

I scrambled toward the column, a shot blowing the back of a chair to smithereens. The shots were getting more frantic, and she was able to get off another before I made it to my destination. The column was brilliantly crafted, with long, deep ridges I could use as handholds. Once I had my initial grip, I climbed as fast as I could and then threw myself over the upper-balcony railing.

Instead of a bullet waiting for me, Mocking Bird slammed the butt of her long gun in my face. I fell backwards against the railing, head spinning and vision blurry, and she held the gun lengthwise against my throat and pushed down until I couldn't breathe.

"It didn't have to be this way, Michael," she sneered. "I was never contracted to kill you. But now you've given me no choice."

I tried to wiggle free of the gun, but she was stronger than she looked, and her unnaturally sharp nails were digging into the gun to make sure it stayed still. Her eyes were burning a deep red. Just like a tweeker's.

"It's rather a thrill to kill you," she said with a laugh. "In all my time, I've never killed a Kingman. Usually the Reaper or War take those contracts. Now I get to join their—"

Mocking Bird never finished her sentence, the pressure on my neck disappearing. I rolled away with one hand on my throat, gasping, holding myself up with my other arm.

Mocking Bird was standing still, eyes wide. There was a . . . a talonlike hand that had burst through her chest and was holding her heart. It tore back out through the body, and all I could do was stare.

Dark held Mocking Bird's heart in his hand. With a gentle movement, he pushed her over the railing and watched as her body awkwardly hit the seats below.

My body moved on its own, my mind still trying but failing to process what I had just seen. I punched Dark in the face with a nullified hand as my other reached for the revolver he kept between his shirt and jacket. I yanked it free and pointed it at his head.

My aim was steady. "Heartbreaker."

Dark touched his lips and looked at the flecks of blood on his fingers. "It's been years since I've seen my own blood. I wonder why you didn't get a fistful of . . . ah, yes, how could I forget?" His shook his hand out and the blood flew off his fingers. "I'm surprised it took you this long to hit me."

"What just happened?"

"Are you willing to listen?" he said. "I did warn you that something like this might happen once you began to know more about me."

I glanced down at what was going on below. The princess and Rowan were checking up on Karin and Michelle. Sirash was standing over Mocking Bird's body, rubbing the lantern pendant on his necklace between his index finger and thumb. No one was paying attention to us. If I was going to uncover the truth—about Angelo, him, the Heartbreaker, and whatever had just happened—I needed to hear his story. Killing him would be a waste. And if there was any time to talk, it was now.

"We'll go somewhere private, and you'll tell me everything."

Dark took a bite out of Mocking Bird's heart, tearing into the recently beating organ—pulling and stretching the muscle as if strands of thread were wrapped around his teeth. Dark red blood dripped down his lips and chin as he chewed. And because fat took longer to soften than muscle . . . it was a painfully long time until he could speak with an empty mouth. "Listen carefully, because unlike you, I have no flair for the dramatics. This is the truth. This is how it all began. This is the truth of the Shade family."

40

EGWSF HVBJ
EGWSF LJ DESGV

Dark had finished eating Mocking Bird's heart by the time we reached the Hollow Library. He hadn't spoken or elaborated any further since we left, only promising that he would when we reached our destination. I didn't trust him, but since I kept the revolver aimed at his back, I knew I was safe. For now.

We entered through the front door, Dark muttered a few words to the Archivist at the main desk, and we descended further into the library. He brought me to the Archmage's room and we both took a seat at the table next to each other. Without explaining why, he moved a chair in front of us so that we were in a triangular formation.

"Are you going to start talking?" I asked. "Or are you trying to stall me?"

Dark's eyes were closed. "Give it a minute. I'm waiting for someone."

"Who?"

"You'll see. It's worth it. I promise."

I drummed my fingers against the table, the gun always aimed at Dark, until the door opened and an old woman strode in. She had wide eyes, wispy white hair, and thirteen small star tattoos around her right eye. She took a seat in front of us.

"Michael, this is Nonna. She's the Chronicler for Orbis Company."

I glanced at Dark, hoping for an explanation for her presence. When it was clear I wouldn't get one, I said, "It's a pleasure to meet you, Nonna."

"As it is to meet you."

This woman may have scared me more than Dark. She had yet to blink. And the way she looked at me was . . . surgical. As if she was breaking me down to my basic foundations. Male. Kingman. Heir. Young. In over his head.

"Nonna is here at my request," Dark said, snapping me back to focus. "She's going to help me show you everything that you need to know."

"Do you not remember everything? Does she hold your story?"

Dark shook his head. "No, I remember. I was being literal. She's going to help me show you. It's her Fabrication specialization. It allows someone to share their memories. As they remember them."

"What?" I said with a laugh. "You're fucking—"

"Language, sweetie."

"Huh? Oh, uh, sorry. But there's no way a Fabrication specialization like that exists."

"There are about a dozen like Nonna. All Mercenaries. One of the many advantages that allow us to hold the prestigious position we do," Dark explained. "There's no formal name for her specialization, so we all call it Illusion. But it's not as miraculous as it sounds. Her Fabrications don't allow the user to see memories they've forgotten or interact with them in any meaningful way. Just to share an exact replica of how it's remembered. Including deteriorations."

"So the older the memory, the more spotty it is."

"Correct," Dark said. "I thought about telling you everything . . . but would you believe anything I said at this point?"

I leaned closer to him, gun still in hand. "How do I know this isn't an attempt to manipulate my memories with your Darkness Fabrications?"

Dark played with the glass ring on his hand, hesitated, and then took it off and put it on the table. "You know what this means to me. Take it. Hide it somewhere in the room. In the library if you want to. Nonna and I will wait. If anything happens to you, I'd never find it again."

"You'd find it eventually."

"Maybe. But you think I want to draw that much attention to myself? With my father and the Heartbreaker in this city?"

"You haven't convinced me you're not the Heartbreaker yet." I gritted my teeth. "And even if you aren't, you *ate* someone's heart. What kind of monster are you?"

Dark tapped the side of his head. "Only one way to find out. Are you in? Or do you want to use that gun and let the mystery die with me?"

I looked into his eyes and saw those damn grey monstrosities that he shared with his father. I hated it, but he was right. I wouldn't trust a single word he said, but the truth was in his memories, and there was only one way to see it.

I put the gun on the table. "How do we do this?"

Dark put his hands on my shoulders. "Look into my eyes."

I had a great quip in my mind but let it go and said, "And?"

Nonna took care of the rest.

She put a hand on each of our arms, an explosion of colors came out of her hands, and I felt it instantly. It was like falling backwards into water. The shock widening my eyes and the splash erasing all my surroundings, turning it into black mist. But it was like falling through the air, rather than swimming. I tried to reach out and grab something but found nothing. Then I hit something solid and lay there, waiting for something—anything—to happen.

Dark descended more gracefully, landing on his feet rather than his back. His voice seemed to come from everywhere, as if it was inside my head. "It can be jarring the first few times you do this. Can you stand?"

I rolled over to my side, took a deep breath, and then got to my feet. Everything felt wobbly and disorienting, surrounded by darkness. When the pounding in my head stopped, I said, "Where are we?"

"This is nowhere," he said. "I haven't begun yet. Are you ready?"

"Get on with it."

"If you say so, Michael. Welcome to Naverre."

Dark raised his hands like a conductor, as he did when he made the darkness move in strange ways. Buildings began to sprout up around him, twisting and solidifying into distinct shapes. Slowly, colors began to spread out, dyeing the water a deep blue and the grass an eternal green as if he were creating the scene around us.

I never saw Naverre. Never at its peak, at any rate. Everyone had heard the stories about it. How it had been built onto the cliff of the biggest waterfall in the world: Eighty-Nine Falls. A towering feat of natural wonder that could never be replicated by humanity, even if they had an eternity to do it. The city sprawled down beside the waterfall, with districts and houses built into the mountain for those who didn't want to live in an eternal rainy season. The High Noble Naverre Keep sat at the top of the waterfall, looking down at all those below. For someone who had never left Hollow, the sight of something else left me breathless.

Dark had placed us in the middle of a square underneath the waterfall's spray, next to a cart steadily meandering up the road. The owner screamed something at the horse, but I couldn't make out the words. I held out my hand to feel the spray, yet it never touched me. It went through me as if I wasn't there.

"Is this where you grew up?" I asked.

Dark shook his head and motioned for me to follow the cart. We did so, keeping a reasonable distance from it.

"I spent half of my early life on ships in the Sea of Statues, traveling between the Gold Coast Clan estates and Eham," he said. "It was a blissful, easy life and it was the only time I ever remember my parents being happy. My mother would sing me lullabies, and my father . . . well. It's not important.

"When my mother got pregnant for the second time, she wanted to return to Naverre. My birth had almost killed her. Left her weak and bedridden for a year. As wonderful as Eham is, their doctors know little about any treatments more complicated than a thread and needle."

Dark paused as the cart in front of us emerged from the spray and into sunlight. The High Noble Naverre Keep was in sight. It was all points and height, more subtlety and restraint in the Church of the Eternal Flame than this thing.

"My father was against it," Dark said. "He hated Hollow. Hated everything about it. The nobility and royalty. The food. Even the smell. He always insisted it smelt like rotten eggs. I was so young, I never knew enough to disagree. He was . . . well, you understand how children feel about their fathers. No need to tell you. Eventually my mother won the argument and we returned to Naverre as a family."

We stopped walking as the people in the cart got out. The first was a young boy, black of hair and light of step. A younger, more innocent version of the man who stood next to me. There was a constant smile on his face as he paraded around with a wooden sword.

After him came a familiar man. He looked very much like Dark did now, except tanner and more muscular. But even so young, Angelo was still as trim as he was now, and he also had a smile on his face, albeit smaller and more conservative than his son's. When he was on solid ground, he held out his hand to the cart.

Katherine Naverre, Dark's mother, descended with help. She was visibly pregnant. She had tanned skin, a dagger on her hip, and wore practical and elegant clothes. A perfect representation of noble society in Hollow. Yet, knowing how Angelo idolized her, I had expected . . . something more. She was beautiful, yes, but also mortal and flawed.

"I hate seeing her like this. Happy and hopeful," Dark muttered. "Knowing what happens next."

The front door to the keep opened and a small army of servants strode out. They were all dressed completely identically, down to their hair color and length. After they had arranged themselves in neat rows, four others came outside. They all had dark brown hair, were dressed in fine, elegant clothes that looked brand-new, and were faceless. No distinguishable features, not even a scar or a freckle or a dimple. They were terrifying to look at.

"Memory-loss casualties," Dark said. "I'd have more sympathy if any of them were still alive. But they aren't, and you'll see why soon enough. My grandfather is almost here."

Dark's grandfather, Edward Naverre, was something else. He had owlish features, was as tall as the Corrupt Prince, and had more muscle than all his children combined. His mud-brown hair was cut short and streaked with grey, and he wore a cape that turned purple in the sunlight. Frankly, it was astonishing he looked as good as he did for someone so old.

"I think my grandfather hated us from the very moment he laid eyes on us," Dark said.

I watched the scene unfold. Edward's shadow elongated down the steps toward Dark and the others like creeping darkness that threatened to swallow all nearby light. Even the sun, which had seemed so bright moments ago, had dulled to a pale grey.

"Katherine," Edward Naverre said, softly but distinct. "You have returned."

"Yes, Father," she said. Returning to her noble roots, she curtsied before kissing his hand. "Thank you for having us."

"It is necessary."

Davis and his father were hanging back behind her, more tentative than I had ever seen them. "Father," Katherine began, "let me introduce you to my husband, Angelo Shade, and our son, Davis."

"You didn't give him a Hollow name," he said, voice level. "What a shame. Is he a Fabricator?"

"No," Angelo answered. "Like me, he is—"

"Did I address you, boy?" Edward asked. "Let your son speak for himself."

Katherine urged Davis forward as Angelo clenched his fists.

"I am not a Fabricator, Grandfather," Davis declared.

"Have you been tested?"

"I don't—"

Edward slapped Davis with the back of his hand. Angelo nearly leapt out of his skin, and only Katherine gripping his shoulder kept him in place.

A servant massaged Edward's hand as he said, "Do not speak like a commoner. You are a Naverre and you will act like one. And if you do not, you may find somewhere else to live. Now. Have you been tested?"

"I do not think so, Grandfather."

Edward snapped his fingers. "Servant Thirty-Three. Take Davis to the Fabrication Master for immediate evaluation."

"Father," Katherine said with a hand on her stomach. "We are tired from the long voyage. Can this not wait for another day?"

"No. I need to know whether he is useful or not."

"My son—" Angelo began.

Edward tilted his head. "My grandson will not dwell in mediocrity any longer. My blood deserves better than what little you have been able to give them. Otherwise none of us would be here. Do you understand, boy?"

Angelo gritted his teeth. "Yes."

"Good," he said as he held out his hand. "Now show me."

Angelo had never bowed to anyone the entire time I knew him. He did not start then, either.

When it was clear Angelo would not submit so easily, Edward Naverre turned to Davis. "Grandson, do you understand what is needed?"

"I knew." Dark gave a flourish and stopped the scene. "But, like an imbecile, I followed my father's lead. I imagine that disrespect was all it took for my grandfather to determine my father was a rodent that needed to be exterminated."

"That's all it took?" I asked.

"Yes," he said, and walked toward the keep. "We shouldn't dawdle. There's plenty more to see."

"What's your original specialization? What happened when you were tested?"

Dark stopped near his father, who was frozen in place. "You'll find out in due time."

Hoping more answers would come, I continued on. The scene changed again when we went through the door.

We were in a bedroom, big enough to hold a bed for two, but small enough that it could hold nothing else but the bare necessities. Davis and his father were in the bed, blankets up to their chins, shaking and coughing and looking as if death was coming for them. Dark's mother doted on them, wiping sweat from their brows and urging them to sip water. But currently she held two cups of tea in her hands. Dark stared at his mother, expressionless.

"You know what happens. Do you need to see it?" he asked, in barely a whisper.

I shook my head. "We can move on."

"Thank you," he said, and turned his back to the scene.

We went through the door together, the scenery changing again as we walked.

"My father killed the Naverre family one by one for what they did to my mother and unborn sibling," Dark explained. "Evelyn was the first to die. But you already know that, as well."

Nevertheless, I watched as a faceless woman was shot in the back with an arrow, fell from her horse, and was trampled to death.

"The second-born son, Patrick, was next," Dark said. "He was found hanged in the dining room. He was a troubled child, and no one was too surprised."

His faceless body hung off in the distance, swaying gently like a tree caught in the wind.

"Edgar Naverre was the third. The night after Patrick's suicide, he went into a frenzy during dinner, claiming that the shadows were coming to get him. His father, still upset, told him to compose himself. He was banished to his room until he calmed down, with instructions that none of his servants should check up on him."

We watched as servants pushed another faceless man into a small room against his will. Edward Naverre watched as it happened, a grimace on his face.

Dark walked into the pitch-black room. "They checked up on him a full day later. And discovered . . ."

He let the scene materialize. The door was open, light flooding the room. Edgar Naverre was against one of the walls, red voids where his eyes should have been. Clumps of his hair covered the ground and stuck to his hands. Messages had been scrawled on the walls of his room in blood. They all read the same thing: *Save me from the shadows. Save me from the shadows.*

"Edgar got the worst fate," Dark said when I had taken in the scene. "I never understood why. Even to this day."

"How did Angelo do this?" I asked. "He's not a Fabricator."

"The same way he framed your father for Davey's murder. With help."

"Who helped him?"

"We're getting there."

———————

The last scene was a dinner between Angelo, Davis, and Edward. The table was long and empty, more food than the three of them could eat in days, let alone at one meal. Nearly finished candles were guttering in the lanterns and holders. The rest of the keep waited in darkness, just outside the room, ready to devour the light. Dark took a seat at one of the empty chairs, and so did I.

"Where's the other one?"

"Edgill?" Dark questioned. "He begged Angelo for mercy when he realized what was going on. Angelo spared him, only because he would have felt some remorse in destroying my mother's family entirely. He was weak in that way. Edgill's peace was short-lived, anyway. He burned alive in his keep when Naverre was annexed by rebels. A fitting end for a man who betrayed his family to save his own life. I bet it hurt."

"What happens here?"

"This is where Edward dies, Angelo becomes the world's most dangerous man, and I learned what he was truly capable of."

It didn't happen quickly. We sat at the table watching the three people eat their dinner. No one spoke, cutting and chewing and smacking of lips the only sounds. No servants came to interrupt the monotony of the meal. It was as if they had given up and were just waiting for the inevitable to happen.

Eventually, once Edward's plate was clear, he said, "When will it be my time, Angelo?"

"Tonight," he said after he swallowed. "Do you want to know how?"

Edward leaned back in his seat. "Ignorance is worse than anything else."

Angelo sighed and stood, a glass of deep-red wine in his hand. "You're lucky it's more entertaining this way. The effects of the poison haven't hit you yet. But they will very soon."

"Poison?" Edward said with a laugh. "After what you did to my family, I expected something more sophisticated."

"Oh, have no fear, Father," he taunted. "The poison won't kill you. Just—"

The glass Edward had been holding slipped out of his hand and shattered against the ground. His lips were twitching but he said nothing.

"—paralyze you. Poison would be too easy. Too nice. Especially since the poison you used on Katherine was agonizing. She bled and she screamed until she couldn't any longer. No, your death . . . your death will be painful." His voice never fluctuated. "Davis, come here. Bring your knife."

Davis crept toward his father, a dinner knife in his hands.

"He's not going to . . . ?"

"He is," Dark said. "I've been a murderer since I was ten. And you want to know the worst part? Most days I don't regret what I was forced to do. Do wicked men not deserve to die if the world will be a better place without them?"

Angelo took Davis's hands in his own, so the tip of the blade hovered over Edward's chest. "Do you know why we do this, Davis?"

"No, Father."

"This man killed your mother and sister . . . your sweet stillborn sister who never even took a breath. We are owed blood."

"Mother always said family forgives family."

"Not this time," Angelo said. "There is no forgiveness for men like him, and he would not be merciful to us."

"Shouldn't we be better than him?"

Angelo put a hand on Davis's shoulder. "Yes. But not to these High Nobles. This is what they deserve." A pause. "You may hate me now, but one day you will have to be stronger than everyone else around you so you can oppose my father and determine your own fate. Consider this the most important lesson I will ever teach you."

Together, Angelo and Davis lodged the blade into Edward Naverre's chest. He didn't gasp or wheeze, just stared at them. As Angelo wiggled the blade around, he said, "Blood means nothing. You choose your family, and whatever consequences come with them."

Dark stopped the scene, jittery, and he cracked his knuckles in quick succession. "You needed to see what Angelo was like as a father. How twisted he became after my mother's death."

"What was his goal here?"

"To make me hate them as much as he did." He ran his hands through his hair. "It didn't work. I ran away the next morning. Hid in the back of a cart headed toward Vargo and the Gold Coast. It would be years before I saw Angelo again. By then . . . his perception of the world was so twisted it was too late to convince him to take another path. Though I knew I could save him by driving a dagger through his heart. Put him out of his misery. I remembered that childhood lesson."

I didn't know how to respond, and changed the topic instead. "Are we headed to Vargo next?"

"No," Dark said. "We'll skip the trials and tribulations of my youth. I was exiled from Vargo. I navigated through the Madness Reef with my sanity intact, on three wooden planks roped together. Orbis Company found me in Torda, the city of orphans. You may have heard the stories about my first contract. I'm the man who brought the titan's statue to the surface in the Sea of Statues." He exhaled. "But we're returning to where everything began and ended. In Hollow."

PANDEMONIUM

When the scene materialized we were beneath a large red tent that could rival many of the buildings in Hollow. Stands surrounded a large dirt circle, with two huge supports holding the tent up. A taut length of rope stretched between two wooden platforms, and the crowd was filing into their seats, all faceless. Just like the Navarre children had been.

"I know this," I said, once I was certain. "This is the Azilian circus that came to Hollow four years ago. I was here."

Dark didn't hear me, standing in the center of the dirt circle, taking in the sights. He looked on the verge of tears.

"I was sent to Hollow for a protection contract at the change of seasons a few weeks after the summer festival. It was supposed to be simple, and I was only supposed to be there for a few weeks, three months at most, but . . ." He trailed off. ". . . fate intervened." He took another breath with his eyes closed. "My employer was a man named Vance Yaio. We met for the first time at the Azilian circus. He had front-row tickets, and I had a brief description of him and orders to protect him. I didn't even know how he could afford my services."

"Yaio isn't a name that's ever been associated with any form of nobility in Hollow," I said.

"I know," Dark said. "I knew back then, too. Take a seat over there. The show's about to begin."

As Dark and I took seats in the front row, the faceless people who had occupied them began disappearing like mist when we sat. Before I could ask what we were looking for, Dark pointed to his younger self as he made his way toward the main area. His hair was long and unruly, and despite lacking some of the muscle he had now, he still looked as ferocious as ever.

"That's Vance Yaio," Dark said as he pointed to a man in the front row.

He was easy enough to spot among the crowd. Old, pitch-black hair, and a scar that looked as if it split his nose into two. He was immaculate, not a single eyebrow hair out of place. Acting and dressed as he was, he should have been the focus of every person here, but no one interacted with him. Only a few even looked at him. It was as if he blended into the darkness, stiller than a statue.

When Davis approached Vance, his voice was amplified so we could hear it.

"Vance?" Davis asked.

The man grunted and then signaled for him to sit down. Once Davis was settled, Vance said, "Why do they call you Dark?"

"Because it's better than Davis."

"That the only reason?"

"You requested me. You must have some idea why the Mercenary community nicknamed me Dark."

Vance took a swig from a flask. After Davis declined a swig, he continued, "Did Tai tell you anything about this contract before sending you to Hollow?"

"No, but I didn't ask for any details. Prefer to begin without preconceptions. Client is king, and I'm here to serve."

The ushers were beginning to quiet the audience. Not a single seat was vacant. Azilian circuses were rare and special events, and with ill tidings of a rebel army brewing in the north, everyone thought—correctly—that this would be the last one for a long time. The prince and king had been in attendance, seated in the front row opposite us with Ravens at their sides. The princess had been absent from Hollow. But I remembered seeing them from a distance. They had looked happy. Content.

"Your contract is to find a man named Brooks Davey," Vance said.

"Any details you can give me about him?"

"Yes, after the show."

"The entire circus before *her* performance had been rather underwhelming," Dark said. "A concentrated, coordinated glimpse at the oddities in the world. I'd already seen too much to be impressed with the fire dancers or the beast masters or the jugglers. It all paled in comparison to the Vakacha's rituals I had had the honor to see in person during a . . . well, that's not important. You're not here to hear those stories. Only the ones that concern the Heartbreaker."

The scene changed quickly, skipping over scenes and performances that had awed me as a child. Even if they weren't special to Dark, they had been to me. Hollow had been my prison, and this had been one of my few glimpses of a world outside the city's high stone walls.

"Do you believe in love at first sight?" Dark asked.

"No," I answered.

"Would it shock you that I do?"

"You? Of all—"

"Relax. I don't," he said with a laugh. "I've always seen love as a weakness and avoided it at all costs. I did, however, give in to lust. Frequently. So when I saw Zahra perform for the first time, I thought it was just that. Lust. Attraction. Desire. But hindsight has colored my memories, and no matter how I present her performance, it will seem as if I was in love with her from the beginning. And maybe . . . maybe I was, and even if I wasn't, history has been rewritten by my words and I will declare it to be so. I was in love with Zahra at first sight."

It was dark within the tent, the only light two bright lanterns that hung on each of the poles that had the rope stretched between them.

"What a sight she was," Dark whispered.

I saw the glimmer off the metal pole Zahra was using to balance herself before I saw she was walking across a length of rope no wider than a splinter. As Zahra walked, she came into focus to all of us lucky enough to see her. Her snow-white hair was like Celona during a cloudy night. She was striking and beautiful . . . yet reminded me of a blank canvas, devoid of color. And as hard as I tried to find her shadow, I couldn't.

Her performance oozed authority and presence. She walked that rope, so high in the air, as if she had been born on it. With every step forward, I could have sworn my heart paused to see if she would fall. She never did, and when the audience began to sink into a lull of security that she would reach the other side unscathed, she insulted us by slowly leaning backwards until her back touched the rope. And then . . . and then she let the metal pole fall from her hands. When it thundered against the ground, she smiled and rose from her precarious position without even bothering to put her hands out to balance herself.

The rope might as well have been the floor beneath my feet for all it bothered her. Just one crossover step after another, hands behind her back. When she reached the platform on the other side, she gently ran her fingertips over it and then turned around so quickly that Dark almost leapt to catch her. Even though she was just a memory. But she didn't need his help and we were spellbound by her performance.

Zahra made the crossing between the two poles seven times, each more brazen than the last. Nothing could stop her. Nothing could hinder her performance. She had captivated the audience.

Then she stepped off the rope onto a platform and it was over. Zahra took no deep breaths nor glistened with sweat, simply smiling and waving from above like God. The audience was silent, until it exploded with deafening applause. All I could do was stare at the woman above me.

All around us, people were screaming for more.

Vance didn't agree with their praise. "She dragged her performance

out longer than necessary. Gave the audience too much. Left them satisfied where they should have been wanting. Amateurish."

"I don't know," Davis said. "I was rather—"

"Wipe the drool off your mouth," Vance sneered. "Or should I find
a real Mercenary to do what I need done? Because this does not inspire
confidence in your abilities."

"Forgive me," Davis said as I watched Zahra descend from her stage.
"I was distracted. It won't happen again."

People were beginning to leave the circus now, following the king
and prince's lead. Vance and Davis remained seated. "Tell me more about
Brooks Davey."

Vance handed him an envelope as he rose to his feet. "That should
be all you need. Leave a message for me at the theater when you have
more information. I expect daily updates every sunrise. The sum Orbis
Company is being paid should make that condition nonnegotiable."

Davis tapped the envelope against his thigh. "Client is king."

While Vance shuffled away, disappearing into the crowd, Davis continued to watch Zahra. She was talking to a fit woman with a few scars on
her face and a female teenager who looked as awestruck in Zahra's presence as Davis had been. Davis waited on the edge of their conversation
until there was a moment to interrupt.

"Excuse me," Davis said. "I must express my admiration at your performance. It was incredible."

"Wasn't it?" the teenager said with a smile too big for her face. Freckles covered the bridge of her nose. "How did you learn to balance yourself so well?"

"Practice," Zahra said sweetly. "You could do it with enough training."

"Really?"

"Absolutely."

The teenager looked at the woman with eyes brighter than diamonds.
All the woman could do was shake her head, thank Zahra for taking the
time to talk to them, and then shepherd her young ward home. When

they were out of earshot, Zahra said, "It's always lovely to have admirers of all ages, genders, and . . . sizes. You didn't tell me your name."

"My apologies, occupational hazard. My name is Davis. Also known as Dark of Orbis Company."

"Do you tend to linger in the shadows and brood and be a terrible addition to a party or something? Why else would you let people call you 'Dark'?" A pause. "'Davis' suits you better."

"You are one of the few that think that. And your name?"

"Zahra," the white-haired woman declared. "Formerly of Azil. Now of wherever the road takes me. A wanderer. Not lost."

"You looked at home on that rope up there."

"What a wonderful line. You must have suitors lining up to talk to you." A roll of her eyes. "Poets are better at flirting than you are. And I don't mind telling you, I loathe poets. I find rocks more engaging."

"I'll do better if you give me the chance. I wouldn't have made it this far if I wasn't somewhat impressive."

Zahra turned her back to Davis. "Come by tomorrow at midday. I can always use some entertainment before a show."

"That was our first meeting," Dark said as the darkness began to overwhelm everything. The scene was changing around us. "If I hadn't gone up to talk to her, maybe things would have been different. She would still be alive. But . . . but it's hard to dwell on things like that. I am grateful for the time I spent with her. She knew that she was my one true love."

Scenes and places and people flashed past us. Zahra and Dark kissing for the first time on top of the Church of the Wanderer after she had challenged him to a race to the top. Zahra glancing at Dark when he wasn't looking, running her fingers down his arms when working with Vance woke his rage. Dark bringing Zahra flowers after her shifts in Hollow Castle, Zahra and Dark swinging Alexis like a small child as they walked down the streets, a makeshift family. Zahra and Dark looking at buying a house together, outside Hollow. Dark renouncing his membership of Orbis Company. He had been willing to give everything up . . . for her.

They had been happy. Perfect for each other. Covering each other's flaws and forming the perfect team in the messed-up world they inhabited. Dark had been happy, whole, and human. And with her death, only a monster remained.

MISPLACED

"Do you ever wonder if there's a God, Michael?"

We were standing in nothingness, the next scene twisting into shapes around us. Only Dark was clear. He was staring absently into the darkness.

"All the time," I said. "But what does God have to do with what comes next?"

"Everything," he muttered.

Our surroundings came into focus. We were alone on the streets of Hollow, headed toward the Poison Gardens. Zahra and Davis walked in front of us, shoulders and hands touching. We followed their shadows in silence, listening to their light laughter.

"I was only supposed to work for Vance for a few weeks. Three months at most," Dark said, hands in his jacket pockets. "But because of Zahra and Alexis, I was still here two years later, doing everything in my power to remain in Hollow. No matter if Vance's contracts grew more and more dubious. He considered himself the city's makeshift savior and did what he thought was necessary to protect it.

"At times it was doing simple things: kill this overambitious Low Noble, make sure this marriage didn't happen, deliver liquor to a High Noble to keep him complacent, or rob that merchant . . . but then came a contract that made the others pale in comparison."

"What was it?" I asked.

"He wanted me to stop the killer that was operating in Hollow. The Heartbreaker."

Dark motioned toward the couple in front of us, and we listened.

"People are talking," Zahra said. Her breath was white and wispy in the cold. "There might be a serial killer in Hollow. High Noble Eliphaz's body was found last night, and Eternal Sister Laurel is still missing."

"Vance asked me to look into it today," Davis said as he rummaged in a pocket. "Said there might be clues to the killer's identity at this party we're going to. Especially since High Noble Eliphaz Braven was the last victim. Though his death seemed . . . more personal than the others."

"You really know how to show a girl a good time, don't you? Who needs romance when there are parties filled with murderers to attend."

"Murderer," Dark corrected. "We have no evidence to believe it's more than one person."

"If you say so, Dark. But I doubt my attendance is necessary. Especially since Scales and the High Nobles have implemented a curfew. Anyone out after Lights Out will be detained until their past can be examined by an Evoker."

"I'll get you back before then."

She rolled her eyes. "Sure you will."

"I mean it. I will."

They stopped walking, and Zahra made him face her. She was a little taller than him. "Dark, you are the most wonderful, loving, caring—"

I snorted, and Dark walloped me on the back of my head.

"—man I've ever known. But we both know the moment you go in there, you'll be the Black Death. The Mercenary the world fears. I'd rather you tell me to walk myself home than hear a sweet lie that melts in time."

"You're right. I should tell you everything." He took something out of his pocket. "This is going to be my last contract, Zahra. Vance is paying enough to buy that house we've been talking about outside Braven. We can be free soon."

"Dark," she said softly, something strange behind the word.

"Zahra, I've never been happier than I am with you by my side. I know it can be hard at times, but—"

She patted him on the chest. "But we should hurry to the party. The sooner you're done with this contract, the sooner we can make plans. Undeterred."

Davis hesitated, then nodded and returned his clenched fist to his pocket. They continued walking down the road hand in hand.

"You were going to propose, weren't you?" I asked.

"Yes," he said. "Lingering on these quiet moments is more painful than I thought. Every word I speak about her drives my mind to places that aren't fit to dwell in for very long. Makes my teeth clench." A pause. "We should catch up to them."

Dark jogged after his past self as I waited, trying to determine why Zahra's words had sounded so . . . off. Had Dark misunderstood something about her? Had his memories been clouded by the idea of the woman he had loved rather than the woman she had really been? And why did I have a sinking feeling in my chest . . . that Dark wouldn't have received the answer he wanted if he had asked her to marry him?

I looked down at Zahra's feet. Her shadow was missing once again, and Davis's wasn't. And unlike Edward's in the previous section, it was perfectly normal.

So Dark was trying to trick me. I couldn't blame him. Up until recently I was a living weapon fit to be manipulated by anyone smart enough to say the right words. And while I was still trying to improve, I knew how to spot memories that had been manipulated, and it all came down to the shadow. I'd have to thank Trey and Symon for revealing Light Fabricator secrets to me.

So what did these twisted shadows mean? Mine flickered in and out, which I could only assume was because the Darkness Fabrications had created two different sets of memories for me. Naverre's had been more prominent, almost obnoxiously so. As if Dark was trying to make it worse than it was. Maybe that meant Edward Naverre wasn't as wicked as he appeared to be? Any child would see the man who had killed their mother as irredeemable.

And then there was Zahra's shadow. It was gone without a trace. Was she fake? Exaggerated to an unrecognizable shape? Or had she been cleared of any darkness until only the perfect memory of the woman he had loved remained? Whatever the truth was, I'd have to uncover it. Else I would just be a pawn for Dark and his twisted desires.

I held those thoughts in my head as I caught up.

The party Dark was attending was hosted by High Noble Maflem Braven, the new head of the family after his father's death. Somehow he had convinced Scales to cordon off the Poison Gardens for it. Because nothing showed off your power and arrogance more than throwing a party somewhere that could be lethal and required absolute trust in your host.

Davis wasn't dressed any differently for this extravaganza and strolled past the guards with little pushback. Like me, they quickly realized saying no to a Mercenary was far worse for their health than annoying their employers. Especially with a flintlock pistol strapped to his chest and a hatchet swinging at his side. Zahra muttered apologies, almost by rote, as she passed them.

Like all parties, there was a theme to this one: death. It was all rather morbid, with bowls crafted from skulls and plates from pelvises, finger bones sharpened to knives, rib cage lanterns, and femurs strung together over the garden like a spider's web. There were even servants pretending to be dead. Some were hunched over as if they had been stabbed, while others were on their knees, staring up as if their eyes had rolled back into their heads and only the whites could show. Everyone in attendance wore black, and there were more drunk nobles than flies. It was typical of High Nobles. Too much money and time on their hands.

But more surprising than anything was seeing Davis and Zahra approached by Bryan Dexter, the head of the Evoker Division. He looked more normal in Dark's memory, more put together and less stoic. But still as fierce, having recognized and spotted Dark at a glance. It was hard not to be at least a little impressed.

"Mercenary," Bryan said. He marched over to Davis. "Orbis Company, correct?"

Davis didn't respond, taking two glasses of wine from a nearby servant instead. He handed one to Zahra and sipped from the other.

"What brings you to Hollow?" Bryan asked, a little more politely. "A contract?"

"Yes, two years ago. Just can't get enough of that fish gut smell." Davis took another sip. "Go away. Silence is more entertaining than conversation with you."

"What do you know about the murders that have occurred throughout Hollow in the past week? I've seen you lingering at the crime scenes."

"And that's my cue to find some other entertainment," Zahra said as she patted Davis on the back. "Find me?"

"Of course," Davis said as he watched her go, the tips of their fingers the last thing to separate. When she was gone, Davis returned to the annoyance in front of him. "You'll have to be more specific. People are murdered in Hollow all the time."

"High Noble Eliphaz Braven, Eternal Sister Laurel, Merchant Reo, and the Braven family servant Charles."

"Can we not discuss this another time?"

"I'd prefer to talk now."

"Yes, well, shame you have no authority over me, isn't it?"

Bryan put his hand on the hilt of his sword—a stupid attempt at a show of force when Davis's gun was visible. As if he stood a chance against Dark. Even back then. "Why are you here, Mercenary?"

"Investigating," Davis answered honestly. "Just like you."

"The serial killer?"

A shrug. "Maybe."

"What do you know? Tell me."

"You're quite desperate, aren't you?" Davis said with a laugh.

"Yes," he admitted. "There's a lot of attention on these deaths. I need something—anything. Whatever you know, tell me. Please. I'll give you anything in return."

"Anything?" Davis said with a lick of his lips. So he'd been like that back then, too. "Dangerous words. Are you sure you mean them?"

"Absolutely."

Davis draped his arm around Bryan and held him close. "I won't want anything too bad. Just some information on a few members of Scales. No one above you or in your division. Just so it doesn't weigh down your heart."

"Fine, now tell me: Who are you here to investigate? Who knows about the serial killer?"

"A man named—"

The moment shattered around us, like ice. Pain splintered through my body and consolidated in my mind. It was so bad, I had to close my eyes, put my hands over my ears, and hope it would stop. I didn't know how long I stood like that for, but I only opened my eyes when the pain began to fade.

Everything had changed. Dark was walking through the Scales Head-quarters hallways in mid-sentence. "—we knew we'd made a mistake. While we had been focused on . . . Michael, what are you doing?"

"What happened to the party in the Poison Gardens?"

Dark looked at me, head slightly tilted sideways. "We haven't been there for a while. Are you getting disoriented? It can happen—"

"Everything shattered around us," I said. "Did you not experience that?"

"This may be too much for you. We can pause and return later when you feel better. You've already seen enough to believe the rest of the story."

"No," I said through gritted teeth. The throbbing in my head wasn't completely gone, it was now a mild ache behind my eyes. "Just give me a second to reorient myself and I'll be fine."

Dark crossed his arms. "Well, be quick. I don't like dwelling in my memories for too long."

Something had happened. We had skipped memories and Dark hadn't realized. Which meant Dark must've lost those memories at some point.

What was the trigger? He had been about to say a man's name when the skip had happened. If it was the same as with Dawn, then the memory of this man would consistently prompt us to skip anything associated with him. And if we were skipping it, it was bound to be important. Was there a way to trick Dark into explaining . . . ah, maybe that was it. It was a *specific* name. If I got Dark to refer to him as something else, we should be fine. I had been able to remember the girl in red even though I couldn't remember Dawn.

"Dark," I said. "The person you wanted to talk to in the Poison Gardens. Did they have a pseudonym?"

He scowled at me. "Why does that matter?"

"Humor me."

"We called him Icey."

"Icey," I muttered. "Why?"

"Have you been paying attention to anything, Michael? It's pretty obvious."

"I'm just making sure I didn't miss anything. Could you refer to him as Icey from now on? It's easier to keep track of."

Dark waved me forward and we continued down the halls. His younger self was in front of us, standing in a doorframe.

"As I was saying," Dark began again, "after Icey escaped we knew we had made a mistake. Our only lead to catch the Heartbreaker was gone and we had no idea who they would strike at next. Imagine our surprise when we learned it was too late. The Heartbreaker had already begun his last hunt."

I peeked around the door. A woman was lying facedown in a pool of blood, a red hole in her back, and splintered rib bones floated on the blood around her. Bryan Dexter was on his knees beside her, pounding the bloody floor and splashing the walls as he screamed. Like all the other crime scenes I had seen, a message was written on the walls: *Welcome to the greatest show in Hollow! I have White Rose and the blue-eyed girl. Save them if you can. I'm waiting for you both where the past can be seen.*

This must've been . . .

"Bryan Dexter's wife," Dark finished my thought. "We didn't know it at the time, but she had died the day before. Because Bryan and I had been looking into the Heartbreaker, we had been chosen for the grand finale. Zahra and Naomi were missing, and we had to play the Heartbreaker's game to have a chance at saving them."

"Where can the past be seen?" I asked.

"The Kingman Keep observatory, but I didn't go there. I knew it would be impossible to save Zahra if I played by the Heartbreaker's rules. I had to become something he feared if I was going to save her."

Our surroundings changed once again. We stood on a cliff overlooking a swirling pit of darkness below. A terrible storm was approaching. "I'll be honest, Michael . . . This is the part where you may want to look away. Where you may pull the trigger out of disgust at what I have done. Are you sure you want to know, Michael? Once you know, there's no going back. You're a part of it."

"A part of what?"

"The pain I've inflicted on the world," Dark said, pacing along the cliff's edge. Rocks crumbled off it and into the void below. Thunder rumbled in the distance. "Either you'll be complicit in my actions, or you'll be trying to kill me and ridding the world of the great evil I represent. Are you sure you want to know what I did?"

I steeled myself. "Would I be here if I didn't?"

"Remember, I gave you the chance to save yourself," he muttered, extended his arms, and fell backwards over the edge into the void below. The mist swallowed him whole, and there was no trace of him as I peered over.

I should have followed my Mercenary mentor off the cliff without hesitation. But if I continued down this path, I would see only what he wanted me to. And after everything I had been through . . . I knew I had to cut through the lies to find the truth. My nullification powers had let me do it once in my mind, so maybe they'd be able to help me out again in Dark's.

I nullified my body, took a deep breath, and then tore open a door at the edge of the cliff. A blinding light shot out of the tear as more rocks fell into the void below. Before the entire cliff crumbled, I dove into the makeshift door and plunged into the memories Dark didn't want me to see.

ILLUMINATED

I landed in a place between dreams and reality where a black sea stretched on as far as the eye could see. The water was hard beneath my feet as large bubbles floated up around me like dissipating smoke. There was no sun or moon in this place to light what lay below the sky, just a million twinkling stars flickering in and out at random and a lighthouse's beacon that swept back and forth across the endless horizon. Something monstrous rumbled and roared far away, as if warning me to make my detour quick.

Moving paintings were on the outer shell of all the bubbles around me. Some depicted Dark as a wide-eyed child leaning over the side of a great ship as it sailed into the unknown. Some showed him with Alexis, caring for her like an older brother, while others showed him climbing a shadow that eclipsed the ocean below, as if it were a mountain in the middle of the sea. There were too many options. Too many memories that might look important from the outside but would be hollow when I saw them. To know a man well enough to see him unimpaired took a lifetime. People changed constantly. Sometimes for the better and sometimes for the worse. And if I were going to determine whatever Dark was hiding, I would have to be lucky or somehow figure out what he . . .

And then I saw a bubble just out of reach that showed Dark in Angelo's house in the Narrows. That was one memory I had to see. I dove into it recklessly, tumbled across the floor, and then smashed against one of the walls in the kitchen of a place I had once called home. There was nothing in the direct vicinity that gave me an indication when this meeting had happened, only that it had occurred while the four of us had been living together.

Father and son sat at the table. Neither had food or drink in front of them, just two flintlock pistols and a revolver fit to kill a king. They sat in uncomfortable silence playing with their guns, both too proud and angry to be the first to speak, until Dark decided enough was enough.

"I'm surprised your Kingman whelps aren't here," he said.

"Two of them are at work," Angelo said. "And Michael is . . . well, Michael is being Michael. No doubt he's doing something he'll later regret."

"Is he dumb or something?"

Angelo chuckled. "I like to think of him like the number zero. Full of possibilities and opportunities if given the right guidance. But he'll never grow if left to his own desires. He's too focused on the past."

"That's ironic, coming from you." Dark leaned back until his chair was tilting. "I'm here to pay respects to my mother."

"Really?" he said, slightly offended. "Why? You haven't any other year since her death."

"I'm going to propose to someone soon."

"Ah." Angelo took his hands off his guns. "Does she know about me?"

"I told her my parents were dead."

"Probably for the best," he said with resignation. "What's her name? Is she a noble? A citizen? A soldier?"

"Her name is Zahra," Dark said. A shadow of light behind him fizzled for a heartbeat when he said her name but disappeared before forming completely. "She works as the lady-in-waiting for the princess. She's from Azil."

"Like father, like son. Shade men are always falling in love with those above our lot in life," Angelo mused. "So you're here for your mother's blessing?"

"I wanted to tell her."

"Same thing." Angelo rose, pushed the table out of the way, and then ripped the rug up to expose a trapdoor. He opened it and then said, "She's down here."

What the . . . ?

Dark was wordless as he descended the ladder and his father followed. As did I, but when I tried to get close to the trapdoor, a howling black wind pushed me away from it. Dark's mind didn't want me to see whatever was down there, yet I put my forearm in front of my face and tried to focus the warmth to nullify whatever this was, refusing to relent. But the wind was too strong and whipped me out and upward as if I were stuck in the middle of a tornado.

I returned to the sea of darkness with a less-than-graceful impact. I groaned in pain but got back up without delay. I'd find another memory to inspect and find the . . .

Every memory bubble around me popped simultaneously.

An army of shadows crawled up from the depths of the sea hands-first, jutting out like newly bloomed flowers. They were the same size as Dark and lumbered toward me with an unwavering tenacity. I ran away from them as best I could—spinning, leaping, and sprinting—but they sprouted up all around no matter where I was.

They encircled me. They made clicks from their mouths like a woodpecker hammering against a tree. I had expected Dark's mind to fight against me at some point, but I hadn't expected it to happen so quickly. I had no idea where to go or what to do. If I nullified the area, would I get rid of them? Or would it kick me out of here without knowing everything? It was all so complicated, and I was running out of time to find answers as they crept closer.

But this was Dark's mind. Maybe there was . . . it was *Dark's* mind. And a perfectly brilliant solution came to me so suddenly that I nearly doubled over laughing.

Since when had Dark ever considered me a threat?

What were the odds he would see me differently in his mind?

"My name is Michael Kingman!" I shouted to the shadows. "I'm Dark's apprentice!"

They stopped and their clicking ceased. Some of them tilted their heads, while others turned their heads to those around them.

"Kingman?" one asked curiously.

I nodded. "Michael Kingman."

They chanted my name in unison like a child who had learned a new word. And then, when they grew tired of saying it, all of them melted back into the sea below us and memory bubbles returned as if they had been there all along.

I put my hands on my hips and exhaled in relief. The rules were different here. I could find the truth if I remembered where I was. So what might lead me to it? Angelo was a dead end. They interacted too rarely for me to get anything out of their meetings besides more questions. Which meant Zahra was the solution. But I didn't see her in any of the memory bubbles around me. Where was she? Where had Dark hidden his memories of . . .

The ring. That stupid ring held all the answers again. Yet this time it was the inscription: *To the light of my life, forever will I be yours.*

And what other light was there in this place besides the lighthouse? All his memories of her had to be hidden there. I ran across the black ocean toward the lighthouse, weaving around any memory bubbles. The lighthouse was surrounded by rocks jutting inward yet had a small stone staircase weaving around it to a door at the base covered in chains and locks. Words were etched into the metal: *Do not open.*

I kicked at the locks and they remained perfectly intact. I kicked at them again and none of them so much as budged. And I kicked at them repeatedly until I finally had to stop to catch my breath. I put my hands on my knees and stared at the door. Like everything else in this place, there was a logic behind what I could and what I couldn't do. Dark didn't want anyone—himself included—to know what was behind this door, so how was I supposed to get through it? Was there a phrase I could say that could make the chains break? It had worked with the shadow army, so maybe it could work again.

It had to be the truth. It broke chains and set us free, and even if we refused to admit that, once we knew it . . . we couldn't get it out of our head. But what was the truth Dark was hiding about Zahra?

"Zahra never loved Dark," I said.

The chains remained sturdy.

"Zahra was going to reject Dark's proposal."

Not even the wind rattled the chains.

I squatted down in front of the door. Dammit. I was certain one of those statements was going to be the answer. What was the truth Dark didn't want to admit? Why had he manipulated his memories of Zahra? What was I missing? I chewed at my thumbnail in frustration. The answer had to be something to do with Zahra's love for Dark . . . Oh, maybe it wasn't as simple as I had assumed. Maybe it was just sad. And maybe Dark and I shared a fate neither of us wanted to admit.

"Zahra loved Dark with all her heart," I said as I rose to my feet. "But they were incompatible. He was willing to trade his freedom for her, but she wasn't willing to do the same for him. So no matter how much either of them wanted to remain together . . . both knew it would come to an end one day."

The locks shattered like ice and the door to the lighthouse's inner sanctum cracked open.

I pulled open the door and climbed up the circular staircase, thinking of Serena with every step I took. The staircase gave on to an area surrounded by steep cliffs with a small house and a pond in the middle of it. Only a singular stone path to the house was devoid of flowers. Zahra sat at a wooden table outside of the house, and she waved me over once she saw me. I went over with a jog and she greeted me with a hug when I arrived.

"Brilliant," she said when we separated. "Dark doesn't realize your full potential. But I had an idea you'd find me. You're too persistent to ignore the signs something was wrong with how it was presented."

We sat down at the small table. "What is all of this?"

Zahra crossed her legs. "Think of this as the very center of Dark's heart. And to answer your next question: the place that you came from is the part of Dark's mind that he tries to ignore or forget."

That answer made sense with what I had seen. "Are you the real Zahra?"

She shook her head. "The real Zahra is dead. I'm Dark's memory of her, and although it's rose colored—apart from Alexis's, which has issues of its own—I am the closest thing to the real Zahra that was."

"If you're Dark's version of Zahra . . . does that mean you won't help me figure out what he's hiding?"

"No, I'll tell you everything I can. It's just . . ." She put her hand under her chin and looked away. "I loved him so much. But our relationship was doomed from the start. Then I was murdered, and he became a being focused on vengeance. He needs to be stopped before he does something irredeemable." She paused. "If he hasn't already."

"I don't know if anything can save Dark at this point."

"Nothing may. But wouldn't you rather be the man who sees the good in everyone than the one who only sees the bad? Where would you have been without your friends during the Endless Waltz?"

I crossed my arms. "Fine. I'll try. But I'm not promising anything."

Zahra leaned across the table and touched my hand. "Thank you, Michael. Ask whatever you want to. But hurry. He'll notice if you're gone much longer."

"If I need to stop him, what should I do?"

"Dark's manipulated many of his memories with Fabrications to change me from a flawed woman that he loved into a martyr that gave him purpose. So you'll need to make him remember the real me by nullifying them," she answered without hesitation. "If he's forced to face the reality of what we were, then he can't hide behind vengeance anymore."

"Wouldn't that make him more dangerous?"

Zahra brushed her hair behind her ears. "It could, but it's also the only thing that can force him to stop living in the past."

I played with my father's ring. "So it's a gamble. Either I let him stay as the monster I know or turn him into something I don't."

"No matter what you choose . . . it won't be an easy decision to make."

Rocks began to fall off the cliff into the garden below and everything shook when they hit. Zahra jumped to her feet and offered me her hand. "It's time to go, Michael. He's starting to realize something's wrong."

"But I haven't asked anything! Why did he eat that heart? Is he the Heartbreaker's successor? And why is he at war with Angelo?"

Zahra dragged me toward the pond. "He'll answer those questions himself. You have too much leverage for him to try and avoid it any longer."

"Wait, one last thing." I stood on the edge of the pond. "Does this kind of place exist in everyone?"

Zahra smiled and it warmed my heart. "Yes. Are you wondering what's in yours?"

I nodded slowly.

"It's what you want more than anything else. A physical representation of a person's strongest desires. For Dark . . ." She trailed off, looking around. "It's to have me and that house in the countryside he always wanted. Even if I never did."

"Zahra, I'm—"

She shushed me and gripped my shoulders. "I don't exist, remember? The real me is free and off on her next adventure. So don't be sad. Death is just another part of life."

I stood straight. "I'll do what I can to save Dark from himself."

"Thank you, Michael." She hugged me again. "But it's time to go. Take a deep breath before you hit the water. It'll be a bumpy journey back."

"What're you—"

She pushed me into the pond, the water enveloped me like quicksand, and I fell into whatever lay below. I had learned what Dark had been hiding from me. And now it was time to find out everything else.

44

THE PRICE OF POWER

Air rushed past as I skydived toward the darkness below, with no way to slow down. I didn't hit anything, but I was in freefall toward whatever was waiting for me. Thanks to Zahra, I knew Dark had manipulated his own memories to make his resolve stronger, so I doubted things would be clearer now that I was on the guided tour again. I'd have to brace for pain as I tried to piece together exactly what had happened. What Dark had done to get to the point of ripping other people's hearts out . . . and why he had eaten one. Was he in fact the Heartbreaker's successor?

I crashed down, hard. My body shook from the force of it. Davis was standing in front of the faceless statue in the Church of the Wanderer. He was speaking to someone just out of sight who was leaning against the door without a lock at the back of the church. None of his features were visible . . . but not in the featureless way I was used to. They had been replaced with wispy shadows that were constantly in motion. Dark hadn't forgotten what this person looked like but instead clouded them with darkness. Why had he made it so obvious?

"That's where he is?" Dark asked the stranger, arms folded.

The shadow man nodded. "Don't underestimate him. He's survived this long for a reason."

"And once I kill him . . . all I have to do is . . ."

"It'll give you what you need to kill the Heartbreaker. A non-Fabricator won't stand a chance against one of the beast Immortals. The only reason you have a chance at this one is because he's been weakened and drugged for years."

"I'll do whatever it takes to save her." Dark paused, looking at the shadow man. "Do I have to do something special to kill them?"

"Tear out their heart. Be aware, he'll be severely weakened once it's been torn out, but he won't die until you either destroy it, destroy his mind, or inherit his powers. A beast Immortal's power is concentrated in their heart, but all it takes is a single bite to cut the thread."

"Wonderful," Dark muttered as he looked at his hands. "After I do this . . . do you know where the Heartbreaker will be?"

"He's been using the tunnels that run through the East Side. Exits and entrances are hidden all over the place and he's likely holding your loved one directly under the colosseum. After you kill him, flood the whole thing. So no one else can use them in the future."

"Thank you. Now, what do you want?"

"For all the Immortals to die. It's the only way I'll be free from his curse."

I fell back into more nothingness, abandoning the scene. This fall wasn't as pleasant as the last one, my body flopping around like a fish out of water. And the impact when I landed knocked the breath out of my body again, reducing me to a hollow husk.

I was somewhere underground, with barely enough light to distinguish anything other than stone, hundreds of swords stuck in the ground, and red flowers that gave off a faint smell of citrus and vanilla. The air felt wet and sticky, and Davis was standing, hatchet and gun in hand, in front of a massive shadow that loomed over him. There was a deep rumbling coming from it and the sound of chains rattling around them while Davis screamed until his voice was hoarse.

I was falling again. It was starting to give me a headache. Where was Dark? Why was I stuck in this endless dive while he wasn't? Was it because of my detour?

The third impact didn't hurt as much as the previous two. Davis was limping down an alleyway somewhere in the Underside, one hand clutching his side as his other held a freshly dripping heart. The tips of his fingers seemed to have been bitten by frost, and he collapsed against a wall, holding up his prize.

"There's no going back once I do this," Davis muttered. "Will Zahra want to be with me if I become a monster to save her?" His eyes hardened. "Better to be alive and angry than dead and remorseful. Time to see what having unconquerable power is like." He hesitated. "Forgive me, Zahra."

When he sunk his teeth into the heart, I fell through the darkness again.

My fourth landing put me smack in the middle of the colosseum. Back when it was still standing. Dark was waiting for me, his eyes focused on his previous self. He was bloodied and broken, and his eyes were burning red, yet he hobbled toward his goal. As if pulled by an invisible force toward Zahra.

"Where were you?" I groaned as I returned to my feet. "Didn't feel like falling with me?"

"No," he said.

"I have questions."

"Let me save you the trouble. I was born a non-Fabricator, just like Angelo. I stole my powers from another and have been steadily stealing more and more ever since."

"How?"

"You have to eat the heart while it's still beating to inherit the power. That's why I ate Mocking Bird's. Thanks to her, now I can use Shadow magic, in addition to Ice and Darkness."

I was slack-jawed. "That's unnatural. I don't—"

"Do you have another explanation for being born with none but now having multiple specializations?"

He knew I couldn't. "So what does that make you? A Fabricator? A Weaver? Something else?"

Dark looked at me, incredulous. "How do you know about Weavers?"

"Did you really think I was going to remain ignorant?"

"Honestly? A little," he said. "But I'm not a Fabricator or a Weaver. The Thebians call me a Spellborn."

My heart nearly leapt out of my chest. Hadn't Domet mentioned that name to me before when he was teaching me about Fabrications? If only I had inquired about them at the time rather than let him dictate what was important for me to know.

"Spellborn have the abilities of both Fabricators and Weavers, letting us create *and* manipulate. Think of us as people who have total control over our specializations to the point where even our magical cost can be different."

That explained why Dark had an overwhelming presence whenever he used magic. He truly was a force of nature. And if the cost was different, then it only confirmed my suspicions that everything I had seen here had been manipulated by Dark to hide information. "If that's true, then why have we come across faceless people in your memories?"

"Because being a Spellborn lets me have access to Fabricating and Weaving. I lose memories when I use Fabrications. I need physical pain to use Weaving. And there's another cost when I use Spellborn abilities."

"Are you going to tell me what that is?"

Dark huffed. "Not a chance."

I didn't think he would, but it was worth asking. I'd find out the cost on my own. "Would you become a Nullification Spellborn if you ate my heart?"

Dark shook his head. "It only works with certain hearts. It's an effect of a different version of magic, one that doesn't need to be inherited through a bloodline. And there are only . . . well, now there are only nine others. Besides mine. If someone ate my heart, I'd imagine they'd gain all three of my specializations."

"So . . . how can you tell which hearts will pass on these powers?"

Dark went after his past self. "That'll become clear."

My headache was getting worse, but I followed. All the answers I wanted were within reach. We entered the colosseum's tunnels. The last time I had been here everything was collapsed and destroyed, and it hadn't looked much better only a few years ago. The cold, tight corridors were dripping with water and reeked of something that made me long for lavender. I felt safe only because we were following memories and couldn't be harmed.

"Can you tell me about the shadow man you met in the Church of the Wanderer?" I asked as we continued to walk.

"Ah," he said softly. "Didn't realize you saw that."

"I did. And I'm curious about what made you manipulate your memories so you couldn't remember any of his features."

"It was at his request."

"Since when do you do things at others' requests?"

"He gave me so much, it was only fair I do something in return. Besides"—Dark made a weird noise with his mouth—"some information is safer not knowing."

"Did you keep their name? Or is that gone, too?"

Dark stopped walking and looked back at me. "Don't you have better things to worry about than a man who helped me? This is not a fight you want to get into."

"I'll decide that for myself."

"I called him 'A.' Happy? Or will you continue to annoy me with your endless questions?"

I saluted him. "After you, master, sir."

Dark grumbled to himself but said nothing. As short-lived as this was going to be, it was fun having some advantage over Dark. Best to make the most of it while I could. After a little more walking, we entered a spacious room that had originally been used to house gladiators. The far wall had cells stacked four high against it. All the metal was rusted and peeling, and the area smelt of rotten eggs and iron. There was a small fire beginning to die in the center of the area. What little light there was revealed a woman lying on her side in one of the cells.

Davis ran to her, screaming Zahra's name.

Only to be blasted away by a plume of flame. His body skittered across the ground as another stepped into view. I didn't recognize him, and, honestly, that made me ecstatic. The man was scarily muscular, had burning red eyes with vertical slits, and had a smile sharper than an animal's. He was covered in burn marks and liked to poke at them as he walked, giggling the entire time.

"Not. Your. Time," the man said with a lightness in his voice. "Why. You. Here."

Davis didn't respond, screaming as he flung long icicles with one hand. The Heartbreaker dodged them with as little movement as possible, watching as they shattered against the wall behind him.

"That. Is. New," he said. "You. Killed. Him. Who. Exposed. Secrets?"

Davis spat blood, then raised his hatchet and flintlock pistol.

"Show. Me. Powers."

The Heartbreaker exploded into smoke and fire. Davis slammed his elbow against the ground, and an ice wall shot up from the floor to block the encroaching flames. The ice and fire clashed, steam rising from where they met. Davis was breathing heavily, glancing around.

The Heartbreaker leaned in behind Davis so his lips brushed against his ear. "Not. Bad. Interesting."

Dark whipped around, but it was too late. The Heartbreaker lifted him off the ground by the neck like a curious child with a new toy. Fire nipped at the ice Davis tried to generate, so he lifted his gun to the Heartbreaker's chest and then pulled the trigger. The gunshot echoed off the walls while the bullet went through him and lodged into the ground below them. There was a small fiery hole where it had collided with the Heartbreaker.

He kept giggling and squeezed Davis's neck harder. Davis swung his hatchet at the hand holding him up. It passed through it and came out the other side so hot, Davis croaked before dropping it. Yet he remained suspended in the air, strings of flame holding the severed parts of the arm together. The Heartbreaker's arm repaired itself while Davis continued to struggle.

"I. Overestimated. You." A sigh. "Make. This. Quick."

Davis exploded into ice, disappearing for a moment and dropping to the ground. The Heartbreaker's hand froze solid, and he said something in a different language as he thawed the ice. Steam rose around them as Davis knelt on the ground, weaponless.

"Maybe. I. Wrong."

"Shut up," Davis muttered.

The Heartbreaker licked his lips. "I. Want. Fun."

"Shut up," Davis repeated, louder.

"Which. One. Yours. White. Or. Blue."

"Shut up!" Davis screamed, and threw a wave of ice toward the Heartbreaker.

The Heartbreaker smiled and returned a massive blast of fire of his own. From his mouth.

The two forces of nature collided halfway between the two men with an audible *thump*, sizzling and steaming and crackling. Both men held their ground with some effort. Neither was strong enough to push back the other.

"You snapped," I said to Dark as we watched the stalemate.

"Yes," he answered, eyes straight ahead.

"What did you lose?"

"Everything."

The Heartbreaker scowled as his body began to shake. Hardening, as if metal . . . metal scales began to cover his body. His features became angular, more animalistic than human. Two veiny membrane wings popped out of his back and then a tail, eerily familiar to that of the Wyvern I had faced during the Endless Waltz, thumping against the ground before gently moving back and forth like a cat's. And then . . . then *it* happened. The Heartbreaker's body transformed . . .

. . . and by the time he was finished, a fire-breathing dragon stood in front of me.

I nearly pissed myself. There was no denying it this time. This was a dragon, straight out of the stories. And it stood in front of me, clear as day. With a barbed tail, and bright red scales, and . . . and flying fuck was it big.

"Thirteen hearts . . . ," Dark said, ". . . for the thirteen magical beasts that reside in this world. The Thebians may call us Spellborn, but the rest of the world has a simpler term—'dragon.' Because once you eat a dragon's heart, you become one."

My heart was in my throat. It felt like it was about to burst. If it even could in this place.

"Tell me this is just your imagination. Or your memories have been corrupted. This is some sort of illusion. Dragons can't . . . Dragons aren't . . . *You* can't be . . ." I trailed off, my words lost.

"All nightmares have some basis in reality."

"I thought dragons would be the exception."

"If only we were so lucky." He looked down at me with pity. "So, Dragonslayer, do you think you're still worthy of that title, or will you renounce it in shame?"

I slapped myself. Monsters were real. Dragons were real. And Dark was one of them. But at least I knew the truth. No matter what he was— or what Angelo might be—I would be the poor fool standing in defiance of whatever went bump in the night. Nothing could make me waver. I met Dark's eyes. "I've never been worthy of anything . . . but to be born great is kind of boring, isn't it? I'd rather claw my way to the top with trails of blood marking my defiance than follow the path fate dictates for me. And after everything I've been through already . . . do you truly think a sweet lie would be my peak?"

Out of nowhere, and despite the fact that Davis now faced down a dragon, his ice began to gain ground on the fire. It crept toward the Heart-breaker, and there was nothing he could do to stop it. Blood was trickling out of Davis's eyes, and he was lost to his rage. How had he not become a Forgotten in this moment? And then, instantly, the duel was over. The Heartbreaker was frozen in ice, encased completely from tail to toe.

Davis didn't hesitate: he sprinted toward the beast. He snatched his hatchet off the ground and then leapt onto the thick ice, lodging the tip of the hatchet into it. He used his free hand to yank it out and waited for the ice to turn to scales and elongate into talons before plunging the hatchet into it again. He dug around a little, dyed the ice red, and then pulled out a beating heart. He froze over the hole he had created before he jumped off.

"I don't know if I can watch this part," Dark whispered.

"It's Naomi in that cell, isn't it?"

"Yes," Dark said, tears falling freely. He looked away and stopped the scene before his past self reached the cell and learned who was in there. "Zahra was already dead . . . I just didn't know."

"Is there anything else I need to see?" I asked, trying to make sense of it all.

He wiped the tears away. "One more scene . . . and you will know everything."

Dark didn't show me any of the aftermath. How he had found Zahra's body, or how he had brought Naomi back to Bryan, or what he had done with the Heartbreaker's heart. When the background came into focus, we were in the Hollow cemetery, standing in front of a pyre. Zahra's body was carefully arranged, arms crossed over her chest and coins covering her eyes. Hundreds of flowers surrounded her.

Davis hovered around her pyre, torch in one hand and a lock of white hair in the other.

"Alexis didn't want to be there for it," Dark said. "I didn't blame her. Saying goodbye to loved ones can be . . . difficult. I didn't know it at the time, but she was applying to join Orbis Company while I did this. To make sure she wouldn't be left alone."

"She was so young when she joined."

"No younger than me," Dark said. "Hopefully she escapes my curse."

Davis lit the pyre and it caught quickly. Smoke billowed out like a torrent and obscured everything, including Vance approaching him. Davis only acknowledged the man when he was within arm's reach, his focus on the pyre.

"I'm sorry it ended this way," Vance said, arms folded behind his back. He stood straight as an arrow.

"She deserved better."

"Many do. It's a shame she was caught up in something like this." He cleared his throat. "Did you finish it? Is the Heartbreaker dead?"

"I tore out his heart," Davis mumbled.

"And the informant I sent you to?"

"Same end."

"I'm assuming you ate his heart, correct? To kill the Heartbreaker?"

Dark looked over his shoulder. "Did you know what he was?"

The cemetery darkened, as if clouds obscured the sun. "Obviously. All the contracts I've given you have been building to this moment. I had to make you strong enough for what is to come. Your father is a failure, but—"

"My father?"

"Yes, your father. I raised him, you know. But the fool ran away before he was ready to help me. He did come begging for my help once or twice, and he promised me a great deal in return for my aid. You."

Dark faced the old man as he tucked the lock of Zahra's hair into his pocket. "You helped my father? With what?"

Black tendrils began to come off Vance as the monster within showed his canine teeth. "Nothing in Naverre was possible without me. Except for that last murder. He wanted to do that personally. With his own hands. I even helped your father dispose of a prince who was watching Celona and its moon-fall a little too closely. A shame that Kingman got involved—"

"You . . . You're the monster my father tried to warn me about. My grandfather," Dark interrupted. "You're the reason Angelo made me help him kill Edward."

Vance bowed. "You caught me. But worry not, Dark. As tragic as this death was, it is for the best. She could never live among us. She would have been a peasant among gods. There will be others and—"

Davis's hand punched through his chest, gripped his beating heart, and then ripped it out. It came out with a sickening *plop* as the old man fell to his knees, awestruck.

"What . . . Why . . . would . . . Why did you do this?"

Dark inspected the black heart in his hand. "You were the darkness dragon, correct? I've always been curious about what it would be like to use those Fabrications."

"I was about to give you everything, and you've thrown it away . . . for what? Revenge?"

"Something like that." Dark kicked his grandfather over onto his back. Vance struggled to breathe.

"I made you strong enough to walk among the Immortals—"

"Enough." Davis squeezed the beating heart in his hand, and the old man spasmed on the ground. "Was it worth it? Whatever it was you wanted me to be, it won't happen. Instead, you've given me purpose."

"Purpose . . . ?"

"I'm going to kill them all," Dark said casually. "No more dragons. No more Immortals. You told me there are only eleven left, including us. It's an easy enough genocide to accomplish."

"Imbecile. The Heartbreaker was the worst of us. The others will stop you."

"Did you tell the Heartbreaker to target Zahra?"

Men of the Shade family never groveled, and Vance was no different. "Yes. Because who cares about some mor—"

Vance never finished his sentence. Davis crushed his head beneath his boot and then wiped the sole clean on the grass and faced the fire. As the flames devoured the pyre, Davis took a bite out of the black heart and chewed slowly.

The scene around us collapsed, and I was shot into the air as if guided upward by an invisible force. There was nothing else to see in Dark's memories. I had seen everything I needed to, and I truly wished I hadn't.

45

SCORCHED GROUND

"Genocide."

The word was hollow on my tongue.

Dark motioned for Nonna to leave.

"Genocide," Dark repeated. "I'm going to kill them all. Partially to avenge Zahra and partially to prevent anyone from ever getting ahold of their hearts. I stole a dragon's power, who's to say others won't, too? Who's to say my father won't? He's dangerous enough, even without any magical abilities. Imagine if he gained some."

I couldn't. I couldn't imagine anything right now. My head was still spinning, struggling to understand—comprehend—what I experienced in Dark's memories.

"Prove what I just saw wasn't an illusion."

Dark did. He laid his hand flat on the table, and I watched as it began to morph. The nails grew longer, sharper, and harder, and his skin began to harden and fold over itself as if to make layers of scales. His eyes started to burn red . . . and then Dark exhaled and shook out his hand, and it returned to normal. Human.

I couldn't stop myself from laughing. "Only the hand? C'mon, Dark. Turn into a dragon! Do it. Do it!"

"I don't want to," Dark said. "The cost is too high, and I have too much left to do before I die."

"That sounds like an excuse."

"It does. But if I forget about Zahra, I lose my purpose. What do you think I would be like then? What would I do with the power I have? Right now I want to take down as many of the remaining dragons as I can before one gets lucky. They deserve to die, just like any other mortal, and I'm going to make sure they do."

"It's still genocide."

"Yes," he said. "I told you I'm not a good person. I'm a monster. But I will carry that evil and do what is right to spare others my pain."

"You sound like Angelo."

Dark opened his mouth in immediate protest. To yell and scream. But instead he softly said, "When I die, the world will be a better place. He doesn't want to die. He wants to be reunited with my mother. That's the difference."

I ran my nullified hands over my face. What was I supposed to do after hearing *that*? Did I let him remain the monster I knew? Or nullify his memory manipulations and make him something else? Dammit. Where were the heroes? Where were the ones who could rise above all evil and hatred and . . . and I already knew the answer. They had died, nobly or stupidly. And only people like Dark and me were left behind. The bad pretending to be good. Those who wanted to be better but always came up short.

"I suppose that's your answer," Dark said as he motioned to the gun lying on the table between us. It had been sitting there since he began the last part of this tale. Neither of us moved for it.

It didn't matter anymore. I wasn't going to stop him or nullify his memory manipulations yet. His war was his to fight . . . and part of me agreed with him. These Immortals were unnatural, and they influenced history and the world as they saw fit. Wasn't it time that they lost that power?

"There's one thing I still don't understand," I began. "If you killed the original Heartbreaker—the Fire Dragon—then who is doing the killing now? I'm assuming you're not lying that it's not you."

"I'm not," he said. "And I never killed the Fire Dragon, only tore out its heart."

"Nothing can live without—" I remembered what the shadow being in the church had said about dragons not dying until their heart or mind was destroyed. "What did you do, Dark?"

He hesitated. "I wanted him to suffer. To feel a fraction of the pain that I did. Killing him was too easy. Too simple. So I imprisoned him in Hollow and left him to suffer for eternity."

"Seriously? You imprisoned a heartless dragon in Hollow? Where?"

"I don't remember."

"What do you mean you don't remember?"

"I'm not sure whether it's from magic use or a Darkness Fabrication, but I've forgotten."

Could it be another thing in his memories he manipulated? At least he was honest about this one. "You're telling me you tore out a dragon's heart, imprisoned it, and left it to suffer for two years, and now it's loose in Hollow?"

"Yes. But I set up countermeasures for this. I left myself a trail of memories that would lead me back to the dragon's prison if I ever forgot."

I ran my hands over my face.

Dragons. Part of me still wanted to disbelieve it. That dragons were real. As if that weren't bad enough, it wasn't just a dragon that was hunting us. It was a vengeful dragon serial killer whose heart had been stolen by Dark.

It was a complete disaster in the making.

"Are you sure?"

Dark motioned for me to elaborate.

"That we're dealing with dragons? That it's not large reptiles? Ancient beasts that—"

"Michael, I'm one of them. I can freeze anything with a touch. I can make darkness move like something straight out of your nightmares. We have a shattered moon in the sky. Magic exists and you can nullify it. Why does the idea of dragons make you angry?"

"Because," I said drawing out the word, "if dragons are real, then what else is? Titans? Gigantic sea monsters? An afterlife for the good and bad?" The last one I said without emotion: "God?"

"Does one of those scare you more than the others?"

I rose from my seat and began to pace. "Isn't it obvious? Inheriting the Kingman legacy and deciding to end the rebellion is one thing—those are my choices—but my family is at war against God! How am I supposed to win that?"

"You can't. So don't try to. It's not your fault you were enlisted into a pointless war when you were born. Abandoning impossible quests doesn't make you a villain."

"I wish I could, but the Kingman family is supposed to hold those in power accountable. What is God but another Royal who doesn't understand the lives of those beneath them? Who makes them answer for their inactivity, their crimes, their decisions? It's what the Kingman family is sworn to do!"

I expected Dark to laugh, but when he didn't, it caught me off guard. "We all make our choices, Michael. Make sure you're willing to face the consequences of that one before committing."

My voice was smooth and true. "If I ever meet God, I'm going to punch them in the jaw and hope I break something. I won't back down before a bully, even if the fight is unwinnable. That's my choice."

"I thought *I* was the insane one."

"No, it's always been me. Now, how do we kill this dragon before it hurts anyone I care about?"

"We don't." Dark took a breath and continued. "I've tried everything

I can think of to find the Heartbreaker, and I've failed. I only found him last time because I was tipped off. But I beat the Heartbreaker once, and I will do it again."

"So your plan is to walk into their trap and hope we survive it?"

"No, my plan is to protect everyone inside Kingman Keep. He's a dragon, they can be overwhelmed. I tore out his heart once already, so he's already severely weakened. And he can't fully recover unless he gets a replacement . . . and now that Mocking Bird is dead, I'm the only one in Hollow with a dragon heart." Dark's eyes flickered red. "When he comes for me this time, I'll make sure he stays dead."

"What about his original heart? Couldn't he just find that one? It's out there if he's still alive."

Dark shook his head. "There's absolutely no way he'll find it. That thing is so well hidden I doubt the person who has it even knows."

I gripped the edges of the table. "How does he even have the strength to hunt people down? I thought tearing out a dragon's heart made them utterly useless and weak?"

"It does." Dark exhaled. "My best guess is that he's using human hearts to sustain his energy when he can. But they wouldn't last long. A few hours at most—maybe less if he's using his powers. That's probably why he initially targeted the weak. Everyone else would be too strong for him to fight against until he got used to what his limitations were."

"Could he have someone helping him? A successor or something?"

Dark looked at me like I was a moonstruck fool. "He was imprisoned for the past two years. That's not really conducive to making lasting relationships."

And yet I couldn't get what happened in the tweeker den out of my mind. How did he kill everyone inside and then get outside in a few heartbeats? Was he really that strong? Even with limitations? Would I stand a chance against him if I didn't have Dark with me?

"Whether you like it or not, we lost our chance to end this early. Now the best thing to do is wait for an opportunity."

"I'm tired of being on the defensive."

Dark leaned forward across the table. "Don't be an idiot, Michael. Be smart. Be safe. Let the dragon come to us. Trying to hunt it—to follow my trail of memories—is a waste of time. They've already escaped."

"At least tell me the first clue in the trail."

"Braven knows where the flowers grow." A pause. "Though I suppose that clue is useless now, too, eh? When you're ready, I'll be at the keep."

He left the room. I stifled a yawn and then rubbed my eyes. When was the last time I slept or rested? Could I keep going? Did I have a choice? There was so much to be done.

I left the Hollow Library, feeling more at ease once I was outside with the late-morning sunlight on my skin. It made me feel human again and was the boost I needed. I had to keep moving forward.

Now that I knew the Heartbreaker was a dragon, I wanted to know more about what I was dealing with. I had to know what went bump in the night and, more importantly, how to kill it. There was only one man who could give me the answers I wanted.

And after hearing Dark's story, I knew where the past could be seen. And where the Archmage would be if I ever wanted to know more about immortality.

The answer was Kingman Keep. Or, to be more specific, the broken observatory at the top of it. It was one of the highest points in the city, and the best place to see the stars and moons at night. They looked so close, as if they could be touched with an extended hand. And if history were to be believed, Kingman Keep was where the Hollow and Kingman families had decided to rebel against the Wolven Kings.

———————

It was exactly as other observatories were, albeit more run-down and neglected. The Archmage was examining the broken telescope at the center of it when I arrived. Half-burned books and charts were all around him, spread out too carefully for it to be random. I wondered how he had gotten here without any of us noticing below. Maybe he jumped up from the outside.

"Archmage," I said. "Amaranths."

The thin man took his eye off the telescope and then pulled up his right sleeve. "Immortality . . . I don't give out that code often. Are you one of my apprentices?"

"No, I'm Michael Kingman. You told me to find you in a place where the past can be seen if I wanted to learn how to kill an Immortal."

"And why do you want to know that?"

"Because the Heartbreaker Serial Killer is back and terrorizing Hollow. They're a dragon, and I need to know how to kill them. Can you help me?"

The Archmage yawned, then motioned for me to take a seat at a nearby table. "Let's get to work."

THE PRICE OF
IMMORTALITY

"So," the Archmage began, pulling out two journals, a jar of ink, and some quills from his pockets. "What do you know about immortality?"

"I know there's two kinds. True and beast. Beast Immortals can't die from sickness or age, but they can die like any other mortal. You suggested I shoot them in the head."

"It's good advice."

"Dragons are beast Immortals, yes?" I asked.

The Archmage paused in opening his jar of ink. "Do I have to show you a dragon's body, or will my word suffice?"

"Just making sure," I said. "I know nothing about true Immortals. Except that they exist. How many are there?"

He paused, dipping his quill. "Hard to tell. When you live long enough, you meet some. But even I'm unsure which are true Immortals and which aren't. No one wants to reveal what they are. It's all power plays and foolish games."

"What are *you*?"

"I don't know."

"You don't know? How is that possible?"

"Because I'm a Forgotten? Calm yourself. I'll check. I keep the most important information near my heart." The Archmage pulled down the collar of his shirt and looked. More words were inked on his chest, but it was hard to make them out with only a single lantern on the table. "Says I'm true. That's a shame."

"How do I kill true Immortals?"

"It's complicated. Are you here to learn how to kill a true Immortal or a dragon?"

"Can you tell me about both?"

He ran his hand through his hair. "So much talking. You're not even my apprentice."

"Consider me an investment for the future. Didn't you want to kill Immortals? I'm a Kingman, and I'd make a damn fine weapon."

"I should have brought something to eat," he said mindlessly. "Do you know what they call the Kingman family in the Warring States?" Before I had a chance to answer, he continued, "The Thronebreakers. In Eham they call you the Nooses of Fate after what the Seafarer did. In Azil you're known as the Corrupters, for obvious reasons. And those are just the ones I remember. Do you notice a trend?"

"We're known all over the world."

"You are. For trying to shape it to your will." A breeze blew through the observatory, ruffling his papers and my hair. "Did you know Immortals didn't appear until the Wolven Kings fell and your family took the stage? As if they were created to counter the foolish ideology, passed down through the generations, that one family could make a difference if they stuck to their beliefs."

"What are you trying to tell me?"

"Your actions have consequences. Your family, despite trying to do good, messed the natural order up. One family isn't meant to have such renown, and it makes everyone else complacent. And we only began to see the consequences of that when you were no longer around."

"Good thing we've returned, then."

The Archmage leaned back in his seat, hands behind his head, and stifled a yawn. "Everything ends eventually."

Not the Kingman family. Not as long as I drew breath. "Are you going to tell me about true immortality and dragons or not?"

"I'm a teacher, I'll get to my point eventually, and I will tell you what you want to know. So long as you promise that once you've accomplished your ends, you will consider letting the Kingman legacy end with you."

I hadn't expected him to say that. I told him as much.

"I worry for the future with the Kingman family around."

"But you're fine with Immortals?"

"No, but if you're here to learn how to kill them, I imagine you won't stop until they're all gone. Then it'll just be you, your family, and that dangerous ideology."

"I'm not promising to end the Kingman legacy."

"Consider it. That's all I'm asking."

I told him whatever he wanted to hear and then folded my arms. "Tell me."

The Archmage flipped to a page in his journal that had been marked with a big X at the top. "We'll start with dragons. There are thirteen in total—one for each of the primary Fabrication specializations."

"Primary Fabrication specializations?"

"Yes," he said matter-of-factly. "The basic specializations. You probably know them without realizing. Fire, Lightning, Sound, Wind, Light, Dark—"

"Light and Darkness are rare, though."

"Basic does not refer to their rarity but whether or not they are building blocks for different specializations. Take the Poison specialization. At first I thought it was another basic specialization, but that's not the case.

Whenever there's a Poison Fabricator, their parents are always Smoke and Fire. No exceptions."

"But that means—"

"Magic is evolving. Slowly and steadily. Every day we discover new specializations that we didn't know existed decades ago. Who knows what we'll see in the future?"

I was awestruck. Magic was supposed to be wondrous but static. The boundaries of it could be pushed, but Domet . . . but Domet had said magic hadn't changed. That the user had to be clever. This explanation undid that. Had he lied to me? I was laughing at the thought. After everything he had done, why did I still trust anything he said?

"Let me ask a hypothetical, then. If you had a child that was a Light Fabricator and a mother that was a non-Fabricator, could you determine what the father was?"

The Archmage tapped a finger against his temple. "You could narrow it down. Fire is the most likely, but you couldn't eliminate any of the specializations in the same family tree like Lava or—"

"Lava?" I interrupted. "You mean that stuff that comes out of volcanoes? Fabricators can have that specialization?"

"The Princess of Hollow can force people to kneel to her. Is lava so much harder to believe in?"

I gulped and looked aside, trying to calm my blush. "So there are thirteen dragons. Do you know who they are and what they want?"

"I don't meddle in the affairs of other Immortals. But . . . I know a few. The Ice Dragon is—"

"Dead."

"Ah. Unfortunate. I rather liked him. The only other dragon I know the identity of is the Nullify Dragon. But he hasn't been seen in years. Last I heard, he went by the name Idris Ardel and was an Evoker for—"

"Idris Ardel is a dragon?"

He arched an eyebrow. "You know him?"

"He was the lead investigator for Davey Hollow's murder."

"If you ever see him, say hello for me. He was the one who sought me out once I became immortal. He taught me a lot, and warned me about even more."

I massaged my temple. "What do they want?"

"Each has their own motives and desires, which change over time. At one point the Lightning Dragon wanted to be a god, but now I think she's started serving one of the prophets. Being immortal can be boring, so they find ways to entertain themselves."

I thought of Domet. And then of Dark and the genocide he wanted to commit. "Do you think humanity would be better off without them?"

"Humanity would be better off without a lot of things, but without dragons . . . I'm unsure. They have a purpose in nature, I just don't know what it is. I worry who or what would fill the void if they went away."

"Maybe the world would be more peaceful?"

He laughed, and I rolled my eyes. "The world thought the same when the Wolven Kings fell. But you can believe in a delusion if you desire."

Whether I would sit back and watch Dark commit genocide wasn't up for discussion today. The Heartbreaker had to be stopped, no matter if it meant playing into Dark's plans. But I couldn't just keep my eyes on the present, I had to look toward the future, too.

"Tell me about true immortality."

"True immortality," he said, as if savoring the words in his mouth like a fine wine, "is a disease. A curse. A flaw. But most of all . . . a refusal. It's the belief that even in the face of death someone can return to life if they want to."

"What?"

"It happens on the verge of death, and what the Immortal sees varies for each person. But so long as they refuse to die, and drag themselves back to life . . . they will return. Immortal."

"That's it?"

The Archmage closed his journal gently. "No. It requires a burning passion. A goal that one must accomplish that warrants utterly rejecting the natural order of things. Not many have that. You'd be amazed how easy it is to die. Life is oh, so cruel and oh, so . . . painful."

"You're omitting key details, aren't you? That's too simple."

The Archmage stared me down. "I'm glad it's so obvious to you. I have no intention of creating more people like me, so excuse me if I don't tell you every secret. The refusal of death is the information you needed to know. Or else you would have no way of killing them."

"What do you mean?"

He leaned his elbows on the table, looked me in the eyes, and said, "If you want to kill a true Immortal, the key is to fulfill their undying wish and to strike while they're happy. Or risk having their desire change and have them remain immortal."

So Domet had been telling the truth about that. He truly couldn't die until his desires were satisfied. Was proving my father's innocence what he actually wanted, or did it have to do with Angelo Shade and the regrets he had when he told him about the secrets of immortality and how to bring—

"Do you know how to bring someone back from the dead?" I asked.

The Archmage was taken aback. "That's impossible. Once someone dies, they're dead for eternity."

"I heard differently," I said. "Are you sure?"

"I'm not omniscient, so, it's possible, but . . ." He started laughing, and laughing, and laughing. "What a mess this world would be if the dead could return. As if immortality isn't enough of a headache."

"What did you desire so much that you ended up immortal?"

The Archmage rose to his feet, gathered his belongings, and said, "I would tell you if I knew. The answer is probably somewhere in my journals, but I have no idea where. If you ever find out, let me know."

"Wait," I said, remembering what I had seen during Joey's surgery. "Did you ever teach any of your apprentices how to perform heart surgery?"

"Any fool with sharp-enough tools can take a heart out without damaging it. But to put one back in? And have the host live? They would need as much experience as I have. More than can be learned in a normal lifetime."

That didn't help me figure out if the Heartbreaker had an accomplice. Someone had to be putting human hearts into him. He couldn't be doing it himself, right?

"Thank you for telling me so much. I wish there were a manual for all of this," I said with an awkward laugh. "Every time I seem to get a grasp on what the limitations are, it changes. And that's just concerning Fabricators. Not to mention Weavers or Spellborn or whatever else is out there."

"I felt the same when I began researching magic." He held up his quill. "Things became much easier when I realized this is the base of all magic."

"A quill?"

The Archmage exhaled like a summer breeze. "I meant its substance." He continued when he noticed my confusion. "'Substance' is a term that we researchers use to describe something that takes up space. This quill is substance. As are you and me and this keep and even this table we're sitting at. It's all substance, just different sizes and weights and what makes up different things."

"So magic is in everything?"

"No. Magic influences everything." He pushed his seat in. "Let me explain in terms of Fabricating. Each Fabricator has a specialization that they can create, correct?"

I nodded.

"Think of the process of using magic like firing a gun. It takes gunpowder and heat to shoot the bullet, and our bodies are like that with magic. Our magically laced blood is the heat that causes the gunpowder—our memories—to explode into our specialization. Be it flames or lightning or a nullification area. Other magic types do something different to matter, depending on your specialization, and have a different cost. Weavers manipulate substance. Insatiables destroy substance. Abyss Walkers transfer substance and—"

"Wait, what are Insatiables and Abyss Walkers?"

"I literally just told you what they are. Destroy and transfer."

I blinked a few times, trying to figure out if my brain was still working. After what I had learned with Dark, this conversation was like having someone smash me in the side of the head with a hammer after I was already wounded. "So what countries are those magic users from? Weavers are from the Thebian Empire, Fabricators are from Hollow, and Spellborns are just wandering cannibals."

"Abyss Walkers are nomadic, so it's hard to narrow them down to a single country." The Archmage pulled down his shirt. "I don't think I know where Insatiables are from." He paused. "That's a rather large gap in my knowledge. Did I deliberately hide it from myself? Interesting."

I couldn't let this opportunity go to waste. What was the next logical question? "Are the abilities of Insatiables, Abyss Walkers, and Weavers passed through blood like Fabrication is?"

The Archmage shook his head. "Fabrication is through the bloodline. Spellborn are through cannibalism. I don't know how Abyss Walkers or Insatiables get their powers. But for Weaving, some of the more basic specializations can be taught. The rarer and more powerful ones are harder to figure out."

And there was the answer to why the Thebian Empire wasn't a kingdom like Hollow. Was their entire army taught how to use magic or was it only a select portion? "Does that mean I could learn how to use Weaving?"

"Yes. In fact, plenty of nobles pass off Weaving as Fabricating. Some of the High Nobles actually hire Weaving Masters to teach their children a specialization that makes sense in their family, or else their marriage desirability would decrease drastically."

"What?" I spat out.

The Archmage looked at me flatly. "I felt that I was quite clear."

"You were. I just . . . didn't think that was possible. But it makes sense. What good is a noble in Hollow society without magic?" Both things would be something to investigate once my life calmed down. Maybe Gwen could learn Weaving to make up for her lack of Fabrications. "How many countries have different kinds of magic?"

The answer fell off his tongue without weight.

"Can you repeat what you said? I missed it."

The Archmage's eyes narrowed and he became more alert than he had for our entire conversation. He even set his quill down. "Do me a favor. Watch my lips very carefully."

The Archmage said something—his lips moved and a sedated breath lingered underneath the words—but before they could reach my ears, the wind carried them away with a strong gust.

"Why are you speaking so softly?"

And he laughed at me, a sound that was light and airy, as if it belonged to a child rather than a full-grown man. "If you couldn't hear what I said, then you've forgotten it. And since the words are so specific, there's nothing your mind can replace it with, so it has to erase it outright." His laughter grew louder. "And you want to hear the best part? If you know what I've said, then that means you figured out one of the great mysteries of the world!"

I stared at him, speechless.

"Congratulations, Michael. I don't know how or why, but you figured out a secret only a handful of people know. Then your mind forgot it and you can never relearn it. What an unparalleled cruelty."

"What did I figure out?" I gripped the edge of the table. "Wait. Whatever I learned must've happened before the day I lost recently, otherwise my mind wouldn't have had to take all of it from me, correct?"

The Archmage nodded. "That's a safe assumption."

"So when did I learn this mystery? Was it sometime as a child? Or in the years after my father's execution?" I tightened my grip on the table. "How important is it, truly? Could it mean the difference between life and death if I go to war with Immortals and dragons and whatever else is out there?"

"If you want any chance of winning, you'll need the whole truth. Not just the fraction of it that I know."

"How am I supposed to solve a mystery that I can't remember?"

The Archmage calmed himself, tore a page out of his journal, and wrote long, frantic sentences on the page. Then he folded it in half and wrote *The Last Secret is hidden at the Institute of Amalgamation* on it. He handed me the folded paper from across the table. "This is everything I know about that secret. If anyone has answers, the people at the Institute of Amalgamation will."

I repeated my previous question.

"That's the beauty of it: you don't have to. If what you've said is true— that you're hunting down Immortals and dragons—then you'll attract too much attention from them if you go to the Institute of Amalgamation. Especially after they discover we've met. But if you send another in your stead . . . well, the truth might finally come out."

"Why can't you solve it? Why put this on me?"

"Because I've tried to and failed," he said. "By the time I figure out where any relevant information might be, it's conveniently gone by the time I arrive. Immortals keep track of other Immortals, and, sadly, I've ended up on the do-not-talk-to list for a lot of them. Apparently, they don't like certain secrets getting out."

"This is insane," I muttered. "The Institute of Amalgamation is on the other side of the continent. How can I ask someone to travel that far to solve a secret I can never learn?"

"I don't know. But it sounds like the perfect quest for someone who wants to escape from their life or someone who lacks purpose. Do you know anyone like that?"

Not off the top of my head. Not with everything going on. This was all too much for me right now. I stuffed the letter into my jacket and then ran my hand through my hair. The mystery could wait to be solved. Even if I didn't understand how I of all people found the answer to one of the world's greatest mysteries. I was a fool, not a scholar. And yet . . . why did I always seem to be at war with my memories?

The Archmage gave me a wave as he left. "If we ever meet again, don't be offended when I don't remember you. It's not personal."

I put my feet up on the table and rubbed my face. I knew more than I did before, but there was still so much I didn't. Like what Domet desired so much that he ended up immortal, or whether Angelo Shade's true goal really was to bring Katherine back to life. But knowledge was power. And this knowledge was a weapon.

I stared at the city below me for a lingering moment, taking in all the midday festivities. It looked so peaceful, and for a moment I was at peace, too.

———

I climbed down the outside of Kingman Keep to avoid Dark—almost falling to my death only twice—and set off to end a war.

Even before a major state event—the princess's coronation—with a serial killer and a king killer running loose in the city, security in the Upper Quarter was downright terrible. I was able to sneak in using my usual route, which I'd used repeatedly during the Endless Waltz. They were all too busy dealing with the banners and parade route and stalls and whatever else the nobility decided was mandatory for the celebrations, even though Hollow was under a soft siege.

I didn't bother knocking on Domet's door but walked straight into his main room. He was sitting surrounded with books, a goblet of clear liquid at his side. More liquor, so early? Disgusting. Looking up, Domet said, "Michael?"

"You stole me out of the castle after King Isaac killed himself. Can you smuggle me into it again? I need to speak to the princess."

"Why?"

"Because she's going to help me kill the emperor. We're ending this rebellion together."

SECRETS EXPOSED

Domet helped me without asking for anything else, not even for details about my plan to kill the emperor. Not that I could give them to him if he asked. I'd lost that day in my memories, and only thanks to Trey had I remembered how the plan began. Hopefully all the other steps I'd put into place would run smoothly without me remembering them.

And it all began with the princess. I had to convince her, today, that I hadn't killed her father. If I failed, well . . . then I didn't entirely know what would happen. I might be executed. Hollow might fall. The nobility might be burned alive in their keeps or be beheaded on the steps of the Church of the Wanderer until the stones were stained red. Many unpleasant things. Though not helping Dark commit genocide wasn't a terrible outcome. When did life become so complicated?

Thankfully for me, I had other things to focus on. Domet led me into an alleyway near his house. After moving a discolored stone, he revealed a ladder and then a dark tunnel beneath that headed in the direction of Hollow Castle. He took a lantern from the wall, lit it, and moved the stone back into place, then we walked down the secret passage to the castle together. Only a flickering flame lit our path.

"Where does this tunnel emerge?" I asked.

"Depends. Where do you want to go?"

"Infirmary," I said. "Three Ravens were injured during the confrontation with the Waylayer in the College of Music. Serena will want to be close to them, and Efyra will want her to be, too. Reduces the number of places they need to protect."

"Good reasoning," Domet said with some hesitation, which was odd. "I heard about what happened in the College of Music. Bold. Very bold, Michael. Surprised they didn't kill you. But I was wondering, who tore out the Waylayer's heart? Was the Heartbreaker there?"

"Does it matter? Famine is dead either way."

"Everything matters to me."

I had to work with Domet to get into the castle. That didn't mean I had to tell him everything I knew. He clearly didn't share everything with me. "Not sure. Hit my head trying to rush the Waylayer and passed out. When I came to, they were dead and Sirash was taking care of me."

If Domet knew I was lying, he didn't call me on it. "Shame. I would have liked to know more."

I held my tongue and kept walking, and eventually the straight path twisted, rose, then split off into multiple directions. It was worse than the dungeons beneath the castle. But rather than my sight being obscured with steam, all I saw was darkness. I could hear people talking on the other sides of the walls. Judging by their conversation about the difficulties getting fresh food and the proper way to spice a chorizo soup, we must've been near the kitchens. Their voices sounded clearer than Domet's voice next to me.

"You may overhear some secrets you have no right to while we creep through the castle, Michael."

"And?"

"Just be aware. Haven't you ever wondered what the people you know are like when no one is around?"

"After what happened with Angelo, more than you can imagine."

Domet brought me up a creaky wooden ladder and into a wider tunnel. Unlike the others, this one had tiny holes in the wall that allowed light in. Two people between them, on the other side, were discussing something, but I couldn't make it out. Domet urged me to look through.

The Corrupt Prince was sitting at a table alone, surrounded by food and servants. He was picking at his meal like a child. A bite here. A nibble there. A look of disgust on his face when he didn't enjoy it, and anything that brought about that reaction was quickly removed from his sight. Someone was at the other end of the table, but I couldn't see them.

"My sister wants to marry me off? Truly?" the Corrupt Prince asked as he cut through a strip of pork. "Who does she think she is?"

"The future queen, my prince."

The voice was feminine. A Raven maybe? It wasn't Efyra or any of the ones I was more familiar with.

"So?" the Corrupt Prince said. "Am I not Royalty, too? Do I not have a say in my future? In who I bed? Who becomes the mother of my children? Who contributes to our bloodline?"

"Not if the queen-in-waiting chooses to make the decision herself. But she will likely consult with you. I have heard her mention High Noble Danielle Margaux, High Noble Claire Castlen, and Captain Emiri of the *Departed Sorrow,* from Eham."

"Brilliant," he said between mouthfuls. "A cripple, a flat-chested bitch, and a fishwife. Tell Serena that if she marries me to any of them, I'll bed them, wait until they pop out my heir, and then strangle them in their sleep, and I'll continue to do so until she lets me choose my own wife. That seems fair, does it not? I get an heir and am not forced to spend my entire life in perpetual boredom."

None of the servants seemed bothered or at all surprised at the Corrupt Prince's statement, even though the women were all High Nobles and one was the most notorious pirate captain in the Sea of Statues.

The unknown woman wasn't, either. "I do not think the princess will agree to those terms."

"Why not? It's not as if she cares. It's all a façade. I could kill unlucky who-gives-a-shit here with my knife," he said as he grabbed a nearby servant's wrist and yanked them close to him, "and play with their guts on the table, and all my fair sister would do is scold me and return to her latest obsession."

"My prince . . ."

"'My prince, my prince, my prince.' Do you know any other words?" Adreann mocked. "Is that not true? Has the Two-Faced Bitch suddenly developed a generous streak? Or is she still obsessed with Michael Kingman?"

"Michael Kingman is a special circumstance, he is—"

"He's a parasite in my city!" the Corrupt Prince screamed as he clenched his knife tightly. All the servants suddenly streamed out, doors creeping closed behind them. "Efyra should have disposed of that entire family after Davey was murdered. But Serena is unable to do what is necessary."

"Then do it yourself."

"Hmm. Maybe I will." The Corrupt Prince collected himself. "I think I know who I want to marry." He sucked on his teeth. "Bring me Jasmine. I will require her expertise in setting up the initial meeting."

"As you command, my prince."

I didn't need to hear any more of that conversation. My face was flushed enough as it was. When we got a little bit away from them, I turned to Domet and said, "Surprise, surprise. The Corrupt Prince still wants to kill me. That's not a very well-guarded secret."

"If that's the only thing you learned from that conversation, you're a bigger fool than I realized."

Domet brought me to another area with small holes in the walls, Efyra on the other side kneeling in front of a picture of King Isaac. She was disarmed and openly crying. Her hair was disheveled, her skin glistening with tears or sweat, and looked—even if it was for a single moment—vulnerable.

"Isaac," she said, "I don't know if I can do this on my own. Serena is distant and cold. Adreann is growing ever more aggressive and bold. And Chloe . . . God above, Chloe had her eye torn out by a Waylayer yesterday. How am I supposed to keep this country afloat when I can't even protect you or Chloe?"

Efyra's sobbing became more intense, and after a moment I walked on. Everyone had the right to grieve.

"It's always those that appear the strongest that are the weakest when they're alone," Domet said as we walked further through the castle's hidden tunnels. "Funny how that is."

"Says the incredibly rich noble that can't go a day without a drink."

"Says the fool who lies to those he loves and deludes himself that it's to protect them."

We overheard more conversations on our way to the infirmary on the lower floors of the castle. Two Low Nobles got into an argument about whether it would be safer to bring their families to Hollow or the Gold Coast, given that the rebel forces were sweeping and looting the rest of the countryside. They never reached an agreement, and both ended the conversation thinking they were right.

In the casual dining hall we overheard a group of merchants discuss whether it was worth attempting to travel to New Dracon City after the princess's coronation. Something was going on there, but no one knew what. There were scattered rumors about limited communication and a declaration that the city was preventing anyone from leaving once they entered.

Right before we reached the infirmary where I guessed the princess would be, I caught the tail end of a passionate affair between two individuals who clearly had never been warned that sneaking away to fuck in the castle might result in them finding a murder. Domet didn't appreciate my joke nearly as much as he ought to have.

He brought me to the end of a hallway. A chain hung from the walls, just like the one that led me to the royal chambers from the Star Chamber. "Are you sure you want to do this?"

My answer was to pull the chain, watch as the wall swung open, and enter the multi-bed infirmary. Serena was standing next to Chloe's bed, revolver pointed at me. She was still dressed as Red, her own eyes were red from crying, and she had deep-set bags under her eyes from a lack of sleep. Karin, Michelle, and Rowan were nowhere to be seen.

"Are you going to shoot me, Serena?" I asked as Domet emerged from the secret passage, too. "Or can we talk?"

The princess lowered her gun. "Why are you here, Michael?"

"To end whatever this is between us. Peacefully."

"Peacefully?" she repeated. "Is that what you'd call shooting at me while I'm onstage? Or barging into an infirmary, unannounced and un-invited, while I check in on one of my Ravens? Or leveraging your rela-tionship with Domet to trick us into having a meal together?"

"In Michael's defense, Princess, I was only—"

"Silence, Domet!"

He went silent, knees buckling at an invisible force pressing down on him.

Serena began to fiddle with the revolver in her hands as Chloe stirred. "But you are correct, Michael. It is time we ended this once and for all."

I didn't like where this was headed but still said, "What do you sug-gest?"

"How about a little roulette? Winner lives, loser dies."

THE KING KILLER AND
THE TWO-FACED QUEEN

We sat across from each other at the table in the middle of the infirmary, the gun that had killed her father and brother between us. Domet was standing off to the right of Serena's chair, trying his best not to let me see that he was shaking. I couldn't quite blame him. Serena was as much a part of his plan as I was, and she was clearly lost to grief.

The Princess of Hollow reached across the table and picked up the gun. "Ready?"

I nodded. The rules were simple. There was one bullet in one of the chambers. We'd each take turns firing at our own temple until there was only one person left. The princess had added the rule that once, and only once, you could point the gun at the other person instead. It meant you were only pointing the gun at yourself twice and your opponent once, and ensured you never knew if you were safe.

"We don't have to do this, Es, we—"

"Don't you dare call me that, Michael. You lost any right to use that name when you killed my father," she seethed. "And, yes, we do. You were right. This ends tonight. I refuse to go on, knowing the monster that killed my father is still alive."

"But you're fine with putting your brother in charge?"

"Adreann is flawed—quick-tempered and blunt—but good-hearted. If it comes to it, he'll do what he must."

I held my tongue. The princess was either delusional or blind to her brother's true nature, but she was still smart. By making this a game of chance, she wouldn't suffer any repercussions from Orbis Company if I died. I was on my own here. If I wanted to survive, I was going to have to outplay the princess. Behind her, Chloe was beginning to awaken, her sword lying against her bed.

If I killed the princess during this game, even to save my own life, would she let me live?

Even if I won, the odds of me walking out of here alive were terrible.

The princess spun the bullet chamber.

"How do I know it's not fully loaded? You could make me go first so I shoot myself in the head."

Serena huffed and slid it across the table. "Check it yourself."

I opened the chamber and looked inside. Sure enough, there was only one bullet chambered. I inspected it, twisting the bullet over and around my fingers for a few moments before slipping it back into where it ought to be.

"Domet," I said, cylinder still unhinged and gun in hand. "Are you really going to let her go through with this? If she dies, the Corrupt Prince will rule, and it'll be on you for not acting when you could."

Domet was shaking. He looked at the princess, and she met his stare. "High Noble Domet," she said softly. "Let me help you decide."

The Immortal fell to one knee, cursing and demanding she let him stand. Serena ignored him and returned her attention to me. And what a sight we made. Neither of us had reached our third decade and yet we were gambling our lives like it was nothing.

"Enough idle chitchat," the princess snapped. "Gun. I'm going first."

I clicked the cylinder back in place, spun it, and slid it toward her. "If you insist."

The princess picked it up, put the barrel to her temple, looked me in the eyes, and then pulled the trigger.

A click and it was over.

Chloe's eyes darted open at the sound, and she sat up in her bed. The blanket that had been covering her fell to the side, exposing wet clothes that stuck to her body. There was dried blood around where her right eye had once been. "What're you two do— Your Highness! Dammit!"

Chloe's hands and body shook, and she fell back down on her bed, immobile.

"Even her?" I asked.

"Your Highness! Please!"

"Even her," Serena answered. "No one interrupts this."

Chloe had closed her eye. I couldn't blame her. She hadn't asked to be here. She didn't deserve to have to protect the princess from herself after losing her eye to a Waylayer. But I was lucky that Chloe was with us rather than her mother. Efyra would have encouraged the princess to make it look like we were playing gun roulette and just shot me in the head to save time.

Serena Hollow, heir to the throne, passed me the gun. "Do you really think your father would have wanted this?" I asked. "He knew you would be a better ruler than he ever could—"

"Don't speak of my father!" she screamed, face going red. "Don't you dare speak of the man you killed as if you knew him! Or cared about him! I've heard what you've said about him in the past! You wanted revenge against him for years. Especially after he gave you that brand."

I touched it with my free hand. She was right. I couldn't deny that. But that was the past. Before I understood what happened between my father, Charles Domet, and Angelo Shade. If I had really wanted the king dead, I would have shot him in his suite. I could never forgive him, but I'd been ready to move on. And then, with his last action, he had damned his daughter to go down the path I had. And that path had only one outcome.

With the barrel of the gun against my temple, I met her eyes. "We shouldn't be doing this, Serena. Not us. Not when we've already lost so much. We should be together. Just as we were in the past."

"I don't *need* you. I turned all my flaws into strengths. I don't need your help in front of crowds like I did as a child. Nor do I need your constant support with my Ravens. I am as strong and wise and caring as my ancestors. But, unlike them, I've done it without a Kingman."

"If that's true . . . then why is your nickname the Two-Faced Queen?"

She didn't say anything.

I took a deep breath and then pulled the trigger.

Again nothing.

As I slid the gun to her, I said, "Is this what you really want? We keep doing this until only one of us walks away? There are only three Hollow and four Kingman left alive right now. Do we really need to lose another? Or risk losing both families to a blood feud?"

She didn't hesitate, putting the gun to her temple again. "Blood must be repaid in blood."

My heart ached. I thought of my father and my ancestors and what they might think of this. Hollow and Kingman, together since the dawn of the country, trying to kill each other. How far our families had fallen.

"What happens if I die?" I questioned. "Do you really think my friends, family, and company will just accept it? They'll figure out what happened eventually and overthrow the country you want to build. And what happens if *you* die, Serena? Do you think your brother and the Ravens won't come after everyone I love in retaliation? How many people have to die before we can end this cycle of revenge?"

"Only you," she said, and pulled the trigger.

Another click.

I watched as the gun returned to me.

"Only you need to die, Michael."

This was pointless. I wasn't going to get her to listen while the odds were in her favor. If she was going to see reason, it was only going to be when she truly realized the stakes. So I took the shot quickly, without thinking, the gun in my hand and the trigger pulled before anything else was said.

Another dud.

Two shots left. The odds were fifty-fifty now. Chloe and Domet our uncomfortable silent witnesses. It was one thing when the odds were fifteen or even twenty-five percent. But now that it was completely even, I wondered if she could really sit and watch and wait for one of us to die.

The princess aimed the gun at me, a smile on her face. "This is it, Michael. This is the bullet that's going to kill you. This is my revenge. You've ruined my life, so it's only fair that I be the one to end yours."

"And if it doesn't?" I asked.

"And if it doesn't what?"

"If it doesn't kill me, are you just going to sit there and let me shoot you?"

Chloe opened her mouth to say something, but the princess interrupted, "Any last words, king killer?"

After another deep breath, I took a shot in the dark, hoping to find the girl I'd known years ago. "It was you, wasn't it, Serena?"

Her face scrunched up and her mouth made a narrow line.

"You were the woman who comforted and sang to me after Jamal died. Even after ten years, you didn't want me to be alone because you cared—"

She pulled the trigger.

It turned over.

Serena stared at the gun, hands suddenly shaking again.

There was only one shot left and it was my turn.

"Princess!" Chloe shouted, wriggling to get free in vain. "We need to—"

Chloe's body convulsed, frozen even tighter in place. The princess had clamped her Fabrications down on her. Just to make sure she couldn't interfere. Like Domet, she couldn't even speak.

The princess very slowly slid the gun back to me, her auburn hair fallen over her face so I couldn't see her eyes.

I took it in my hand and took aim.

"Do you really want to die because of this feud, Serena? I didn't kill King Isaac. And my father didn't kill your brother. I know you probably don't believe me, but it's the truth."

She sat in her seat, shaking and silent.

"You've always been able to tell when I'm lying. So you know I'm telling the truth."

"I can be wrong."

"But you're not wrong, Es."

"Don't call me that." Her voice wavered like rising smoke. "Do what you must."

I stood up and the chair squealed. My aim was still on her. "Is this what you really want? Do you want to die for the notion of revenge, over something I didn't do, Serena? I'm trying to protect this country as our fathers did in the past. Trust me. I didn't kill your father and my father didn't kill your brother."

"Who did, then?" she asked, suddenly laughing slightly. "Who, if it wasn't you, was responsible for killing my father?"

"He killed himself!" I said. "He thought he was a useless king who was hated by his own family and by everyone in the city. He thought he had nothing left to give. But he had faith in you. He knew you would be the greatest queen this country had ever seen."

"And my brother?"

I paused. "That's a much longer story. My father tried to save your brother from an assassination, and he failed. The people behind it have gotten away with it for far too long, but I'm going to get revenge for my father and your brother. I promise."

"You promise?" she said, laughing. I still couldn't see her face or eyes. "I don't believe you. All you're trying to do is make me believe in you right before you kill me. An unparalleled cruelty."

I didn't respond.

"Kingman!" Chloe shouted in a strained voice. "Princess! Please release me! Let me explain. Michael, isn't what you—"

"Enough," she said, rubbing her left wrist. "This ends tonight. One way or another. Right, Michael?"

Serena Hollow, my first love and heir to the Hollow throne at age nineteen, was now at the end of the same barrel of the gun that had killed her father and brother. And she faced her death with pride, moving her hair out of her face so she could stare straight at it, exposing her tear-stained red eyes. Chloe couldn't watch and had her eye closed, waiting for the bullet to kill the Princess of Hollow. Domet was as he always was: an observer. Useless to prevent another Hollow or Kingman from dying.

I put the gun to my temple. "You're right, it does."

I pulled the trigger and Serena screamed.

The cylinder turned over for the sixth time as the princess stared at me in horror and confusion. I put the gun down, reached into my jacket, and pulled out the bullet I had pocketed when I checked it. I placed it between us, in the middle of the table. Chloe and Domet both let out loud gasps as I canceled out Serena's Fabrications.

"I'm done with this blood feud between our families," I stated. "Now it's your choice if you want to be done with it, too. But if you'll all excuse me, I have a serial killer to stop, an emperor to murder, and a city to protect. If you're ready to trust me, unite the provincial armies and get ready to command them. You'll need them tonight."

I took the gun and all five bullets from the case for it with me as I left the room with Domet. The Raven and the princess were silent. As I returned to the hidden tunnels within the castle's walls, I heard both crying.

"Did you plan that?" Domet asked when we were alone.

"When we get out of here, go to Kingman Keep and tell my family to get ready."

"I'm not your errand—"

"Did I stutter?" I looked straight into his eyes. "I am Michael Kingman and you will do as I say. Or do you have faith in someone else doing half of what I'm capable of? You created me. You wanted this. Sit back and enjoy the show."

I left Domet standing in the tunnels, mouth agape. As chaotic as my plan had been, it had ended as well as it could have. I didn't know if this had changed anything between me and Serena, but I had to have faith in the little girl I had once known, and the good that had been in her heart.

By tomorrow the rebellion against her would be over, once and for all.

NAP IN THE COUNTRYSIDE

I had dreamed about leaving Hollow for so long, yet my stomach churned as I stepped outside the walls for the first time in my life.

They shut the southern gate behind me as quickly as they could. Being a Mercenary had forced them to let me out, but it didn't mean they had to leave the gates open in case I changed my mind. And as I gazed off in the distance toward the rebel encampment, I couldn't help but wonder if I had made a huge mistake.

Trey had told me my plan hinged on being caught or imprisoned by the rebels, and walking toward their base was the easiest way to accomplish that. But that was assuming they didn't gut me outright as I approached. Up until now only Mercenaries had been able to walk freely. Good thing I was one. It also helped that the emperor had spared me once, long before I had become a king killer. Now that I'd become a symbol, someone believed to have struck against the nobility, I thought she might welcome me with open arms.

I walked through the farmland, getting stopped nearly a dozen times by people warning me to turn back. Instead, I ended up taking a nap in a sunny field, resting until I could no longer feel the warm light on my skin and dusk had arrived. It wasn't nearly long enough to make me feel whole again, but it would have to do.

Past the farmland was a seemingly endless stretch of plains, burned and ruined and turned to ash. With the sun setting in the distance, I was surrounded by rebels on horses with spears and flintlock pistols. Their eyes were focused on my brand. "On your knees, Kingman!"

I did as they told me to. My arms were tied behind my back and they led me on a leash behind their horses to their encampment, all blissfully unaware there was a loaded revolver strapped to my chest.

Time to live up to my reputation.

ILXU HVBJ ILXU
LJ VLKFSXLXK

Fake your true feelings and remain calm.

It's the most common advice given to captives and what I had done in the dungeons below Hollow Castle, waiting to die like a good little sacrifice. This time was different. It felt different, with the sky above me and people—actual traitors—around me. My rebel captors walked me straight through the center of the camp. A small impromptu parade that drew everyone's attention. Some saluted me. Others stared as if I were a mythical beast they'd never expected to see in real life. A few held weapons. But those were former nobles, still wearing their sigils proudly on their chests, holding on to a status that should have meant nothing here.

Hypocrites.

I was led to a large makeshift building of broken timber and cut stone with a thatched roof. It was a single room with animal furs on the ground, holding a bed and some chairs. There was a small firepit in the middle, with more chairs all around it. A dirty man who smelt strongly of citrus was sitting in one of them, stocking the fire with tinder and sticks.

He saw me and gave an oddly straight smile, then squished my cheeks and said, "Michael Kingman. What a sight you are now. So pretty. So noble. So . . . fracking wonderful. I could kiss you. A dead king, what a gift!"

"Release me, I'm here to join you."

"Are you, now?" a soothing voice asked behind me.

The emperor, Emelia Bryson, walked past me. She was dressed in noble regalia, albeit styled to fit her personality, with cropped sleeves and copper earrings. The scar that ran from her ear to her neck was as prominent as ever. As was her beauty, so striking that wars could have been waged over her as the old song claimed. And yet to me . . . she was nothing more than a feral cat who had grown too arrogant.

She took a seat on the bed, crossed her legs, and then said, "Last we spoke, you were set on trying to defy me. Why the sudden change?"

"I realized how dangerous Domet was."

"Doubtful," she said. "Domet wasn't enough to turn you. Did you learn what the Heartbreaker was? One of those Immortals?"

My mouth might as well have been touching the ground. "How do you—"

"You've had two months to learn the truth. I've had ten years. I know a great many things, Michael, and I wouldn't have let you live in the graveyard if I didn't think you'd join us eventually. Domet and the other Immortals, left unchecked, will continue to dictate Hollow's future as they have for a millennium. The king, the prince, and the princess are all puppets whose strings must be cut before we can rebuild. We are Hollow's only hope. No one else will stand against them."

"There's another," I said with gritted teeth. "And, unlike your rebellion, he isn't killing innocents."

Emelia leaned so close, I could smell the floral perfume she wore. "The Black Death? Are you sure about that? And as much as I would love to work with him, the Mercenary only cares about killing the beast Immortals. They are nothing in comparison to the true Immortals."

I stared into her dark eyes. She knew about Dark—his goals and maybe how he had gained his powers—and she was using the same terms as the Archmage. Where had she learned all of this? I asked.

"Those secrets aren't impossible to find if you know where to look . . . or who to ask."

"So who *did* you ask?"

Emelia smiled at me. "You have a lot of questions, I know. But, truthfully, isn't all *this* merely a façade, Michael? If you prove you're one of us, that you really want to end the old generation, then I'll answer all your questions."

"And how do you expect me to do that?"

"Listen," she said, and left the tent.

The lemon-smelling man took care of the rest.

He brought in dozens of people, all of whom believed joining the rebellion was their only hope. All of them had stories, all of them stirred my sympathy and explained why they were willing to destroy Hollow.

Two children from Naverre told me how, a week before it fell to the rebels, their parents had been executed by the High Nobles. For stealing four apples from the garden.

A grandfather had grown up in the countryside around Vurano until it was destroyed. The king had abandoned them, and bandits had taken over and set up tolls on every major road. They'd taken everything from anyone who tried to pass. If you couldn't pay them, then your life or freedom was taken instead. Some of his friends had survived the Mercenary attack only to die in the ditches beside the road, and those were the lucky ones. Others had been shipped down to the Skeleton Coast, never to be seen again.

A woman told me she had been engaged since childhood, only for her fiancé to show Fabricator abilities. He was whisked away to a High Noble Fabricator army and she spent years trying to find him, only to discover he had forgotten her. He died in Naverre—burned alive in the keep with the other nobles—and she fought on against the inequality of our society. Just like Trey did.

A man had nursed a Low Noble back to health, contracting the infection himself and losing an eye to it. Instead of thanks or compensation, he lost his job because he had been unable to perform his duties while he recovered. From there it was a slippery slope. He lost his wife and children, his home, and then everything else. Joining the rebellion was the only option he had left: it wasn't about revenge for him, only survival.

Most of them, when I asked, didn't consider themselves heroes. They didn't even like what they were doing. But they didn't see any other option, if there was to be hope for the future. Even if they weren't a part of it. They would destroy the old, corrupt ways and let the survivors figure out who was fit to rule the ashes. It was as if they were a force of nature rather than a collective of people with dreams and aspirations.

How was I supposed to reason with that? Would even killing Emelia stop them?

When the lemon-smelling man stopped bringing people to me, he gave me water, a piece of stale black bread, and some old stew that had been sitting around for too long and had indistinguishable brown chunks in it. We ate in silence until I asked, "Why did you kill the boy that was with me in the graveyard?"

The lemon-smelling man sucked at his teeth and put the empty bowl on the ground. "We did what Em ordered."

"Did she think killing my friend would make me want to join you all?"

"You're here, aren't you?" the man asked. "You could ask her yourself, but I imagine she wanted you to have some motivation. Even if it was to avenge him."

"Motivation?" I said, spitting the word out.

"We all need it. Death and revenge are usually the best. And after what happened to your father, it's no surprise you went into hiding. That boy's death brought you back into the open. Or do you think you'd still be here if he were alive?"

"Jamal deserved better than that."

"A lot of people do. Or does his life mean more, just because you knew him, than hundreds and thousands of others'?"

I closed my eyes and exhaled. "When is Emelia coming back? She said she would answer my questions."

The lemon-smelling man pulled me to my feet. "I'll take you to her."

There were crowds around the house I'd been in. Upon seeing us, they dispersed like mist when a hand was run through it, returning to whatever they were supposed to be doing. A few of the former Low Nobles kept watching me until I looked in their direction, as if hoping to taunt or intimidate me.

We walked to another run-down stone building in the middle of the camp, the accumulated flags flying around it with the rebel symbol at the apex, so it could be seen from Hollow. There were men and women armed with pickaxes and covered in dust and dirt resting around the building. They were different from any of the other rebels I had seen, most suffering from a hacking cough that made me wish for a drink myself.

Inside, it was devoid of any luxuries or comforts, except for lit lanterns, buckets of water, and well-worn tools. My rebel escort dismissed anyone we ran into, sending them outside to get water or food or rest. They were happy to comply, eager to stop their backbreaking work. We went down a set of stone stairs and entered an underground cavern. The entire area was overgrown with various fauna that liked the darkness, with a single path for us to traverse. Tunnels branched off the main path, into the stone around us, but all I could see was darkness within them.

Emelia was waiting for us at the furthest end, in front of a pool of calm water and a massive weathered painting. The painting was of a familiar-looking man with strange red tendrils coming out of his body, screaming as he held his hands over his ears. The shattered Celona and perfectly whole Tenere were above him. It was possible to see there had been other people in the painting once, all connected by the red tendrils, but age had destroyed the details.

"Do you recognize him, Michael?" Emelia asked as I went to her side. The lemon-smelling man waited behind us, tapping a flintlock pistol against the side of his leg. As if tempting me to try something.

"Kind of," I said. "He looks familiar."

"Look again."

I cracked my knuckles and took another look at the man. His eyes were a fading gold, his jaw was strong and prominent, his eyebrows were thin, and his mouth was . . .

It was Charles Domet. Younger, but definitely him.

"Scary, isn't it?" she asked. "This painting is more than a thousand years old. What does that make Domet? Just how old is he?"

"What is this supposed to be a painting of?"

Emelia pointed at a gold plaque underneath the painting. The first and third sentences had been scratched off recently, likely thanks to a dull knife. But the second one was clear: *The Lifeweaver.*

"The Lifeweaver?" I said out loud.

"It was Domet's original title. Back when he was mortal."

I glanced at the shattered moon. So he had still been mortal when the shattered moon was in the sky. Had it shattered before him? I wouldn't get the answer to that question, so I asked another: "What else was written on the plaque?"

"Information too valuable to leave out in the open."

I thought back to the name Angelo had whispered in front of the sarcophagus. "Was his real name on it?"

Emelia smiled softly at me. "Along with a clue as to what binds him to life."

"You know what he regrets?"

Her smile vanished. "I think so. It's not as simple as . . . actually, I don't think I should tell you yet. I wouldn't want you to run away with all my carefully curated knowledge. If you want the rest, you'll have to submit to me and my cause."

The title alone was more information than I'd had about Domet before. Was there a chance he was a Weaver with the ability to manipulate life? Did he have a hand in creating Immortals? I didn't know, but it would give me a place to start my research—when I had the time. After I killed Emelia and the Heartbreaker and got Serena to accept the truth about King Isaac.

"Tell me, then," I said as I turned to Emelia. "What did Domet do, besides live for a very long time, to justify you starting a rebellion to try and kill him?"

Emelia took a seat on a large boulder near the pool of water. She tossed smaller rocks into it and watched the ripples. "Domet is a living, breathing, and evolving curse on Hollow. He has influenced events and people for generations. Does someone like that deserve to continue living without consequence?"

"Whatever he once was, Domet is currently an alcoholic and an observer. He's harmless."

"Harmless?" she repeated. "Are you blind or just stupid? Domet is the single most powerful person in this country. It doesn't matter if he's in a lull right now. One day he will return to his former self and when he does, Hollow will burn. Just like it did when the Wolven Kings ruled."

"Are you suggesting Domet overthrew the Wolven Kings?" I asked, trying to contain my laughter. "Because there's enough history about their defeat to prove that wrong. The First Kingman and Adrian the Liberator—"

"No, he didn't help overthrow them. I believe he was one of them."

I couldn't control myself. I howled with laughter, nearly doubling over with tears in my eyes. Neither Emelia nor the lemon-smelling man appreciated it.

"You think Charles Domet was a Wolven King? Seriously?"

"You're quick to mock, but do you know what the Wolven Kings did when they ruled? What they were like?" Emelia asked as the edges of her mouth twitched.

"No," I said as I caught my breath. "I don't concern myself with the losers of history."

"The Wolven Kings were the worst of humanity. They waged war across the continent, against each other, simply to prevent the others from amassing more power. The Ash City, the Desert of a Thousand Craters, and the Sword Graveyard are only a few of the scars their battles left behind. If there was a chance one of them was still alive, do you really think we should let them be? Even if they're seemingly harmless?"

"What makes you think Domet was one of them?"

Emelia pointed to the plaque with one hand and then tapped her chest, over her heart. "Because it explains his regrets."

"Which are?"

"I'm not telling you—not yet."

This was getting ridiculous. Emelia was expecting me to believe everything she said without a shred of evidence. And I was going to need overwhelming evidence to believe a word of it. Domet was definitely something old and powerful . . . but not a Wolven King.

"If you won't tell me anything, then why should I believe you?"

The lemon-smelling man pointed his flintlock pistol at me as Emelia said, "Because either you're with us or you're working with him."

Why was everyone so dramatic nowadays with all these ultimatums?

"You really think your man can hit me from that distance?" I mocked. "Because *I* don't."

Emelia stared back at me, smiling. "Do you really think I'd let you keep that gun strapped to your chest if I didn't have a way to stop you?"

I felt myself pale.

"Might as well lay your cards on the table for all of us to see."

Slowly, I reached under my shirt and pulled out the revolver. It was loaded and felt heavy in my hand. I had a better shot at the emperor than her man did at me. Assuming she wasn't lying about having a way to stop me. I kept a tight grip on it and tried to remember the plan that had brought me here. I was sure this wasn't how it was supposed to go.

If only I could remember what Trey was going to do.

"If you're going to shoot me"—she crossed her legs and leaned back—"best not miss."

"You're not scared to die?"

She shook her head. "If anything, I was disappointed when they found me not guilty at my trial. It would have been a perfect chance to test my beliefs."

My mouth dropped as I realized what she intended. "You mean to fight fire with fire. Do you think if you die, you'll return immortal?"

"Yes," she said, unwavering. "I've made all the necessary preparations. All that's left is to die and see if my will is strong enough to defy death. Care to help me find out?"

"You're insane," I said, backing away from her.

"I am necessary." Emelia rose to her feet, straightened her clothes, and then held her hands out to me. "I will save this city. No matter the cost. Now, what will you do, Michael? Will you risk it and shoot me? Knowing that I might return . . . ?"

Emelia didn't have to finish her sentence. If she returned, immortal, her cause would be stronger than ever. She would rise up again having defied the old generation. How powerful would a martyr be if they returned to their cause after dying for it?

As Emelia tapped her chest, she said, "Aim for the heart."

"And if I won't?"

"Then pledge your allegiance to our cause. Help me end his rule."

"Any other option?"

The lemon-smelling man coughed meaningfully behind us, gun still pointed at me.

So it was either kill, die, or submit. I hated all those options. I had come here to kill her, but if she returned—

"What will it be, Michael?" she pressed.

What was I supposed to do? What was the right answer?

Shi—

A small black boy was running toward us, shouting, "Sir! We have a blunder!"

The lemon-smelling man lowered his gun and turned toward the voice. "What?"

"Intruders, sir."

"Where?"

"Right here," a deeper voice said.

A gun went off. The lemon-smelling man dropped his flintlock pistol and held his neck as blood began to flow freely. He was gurgling as he hit the ground. Trey put his foot on the man's chest and pointed another gun at the emperor herself. The cavern was filled with the sounds of a man drowning.

And just like that, my big damn hero arrived.

Emelia tilted her head to the side as she stared at Trey and Rock. "This is unexpected."

Trey waited for the lemon-smelling man to be still before advancing toward us, another loaded pistol in his other hand. "Are you the emperor?"

"Yes."

He took a step forward. "Did you lead the attack on the Militia Quarter?"

"Yes."

Another step. "Did you meet Michael in the graveyard that day?"

"Yes."

Trey was close enough to her to make sure his shot wouldn't miss. "Did you kill a small boy that day?"

"Yes." She clicked her tongue. "Who are you?"

"Nobody."

"Trey! Wait, don't—"

Trey shot Emelia in the head, her blood spraying the immediate area red.

Her body hit the ground with a *thud* as the gunshot echoed throughout the cavern. Her eyes were vacant, her fallen body in an unnatural position, bits of her brain and skull littering the ground. There was no mistaking she was dead. Domet might not even be able to come back from that.

Her will hadn't been strong enough to defy death after all.

Trey was breathing shallowly. "Do you think it hurt?"

"I don't know," I said as I went to his side. "What took you so long?"

Trey remained still, staring at the emperor's body.

"We were in the middle of preparing dinner," Rock said. "Came as quickly as we could."

"Revenge doesn't feel as good as I thought it would," Trey muttered to himself.

I put my hand on his shoulder. "We should go. Before someone realizes what happened here."

"I thought it would make me feel better." He spat to his side. "To think I almost traded my freedom for *this*."

"Are you two done?" Rock asked. "We need to move. I may have done something stupid earlier."

We both looked at him. Avoiding our gaze, he said, "I may have added a generous dose of one of my miracle cure-alls to the camp's dinner. One that's more or less pure obsidian root."

"Obsidian root is a laxative. How much did you put in?"

Rock smiled broadly. "So much. This camp is going to be a river of shit."

I laughed, and even Trey had to press his tongue against the inside of his cheek to stop himself from joining me. But when my laughter stopped, another's continued.

A laugh that was higher-pitched.

I gripped Trey's shoulder tightly as we both turned to stare at Emelia's body. The blood and bone and brains that had splattered across the area were trickling back toward her, re-forming as if Trey had missed his shot.

I had only ever seen this happen once before. With Domet. A true Immortal.

Emelia sat up, smiling from ear to ear. She stared at her hands for a moment before running them over where her wound had been, discovering nothing. Not a hair out of place or a speck of blood. "It seems . . . ," she began, voice raspy, ". . . that my quest is just."

"Michael," Trey growled. "Give me your gun."

"It won't work," I said. "Didn't you see what just happened?"

Trey threw his guns aside, pulled out another, and shot. The bullet hit Emelia's chest, right in the middle. She laughed as she dug her fingers into her body, plucked out the bullet, and then flicked it back at us. The wound was already healing by the time the bullet hit the ground.

She was no longer mortal.

Emelia rose to her feet. "I feel so refreshed."

"Trey!" I screamed as I pulled him away from Emelia. Rock was already running away. Our adventure in the Tweeker Keep had taught him a lot. "We need to go! The plan failed and we can't stop her like that!"

"What . . . what is she? There has to be—"

Emelia smiled at him. "There isn't. But you've given me the power to end this war once and for all. Tomorrow morning Hollow will fall and a new generation will be reborn from the ashes."

Trey wrenched away from me and faced Emelia. "You think I'll let the woman who murdered my brother take control of Hollow?"

"Who said you have a choice in the matter?" she asked. "What is some nobody against an army? Especially when the gates will open for us and the city will greet us with open arms."

"You're just another delusional, power-hungry noble standing in the way of progress. You've become exactly what you said you hate. Thanks for keeping me focused."

Emelia smiled at him, showing all her teeth like a mocking monkey. "I can't wait to see you again."

We ran. Through the underground cavern, up the stairs, and then into the encampment, where nearly half the army was running around or squatting behind whatever protection they could find to relieve themselves after Rock's culinary efforts.

"How are we getting out of here? Did you two come up with an escape plan?" I asked as we passed a rebel on the ground groaning and holding his stomach.

"We need to signal the cavalry," Rock said.

I didn't have time to question what that meant. "How?"

"By doing what I do best," Trey said as he approached three barrels of gunpowder. He took a length of fuse from his pockets, wedged one end of it into the barrel, and then uncoiled it so we were as far away from the gunpowder as possible. He took out a piece of flint and a dagger and struck them together until it caught fire.

As the fire began to travel down the fuse, Trey nudged us. "Time to get going."

It was chaos when the explosion went off. The diarrhea had been enough for the rebels to handle; with the fire that was quickly spreading through the camp as well, they had no chance of mobilizing the army. Rock brought us to a quieter section of the camp where horses were normally stabled, only to see the stalls were empty.

"They should be here," Rock said. "Else it's going to be a long run home."

"Who should—"

I was cut off by the thunder of hooves approaching. Three riders on horses stopped in front of us. Dawn, Kai, and Olivier. The cavalry.

"All aboard," Olivier shouted. "Rock, untie Kai's horse from mine, then hop on with High Noble Margaux. Trey, you're with High Noble Ryder. Michael, with me."

Rock did as he was told as Trey took the reins and lead from Kai. I hoped he knew how to ride a horse, or at least learned quickly.

"You coming?" Olivier asked with an outstretched hand. "Or do you want to find your own way home?"

I wasn't stupid enough to run my mouth, so I took his hand. I was up and on his horse, one arm around his waist, gripping for dear life. Horse riding was never my thing as a child. Too much rocking and soreness and dealing with something with a mind of its own. I was glad not to be in control as we took off at a blistering pace. Horns sounded as soon as we hit the plains and riders took off after us.

So much for a clean getaway.

I held the revolver in my hand. Five bullets.

"If they get closer, shoot them! Make it count!"

I nodded and turned around to aim. Too far away. Too hard to aim true on a horse. I would almost certainly miss. That didn't stop our pursuers from trying. Two fired, and the bullets blew up dirt when they connected with the ground.

We were already halfway there.

"We need the gates open!" I shouted to no one in particular.

"Gwen is handling that!" Dawn shouted back. A bullet bounced off her back—a metal twang echoing around us—as Rock cursed loudly, curling up tighter in front of her. "We just have to give the signal when we're close!"

"What's the signal?"

"This," Kai said, and then took a deep breath.

The sound that came out of his mouth scared the horses and forced us all to hold on tighter. Two of the rebel riders were bucked off as their horses ran away. Kai had given a sharp, piercing howl that made my ears ring long after it was gone. I could hear only half of what anyone was saying and watched as the southern portcullis was slowly lifted, room enough for us to roll under. Far too low for the horses. We would have to—

Dawn jumped first, carrying Rock with her. She hit the ground with a *thud* and then shoved Rock under the gate, following close behind. Trey and Kai were next. Neither as graceful as Dawn. Both hit the ground hard, and they were slow to recover and roll under the gate, but did so together.

I jumped, rolled a distance on the ground, and then groaned in pain. It felt like I had been stabbed in the side again. Olivier wasn't as lucky, misjudging his timing and landing awkwardly on one leg with a distinct *snap.* He fell to the ground, bone sticking out of a place it had no right to be.

Dawn screamed at us to get under the gate.

The rebel riders were close.

"Michael! Go! Get under!" Olivier shouted. "Leave me!"

Like that was going to happen.

I staggered over to Olivier—the sound of hooves pounding into the ground getting louder and louder behind me—and threw his arm over my shoulder, and we limped to the gate together. I stuffed him underneath it without much care, took one last look at the rebels, and then followed.

The gate crashed down behind me, and I lay on the ground trying to catch my breath. The gate guards were checking up on Dawn and Kai, much to the annoyance of both of them.

"You should have left me behind," Olivier said as Dawn inspected his leg. "Why put your own life at risk? For me? I'm a dead man walking, whatever happens."

"Yeah, and you're going to die from that sickness," I said as I sat up. "Have the decency to say goodbye to my mother before you go. She deserves that much. I don't want to lose anyone else without having the chance to tell them how I feel. Understand?"

He hesitated, wincing as Dawn tried to adjust him. "Guess I'll have to wait a little bit longer to hear how much you hate me, then."

"Look forward to it, old man."

Gwen tackled me back to the ground. And then hit me. Repeatedly. "What was that plan, Michael? Give yourself up to the rebels and hope Trey and Rock got there in time? What if they'd killed you on sight?"

"I knew Emelia wouldn't."

"I hate you so much." She ran her hands over her face. "Please just tell me the emperor is dead and we can go tell the princess. She's at Kingman Keep, waiting for you to return. Let me tell you, that was an unpleasant conversation to have."

I didn't respond.

"Michael? What happened?"

"The emperor is alive. Our plan failed," Trey said, choosing his words carefully.

This time it was Kai who responded. "You mean we did all of that for nothing? Nothing? Do you know how much danger Hollow is in now?"

"Hollow was in danger anyway. The emperor is attacking Hollow tomorrow morning."

"That would be suicide," Dawn said. "Everyone is on edge because of the princess's coronation. We have more guards on duty tonight than any other. Why would she choose that morning?"

"Because she has an easy way in," I said. "She said the gates would be open when her army approached."

Kai clicked his tongue. "Only a High Noble could authorize that."

"Or a persuasive woman saying High Nobles were in trouble," Gwen said as she tapped her foot.

"Who could it be? Any High Noble acting unusual?"

"Some would say Dawn and I are. Associating with the Kingman family again," Kai stated.

"Not some," Dawn corrected. "Almost everyone. My parents included."

I took a deep breath and toyed with my father's ring. "Let's return to Kingman Keep. We'll tell the princess what happened. Hopefully she listened to me and readied the provincial armies."

"You have a lot of faith in her," Dawn said.

"Should I not?"

"Most wouldn't. You know what the nobles call her?"

"I do . . . but she'll always be Serena to me."

We began our walk to Kingman Keep. Gwen and I half carried Olivier, his arms over our shoulders. Kai and Dawn had a quiet conversation as Trey and Rock—mainly Rock—laughed and joked about everything. If I hadn't been focused on other things, I would have joined them. Trey was smiling, ever so slightly. It was the first time I'd seen that since Jamal's death.

My mother and Efyra were waiting for us outside of Kingman Keep, in the middle of a very loud and very heated argument. Chloe was resting on a nearby bench, eye closed.

"—and forget Orbis Company. Let them come after us for killing that traitor."

"If you think you can attack Michael without my intervening, you seriously underestimate me."

"I've always wanted to put you in your place. This will give me the chance."

"Then do it."

"Oh, I—" Efyra stared at us as we approached. "Michael Kingman! On behalf of Hollow and the Royal Family, I hereby arrest—"

My mother shoved her out of the way to get to us. "Father," she said. "What happened?"

Olivier grumbled something inaudible. Then, more clearly, he said, "Misjudged a jump. But I'm alive. No thanks to my own doing."

"Where's the princess?" I asked.

"Inside. She came here with most of the Ravens. Charles Domet, Lyon, and Kayleigh are all here, too. Apparently Dark forced them to come here, and Naomi is beyond annoyed she got left behind. What's going on, Michael? What—"

"I'm ending this here." Efyra was standing in front of the entrance, sword drawn. It glimmered in the moonlight. "Sometimes rules have to be broken to—"

I drew my revolver and stood in front of Efyra.

She recognized it immediately. "How do you have that, Kingman?"

"Mother," Chloe said from the bench, "let him pass. If you want the answers to those questions, go with him. Her Highness will explain."

"What?"

Chloe stood, wobbling slightly, walked to my side, and took my arm. "Walk with me, Michael. There's work to be done."

Efyra Mason didn't move a muscle as we walked past her. Not a twitch or a blink or a quiver. Only a thousand-yard stare as her only daughter willingly embraced the king killer.

When we were inside, Chloe said, "Consider this my thank-you."

"Did you get Serena to believe me?"

"No," she said as we opened the door to the great hall. "Only to listen."

"Will it be enough?"

"For you? Maybe."

I readied myself for the conversation that would come. "Serena, I think—"

Destruction interrupted me.

Beorn's body hung from the rafters by a hook through his jaw, blood dripping down to the floor below. There were too many pools of it to count. To ignore. His heart had been torn out, and no one else was around.

Chloe pointed. Written in blood on the wall were the words:

Five have been taken. All will die if you refuse to play. Time for the main event. Bring the heart of the Historian to your grave by Lights Out if you want a chance at saving them, Kingman.

THE CONTESTANTS

We found Lyon unconscious in the pantry, his wrists tied behind his back. He was unhurt except for his torn shirt and a multitude of thin, jagged cuts across his chest. The Ravens who had accompanied Serena here, Hannah and Rowan, were in a room near the great hall. Both alive and angry. The Ravens cut Beorn's body down and covered him with linen in an attempt at some sort of dignity.

Once we brought everyone inside, we had a list of those who were missing: the Princess of Hollow, the pregnant Kayleigh Ryder, High Noble Charles Domet, the Mercenary Dark, and Naomi. All had been here and safe moments before we arrived when my mother and Efyra had gone outside to argue. Now all were gone. All targeted by the Heartbreaker Serial Killer for the grand finale. Along with two still-unknown participants.

"Where's Kayleigh?" Lyon asked as Gwen attempted to attend to his wounds. It took our mother, Olivier, and Chloe to hold him down when he heard.

No one had spoken much since Chloe and I found Beorn and the message. Only what was necessary. Search the keep. Identify who was missing, and who needed aid. An eerie silence hung over us all as Lyon asked his question again, much more forcibly.

"I don't know," I said. "The Heartbreaker must have taken her somewhere. But I don't know where."

"Then who does?"

Trey and Rock were sitting at the table together while Efyra sat against a nearby wall, completely defeated, muttering, "She's dead," as the other Ravens attempted to encourage her not to give up. Kai and Dawn spoke together in hushed tones.

That made me the bearer of bad news. "Everyone who might have had an idea was taken."

"What do we do, then?" Lyon said, voice rising.

"Find the Heartbreaker and stop them."

"How? Gwen told me about this killer, Michael. One of those taken survived. Out of thirteen. And she wasn't meant to. Those aren't odds I like. Especially not when they concern my pregnant fiancée. So tell me something that will make what just happened better."

"I'm going to save everyone. Without having to play their game. No one else dies."

Lyon laughed at me, and it struck something primal in my chest. A tightness around the heart that made me blink rapidly to prevent the tears from forming. He laughed longer than he needed to. And no matter what kind of look he received from my mother and sister, Lyon only stopped when he wanted to. When I was nearly broken in front of everyone.

"You're going to save everyone? Without playing their game? You saved our mother—I'll give you credit for that—but you can't stop a serial killer! You weren't even able to hear them take everyone captive as you stood outside! You're a fuckup pretending to be a hero!"

"Lyonardo Kingman!" our mother shouted. "Apologize this instant."

"He did one good thing. That doesn't make him a good person. Do you know what he does? The way he acts when no one's looking? The lies he spreads? We could have walked away from all of this if it wasn't for him!"

"Kayleigh is missing and you're upset. I understand that. But Michael is your brother and you will not speak to him like that. Do you understand me?"

Lyon looked at me. "I regret saving your life. I wish you would have died on those steps. It would have saved us so much pain. If something—anything—happens to Kayleigh and our unborn child, I will never forgive you, Michael."

No one had a response to that. Not me, my mother, my sister, or my grandfather. All I could do was cry. Lyon left Kingman Keep before my tears stopped, mumbling about how he would play the game the Heartbreaker set up for us and save Kayleigh on his own.

And just like that, the two contestants were clear. The Kingman brothers.

Gwen said nothing as she hugged me and let me compose myself.

I wiped the tears away. I had to move forward. People were depending on me. There was no time for sadness, only action.

"We need to figure out where the Heartbreaker's game begins," I said as I gave Gwen a tight squeeze. "It's the princess's coronation, there are celebrations everywhere. It'll be—"

"It doesn't matter," Efyra said, breaking her mantra of "She's dead." "The country is doomed. The rebels are about to attack, and we have to deploy the army."

"They should be ready. Or did Serena not tell them to prepare?"

"They're ready," Efyra said as she went to her feet. "But only Her Highness can unite them. Otherwise they listen to the High Noble families that maintain them."

"That wasn't how it used to be," my mother said. "The Kingman family or a majority vote from the High Nobles used to be able to appoint a war general."

"That changed a month after your husband's head rolled down the steps."

My mother remained calmer than she would have if Lyon hadn't just thrown a tantrum in front of everyone. "What does that mean?"

The answer came to me and I said it out loud, in horror. "It means the Corrupt Prince is about to take the throne. To unite the army now, they'll have to call an emergency meeting and transfer power to the prince or watch the city fall to the rebels."

"Correct," Efyra said, her disdain clearer than the bloodstains on the walls. "You didn't even manage to kill the emperor. What a worthless, pathetic waste of breath you are. Your brother was right. You should have died that day."

The joke was on her. My heart was already broken, and her insults might as well have been a breeze in the wind. This country might be on the brink of falling to the rebellion or the Corrupt Prince, but I could still save everyone. I could still do something good.

Thankfully for the city, Gwen was the hero it needed.

"Efyra, I have a plan," she said. "And before I say it, remember that I saved your delusional ass. Once this is over, I expect my family to be returned to its High Noble status."

Efyra waited for Gwen to continue, arms crossed and face expressionless.

"Call the High Nobles to an emergency meeting. We'll dye my hair and dress me up like Serena. Everyone used to say we looked like sisters when we were younger, and I had the same etiquette and political training as she did. If it works, I can command the army myself. If it doesn't, I'll still buy enough time for Michael to find Serena. I'd rather let Hollow burn to the ground than let Adreann take control."

"If the High Nobles discover you're impersonating the princess, they will execute you. I won't protect you from them or the prince, and I will not risk my life for you."

"I'm aware of the risks."

"You trust your brother that much? That he'll find and stop the Heartbreaker with nothing more than an old gun? That he can do it all without having to murder this Historian?"

Gwen didn't blink. "After what I've seen him do, only a fool would bet against him."

"So Lyon is a fool?"

"Lyon is angry that Kayleigh is missing. Michael may have his faults, but he's already done what others consider impossible. He cured our mother and found the man behind Davey Hollow's death in a week. Once he stops the Heartbreaker—without murdering this Historian—maybe you should listen to what he says about King Isaac and Davey."

"Never."

"We'll see how you feel in the morning when the rebel army has been stopped, the princess is still on the throne, Hollow is still standing, and everyone is alive."

Efyra rolled her eyes, and our mother began to insist she should be allowed to accompany Gwen to the meeting, and my sister gave me a hug. "You've got this, Michael. Don't be afraid."

"Too late." A pause and an exhale. "Why would you risk yourself like this?"

"I'll do whatever I have to to make sure that asshole doesn't take the throne. Besides, isn't this what Kingman do? The right thing?"

"I don't like when people use the Kingman legacy against me."

"You wouldn't," Gwen said as she stepped back. "You're a hypocrite sometimes, twisting facts to fit the narrative you wish to present. But you do the right thing. Usually. Our ancestors would be proud."

I let the insult slide. "I suppose today is the day I become a true King-man. Save the city and all that nonsense."

"Yes," she said with a smile. "Try not to mess it all up."

Gwen left with my mother, Efyra, Chloe, and the Ravens. Efyra ordered me to bring the princess to the Poison Gardens if I was successful. A Raven would wait there until sunrise. Chloe had wanted to stay and help me find the princess, but with Gwen taking the role, she had to be at her side. Regardless of her injury.

Before my mother departed, she gave me a kiss on the forehead and said, "Never forget you are your father's son, Michael. You can do this."

And then it was me, Trey, Rock, Dawn, Kai, and Olivier.

"Trey," I said, "I need a favor. Can you look after Rock and Olivier while I go hunt this killer?" Trey pressed his tongue against the inside of his cheek. "Please. I don't want to have to worry about—"

"Your brother. That was how I treated you when you told me Jamal died, wasn't it? It was . . ." He paused. "Ugly."

I made a face at Dawn, who was smiling. What was he saying?

Trey walked over to me. "I'll do better. I'll help you stop this killer. If the city falls, my people will suffer, too."

"What happened to bringing me down if I stand by the princess?"

A shrug. "I hate the rebels more."

"But—"

Dawn put me in a headlock and then said, "Michael is trying to say we would be happy to have your help."

"Where do we begin?"

I slipped out of the hold. "I'm going to kill the Historian and you're going to make sure I have the opportunity to."

Everyone was caught off guard. But it was Dawn who said, "Michael, you just said—"

"I know what I said," I stated. "I lied. They needed a Kingman who could do the impossible, in that moment, and I gave them one. But in truth this city needs a villain to save it. I can play that role well enough. Let history remember me as it will." I thought of my father and his last act. "None of you have to help me now that you know the truth. I won't blame you."

Trey shrugged. "I never wanted to be a hero anyway."

"If one person has to die for the greater good, then so be it," Kai said. "The heroes our parents idolized failed them, so I suppose it's up to us."

Dawn was more tentative, curling her hair around a finger. "There's no other way?"

"Would you ever forgive me if my pride blinded me and I said I could save this city and it fell instead?"

A deep breath. "Alright. Any idea who this Historian is?"

"He's Rian Smoak, a Scorcher and dragon Historian for the Church of the Eternal Flame. And I suspect he's very likely a dragon in disguise."

COLDHEARTED

There was only one place Rian could be during the pre-coronation celebrations: the Church of the Eternal Flame. Most members of the congre-
gation spent their nights melting gold and performing whatever initiation
or advancement ceremonies they did to draw attention away from the
castle. There was always too much fire, and it made not only the Upper
Quarter but the Sword and the . . . the . . . the whatever district I passed
out from blood loss in smell like smoke, too. It was easy to sneak into
Rian's office with them so preoccupied, only to discover it abandoned.
There was an invitation to the Royals' coronation party on top of a stack
of books.

That was awkward. At least we could have snuck into the church
without raising too much suspicion, but the same couldn't be said of the
castle. Not after the king's death. Not during a massive celebration with
heightened security. And when the person doing the sneaking was . . .
well, me. But I had already done it once, how hard could it be to do
it again?

Turns out, incredibly difficult.

Instead of letting Advocators handle security around the castle, they had brought in Wardens. The metal monsters were almost as intimidating as Mercenaries, to the general public, and they were one of the few things that could send me in the opposite direction at a single glimpse or mention.

Today they were everywhere.

There were five outside the main entrance to the castle, checking for a brand on the neck of every person who approached. There were two more at every other way in. A few were patrolling along the river. More concerning was that no one seemed to care about the increased security, some even reveling in it—while an army was preparing to invade Hollow and burn it to the ground. Always so foolish. So ignorant.

The four of us—Kai, Dawn, Trey, and myself—were watching the main entrance from a distance. True to their titles, Dawn and Kai were dressed for a noble event. Trey and I weren't. We were still working on our plan, since storming the castle in search of Rian would definitely cost Trey and me our heads.

Which meant we'd have to use Domet's secret entrance. After raiding the High Noble's house for supplies and new clothes and a quick bite of food—his servants were helpful in our search and delighted to be doing something that wasn't cleaning or dusting or waiting for Domet— we walked through the underground tunnels to the castle. Instead of taking the infirmary entrance, we left the secret tunnels in a hallway off the beaten path. I was the one who closed the full-sized painting behind us after helping Kai through, making sure there was no indication that it was a hidden entrance.

I had to give Domet some credit, he knew this castle better than anyone else.

Trey fiddled with the extravagant feathered hat Dawn had insisted he wear. "Where would the Historian be? What do the nobles even do during a coronation? Have an eating contest? Watch gladiatorial combat?"

"There's no gladiatorial combat," Dawn said quickly. "Not this year."

"And the eating contest?"

Dawn and Kai were silent.

"You're kidding me," Trey said, mildly amused.

"It's not really an eating contest per se. More like a . . . a . . ."

"Exotic cuisine sampling," Kai finished. "The Corrupt Prince brought in some of the finest ingredients and chefs for tonight. The more exotic, the better."

"More rhubarb pie bullshit," I mumbled. "Is the Eternal Flame participating in this exotic cuisine sampling, too?"

"Yes. They'll be taking a small portion of whatever is cooked and burning it as a sacrifice to God."

"Ridiculous. All that money and food could be used for better things."

"Michael"—Dawn put a hand on my shoulder—"this isn't the time. We have to save the city from an invasion before we can make it better."

"You're right," I said through gritted teeth. "Let's go to the party."

And what a party it was. The Endless Waltz had been a level of extravagance I'd never seen before, but this . . . this made it look like a tweeker den. Everything was pale blue and white, from the crystal goblets and the snowflake-patterned plates to the Ice Fabricators who were gently showering the guests with snowflakes from above. Rather than make people suffer outside, they had brought only the best part of a bad thing indoors.

High and Low Nobles were mingling freely in the grand ballroom, the bodyguard balcony still as raucous as ever. And members of the Church of the Eternal Flame had more of a presence here tonight than during the Endless Waltz, black and red flames as common as the party's theme. I couldn't smell smoke or see Rian's potbelly anywhere, though. Where was he?

Trey elbowed me in the side. "Michael."

"Wha—" And then I saw.

The Corrupt Prince was staring at me from across the room. His Throne Seekers surrounded him, chatting and vying for his attention. But the giant of a man never took his eyes off me. He tapped his scarred cheek and then broke off his gaze, returning to his allies.

"The Corrupt Prince knows I'm here," I whispered loud enough for my friends to hear. "We need to find Rian. Quickly. Kai and Trey, you two search the left side. Dawn and I will search the right."

There was no argument and we went to work. Kai and Dawn were able to slip in and out of every group within the party, whether they were in the middle of a conversation or not. Since Dawn was so lively, few people even glanced at me while I was on her arm. Those who attempted to court Dawn never lasted long—a night, maybe an entire day if they were lucky. My disguise should have been perfect. But every once in a while the Corrupt Prince glowered at me until I met his gaze, then he smiled, tapped his cheek, and looked away. I had no idea what he was planning, and the fact that he was *waiting* made it worse.

The Corrupt Prince was not one to think about the consequences of his actions, let alone be patient. So his not acting on impulse was concerning. Maybe he knew taking me down here wouldn't help him in the long run. Maybe he was getting more tactical. Smarter. Calmer. Neither option was good for me.

While we were in the middle of a truly boring conversation with High Noble Dara Hyann about his concerns over the economic troubles in New Dracon City, I slipped away to get some food. Who knew when I would get another opportunity? I began to stuff my face with pickled herring, sausage and lentil stew, and sticky rice cakes. Despite how high-quality it all was, I didn't savor it. I just wanted the pain in my stomach to stop.

"So you're the latest one, eh?" a young man said as he approached the table full of food. When I didn't respond—a mouthful of pork my excuse—he clarified, "You're courting High Noble Margaux?"

I nodded and continued to eat. The noble did what they do best and continued the conversation on his own.

"We failures nicknamed her 'the Intangible.'"

After swallowing, I said, "Here I thought nicknaming her 'the Girl in Red' was bad."

The noble looked at Dawn. "But she's wearing trousers. Brown ones."

"Not all the time."

For a man dressed entirely in blue, though, that thought may have been preposterous. He rallied well. "Still. Be wary of High Noble Margaux. There's a reason she earned her nickname."

"It wasn't just bitterness?"

"No . . . well, perhaps some," the noble said. "We realized we were all just distractions. Flings she was quick to get out of her system. That woman . . . she's not thinking about the future. All she cares about is having fun."

"What's wrong with that?"

"Nothing," he said quickly. "But . . . I courted her for three months two years ago. I was in love—the all-you-can-think-about kind of love. The love that makes you content to sleep because you know you'll dream of her. I was *so* happy." The noble closed his eyes. "Until one day I went to meet her for a picnic, and she forgot who I was. Nothing of me remained. Then I found others who told similar stories." He opened his eyes. "She clings to certain memories like a child who has bottled fireflies, but everything else is a dream that disappears when she awakes."

I chewed slowly but listened intently.

"She hides her constant memory loss well, but I don't think it's much longer before she becomes a Forgotten." He put his hand on my shoulder. "Just know that if you love her, it will be wonderful and amazing, but it won't be forever. Guard your heart, friend."

I nodded and continued to eat as I watched Dawn mingle with other nobles. Full of laughter, a smile almost wider than her face allowed, and legs that might as well have been carved from steel, thanks to her Fabrications. At the rate she was using them, how much longer did she have before she became a Forgotten?

I stole her away from the conversation she was having with a pull of the wrist and a motion to the dance floor. She followed without question despite confusion. The musicians were playing a slow, sad song that most people had chosen to opt out of, eagerly waiting for a waltz to begin to show off their skills. I pulled her close, put my hands on the small of her back, and danced—or tried to remember how to dance. It had been well over a decade since I had participated in one.

"Everything well?" she asked quietly, leading us. "Did someone say—"

"Be honest with me. How close are you?"

Her eyes narrowed. "How close to what?"

I leaned close so I could whisper in her ear. "How close are you to becoming a Forgotten? Please. Tell me the truth."

Dawn couldn't meet my eyes.

"Dawn."

"If I'm lucky? A month or two." She paused. "If I'm not? A week or two."

My heart skipped a beat, and everything slowed down around us. "I don't . . . Why didn't you tell me sooner? At Margaux Keep you were so . . . you said the journals would . . ." And I trailed off, unable to find the right words. "Does anyone else know?"

"Kai suspects but hasn't asked," she said with a forced smile. "I don't think he wants to. If he did, he'd be forced to stop me from being who I want to be. And he knows that I consider losing what little freedom I have worse than becoming a Forgotten. I want to live my life my way."

"No matter the cost?"

"No matter the cost. That's the beauty of life. We all have the right to choose what we want to do with what little time we have." She put her head on my chest. "If I become a Forgotten tonight trying to save this city . . . will you still be my friend when morning comes?"

"Always."

And so we danced until the song ended without saying anything else.

Afterward, Kai and Trey came over to us as we left the dance floor. Trey whispered, "We spotted Rian heading toward the throne room."

We all took off briskly toward the throne room. It became a jog and then a full-out sprint once we were out of the public eye. And there was Rian Smoak, standing in front of the stone throne, which had been decorated for the coronation at dawn. He was wearing the typical flame-trimmed robes of his order. His potbelly was prominent, he smelled of a pungent smoke that lingered in the air, and whatever he was drinking had dyed the goblet a dark red.

"Michael! Wonderful to see you again. Are you here to help the queen-in-waiting with her coronation?"

I stopped within arm's reach of him. "Rian, are you a Spellborn?"

It was only there for a moment—shorter than a standard blink—but even he couldn't stop his face from recoiling in shock. Not at the question but at the fact I had figured out a truth I shouldn't have. I had seen it before when I confronted Angelo in the dungeons.

Before he could explain, I did what had to be done.

I drew my revolver and shot the dragon between the eyes.

SMOKE

Rian Smoak exploded into smoke before the bullet collided with him, and it lodged in the wooden floor behind him instead.

As if it was going to be that easy. Not for me. Never for me.

As Rian re-formed exactly where he had been, Trey drew two flint-lock pistols, Kai clicked his tongue, and Dawn steeled her body completely. We had beaten a false dragon once before, how hard could a real one be?

"I suppose she sent you to take my heart, didn't she, Michael?" Rian asked. Smoke was still coming off him like steam. "I knew she would come for me eventually. I thought she'd come for me herself, but that was never her style. It was his but not hers. Always quiet and never heard, always in the background."

"*She*?" I asked. "The Heartbreaker is a man."

"The Heartbreaker is one of the most infamous serial killers in the world. Do you really think it's just one person?"

My mouth hung open. Dammit. I had suspected but didn't have confirmation until now. Two people acting as one was the only thing that explained all the inconsistencies while we had been chasing them. Rian laughed at me.

"The Heartbreaker you must be familiar with is Luis Valenti, the man who stole fire. He was the worst of us. Where most of my family sought to dictate or aid this world, all he wanted to do was have fun. We knew how inhumane he was before, but none of us could have predicted what he'd become. The only thing that could excite him once he became immortal was murder and the thrill of being caught."

"And her?"

"That's a more tragic story," Rian said softly. "Her name is Anna Valenti, the woman who listens to everything. She was a nurse in the Wolven Kings War, and the poor child who ended up treating a young, charismatic man named Luis. He made her fall in love with him . . . and then abused her until she thought no one would ever love her like he did." Rian closed his eyes. "When the time came for all of us to become monsters to end a war . . . Luis manipulated her into joining our family." He opened his eyes and all I saw was an endless ocean of regret. "She didn't want to lose him, so she became a monster to remain at his side."

"What do you mean she became a monster?"

"Do you know what I am, Michael?"

"I do," I said, the revolver still in my hand, knuckles white from strain.

Rian put his hand over his heart. "Then you know where our powers lay. How do you think we became what we are? We ate our predecessors' hearts to help end the Wolven Kings' tyranny." He hesitated and then added, "Most of us won't claim to be good people, but we did what was necessary."

"Necessary?" I shouted. "Ending a war a thousand years ago doesn't excuse that you left the Heartbreaker alone for so long! Why didn't you stop him once it was over?"

"Because one does not win wars with pleasant words and handshakes. Sometimes blood must be spilled." He looked away from us. "Sometimes we need monsters to do what civil people cannot."

"Spoken like someone who's always held power," Trey mumbled.

"And you four are any better? You're playing by their rules. To kill me for . . . what exactly does she hold of yours?"

"Everything."

"She has the princess. That explains why High Nobles are trying to slip out of this party unnoticed. I'm surprised she didn't try to send the Mercenary after . . . Oh, well I suppose she has him, too. Interesting. That just leaves you."

"Will you help me stop them?"

Rian shook his head. "I'm sorry, Michael. I won't help the Mercenary. Left unhindered, he will soon become as dangerous as the Wolven Kings were. He must die for the world to avoid ruin."

"And the others? What are they? Necessary sacrifices?" I clenched my fists. "If Serena dies, then Hollow will follow soon after!"

"Losing the princess will be a tragedy"—Rian put his hands on his hips and looked down—"but this is the way the world works. There are the remembered and the forgotten. And not every forgotten is unremarkable. Some are erased on purpose. Maybe it's time for Hollow to be reborn."

"I will not let my home be destroyed for the greater good."

"Then that's it."

"I suppose it is."

Rian was pacing, his movements lighter than air. Smoke was coming off every part of his body now, tendrils dancing like wind blowing falling snow. His features seemed to elongate, turning more beastlike, teeth growing sharper and nails that might as well have been talons. His eyes were glowing, burning red. It must have been a dragon thing, because both Mocking Bird and Dark did the same when they used their magic. I didn't know why I hadn't noticed that sooner. Had I missed others who had done the same? How many of these remaining immortal dragons were hiding in Hollow, steering us toward the fate and society they desired?

I didn't agree with Dark committing genocide, but right now I wasn't going to let one old person condemn Hollow to destruction.

"Are you sure you want to do this, Michael?" Rian's voice was a deep growl. "I won't go quietly. You won't be the first noble fool to fall at my feet."

I didn't blink, my gaze focused on Rian. Smoke was obscuring most of his face now. Except his eyes. Those were still visible and bright red. And just outside the smoke, something coiled like a snake before thumping against the ground.

"This will—" Rian began before I interrupted. I sprinted toward him and then leapt with a nullified fist. It went through him, a handful of smoke my only reward. Then his tail tripped me, and I fell face-first into the floor, cursing as I reoriented myself.

Smoke was circling the room now, Rian's voice coming from every-where and nowhere. "Children. Novices. Did you really think that would work? I've fought Fabricators for hundreds of years! You can't surprise me."

"We'll see about that," I muttered, trying to find the warmth in my chest. I had nullified a large area before and could do it again. But the moment I did, it would take Dawn out of the fight. Without her Fabrica-tions she wouldn't be able to stand. It was my last resort, but one I sus-pected I'd have to turn to.

"How do we hit him?" Trey yelled, watching as the smoke approached like fog.

"You don't," Rian said.

A hand came out of the smoke, covered Trey's face, and then slammed him down to the ground. It was so overwhelming, there was nothing Trey could do to stop it. Even Dawn's last-ditch effort to stop the hand was fu-tile, grabbing a fistful of smoke as the cloud distorted and twisted before engulfing her completely. I heard her body hit the floor.

Kai was taken out soon after, punched in the stomach so hard, he puked as his knees touched the floor. Flies would have put up more of a fight than we did. But now nothing was stopping me from nullifying this area. I took a deep breath, focused on the warmth in my chest, and then expelled it outward. There was no sign that I had done anything. No gust of power, or wind, or light, or anything. But the smoke simply cleared to reveal Rian Smoak's new form.

Rian Smoak was still wearing his black robes with a flame trim. His arms, his legs, and the right side of his face were covered in shiny silver scales. His nails, toenails, and teeth were long and sharp. A pair of tattered bat-like wings had erupted from his back, and a long tail gently waved back and forth on the ground behind him. He wasn't fully transformed, but it was going to be hard to claim that dragons weren't real now. Of course, this had to be one of the many things in my life I was wrong about. As if there weren't already enough.

"Not a complete novice, then," Rian said. "And here I thought you still didn't understand how your powers worked."

"I learn quickly."

"So Domet told me. Shame you didn't listen to his warning about me."

"What warning?" I asked as I started to pace. I was too far from him to try a shot now. The odds were I'd miss, and with only a few more bullets left, each of them had to count. But if I could get a little closer . . .

A laugh. "Do you misunderstand all of Domet's mannerisms and words?"

"I don't," I said, the thought of the note from the Waylayer in my head. "I know exactly what Domet is. A suicidal Immortal."

"He's more than that," Rian said softly. "Much more. It's a shame you don't realize who you're dealing with. How much he cared. How far he was willing to go and why he wants to die so badly."

"Do you know why he wants to die?"

"Obviously. But am I going to tell you? No. But I'll tell him goodbye for you."

Rian rushed me and I shot. The bullet hit him in the shoulder, but he didn't stop. I tried to parry. I tried to do anything, but I was overpowered in an instant. He slammed me down, my ears were ringing, and my vision was blurry as Rian stood over me.

I could hear shouts and footsteps off in the distance. I had been a fool to try this, but if I could just hold on a little—

Rian picked me up by the throat.

I couldn't breathe and clawed at his hands, trying to get him to drop me. Kicking at his face and body. Nothing worked. I was like an ant trying to move a mountain.

"You Kingman always try to interfere in the affairs of Immortals," Rian taunted. "Who was the last one to try and kill one of my siblings? What was their name? Cora? No, Cordelia? I stomped them like the insect they were, and you won't be any different."

I tried to claw out his eyes and was only met with laughter.

Rian held up his hand, nails sharper than any surgical instrument. "Since you came for my heart, it only seems fair that I should take yours."

Something was cracking and scraping against stone out of view. I just had to hold on a little longer. Someone would come to save me. I knew it. Wardens. Advocators. Ravens. Mercenaries. Someone. Anyone.

I didn't want to die without telling—

"Goodbye, Michael Kingman. Say hi to God."

My eyes closed as Rian's hand thrust for my chest.

I fell to the ground, my body heavier than it had ever been before.

And I opened them to see Dawn was on top of me, a slight smile on her face and a hole where her heart had been.

With her last act, Dawn brushed a strand of hair out of my face. "Told you no one decided my fate but me."

Then her eyes went vacant and her body limp.

Rian was staring at her, holding Dawn's heart in his hand as if he were about to recite poetry to it. "Where did she come—"

A bullet through his mouth cut him off. Her heart fell and he went to his knees, one hand on the back of his neck while the other covered his mouth. He was gurgling blood.

I carefully rolled Dawn's body off me until she was lying comfortably on her back, her eyes closed. Then I stood over Rian with the revolver against his forehead and his hands desperately trying to keep the blood in. "I hope this hurts and I hope you're scared of dying. Tell God that if they get in my way, they're next. Everything dies eventually."

I pulled the trigger and was greeted with a face full of smoke.

My screams filled the room as I tried to grab the smoke around me. Even nullifying the area again did nothing but take another one of my memories. Rian Smoak had escaped, and Dawn was . . . Dawn was . . . Dawn . . .

My hand shook as the gun in my hand moved closer to my temple. I had failed. Again and again and again. I couldn't do this—

"Michael?" Kai sat up with a groan. I lowered the gun back to my side. "What happened?"

Trey was stirring next to him. He saw the scene and put his hand over his mouth as his eyes went wide. There was so much blood. On me. On the floor. On Dawn . . . on Dawn's . . .

"Michael," Kai repeated, his voice shakier. "Why is Dawn lying there? Where's Rian? What's going on?"

I couldn't find my voice.

"Michael!" Kai shouted. "Why can't I hear Dawn's heartbeat?"

It came out like a croak: "Rian tore out her heart. She's dead."

Kai screamed, scrambling toward his best friend, saying, "No. No. No," over and over again until his voice was hoarse. He checked for a pulse, and when he found nothing, he screamed again. A scream that would haunt my dreams.

I slumped down on the floor, mindless, with an itch in my temple that wouldn't go away.

Trey put his hand on my shoulder and didn't move it away when I put mine over it.

"He should have killed me," I whispered. "I failed her."

"But *she* didn't fail *you*. She saved your life. A lot more people are going to die unless we stop the Heartbreaker. This isn't the time to give up."

"It shouldn't be on us to save the city."

"But it is," Trey said. "If life were fair, Jamal would still be alive. But he isn't, so it's time to move forward."

"We don't have Rian's heart. Everyone's going to die regardless of what we do."

Wordlessly, Trey picked Dawn's heart off the ground.

I just looked at it. "She deserves better than that."

"We do what we must to survive. Don't let her sacrifice be an excuse to give up."

I rose to my feet, weary. Kai was crying over Dawn's body.

"Kai, I'm sorry," I said. "I have to go stop the Heartbreaker."

He paused long enough to say, "I need to stay with her. She shouldn't be alone."

"No, she shouldn't."

"Michael," he said as he wiped some of the tears away. "Don't let this be in vain."

There was that familiar weight on my shoulders. Trey quickly wrapped Dawn's heart in a handkerchief from his pocket. All the gunshots had attracted attention to the throne room and people were coming. I didn't have time to say goodbye to Dawn before we had to run.

Trey took the revolver from me, and I didn't stop him.

BURIED ALIVE

Neither of us spoke until we passed the gates to the King's Garden. Slushy snow lingered on the ground, wet and icy, and the wind was unforgiving. Rain dripped off the buildings into puddles in the street. My senses were dulled, everything indistinguishable and barely in focus. It was as miserable outside as I felt, and all I wanted to do was find a ditch to crawl into and . . . and . . .

"I go to Jamal's grave every other day or so. It's one of the kids' jobs to bring me, since I can't remember where it is anymore," Trey said, hands bundled in his jacket. "Helps ease some of the pain to visit. Makes me feel less like a failure."

"Does it really?"

"Not in the slightest."

We watched our breath steam up and away. When we reached the point where the manicured gardens blended with uncontrollable nature, with toppled-over trees and twigs that snapped beneath our heels, I knew we were close.

"How do you want to handle this?" Trey asked.

I held out my hand for my gun and checked how many bullets were left. "Two bullets," I muttered. "Just enough to shoot the Heartbreaker in the head twice."

"Will that be enough? Rian—"

"Rian bled any like other mortal. He feared death like any mortal. I'm going to make the Heartbreaker feel the same."

Trey checked the flintlock pistols strapped to his chest while staring at a trail of blood leading toward my grave. "Michael, we have a problem."

Because of course we did. At least this time we hadn't been caught off guard. From this distance, I could see that two people were standing in front of my grave. One was tied up and the other had an open wound down their forearm—blood dyeing the snow below—as they held a sword against the back of their captive's neck. Identities and specifics were being obstructed by their winter clothing. Lousy winter. Always making life harder.

"How do you want to handle this?" Trey asked.

"Thinking about shooting first and sorting through the bodies later."

"Usually works. Might not this time."

"Why not?"

Trey cleared his throat. "Because that's Lyon and the Recorder over there."

I sighed instead of cursing.

"Lyon!" I ran toward the grave. "What're you doing?"

Lyon yanked Symon off the ground, sword against his neck. Symon's hands were tied behind his back, and, incredibly, Lyon had found a way to silence him. A piece of cloth down his throat, a length of rope over his mouth, and Symon was clearly livid about it.

"Michael? What're you doing here?" Lyon asked, his voice calmer than it had any right to be. "I thought you weren't going to play the Heartbreaker's game."

"I lied."

"To Ma and to Gwen? Do you even know what the truth is anymore? Not that it matters. I have the Historian. I'll save Kayleigh myself."

Trey held up the heart we had brought. "The Heartbreaker asked for the Historian. Not the Recorder. We brought the right one."

Lyon lowered the sword from Symon's neck slightly. "You're wrong."

"We're not." I tried to approach Lyon but stopped when he tightened his grip on the sword. "Let him go."

"Why should I take that risk?" he questioned. "You have a heart. I have a heart. Maybe one of us will be right."

"Can you really live with killing someone who may be innocent?"

Lyon stared me down. "All I do is kill people. If I must add another name to my skin to save Kayleigh and my child, I will do so without hesitation."

"Lyon, please," I said softly. "Enough blood has been spilled tonight."

"I would burn this city to the ground for them." My brother exhaled. "I'm sorry you had to see this."

"Lyon, don't—"

A flash of light whizzed past me and collided with Lyon's chest. He flew backward, slamming into my grave as the sword in his hand skittered to the side. Symon scrambled away from Lyon and toward us. Trey was still standing as if he had thrown a spear, breathing shallowly. Thankfully for us all, Trey was calm and focused enough for the both of us.

"I could have talked him down," I muttered.

"No, you—"

And he stopped, watching as Lyon slowly returned to his feet as if pulled by invisible strings, blood trickling down his forehead. Lyon went to pick up his sword and then held it in his right hand, glancing at each of us.

"You three will not stop me from saving my family."

All the blood in the area flew upward, hovering in the air like rain droplets stopped in mid-motion before coming together at our feet and wrapping around our necks, waists, feet, and arms like a snake. It hardened in place almost instantly once it was in place and felt as if thousands of tiny thorns covered it. The blood choked, bound, and forced all three of us to fall to our sides, struggling to get free.

"I never wanted to be the heir," Lyon said. "Not even when Da was still alive. But I was always expected to do what was right. To bleed for this city . . . until the princess gave me an out. These last few days have been paradise. I was finally free from this curse on my blood."

"You've been a Fabricator?" I groaned. "This entire time?"

"Da figured it out when I was very young. Something about how I bleed made him suspicious. The usual tests didn't work, but when it was confirmed what I was, he taught me how to control my powers in secret. He was worried . . . that people might not see me as a hero because of it. It's not very befitting of a Kingman to have the ability to manipulate blood, is it? It seems villainous."

I nullified my body, letting the warmth spread out over any part that the blood was touching, but it didn't go away. If anything, my constraints got tighter.

Lyon stepped over me, sword still in hand, and then looked down. "Don't bother struggling. It won't break easily. Every person's blood has different properties and lets me do different things. Can you guess what our family's blood is the best for?" He paused for effect. "Binding. Obstructing. Holding captive."

I wiggled on the ground, cursing. Trey was doing the same, albeit glowing from his Light Fabrications. Symon was still, eyes wide at my brother and the sword in his hand. He looked like someone who knew his fate.

"I'm sorry I never told you and Gwen," he said. "But I never thought I'd have to use them again after the riots. I killed so many that night . . ." Thorns of blood formed on his sword's blade. "Ironic . . . that once again I'm using them to save my family . . ."

"Lyon! Stop this!"

My brother put the tip of his sword against Symon's chest and ignored my shouts. He looked Symon in the eyes as he said, "If it brings you some comfort, I will remember you. Long past my dying breath."

Not again.

No one was going to die here. No matter the cost to me.

I *repelled* the warmth in my body, blood losing its form, as I screamed and punched my brother solidly in the jaw. He hit the ground with a thud and lay still as I stood in his place. My knuckles burned and ached, but in the cold and snow it was all a dull numbness.

There was no time for his bullshit, his insecurity, or whatever this clusterfuck had been. He could either make things better or get out of the way.

"Are you done?" I asked.

"I can't lose them."

"You won't. Trust me. For once in your life."

I undid Symon's restraints, eyeing my brother on the ground. He refused to look at me. Symon pulled the gag out of his mouth and then said, "Anyone want to explain why I was just kidnapped and almost killed by a Kingman?"

"Not really," I said.

Lyon was shaking on the ground, muttering and sobbing to himself. Trey had a gun aimed at him, just in case.

Symon wouldn't drop it. "I think I deserve an explanation."

Thankfully, Trey gave him one. "Lyon thought you were the Heartbreaker's target, so he brought you here to get murdered to save his pregnant fiancée who was taken. Along with the princess, Dark, Domet, and Naomi."

Symon opened his mouth, paused, and then said to me, "I leave you alone for one night and you get caught up in this? How could you not come and get me? I have a right to record your story. How dare you let me miss all the good bits."

"Sorry," I said. "Must've been caught up trying to stop a serial killer and forgot about your story. How rude of me."

"Apology accepted."

I was about to say something quite uniquely rude when I was interrupted by a very familiar voice. "Mi-chael King-man. So. You. Came."

Trey and I pulled out our guns at the same time, turning in the direction of the voice. Nothing was there. In fact, there wasn't anyone anywhere. It was as if the wind had carried their words to us.

"You. Brought. Friends." A harsh gust of wind howled through the graveyard. "How. Quaint."

Trey held up the heart as I said, "I have the Historian's heart! If you want it, I want those who you've taken released. Or else I'll crush it!"

Laughter echoed around us. Even Symon, who was normally so composed, wasn't reaching for the pen and ink he kept in his pockets. He was too terrified. Seemed even those meant to record history had their limits.

"Just release Kayleigh!" Lyon pleaded. "Please!"

"Beg."

Whatever pride Lyon had, it was gone as he fell to his knees, put his forehead against the snow, and screamed, "Please let Kayleigh live!"

There was no response. Not even a gust of wind. Until, softly, a voice said, "Lyon? Is that you?"

Kayleigh was walking toward us, barefoot and blinded by a cloth over her eyes. Lyon ran to her, jumping over graves and sticks and stones, and didn't stop crying until he held her in his arms again.

"Lyon?" she asked as she returned the hug. "I was told not to take off the blindfold until I was out of the gardens. Is it safe to yet?"

My brother calmed Kayleigh down by running his hands through her hair. "It's okay, you're safe. We're not out of the gardens yet. Here, take my boots. I'm fine without them."

Kayleigh didn't complain, slipping into my brother's boots, which were much too big on her and slapped the ground with every step. My brother only nodded to me before leading her away. He had what he had come for, and now it was my turn to do the same.

"Where are the others?" I shouted once Lyon and Kayleigh were out of view.

"Leave. Heart. Grave."

"How do I know the others are still alive?"

"Not. Fun. Otherwise."

"Where are they?"

No response.

Trey put his hand on my shoulder. "I think we have to play their game, Michael. We already got one."

"This is bullshit," I snapped.

"Only if we lose."

"Fine," I said as I took the heart from Trey. I laid it gently over my grave and hoped Dawn could forgive me. I was doing my best. "The heart is on the grave! Where are the others?"

"Church. Wanderer. Hurry."

I looked around. Still no one. Where was the voice coming from? What was I missing?

Trey grabbed my sleeve. "Michael, we need to go."

"What if they're lying?"

"Then we find them and make them pay. But standing here, waiting for them to show up, is useless. We're going to play their game and win. Trust me?"

I spoke without thinking. "Always."

"I'm coming with you," Symon declared, as if he were a small child asserting himself to his parents. "I have a right to your story, Michael, and I will have it."

Trey and I shared a glance before we did the only reasonable thing. We overpowered Symon easily—years of sitting and writing doing him no favors in this situation—and bound him in the same restraints he had been brought in. We needed fighters with us, not writers.

Trey threw Symon over his shoulder and we left my grave. I tried to be alert for anyone approaching as we ran off toward the Church of the Wanderer, but, without me seeing how, Dawn's heart was taken from the grave.

A disturbed pile of snow and a clean headstone were all that remained.

55

ENDLESS BELLS

After we dropped Symon off in a refugee camp, with very strict instructions not to untie him until morning, we made our way to the Great Stone Square. It was full of people, lights, noise, and food. Everyone went to the colosseum for the executions and free food, but no one enjoyed it. A coronation was different. There was a celebration for everyone, regardless of class, wealth, or citizenship. The only day of true equality in Hollow. Even the two churches—Wanderer and Eternal Flame—came together to throw a joint celebration. And the rebels were going to ruin it by destroying this city. Unless we stopped them.

Which was a problem for after we'd taken care of the Heartbreaker.

The two of us made our way through the crowds as best we could, trying not to trip over all the gangs of children that ran through the streets pelting anyone they saw with brightly colored powders. Some elders, not to be outdone by those they had watched learn to walk, responded with attacks of their own, dyeing the children and street a majestic purple. They shrieked as they shielded their eyes, not used to being outwitted.

Some chose to continue their attack, while others kept running to chase after unsullied targets.

There were vendors and people and games everywhere, and a metal tree in the center of the square that many had tied prayers to. Large pots of dye sat unattended every few steps to make sure the city at the end of the festival would make the Rainbow District look dull. Not wanting to test my luck after everything that happened, I covered my treason brand with a bright blue streak of powder. I would have gone with red—to keep with tradition—but for some reason that was the only color not offered for use. I couldn't help but wonder if Serena had made that decision or not.

It was all one giant lump of controlled chaos. Despite the food vendors who called to us to stop and enjoy the coronation delicacies that would be available only tonight, we persisted toward the church. By the time we made it through the Great Stone Square, I was plastered with so many different-colored powders, I looked as if a sadistic jester had done my makeup. Trey had escaped with only a splattering of colors rather than a messed-up palette. Not wanting to look like a madman, I tried to clean some of it off my body in large pots of water as Trey took a moment to collect himself.

When it was clear the water just seemed to fix the colors in my skin rather than wash them away, we climbed the stairs to the church with no idea what the Heartbreaker had left for us. The Church of the Wanderer didn't burn a wooden statue like the Eternal Flame or hold a Fabrication tournament like the nobility did in the castle. There was no grand celebration to ruin here. So where would the Heartbreaker have left the hostages?

When we reached the top, a barefoot monk was standing near the entrance. He was dressed in white robes and a head scarf that looked like it had been put on in a rush, haphazardly looped around his neck with one end way too long and the other way too short. A permanent smile seemed etched on his face. Without doubt, he was a member of the Church of the Wanderer. They were the only ones foolish enough to wear such light clothing when it was so cold out. Their traditional nomadic dress only ever benefited them in the warmer months.

"Michael Kingman! In the flesh!" the monk said as he skipped over to me. "If you have a moment I would love to— Oh, is that dried blood below all that dye? Are you well? Do you need me to take you to a hospital?"

"No hospital," I said as we entered the church. It was quieter in here, despite the celebration going on outside and all the refugees inside. "Where's the Reclaimer?"

"Away," the monk said. "What do you all want with her?"

"We have reason to believe the Heartbreaker brought hostages here."

Without hesitation the monk said, "The Reclaimer isn't here. She went out to visit some of the refugees who are still in hiding. Can I help?"

"Has anything unusual happened tonight?"

The monk tapped his bare foot against the cold stone. "How would we know? We're overwhelmed with refugees here. Every day something new happens."

"What about people in places they shouldn't be?" Trey asked.

"Not really. Some people try to sneak food out of the kitchens, or walk the halls in the middle of the night, but after everything they've been through . . ."

I couldn't stop looking around the church as the monk attempted to remember any unusual happenings. There were parents covering their children with blankets, friends feeding those who had lost limbs and were unable to do it themselves, and people with the Corruption who sat unmoving as they stared off at nothing. So many people. So many hurt from war. How could the Heartbreaker go unnoticed in this—

Oh. That was it.

"Is there anywhere in the Church of the Wanderer that is always restricted to the public? A sacred place?"

"We're not the Church of the Eternal Flame. Everything is open for any who need it. But I suppose no one goes into the old bell tower anymore. Not since Hollow built the new ones run by the Watchers."

"That's where they are."

"If the Heartbreaker was here, I doubt they would have left something in the bell tower," the monk said. "Only the Reclaimer has the key to it."

"Humor me."

"Fine."

I couldn't help but smile as we went to the bell tower. The door was slightly ajar, key still in the lock. The monk pocketed it without comment and led us up the tower. The steps were steep and jarring, and there was an odd, overwhelming smell that I couldn't place. Like a forgotten memory. When we had all climbed up, slightly out of breath, the monk opened the main door.

That was when the fuses were lit.

Four lines sparked to life and flames began to travel down a length in twisting patterns toward a group of barrels stacked together, two wiggling bodies bound with rope in front of them. A man and a woman.

There was no time to think.

Only act.

Trey shoved the monk out of the way and went for the body on the right. I sprinted toward the fuses, attempting to stamp them out, to no avail. There was no dirt or water or anything I could throw over them. Just my feet. The monk cursed loudly and then sprinted down the stairs.

A hero he wasn't.

The fire was getting closer to the gunpowder.

"Trey! Tell me good news!"

"I can't. I . . . can't. The knots . . . Too tight."

I knelt and tried to pull up the fuses. My nails dug at the edges but were unable to grasp them before the fire burned through my grip and singed my fingers. Not much longer. A few heartbeats before the *bang*.

"Trey! Hurry! I can't—"

"Dammit!"

Trey took the woman in a tight hug and threw himself over the edge. I heard him hit the ground much softer than he should have. One innocent was out of danger. Hopefully. Only one to go.

I realized it was Domet only as I dove to shield the Immortal. The fire reached the barrels and the bell fell through the floor as an explosion rang out around me.

56

FLOWERS FOR
THEIR GRAVES

Still alive. That was a good start.

Everything hurt, but recently it was hard to remember a time when it didn't. This pain would be temporary, and worth it if I saved everyone. The bell tower had collapsed into the church, crushing the central pews. The bell was upside down and lodged all the way into the ground as if a hole had been dug for it. The refugees were huddled against the wall. The fleeing monk had gotten everyone out of the way. I had misjudged him.

Domet was within arm's reach, groaning and clutching his stomach with an arm that was bent at an unnatural angle. He was badly burnt, his skin was wrinkled, mangled, and oozing pus and blood. Considering how uninjured I was, he must've shielded me rather than the reverse. I would have had some sympathy if I couldn't already see his body healing itself, straightening and smoothing his injuries.

Domet was laughing.

"I told them you would come," Domet said. "They've faced other Kingman before. They didn't realize you were different. Your ancestors never scared me." A pause. "You do."

"Enough," I groaned as I went to my knees. "I haven't won anything yet."

"Not yet, but you will. Don't you see, Michael? I've created an Immortal's natural enemy. Someone with the power to stand against anyone or anything."

"I'm mortal," I breathed. "I'm a fool living on borrowed time. I will fall eventually."

"But not today," he cackled. "How far will you rise and who will you destroy before you die?"

My eyes watered from the pain, but I pushed through it and towered over the Immortal.

"Just so your adventure doesn't end here . . ." Domet extended his hand and opened his closed fist to give me what he was clutching. A red flower petal. It seemed fragile in my palm and I didn't know its significance. I told Domet as much.

"Ask your friend. I got it from the Heartbreaker," Domet said with closed eyes. "Now, if you'll excuse me, I have the hurt High Noble to masquerade as. Do you think they'll all believe your Nullification Fabrications protected me? Oh, I hope so. Your legend will grow after tonight."

"Whatever you say, Lifeweaver."

Domet's eyes snapped open. "How do you know that name?"

"Someone told me."

"Who?"

I laughed. "As if I'd tell you. I like having some—"

"Tell me, and I'll tell you about the *obligations* that prevented me from choosing Gwen as my weapon. You were my backup, you know, and aren't you a little curious why?"

It felt as if I had been struck by lightning. My lips curled upward slightly as hundreds—thousands—of questions ran through my head. Gwen had mentioned things stopping her from leaving Hollow before, but I had always assumed . . . I exhaled and calmed my mind down.

"Once this is over, I'll ask her myself."

"If she hasn't told you by now, why do you think she ever would? You need me, Michael. I have information you can never access otherwise."

It would have been so simple to accept his deal. To give me whatever I wanted. He lied constantly and tried to twist me into doing his bidding. I wouldn't have come this far without him. But . . . but just as Jamal's death had forced me to confront my magical abilities, Dawn's death had forced me to seek what I wanted. To be free from the chains that held me down, no matter what kind they were or what hardships would find me without their support.

I gave him the one-finger salute. "Goodbye, Domet."

He shouted at me to reconsider, but I left the madman to heal and plot and scheme by himself.

The barefoot monk from before limped over to me, using a broken piece of the pew as a cane. Before he could speak, I asked, "Are you all well? And are all the refugees unharmed?"

"No major injuries. Not sure about your friend yet," the monk said. "Got everyone out of the way in the nick of time. God willing."

"Good," I said. It hurt to move. What I wouldn't do for some sleep. I showed him the red petal. "Do you know what this is?"

After only a glance, the monk said, "No idea."

I cracked my neck, mumbled about checking up on Trey, and left the monk behind. There was a crowd gathered where Trey had landed, a few of the stone steps cracked. Most of the festivities had stopped, replaced with whispers that Hollow had missed that a piece of Celona was falling from the sky. I pushed aside anyone in my way to get to Trey and the woman he had saved.

Naomi.

She was on her back, shuddering with pain, but conscious. Trey was on the ground next to her, less injured. Both were alive. I squatted, held out my hand, and said, "Can you walk?"

Trey clasped my hand and pulled himself up. "Assume I can until I say otherwise."

"Will do. Nice move up there."

"'Painful' might be more appropriate. Even with Naomi's Wind Fabrications slowing us."

"Naomi, how about you?"

She opened one eye to look at me. "What took you so long?"

"Since when do you need someone to save you?"

"Shut up and help me up."

We did, as the crowds stared. Not wanting to ruin the rest of their night—fully aware the rebels might do it for me unless I stopped them soon—I shouted, "I apologize for the inconvenience, fine citizens of Hollow. Please return to your festivities. Eat to your hearts' content, drink so much your bellies burst, and be daring . . . like it is the last night of your lives."

"What about the midnight service?" someone bellowed.

I looked back at the church. Part of the roof was caved in and the top of the bell tower was no more. It was a mushroom stem with its head ripped off. The dust from the collapse was spreading out over the area, illuminated by the pale light from the Moon's Tears on the church.

"A barefoot monk will be here momentarily to let you all know. I have no doubt that he will be able to perform a sermon from the top of the steps if need be. His voice carries very well."

We retreated before any other questions could be asked. Despite the explosion in the bell tower, most seemed to return to what they had been doing. Some fine Hollow resilience right there. Everyone was too used to random objects falling from the sky to be scared. Nothing could stop the party. Except the rebel army.

When we found a place to talk, Naomi sat down on the ground and massaged her shoulders. I showed them the petal Domet had given me. "Any idea what this is? Domet said he stole it from the Heartbreaker."

Naomi was the first to respond. "A flower petal. Sometimes you give whole ones to people you want to court as a sign of affection."

"And people say *I'm* the asshole."

"If you hadn't left me in that basement, maybe I wouldn't be so angry right now."

"Oh, I'm sorry," I said with hands extended. "I checked on you before I left, but Chloe had just lost an eye and a Waylayer was coming to kill the princess."

"You still left me behind."

"What else was I supposed to do? It was an emergency!"

"You could have woken me up and taken me with you! I would have done that for you!"

"You were unconscious! Chloe was missing an eye! I had to get help! Why are you blaming me for doing the right thing?"

"Because it's your fault I was at Kingman Keep when I was! *You're* the reason the Heartbreaker kidnapped me! I hate—"

"It's a poppy petal," Trey interrupted.

Naomi and I glared at each other and took a breath, and then I said, "So are we looking for somewhere poppies grow? They could be using—"

"You don't understand," Trey said. "People use poppy pods to create opium outside Hollow. But here, poppy extract is one of two key ingredients that, mixed properly, crystallize into the drug we know as Blackberries."

"What's the other ingredient?" I asked, softly.

Trey was laughing almost hysterically as he ran his hands over his face. "I've seen Blackberries being made before. Never understood why they felt the need to combine anything with opium. It's strong and addictive on its own. And it never made sense that tweekers had red eyes. Not until today."

"Trey? Talk to me."

"Think, Michael," Trey responded. "Who have you seen with red eyes? What do you think the other ingredient is?"

Dark's, Rian's, and Mocking Bird's eyes had all flashed red when . . . but no, it couldn't be . . .

"Tongue-tied? Let me spell it out for you, then. Blackberries are made from a combination of poppy extract and blood. Dragon blood."

"But that means—"

"That my supplier is either holding a dragon captive or it's volunteering its blood to make Blackberries. If we find the production facility, then we'll find the Heartbreaker."

Silence between us.

I took a deep breath, steadying myself. "You told me you knew who the Blackberry supplier is. Is that true?"

"You won't like it."

"Try me."

"It *was* High Noble Eliphaz Braven, who used to be the head of the family. I know because I used to work for him. Desperate times called for desperate measures, but something changed two and a half years ago. The Bravens got out of the Blackberry trade."

"Who took it over?"

"High Noble Alexander Ryder."

REDEMPTION

The three of us went to go meet with High Noble Alexander Ryder carrying loaded guns.

I gave my name to the friendly guard at the main entrance to Ryder Keep. With a smile and a few jokes, the Ryder house guards brought us to a plush and clean room designed for meeting without bothering to inspect us. A privilege I attributed to the fact that my brother was marrying Kayleigh.

The last time I had met with someone so influential and powerful, one of us died. I could only hope this time would be different. For some reason I doubted it. Trey was certain High Noble Alexander Ryder was responsible for the plague of Blackberries, and I had an uncomfortable feeling that if I had the opportunity, I should put an end to it.

Before I could determine what I was going to do, High Noble Alexander Ryder entered the room. There was a slight flush to his face and a wine goblet in his hands. The blond man was once again dressed in yellow and black, which highlighted the ugly scar across the bridge of his nose.

His pant leg was tucked into one of his boots and his jacket was unbuttoned more than was ever acceptable by High Noble standards.

"Michael!" High Noble Alexander said, opening his arms for a hug. "It's been too long. How have you been? And where's your brother and my daughter? They should have been here a long time ago."

I stayed seated. "I'm not sure. They might be at the Great Stone Square to enjoy the festivities."

"Kayleigh loved the Ehamian noodles there as a child." High Noble Alexander Ryder put his hand over his chest. "Excuse my manners. Michael, do introduce your two friends. They both look familiar."

"This is Naomi Dexter and Treyvon Wiccard."

Alexander Ryder bowed slightly to them. "Pleasure to meet you both. Any friend of Michael's is welcome in my home. My family remembers the old ways."

All three of us were shifting uncomfortably in our seats. Trey most of all. He had worn a mask every time he had bought Blackberries, to conceal his identity, but he was fairly certain his voice would give him away.

"I'm surprised to see you're still here. I thought the princess was holding a meeting with all the High Noble families tonight."

Alexander Ryder flopped into one of the many comfortable chairs in the room. "My wife went in my place, since I . . . began to celebrate rather early. But what do you need, Michael? Is everything well at Kingman Keep? I know Efyra was—"

"Are you supplying Blackberries to the East Side of Hollow?"

Alexander Ryder stared at me as he put his wineglass down on a side table. "That's a very serious accusation, Michael."

"Is it true?"

"It is not."

"Liar," Trey said. "And his shadow is normal, so his memories haven't been manipulated to hide the truth from him."

"This is a joke?" Alexander asked. "There's no other way you could think it appropriate to walk into my home and make these accusations.

Michael, I was your father's friend. Do you really think I would stoop to dealing drugs? Trust me. I am a good man."

"Every man I have looked up to in my life has lied to me," I said. "My father when he tried to protect me, my grandfather when he lied about how much time he had left, Angelo when he was raising me, and Charles Domet every day we meet. They all thought they had good reasons. No doubt you do, too. So prove me wrong. Show me that you're not just about to be another addition to that list."

"Michael, I—"

"Tell me why you did it," I said without a trace of anger in my voice. "Tell me why you've poisoned so many people. Show me how a good person could do that and still expect mercy."

I drew my revolver and let it hang between my knees.

Alexander Ryder said nothing.

"If you refuse to tell me your truth, then listen to mine."

With a gun in my hand, I told Alexander Ryder everything. The Heartbreaker and the hostages, Dawn's death, Kayleigh's release and Lyon's near fall from grace, the Church of the Wanderer being destroyed, and how I had to find the killer or this city would fall. All I needed was the Heartbreaker's location. A piece of information only he, Dark, and High Noble Maflem Braven had.

When the story was over, Alexander Ryder was painfully sober. While I talked, he had become more himself, straightening out his hair, re-buttoning his jacket, and correcting his pant legs. After an audible gulp, he said, "I'm sorry."

I motioned for him to elaborate.

"I've been supplying Blackberries, and I am sorry for it."

"Why?" Trey asked softly. "You had a chance to end it. Why didn't you? How much blood is on your hands?"

"Does it matter? Will my justifications make it better? I poisoned the city I was supposed to heal. There is no redemption for me. Only shame."

"I need to know." One of Trey's flintlock pistols was in his right hand. The High Noble hesitated, drawing breath slowly as he looked Trey in the eyes. "I thought that if I could raise enough money I could bribe the rebels to give up their cause. The lives of many outweighed the lives of a few."

"Liar," Trey whispered. "I don't know why you're still lying, but you are. What are you still protecting?"

A small smile. "The future."

"I don't care *why*," Naomi said from behind us. "Where is the dragon imprisoned?"

"Beneath the Great Stone Square. He was always there, I never moved him."

"How do we get in?"

"There are three ways. Through the cellar of the Church of the Wanderer, through the castle dungeons, and . . ."

"And?"

"And through the Kingman Keep crypts."

"Where's the crypt entrance?"

"The Failure guards it."

Then it would be easy to find. Whereas dealing with High Noble Alexander Ryder would not. I asked Naomi and Trey to meet me outside as I settled this . . . problem with him on my own. A part of me expected Trey to protest and remain, but he didn't. Like me, there wasn't enough anger left in him for this fight. If Trey had wanted to get revenge against him, he would have a long time ago. This was merely an insect on our arm, when we were parched in the middle of a desert with no water in sight.

Trey left me one of his flintlock pistols in case I needed it.

"A decade after your father's death, I still think about him daily."

I said nothing.

"He was a good man. Smarter and braver than I ever was. I miss him. I wonder how he would have handled this. Would we have fallen as far as we have without him? I doubt it."

"I don't know."

"He was the best of us," Alexander said before he downed the rest of his drink, savoring it before the swallow. "Will you decide my fate yourself? Or will you force me to redeem myself?"

I laughed, my hand over my mouth to deafen some of the noise. "You think I'm going to kill you or let you kill yourself for a chance at redemption? Is that what you think suicide is? Redemption? Because let me tell you what it is: it's passing on pain and suffering. I carry King Isaac's pain. As does the princess. Because we feel like failures because we couldn't help him. That he thought that was the only option he had left." A pause. "Is that what you want to leave behind for Kayleigh? Karin? Kai?" And this last part I wanted to hurt, so I said it slowly: "For Joey?"

Alexander Ryder had tears streaming down his face.

I rose from my seat. "I'm going to go and stop the Heartbreaker. Once they're dead, so is your Blackberry business. I expect you to do better. Try to be like my father, rather than whine about how much you miss him. Your entire generation is a disgrace."

It occurred to me, as I left, that Alexander Ryder might be dead in the morning. That the guilt might be too much for him to bear or if he thought his actions were irredeemable. That he might ignore my words. It was his choice, I wouldn't wait for him to decide. The lives of the many outweighed the lives of one.

If he chose death, I knew I could carry his pain on my shoulders. Hopefully his children could, too.

58

THE UNWORTHY

It was Lights Out when we approached Kingman Keep. The city was still alive with festivities and fireworks, and I was exhausted as we made our way through the servants' entrance feeling so heavy and stiff that I massaged my shoulders for any relief. Trey and Naomi were scarcely better, all of us broken yet refusing to give up. As it should be.

Olivier was the only person awake at the table, his leg bandaged and wrapped, drinking wine straight from a bottle. Rock was resting his head on Olivier's shoulder, a blanket covering him as he snored lightly. The infection covered half of Olivier face. He didn't have much longer.

"Is he okay?" I asked as I took a seat next to Olivier.

"Yes, just tired," Olivier said as he tightened the edges of the blanket around Rock. "I don't think he slept very restfully before he came here."

"I wouldn't imagine so." I watched Trey and Naomi take a moment to drink some water and take care of their wounds. "How about you?"

Olivier closed his eyes and leaned back in his seat. "Exhausted."

"Any desire to help us stop a dragon serial killer?"

"I don't think I'll be of much help with a broken leg and—" Olivier coughed up more clumps of ash into his hand. "Whatever this is. Being a hero is a young person's game."

"Seems so." There was a lump in my throat that came out of nowhere and eyes that seemed itchier than normal. "Will you be dead by the time I get back?"

"Don't think so," he said. "Planning to keep breathing until your mother returns. She deserves a goodbye. Only wish I had come here sooner. Been there for all of you. Sorry I wasn't."

"You did what you thought was right. We all do."

"Here I thought you'd insult me." Olivier chuckled. "One last dagger in the heart. Still, I'm sorry, Michael. If I had known . . . no, I shouldn't lie. I would have come as fast as I was able. But there were too many people looking up to me to abandon them all just for my family."

"I understand," I said as I got to my feet. Trey and Naomi were ready to move on. "I mean that. Now do me a favor and don't die while I'm gone, old man. My mother, Gwen, and Lyon will be back by morning. Can you wait that long?"

"I think so."

I gave my grandfather a fresh bottle of wine before leading the way down into the Kingman crypts. There was an odd warmth down here that kept my skin from prickling. The way was narrow and water dripped from the walls, seeping through from the river raging nearby. The pathway was covered with water—not enough to nip at our ankles, but enough that water splashed against the backs of our calves with each step we took.

When we began to pass plaques about my family, my heart began to race. This place elicited different reactions from every member of my family. My mother had spent the most time down here, ensuring a place for my father was prepared.

Lyon was next. He'd walked through the crypts memorizing our ancestors' names. From the Conqueror to the Chosen. The only exception had been the First Kingman, who wasn't buried here, and no one knew why. And after a little research, Lyon had discovered even their name had been misplaced by history. Archivists only referred to them as the First Kingman. Nothing else. Learning that had felt . . . odd to all of us. What did it mean for our legacies that someone so famous could be erased? Would our names all disappear eventually?

Gwen had spent the third-most time inside. She had visited once, sitting at the entrance of the crypts as she whistled to see if it went on forever. When it eventually stopped, Gwen had taken a deep breath, closed the door, and said that the next time she visited the crypts would be when she was laid to rest herself. No sooner.

And then there was me. I had never set foot in this strangely warm place before. I had never helped create a new niche for one of my family, as my mother had, nor desired to remember my ancestors like Lyon, nor known where my story would end like Gwen. I had never paid my respects to the dead in a traditional way, not even as a child. For some reason . . . for some reason this place was . . . was terrifying to me. Not because I feared dying. But because I feared I wouldn't be welcome within these walls. That I wasn't worthy to be buried next to my near-mythical ancestors.

I feared being a failure compared to them.

If I survived this ordeal, maybe that would change.

"I will never understand burying the dead," Naomi muttered to herself. "Who thinks this is better than turning to ash?"

"People who want to be remembered," Trey said. "Not that an addict can be, or have you given up Blackberries? Might as well, since we're about to get rid of the source."

Naomi stuck out her tongue so we could see that nothing was in her mouth. "Joke's on you. I already did."

"Did it take divine intervention?"

"Nope. Just my father's death."

"Ah. I'm sorry for your loss." He kicked a rock down the tunnel. "Does water truly taste as dry as ash after you stop using? My mother used to complain about that all the time every time she tried to quit."

Naomi rubbed her father's locket. "It's sour. As if I were eating a lemon."

"Maybe ash is just for tweekers, then," Trey said as we reached a wrought-iron gate. It didn't have a lock on it, and yet he hesitated to open it. "Michael, what's past here?"

"The special Kingman."

"The special Kingman?" Naomi repeated.

"We just passed the section where those who failed to emulate our family values are buried. Not forgotten, but not honored, either. This is where those who were found worthy are laid to rest. Finally at peace and surrounded by family for eternity. Or so I've been told."

"But we didn't pass any burial statues."

"No, we didn't."

Naomi opened her mouth, paused, and then said, "Oh. Your family is all kinds of fucked-up."

"We're made aware, from a young age, what's expected from us. The family legacy." I opened the gate. "Lyon rebelled against it, Gwen avoided it, and you already know what I did."

I was already through the gate when Trey said, "They fucked him up real good."

I let that one go, more preoccupied with coming face-to-stone-face with my ancestors.

I could feel their gaze as I stepped into the main area with the ever-lasting flame in the middle of it. There were three paths that led off it, each guarded by one of the First Kingman's three children: the Conqueror, the Cartographer, and the Builder. Each of their statues was imposing and held a meaningful item. A sword for the Conqueror, a quill for the Cartographer, and a hammer for the Builder.

"Which path do we take?" Naomi asked.

"The Conqueror is in front of it. The Failure Alexander Ryder spoke of is of his lineage."

"Whose descendant are you?"

"The same."

We took that path together, the everlasting flame lining the ceiling to warm and light the area. Stone statues surrounded us. Watching. Judging. Waiting. I could recognize most of them at a glance. The Explorer was in a dramatic pose, his head tilted upward and a hand over his heart. His body wasn't here but lost in the Azilian Jungle. Past him was the Golden Kingman. A woman who had revolutionized the Hollow economy, standardizing the currency we continued to use to this day. And past her stood the Noble Kingman with his hands up, presenting a crown to all those around him. He had created the Kingman symbol.

Finally we reached the Failure. Otherwise known as the Kingman Who Failed. Half of his stone face was missing, and the other half was smoothed out, making it featureless, much like the faceless statue in the Church of the Wanderer. His daughters, the Inflamed and the Skipped Over, were at his side.

"This is the Failure? It looks as if he—I think it's a he—he's been erased from history. What did he do to earn that name 'Failure' and still end up in this section?"

I began to inspect the statue and surrounding area. "He lost his king. Gerald Hollow, the Lost King, went to pray in the Church of the Wanderer one night and disappeared. No one knows where or how, even decades later. He was blamed, though even my family understood it wasn't his fault. History did not."

"Brutal," Naomi said. "And I thought *you* had a stick up your ass for no reason. What's it like to grow up with all this hanging over you?"

It was an overwhelming weight on my shoulders. An unrelenting pressure to do right. A guilt that I was letting everyone down whenever I made a mistake. A legacy I felt I had to contribute to.

But this wasn't the time or place for my insecurities. I had to keep moving forward. "Help me look for something that might open up a hidden passage."

They did. We searched behind all the statues and found nothing but wet, slick brick. The statue itself had no holes or bumps or raised surfaces that might be a switch. There wasn't even an indent or cutout that I could fit my ring into. That key clearly wasn't going to work twice. Assuming my ancestors or the Royals were even responsible for this secret prison. But if an entrance was down here, they had to be. Who else could have built it?

"I can't find anything," Naomi declared.

"Neither can I," Trey said. "Is there any other Kingman who High Noble Alexander Ryder could have been referring to?"

"No. This is the Failure. That was his legacy."

"Are you—"

"I'm sure!" I screamed, face hot.

Naomi and Trey stared at me, silent and unmoving.

"I . . . I'm sorry. I'll go look around at the other statues. Shout if you find anything."

I left their side quickly and headed toward some of the older statues. My direct ancestors were descendants of the Failure and, except for my father, none of them could be considered an embarrassment. Not with titles like the Mother and the Unneeded. But as I searched the other statues, I knew this was a pointless quest. No other members of my family had been considered failures by history. Only one. Only the . . .

Oh.

There was another. Not a failure in the eyes of the public, but might my family have seen what they had done differently?

When there was no statue of hers where it should have been— between the Heartbroken and the Hanged—I knew I had found the correct failure. Niamh Kingman, The Kingman Who Walked Away during the War for the Bloodline. I couldn't help but laugh. So losing a Royal or killing one could earn you a place in these crypts, but running away wouldn't. And a few months ago . . . that was exactly what I had wanted to do.

"Was it worth it?" I asked my ancestor who had lost her place among family. "Would you do it again if you knew the consequences? What was worth abandoning our family?"

I pushed the direct center of the wall, behind the spot where Niamh

Kingman's statue should have been. It rumbled and rose to expose a hidden passage.

"Niamh Kingman," I muttered as the secret passage was fully open. "I won't forget you. Us failures have to stick together."

I shouted into the abandoned crypts for Trey and Naomi. We had our entrance to the dragon prison, and now all we had to do was survive.

59

HUSBAND AND WIFE

"Do we have a plan to kill the Heartbreaker?" Naomi asked as we walked down the cramped passageway. The sides were still wet, water dripped down from the ceiling, and everything smelled damp.

"Nullify the area, shoot it with everything we've got, and then release Dark and the princess so they can finish it off. We might be able to fight Luis on our own if he's weakened, but having failed to kill Rian, I don't want to take any chances with Anna. Dark and Serena are stronger than us."

"Who are Rian, Luis, and Anna?"

Trey answered. "Luis is the Heartbreaker you're familiar with. Anna is his traumatized partner who helps him murder people—also a dragon. And Rian's the dragon who already kicked our ass tonight."

"And he's not working with the Heartbreaker?"

"No," I said. "But he's not helping us, either. He killed . . ."

"He killed Dawn," Trey said as her name got caught in my throat.

Naomi stopped in place, opened her mouth, and then caught back up to us. "How?"

"He's a Smoke Spellborn. It's what the Thebians call those who have the powers of a dragon . . . and it was as if his body was made of his specialization. Never seen anything like it."

"Does that mean Anna and Luis will have the same abilities? Are their bodies made up of their specializations, too?"

"Probably," Trey said.

"But," I said, "they can be hit when I nullify them."

"And if you don't?" Naomi asked.

Trey and I didn't respond.

"So if Michael goes down, we're doomed."

"We're doomed even if he doesn't," Trey said with a smile. "But who wants to live forever, anyway? Not the three of us, clearly."

And when neither of us disagreed, we all realized it was true. Thankfully, rather than having to confront how problematic that was, we entered a large cavern with an underground lake and an island in the middle of it. There were two waterfalls on opposite sides of the lake, one that let the water in and then another that let it out. The pathway we had taken stopped at a creaky wooden dock, a single boat moored to it.

"This is . . ." Naomi said, trailing off as she stared at the sight in front of us. "Do you think this lake is man-made or natural?"

"If it's man-made, it would have taken decades to build," Trey said.

"Has to be man-made," I said.

Naomi turned to me. "Why do you say that?"

I pointed to the vaulted ceiling above. It was the same stone as the Great Stone Square had been built with. "They built the Great Stone Square directly over it."

"Was the Kingman Builder responsible for this?"

I shook my head. "The Archivists don't know who built it. It was here before the Kingman and Hollow took power. And history is . . . loose during the Wolven Kings' rule."

"What does 'loose' mean?" Trey asked.

"It means 'We have no idea what happened before the Hollow family took power, but we don't like to admit it.' They know what happened before the Wolven Kings took control, just not during. There's more than two hundred years of history missing."

"Pathetic."

Naomi tentatively put her foot on the boat. It wobbled but floated. "We should be able to row out."

"I hate boats. And water. And getting wet."

"Would you rather swim?"

Still needed to learn how to. So all I could do was get on the boat as carefully as I could and hold on to the sides for dear life. Once Trey and Naomi were in, we kicked off the dock and began to row for the island. Naomi steered as Trey and I rowed. Trey created a ball of light to guide our way.

For a mostly still body of water, there seemed to be a lot of motion underneath the surface. It was hard to see through the murky water, and if I was a braver man, I might have leaned further over the side of the boat to get a better look. But I wasn't, and before I could ask Naomi and Trey if they thought anything was weird with this lake, something vast opened beneath us.

An eyelid, to be exact.

That eye was bigger than I was. Our boat was over the iris and pupil, so all I could see was the stark white of the eye. My heart stopped, my breath froze, and I couldn't even croak out a warning.

Then it closed again as if nothing had happened.

We were over halfway to the island and I kept rowing rather than risk upsetting or disturbing whatever that thing was below the water. But though I kept my calm on the boat, it was a relief to reach the island, and I sagged to the rocky ground.

Naomi was tying the boat to a broken piece of timber lodged in the sand. "You really don't like water, do you, Michael?"

"There was something *in* the water."

"When did you become scared of fish?" Trey asked.

"It wasn't just a fish! An eye opened beneath us! It was bigger than I am!"

Naomi and Trey glanced at each other. Then Trey said, "I think learning that dragons are real may have broken you. Not all those bedtime stories are real. Besides, if something was really that big, where's the rest of its body? The lake isn't that large."

"I don't know, but I know what I saw. It makes sense, doesn't it? How do you contain a dragon down here? With something worse. Something scarier. Something more monstrous."

They both gave me another concerned look.

After clearing his throat, Trey asked, "When's the last time you slept, Michael?"

"Voluntarily or forcibly?" I said with a chuckle.

Neither found it funny, and Trey asked again.

"I . . . I don't know. A lot has happened."

"Do you need a moment to compose yourself before we head up there?"

Yes.

"No." I forced myself to speak that word. "I'll be fine. We can't afford to waste time."

"Are you sure?"

No.

"Yes," I said with more conviction. "Maybe I was seeing things in the water. Forget I said anything. Let's go and find the Heartbreaker."

They didn't push the issue and I was thankful for that. The three of us made our way up the beach toward the center of the island. Light spotted in through the cracks in the Great Stone Square above, and the closer we got to the center, the more oddities we discovered. There were ruined mud houses and burnt skeletons that turned to dust when stepped on. Some sort of battle had occurred here a long time ago, as evidenced by hundreds of swords stuck in the ground in a field of red poppy flowers to form a makeshift cemetery. A single pathway that led toward the stone pillar in the center wasn't obstructed with swords. There were bodies—all heartless and decaying—along with tables with crushed glass and Blackberries on them. This must have been the production area. We picked our way through it.

When we were close to the stone pillar, which was streaked with green crystals, we realized that we had reached the dragon's prison. A part of the stone had been hollowed out to create a single jail cell, complete with bars and chains to hold someone. It was also covered in the Moon's Tear flowers, lighting the area in a dull white light. The shadow of a man fidgeted in the cell.

We only saw who it was when Trey's ball of light came closer.

It was Dark, chained up and gagged with a cloth.

The Princess of Hollow was slumped against the pillar, her hands chained up over her head.

Neither was using their Fabrications. But the crystals in the pillar lit up like exploding fireworks whenever either of them squirmed or shifted. Was it limiting their ability to use magic or something?

There was no one else here—

—until a man crashed down from above, surrounded by a wall of flames.

I raised my forearms in front of my face, my body nullified before the heat touched us. Trey and Naomi took shelter behind me. When the smoke and dust cleared, we all got a closer look at the Heartbreaker Serial Killer.

Luis Valenti was gaunt and shirtless, and he smiled wide to show his sharp teeth. His skin was covered in dark holes and small bruises, except for the jagged scar over his heart. The stitching was fresh, blood oozing from it. Yet, unlike Rian, he was still completely human.

"I wondered when you would come for them, Michael Kingman," the Heartbreaker said slowly. "You even brought Naomi Dexter back to me. How thoughtful of you. And the nobody seems uninteresting." A pause. "I'll save him for last."

I pulled out my revolver as Trey drew his pistols and Naomi her sword.

"How bold! Greater men and women than you three have tried and failed to stop me."

None of us responded and stayed perfectly still.

"Not feeling talkative? How disappointing. Don't you three have questions? I love talking to my prey. Ask me anything."

Curiosity got the better of me. "Why did you want Rian's heart?"

"Because I needed a new one. Mine was stolen from me and only another dragon's heart will do. Human ones only last for a short time. Though it has been wonderful to take revenge against the Mercenary who tore out my heart and imprisoned me here two years ago. The hearts of those who stole my blood kept me going until you got me a suitable replacement. Thank you, Michael."

I could feel Trey avoiding looking at me. We had a chance, then. But how long would it take for Dawn's heart to burn out inside his body? Could we survive for long enough? Rian had decimated us so quickly.

"Any more questions?" Luis asked as his arms were engulfed with flames.

"Is there a key to that cell and those chains?"

Luis held up a small key in his left hand before putting it in his pants pocket. "Just to make things interesting. Anything else? Naomi? Curious about your mother's last words?"

"No," Naomi said, grip white on her sword. "But I imagine it was more colorful than you were used to."

"Not really. You'd be amazed at the names people call me before they die."

"You must have had an extensive vocabulary ready when Dark nearly killed you, then," I said. "I bet you whined for mercy."

The Heartbreaker's smile fell. "You'll die first."

"Come and get me."

"As you desire, but where are my manners? I haven't properly introduced you all to my wife. Darling! Come on out!"

A woman appeared behind us, moving with a sharp, distinct sound. *Clap. Clap. Clap.* I recognized her at once. It was the Reclaimer from the Church of the Wanderer. Ah. That made sense. She was a recent arrival who was skilled with surgical procedures. And it answered the question of who was putting Luis's hearts into him.

I opened my mouth to ask if the Reclaimer had been stalking us this past week, but nothing came out. Everything was quiet. All those little sounds I hadn't noticed until they were gone. The rush of water, the clatter of stones, and even our voices. She must've been a Sound Spellborn. That would explain how she had spoken to us near my grave but not been visible.

How were we supposed to win a fight against two dragons while being unable to communicate?

"I know you all met in that lovely tweeker den," Luis said. "But let me formally introduce you to my wife and co-conspirator, Anna Valenti—the dragon who controls sound. We've been married for . . . oh, what has it been, darling? Five or six centuries now?"

"A millennium, my love."

"A millennium! You three whelps are barely a decade out of your mother's womb and you think you can challenge us? We are gods who walk the earth."

If they could have heard me, I would have told them Kingman don't bow to God or believe in stupid stories about fire gods or water gods or storm gods or *anything*. With a gun, anything could be killed. If they were naïve enough to not have learned that rule by now—thinking themselves above what foolish mortals could create—then they would soon enough be just like everyone else.

So instead of telling them that with words, I flipped them off.

Luis Valenti wasn't happy. "How childish."

"The Kingman likes to pretend to be brave, my love. But he will scream like all the others."

"Yes, he will. Darling, entertain his friends while I deal with the Kingman, will you?"

"Of course, my love."

I nullified my body just before he hit me with a rush of fire. He grabbed me and dragged me up and up and up into the air until we nearly touched the ceiling. My clothes began to singe and burn, and there was laughter within the fire, a deep rumbling that was wholly inhuman.

"This will be entertaining," Luis Valenti said within the fire. "Nullify this."

He dropped me, and I hurtled toward the ground.

I clawed at the air, trying to grab anything. I tried to kick and maneuver my way to land in the lake, but it wasn't possible and I was falling so fast . . . until a gust of wind blew me toward the lake and cradled me as best it could to slow my fall.

White smoke was rising from where Trey and Naomi were. I could only hope they were—

I convulsed as I hit the water, breath knocked out of me as I sunk deep into the lake water. Everything was numb. My arms and my legs wouldn't move. The only thing that would were my eyelids and my lips as I watched the bubbles escape toward the surface.

I was helpless, sinking into the lake, and when my eyes finally closed, an overwhelming warmth greeted me like a long-lost friend.

GYSEWVLYE

It was not a sea of darkness or light that was waiting for me this time but the inside of a church. It was unlike both the Church of the Wanderer, with its abundance of dull stone, and the Church of the Eternal Flame, which glittered with gold. Everything was made of pure-white marble. From the pews and altar to the floor and the walls. Two featureless stone statues were sitting in one of the pews—a woman and child—who looked as if they had fallen asleep waiting for a night that would never come. A massive copper door covered much of the length of the entire wall, with three much-smaller doors next to it. One was blue, one red, and the other black. There were no windows, and yet everything shone brilliantly clear. Darkness had been banished from this place and everything was perfect except for a small crevice in the direct center of the copper door, as if someone had taken a knife and tried to dig their way through it.

My mind was clearly getting more elaborate in coping with death. It had too much practice. But if I could wake up before I died, I still had a chance. I pinched myself and felt pain but didn't wake, so I looked around for another way. And saw my friend waiting for me.

Dawn was sitting in the pew closest to the copper door in a brilliant gold-and-purple dress. Because of course she wasn't wearing red. Her hair was elaborately pinned and a pair of simple gold slip-ons lay on the ground. She was sitting on the pew cross-legged as she plucked and ate fresh white grapes from a vine. Dawn motioned for me to sit down next to her.

"Grape?" she offered.

I shook my head. "Never was a big fan of them."

"Pity," she said as she ate another. "We really should stop meeting like this."

"My mind likes to torture me. But all this seems excessive. A simple white background would have been enough. It was last time."

"Maybe. But when I got here there were grapes. Made waiting for you bearable."

I put my hands behind my head and leaned back in my seat. "Any idea how I wake up this time? Last I checked, I was drowning."

"Absolutely no idea." Another grape went into her mouth. "Anything you need to say before I depart fully? This may be our last chance to talk."

"I'm sorry," I said after a long pause. "You died because I wasn't strong enough, it's all my—"

Dawn chuckled and swallowed her grape. "I saved your life because I chose to. Because *I* was strong enough to protect me. Don't imagine me as some damsel in distress. I knew what I was doing."

"I'm still sorry."

"I know. But it is what it is. I never wanted to be a Forgotten, and I always wanted to choose my fate. I've managed both."

"Except now you're dead."

"Losing all my memories would have been the death of me, too." Dawn shuffled in her seat. "Can you do me a favor?"

"Anything."

"One last story before I go?"

"How can I refuse? But I don't know if I have any left."

She smiled at me and kicked her legs as if splashing water. "Who said *you* were going to tell it, Michael? This time it's on me."

Her story began on a cool night, in a noble keep surrounded by a hedge maze. She told me of how a young girl who had never seen much of the outside world had been woken up in the middle of the night because, unexpectedly, one of her friends was coming to stay the night. This was magical to her, as her days were so routine—wake, eat, go to the doctor, eat, return home, read and paint in bed, eat, and then sleep—and her only adventures came in dreams. So she was wide-awake when a young boy with amber eyes, no older than eight, entered her room. The servants had already set up a makeshift bed for him in the far corner of her room, and he fell on it with a *thud* and let out a large yawn.

"What did you do this time, Michael?"

The boy rolled over to face her, still yawning. "Couldn't sleep. Bothered my da as he was trying to work. Thought sending me here would be best."

"You look pretty tired."

He hit his cheeks a few times, then swung his legs over the bed as he wore a mischievous smile. "So says you. Wanna go explore?"

The girl made a sweeping gesture to her legs. "You're not strong enough to carry me, and we both know it."

"Just because it didn't work yesterday doesn't mean it won't today." He flexed his muscles. "I've been getting stronger, ya know? Serena says so."

"Serena would praise you if your nose was cut off, you had warts all over your face, and you bled from your ears whenever you sneezed."

"No she wouldn't. Serena doesn't lie," the boy said quickly. "And I'd be disgusting if all that happened to me."

Dawn laughed. "Have no fear. Serena will always find you handsome. Even with warts."

"Who thinks warts are handsome?"

"Someone in love with a person who has them," a third voice said from the window. An older boy sat in the windowsill. He had a circular birth mark on his temple that was nearly obstructed by the tangles of red hair that fell over his forehead. He was dressed in a plainer and darker way than usual, as if trying to blend into the night. A permanent smile was etched onto his face.

"Davey? What the frack are you doing here?"

"Michael!" Dawn's younger self said from her bed. "You're not supposed to curse!"

" 'Frack' isn't a curse," my younger self stated. "It's a nothing word my da says when he's surprised."

The girl in the bed stuck her tongue out at him as Davey Hollow, the future prince, crept into the room. The young boys embraced before Davey bowed to Dawn. Even when he wasn't in public, the young prince remembered his duties and training.

"My apologies for the sudden intrusion," he said with an air of authority despite his age. "But I was going to see Michael in Kingman Keep and saw him come here instead. I try not to make a habit out of breaking into keeps uninvited."

"I do it all the time. No one cares."

"Literally everyone cares, Michael," Dawn said. "Do you know how many guards have been warned about you?"

"Whatever," my younger self said. "Davey, what is it?"

He glanced around the room and then whispered, "I think I figured out who shattered Celona."

We laughed at him.

"Yeah, right," I said. "Do you know many people have tried to figure it out? I wonder how they'll all feel when they discover a nine-year-old boy did it?"

"Some things only make sense when one is young. Are you going to help find the proof I need or not?"

"Where's the proof?"

"In the castle," he said confidently. Then added, "I think."

"You think? What're you even looking for?"

"A door that cannot be opened by mortals."

"How *very* specific. Will we search for a dragon afterward?"

Davey clenched his teeth. "You're the only one who's explored the castle as much as I have. Are you going to help me or not?"

My younger self wanted to go with Davey—I knew that—but something else forced him to stay.

Dawn.

She was smiling from her bed, white-knuckled hands gripping the blankets. "Go," she said, forcing a smile. "Tell me all about it when you return."

"Are you sure?"

Davey was already back on the windowsill, urging me to join him.

"Absolutely," Dawn said. "We can't both miss out on the adventure. And what's a single night? We have the rest of our lives to spend time together!"

"I'll be back by morning," I said from the end of her bed.

"I know."

And then I was standing back in the bright white church again. I was reaching toward Dawn's bed, mouth agape. I had no memory of that event, and I was supposed to remember everything now. So why didn't I remember that? It couldn't be Darkness Fabrications. My shadow wasn't corrupted anymore. What had happened to that night? Where did those memories go?

As I stood there Dawn said, "I thought you might want to hear that story."

"Why don't I remember it?"

"I don't know. Even I didn't remember it until recently. But I know you needed to recall it."

"What did Davey and I do that night?" I muttered to myself.

"You'll remember eventually," she said. "Especially now you know to. I can't have been the only person you two saw that night."

"But why don't I remember it? I'm supposed to be whole—"

I looked back to ask Dawn but saw her eyes were closed and she was breathing softly, as if napping next to me. I went to her side, setting aside my feelings, and took her hand in mine. There would be time for new mysteries later. Right now she was the most important thing in the world. Dawn squeezed my hand and put her head on my shoulder.

The massive copper door in front of us rumbled open just enough that Dawn could walk through it. Beyond the door was a blinding light.

Dawn sighed, let go of my hand, and slipped on her shoes.

"May I walk you to the door?"

"No," she said, voice unwavering. "I want to do this on my own."

"I'll miss you, Dawn."

"I know you will. Don't forget me again if you can help it."

"I'll do my best."

Dawn stood in front of the door and took a deep breath to calm her shaking hands and legs. Her movements had always seemed heavy and brutish, but now they had a lightness most dancers would be jealous of. "Michael, can I give you some advice before I go?"

She didn't need to ask, and I told her so.

With a warming smile Dawn said, "Kick like a frog."

Then she walked into that brilliant light, which overtook everything around me, and all I could do was focus on the small bit of warmth deep within my chest and the tears streaming down my face as I said, "Good-bye, Dawn. You were the big sister I never had. Thank you for every-thing."

INFAMOUS

My peace was shattered when my eyes opened again. I was deep in the water and my throat and lungs were burning. My back was against the metal floor of the lake and I watched a few last bubbles flutter toward the surface. There was no time to mourn or hesitate. I launched myself off the bottom of the lake and then, half on instinct, kicked like a frog. To my own amazement, I started to rise toward safety. A last parting gift from one of my oldest friends.

I could feel the eye of whatever lay in this lake on me as I made my way to the surface and broke through to take a deep, long breath. Pain and pleasure mixed together.

Luis Valenti was waiting for me on the shore, lip curled and body still aflame.

"Want to come for a swim, Heartbreaker?" I shouted. "The water's not too bad!"

"I'm going to eat your heart, Kingman."

"Come and try it!"

Luis Valenti flew over the water, igniting in a ball of flame. He grabbed me out of the water but this time I was prepared. I was nullified already, and I twisted my body around his until I had him in a headlock. We flew up into the air again, but he was coughing and gagging as I tightened my grip.

The flames around us grew brighter, changing from red and orange to blue and then white. He was flying more erratically, weaving over the lake in no pattern as I squeezed the air out of him.

Luis flipped over until I was hanging from him, one arm locked around his neck, my legs around his waist. We plummeted toward the lake together.

"This all you got, Heartbreaker?" I taunted. "Scared to take your dragon form? You're pathetic!"

Two veiny, membranous wings snapped out of his back and almost broke my grip and sent me back into the lake. Again. Our fall became a glide and I tightened my hold around the Heartbreaker, then threw my wet elbow into the back of his neck. It whapped against him and he grunted in pain before we crash-landed together on the rocky beach.

Luis took most of the impact, and yet I still ended up a distance away from him, bruised and aching. The Heartbreaker was on one knee, coughing harshly, and I made it to my feet with fists raised before he did. Water still dripped from my wet, clinging clothes.

The Heartbreaker was halfway between his human and dragon forms. His body was covered in thick red scales that shone in the dull light. His nails were talon-like, his teeth predatory, and a long tail waved back and forth from behind him. He coughed as if he was dying.

"How's your new heart doing, Luis?" I asked. "Tired? Want a break?"

"I'm going to make your death hurt, Kingman," Luis said between coughs. "I'll eat your heart and drag your dead body out in front of your friends. Then, when they've shared your fate, I'll cut off your head and display it in front of Kingman Keep."

And people said *I* was dramatic.

"Big talk for a man on his knees."

He breathed fire on me, having forgotten what I was. I nullified my body, put my forearm in front of my eyes, and pushed through the flames. Heat and light rushed past me, obscuring my vision and drowning out anything else. So long as I kept walking forward, mind focused on maintaining the warmth in my body, his magic couldn't stop me.

He must've realized his plan wasn't working, as he rushed me, screaming obscenities.

This I could counter. So clumsy. So easy to grab his wrist, twist it behind his back, and plant my knee in his chest to drive him to the ground. I grabbed his tail with the same hand and held the sharp end of it against his neck as my other choked him. He was wriggling and squirming under my weight, but I could feel the strength leaving his body with each blood-flecked cough.

"How does it feel to be on the other side? Does it hurt? Do you feel helpless?"

"Why"—*cough*—"does my"—*cough*—"heart hurt so much?"

"Because it's not a dragon's heart," I said. "You were too confident. Exerted yourself too quickly. You must've forgotten in your immortal life the one rule that all of us learn as children: walk before you run." I gripped the Heartbreaker's neck tighter still, and he thrashed. "That heart belonged to Danielle Margaux. Her friends called her Dawn. And she was stronger than you. She was stronger than anyone I've ever known."

The Heartbreaker was losing his dragon form, reverting to a human's again. When his tail disappeared, I started to wring the life out of him with both of my hands and held on until his eyes rolled back in his head, his limbs went limp, and he was still.

So that's what it was like to kill someone.

I climbed off him, took the key to Serena's chains out of his pocket, picked up my revolver, and then shot him in the head. I wanted to take no chance of him coming back from that, but just to make sure I rolled his body into the lake. When it sank like a rock I knew it was over.

As I caught my breath, I checked how many bullets I had left. Only one. I'd better make it count.

I ran up the beach toward the stone column, and when my steps stopped making any sound, I increased my pace.

Trey and Naomi were standing back-to-back, as I had left them. The Reclaimer wasn't in sight. The area was buffeted by strong gusts of wind, and Trey had stuck balls of light around the area to banish the darkness. Neither of them saw me coming. They were too focused on looking up.

I shouted to them but no sound came out. So their magic wasn't just limited to those she chose to affect—it must work on an area, much as my Nullify Fabrications did when I expelled them. How could I beat that? I had been lucky with Luis—his body couldn't handle Dawn's heart—but the Reclaimer wouldn't be so easy to defeat. I needed to free Serena and Dark to stand any chance, otherwise this fight would go the same way as the one with Rian.

I ran past Trey and Naomi toward Serena, only to be slammed down by a backhanded blow from the Reclaimer. The key remained safely in my hand as she stood over me, snarling.

"Running away from my love already, little Kingman?"

Sounds returned in an instant. She probably expected to hear me beg or cry or whine, but instead only heard heartbreak. "I killed him."

The Reclaimer stayed perfectly still as tears streamed down her face.

"He's dead, Anna. I don't know what he did to you to make you like this, but you're free now. You may never be able to make up for what you've done, but wouldn't seeking redemption be better than death?"

She muttered something under her breath.

"Anna?" I said as I crept closer. "Did you—"

"Murderer!"

She screamed so loudly, it shook everything around us. The walls of broken houses vibrated around us and then crumbled completely. Out of the corner of my eye, I saw Trey and Naomi on their knees, covering their ears. Dark and Serena were struggling to protect theirs from the sound.

So much for redemption.

While the Reclaimer was distracted, I tossed Naomi the key to Serena's chains. She snatched it and ran to unlock the chains while the Reclaimer was focused on me. She even ignored Trey, who was aiming one of his pistols at her. She opened her mouth—

My ears popped as I flew. An invisible force whipped up nearby swords and they hurtled toward me like a hurricane of steel. Did she hit me with a blast of sound or something?

My back collided with a wall as all the flying swords followed suit. A sharp pain ran from my right bicep down my arm to the tips of my fingers. It went numb, and I glanced down to see a sword lodged through it and the stone wall behind me. Everything around me was spinning and I felt like I was going to throw up.

The Reclaimer, still in her human form, stared at me as she said, "I'm going to kill them all and make you watch."

Trey shot and hit her straight in the chest. But the bullet passed through her without doing any damage and she turned on him, slapping one hand over his face and using it to slam him into the ground. He lay still. I couldn't even see the rise and fall of his chest.

No. No. No. This wasn't happening again.

Naomi had just undone one of the chains on Serena's left arm when she was dragged away by her hair. She kicked and screamed wordlessly, right before the Reclaimer hurled her away and out of sight. I couldn't hear her land with a splash or a crash or anything.

This couldn't be happening again.

A weight fell on me as Serena rose to her feet. She was free and she was livid. The Reclaimer had been forced down to one knee, the full weight of Serena's unrestrained power coming down on her. But the Reclaimer was laughing as her body slowly morphed. Scales formed over her skin as her nails and teeth became sharper. A tail whipped out behind her and a single wing sprouted from her back. Unlike the others, she didn't stop until a one-winged, fully grown dragon stood in front of us.

And she was huge. Easily forty feet high, with a wingspan twice as large. It made the Toothless Wyvern from the Endless Waltz look like an ant in comparison. How were we supposed to stop that thing?

Buildings around us buckled and fell from the weight of Serena's Fabrications. The dragon seemed unfazed by it, slowly walking toward the princess, shaking the ground with every step it took.

Serena faced it, unwavering before the towering creature.

"Do you think I am impressed by a little weight on my shoulders?" the dragon growled.

Serena put her fingers in her ears as the pressure on the dragon increased. I had to nullify my body just to be able to breathe and the stone column that held Dark started to shake.

The dragon bellowed with enough force to blow the princess back a step or two, her hair streaming behind her.

I seized the sword that had skewered me and tried to wiggle the blade out of my bicep. Every movement brought such pain, I had to stop to avoid passing out from it.

"How long can you keep this up?" The Reclaimer laughed. "How many memories are you losing to exert a little pressure on me?"

Serena mouthed something to the dragon that made her laugh again.

"So much misplaced faith in someone so useless. What do you think he can do? Stall for more time? The moment your Fabrications fail, you will die."

The princess looked at me and mouthed four words: "Nullify and catch me."

Catch me? What did she mean? Whatever her plan was, I'd follow it. I did the first part as I was told. Focusing on the warmth in my chest, I expelled it outward and knew my hearing was back when I heard a stone crash to the ground right before the dragon's tail whipped Serena into the stone column. The force knocked the stones out of place, breaking the column in half, and an earsplitting groan echoed above us. The ceiling began to shake as bits of dust and pebbles fluttered to the ground below and a large crack spread throughout it.

And then the Great Stone Square above us split in two and collapsed. Onto us. Oh, fuck.

Besides the dragon and potentially Dark, I was the only one still moving. And as the giant slabs of stone, wooden timbers, and colored cloth fell toward us, I had to become the hero I was supposed to be.

No pressure.

First step: catch the princess.

Well, I suppose I had to free myself first. I gripped the hilt of the sword stuck in my bicep and yanked it out in one really fucking painful motion. I blinked back tears and the darkness and then did as I had been ordered. Revolver in one hand and sword in the other, I ran up an angled wall in the direction of the fallen column and saw Serena flying—no, floating—through the air more gracefully than seemed possible. Naomi must also be conscious somewhere.

I leapt into the air to catch her, which became more like a collision with a *crack* before we tumbled to the ground together.

Serena was wheezing at my side as rocks continued to fall from above. They were tumbling more toward the dragon than to us, as if something was funneling them that way.

With an arm around my shoulders, Serena said, "I think you broke another of my ribs. I can't breathe very well."

"Want me to kiss it to make it better?"

"No, dumbass."

"Thanks for not calling me a wiseass. That always felt wrong."

"I hate you, Michael Kingman. Help me to my feet."

I did, despite my body screaming at me to remain where I was. The dragon was roaring as she slapped and snapped at the rocks hurtling at her . . . and in the shadows behind her, Dark stepped out of his prison, finally unshackled. I blinked, and shadows swarmed the dragon, binding its arms and legs with wispy black chains. Ice creeped up from the floor to freeze it in place, and Dark's eyes went redder than rubies. Redder than fire. Redder than blood.

The Mercenary cracked his neck and then shouted, "You should have killed me when you had the chance, Anna!"

The dragon kept roaring, but it sounded more like crying now.

"You and Luis should have run away once he escaped. Maybe I wouldn't have noticed if you'd taken up your sick, murderous desires somewhere else. Maybe you wouldn't be in so much pain right now. Maybe you wouldn't be about to die."

A wooden beam pierced the membrane of the dragon's wing. Her scream was so sharp that I heard a ringing in my ears long after it ceased. The princess gripped my shirt tightly.

"It hurts, doesn't it?" Dark cackled, the ice and darkness enveloping the dragon's body. "I can see why you and Luis enjoyed tormenting those weaker than yourselves. It feels good completely controlling someone! Let me offer you a choice. Would you like to freeze until your heart stops or have darkness slither down your throat and rip it out?"

The dragon continued to thrash, but now more pieces of the Great Stone Square above were hitting her. Two large stones pinned her wing down. Another cracked against her head so sickeningly the hairs stood up on my arms and neck, and then another, and the dragon's body toppled bonelessly across the ground so flat, it could have been gutted and skinned for a High Noble's rug.

"Tell me how you want to die, monster!"

There was no response as ice encased her body from the neck down. "Tell me!"

I took Serena's arm off my shoulder and said, "I have to go and do something stupid."

She put her arm back around me. "Then do it."

We limped closer to the dragon as the last stones from above tumbled onto her, encasing her in ice and rock. Only her head was still exposed as Dark continued to gloat about his victory over her. As if he were a poor farmer's boy who had become a Dragonslayer to save his love, rather than the genocidal terror he was.

I put the dragon out of her misery as soon as I was within range to make the shot.

The Reclaimer reverted to a human when she died, and it was almost over. There was only one monster left to deal with.

Dark jumped down from where he had been, eyes still inflamed. "Her life wasn't yours to take, Michael. You had no right. She and Luis murdered—"

"Death is death, Dark. Making her suffer wasn't going to bring Zahra back. Let it end here."

"I was owed revenge."

I gestured to the dead woman. "You have it. His body is at the bottom of the lake."

"They should have suffered more."

I held out to Dark the revolver that had killed two Royals. "If I have robbed you of it, aim for my head. I think I've worked hard enough for you to earn a quick death."

Dark breathed in and out through his nose, hands clenched tightly.

"Might as well shoot me, too," Serena declared. "Leave no witnesses."

"I wanted to take revenge my way, Michael."

My hand that held the revolver was shaking slightly. "Then take it out on me or move on."

Dark cursed, and then rubbed his eyes. They reverted to their normal grey. "If you ever disobey me again, I will kill you. Your life is in my hands until Orbis Company sees you as a full member."

"Maybe I can help with that," Serena said. "Once we're out of here, Michael's life will be his own again. I have seen enough to accept Michael's statement that my father . . . that King Isaac killed himself. He will always be a Mercenary, but you won't be able to hold his life over him anymore."

Instead of confining me, Serena's arm around my shoulder suddenly felt comforting.

Was this what freedom felt like? I was sure I was forgetting— Oh, shit.

"Not to ruin the moment," I began, "but we need to find Naomi and Trey and get out of here. The rebel army plans to invade Hollow, burn it to the ground, and murder everyone at dawn."

Serena looked at me as if she were about to take it all back. "Explain."

I gave her the quick version, and it still felt too long. Dark left us halfway through, more focused on getting the dragon's heart for himself. Out of the corner of my eye, I saw him flip over the Reclaimer's body and carve her heart out.

"So one of two things is happening currently," Serena said once I was finished. "Either Gwen has convincingly taken my place and is commanding the provincial armies or . . ."

"Or?"

"Or she's about to be executed for impersonating me."

"You Royals and High Nobles really need to stop executing so many people."

Serena gave me a sideways glance. "Save that complaint for another day. Help me get out of here, we need to hurry."

"I have to find Trey and Naomi before we leave. They're family, and—"

"We don't have the time. Hollow is under threat, Michael. As is your sister's life."

"Family doesn't abandon family. No matter what."

Serena shook her head at my stubbornness. "Find them quickly."

"Find who quickly?" Naomi asked, stumbling toward us while holding up Trey. Both were covered in dirt, dust, and dried blood but were wholly alive, and that was all that mattered. "Were you all worried about us? How sweet. I thought you might have noticed I saved you from a fall, and that thanks to me, those rocks didn't crush you all."

"Thank you, Naomi. You will be generously compensated when this is all over. If you'll excuse—"

"How are you doing, Trey?" I interrupted.

A groan as Naomi sat him on a fallen rock. "Two dragons have slammed my head into the ground tonight. It hurts."

"What he's saying is he'll be fine," Serena said. "We need to go."

Naomi and Trey waved us off, content to sit down for a bit longer. People were beginning to gather around the hole above with a still-dark sky as their background, looking down into this underground cavern. Dark already had the Reclaimer's heart in his hand and was eyeing it up like a snack. I didn't have the time to deal with him right now, so Serena and I left. We walked down to the beach together, she boarded the boat, and I pushed it off the sand into the water and climbed in behind her.

If we hurried, there was still time to stop the rebellion.

NOBLE NICKNAMES

Kingman Keep and the Isle were empty when we left the crypts, the sky beginning to lighten as the moons set. Only a few Advocators stood around the hole where the Great Stone Square had been, blocking it off for now. Neither Serena nor I had much strength left, and we had started to leave a light trail of blood behind even after we had bound my wound. The Poison Gardens were close but still so far, and I didn't know how much further I could carry her. But I would for as long as I could.

Serena was more important than anything.

We were halfway through the Commerce District when Serena spoke again. "Do you know which Raven will be waiting for us in the Poison Gardens?"

"Not Chloe. She's with Gwen."

Serena took a deep breath. "Hopefully, Rowan or Karin."

"Playing favorites?"

"No, I just want to know they are safe."

"You consider them family?"

"Yes," she said simply. "I grew up with Karin, and Chloe might as well be my twin. We were together almost every day after your father . . . after Davey died. She kept me sane. And Rowan kept me grounded and cared for me in a way I hadn't thought possible. She treated me as a person rather than a surrogate for the crown."

"What about the others?" I asked as we passed an unconscious drunk slumped against a wall.

"Jasmine, Hannah, and Efyra are from the older generation. It was always hard to connect to them. I was never anything but the princess to them."

"And the four-feathered Raven?"

"Michelle?" Serena questioned. I nodded. "I trusted you more after hearing what happened to my father than I ever did her."

"Seriously? What'd she do?"

"She's a Cityborn and has made it quite clear that her allegiance is to the throne."

"Isn't that a good thing?"

"Only if I'm sitting on it."

Oh.

"Let's hope she's not the one waiting for us in the Poison Gardens," I said, eager to end that conversation.

"Yes, let's. My patience has run out for the night and I doubt she will help me regain it."

We stopped talking as we entered the Poison Gardens. As always, it was filled with poisonous flowers and roots and stems. Anything that could kill someone, from spotted parsley to hemlock. It was never locked or monitored, though there were cages around some of the deadlier items. I always wondered how often something from here had killed someone in Hollow.

There was little time to dwell on that thought as we saw a figure off in the distance. She wore plate mail and was standing in a field of lilies of the valley. A battle-ax was across her back.

"I have her!" I shouted toward them.

The Raven faced us, showing the six peacock feathers woven into her hair. Jasmine Andel, the highest-ranking Raven besides Efyra herself. Why send a cub when a lioness would do?

"Kingman? Serena?" Jasmine Andel questioned tentatively. "Is that really you?"

"Jasmine, it's me," the princess said, as if she had been holding in a very long breath.

The Raven ran toward us, every step thundering under the weight of her armor. I put Serena down on a nearby bench and let Jasmine inspect her. My own body was shaking, but I had done what I had set out to do. It was finally time to rest.

"Are you injured?" Jasmine asked as she poked and prodded Serena's body.

Grunts and winces and sharp intakes of breath were the princess's responses. "Has the army been deployed? The rebels will attack Hollow soon. We don't have much time."

Jasmine Andel paused before she said, "No, it's not been deployed, Serena."

That sent a jolt through my body. "Why not? Gwen's plan—"

"It failed."

I couldn't ask the next question, too fearful of the response I would get. Serena asked for me. "What happened?"

"The High Nobles saw through Gwen Kingman's ruse, Serena. They assumed that you were dead and that Gwen was trying to usurp the throne. Gwendolyn and Juliet Kingman were executed immediately, without trial. No formalities, just an ax."

My body shook. Serena asked what we were both thinking. "Does that mean—"

"King Adreann now sits on the throne. Long may he reign."

I clutched the sides of my head and screamed so loudly, birds flew out of the nearby trees and away into the foggy haze.

I had failed. Again. Everything I had ever done ended up in failure, there was no point in me—

Serena slapped me on the back, and I steadied myself. "Breathe, Michael. This is not over yet. Jasmine, take me to the castle. I will explain to the High Nobles and condemn the executions. We can still save Hollow. We can still . . ."

Jasmine Andel had drawn her great-ax. The edges of it seemed to twinkle in the emerging morning light. "I apologize, Serena."

"Ah. That's why you've been calling me 'Serena,' not 'Your Highness.' Are you acting on my brother's orders?"

"No," the Raven said. "This is my own choice. I saw what befell Hollow when King Isaac refused to bow to the rebellion. You would have gone down the same route, but sacrifices must be made for the greater good. Your brother knows that and is on his way to negotiate peace with the emperor now. Some High Noble families will fall, but I have faith that power in Hollow will remain in the hands of those who deserve it. You are an obstacle in the path to peace."

Serena looked up at the Raven towering over her, still clutching her side and breathing shallowly. "I always knew there was a traitor within the High Nobility. Never determined who it was. How pathetic of me to forget not all Ravens discard their family ties."

"How ironic, when your own family blinded you, and you held on to outdated ideals."

"Do you really think the emperor will let the Andels retain even a semblance of the power they have now?"

"Yes," she said. "We have an agreement."

"I gave the emperor too much credit, then. I wonder what she's really after, since it's not equality."

"Hollow will see in due time." A pause as she raised her ax with one arm. "Goodbye, Serena. Tell your father I miss him."

Then she swung at Serena's neck.

I caught the handle of the great-ax underneath the blade before it collided.

"Princess," I growled as I kept the ax from cutting her head off. "Any desire to help me here? Perhaps by bringing the Raven to her knees with your Fabrications?"

"She's a Nullification Fabricator, too."

Oh.

Jasmine Andel punched me in the gut with her gauntleted hand, and the air left my body. By some luck I kept my grip on the ax. I clenched my free fist, ignoring the pain shooting to my fingertips from my bicep, and punched the Raven in the jaw. She barely acknowledged it.

"You hit like a child."

Her second punch sent me to the ground, gasping for air. She kicked me over, put her foot on my chest, and pushed down with it. The blade of her ax was against Serena's neck. And with my revolver empty, we were helpless.

I refused to die like this. Not here. Not after everything I had done.

But there was nothing I could do on my own.

I had an idea, an inkling of how to win. There was the faintest chance it would work so long as the princess was still the person I remembered.

As I tried to force Jasmine's foot off me, I reached for the revolver I had left tucked against my skin and waistband. I withdrew it slowly, careful not to alert Jasmine. Then, with it firmly in hand, I started to laugh.

Jasmine took some of the pressure off my chest. "Have you finally gone insane, King—"

I pointed my revolver at her. "Nullify this."

The gun clicked over as Jasmine jumped off me and to the side. When she realized nothing had happened, she snarled and said, "What a pathetic—"

Serena stabbed her in the jugular with her lucky knife, the one affectionately nicknamed Lucky, which I had given her when we were children.

She had always kept it strapped to her left ankle, and thankfully it had remained there.

Jasmine tried to pull the knife out, only for Serena to grab the other side of her neck and hold it in place. Blood was coming out of her mouth. Sputtering and dripping and, likely, drowning her. Serena guided her fall, onto her back, and kept her grip firm.

"This hurts, I know," Serena said. "You will not die alone, and as long as your family was not involved in this foolish coup, they will not be harmed. Consider that my mercy."

Jasmine—intentionally or not, it was hard to tell—spat blood onto Serena's face. Yet the princess remained firm, knife still embedded in Jasmine's neck. She didn't look away.

"Tell my father I love him. You will not be remembered."

With that, Jasmine Andel, the six-feathered Raven, twitched one last time and then died.

Serena stood, cleaned her knife off on her clothes, and then wobbled.

I caught her before she hit the ground and held her until she stopped shaking.

"Michael," she said quietly. "I'm sorry. Your family . . ."

There was a lump in my throat. "I don't want to dwell on it now. Can we stop Adreann from taking control?"

"Not if he's already been crowned."

"What about stopping him from giving control to the emperor?"

"That we can do."

"How?"

Serena closed her eyes. "By not letting a single rebel set foot in Hollow. Can you carry me to the southwest gate?"

Easily. What was a little more pain at this point? As if it could begin to compare to what my heart was going through. It was in denial that what Jasmine had said was true. That my mother and sister were . . . were . . . It didn't seem possible.

"Do you have a plan to stop them?" I asked as we walked down the empty streets together. Mist hovered over the city, a lingering remnant of winter that refused to go away.

"Kind of," she said, and didn't elaborate.

The southwest gate was wide open when we arrived, with no guard in sight. No doubt Jasmine's doing. Everything had been prepared for the rebel attack. After we crossed the boundary between Hollow and the outside world, Serena stopped leaning on me and stood up as straight as she could. No words were spoken as we walked farther away from Hollow.

Off in the distance, we could see dust being kicked up near the rebel base. A host of horses and soldiers were inbound.

"You should go," Serena declared. "Warn as many people as possible."

"What are you going to do?"

She refused to look at me. "Hold them back for as long as I can. I don't know how many I can kill or stop before I become a Forgotten . . . but . . . but if I can be an example . . . Hold them off. Then maybe the High Nobles will understand they have to fight back, not kneel to their demands. Maybe even Adreann will see it."

"Serena, that's ridiculous. You can't—"

"Give my life for Hollow?" she said as tears streamed down her face. "Is that not what queens do? Even uncrowned ones? This is for the greater good."

"You'd be giving up your position to Adreann. Do I really need to explain how stupid that is? You know what he's really like, don't you?"

"He's the only family I have left! He'll grow up once he learns what I've done. See how a Royal is expected to behave. He didn't have an easy childhood. No one was there for—"

"None of us had easy childhoods. That doesn't excuse his behavior."

"Michael," Serena said, the morning sun rising behind her. "I am doing this. Nothing you can say will convince me otherwise. Now leave. I command you to."

I laughed at that. "Command? What gives you the right to do that?"

"I am Serena Hollow, the queen-in—"

"Former."

"Former queen-in-waiting," she corrected, annoyed. "This is my choice, and I cannot see another way to help Hollow. This is my last act as Serena Hollow. Let it be a noble one."

Forget all the assholes who had ever said I was overly dramatic.

I took Serena's hand. She was caught off guard, and I had time to say, "If you're going to throw your life away and become a Forgotten in a foolish attempt to protect Hollow, I might as well be here to drag your ass out afterward. What kind of Kingman would I be if I let my Royal do this alone?"

"A bad one," she admitted. "But this is my duty, not yours."

"My duty is to protect you. We do this together or not at all. I failed your father. I won't fail you."

The horses in the distance were barreling toward us. They'd be at the gates before the sun had fully risen.

"So be it," Serena said as she squeezed my hand.

"So be it." A pause. "Serena, can I tell you something? I've wanted to for a long time, and I'd like you to know before you lose all your memories."

"If you must."

"I loved you for most of my childhood."

Serena snorted, and it was far from elegant. "Really? This is the moment you choose? And even though we were Hollow and Kingman? Our families intermingling is literally the first thing they teach us is forbidden, and you chose to ignore that?"

The army was led by a brilliant grey horse with a rider in heavy leather armor and a metal wolf's-head helmet. The emperor herself would soon be in front of us. What a shame I was out of bullets.

"Yes," I eventually said. "What can I say? I always had selective hearing."

"Yes, you always did. You might want to nullify yourself now. I'll wait until the last possible moment before I bring them down to their knees. I want to get as many as possible."

A warmth covered my entire body. "Are you scared?"

"Absolutely."

"Glad it's not just me."

"Michael, if we somehow survive this, can you make sure I remember something?" Serena asked, her voice serious and stern.

"Anything."

Still holding my hand, Serena pulled back her sleeve so her left wrist was exposed. Written in sloppy, childish handwriting was the name *Ike*. My heart nearly burst. It was a memory tattoo of my nickname. On her wrist. The name only she knew I answered to. Did that mean she . . . ?

Serena pulled it back down, laughing to herself. "Guess I had selective hearing, too. Only I was more impulsive and headstrong than you, and slightly foolish for believing in true love. Got it without anyone knowing, and I cover it with cream to conceal it in public. It's always been you for me, Michael. No one else. And, yes, that auburn-haired woman was always me. You're an imbecile for not realizing sooner."

"Es, I—"

"Don't get sentimental on me now, Ike," Serena said with a smile. We could see the riders, clear as day. "Just keep your promise."

I took a deep breath and held her hand tighter.

The sound of hooves thundering against the ground blocked out all my thoughts. Except for one.

I should have ki—

"Friends incoming!" a voice shouted from the approaching army.

Wait, what?

The horde slowed, and the lead rider, the one with the brilliant grey horse, stopped in front of us, dismounted, and then pulled off their helmet. It wasn't the emperor but the handsome Skeleton whom I had run into during Dawn's courting event and at the Thebian embassy.

"Princess Serena, it is a pleasure to finally meet you face-to-face without a curtain separating us," the man said as he approached us.

Serena let go of my hand, and then said, "Who are you?"

The man knelt in front of us and put his helmet against his chest. "My sincerest apologies, Princess. My name is Jay Prince, one of the twenty-one merchant princes of New Dracon City and primary benefactor of Regal Mercenary Company. Regal Company, give greetings to the Princess of Hollow!"

In one coordinated moment the entire horde in front of us saluted Serena and shouted, "It is an honor, Your Majesty!"

"I . . . I do not understand. What are you doing here? Where is the rebel army?"

Jay Prince returned to his feet. "We routed them, Princess. They were planning to attack Hollow and, by the grace of God, we arrived just in time to stop them. We even disposed of the so-called emperor. Ciara! Our gift to the princess, please!"

A woman with short blond hair threw a dripping sack to Serena. She caught it, undid the rope around the top, and looked inside. There was a burnt, nearly unrecognizable head in it. The smell alone made me gag and brought back unpleasant memories from the Militia Quarter. It could have been the emperor, but having already seen her escape death once, I doubted it. She was still alive somewhere. The bigger question was whether this present was a mistake or a manipulation.

Unlike me, Serena was still able to speak. "I . . . You . . . My . . . Why are you here? Why did you do this service for Hollow? New Dracon City has not been an ally of ours since the Gunpowder Wars."

"I've been here awhile. I was one of your suitors at Margaux Keep, but at the time . . . I think you were too preoccupied with other people for me to stand out." Jay flashed that easy smile of his. "But when I heard from an old friend of mine that Hollow was in danger, I had him bring Regal Company from New Dracon City under my orders. His name is Angelo Shade."

How had I forgotten that bastard? I should have seen this coming. He had even told me this would happen. I thought it was a bluff. I hadn't realized he had been waiting for the perfect opportunity to strike. But what was his endgame?

Serena composed herself better than I did. "You are correct. What did he promise you for aiding us?"

"Nothing. I did this out of the generosity of my heart," Jay Prince said with another smile. "But I would like to use the opportunity to propose something to the benefit of us all. Marry me."

What?

"Excuse me?" Serena asked.

"Marry me," Jay Prince repeated. "I understand your situation. The emperor is dead but most of her lieutenants escaped and they still have Naverre under their control. Who knows what Castlen and Braven are like? When's the last time you received word from them? You need an army, and I can provide one of the strongest and fiercest the world has ever seen. With my help you can unite Hollow, drive back all those who oppose you, and return Hollow to the golden age."

The army of Mercenaries didn't holler like Orbis Company in the church. Instead they stood perfectly still, their mere presence speaking for them. Credited for more destruction than some empires or kingdoms, Regal Company was something unseen before in Hollow. A controllable natural disaster.

"And what's in it for you?" Serena asked, her fists clenched tight. "What do you want?"

Jay's answer was simple. "To be a king. To prove that even a former Skeleton can rise to unimaginable heights. I have seen the worst of this world, and now I seek to reform it."

"I would have conditions," she said. "There would be a formal treaty. Promises, investigations into your person, and more."

"Anything you desire, Princess."

The princess hesitated. Was Serena seriously considering his offer? She didn't even know if she was still a princess. All this would be for nothing if Adreann had the throne.

"There has never been a Mercenary king before. It would be unprecedented."

I could have sworn Jay Prince glanced at me before he said, "There's a first time for everything."

Serena rubbed the tattoo on her left wrist and said nothing.

Jay Prince took her hand in his own. "Whatever objections or concerns you have, we can work through them. You will be in charge. I will simply lead your army and sit next to you. If you want, write it into law that I myself can never rule if something ever happens to you."

"Es, you don't have to—"

She interrupted me. "My duty is clear."

Jay Prince beamed.

"There will be many conditions and promises, but I accept your proposal." She looked over her shoulder toward Hollow Castle. "Now, would you escort me home? It seems to have been a busy night."

"With pleasure," Jay Prince said as he motioned his Mercenaries forward. To his army he shouted, "Make a path to the castle! Harm no one! For Hollow!"

"For Hollow," Serena muttered.

The Mercenaries ran past us on both sides, moving more like a river than people. I closed my eyes and put my hand over my heart to make sure it hadn't shattered. When I found it still beating, I ignored all the pain at the sight of Serena walking away with Jay. And off to war we went.

A NEW ROYAL

Turns out, with an army of Mercenaries behind Serena, no one wanted to stop her march to Hollow Castle to take back her throne. Not a single member of Scales, or the castle guards, or any poor fool unlucky enough to still be on the streets after last night's celebrations. Jay Prince and Serena rode together on his horse, and I walked next to it like a jester without a hat to indicate his position. When she threw open the doors to the throne room, all eyes were on her.

All eleven of the High Noble families were in there, along with the remaining Ravens and some Low Nobles lucky enough to get an invitation. My mother and sister were nowhere to be seen, and the last of my foolish hope that they were alive fizzled out. Adreann was kneeling in front of Efyra, a crown in her hands and a gold cape draped over his back. Efyra gasped when the doors opened and she saw Serena, and the crown tumbled out of her hands. The room filled with hushed whispers.

Adreann was shouting before he was on his feet. "What are you doing, Efyra? Can't you even—" He turned and saw his sister walking toward him and his anger evaporated, leaving a sweet smile behind. "Serena! You are alive! I knew the—"

Serena moved two fingers in his direction and he fell to his knees, body shaking from an invisible force pressing down on him. She picked the crown up off the floor and held it tightly as if trying to bend the metal to her will.

"Efyra, where are Juliet and Gwendolyn Kingman?"

"They are in custody, Princess. Prince Adreann was—"

"Have them released," Serena ordered. "See to it yourself. Immediately."

My knees buckled and I almost dropped to the ground.

Jasmine Andel had lied to us. Thank God.

Efyra had always been a good soldier. She bowed to Serena and held her tongue before scurrying off to get my family. With her gone, Serena made her way to the throne. Chloe emerged from the crowds and marched up the steps to stand to the left of the throne, where the princess sat with her legs crossed and twirled the crown around with her finger. Given the dirt and bruises covering her, she looked like the last person who should sit there.

"As you can all see," Serena began, "my enemies have spread lies about my death."

No one responded.

"You may have heard, I was kidnapped by the Heartbreaker Serial Killer last night. No? Judging by your expressions, you were not privy to that information. A shame. While you all were here, about to crown my brother, I dealt with the killers. They're dead and we are free from their reign of terror. Forever."

The Corrupt Prince continued to squirm in place, the pressure forcing him to brace his body with his forearms.

"This is the part where you applaud me."

They did so without hesitation. Jay Prince and his Mercenaries joined in for good measure until she raised her empty hand and they quieted down.

"Thank you. I appreciate your boundless support. After the Heartbreaker was dead, I went to the Poison Gardens to meet a Raven who was supposed to escort me back here before any of you were any the wiser. I wouldn't want to worry you about silly things like catching serial killers or ending rebellions when you are all so busy doing . . . whatever it is you do."

If only Trey had been here. He would have loved this. The High Nobles around me were cowering like caged animals. No one could meet her eyes, let alone speak.

"Consider my surprise when Jasmine Andel told me my brother had been crowned in my short absence before she tried to kill me."

That got a few reactions from the crowd. Mainly curses and the slamming of fists against palms. It seemed the princess had many supporters, and plenty of unfriendly eyes turned on the High Noble Andel family in the corner.

"Do not fear. She's been dealt with. As has the rebellion. The Mercenaries who graciously escorted me here routed them right before they attacked. Isn't that wonderful?"

They clapped without being told to this time.

"You are all so kind," she said. "But, as you can imagine, these recent attempts on my life have left me wondering who my allies are. Let this be the singular moment of mercy I grant all of you. I am not my father. I will not destroy families for petty revenge. If you were involved in Jasmine Andel's coup, leave now and no harm will come to your family. If you do not, I will scorch the earth beneath your keeps and make sure you regret crossing me. Do we all understand?"

"Yes, Princess Serena!" the High Nobles shouted. They knelt before her, willingly. In the corner I saw the Andels glance at each other before scurrying out of the room like the rats they were. The Throne Seekers, Castlen family, and Sebastian Margaux—Dawn's stepbrother—were close behind.

Serena continued. "Adreann, we will talk in private." She exhaled. "Now. On with my coronation. As you all know, I have the power to elevate a family to High Noble status if I so desire. And I do."

One of the side doors opened, and Efyra and my sister and mother were standing in the doorway. They looked a little dingy but healthy and whole, and that was all that mattered. I would have run over and hugged them if I could, but the crowds of nobles and Mercenaries made it impossible.

"Juliet Kingman, come forward, please."

My mother was not one to show fear, and she approached Serena as a Kingman would: head held high and eyes unwavering.

Serena stopped spinning the crown and leaned forward in her seat. "Ten years ago my brother, Davey, was murdered. We executed your husband for it, but recent evidence has led me to question that verdict. I cannot bring him back, but I can restore your family's legacy. If you so desire, will you and your family retake your rightful place?"

"We live to serve, Princess."

My mother took her place to the right of the throne, and it felt like a dream.

"If anyone has an objection, voice it now," Serena commanded those below her.

One of the braver High Nobles, Cyrus Solarin, stepped forward. "Princess, if the Kingman family is restored, is Michael Kingman still the primary suspect in King Isaac's murder?"

"Michael Kingman," she said slowly, "is innocent. I saw Michael trespassing in the castle that night, but he was not there to kill my father. King Isaac killed himself. He had suffered much after Davey died, and it became too much for him to bear."

"Princess!" Efyra shouted. "Your father—"

"My father was hurting. We're all to blame for not being there. His death is on all of us." A pause. "But now he is at peace with Davey. And that is all that matters."

"For King Isaac," Alexander Ryder said, stepping into view with a glass of wine. So he was still here. "Let his pain be a reminder to us all that we are mortal and flawed."

The entire room raised the nearest glass to them and drank in unison in a toast of remembrance.

"There is only one last thing to do," Serena said. "My declaration of purpose for my reign. My dream is simple and clear: I will end the rebellion and reunite Hollow. Our fractured days are over. We will return to the world stage and make them remember us. Do I hear any objections?"

"No, Princess!" the Hollow Court shouted.

"Then let my purpose stand." She stood, holding the crown out to the crowd. "Michael Kingman, if you would do the honors."

There is a tradition in Hollow that whenever a new king or queen takes the throne, their Kingman will place the crown on their head. A unification of sorts, to show that their lives are tied together. I hadn't expected Serena to remember it, but as I pushed through the crowds and took the crown from her hands, I glimpsed the tattoo on her wrist again. It had been there for years.

"Serena . . . I can't be—"

"I know. But you are now," she whispered. "Don't make me ask another. Please."

She knelt in front of me, facing the crowd, and I slowly walked around her to hold the crown over her head in my shaking hands. Ten years ago this had been my dream. Now it was my nightmare. But as I placed the gold crown amidst the tangles of her auburn hair, I remembered the words that needed to be said: "Rise, Queen Serena Hollow! Long may she reign! Long shall she be remembered!"

She rose to a thunderous standing ovation, the kind that shook the castle and could be heard across the city. It all turned to white noise as I looked at Queen Serena Hollow, eyes focused as she stared straight ahead, wondering if she was scared of what was to come next. The rebellion had been stopped, the Heartbreaker was dead, her life and throne were preserved.

But at what cost?

64

FAMILY BONDS

When the ovation died away, and the final formalities began, I ran to Gwen. She shoved people out of the way to hug me, and she was right. With her hair dyed and dressed like the princess, they were nearly identical.

I would have ugly cried when we embraced if we weren't surrounded by potential enemies. That didn't stop Gwen, and suddenly I felt loved in a way I had forgotten about. When it became painfully clear no one cared what we did, my mother joined us. Serena, now embroiled in all the pomp of her coronation, whispered something to Chloe, who walked toward us with a tempered ferocity.

"I thought you were dead," Gwen said once she stopped hugging me.

"I was told you and Ma were dead," I responded with a smile.

"Lyon? Kayleigh?"

"Both safe and alive. What happened?"

"The ruse didn't last long. The Corrupt Prince figured out I was an impostor within a few sentences. I wasn't expecting him to be so . . . intelligent. We were nearly arrested."

"'Nearly'?"

"Nearly," my mother said. "It was all chaos. The Ryders, Moraleses, and Solarins jumped to our defense. The court demanded an explanation. Only the Andels and Castlens wanted us executed on the spot."

"The Moraleses and Solarins defended us? Why?"

"I don't know," my mother said. "Once everyone calmed down enough to speak, we told them Serena had gone to face the Heartbreaker and had sent Gwen to mobilize the army because the rebels were about to attack Hollow."

"Except the army wasn't mobilized."

"No," Gwen said, "it wasn't. The Corrupt Prince saw his opportunity. He insisted that only the princess could mobilize the army, and if it was essential, the only option was to crown him."

"We tried to prevent it," Chloe said. "But it was all for naught. People were scared and we were outnumbered. If the High Noble Margauxs had been here, then maybe we would have stopped it, but they left as soon as they heard High Noble Danielle Margaux had been murdered."

I felt a sting in my chest, and on seeing my face, Gwen asked, "Michael, do you know what happened?"

I told them as best I could. I omitted the part about Rian being a dragon, not wanting to explain that detail just then. His being an extremely powerful Spellborn, and admitting that I had lied to them, was enough. I had gone to the castle to murder him, and I didn't shy away from that fact. It was my fault Dawn was dead.

Chloe was the first to speak. "High Noble Antoine and Camille Margaux will want to hear your testimony. High Noble Kyros Ryder was too distraught when Evokers questioned him."

"I'll do whatever I can."

My mother and sister were refusing to meet my eyes.

"I'm sorry I lied to you both. I . . . . I did what I thought I had to. I didn't want anyone else to bear the weight of it. It was—"

My mother held me tightly, ran her hand through my hair, and said softly, "Silly boy. When will you learn you're not alone? These decisions aren't always yours to bear. Remember your family. Remember your friends. We are stronger together."

I returned her hug, scared that if I let go, she would vanish. "Ma, we need to go home. Olivier is dying."

"He's been dying all week, Michael."

"No, it's gotten worse," I said, easing away from her. "Last night the markings covered his entire body. He doesn't have much longer."

My mother went pale. "We can continue this conversation another time. Let's go."

Before I could leave, Chloe put her hand on my shoulder and said, "Can I speak to you for a moment, Michael?"

I waved my sister and mother on, and Chloe saluted me. "I owe you a debt of gratitude, Michael Kingman. You saved Naomi's and the princess's lives and I will never forget that."

"Please don't salute me. Makes me feel more important than I am."

A smile as she lowered her hand to her side. "If you say so."

"But you could answer a question for me. What do you know about Jay Prince? He said Angelo Shade sent him here and he offered Serena his support . . . in exchange for marrying him. He wants to become a Mercenary King by marrying Serena."

Chloe frowned. "I know very little. Rumors and stories, primarily."

"And?"

"And I am hesitant to give my opinion one way or another. Their engagement will expose his true character. Royal engagements and weddings are not trivial affairs."

"I don't trust him."

Chloe glared at me with her one good eye. "You saw the tattoo on her wrist, didn't you?"

"That obvious?"

With a sigh she said, "Yes. Whether you both feel the same now is inconsequential. I would suggest forgetting what is written on her skin. Let her do what she must without causing her distress. Just because she is stone-faced in public does not mean she doesn't weep in private."

"I . . ."

I didn't know what to say. My mind was too full and too confused. Maybe tomorrow I could think clearly. Not today. I said as much, refusing to commit to anything no matter how much Chloe tried to make me swear upon my family that I would let the queen do as she saw fit. When she grew tired of arguing with me, we parted ways: me to Kingman Keep and her to dispose of a bird's body in the Poison Gardens.

———

I ran back to Kingman Keep as fast as I could. Rock was waiting for me outside. "It won't be much longer," he said, and we entered our home together, my run turning into a light jog.

Olivier was in the middle of the great hall. His entire body was covered in red markings that moved like living flame underneath his skin, and his feet had already begun to combust, the fire spreading up his legs like a fuse. He was surrounded by my family at a distance: my mother, Gwen, Lyon, and Kayleigh. Even Dark, Trey, and Naomi were in the room, off to one side, and I went to stand by Gwen. I squeezed my sister's shoulder. My mother was being held by Lyon as she cried openly, desperately trying to get away from my brother's grasp so she could hug her father one last time. Even if he was on fire.

Olivier was talking to her quietly, a smile on his face. "Don't cry, my love. I have lived a long, long life. I go with few regrets."

My mother couldn't form words, just a garbled whimper.

"Is there anything I can get you, Grandfather?" Gwen asked as the flames continued up his body.

"Your presence is more than enough," he said before coughing harshly. "It doesn't hurt as much as I thought it would. And it's a nicer way than dying with dozens of others in a mass grave."

"Life is full of surprises," Kayleigh said with her hands over her stomach.

"Oh, it is. If there is an afterlife, I am excited to see my wife again. It's been too long." Olivier turned to my mother. "She would be so proud of you, Juliet. Look at these amazing children you have. So strong. So intelligent. So compassionate." A pause. "I am so proud of you all."

"Please, Papa. Let me say goodbye. The flames won't hurt me."

"Yes, they will, Juliet." Olivier looked down as the flames reached his waist. "I'm sorry, Juliet, but this is the way it has to be. I won't let you get hurt trying—"

Funnily enough, no one thought to prevent me from doing something stupid. So I crossed the invisible barrier they had formed and charged my grandfather.

"What are you—"

I enveloped him in a tight hug, letting my warmth cover his entire body. It wouldn't be enough to stop the flames from killing him, but it would let us say a proper goodbye. My mother realized what I was doing instantly, stomped on Lyon's toes to free herself, and then joined me in hugging Olivier. The flames didn't so much as singe her.

"Thank you, Grandfather," I said. "For everything."

"Michael, your memories! Stop this. I'm not worth it."

"This memory is worth whatever the price will be."

Olivier hesitated, putting his hand over his daughter's head one last time as she sobbed into his chest. "Ah, thank you, Michael."

Gwen and Lyon joined us, and so we gave our grandfather a proper farewell. As the flames crawled up his neck, he said with a smile, "I don't feel scared anymore. What a wonderful life this has . . ."

The flames consumed his entire body as my mother whimpered, "Papa. Please don't go. I still need you."

But he was gone. Charred bones were all that was left where his body had been, and the light shone through the windows onto his remains. And just like that, my family returned to the size it had been one week ago, albeit with another gap that could never be filled.

CROSSROADS

Dawn and Olivier were laid to rest on the same sunny day, a week after their deaths, when spring had come and remained, and the city had calmed down.

Olivier was given a spot in the Kingman Keep crypts near the spot where my mother would be buried when it was her time. After everything he had been through, we thought it was the least we could do. To let him be surrounded by family. There was little ceremony or celebration, and my mother did most of it herself. She claimed it was a daughter's duty, though we all offered to help. She never needed it until we all went to pay our respects and see his statue in place, when her tears so overwhelmed her that she needed our support.

Dawn, on the other hand, was burned in the Royal Gardens on a pyre fit for a king. When Serena learned what she had done, she accorded her the highest honors possible. Most thought it was a reflection of how young Dawn had been, a formality to honor her, not because she was a hero.

Gwen, Naomi, Trey, and I were in attendance. Trey had initially refused to come, but on the day of the cremation he showed up at Kingman Keep in his best clothes. When asked what changed his mind, he said, "I don't want to be a hypocrite. I must acknowledge the good as well as the bad."

The funeral was simpler than I'd expected. No food, or fireworks, or anything lavish, really. The family had asked that the High and Low Nobles wear the Margaux family colors—gold and purple—to honor Dawn, and everyone did, including Serena, her betrothed, and the Corrupt Prince.

The queen lit the pyre herself and even said a few words before doing so.

"Welcome, distinguished members of Hollow Court," Serena began, torch in hand. "We are gathered on this sad day to mourn the passing of High Noble Danielle Margaux."

Antoine and Camille Margaux were devastated and held each other. Dawn's brother, Sebastian, was statuesque as he stared ahead, unflinching.

Everyone else was gathered in a semicircle in front of the pyre. We were at the very back, doing our best not to draw any attention to ourselves. Although Serena had promised I was no longer under suspicion of murdering her father, and had said as much at her coronation, with all the other commotion she hadn't been able to put out a public statement saying so. A great many things were awkward until she did. I wouldn't have been there if it wasn't for Dawn.

"When I was fourteen, Dawn and I talked about how we would be remembered," Serena said. "I wanted to be a great queen, one my parents could be proud of. One that would serve the people. One that would be above all the nonsense. Dawn wanted to be free. To choose how she lived and died, and to never bow to anyone. Those of us who were close to her know that's what she did, and she was full of life for it. She lived her life her way. She danced with whom she wanted, spoke with whomever she wanted, and fought as if every day were her last. So it comes as no surprise to me that she died with a smile on her face.

"I would love to tell you all we caught her murderer . . . but we haven't. There were no witnesses. No discernible reason for her to have been in the castle where she was found. We are without leads. Without hope of catching whoever stole away her light.

"But," Serena said as she looked down at Dawn, "I have hope. If Hollow is anything, it is resistant, and it is stubborn. We will find her murderer and make them pay. No matter who is responsible. So I ask you all to remember her name. To speak it until the murderer themself hears it and fears for their life. She will not go unavenged. And I will make sure of it."

Dawn's stepbrother fell to his knees sobbing, fists slamming into the ground hard enough to draw blood.

"Danielle Margaux, you will be remembered." Serena tossed the torch onto the pyre, and it caught in the blink of an eye. "Always."

The flames licked up around her body, the smoke drifting upward and away. I held my tears in, just in case someone was watching. I had to be strong for just a little bit longer. When I was surrounded by family, I could be vulnerable. Right now I had to be a symbol for everyone else.

I had added Rian to my list of bastards who had escaped justice so far, whom I intended to kill. He wouldn't escape or harm anyone else. I would make certain of that. Two dragons had already met their end because of me, what was another?

"Michael, if you outlive me," Trey said as he leaned against a tree, "bury me next to my brother."

"Only if you tell stories about me when I die. Make sure the world knows my name."

Naomi clawed at the back of her hand. "If I die, will one of you make sure there's no trace of my body? Scatter my ashes to the wind."

We agreed to each other's terms and watched the fire engulf the pyre. When the timbers began to crack, I closed my eyes and said goodbye to a better friend than I'd deserved. As it finally began to die down, Chloe walked over to stand with us and remained until Fire Fabricators accelerated the burn and made it ashes and embers.

"Thank you for being here," she said. She had chosen to let the scar where her eye had been be seen by the world. But more interesting was the two feathers now hidden in the frizzy black tangles of her hair.

"Congratulations on the promotion," I said.

"Having more feathers in your hair just means you've lived longer than your peers."

"Sometimes surviving is its own victory."

"On days like these, it just feels like failure," she said with a sigh. "Naomi, can I talk to you for a moment?"

They left, and when it was just Trey and me, he said, "I think it's time to leave."

"Thanks for coming with me."

Trey hesitated and then said, "What happened with the Heartbreaker doesn't change our fates, Michael. You crowned her. You confirmed your place at the queen's side."

"Can't there be a solution where both of us are happy?"

"I don't see one. I won't trust a woman whose ancestors have shown they don't care what happens to people like me. Even if you believe she's different. That she'll do better."

"Then trust in me that I'll make sure she does better."

"You're a Mercenary. One that doesn't even have a say in where he goes. How can I have faith in someone who isn't free? Will you even be in Hollow for much longer?"

"I will be if I pass my Mercenary advancement test."

"And if you don't?"

"Then I'll keep trying until I do."

"And what happens in the meantime? Am I supposed to do nothing but hold out hope for your return? Because that's not happening. I am not waiting around to be taken advantage of." Trey lowered his voice. "We're good, Michael. That won't change. But this isn't," he said, gesturing to the nobility around us. "I want to save future generations from pain."

"You'd start another rebellion? You'd become what you hate."

"No," he said. "I won't kill innocents. I don't want power for myself, unlike the emperor . . . who I assume is still out there. I want power spread out equally among all citizens of Hollow."

"And how are you going to do that?"

"I've always thought I had to stain my hands red with the blood of tyrants—and I will if I have to—but do you think there might be another way? Can I change this city without wiping out all those who benefited from a corrupt system?"

"Every revolution I've ever learned about ends in death for those who once had power."

"Then maybe mine will be the first not to," he said softly. "For Jamal. For you. For Dawn and Kai and Naomi and everyone else who has inherited broken ideals. We are our parents' children, but that doesn't mean we're tied to their fate." Trey looked up at the clouds. "We can change the world."

My friend stood under the bare birch tree with his arms behind his back. I finally understood why we couldn't walk down the same path. Trey had always called himself the villain because he wanted to rebel against Hollow and those in power—but he was trying to save this city from repeating its past mistakes. I was trying to return it to what it once was: a time when Kingman and Hollow ruled and foolish ideologies were passed down throughout the generations. And that was when I realized the undeniable truth:

Trey was the hero I had always wanted to be, and I was the villain.

Trey hugged me. Tightly. "I hope when we see each other again we'll be able to reminisce like old friends. But whatever happens, know that I love you, Michael. You're the only family I have left. I'd die for you . . . but . . ."

I returned his embrace. "I love you, too, Trey. No matter what happens next."

When we separated, our feelings and fates were clear. Trey left as I waited under the tree for Naomi, wiping whatever was leaking from my eyes. When she returned, she looked worse than I did.

"Did confessing your undying love to Chloe go badly?" I asked.

"I didn't tell her, you insufferable asshole . . . I . . ." Naomi blinked a few times in rapid succession. "Chloe offered me the first-feather Raven position. The queen has the numbers to induct me. Says they know I'm loyal after what happened with the Heartbreaker and . . . they want me to be one of them."

"Naomi, that's . . . it's your childhood dream."

The wind began to pick up around us and shook the branches in the tree above. "I had already come to terms with being rejected. I'd moved on, found a new goal. And now . . . now that my mother and father are both dead, and their murderer avenged . . . I am given the very thing that would have made them proud of me."

"What are you going to do?"

"Live," she breathed. "I told her I'd consider it, and she was fine with that for now. If I do want to join them, there's some event coming up that I'll have to participate in."

"I hope whatever you choose to do makes you happy."

Naomi glared at me. "Thanks for being so supportive, Michael. Have you left Hollow with Orbis Company yet? Can't wait to be rid of you."

I couldn't help but smile. "There's always a place for you in Kingman Keep. I think my mother likes the bustle of company."

"That's because your mother is a nice person. Unlike you."

I held out my hand. "Friends?"

"Prude," she muttered before giving me a hug. "Friends. Sadly."

Naomi insulted me a few more times before leaving. I lingered at the funeral a little longer than I'd wanted to, hoping—wondering—if I might get a moment to talk to Serena. But, as was expected for the Queen of Hollow, she was always surrounded by either Ravens, High Nobles, or her soon-to-be husband. When I spotted Symon looking for me—furious he hadn't yet heard all the details about what had happened—I left to ask a friend a favor that I would never be able to repay.

———————

Living in Hollow had taught me two fundamental truths. The first was that history was fickle and could be rewritten and shaped by those in power. The other was that there was always another secret lying below the surface, and as a fool for the truth I couldn't let any mystery concerning the Heartbreaker go unsolved. And there was still one thing I didn't understand after thinking about it repeatedly. Why had Alexander Ryder flooded the East Side with Blackberries?

I had a feeling Kai might know why, so I went to visit them in their keep. The servants took me to the room he shared with Joey, where they had been holed up ever since Dawn had been murdered. The only time he had left was if it had something to do with the investigation into her death. Every meal was brought to them.

I knocked on the door as I opened it with my other hand. "Kai? It's Michael. I'm coming in."

Kai sat upright in his bed as I entered the room. Dying light poured in from all the windows and made Kai look frailer and weaker than I had ever seen him before. Joey was on the floor of the room, livelier than ever before as he played with his wooden toys.

"You weren't at Dawn's funeral."

Kai clutched at the blanket that covered his legs. "I was too ashamed to go."

"It wasn't your fault, Kai," I said. "If anyone should feel guilty about how Dawn died, it should be—"

"I can't remember her name," he interrupted.

"Oh." I took a seat on the edge of the bed. "*Oh.*"

"I don't know when it happened." Kai looked as if he was on the verge of tears and spoke without breaths. "But I couldn't bear to be with you all or her family or the queen or any of the other High Nobles as you all talked about how much you missed and loved her while I was supposed to be her best friend and I can't even remember her name anymore!"

"I'm sorry, Kai."

He pounded his palms against his head. "Why did my Fabrications have to take that memory away from me? Wasn't it enough when they took my sight? Why does my magic seem so bent on making me miserable? Can't I be happy?"

"Some days I think it takes the most ironic thing from us out of spite."

"It definitely does."

"It won't make you feel better, but"—I took a deep breath—"I know what you're going through right now. My Fabrications took my father's name from me a while ago."

Kai's voice was barely a whisper. "What? When?"

"Church of the Wanderer. When I escaped my execution and went after Angelo." I leaned forward, fingers interlaced. "I didn't realize until a long time after and haven't told any of my family out of shame. It's amazing how long you can go only hearing 'your father' until you become suspicious when the last time you heard his name was." I paused. "What does Dawn's name sound like to you?"

"'Your best friend,'" he said meekly. "And it's like a knife to the gut every time."

"I think it always will be."

Kai grabbed a nearby pillow and screamed into it. When he settled, he threw it against a wall and then asked, "Do you know where Rian is? We're going to hunt him down, right?"

"You know I won't let him get away with what he did, but we don't know where he is. Right now all we can do is wait for him to reappear."

"I don't want to wait," he growled. "He murdered my best friend! He tore out her heart and . . . and . . ."

"I know, I know. I feel the same, but . . . Dammit. I'm sorry, Kai. We can't do anything right now." I rubbed my eyes. "Just trust me that I'll get it done when I can."

"You'll get it done? Why does it sound like I'm not invited?"

"Because you're not."

Kai threw his covers off and swung his legs over the bed. "Michael! I have every—"

"You do! I'm not saying you don't, but I need a favor from you. One I can't ask anyone else. It's more important than getting revenge on Rian." I exhaled. "There's a war coming, Kai. One bigger than the rebellion or the Gunpowder War, and we need to be ready."

"What are you talking about, Michael?"

I remained silent as I inspected Joey. The young boy's hair and skin were getting darker, filled with life once again. And as Joey made roaring noises as he flew his toy dragon around him, my suspicions were confirmed. His eyes were no longer the same shade as Kai's. They were a bright red.

The Fire Dragon's missing heart and the reason why Alexander Ryder had plagued the city with Blackberries was right in front of me. It wasn't for this country's future as he had tried to claim . . . it was about his son's future. Joey had the Fire Dragon's heart inside of him, and whatever kind of magic associated with it had cured him. Just like my father, Alexander had done whatever it took to save his child from death. Even at the cost of hundreds or maybe thousands of others.

And without realizing, Alexander had made Joey the target of Dark's revenge. I doubted Dark would let Joey live simply because he was a child. He had made it painfully clear that all dragons were going to die. Which was why I was here. I had to save Joey from him.

"Did your father ever tell you why a heart transplant was the only way to save Joey?"

Kai was caught off guard by the question. "No, why?"

"Joey has the Fire Dragon's heart inside him."

"What? Michael, that's impossi— How would my father have found it?"

I stood up and then sat back down on the bed next to Kai. "I think it's better if you ask him yourself. It's not something I feel comfortable telling you. I think, if possible, we deserve to hear about our parents' flaws from themselves so they can teach us to be better than they were."

Kai nodded shallowly. "Dark's going to come after Joey, isn't he?"

"Likely."

"How are we going to protect him? Dark's a monster. And he's only getting stronger."

I reached into my jacket pocket and pulled out the Archmage's letter. "That's where my favor comes in. But it's not really a favor . . . more like a massive debt I'll owe you." I slapped the letter against my thigh. "I have a message from the Archmage in my hand that contains the first clue to one of the world's greatest mysteries. I need you to go to the Institute of Amalgamation and solve it. I would do it myself, but ironically I'm the only one who can't."

"Why not?" he said quickly.

"Because I've already solved a part of it, but every time I remember it, I forget it. My memories aren't altered . . . they're simply gone. So someone has to do this in my place."

"And you thought that it would be me?" he asked bitterly. "Because I have nothing else to do? I know I told you I didn't know what I wanted to do with my life, but that's no—"

"I'm asking you to do this because you're the only person I can trust to do it." I played with my father's ring. "And honestly, if you take Joey with you, the Institute of Amalgamation is far enough away from Dark that I won't worry about either of you. For now, it's outside his reach."

"If I do this," he said softly, "I can't really walk away once I start down this path."

"No, you can't."

Kai put his right hand under his chin. "My best friend would've done it in a heartbeat. She always wanted to leave Hollow but never got the chance. I would travel a lot of the world if I went to the Institute of Amalgamation. It's far away."

"Don't do this for Dawn, Kai. Do it because you want to. If you don't, I can maybe—"

"I'll do it," he interrupted. "To protect my brother." A mischievous grin spread across his face. "Besides, wouldn't it be funny if a blind man solved one of the world's greatest mysteries? I bet the Archivists would pull their hair out."

"I bet they would, too."

Kai took the letter from me and drew a deep breath. "So, any idea what this great mystery is?"

I nodded. "I've been trying not to think about it too much—just in case I forget—but . . . but I have a feeling it has something to do with where our magic came from. It's the only way to explain why my memory loss occurred when I tried to learn how many countries had magic in them. There's no record of how it started or where it came from, and I think the Immortals have been trying to make sure it remains hidden. Knowledge is power, so knowledge about the origin of magic must be more important than anything else."

Kai fell back onto his bed. "The man who discovered the origins of magic . . . I like the sound of that title."

And so we chatted and caught up for as long as we could, not knowing when we would get the chance to again. Our paths were going to diverge to two different sides of the world, but hopefully we'd meet again somewhere in the middle.

66

THE TRUTH

It was impolite to show up unannounced and without a gift, so I brought brass knuckles to Angelo's house. I would have preferred one of the twin revolvers, but Dark had taken possession of them, and I didn't want him to know about the little visit I was about to pay his father.

I had never knocked to enter before, and just because I was a few months removed from calling this place home didn't change that trend. I made a ruckus as I entered. Stomping my feet and pounding my fists against the walls. There was no point in sneaking up on him.

This was my declaration of war.

The too-small kitchen table was covered in books, the counters were empty, and the stove was shining. Without three children living with him, Angelo had returned this place to the mausoleum it had been before we arrived. Especially with the portrait of Katherine Naverre hanging opposite the entranceway.

Angelo set his book down upon my arrival. "I've been waiting for this."

I took a seat at the table, moving things out of the way so we could look at each other. "Sorry I'm late."

"Are you here to join me? To grovel? Or to continue your pointless war?"

I tapped my brass knuckles against the wood. "Do I look like I'm here to reconcile? You're responsible for the deaths of my father, Davey, and the entire Naverre family. I'm not going to let you get away with what you've done."

"How much do you know?"

"Vance Shade, Zahra, Edward Naverre."

"Ah," he said with his perfect smile. "I'm so proud. You've grown up and learned to do the necessary research. Imagine what could have happened if you had done the same before confronting the king. Maybe Isaac would still be alive." His smile vanished. "So what do you want, Michael?"

I pointed to the trapdoor beneath the table I had seen in Dark's memories.

Angelo stared at me, unfazed. "How?"

"Does it matter?"

"No," he said as he rose to his feet. "I suppose not."

Angelo pushed the table out of the way and let the books fall to the floor. He yanked up the carpet, opened the trapdoor, and descended the ladder. I followed without hesitation.

When Dark had told me that Angelo's love for Katherine was catastrophic, I brushed it off. Too eager to learn more about what Dark was and what his goals were when confronted with the knowledge he could turn into a dragon. But that was ignorant of me.

I had assumed I knew what catastrophic love was. Love that made logical men emotional. Love that was patient and kind and heartbreaking. Love that made couples travel across the world all for a glimpse of each other. But that wasn't Angelo's love . . . His was world-breaking.

"Michael," Angelo said with a drawl. He lit a lantern on the far wall. "Let me introduce you to my wife, Katherine."

The light illuminated the blurry haze I had seen in the darkness. A coffin stood upright against the wall and Angelo opened it with a sickening smile. Katherine's body had been embalmed and wrapped in cloth yet wore a frilly yellow dress that had withered away. Angelo had surrounded her with flowers and perfume to lessen the stench of decomposition, but down here it was too concentrated for me to stop from gagging. Only divine intervention stopped me from losing the contents of my stomach all over the floor.

"Isn't she gorgeous?" Angelo asked, his back to me. "She always loved that yellow dress of hers. So it seemed only fitting to bury her in it."

"You're insane," I said. "Is this how you remember someone? By refusing to let them rest?"

Angelo looked over his shoulder. "She *is* resting, Michael. But it will not be forever. We will be reunited in due time."

"What are you . . . ?" I trailed off. "So you really do want to bring her back. And because of Domet you know how."

"Yes! Congratulations, Michael! You figured it out!" Angelo howled with laughter. "It's wonderful to talk to you openly about this." He motioned for me to continue. "C'mon! Ask the next logical question!"

"How?"

"That's not the next logical question, Michael. Do you really think I'm foolish enough to tell you what I'm going to do?" He crossed his arms. "Try again."

I took a deep breath and steadied my mind. "If your goal is to bring Katherine back, why do all this? Why take us in? Why kill Davey? Why . . ." I tilted my head back and cursed. "Both Domet and the Archmage fear the idea of bringing someone back to life. How severe is the cost to do it?"

Angelo ran his hand down the side of the coffin. "Immortality is a momentary abstraction that will eventually be corrected, but bringing someone back from the dead defies the laws of nature. So its cost is all-encompassing." He looked at Katherine longingly. "It's taken me nearly two decades to get all the pieces in place. But now I can finally begin the main event."

I cracked my neck and then raised my fists. "The exit is behind me. Do you really think I'm going to let you out of—"

Someone wrapped their hand around my neck, sharp nails pressing against my skin as they put a knife against my spine.

"Hello, Michael," Emelia whispered into my ear. "I hope you didn't miss me too much."

At least this let me confirm Emelia was still alive.

"So you two—no, Jay Prince must be an accomplice, too—are all working together. Does that mean . . . Did you start the rebellion just to have Jay rush in and save the city? Was that why the targets never made sense? Was it just to sow chaos and create leverage for Serena to accept Jay's proposal?"

Emelia's voice was like a mockingbird's song. "Would you believe us even if we said no?"

Naomi's old words were a painful reminder of past mistakes. "What is the connection between a sacrifice who wants to kill an Immortal, a Skeleton who wants to be king, and a man who wants to bring his wife back from the dead?"

Angelo closed Katherine's coffin and then wrapped chains around his arms so he could pull it behind him. It should have been impossible, but he did it with ease. "That's up to you to figure out. I wouldn't want to make it too easy, would I? But I'll give you one last piece of fatherly advice. If you want to save your loved ones, stay away from Serena and run as far away as you can with Orbis Company. Maybe then you'll escape your tragic fate."

"You really think I'll abandon them?"

Emelia shoved me against the wall and held me in place as Angelo lumbered past me with Katherine's coffin. Rather than climb up the ladder to his house, he continued down into the darkness out of sight. But before he disappeared, he said, "You will if you love them."

When Angelo was gone, Emelia released me. She crept back up the ladder with a giggle, knowing that even I wasn't stupid enough to pick a fight with an Immortal.

I followed Angelo down the tunnel he had vanished into but never caught up to him. It exited outside of Hollow near an abandoned farm. There was nothing in it except for a letter dated nine years earlier and a small vial filled with a translucent red ball that flickered like a firefly.

Gwendolyn,

Firstly, congratulations on finding this place—assuming I didn't lead you to it—but I regret to inform you that it's too late to stop me. By now a chain reaction will have begun and I will be in the final stages of my plan to bring back my beloved. Lyon will have renounced his Kingman heritage for love, Michael will have razed Hollow Castle and declared war on the Royal Family, Serena will be engaged to Jay Prince, and your Royal—Adreann—will be the Lifeweaver's immortal killer.

I assume, of course, that Domet has refused to tell you what the cost is to bring someone back to life. Smartly so, after his slipup with me and Vance. So consider the memory I've left behind for you a final parting gift from your foster father. If you can find a way to see it, you'll know what the price is and realize why you should let me bring back Katherine. It's the only way to stop Michael and Serena from shattering Tenere. My love may be catastrophic, but theirs is apocalyptic. Kingman and Hollow aren't meant to be together for a reason.

So tell the Wolven King you're working for to stop interfering with my plans. We wouldn't want another Celona, would we?

Yours truly,
Angelo Shade

The postscript was written in fresh ink.

P.S. Congratulations, Michael, for proving me wrong. I always thought it would be Gwen who would oppose me. But even I can't get everything right. How far will you go to protect Serena from Jay Prince? And Gwen from a Wolven King? Or will you do the smart thing and walk away?

My mind snapped, so my body moved on its own, grabbing the letter and vial before sprinting back to Kingman Keep to find Gwen and, hopefully, get answers.

THE KING OF STORIES

"Hello, Gwendolyn," Symon said as he pushed open the door to her tower room. The youngest Kingman stood in front of her bed with her back to him, airing out blankets in front of an open window. Her hair was tied back, and her clothes were wet from doing the laundry in the river. "I've come for my answer."

"I don't have the patience for this right now."

"Why not?" he asked, creeping closer. "Are you that nervous about me finding out who you're working for?" He paused for dramatic effect. "You're a foreign spy, aren't you? It's the only thing that makes sense."

"I'm not."

"Then what are you?"

"Why do you care so much?" she whined, turning toward him with hateful eyes. "Can't you just f—" Gwen's eyes snapped up at the sight of a small rock falling from the ceiling. She dropped the blanket she had been carefully folding as the rock shattered on impact with the floor. "Symon, you need to leave. Right now."

"I'm not leaving until I get what I want."

Gwen turned to him, put her hands on his shoulders, and pushed him away. "Just trust me! You need to leave immediately!"

"This is ridiculous," he said, struggling to stay in the room. Gwen was by far the strongest member of the Kingman family, but this wasn't the first time he'd had to wiggle his way out of trouble. "There's no need for force. Just tell me who you're working—"

The air in front of Gwen's bed shattered like glass and it forced Symon to the ground as if he were knocked down by an explosion.

Two massive hands emerged from nothing and grabbed the sides of the crack before pulling them apart until it was big enough for someone to fit through. Something other than the room was in the background, but Symon couldn't concentrate on what it was, as he was too focused on the man climbing through the crack. His face was completely smooth, as if erased by fire—not an eye, nostril, lip, or scar dared blemish it. He wore loose white trousers, a bronze sash around his waist, gold sandals, a necklace of wolf teeth, and a leopard skin draped over his shoulders. As Symon knelt before the intruder, he couldn't help but tremble at the man's towering presence. It was as if he were in the presence of a titan.

"Symon!" Gwen wailed, desperately trying to push him out of the room. "Run! Please!"

All of Symon's muscles were locked in place.

"Gwendolyn," the man sang. "It's time for us to leave. The Lifeweaver's immortal killer has discovered us and we must prepare for my brothers." The intruder looked down at Symon. "Who is this?"

"No one," Gwen pleaded as she tried to shield Symon. "He doesn't know anything."

The faceless man shoved Gwen out of the way as if she were a fly. He knelt in front of Symon and picked a stray hair off Symon's red robes. "Who are you, Archivist?"

"My name is Symon Anderson," he said, voice trembling. "I'm the King of the Stories." Symon gulped. "How can you speak without a mouth?"

"Just because you can't see it doesn't mean I lack one." The intruder grabbed Symon by his collar and held him up in the air. Symon remained perfectly still, unable to fight back despite his mind screaming at him to flail, kick—anything. One of his quills fell out of his sleeves into his hand and, using all his strength, Symon slowly raised his right arm. "I've read some of your work," the faceless man said. "Your analysis on the problematic aspects of a monarchy government was masterfully crafted. I admired how you tried to come up with a solution that might alleviate some of the struggles of this country's peasant class. It's a shame your peers refused to bring it to the Hollow Council."

"That was the first thing I wrote as an Archivist." Every word was a struggle. "Who are you?"

"I have many names and titles. But the only one you will recognize is that I am Gwendolyn's employer." The man exhaled. "I'm sorry you saw me here today." A pause. "Are you scared of heights?"

Symon shook his head. Just a little further and his arm would be close enough to stab the faceless man. He would not die here. He had survived his brother's torture with fire and small, dark places. He had become a Recorder younger than any other in written history. He was not going to die before writing the greatest story ever told.

Gwen pounded her fists against the man's back. He shoved her away again without a lingering glance as he strolled over to the open window. A spring breeze fluttered Symon's robe. Conversation and laughter from merchants, refugees, and passersby drifted up from the streets below.

"Then this will be the easiest way for you to go," the man stated. "I'm sorry again that this has to happen to you. It's truly unfortunate. You would have been one of the best Recorders in history."

"Why are you doing this?"

"You've seen me."

Symon gritted his teeth. "Then take my eyes, not my life."

"If only it were that simple. You'll still have the memory of me, and my enemies are adept at extracting them whether you remember this meeting or not. Sadly, death is the only solution that keeps me safe." Gwen jumped onto his back, clawing at his neck with her sharp nails. It was soon covered in long red marks, but the faceless man didn't shift his attention away from Symon. "I want you to know before you go that you were right."

"About?"

"The Kingman family shattered Celona."

It was a dying comfort and yet Symon still felt content that his hypothesis was right. The Kingman family was nothing but trouble. "How are you certain?"

The faceless man's skin moved as if he was smiling. "Isn't it obvious? I was there."

Symon stabbed his backup quill into the intruder's face right where his left eye should have been.

The faceless man chuckled, plucked it out, and wiped away the tear of blood, then snapped the iron quill in half as if it were a twig. The quill that had created a thousand tales turned to powder in his hand. "I admire your will to live. Most can barely speak in my presence. So let me tell you one last thing. You may know another title of mine: Wolven King. Now, goodbye, Symon. Enjoy the view if you can."

Gwen screamed as Symon was thrown out of the window. He clawed in her direction as he flew farther and farther away. When it was clear there was nothing around for him to grab, Symon tilted his head to the side and admired the Hollow skyline from the castle's bizarre amalgamation of architectural styles to the Hollow Library's beautiful brass clock tower at the top of it. Its chimes woke him every morning after he fell asleep reading and lulled him to bed when it signaled the library would be closed to outsiders. He felt the cracked leather spines on his fingertips and smelt the dust locked in every page whenever he discovered a lost tome in those dark halls. The library was his home, more so than that idyllic little mining village ever was. He would have regretted missing out on all the beauty in this city for a long life underground.

"Farewell, my love," the King of Stories whispered with a smile.

Then his back hit the ground and nothing remained.

FACELESS

"Ma! Where's Gwen?" I shouted as I burst into the great hall carrying Symon's mangled body. Bones jutted out of his legs like blooming flowers, blood leaked from his tear ducts and ears, and broken glass and ink were interwoven with the threads of his red robes. My hands were stained black the moment I picked him up.

My mother had a basketful of laundry in her hands. "She's in her room. What's wrong? Wait. What happened to Symon?"

In my frazzled state, I screamed out a few words—"Wolven King" . . . "Angelo" . . . "Tenere" . . . "found him"—as I placed Symon's body on the table and then ran past her. She dropped her basket and went to the Recorder's side, screaming for Rock and Naomi. Symon's breath had been weakening when I found him in the middle of the street.

I flung open Gwen's door. Her window was open, and a soft breeze blew through it. Gwen was standing in front of a tear in the air that pulsated like a beating heart. A faceless man with black grey-streaked hair was on the other side. There was a black sand beach in his background. The Skeleton Coast? Or maybe Eham?

Four steps separated us.

Three left as Gwen was yanked toward the strange man.

Two left as her body crossed the threshold.

I dove toward her. The tips of her fingers brushed against mine as she smiled painfully and whispered, "All debts have to be paid."

The tear snapped closed and I crashed into her bed. If I had been a heartbeat faster, I could have pulled her back or gone through the tear with her. As I kicked and screamed profanities at my inability to protect my sister, a pile of rocks fell out of nowhere onto the spot where she had been standing before going through the gate. It stopped my tantrum instantly. Had taking Gwen from here come with a cost like Fabricating and Weaving? If so, what was it? Abyss Walking made the most sense from what little I knew, but I didn't want to assume Weaving or whatever an Insatiable did couldn't be responsible either. Or could it be one of the others I didn't have a name for?

But, more importantly, which country was this magic from?

Where did I have to go to get my sister back?

A sheet of paper was nailed into her bed frame.

> *I'm sorry I'm leaving without a goodbye. I love you all. Don't come looking for me. My employer already killed Symon and I don't want to lose anyone else. I'll be back when I can.*
>
> *Love, Gwen*

"Michael?" My mother's voice was wavering as she entered. "What happened?"

"Is Symon alive?" I countered.

"Yes. But I don't know for how long. Naomi is taking him to a surgeon. Where's Gwen?"

I gave her Angelo's letter and then sat on the edge of the bed, my face in my hands.

"This is . . . I don't . . . What does it mean Gwen is working for a Wolven King? They've been dead for over a thousand years!"

I told my mother what little I knew, and when I was done, she sat against a wall, staring out the window. In a whisper she asked, "What are we going to do?"

"I don't know, Ma. But I do know Angelo's letter wasn't completely right. He didn't predict I would become a Mercenary." I held up the small vial with a red ball in it up to the light. "I'm going to pass my advancement, then go find Gwen and someone who can show this memory to me. Our fates can be rewritten."

And for the first time in my life, I was confident I could turn a hopeful delusion into reality.

ORBIS COMPANY

The vote for my advancement within Orbis Company's ranks had been delayed a week, partially because of what had happened to Beorn and partially because Dark had gone missing after the Heartbreaker's death. When he reappeared, all he had done was shrug no matter how many times he was asked where he had been.

Only Alexis still tried to pry answers out of him, but not even she could.

By the time the vote took place I was in a much better mental state, albeit still nervous at what it would mean to fail. But I tried not to dwell on it too much and kept myself busy. Funerals and too much pain to move made that easy.

Dark brought me to the Lone Wolf, into a back room that was filled with the rest of Orbis Company. They were all gathered behind a long table facing a single chair. I recognized a few of them—Haru, Imani, and Alexis—but most of them were strangers to me, and that didn't calm my nerves. Not when my future was, once again, coming down to a vote.

Dark instructed me to sit in the lone chair while he took his seat between Imani and Alexis. There was a dagger in front of each of them.

Once we were both settled, Imani stood and began proceedings. "Orbis Company, we are gathered here today to decide if Michael Kingman, apprentice Mercenary in Orbis Company, has shown enough potential to be elevated to a full-fledged member. I will say a few words on his latest contract and then we will proceed to his examination."

There were nods around the room.

"Michael Kingman was taken in as a Mercenary prior to his execution for his supposed murder of King Isaac of Hollow. We had reason to believe that Michael was in fact merely in the wrong place at the wrong time. Dark has told us, and I quote, 'Michael is a small dog with a big ego and obsessed with not tarnishing the Kingman family's legacy any further. There's no reason to believe he killed King Isaac of Hollow.'"

Please. I was at least a medium-sized dog. How rude of them to say otherwise.

Imani continued. "In the past week, Michael and Dark were tasked with investigating the refugees coming to Hollow for High Noble Maflem Braven, now deceased. They investigated but then confronted High Noble Maflem Braven after a few of the refugees were murdered in the manner of the Heartbreaker Serial Killer who ravaged Hollow two years ago and is credited with assassinations including Berserker Rami and Mercenaries Bottles and Flowers of Machina Company. The confrontation ended up with High Noble Maflem Braven being thrown from the Hollow battlements."

"Let the record note that I threw that maggot off. Michael was simply along for the adventure," Dark said. "Any repercussions for killing an employer should be on me. Not him."

"Noted," Nonna said at the far end of the table. How did this woman stare so long without blinking?

Imani cleared her throat. "After being arrested—"

A dainty woman who reeked of perfume and was covered in jewelry snorted loudly. Everyone stared at her. "What?" she said with a grin.

"Dark was arrested? That's hilarious. When was the last time that happened? Vargo? Are we really going to skip over that little tidbit?"

"Yes," Imani said. "As I was saying. After their arrest and an audience with Queen Serena Hollow, Dark and Michael accepted a new contract: finding the Heartbreaker and Waylayer who were operating in this city. I think we all know what happened from there. Does anyone need any clarification before we commence the examination?"

Haru raised his hand. "I want the record to show that Michael and Dark avenged Mercenary Beorn Orbis."

Imani looked toward the old woman, who said, "Already noted."

Haru nodded and lowered his hand.

Imani took her seat. "Unless there's anything else, we should continue. Since Michael has not met everyone, I suggest everyone state their name and position within Orbis Company before asking their question. Who would like to go first?"

Haru rose to his feet, looking as if he was on the verge of tears, and said, "Haru Orbis, the Weapons Master of Orbis Company. My question is simple: How did the Heartbreaker die? I want to know the details. I want to know if it was painful."

"I choked him to death." I looked at my hands. "I watched the life leave his eyes, shot him in the head, and then threw his body into the nearby lake. He died begging for mercy."

Haru took the dagger that was lying on the table in front of him and stabbed it into the wood. "For Michael Kingman."

It was the dainty woman's turn. Her eyes were the same shade of blue as Naomi's, which meant she was a Thebian. "Cassia Orbis, Orbis Company's navigator, geographer, and mapmaker extraordinaire. How much do you know of the outside world, Michael? What are the differences between the masks that the Vargo and the Medceli clans on the Gold Coast wear?"

"I don't know."

"What lies beyond Eham in the Eastern Sea?"

"I don't know."

Cassia rolled her eyes dramatically and then folded her arms. "Can you at least tell me what the title of the leader of the Thebian Empire is?"

Naomi had told me it recently. I knew she had, but the word escaped me at that moment. I said as much.

"Then my vote is clear. Letting you into the world unsupervised would be disastrous. There's more he still needs to learn." Cassia sat back down. "Against Michael Kingman."

I exhaled as another rose to ask their question. A big dark-skinned man who wore a stark white apron over his clothes. His voice was smoother than I'd expected. "Titus Orbis, the cook of Orbis Company. Do you have a favorite food? If so, what is it?"

"Candied nuts."

"Interesting. How do they season them in Hollow?"

"With cinnamon and chilies."

"Haven't seen that variation before. In New Dracon City it's only sugar, and on the Gold Coast it's ginger and garlic. Tell me, why is it your favorite?"

"It reminds me of a friend."

Titus smiled. "Do you know how to make it?"

I nodded.

"Good. I require you to make me some once we're done with all this." Titus took the dagger in his hand and stabbed it into the wood. "For Michael Kingman."

A blind man stood next. "Otto Orbis, Fabrications Master of Orbis Company. At such a young age, your reputation precedes you. People whisper about you in the streets. But all I see is a child in over his head, struggling not to drown. Prove me wrong. How were you able to catch the Raven's lightning in the Church of the Wanderer?"

Dark glared at me. We must have gone over this during that day I forgot about. He wasn't going to like what I was about to say. "I don't know. Dark trained me about Fabrications—in detail, I think—but I've forgotten the day entirely."

My Mercenary mentor swore under his breath as Otto continued: "So you've had memory issues in the past? At age nineteen?"

I gave him the condensed version of my history. No one at the table gave any response to it, which included no sympathy.

"Then this choice is clear for me," Otto said as he sat down. "The child is too impulsive to be on his own and has yet to understand the price he pays every time he uses Fabrications. Against Michael Kingman."

I rubbed my hands over my face. This wasn't going as well as I'd hoped.

Another Mercenary was already on his feet. A short man who was missing his right hand, but wore multiple pistols. He was dressed exactly as those from New Dracon City had been.

"Gael Orbis. The boom-boom boy," the man said with a yawn. "I refuse to vote for someone from Hollow. Against Michael Man-child."

Alexis had warned me there would be one Mercenary who would never vote for me no matter what I did. Must've been referring to this one.

It was a very heavily tattooed woman's turn. No part of her skin wasn't covered. "Jade Orbis, tattooist of Orbis Company. If you could pick an image or a sigil to encompass everything you stood for, what would it be?"

Without hesitation I said, "A crown being pulled apart by two hands."

Dark was glaring at me again, but Jade was smirking. "Really, now? How come? Didn't think of you as a fan of Tosburg Company."

"I'm not," I said. "That symbol was created in opposition to my family and I want to take it back. Make it into a symbol for me. My sister can carry the Kingman family when she returns. She's more than capable of it. I can become something else."

"What would you like that symbol to stand for?"

"The symbol of the future Mercenary King."

Silence. And then Jade cast her vote with a broad smile. "For Michael Kingman."

"My turn," the elderly woman said as she rose to her feet ever so slowly. "I am Nonna, historian for Orbis Company and a member of the council that records the natural order of events at the Institute of Amalgamation."

The whole not-blinking thing didn't get less creepy the more I saw of her. Wonderful.

"Do you know any attributes, name included, of the one known as the First Kingman?"

"No."

"What about the names of the three Wolven Kings? Or their relation to each other?"

Another "No."

"Oh, dear me, how disappointing. How about God's favorite color?"

She knew my answer the moment she finished her question. There was a chance I could have answered the others. But these? These were impossible. Did anyone know the answers?

Nonna sat down with a frown on her face. "Sadly, I don't think it's your time to be independent yet, sweetie. Try again in another decade. Against Michael Kingman."

Besides the commander of Orbis Company, who sat next to Imani with his hand against his cheek, snoring slightly, the only ones left were Dark, Alexis, and Imani. I could still pass if they all voted for me.

Alexis stood next. "Alexis Orbis, Gun Master of Orbis Company. Do you know why I joined Orbis Company?"

I hesitated. Dark claimed that she had joined to be with him after Zahra died, but . . . but the way she was looking at me and her question suggested I was missing something. Or maybe I wasn't. Maybe the answer was still correct but the reasoning was wrong.

"You joined because of Dark."

"Correct. You have my vote." Another dagger in the table. "For Michael Kingman."

Dark didn't stand but spoke anyway. "My eyes are open. Against Michael Kingman."

Everyone was caught off guard by that. But before the bubble of surprise could grow, Imani rose and said, "Imani Orbis, second-in-command of Orbis Company. Do you know what goes bump in the night, Michael?"

I was completely thrown by what Dark had just done. Was he trying to get rid of me? "Yes."

"Are you scared of it?"

"No," I said. "They die like any other."

"Don't forget that. Ever." A pause. "For Michael Kingman."

Five daggers in the table, and five still lying flat. A tie.

What happened now?

I wasn't the only one confused about what had just happened. Beorn's death had created an imbalance, one that the commander of Orbis Company would have to settle himself. Imani nudged him in the side until he was awake.

The commander, a middle-aged man with sun-soaked skin, grumbled to life. His hair was wispy and dyed from the sun until he was blonder than any of the Ryders. As he cracked his neck, I noticed that he had the words *Hold Fast* tattooed over his knuckles. "Is he a full member or not?"

"It's a tie," Imani said.

"So it's up to me, then."

The commander of Orbis Company rose to his feet, stretched his back, and yawned. "Michael Kingman, my name is Tai Orbis and I am the commander of this company. Normally I am not required to vote on these matters, because I don't really care who or what you are so long as you are great at something once you join us. I don't have a question for you. I have a test."

Tai held out both his hands, fists closed. "Left or right. One has a sun in it and the other doesn't. If you get the sun, you have my vote."

"Seriously? All of this, and it comes down to luck?"

"Yes," Tai said. "You'd be amazed how important luck is to a Mercenary. One without any is useless. You never want to have someone like that at your back when it all goes to shit."

"And if I refuse to play?"

"Then you'll be disobeying my orders. And I will retaliate by disowning you from Orbis Company. You'll be known as a rogue Mercenary with no support system to protect you from Jay Prince or Regal Company." He gave me a toothy smile when my face dropped. "Didn't think I knew about that? I'd be an irresponsible leader if I didn't. How long do you think you'll last against them when they can kill you without any repercussions?"

"Not very long," I admitted.

"Then choose. Left or right."

Did I know anything about the commander of Orbis Company? Which hand was dominant? Had Alexis or Haru or Dark or Imani given me any indication which hand it might be? There had to be some clue I was missing. It couldn't just be luck. This *was* a test, and I was too blind to see how to win it.

"Are you going to pick or just sit there staring at me like a madman?"

Maybe it really was up to luck. "Right."

Tai opened that hand. There was nothing in the palm. "Wrong."

"How do I—"

He opened the other one. The gold sun was there.

I had lost.

I was still an apprentice Mercenary.

I would have to leave Hollow with Dark. And I wouldn't be able to go find Gwen or avenge Dawn.

I sat there, still stunned, doing my best not to let my jaw hit the floor as everyone else continued like nothing important had happened.

"Imani," Tai said as he returned to his seat. "Finish up business, will you?"

"With pleasure, sir." Imani took out two envelopes and placed them on the table. "Listen up, everyone. We have two big contracts and we'll need everyone to get them done in a timely manner. The commander, Nonna, and Haru will return to headquarters. We've all been away too long. Don't want the locals to forget about us."

"What are the contracts?" Dark asked.

"First one is in New Dracon City, it's a—"

"Mine," the asshole with only one hand declared. "Don't care about the job. I'm going. Otto? You in?"

"Absolutely."

"That makes two for that contract," Imani said. "We'll still need a few more. The other contract is on the Gold Coast. It's a—"

"Oh! Me! Me! Me!" Cassia said with a hand raised. "I haven't been near the ocean in over a year. I can barely remember how it looks."

Imani rubbed her brow. "Does anyone care about the details or just where the contracts are?"

There was a unanimous consensus that the locations mattered the most, to Imani's annoyance. I remained silent, waiting for Dark to choose for the both of us. Given how that had just gone, I really was going to be attached to him for as long as I lived. There was little debate, as most of the Mercenaries decided where they were going. Titus and Alexis were joining Cassia on the Gold Coast, while Otto, Gael, Imani, and Jade were headed to New Dracon City.

"The Gold Coast," Dark said, having been prompted to choose by Imani. "About time I went home."

Having wanted to leave Hollow for years, I had to blink away the tears now that it seemed I would have to go. I didn't want to. I wanted to be with my family, now that I had one, and now that was the last thing that would happen.

Imani covered a few more minor details that we all needed to know about. The emergence of new, younger pirate crews along the Gold Coast and an update about the civil war in the Warring States. Both would make traveling harder for us, but it was incomparable to what the rebellion had done to Hollow. Once we were all excused, only Titus came up to me to wish me luck on my advancement next time and to say I would have his vote when the time came.

And then Dark and I were alone.

"Why did you vote against me?"

"Because you aren't ready to be on your own. You're too focused on what you want and on what you think is important, rather than what I told you to improve on. I was trying to help you, and you ignored my advice."

"But I helped you stop the Heartbreaker and a Waylayer. Doesn't that—"

"Count for something?" Dark finished. "It does. But there aren't many of us in Orbis Company, and we have to be able to trust each other. As it is now, I don't trust you to not abandon your Mercenary obligations if something about your family comes up. Or am I wrong?"

I didn't want to lie—for once—so I didn't respond, giving him his answer anyway.

"This will be good for you, Michael," Dark said as he walked away from me. "Get away from your family. See the world and become your own man."

"Who's to say I can't be my own man with them by my side? Why is that worse than being the man you want me to become?" I asked. "Besides, Dark, I have one more question."

Dark stopped but didn't turn to face me. "What?"

"Are you really trying to help me or just keep me where you can see me? Is that what you did with Alexis? Did you force her to be with you because you can't let people go after losing Zahra? How many of them know what you are and what you're planning to do?"

"I don't think even you know what I have planned, Michael," he said coldly.

"You're going to kill all the dragons," I declared. "What else . . ." And then the realization hit me. Meeting Zahra in Dark's mind had given me an easy answer—that Dark was using her death to give himself purpose—and I had accepted it without protest. Especially when Dark told me he wanted to die after he got revenge. But killing all the dragons was what Dark had to do to make himself feel better, just as Angelo had to kill all the High Nobles. Their desires were different. They both cared about their lovers more than anything else in the world.

I was such a fool.

It hadn't been vengeance that I had seen in the depths of Dark's heart—it was a woman pleading for redemption for the man she had once loved. And if that was a representation of what he wanted more than anything else, why had I ever believed his ultimate goal was about revenge? And just like that, I found another connection between father and son.

"You *lied* to me in the Archmage room. Vengeance is just a way for you and Angelo to repair your wounded pride. It's not what you really want," I muttered. "You want to bring Zahra back from the dead. And Angelo wants to bring Katherine back." I gulped. "It's about love. And only one of you can do it. That's why you're opposing each other."

My body was tense as he looked over his shoulder, no smile or grimace evident. Only a gaze that went right through me, sharper than any blade. It reminded me of Angelo when his friendly persona had shattered. My body was cold as ice, and no matter what I did, no warmth would cover my skin. Ever so slowly he said, "Find my father if you want to change sides."

"If I want a third choice?"

A shrug. "Become strong enough to stand on your own."

"I already am."

"No, you're my apprentice."

A calmness ran through my body like a cool gust of wind on a blistering summer day. "You think that matters? Look me in the eyes and see if I'm lying."

Dark reluctantly did. And when I met his grey eyes, I said, "A Wolven King has kidnapped my sister, so excuse me if I'm a little more volatile than usual. If either you or your father hurt my friends and family to bring back Katherine or Zahra—I'll devour your heart."

Four black tendrils writhed around him and his eyes flashed red. "Care to repeat what you said?"

"Did I stutter?"

The tendrils rushed me as I nullified my body. I grabbed the first, batted away the second, stomped on the third, and bit through the fourth so they all dissipated like a lingering breath. And then—to wound his pride further—I expelled the warmth in my body so he couldn't continue his assault with magic. If he wanted to end this now, it would have to be with our fists. I had already choked out one dragon, so I was confident I could do it again.

"I'm your apprentice, Dark. Were you foolish enough to think I wouldn't take after you?"

Dark said nothing, eyes as red as they had been at the underground lake. No longer was I a dog that he could direct without pushback. In that moment Dark finally saw me as a threat. That I might become what he was to save those I loved, just as he had.

And so we monsters stared each other down, each waiting for the other to make the first move.

CATASTROPHIC LOVE

I was almost home when I found Serena waiting for me at the end of the western bridge. There were no Ravens with her, and she didn't even notice me until I said her name. The river running beneath us had held her attention until then.

"No congratulations on my engagement?" the queen said, something I couldn't quite identify hiding in her voice. Bruises covered her neck, purple and splotchy, as if painted on with a brush. "How very impolite of you."

"I'm trying not to lie so much."

"How convenient." Serena hopped off the ledge she had been sitting on. "Walk with me?"

"Always."

Together, side by side, we walked toward the Church of the Wanderer and the giant hole where the Great Stone Square had once been. The Church of the Wanderer had remained semi-intact—the bell tower collapsing had only destroyed part of it—but was closed for the foreseeable future. Losing two Reclaimers in the span of three months had left the church authorities with little faith in the Hollow branch. The monks had all been shipped out to other places, and no one knew when or if the church would reopen. There were no Advocators in the area, either, though it had been full all week, and when I pressed Serena as to where they had gone, all she did was shrug.

"How'd you get away from all your Ravens?" I asked as we got closer to the hole.

"Snuck out," she said matter-of-factly. "No one can really contain me if I don't want them to."

"No one?"

"No one," Serena repeated softly.

"Does Jay Prince know that?"

The Queen of Hollow didn't respond, squatting down to examine some Moon's Tears that had grown up out of the hole. Their light was guiding our way around it. She plucked one, put it in her hair, and then said, "He'll learn in due time."

I felt like I was dancing with a partner who didn't want to touch me. I would have to be blunter if I wanted to get any answers from her tonight. "Are you here to make sure I won't tell anyone about that tattoo on your wrist?"

"I know you won't," Serena said as she stood straight. "Those were a dying woman's foolish last words. Only a queen remains."

She continued to walk around the pit, toward the church.

I followed like a moonstruck fool.

A little further around, one hand holding her hair from blowing in her face and the other over her heart, she looked down to the lake beneath the square. The remnants of our struggle were still evident, the area crushed by falling debris. Most of the wood and metal down there would be scavenged in the dead of night by those brave enough to venture into the pit once Advocators stopped patrolling the area.

We stood there together for a time, staring into it until Serena said, "Was my father scared before he killed himself? Some days I wonder if he was."

"No. Just tired, and hopeful that he was going to see Davey again."

"Some feelings are eternal. I wonder if they will ease with time." Serena closed her eyes, enjoying the cool wind blowing against her face. "This is the part where you tell me not to marry Jay Prince but to run away with you, Michael. In case you have forgotten your cues."

"You wouldn't still be here if you wanted to do that."

"You're right," she said with a smile. "We'd already be gone."

"Why are you here, Serena?"

Serena sat down on the edge of the pit, letting her legs dangle over it. Only when I followed did she answer. "Do you believe in God?"

"You're avoiding my question."

"Humor me."

I exhaled. "It doesn't matter if I do or don't, only that I'll hold them accountable if I ever run into them."

Serena laughed so obnoxiously that it sounded fake. "Why are you like this? Why were your family and its problems ingrained into you like chiseled marble? I would trade away my last name, crown, and lifestyle in an instant if I could."

"I think I was the only member of my family who wouldn't."

"Why not?"

I hesitated, looking up at the stars and moons in the sky. It all seemed so serene. There was no noise on the rest of the Isle with the church in such a . . . half-formed state. The only light came from Kingman Keep. For once, this city seemed at peace.

"I thought it was the only way people would love me," I began. "That my life was worthless unless I used it in service to Hollow. That I had to be a part of something greater, and if I wasn't . . . then I wouldn't be remembered whenever my time comes. Because for some reason that scares me more than anything else. To be forgotten feels more like death than death."

"A mentor told me we die twice. Once with the body, and another when our name is spoken out loud for the last time." Serena ran a hand along the side of her neck. "I was never scared of that, though. Thinking I may never see my family again was worse. I . . . I . . ."

"Do *you* believe in God?"

Serena blinked back tears. "Yes. Because if they don't exist, I'll never see my father or brother again." Her blinking wasn't working. "All I want is a real family again. People to hold me when I'm upset and tell me it'll be okay even if it won't—"

I put my arm around her and held her close and she cried into my chest. As if she was crying for the first time, as I had after King Isaac's death. I suspected this was her first moment of vulnerability in over a decade. There was no lonelier person than the one who sat on a throne, and even I had forgotten that.

It was some time before she was able to speak without sniffling. But I was there until she composed herself and sat upright again, wiped away whatever tears were left, and then said, "My apologies."

"Don't. We've all been there."

"But I am the queen. A higher standard is set for me."

"That's what I said about being a Kingman. Look how *that* turned out."

Serena laughed, as if reassured that maybe things would be alright. "I don't remember when I stopped being a child, but whenever it was . . . God, do I miss those simpler days. The pressure was still there, but it seemed manageable."

"Ten years ago for me."

After a little hesitation, she said, "I think it's about the same for me. When my brother died, my mother and father were never willingly in the same room again, Adreann turned inward, and the people that were always supposed to be there . . . suddenly weren't. I lost so many people so quickly . . . and . . . and I think it broke me."

"Everyone is broken in one way or another. But I'm starting to realize that the beauty of life—the joy of living—is finding others that are broken in a way that covers your weakness, exposes your strengths, and makes you stronger together. That's all love is. Familiar or romantic, there's no difference." A pause. "I can't do it all on my own, and neither can you. Don't try to."

"Asshole," Serena said, not letting me see her eyes. "Stop being so overdramatic."

"Given what's ahead of me, I'd rather be a blind fool than a wise man."

Serena waited for me to elaborate.

"Gwen left Hollow," I said, forcing a smile. "And I failed my Mercenary advancement test, so I can't go find her. I go wherever Dark does. I don't know when I leave or . . . if I'll ever return to Hollow. And I . . . I . . . This messed-up city is all I've ever known. I've always wanted to leave. And yet I'll miss it. For some reason."

This time *she* comforted *me*. A gentle touch and a soft lullaby that made me feel at ease. When I could focus again, I said, "Guess both our lives are about to change."

"Guess so. Do you know where you're going?"

"The Gold Coast."

I hadn't even finished before Serena started laughing. Loudly.

"What?"

"Chloe, you lovable bitch," Serena muttered. "She tried to tell me earlier, but I was focused on other things. Didn't realize what she was saying."

"Kind of like me right now."

"Michael, the Royal wedding is going to be held on the Gold Coast. In my mother's hometown. And Chloe was quick to tell me that we would be hiring Mercenary support until we are certain that Jay Prince is trustworthy."

"He's not. But does that mean—"

"Yes," the queen said with a smile. Everything disappeared around us. "You may be leaving Hollow, but you won't be alone. Orbis Company has been tasked with my protection. Are you willing to see another part of the world with me? One last adventure together before we do what we—"

"I finally get it," I interrupted. "Their catastrophic love."

She stared at me with longing eyes. "Michael, our duty—"

I kissed her. And she kissed me back. And it was the worst thing we could have done.

EPILOGUE

I walked into the Church of the Wanderer alone. It was abandoned. The lanterns were dark and the fallen bell remained in the very center, the stone and pews around it obliterated. As I strolled down the center, my fingers grazed the tops of the pews. It felt harsher than I remembered, wood that hadn't been cared for properly. A seat of splinters fit for a guilty man's conscience.

There was no comfort in this hollow ground. Well, at least not for me.

Yet, it still reminded me of that place I had been within my mind. That church where I had said my final farewells to Dawn. It didn't exist, but this was the closest I was ever going to come to it with my eyes open and my mind focused. There were things that still needed to be said, feelings to be resolved, and tears to be shed without people being concerned about my emotional stability.

Thankfully, the church had been evacuated, and no one would be here anytime soon. No one would know I had ever been here. No one would remember this moment. No one would record these words. It was just for me.

I gingerly sat down in the first pew. The faceless statue was my only companion.

I took a deep breath, laced my fingers together, and hesitated.

My mind felt unfocused, yet my words came out clear and strong.

"Dear God, I think it's time we had a conversation."

ACKNOWLEDGMENTS

Well, here we are, nine-ish months and a pandemic later. And if you're here immediately after reading the first book—congrats! That's a much quicker wait. This book was relatively easy for me to write—which is wild, considering second book syndrome usually hits most authors. But don't worry, book 3 will make up for that lapse in pain. This book was written in 2018/2019 before *The Kingdom of Liars* was out, so while writing it, I avoided most of the stress associated with 2020. It was a gift, and I'm thankful for that opportunity.

Obviously, there are a lot of people to thank for helping me get this book out. My agent, Joshua Bilmes, continues to be my biggest supporter and strongest advocate. I will always be eternally grateful for how much he believes in me, Michael, and my career as a writer. My thanks also extend to John Berlyne at Zeno Agency and everyone else at JABberwocky Literary Agency.

My US editor, Joe Monti, was the driving force behind my writing book 2 before the first was out. His compassionate guidance let me write in a place and time where the only voices in my head were my editors' and my agent's. For that, I am so grateful. My UK editor, Gillian Redfearn, continues to help me appear smarter than I am thanks to her careful edits. I also appreciate her pushing me to lean into the darker elements of this novel. Especially that one scene. Is it bad I ate a rare steak to get an idea about what to write?

Thanks again to my wonderful cover artists, Richard Anderson and Benjamin Carré. Both knocked it out of the park, as always. It takes a village to get a book to print, so thanks to Caroline Pallotta, Allison Green, Iris Chen, Kaitlyn Snowden, Alexis Leira, Alexis Minieri, Alexandre Su, Stephen Breslin, David Chesanow, Regina Castillo, Linda Sawicki, Andy Goldwasser, and John Vairo for all their hard work. Thank you also to Lauren Jackson, Madison Penico, Brendan Durkin, and Will O'Mullane for their support.

The book community is wonderful and welcoming, but also lonely at times while being a debut, so thank you to some of the authors and community members who showed me early support: Brandon Sanderson, Tamora Pierce, James Islington, Edward Cox, Jeremy Szal, Joshua Palmatier, Gerald Brandt, Troy Bucher, Menachem Luchins, and so many others.

As always, there are a bunch of people outside of publishing who help me stay sane and keep writing despite all the nonsense in life. Thank you to my mother and father, my grandparents, my family, the Church of the Overlord, Bot's Ambassadors and their plus ones, Kyle VanLaar, Penny, and Erin McKeown.

Lastly, thank you to the readers who have continued with the series. The jump from first to second doesn't always bring everyone along, but I'm happy to have you here. I hope you enjoyed this book and will enjoy the next. We'll watch a moon shatter together. Thank you.

Turn the page for a preview of

THE VOYAGE OF
THE FORGOTTEN

the epic finale to The Legacy of the Mercenary King trilogy . . .

CHASING SUNSETS

"I love you, Serena. Always have, always will."

The Queen of Hollow's glass goblet slipped out of her hand and shattered on the balcony floor. That wasn't the reaction I had been expecting, but it was better than being slapped. Or so I told myself, if only to make myself feel better. Saying I love you and getting silence in return was perhaps the most humbling thing I had ever experienced.

If my sister had been with me, Gwen might have smacked some sense into my delusional head. There were very few rules the Kingman family were expected to obey without question. Not falling in love with the Royal we were bound to protect might have been higher on the list than not killing them. But, I suppose, I had always been a slow learner. Hollow didn't know me as Michael dumbass Kingman because of my sparkling personality and sound judgment.

I felt like a child in a costume, picking at my fancy clothes as Serena stared at me, green eyes wide and lower lip trembling. She was beautiful any way I looked at her. From the freckles over the bridge of her nose and her braided auburn hair to her long pale blue dress and the black cosmetics she wore around her eyes. I wished I could be beside her for forever and a day.

Trying to deny it for so long was, perhaps, the greatest lie I had ever told myself. Finally telling her the truth was my attempt at rectifying that mistake.

"Are you going to say anything?" I asked, holding my left wrist. "I know I probably should have told you sooner—"

"We've spent every night together since that night!" she shouted. And then lowered her voice, trying not to attract any of the other guests' attention. "Why would you choose now to tell me? We're at Adreann's wedding!"

"Look," I said. "It's bad timing. I'm aware. But I had to let you know how I—"

"You run away whenever I try to talk to you about our relationship. Literally. You dove into a lake rather than talk about your feelings—let alone have a conversation that wasn't about Angelo, saving Gwen, or our duty. And now you want to tell me you love me? And that you always have and always will? Were you always this much of a dumbass or did you take one too many hits from Dark recently?"

"I was struggling to understand my feelings," I explained. "After what happened in Hollow, I was . . . I didn't know what to do. We're Kingman and Hollow. There are precedents we must follow." And there was the whole warning from Angelo, that if I stayed with Serena she would die. That our love could shatter Tenere. "Yet . . ."

"And yet," she repeated, turning away from me so her elbows rested against the balcony's railing. "And yet. And yet. And yet."

All of Vargo, her mother's city, was in front of us. Unlike Hollow, which showed the impact of many generations on the city, Vargo was too uniform to look natural. It was as if every hundred years or so the city was razed to the ground and built anew in whatever direction the current ruler desired. The current theme was sprawling, tall, and built around a shimmering pink lake with a palace in the middle of it. Every building was perfectly symmetrical, the flat, clean architecture easily replicated hundreds of times. Past the city itself was a port bigger than the rest of the city, with more twists and turns and docks than the Narrows in Hollow. We could hear sailors shouting.

"We should have had this conversation a month ago," she said, when the silence became unbearable. "Not now. Not here. I've already accepted my fate. It's too late to change it."

"Serena," I muttered.

She swept the broken glass over the railing with the side of her foot. The pieces fell into the water below us like glittering shooting stars. "Michael, I've been in love with you for as long as I can remember. But I was a child then . . . and now I'm a queen. I must do what is best for Hollow. Regardless of my feelings."

"Do you really think Jay Prince is what's best for Hollow? He's in league with Angelo Shade!"

"I'm aware," she said icily. "I'm not a fool, but they'll try to get the throne with or without me on it. Adreann wants it now more than ever. Marrying that rebel bitch has only deepened his hunger. At least this way I can stand in their way and keep them in sight. I would not have let the engagement get this far if I thought Hollow was in danger, but I have something they need that I can barter with if things become truly desperate. Or do you not trust my judgment?"

"I do, but—"

"But nothing. This is how it is. How it must be."

I didn't respond, a thousand schemes and plans running through my head to set her free. But when she gave me a lingering kiss on the cheek, it felt like a final goodbye rather than a lover's embrace.

"You'll always be my Kingman," she whispered with a forced smile.

She returned to the celebration before I could reply, disappearing into the crowds of masked partygoers. I closed my eyes, letting the wind blow against my face, and then unclenched the hand around my left wrist. Where my palm had been, there were two letters in black ink over irritated red skin: *Es*. It was Serena's noble nickname. A tattoo I had just recently got to match hers of mine. It was meant to be romantic. Instead it was pathetic. I wrapped it back up in a bandage to hide my shame, donned my mask, and went back inside. There was no rest for a Mercenary. Not even a heartbroken one.

This party was no more threatening than any of the ones I had been to in Hollow. All that differed were the asinine rules everyone was forced to follow. And in the Gold Coast, nothing was held in higher esteem than one's mask. They were strictly regulated to show class, age, profession, and marital status. There were ten creatures to represent the ten families that originally made up the Vargo Clan: the rat, the dog, the shark, the snake, the monkey, the spider, the wasp, the eel, the cow, and the dragon.

Servants wore wooden masks of varying intricacies, indicating their own hierarchy, while guests were given simple colored masks based on where they were from. Mercenaries wore daemon masks. Gnarly things with obnoxious sharp teeth and horns. That was the only thing that made sense in this twisted new dance I had been forced to participate in.

I patrolled the party, one hand on the sword hanging from my hip, keeping an eye on Jay Prince and the noble siblings of Regal Company. Dark and Alexis were doing the same, while Titus was stationed in the kitchen to make sure nothing was poisoned. Meanwhile dear, sweet Cassia was being selfish, as usual. Rather than use her renowned abilities to help us, she had decided to continue reading the map she had been obsessed with throughout our trip to Vargo. It was old and brittle and written in a strange language that reminded me of the strange script I had seen in the Royal Crypts, but I had been unable to get a good look at it. Even with all the noise and festivity around us, she was studying it in one corner of the room.

Most of the party was focused on Jay Prince and he was kept surrounded, most feigning excitement about having a Merchant Prince engaged to their clan leader's daughter. As if they hadn't fought with Hollow against New Dracon City during the Gunpowder War. Their memories were fickle tonight.

Someone clinked a knife against their glass and drew everyone's attention. Erica Hollow stood on an elevated platform with Serena by her side. Erica Vargo looked nothing like Serena or Adreann—having a bigger forehead, a thinner body, and a bright blond braid of hair that went down to her shoulder blades. But her penetrating green eyes were the same as her children's. She wore leather pauldrons over a simple black shirt and pants, a golden cape behind her, and three strips of white war paint over her right eye. In Vargo, the leader's goal was not to dress to impress, as it was in Hollow. It was to remind everyone who was in charge. Survival of the strongest was not a belief here, it was a daily practice.

"Dearly beloved, we are gathered here today to celebrate my son's wedding," Erica said overly sweetly. "It is a historic event that will unify many countries and wipe away decades of bad blood. Love can build bridges, especially when hate is all that's usually seen."

People didn't clap in Vargo, snapping their fingers in agreement instead.

"Sadly for us, my son is already celebrating their union with his new wife." Erica twirled her finger around the rim of her glass. "But, thankfully, my daughter and soon-to-be son-in-law are here. Jay Prince, would you join us onstage?"

Jay adjusted his coat and walked toward Serena and Erica. His black hair was kept short, his ears would have made an elephant feel self-conscious, and half of his face was covered in bone tattoos. When he reached Serena, he bowed deeply and then kissed her hand. I gritted my teeth and tried to remind myself of my duty rather than my hopes.

"Hollow has its own wedding rituals . . . as does Vargo and New Dracon City," Erica stated, putting her hands on Serena's and Jay's shoulders. "We wish to honor them all, but as of right now, we are quite . . . overwhelmed finding a way to do so. Therefore it has been decided to extend the engagement period."

Murmurs went through the crowd as my heart soared. Maybe there was still a chance I could stop Serena from marrying Jay. I had spent some time trying to figure out his connection to Angelo Shade, but there was nothing tangible to act on. All I knew was that they trusted each other completely. Dark wouldn't or couldn't confirm anything else. He liked keeping secrets too much.

"How long?" a rat-masked man shouted from the crowd.

"Thirty days," Jay said. "We hoped we could have the preparations complete by the end of the month, but we were both woefully ignorant of Hollow's strict laws and regulations for royal weddings. Prince Adreann's wedding only made matters more complicated."

Serena took Jay's hand. "Just as we were ignorant of how many of the Merchant Princes and High Nobles would feel slighted if they were not given enough time to attend. Vargo, for all its size, isn't even able to house all of them at the present moment. But in thirty days it will be. Or so we hope. We have builders working day and night."

"Does that mean you will be married during the upcoming solar eclipse?" a snake mask called out.

"Yes," Jay said, raising their intertwined fingers. "The astronomers even say that it will last half a day, giving us plenty of time to complete the full ceremony. It will be an unparalleled omen, befitting our legendary union." He smiled lovingly at Serena. "The skies above will stop, and learn what true love is."

I nearly gagged as others around me cooed and swooned at the handsome man's words.

As Jay and Serena answered questions, I felt a tap on my shoulder. It was Chloe. The one-eyed woman had two peacock feathers woven into her hair. She wasn't in her normal plate mail, had a decorative spear across her back, and had shaved the sides of her head and cut her hair into a neatly maintained black streak. No longer was she the fragile girl who would blow away in the wind I had met at the Shrine of Patron Victoria. She had morphed into someone capable of standing next to the queen of Hollow.

"Can I steal you for a moment, Michael?"

I nodded and followed Chloe out of the ballroom and into a servant's hallway. It was cramped, but people were still able to pass us with covered and sparse plates, full and empty wineglasses, and everything else needed for a party. It all smelt wonderful, but for some reason I kept remembering the smell from the rebel attack on the Militia Quarter. Serena's rejection must've sent my mind to unfit places.

"Serena told me what happened before she took the stage," Chloe declared without fanfare.

Because of course she did. Fan-fucking-tastic. I crossed my arms. "Are you here to be my shoulder to cry on or something?"

"No," she said. "I'm here to make sure you don't do anything stupid. Until they're wed, you are the most dangerous man in Hollow. You do one wrong thing, and we could have a massive war on our hands."

"Angelo Shade would be offended to hear that. He's been trying to bring down Hollow for a long time," I mumbled. When she raised an eyebrow at me, I sighed and continued, "What do you think I'm going to do? Kill Jay?"

Chloe stared at me. "I wouldn't put it past you."

"I'm not a monster."

"You are a Kingman who thinks his Royal is making a mistake. Your ancestors are famous for doing whatever it took to stop them in a similar situation."

I played with my father's ring, always amazed how such a small thing could bring me comfort. If my father hadn't given it to me before his execution, would I even be here? Or would I have fallen for Angelo's schemes and lies?

"I am not my ancestors. What do you want me to . . ." I trailed off, the smell of sulfur distracting me again. People were shouting and screaming from the party, and it had been a while since any servants had crossed paths with us. "Chloe, I think—"

She was already running toward the ballroom door, slamming into it with her shoulder. It didn't budge. Smoke was coming in through the slit at the bottom, pungent and grey. Gunpowder smoke or fire smoke—we could hear people frantically pounding on the other side.

Chloe electrified her arms, shot lightning at the hinges, and then rammed the door with her shoulder again. It fell back into the room, smoke clouding our vision as people ran past us. They were all screaming, some of them without their masks. We pushed past them all and into the ballroom proper. The servants were swinging swords and aiming guns at Erica, Serena, Jay, and the other Mercenaries in the room.

Black tendrils slithered over the ceiling, periodically yanking someone upward until they slammed against something hard with a sickening snap or crack. Dark, as always, was a conductor of death, using his magic to control the battle around us as Alexis used her flintlock pistols to stop anyone from getting close to him. The noble siblings, the commanders of Regal Company, cut through friend and foe alike trying to join Jay, Serena, and Erica, though they didn't need their help, easily pushing back anyone who got close with Serena's Fabrications and Jay's bare fists. The only one not doing something to help was Cassia. She didn't even look bothered by the smoke in the corner of the room, still examining her antique map.

"Who are we fighting?" I asked as I punched someone in the jaw, sending them to the floor.

Chloe threw a bolt of lightning at a man with a gun, blasting him away from Serena and the others. "Does it matter? Stop anyone who gets close to them!"

Easier said than done. For every three people I knocked down or away, at least one was a civilian. And since it was impossible to tell who was who at a simple glance, I didn't feel comfortable enough using the sword attached to my hip. I may have done questionable things in the past, but so far I had only killed people who were unmistakably evil.

"Enough!" Serena shouted. "I'm ending this."

Everyone bowed before her, forced to their knees as an invisible weight pushed down on us all. The world around us was shaking as her Fabrications rendered any opposition futile. She was a titan among us mortals.

I nullified my body as quickly as I could—the only other person in the room who wasn't on the ground. But then something happened. Serena blinked and everything stopped—the screaming and sobbing, the gunfire and clang of metal, the inhale and exhale of deep breaths. A silence that lingered in the depths of all our lungs. The world darkened around us as my skin prickled. All I could see was her, but something was wrong. It was like being in a dream, only to discover it was a nightmare all along.

Serena looked at me, visibly confused. Her confidence and poise disappeared in a moment. "Who—"

A bullet hit her, and I screamed as Serena fell.